PRAISE FOR JEFFREY ARCHER

"A sprawling blockbuster!"   —*Publishers Weekly* on *Kane & Abel*

"Archer provides a fine read with keen sense of the good and the bad in people and the importance of kinship . . . [He] masterfully creates a great villain in Elliot, who jumps off the pages in all of his vengeful and shady glamour."—*Los Angeles Times* on *Sons of Fortune*

"One of the top ten storytellers in the world!" —*Los Angeles Times*

"There isn't a better storyteller alive."   —Larry King

"Archer is a master entertainer."   —*Time*

"Cunning plots, silken style. . . . Archer plays a cat-and-mouse game with the reader."   —*The New York Times*

"A storyteller in the class of Alexandre Dumas . . . unsurpassed skill . . . making the reader wonder intensely what will happen next."   —*The Washington Post*

"Archer plots with skill, and keeps you turning the pages."
                            —*The Boston Globe*

"A master at mixing power, politics, and profit into fiction."
                            —*Entertainment Weekly*

KANE & ABEL

SONS OF FORTUNE

KANE & ABEL

SONS OF FORTUNE

JEFFREY ARCHER

St. Martin's Griffin ✹ New York

ISBN-13: 978-0-312-36686-5
ISBN-10: 0-312-36686-8

Kane & Abel was originally published by Simon and Schuster in 1979.
Ballantine edition / 1980
HarperPaperbacks edition / August 1993
St. Martin's Paperbacks edition / March 2004

Sons of Fortune was originally published by St. Martin's Press in 2003.
St. Martin's Paperbacks edition / December 2003

First St. Martin's Griffin edition: September 2006

10 9 8 7 6 5 4 3 2 1

KANE & ABEL

TO MICHAEL AND JANE

Two men have made this book possible, and they both wish to remain anonymous. One because he is working on his own autobiography, and the other because he is still a public figure in the United States.

PART ONE
1906–1923

CHAPTER ONE

April 18, 1906
Slonim, Poland

She only stopped screaming when she died. It was then that he started to scream.

The young boy who was hunting rabbits in the forest was not sure whether it was the woman's last cry or the child's first that alerted his youthful ears. He turned suddenly, sensing the possible danger, his eyes searching for an animal that was so obviously in pain. He had never known any animal to scream in quite that way before. He edged toward the noise cautiously; the scream had now turned to a whine, but it still did not sound like any animal he knew. He hoped it would be small enough to kill; at least that would make a change from rabbit for dinner.

The young hunter moved stealthily toward the river, where the strange noise came from, running from tree to tree, feeling the protection of the bark against his shoulder blades, something to touch. Never stay in the open, his father had taught him. When he reached the edge of the forest, he had a clear line of vision all the way down the valley to the river, and even then it took him some time to realize that the strange cry emanated from no ordinary animal. He continued to creep toward the whining, but he was out in the open on his own now. Then suddenly he saw the woman, with her dress above her waist, her bare legs splayed wide apart. He had never seen a woman like that before. He ran quickly to her side and stared down at her belly, quite frightened to touch. There, lying between the woman's legs, was the body of a small, damp, pink animal, attached only by something that looked like rope. The young hunter dropped his freshly skinned rabbits and collapsed on his knees beside the little creature.

He gazed for a long, stunned moment and then turned his eyes toward the woman, immediately regretting the decision. She was already blue with cold; her tired twenty-three-year-old face looked middle-aged to the boy; he did not need to be told that she was dead. He picked up the slippery little body—had you asked him why, and no one ever did, he would have told you that the tiny fingernails clawing the crumpled face had worried him—and then he became aware that mother and child were inseparable because of the slimy rope.

He had watched the birth of a lamb a few days earlier and he tried to remember. Yes, that's what the shepherd had done, but dare he, with a child? The whining had stopped and he sensed that a decision was now urgent. He unsheathed his knife, the one he had skinned the rabbits with, wiped it on his sleeve and, hesitating only for a moment, cut the rope close to the child's body. Blood flowed freely from the severed ends. Then what had the shepherd done when the lamb was born? He had tied a knot to stop the blood. Of course, of course. He pulled some long grass out of the earth beside him and hastily tied a crude knot in the cord. Then he took the child in his arms. He rose slowly from his knees, leaving behind him three dead rabbits and a dead woman who had given birth to this child. Before finally turning his back on the mother, he put her legs together and pulled her dress down over her knees. It seemed to be the right thing to do.

"Holy God," he said aloud, the first thing he always said when he had done something very good or very bad. He wasn't yet sure which this was.

The young hunter then ran toward the cottage where he

knew his mother would be cooking supper, waiting only for his rabbits; all else would be prepared. She would be wondering how many he might have caught today; with a family of eight to feed, she needed at least three. Sometimes he managed a duck, a goose or even a pheasant that had strayed from the Baron's estate, on which his father worked. Tonight he had caught a different animal, and when he reached the cottage the young hunter dared not let go of his prize even with one hand, so he kicked at the door with his bare foot until his mother opened it. Silently, he held out his offering to her. She made no immediate move to take the creature from him but stood, one hand on her breast, gazing at the wretched sight.

"Holy God," she said, and crossed herself. The boy stared up at his mother's face for some sign of pleasure or anger. Her eyes were now showing a tenderness the boy had never seen in them before. He knew then that the thing he had done must be good.

"Is it a baby, Matka?"

"It's a little boy," said his mother, nodding sorrowfully. "Where did you find him?"

"Down by the river, Matka," he said.

"And the mother?"

"Dead."

She crossed herself again.

"Quickly, run and tell your father what has happened. He will find Urszula Wojnak on the estate and you must take them both to the mother, and then be sure they come back to me."

The young hunter handed over the little boy to his mother, happy enough not to have dropped the slippery creature. Now, free of his quarry, he rubbed his hands on his trousers and ran off to look for his father.

The mother closed the door with her shoulder and called out for her eldest child, a girl, to put the pot on the stove. She sat down on a wooden stool, unbuttoned her bodice and pushed a tired nipple toward the little puckered mouth. Sophia, her younger daughter, only six months old, would have to go without her supper tonight. Come to think of it, so would the whole family.

"And to what purpose?" the woman said out loud, tucking a shawl around her arm and the child together. "Poor little mite, you'll be dead by morning."

But she did not repeat these feelings to old Urszula Wojnak when the midwife washed the little body and tended to the twisted umbilical stump late that night. Her husband stood silently by observing the scene.

"A guest in the house is God in the house," declared the woman, quoting the old Polish proverb.

Her husband spat. "To the cholera with him. We have enough children of our own."

The woman pretended not to hear him as she stroked the dark, thin hairs on the baby's head.

"What shall we call him?" the woman asked, looking up at her husband.

He shrugged. "Who cares? Let him go to his grave nameless."

CHAPTER
TWO

April 18, 1906
Boston, Massachusetts

The doctor picked up the newborn child by the ankles and slapped its bottom. The infant started to cry.

In Boston, Massachusetts, there is a hospital that caters mainly to those who suffer from the diseases of the rich, and on selected occasions allows itself to deliver the new rich. At the Massachusetts General Hospital the mothers don't scream, and certainly they don't give birth fully dressed. It is not the done thing.

A young man was pacing up and down outside the delivery room; inside, two obstetricians and the family doctor were on duty. This father did not believe in taking risks with his firstborn. The two obstetricians would be paid a large fee merely to stand by and witness events. One of them who wore evening clothes under his long white coat had a dinner party to attend later, but he could not afford to absent himself from this particular birth. The three had earlier drawn straws to decide who should deliver the child, and Doctor MacKenzie, the family G.P., had won. A sound, secure name, the father considered, as he paced up and down the corridor. Not that he had any reason to be anxious. Roberts had driven the young man's wife, Anne, to the hospital in the hansom carriage that morning, which she had calculated was the twenty-eighth day of her ninth month. She had started labor soon after breakfast, and he had been assured that delivery would not take place until his bank had closed for the day. The father was a disciplined man and saw no reason why a birth should interrupt his well-ordered life. Nevertheless, he continued to pace. Nurses and young doctors hurried past him, aware of his presence, their voices lowered when they were near him and raised again only when they were out of his earshot. He didn't notice, because everybody had always treated him this way. Most of them had never seen him in person, but all of them knew who he was.

If it was a boy, a son, he would probably build the new children's wing that the hospital so badly needed. He had already built a library and a school. The expectant father tried to read the evening paper, looking over the words but not taking in their meaning. He was nervous, even worried. It would never do for them (he looked upon almost everyone as "them") to realize that it had to be a boy, a boy who would one day take his place as president and chairman of the bank. He turned the pages of the *Evening Transcript*. The Boston Red Sox had tied with the New York Highlanders— others would be celebrating. Then he recalled the headline on the front page and returned to it. The worst earthquake ever in the history of America. Devastation in San Francisco, at least four hundred people dead—others would be mourning. He hated that. It would take away from the birth of his son. People would remember that something else had happened on this day.

It never occurred to him, not even for a moment, that the baby might be a girl. He turned to the financial pages and checked the stock market: it had dropped a few points; that damned earthquake had taken $100,000 off the value of his own holdings in the bank, but as his personal fortune remained comfortably over $16 million, it was going to take more than a California earthquake to move him. He could now live on the interest, so the $16 million capital would always remain intact, ready for his son, still unborn. He continued to pace and pretend to read the *Transcript*.

The obstetrician in evening dress pushed through the swinging doors of the delivery room to report the news. He felt he must do something for his large unearned fee and he was the most suitably dressed for the announcement. The two men stared at each other for a moment. The doctor also felt a little nervous, but he wasn't going to show it in front of the father.

"Congratulations, sir, you have a son, a fine-looking little boy."

What silly remarks people make when a child is born, the father thought; how could he be anything but little? The news hadn't yet dawned on him—a son. He almost thanked God. The obstetrician ventured a question to break the silence.

"Have you decided what you will name him?"

The father answered without hesitation: "William Lowell Kane."

CHAPTER
THREE

Long after the excitement of the baby's arrival had passed and the rest of the family had gone to bed, the mother remained awake with the child in her arms. Helena Koskiewicz believed in life, and she had borne six children to prove it. Although she had lost three more in infancy, she had not let any of them go easily.

Now at thirty-five she knew that her once lusty Jasio would give her no more sons or daughters: God had given her this one; surely he was destined to live. Helena's was a simple faith, which was good, for her destiny was never to afford her more than a simple life. She was gray and thin, not through choice but through little food, hard work and no spare money. It never occurred to her to complain, but the lines on her face would have been more in keeping with a grandmother than a mother in today's world. She had never worn new clothes even once in her life.

Helena squeezed her breasts so hard that dull red marks appeared around the nipples. Little drops of milk squirted out. At thirty-five, halfway through life's contract, we all have some useful piece of expertise to pass on, and Helena Koskiewicz's was now at a premium.

"Matka's littlest one," she whispered tenderly to the child, and drew the milky teat across its pursed mouth. The blue eyes opened and tiny drops of sweat broke out on the baby's nose as he tried to suck. Finally the mother slumped unwillingly into a deep sleep.

Jasio Koskiewicz, a heavy, dull man with a full mustache, his only gesture of self-assertion in an otherwise servile existence, discovered his wife and the baby asleep in the rocking chair when he rose at five. He hadn't noticed her absence from their bed that night. He stared down at the bastard who had, thank God, at least stopped wailing. Was it dead? Jasio considered the easiest way out of the dilemma was to get himself to work and not interfere with the intruder; let the woman worry about life and death: his preoccupation was to be on the Baron's estate by first light. He took a few long swallows of goat's milk and wiped his luxuriant mustache on his sleeve. Then he grabbed a hunk of bread with one hand and his traps with the other and slipped noiselessly out of the cottage, for fear of waking the woman and getting himself involved. He strode away toward the forest, giving no more thought to the little intruder other than to assume that he had seen him for the last time.

Florentyna, the elder daughter, was next to enter the kitchen, just before the old clock that for many years had kept its own time, claimed that 6 A.M. had arrived. It was of no more than ancillary assistance to those who wished to know if it was the hour to get up or go to bed. Among Florentyna's daily duties was the preparation of breakfast, in itself a minor task involving the simple division of a skin of goat's milk and a lump of rye bread among a family of eight. Nevertheless, it required the wisdom of Solomon to carry out the task in such a way that no one complained about another's portion.

Florentyna struck those who saw her for the first time as a pretty, frail, shabby little thing. It was unfair that for the last two years she had had only one dress to wear, but those who could separate their opinion of the child from that of her surroundings understood why Jasio had fallen in love with her mother. Florentyna's long fair hair shone and her hazel eyes sparkled in defiance of her birth and diet.

She tiptoed up to the rocking chair and stared down at her mother and the little boy, whom Florentyna had adored at first sight. She had never in her eight years owned a doll. Actually she had seen one only once, when the family had been invited to a celebration of the feast of St. Nicholas at the Baron's castle. Even then she had not actually touched the beautiful object, but now she felt an inexplicable urge to hold this baby in her arms. She bent down and eased the child away from her mother, and staring down into the little blue eyes—such blue eyes—she began to hum. The change of temperature from the warmth of the mother's breast to the cold of the little girl's hands made the baby indignant. He immediately started crying and woke the mother, whose only reaction was of guilt for having fallen asleep.

"Holy God, he's still alive," she said to Florentyna. "You prepare breakfast for the boys while I try to feed him again."

Florentyna reluctantly handed the infant back and watched her mother once again pump her aching breasts. The little girl was mesmerized.

"Hurry up, Florcia," chided her mother. "The rest of the family must eat as well."

Florentyna obeyed, and as her brothers arrived from the loft where they all slept, they kissed their mother's hands in greeting and stared at the newcomer in awe. All they knew was that this one had not come from Matka's stomach. Florentyna was too excited to eat her breakfast this morning, so the boys divided her portion among them without a second thought and left their mother's share on the table. No one noticed, as they went about their daily tasks, that the mother hadn't eaten anything since the baby's arrival.

Helena Koskiewicz was pleased that her children had learned so early in life to fend for themselves. They could feed the animals, milk the goats and cows and tend the vegetable garden without her help or prodding. When Jasio returned home in the evening she suddenly realized that she had not prepared supper for him, but that Florentyna had taken the rabbits from Franck, her brother the hunter, and had already started to cook them. Florentyna was proud to be in charge of the evening meal, a responsibility she was entrusted with only when her mother was unwell, and Helena Koskiewicz rarely allowed herself that luxury. The young hunter had brought home four rabbits, and the father six mushrooms and three potatoes: tonight would be a veritable feast.

After dinner, Jasio Koskiewicz sat in his chair by the fire and studied the child properly for the first time. Holding the little baby under the armpits, with his splayed fingers supporting the helpless head, he cast a trapper's eye over the infant. Wrinkled and toothless, the face was redeemed only by the fine, blue unfocusing eyes. As the man directed his gaze toward the thin body, something immediately attracted his attention. He scowled and rubbed the delicate chest with his thumbs.

"Have you noticed this, Helena?" said the trapper, prodding the baby's ribs. "The ugly little bastard has only one nipple?"

His wife frowned as she in turn rubbed the skin with her thumb, as though the action would supply the missing organ. Her husband was right: the minute and colorless left nipple was there, but where its mirror image should have appeared on the right-hand side, the shallow breast was completely smooth and uniformly pink.

The woman's superstitious tendencies were immediately aroused. "He has been given to me by God," she exclaimed. "See His mark upon him."

The man thrust the child angrily at her. "You're a fool, Helena. The child was given to its mother by a man with bad blood." He spat into the fire, the more precisely to express his opinion of the child's parentage. "Anyway, I wouldn't bet a potato on the little bastard's survival."

Jasio Koskiewicz cared even less than a potato whether or not the child survived. He was not by nature a callous man, but the boy was not his, and one more mouth to feed could only compound his problems. But if it was so to be, it was not for him to question the Almighty, and with no more thought of the boy, he fell into a deep sleep by the fire.

• • •

As the days passed by, even Jasio Koskiewicz began to believe that the child might survive and, had he been a betting man, he would have lost a potato. The eldest son, the hunter, with the help of his younger brothers, made the child a cot out of wood that they had collected from the Baron's forest. Florentyna made his clothes by cutting little pieces off her own dresses and then sewing them together. They would have called him Harlequin if they had known what it meant. In truth, naming him caused more disagreement in the household than any other single problem had for months; only the father had no opinion to offer. Finally, they agreed on Wladek; the following Sunday, in the chapel on the Baron's great estate, the child was christened Wladek Koskiewicz, the mother thanking God for sparing his life, the father resigning himself to whatever must be.

That evening there was a small feast to celebrate the christening, augmented by the gift of a goose from the Baron's estate. They all ate heartily.

From that day on, Florentyna learned to divide by nine.

CHAPTER
FOUR

Anne Kane had slept peacefully through the night. When after her breakfast her son William returned in the arms of one of the hospital's nurses, she could not wait to hold him again.

"Now then, Mrs. Kane," the white-uniformed nurse said briskly, "shall we give baby his breakfast too?"

She sat Anne, who was abruptly aware of her swollen breasts, up in bed and guided the two novices through the procedure. Anne, conscious that to appear embarrassed would be considered unmaternal, gazed fixedly into William's blue eyes, bluer even than his father's, and assimilated her new position, with which it would have been illogical to be other than pleased. At twenty-one, she was not conscious that she lacked anything. Born a Cabot, married into a branch of the Lowell family, and now a firstborn son to carry on the tradition summarized so succinctly in the card sent to her by an old school friend:

> And this is good old Boston,
> The home of the bean and the cod,
> Where the Lowells talk to the Cabots,
> And the Cabots talk only to God.

Anne spent half an hour talking to William but obtained little response. He was then retired for a sleep in the same efficient manner by which he had arrived. Anne nobly resisted the fruit and candy piled by her bedside. She was determined to get back into all her dresses by the summer season and reassume her rightful place in the fashionable magazines. Had not the Prince de Garonne said that she was the only beautiful object in Boston? Her long golden hair, fine delicate features and slim figure had excited admiration in cities she had never even visited. She checked in the mirror: no telltale lines on her face; people would hardly believe that she was the mother of a bouncing boy. Thank God it is a bouncing boy, thought Anne.

She enjoyed a light lunch and prepared herself for the visitors who would appear during the afternoon, already screened by her private secretary. Those who would be allowed to see her on the first days had to be family or from the very best families; others would be told she was not yet ready to receive them. But as Boston was the last city remaining in America where each knew his place to the finest degree of social prominence, there was unlikely to be any unexpected intruder.

The room that she alone occupied could easily have taken another five beds had it not already been cluttered with flowers. A casual passerby could have been forgiven for mistaking it for a minor horticultural show, had it not been for the presence of the young mother sitting upright in bed. Anne switched on the electric light, still a novelty for her; Richard and she had waited for the Cabots to have them fitted, which all of Boston had interpreted as an oracular sign that electromagnetic induction was from then on socially acceptable.

The first visitor was Anne's mother-in-law, Mrs. Thomas Lowell Kane, the head of the family since her husband had died. In elegant late middle-age, she had perfected the technique of sweeping into a room to her own total satisfaction and to its occupants' undoubted discomfiture. She wore a long chemise dress, which made it impossible to view her ankles; the only man who had ever seen her ankles was now dead. She had always been lean. In her opinion, fat women meant bad food and even worse breeding. She was now the oldest Lowell alive, the oldest Kane, come to that. She therefore expected and was expected to be the first to arrive. After all, had it not been she who had arranged the meeting between Anne and Richard? Love had seemed of little consequence to Mrs. Kane. Wealth, position and prestige she could always come to terms with. Love was all very well, but it rarely proved to be a lasting commodity; the other three were. She kissed her daughter-in-law approvingly on the forehead. Anne touched a button on the wall, and a quiet buzz could be heard. The noise took Mrs. Kane by surprise; she had not believed that electricity would ever catch on. The nurse reappeared with the heir. Mrs. Kane inspected him, sniffed her satisfaction and waved him away.

"Well done, Anne," the old lady said, as if her daughter-in-law had won a minor equestrian prize. "All of us are very proud of you."

Anne's own mother, Mrs. Edward Cabot, arrived a few minutes later. She, like Mrs. Kane, had been widowed at an early age and differed so little from her in appearance that those who observed them only from afar tended to get them muddled up. But to do her justice, she took considerably more interest than Mrs. Kane in her new grandson and in her daughter. The inspection continued to the flowers.

"How kind of the Jacksons to remember," murmured Mrs. Cabot.

Mrs. Kane adopted a more cursory procedure. Her eyes skimmed over the delicate blooms, then settled on the donors' cards. She whispered the soothing names to herself: Adamses, Lawrences, Lodges, Higginsons. Neither grandmother commented on the names they didn't know; they were both past the age of wanting to learn of anything or anyone new. They left together, well pleased: an heir had been born and appeared, on first sight, to be adequate. They both considered that their final family obligation had been successfully, albeit vicariously, performed and that they themselves might now progress to the role of chorus.

They were both wrong.

Anne and Richard's close friends poured in during the afternoon with gifts and good wishes, the former of gold or silver, the latter in high-pitched Brahmin accents.

When her husband arrived after the close of business, Anne was somewhat overtired. Richard had drunk champagne at lunch for the first time in his life—old Amos Kerbes had insisted and, with the whole Somerset Club looking on, Richard could hardly have refused. He seemed to his wife to be a little less stiff than usual. Solid in his long black frock coat and pinstripe trousers, he stood fully six feet one, his dark hair with its center parting gleaming in the light of the large electric bulb. Few would have guessed his age correctly as only thirty-three: youth had never been important to him; substance was the only thing that mattered. Once again William Lowell Kane was called for and inspected, as if the father were checking the balance at the end of the banking day. All seemed to be in order. The boy had two legs, two arms, ten fingers, ten toes, and Richard could see nothing that might later embarrass him, so William was sent away.

"I wired the headmaster of St. Paul's last night. William has been admitted for September 1918."

Anne said nothing, Richard had so obviously started planning William's career.

"Well, my dear, are you fully recovered today?" he went on to inquire, having never spent a day in the hospital during his thirty-three years.

"Yes—no—I think so," his wife responded timidly, suppressing a rising tearfulness that she knew would only displease her husband. The answer was not of the sort that Richard could hope to understand. He kissed his wife on the cheek and returned in the hansom carriage to the Red House on Louisburg Square, their family home. With staff, servants, the new baby and his nurse, there would now be nine mouths to feed. Richard did not give the matter a second thought.

William Lowell Kane received the church's blessing and the names his father had chosen before birth at the Protestant Episcopal Cathedral of St. Paul's, in the presence of everybody in Boston who mattered and a few who didn't. Bishop William Lawrence officiated; J. P. Morgan and Alan Lloyd, bankers of impeccable standing, along with Milly Preston, Anne's closest friend, were the chosen godparents. His Grace sprinkled the holy water on William's head; the boy didn't murmur. He was already learning the Brahmin approach to life. Anne thanked God for the safe birth of her son, and Richard thanked God, Whom he regarded as an external bookkeeper whose function was to record the deeds of the Kane family from generation to generation, that he had a son to whom he could leave his fortune. Still, he thought, perhaps he had better be certain and have a second boy. From his kneeling position he glanced sideways at his wife, well pleased with her.

CHAPTER
FIVE

Wladek Koskiewicz grew slowly. It became apparent to his foster mother that the boy's health would always be a problem. He caught all the illnesses and diseases that growing children normally catch and many that others don't, and he passed them on indiscriminately to the rest of the Koskiewicz family. Helena treated him as any of her own brood and always vigorously defended him when Jasio began to blame the devil rather than God for Wladek's presence in their tiny cottage. Florentyna, on the other hand, took care of Wladek as if he were her own child. She loved him from the first moment she had set eyes on him with an intensity that grew from a fear that because no one would ever want to marry her, the penniless daughter of a trapper, she must therefore be childless. Wladek was her child.

The eldest brother, the hunter, who had found Wladek, treated him like a plaything but was too afraid of his father to admit that he liked the frail infant who was growing into a sturdy toddler. In any case, next January the hunter was to leave school and start work on the Baron's estate, and children were a woman's problem, so his father had told him. The three younger brothers, Stefan, Josef and Jan, showed little interest in Wladek, and the remaining member of the family, Sophia, was happy enough just to cuddle him.

What neither parent had been prepared for was a character and mind so different from those of their own children.

No one could miss the physical or intellectual difference. The Koskiewiczes were all tall, large-boned, with fair hair and, except for Florentyna, gray eyes. Wladek was short and round, with dark hair and intensely blue eyes. The Koskiewiczes had minimal pretensions to scholarship and were removed from the village school as soon as age or discretion allowed. Wladek, on the other hand, though he was late in walking, spoke at eighteen months. Read at three but was still unable to dress himself. Wrote at five but continued to wet his bed. He became the despair of his father and the pride of his mother. His first four years on this earth were memorable only as a continual physical attempt through illness to try to depart from it, and for the sustained efforts of Helena and Florentyna to ensure that he did not succeed. He ran around the little wooden cottage barefoot, usually dressed in his harlequin outfit, a yard or so behind his mother. When Florentyna returned from school, he would transfer his allegiance, never leaving her side until she put him to bed. In her division of the food by nine, Florentyna often sacrificed half of her own share to Wladek, or if he was ill, the entire portion. Wladek wore the clothes she made for him, sang the songs she taught him and shared with her the few toys and presents she had been given.

Because Florentyna was away at school most of the day, Wladek wanted from a young age to go with her. As soon as he was allowed to (holding firmly on to Florentyna's hand until they reached the village school) he walked the eighteen *wiorsta*, some nine miles, through the woods of moss-covered birches and cypresses and the orchards of lime and cherry to Slonim to begin his education.

Wladek liked school from the first day; it was an escape from the tiny cottage that had until then been his whole world. School also confronted him for the first time in life with the savage implications of the Russian occupation of eastern Poland. He learned that his native Polish was to be spoken only in the privacy of the cottage and that while at school, only Russian was to be used. He sensed in the other children around him a fierce pride in the oppressed mother tongue and culture. He, too, felt that same pride. To his surprise, Wladek found that he was not belittled by Mr. Kotowski, his schoolteacher, the way he was at home by his father. Although still the youngest, as at home, it was not long before he rose above all his classmates in everything other than height. His tiny stature misled them into continual underestimation of his real abilities: children always imagine biggest is best. By the age of five Wladek was first in every subject taken by his class.

At night, back at the little wooden cottage, while the other children would tend the violets and poplars that bloomed so fragrantly in their springtime garden, pick berries, chop wood, catch rabbits or make dresses, Wladek read and read, until he was reading the unopened books of his eldest brother and then those of his elder sister. It began to dawn slowly on Helena Koskiewicz that she had taken on more than she had bargained for when the young hunter had brought home the little animal in place of three rabbits; already Wladek was asking questions she could not answer. She knew soon that she would be quite unable to cope and she wasn't sure what to do about it. She had an unswerving belief in destiny and so was not surprised when the decision was taken out of her hands.

One evening in the autumn of 1911 came the first turning point in Wladek's life. The family had all finished their plain supper of beetroot soup and meatballs, Jasio Koskiewicz was snoring by the fire, Helena was sewing and the other children were playing. Wladek was sitting at the feet of his mother, reading, when above the noise of Stefan and Josef squabbling over the possession of some newly painted pinecones, they heard a loud knock on the door. They all went silent. A knock was always a surprise to the Koskiewicz family, for at the little cottage, eighteen *wiorsta* from Slonim village and over six from the Baron's estate, visitors were almost unknown and could be offered only a drink of berry juice and the company of noisy children. The whole family looked toward the door apprehensively. As if it had not happened, they waited for the knock to come again. It did—if anything, a little louder. Jasio rose sleepily from his chair, walked to the door and opened it cautiously. When they saw the man standing there, they all bowed their heads except Wladek, who stared up at the broad, handsome, aristocratic figure in the heavy bearskin coat, whose presence dominated the tiny room and brought fear into the father's eyes. A cordial smile allayed that fear, and the trapper invited the Baron Rosnovski into his home. Nobody spoke. The Baron had never visited them in the past and no one was sure of what to say.

Wladek put down his book, rose and walked toward the stranger, thrusting out his hand before his father could stop him.

"Good evening, sir," said Wladek.

The Baron took his hand and they stared into each other's eyes. As the Baron released him, Wladek's eyes fell on a magnificent silver band around his wrist with an inscription on it that he could not quite make out.

"You must be Wladek."

"Yes, sir," said the boy, neither sounding nor showing surprise that the Baron knew his name.

"It is you about whom I have come to see your father," said the Baron.

Wladek remained before the Baron, staring up at him. The trapper signified to his own children by a wave of his arm that they should leave him alone with his master, so two of them curtsied, four bowed and all six retreated silently into the loft. Wladek remained, and no one suggested he should do otherwise.

"Koskiewicz," began the Baron, still standing, as no one had invited him to sit. The trapper had not offered him a chair for two reasons: first, because he was too shy, and second, because he assumed the Baron was there to issue a reprimand. "I have come to ask a favor."

"Anything, sir, anything," said the father, wondering what he could give the Baron that he did not already have hundred-fold.

The Baron continued. "My son, Leon, is now six and is

being taught privately at the castle by two tutors, one from our native Poland and the other from Germany. They tell me he is a clever boy but lacks competition: he has only himself to beat. Mr. Kotowski at the village school tells me that Wladek is the only boy capable of providing the competition that Leon so badly needs. I wonder therefore if you would allow your son to leave the village school and join Leon and his tutors at the castle."

Wladek continued to stand before the Baron, gazing, while before him there opened a wondrous vision of food and drink, books and teachers wiser by far than Mr. Kotowski. He glanced toward his mother. She, too, was gazing at the Baron, her face filled with wonder and sorrow. His father turned to his mother and the instant of silent communication between them seemed an eternity to the child.

The trapper gruffly addressed the Baron's feet. "We would be honored, sir."

The Baron looked interrogatively at Helena Koskiewicz.

"The Blessed Virgin forbids that I should ever stand in my child's way," she said softly, "though she alone knows how much it will cost me."

"But Madam Koskiewicz, your son can return home regularly to see you."

"Yes, sir. I expect he will do so, at first." She was about to add some plea but decided against it.

The Baron smiled. "Good. It's settled then. Please bring the boy to the castle tomorrow morning by seven o'clock. During the school term Wladek will live with us, and when Christmas comes he can return to you."

Wladek burst into tears.

"Quiet, boy," said the trapper.

"I will not go," Wladek said firmly, really wanting to go.

"Quiet, boy," said the trapper, this time a little louder.

"Why not?" asked the Baron, with compassion in his voice.

"I will never leave Florcia—never."

"Florcia?" queried the Baron.

"My eldest daughter, sir," interjected the trapper. "Don't concern yourself with her, sir. The boy will do as he is told."

No one spoke. The Baron considered for a moment. Wladek continued to cry controlled tears.

"How old is the girl?" asked the Baron.

"Fourteen," replied the trapper.

"Could she work in the kitchens?" asked the Baron, relieved to observe that Helena Koskiewicz was not going to burst into tears as well.

"Oh yes, Baron," she replied. "Florcia can cook and she can sew and she can . . ."

"Good, good, then she can come as well. I shall expect to see them both tomorrow morning at seven."

The Baron walked to the door and looked back and smiled at Wladek, who returned the smile. Wladek had won his first bargain, and accepted his mother's tight embrace while he stared at the closed door and heard her whisper, "Ah, Matka's littlest one, what will become of you now?"

Wladek couldn't wait to find out.

Helena Koskiewicz packed for Wladek and Florentyna during the night, not that it would have taken long to pack the entire family's possessions. In the morning the remainder of the family stood in front of the door to watch them both depart for the castle, each holding a paper parcel under one arm. Florentyna, tall and graceful, kept looking back, crying and waving; but Wladek, short and ungainly, never once looked back. Florentyna held firmly to Wladek's hand for the entire journey to the Baron's castle. Their roles were now reversed; from that day on she was to depend on him.

They were clearly expected by the magnificent man in the embroidered suit of green livery who was summoned by their timid knock on the great oak door. Both children had gazed in admiration at the gray uniforms of the soldiers in the town who guarded the nearby Russian–Polish border, but they had never seen anything so resplendent as this liveried servant, towering above them and evidently of overwhelming importance. There was a thick carpet in the hall, and Wladek stared at the green-and-red pattern, amazed by its beauty, wondering if he should take his shoes off and surprised, when he walked across it, that his footsteps made no sound. The dazzling being conducted them to their bedrooms in the west wing. Separate bedrooms—would they ever get to sleep? At least there was a connecting door, so they need never be too far apart, and in fact for many nights they slept together in one bed.

When they had both unpacked, Florentyna was taken to the kitchen, and Wladek to a playroom in the south wing of the castle to meet the Baron's son. Leon was a tall, good-looking boy who was so immediately charming and welcoming that Wladek abandoned his prepared pugnacious posture with surprise and relief. Leon had been a lonely child, with no one to play with except his *niania*, the devoted Lithuanian woman who had breast-fed him and attended to his every need since the premature death of his mother. The stocky boy who had come out of the forest promised companionship. At least in one matter they both knew they had been deemed equals.

Leon immediately offered to show Wladek around the castle, and the tour took the rest of the morning. Wladek remained astounded by its size, the richness of the furniture and fabrics and those carpets in every room. To Leon he admitted only to being agreeably impressed: after all, he had won his place in the castle on merit. The main part of the building was early Gothic, explained the Baron's son, as if Wladek were sure to know what *Gothic* meant. Wladek nodded. Next Leon took his new friend down into the immense cellars, with line upon line of wine bottles covered in dust and cobwebs. Wladek's favorite room was the vast dining hall, with its massive pillared vaulting and flagged floor. There were animals' heads all around the walls. Leon told him they were bison, bear, elk, boar and wolverine. At the end of the room, resplendent, was the Baron's coat of arms below a stag's antlers. The Rosnovski family motto read:

"Fortune favors the brave." After a lunch, which Wladek ate so little of because he couldn't master a knife and fork, he met his two tutors, who did not give him the same warm welcome, and in the evening he climbed up onto the longest bed he had ever seen and told Florentyna about his adventures. Her excited eyes never once left his face, nor did she even close her mouth, agape with wonder, especially when she heard about the knife and fork.

The tutoring started at seven sharp, before breakfast, and continued throughout the day with only short breaks for meals. Initially, Leon was clearly ahead of Wladek, but Wladek wrestled determinedly with his books so that as the weeks passed, the gap began to narrow, while friendship and rivalry between the two boys developed simultaneously. The German and Polish tutors found it hard to treat their two pupils, the son of a baron and the son of a trapper, as equals, although they reluctantly conceded to the Baron when he inquired that Mr. Kotowski had made the right academic choice. The tutors' attitude toward Wladek never worried him, because he was always treated as an equal by Leon.

The Baron let it be known that he was pleased with the progress the two boys were making and from time to time he would reward Wladek with clothes and toys. Wladek's initial distant and detached admiration for the Baron developed into respect, and when the time came for the boy to return to the little cottage in the forest to rejoin his father and mother for Christmas, Wladek became distressed at the thought of leaving Leon.

His distress was well founded. Despite the initial happiness he felt at seeing his mother, the short space of three months that he had spent in the Baron's castle had revealed to him deficiencies in his own home of which he had previously been quite unaware. The holiday dragged on. Wladek felt himself stifled by the little cottage with its one room and loft, and dissatisfied by the food dished out in such meager amounts and then eaten by hand: no one had divided by nine at the castle. After two weeks Wladek longed to return to Leon and the Baron. Every afternoon he would walk the six *wiorsta* to the castle and sit and stare at the great walls that surrounded the estate. Florentyna, who had lived only among the kitchen servants, took to returning more easily and could not understand that the cottage would never be home again for Wladek. The trapper was not sure how to treat the boy, who was now well dressed, well-spoken and talked of things at six that the man did not begin to understand; nor did he want to. The boy seemed to do nothing but waste the entire day reading. Whatever would become of him, the trapper wondered, if he could not swing an axe or trap a hare; how could he ever hope to earn an honest living? He too prayed that the holiday would pass quickly.

Helena was proud of Wladek and at first avoided admitting to herself that a wedge had been driven between him and the rest of the children. But in the end it could not be avoided. Playing at soldiers one evening, both Stefan and Franck, generals on opposing sides, refused to have Wladek in their armies.

"Why must I always be left out?" cried Wladek. "I want to learn to fight too."

"Because you are not one of us," declared Stefan. "You are not really our brother."

There was a long silence before Franck continued. "Ojciec never wanted you in the first place; only Matka was on your side."

Wladek stood motionless and cast his eye around the circle of children, searching for Florentyna.

"What does Franck mean, I am not your brother?" he demanded.

Thus Wladek came to hear of the manner of his birth and to understand why he had always been set apart from his brothers and sisters. Though his mother's distress at his now total self-containment became oppressive, Wladek was secretly pleased to discover that, untouched by the meanness of the trapper's blood, he came of unknown stock, containing with it the germ of spirit that would now make all things seem possible.

When the unhappy holiday eventually came to an end,

Wladek returned to the castle with joy. Leon welcomed him back with open arms; for him, as isolated by the wealth of his father as was Wladek by the poverty of the trapper, it had also been a Christmas with little to celebrate. From then on the two boys grew very close and soon became inseparable. When the summer holidays came around, Leon begged his father to allow Wladek to remain at the castle. The Baron agreed, for he too had grown to respect Wladek. Wladek was overjoyed and entered the trapper's cottage only once again in his life.

When Wladek and Leon had finished their classroom work, they would spend the remaining hours playing games. Their favorite was *chow anego*, a sort of hide-and-seek, and because the castle had seventy-two rooms, the chance of repetition was very small. Wladek's favorite hiding place was in the dungeons under the castle, in which the only light by which one could be discovered came through a small stone grille set high in the wall, and even here one needed a candle to find one's way around. Wladek was not sure what purpose the dungeons served, and none of the servants ever made mention of them, since they had never been used in anyone's memory.

Wladek was conscious that he was Leon's equal only in the classroom and was no competition for his friend when they played any game other than chess. The river Shchara, which bordered the estate, became an extension to their playground. In spring they fished, in summer they swam, and in winter, when the river was frozen over, they would put on their wooden skates and chase each other across the ice, while Florentyna sat on the river bank anxiously warning them where the surface was thin. But Wladek never heeded her and was always the one who fell in. Leon grew quickly and strong; he ran well, swam well and never seemed to tire or be ill. Wladek became aware for the first time what good-looking and well built meant, and he knew when he swam, ran and skated he could never hope to keep up with Leon. Much worse, what Leon called the belly button was, on him, almost unnoticeable, while Wladek's was stumpy and ugly and protruded from the middle of his plump body. Wladek would spend long hours in the quiet of his own room, studying his physique in a mirror, always asking why, and in particular why only one nipple for him when all the boys he had ever seen bare-chested had the two that the symmetry of the human body appeared to require. Sometimes as he lay in bed unable to sleep, he would finger his naked chest and tears of self-pity would flood onto the pillow. He would finally fall asleep praying that when he awoke in the morning, things would be different. His prayers were not answered.

Wladek put aside a time each night to do physical exercises that could not be witnessed by anyone, even Florentyna. Through sheer determination he learned to hold himself so that he looked taller. He built up his arms and his legs and hung by the tips of his fingers from a beam in the bedroom in the hope that it would make him grow, but Leon grew taller even while he slept. Wladek was forced to accept the fact that he would always be a head shorter than the Baron's son, and that nothing, nothing was ever going to produce the missing nipple. Wladek's dislike of his own body was not prompted by Leon, who never commented on his friend's appearance; his knowledge of other children stopped short at Wladek, whom he adored uncritically.

Baron Rosnovski too became increasingly fond of the fierce dark-haired boy who had replaced the younger brother Leon had so tragically lost when the Baroness died in childbirth.

The two boys would dine with him in the great stonewalled hall each evening while the flickering candles cast ominous shadows from the stuffed animal heads on the walls, and the servants came and went noiselessly with great silver trays and golden plates, bearing geese, hams, crayfish, fine wine and fruits, and sometimes the *mazureks*, which had become Wladek's particular favorites. Afterward, as the darkness fell ever more thickly around the table, the Baron

dismissed the waiting servants and would tell the boys stories of Polish history and allowed them a sip of Danzig
vodka, in which the tiny gold leaves sparkled bravely in the
candlelight. Wladek begged as often as he dared for the
story of Tadeusz Kosciusko.

"A great patriot and hero," the Baron would reply. "The
very symbol of our struggle for independence, trained in
France . . ."

"Whose people we admire and love as we have learned to
hate all Russians and Austrians," supplied Wladek, whose
pleasure in the tale was enhanced by his word-perfect
knowledge of it.

"Who is telling whom the story, Wladek?" The Baron
laughed. ". . . and then fought with George Washington in
America for liberty and democracy. In 1792 he led the Poles
in battle at Dubienka. When our wretched king, Stanislaw
Augustus, deserted us to join the Russians, Kosciusko returned to the homeland he loved, to throw off the yoke of
tsardom. He won the battle of where, Leon?"

"Raclawice, sir, and then he freed Warsaw."

"Good, my child. Then, alas, the Russians mustered a
great force at Maciejowice and he was finally defeated and
taken prisoner. My great-great-great-grandfather fought
with Kosciusko on that day and later with Dabrowski's le-
gions for the mighty Napoleon Bonaparte."

"And for his service to Poland was created the Baron
Rosnovski, a title your family will ever bear in remembrance
of those great days," said Wladek as stoutly as if the title
would one day pass to him.

"Yes, and those great days will come again," said the
Baron quietly. "I only pray that I may live to see them."

That Christmas some of the peasants on the estate brought
their families to the castle for the celebration of the blessed
vigil. Throughout Christmas Eve they fasted, and the children would look out of the windows for the first star, which
was the sign the feast might begin. The Baron would say

grace in his fine, deep voice: *"Benedicte nobis, Domine Deus, et his donis quae ex liberalitate tua sumpturi sumus,"* and once they had sat down Wladek would be embarrassed by the huge capacity of Jasio Koskiewicz, who addressed himself squarely to every one of the thirteen courses, from the *barszcz* soup through to the cakes and plums, and would, as in previous years, be sick in the forest on the way home.

After the feast Wladek enjoyed distributing the gifts from the Christmas tree, laden with candles and fruit, to the awestruck peasant children—a doll for Sophia, a forest knife for Josef, a new dress for Florentyna—the first gift Wladek had ever requested of the Baron.

"It's true," said Josef to his mother when he received his gift from Wladek, "he is not our brother, Matka."

"No," she replied, "but he will always be my son."

Through the winter and spring of 1914 Wladek grew in strength and learning; then suddenly, in July, the German tutor left the castle without even saying farewell; neither boy was sure why. They never thought to connect his departure with the assassination in Sarajevo of the Archduke Francis Ferdinand by a student anarchist, the event described to them by their remaining tutor in unaccountably solemn tones. The Baron became withdrawn; neither boy was sure why. The younger servants, the children's favorites, inevitably began to disappear one by one; neither boy was sure why. As the year passed Leon grew taller, Wladek grew stronger and both boys became wiser.

One morning in August 1915, a time of fine, lazy days, the Baron set off on the long journey to Warsaw to put, as he described it, his affairs in order. He was away for three and a half weeks, twenty-five days that Wladek marked off each morning on a calendar in his bedroom; it seemed to him a lifetime. On the day the Baron was due to return, the two boys went down to the Slonim railway station to await the weekly train with its one carriage and greet the Baron on his arrival. The three of them traveled home in silence.

Wladek thought the great man looked tired and older, another unaccountable circumstance, and during the following week the Baron often conducted with the chief servants a rapid and anxious dialogue, broken off whenever Leon or Wladek entered the room, an uncharacteristic surreptitiousness that made the two boys uneasy and fearful that they were the unwitting cause of it. Wladek despaired that the Baron might send him back to the trapper's cottage—always aware he was a stranger in a stranger's home.

One evening a few days after the Baron had returned he called for the two boys to join him in the great hall. They crept in, fearful of him. Without explanation he told them that they were about to make a long journey. The little conversation, insubstantial as it seemed to Wladek at the time, remained with him for the rest of his life.

"My dear children," began the Baron in a low, faltering tone, "the warmongers of Germany and the Austro-Hungarian empire are at the throat of Warsaw and will soon be upon us."

Wladek recalled an inexplicable phrase flung out by the Polish tutor at the German tutor during their last tense days together. "Does that mean that the hour of the submerged peoples of Europe is at last upon us?" he asked.

The Baron regarded Wladek's innocent face tenderly. "Our national spirit has not perished in one hundred and fifty years of attrition and repression," he replied. "It may be that that fate of Poland is às much at stake as that of Serbia, but we are powerless to influence history. We are at the mercy of the three mighty empires that surround us."

"We are strong, we can fight," said Leon. "We have wooden swords and shields. We are not afraid of Germans or Russians."

"My son, you have only played at war. This battle will not be between children. We must now find a small, quiet place to live until history has decided our fate, and we must leave as soon as possible. I can only pray that this is not the end of your childhood."

Leon and Wladek were both mystified and irritated by the

Baron's words. War sounded like an exciting adventure, which they would be sure to miss if they left the castle. The servants took several days to pack the Baron's possessions, and Wladek and Leon were informed that they would be departing for their small summer home to the north of Grodno on the following Monday. The two boys continued, often unsupervised, with their work and play, but they found no one in the castle with the inclination or time to answer their myriad questions.

On Saturdays, lessons were held only in the morning. They were translating Adam Mickiewicz's *Pan Tadeusz* into Latin when they heard the guns. At first, Wladek thought the familiar sound meant only that another trapper was out shooting on the estate; the boys returned to the Bard of Czarnotas. A second volley of shots, much closer, made them look up, and then they heard the screams coming from downstairs. They stared at each other in bewilderment; they feared nothing, because they had never experienced anything in their short lives that should have made them fearful. The tutor fled, leaving them alone, and then came another shot, this time in the corridor outside their room. The two boys sat motionless, terrified and unbreathing.

Suddenly the door crashed open and a man no older than their tutor, in a gray soldier's uniform and steel helmet, stood towering over them. Leon clung to Wladek, while Wladek stared at the intruder. The soldier shouted at them in German, demanding to know who they were, but neither boy replied even though both had mastered the language as well as their mother tongue. Another soldier appeared behind his compatriot as the first advanced on the two boys, grabbed them by the necks, not unlike chickens, and pulled them out into the corridor, down the hall to the front of the castle and then into the gardens, where they found Florentyna screaming hysterically as she stared at the ground in front of her. Leon could not bear to look and buried his head in Wladek's shoulder. Wladek gazed as much in surprise as in horror at a row of dead bodies, mostly servants, being placed face downward. He was mesmerized by the sight of a mustache in profile against a pool of blood. It was the trapper. Wladek felt nothing as Florentyna continued screaming.

"Is Papa there?" asked Leon. "Is Papa there?"

Wladek scanned the line of bodies once again. He thanked God that there was no sign of the Baron Rosnovski. He was about to tell Leon the good news when a soldier came up to them.

"Wer hat gesprochen?" he demanded fiercely.

"Ich," said Wladek defiantly.

The soldier raised his rifle and brought the butt crashing down on Wladek's head. He sank to the ground, blood spurting over his face. Where was the Baron, what was happening, why were they being treated like this in their own home? Leon quickly jumped on top of Wladek, trying to protect him from the second blow that the soldier had intended for Wladek's stomach, but as the rifle came crashing down the full force caught the back of Leon's head.

Both boys lay motionless, Wladek because he was still dazed by the blow and the sudden weight of Leon's body on top of him, and Leon because he was dead.

Wladek could hear another soldier berating their tormentor for the action he had taken. They picked up Leon, but Wladek clung to him. It took two soldiers to prise his friend's body away and dump it unceremoniously with the others, facedown on the grass. Wladek's eyes never left the motionless body of his dearest friend until he was finally marched back inside the castle and, with a handful of dazed survivors, led to the dungeons. Nobody spoke for fear of joining the line of bodies on the grass, until the dungeon doors were bolted and the last murmur of the soldiers had vanished in the distance. Then Wladek said, "Holy God." For there in a corner, slumped against the wall, sat the Baron, uninjured but stunned, staring into space, alive only because the conquerors needed him to be responsible for the prisoners. Wladek went over to him, while the others sat as far away from their master as possible. The two gazed at each other as they had on the first day they had met. Wladek put his hand out and, as on the first day, the Baron took it. Wladek watched the tears course down the Baron's proud face. Neither spoke. They had both lost the person they had loved most in the world.

CHAPTER
SIX

William Kane grew quickly and was considered an adorable child by all who came in contact with him; in the early years of his life these were generally besotted relatives and doting servants.

The top floor of the Kanes' eighteenth-century house in Louisburg Square on Beacon Hill had been converted into nursery quarters, crammed with toys. A further bedroom and a sitting room were made available for the newly acquired nurse. The floor was far enough away from Richard Kane for him to be unaware of problems such as teething, wet diapers and the irregular and undisciplined cries for more food. First sound, first tooth, first step and first word were all recorded in a family book by William's mother along with the progress in his height and weight. Anne was surprised to find that these statistics differed very little from those of any other child with whom she came into contact on Beacon Hill.

The nurse, an import from England, brought the boy up on a regimen that would have gladdened the heart of a Prussian cavalry officer. William's father would visit him each evening at six o'clock. As he refused to address the child in baby language, he ended up not speaking to him at all; the two merely stared at each other. William would grip his father's index finger, the one with which balance sheets were checked, and hold on to it tightly. Richard would allow himself a smile. At the end of the first year the routine was slightly modified and the boy was allowed to come downstairs to see his father. Richard would sit in his high-backed, maroon leather chair, watching his firstborn weave his way on all fours in and out of the legs of the furniture, reappearing when least expected, which led Richard to observe that the child would undoubtedly become a senator. William took his first steps at thirteen months while clinging on to the tails of his father's topcoat. His first word was *Dada*, which pleased everyone, including Grandmother Kane and Grandmother Cabot, who were regular visitors. They did not actually push the vehicle in which William was perambulated around Boston, but they did deign to walk a pace behind the nurse in the park on Thursday afternoons, glaring at infants with a less disciplined retinue. While other children fed the ducks in the public gardens, William succeeded in charming the swans in the lake of Mr. Jack Gardner's extravagant Venetian Palace.

When two years had passed, the grandmothers intimated by hint and innuendo that it was high time for another prodigy, an appropriate sibling for William. Anne obliged them by becoming pregnant but was distressed to find herself feeling and looking progressively off-color as she entered her fourth month.

Dr. MacKenzie ceased to smile as he checked the growing stomach and hopeful mother, and when Anne miscarried at sixteen weeks, he was not altogether surprised but did not allow her to indulge her grief. In his notes he wrote: "preeclampsia?" and then told her, "Anne, my dear, the reason you have not been feeling so well is that your blood pressure was too high and would probably have become much higher as your pregnancy progressed. I fear doctors haven't found the answer to blood pressure yet; in fact, we know very little other than it's a dangerous condition for anyone, particularly for a pregnant woman."

Anne held back her tears while considering the implications of a future without more children.

"Surely it won't happen in my next pregnancy?" she

asked, phrasing her question to dispose the doctor to a favorable answer.

"I should be very surprised if it did not, my dear. I am sorry to have to say this to you, but I would strongly advise you against becoming pregnant again."

"But I don't mind feeling off-color for a few months if it means . . ."

"I am not talking about feeling off-color, Anne. I am talking about not taking any unneccessary risks with your life."

It was a terrible blow for Richard and Anne, who themselves had both been only children, largely as a result of their respective fathers' premature deaths. They had both assumed that they would produce a family appropriate to the commanding size of their house and their responsibilities to the next generation. "What else is there for a young woman to do?" inquired Grandmother Cabot of Grandmother Kane. No one cared to mention the subject again, and William became the center of everyone's attention.

Richard, who after six years on the board had taken over as the president of Kane and Cabot Bank and Trust Company, had always immersed himself in the work of the bank. The bank, which stood on State Street, a bastion of architectural and fiscal solidity, had offices in New York, London and San Francisco. The last had presented a problem to Richard on the very day of William's birth when, along with the Crocker National Bank, Wells Fargo and the California Bank, it collapsed to the ground, not financially but literally, in the great earthquake of 1906. Richard, by nature a cautious man, was comprehensively insured with Lloyd's of London. Gentlemen all, they had paid up to the penny, enabling Richard to rebuild. Nevertheless, Richard spent an uncomfortable year jolting across America on the four-day train journey between Boston and San Francisco in order to supervise the rebuilding. He opened the new office in Union Square in October 1907, barely in time to turn his attention to other problems arising on the Eastern Seaboard. There was a minor run on the New York banks, and many of the smaller establishments were unable to cope with large withdrawals and started going to the wall. J. P. Morgan, the legendary chairman of the mighty bank bearing his name, invited Richard to join a consortium to hold firm during the crisis. Richard agreed, the courageous stand worked, and the problem began to dissipate, but not before Richard had had a few sleepless nights.

William, on the other hand, slept soundly, unaware of the importance of earthquakes and collapsing banks. After all, there were swans that must be fed and endless trips to and from Milton, Brookline and Beverley so that he could be shown to his distinguished relatives.

Early in the spring of the following year Richard acquired a new toy in return for a cautious investment of captial in a man called Henry Ford, who was claiming he could produce a motor car for the people. The bank entertained Mr. Ford at luncheon, and Richard was coaxed into the acquisition of a Model T for the princely sum of $850. Henry Ford assured Richard that if only the bank would back him the cost could eventually fall to $350 within a few years and everyone would be buying his cars, thus insuring a large profit for his backers. Richard did back him, and it was the first time he had placed good money behind someone who wished his product to halve in price.

Richard was initially apprehensive that his motor car, somberly black though it was, might not be regarded as a serious mode of transport for the president and chairman of a bank, but he was reassured by the admiring glances from the sidewalks which the machine attracted. At ten miles an hour it was noisier than a horse, but it did have the virtue of leaving no mess in the middle of Mount Vernon Street. His only quarrel with Mr. Ford was that the man would not listen to the suggestion that a Model T should be made available in a variety of colors. Mr. Ford insisted that every car should be black in order to keep the price down. Anne, more sensitive than her husband to the approbation of polite society, would not drive in the vehicle until the Cabots had acquired one.

William, on the other hand, adored the "automobile," as the press called it, and immediately assumed that the vehicle had been bought for him to replace his now redundant and unmechanized pram. He also preferred the chauffeur—with his goggles and flat hat—to his nurse. Grandmother Kane and Grandmother Cabot claimed that they would never travel in the dreadful machine and never did, although it should be pointed out that Grandmother Kane traveled to her funeral in a motor car but was never informed.

During the next two years the bank grew in strength and size, as did William. Americans were once again investing for expansion, and large sums of money found their way to Kane and Cabot's to be reinvested in such projects as the expanding Lowell leather factory in Lowell, Massachusetts. Richard watched the growth of his bank and his son with unsurprised satisfaction. On William's fifth birthday, he took the child out of women's hands by engaging at $450 per annum a private tutor, a Mr. Munro, personally selected by Richard from a list of eight applicants who had earlier been screened by his private secretary. Mr. Munro was charged to ensure that William was ready to enter St. Paul's by the age of twelve. William immediately took to Mr. Munro, whom he thought to be very old and very clever. He was, in fact, twenty-three and the possessor of a second-class honors degree in English from the University of Edinburgh.

William quickly learned to read and write with facility but saved his real enthusiasm for figures. His only complaint was that, of the eight lessons taught every weekday, only one was arithmetic. William was quick to point out to his father that one-eighth of the working day was a small investment of time for someone who would one day be the president and chairman of a bank.

To compensate for his tutor's lack of foresight, William dogged the footsteps of his accessible relatives with demands for sums to be executed in his head. Grandmother Cabot, who had never been persuaded that the division of an integer by four would necessarily produce the same answer as its multiplication by one quarter—and indeed in her hands the two operations often did result in two different numbers—found herself speedily outclassed by her grandson; but Grandmother Kane, with some small leanings to cleverness, grappled manfully with vulgar fractions, compound interest and the division of eight cakes among nine children.

"Grandmother," said William kindly but firmly when she had failed to find the answer to his latest conundrum, "you can buy me a slide rule; then I won't have to bother you."

She was astonished at her grandson's precocity, but she bought him one just the same, wondering if he really knew how to use the gadget. It was the first time in her life that Grandmother Kane had been known to take the easy way out of any problem.

Richard's problems began to gravitate eastward. The chairman of his London branch died at his desk and Richard felt himself required in Lombard Street. He suggested to Anne that she and William accompany him to Europe, feeling that the education would not do the boy any harm: he could visit all the places about which Mr. Munro had so often talked. Anne, who had never been to Europe, was excited by the prospect, and filled three steamer trunks with elegant and expensive new clothes in which to confront the Old World. William considered it unfair of his mother not to allow him to take the equally essential aid to travel, his bicycle.

The Kanes traveled to New York by train to join the *Aquitania* bound for her voyage to Southampton. Anne was appalled by the sight of the immigrant street peddlers pushing their wares, and she was glad to be safely on board and resting in her cabin. William, on the other hand, was amazed by the size of New York; he had, until that moment, always imagined that his father's bank was the biggest building in America, if not the world. He wanted to buy a pink-and-yellow ice cream from a man with a little cart, but his father would not hear of it; in any case, Richard never carried small change. William adored the great vessel on sight and quickly became friendly with the captain, who showed him all the secrets of the Cunard steamships' prima donna. Richard and Anne, who naturally sat at the captain's table, felt it necessary before the ship had long left America to apologize for the amount of the crew's time that their son was occupying.

"Not at all," replied the white-bearded skipper. "William and I are already good friends. I only wish I could answer all his questions about time, speed and distance. I have to be coached each night by the first engineer in the hope of first anticipating and then surviving the next day."

The *Aquitania* sailed into The Solent to dock at Southampton after a ten-day crossing. William was reluctant to leave her, and tears would have been unavoidable had it not been for the magnificent sight of the Rolls-Royce Silver Ghost, sitting at the quayside complete with a chauffeur, ready to whisk them off to London. Richard decided on the spur of the moment that he would have the car transported back to New York at the end of the trip, a decision more out of character than any he would make during the rest of his life. He informed Anne that he wanted to show the vehicle to Henry Ford.

The Kane family always stayed at the Ritz in Piccadilly when they were in London, which was convenient to Richard's office in the City. Anne used the time while Richard was occupied at the bank to show William the Tower of London, Buckingham Palace and the Changing of the Guard. William thought everything was "great" except the English accent, which he had difficulty in understanding.

"Why don't they talk like us, Mommy?" he demanded, and was surprised to be told that the question was more often put the other way around, as "they" came first. William's favorite pastime was watching the soldiers in their bright red uniforms with large, shiny brass buttons who kept guard duty outside Buckingham Palace. He tried to talk to them, but they stared past him into space and never even blinked.

"Can we take one home?" he asked his mother.

"No, darling, they have to stay here and guard the King."

"But he's got so many of them, can't I have just one?"

As a "special treat"—Anne's words—Richard allowed himself an afternoon off to take William and Anne to the West End to see a traditional English pantomime called "Jack and the Beanstalk" playing at the London Hippodrome. William loved Jack and immediately wanted to cut down every tree he laid his eyes on, imagining them all to be sheltering a monster. They had tea after the show at Fortnum and Mason in Piccadilly, and Anne let William have two cream buns and a thing called a doughnut. Daily thereafter William had to be escorted back to the tea room at Fortnum's to consume another "doughbun," as he called them.

The holiday passed by all too quickly for William and his mother, but Richard, satisfied with his progress in Lombard Street and pleased with his newly appointed chairman, began to look forward to the day of their departure. Cables were arriving daily from Boston, which made him anxious to be back in his own boardroom. Finally, when one such missive informed him that 2,500 workers at a cotton mill with which his bank had a heavy investment in Lawrence, Massachusetts, had gone out on strike, he was glad that his planned date of sailing was only three days away.

William was looking forward to returning and telling Mr. Munro all the exciting things he had done in England and to being reunited with his two grandmothers. They had never done anything so exciting as visiting a real live theater with the general public. Anne was also not unhappy to be going home, although she had enjoyed the trip almost as much as William, for her clothes and beauty had been much admired by the normally undemonstrative English. As a final treat for William the day before they were due to sail, Anne took him to a tea party in Eaton Square given by the wife of the newly appointed chairman of Richard's London branch. She, too, had a son, Stuart, who was eight—and William had, in the two weeks in which they had been playing together, grown to regard him as an indispensable grown-up friend. The party, however, was rather subdued because Stuart felt unwell and William, in sympathy with his new chum, an-

nounced to his mother that he was going to be ill too. Anne
and William returned to the Ritz Hotel earlier than they had
planned. She was not greatly put out, as this gave her a little
more time to supervise the repacking of the large steamer
trunks, although she was convinced William was only putting on an act to please Stuart. When she put William to bed
that night, she found that he had been as good as his word
and was running a slight fever. She remarked on it to
Richard over dinner.

"Probably all the excitement at the thought of going
home," he offered, sounding unconcerned.

"I hope so," replied Anne. "I don't want him to be sick on
a six-day sea voyage."

"He'll be just fine by tomorrow," said Richard, issuing a
directive that would go unheeded, but when Anne went to
wake William the next morning, she found him covered in
little red spots and running a temperature of 103. The hotel
doctor diagnosed measles and was politely insistent that
William on no account be sent on a sea journey, not only for
his own good but for the sake of the other passengers. There
was nothing for it but to leave him in bed with his stone hot-
water bottle and wait until he was fully recovered. Richard
was unable to countenance the two-week delay and decided
to sail as planned. Reluctantly, Anne allowed the hurried
changes of booking to be made. William begged his father to
let him accompany him: the fourteen days before the ship
was due back in Southampton seemed like an eternity to the
child. Richard was adamant and hired a nurse to attend
William and convince him of his poor state of health.

Anne traveled down to Southampton with Richard in the
new Rolls-Royce.

"I shall be lonely in London without you, Richard," she
ventured diffidently in their parting moment, risking his disapproval of emotional women.

"Well, my dear, I dare say I shall be somewhat lonely in
Boston without you," he said, his mind on the striking mill-
workers.

Anne returned to London on the train, wondering how

she would occupy herself for the next two weeks. William had a better night and in the morning the spots looked less ferocious. Doctor and nurse were unanimous however in their insistence that he remain in bed. Anne used the extra time to write long letters to the family, while William remained in bed, protesting, but on Tuesday morning he got himself up early and went into his mother's room, very much back to his normal self. He climbed into bed next to her and immediately his cold hands woke her up. Anne was relieved to see him so obviously fully recovered. She rang to order breakfast in bed for both of them, an indulgence William's father would never have countenanced.

There was a quiet knock on the door and a man in gold-and-red livery entered with a large silver breakfast tray. Eggs, bacon, tomato, toast and marmalade—a veritable feast. William looked at the food ravenously as if he could not remember when he had last eaten a full meal. Anne casually glanced at the morning paper. Richard always read *The Times* when he stayed in London, so the management assumed she would require it as well.

"Oh, look," said William, staring at the photograph on an inside page, "a picture of Daddy's ship. What's a ca-la-mity, Mommy?"

All across the width of the newspaper was a picture of the *Titanic*.

Anne, unmindful of behaving as should a Cabot or a Kane, burst into frenzied tears, clinging to her only son. They sat in bed for several minutes, holding on to each other, William wasn't sure why. Anne realized that they had both lost the one person whom they had loved most in the world.

Sir Piers Campbell, young Stuart's father, arrived at Suite 107 of the Ritz. He waited in the lounge while the widow put on a suit, the only dark piece of clothing she possessed. William dressed himself, still not certain what a calamity was. Anne asked Sir Piers to explain the full implications of the news to her son, who only said, "I wanted to be on the ship with him, but they wouldn't let me go." He didn't cry, because he refused to believe anything could kill his father. He would be among the survivors.

In all Sir Piers's career as a politician, diplomat and now chairman of Kane and Cabot, London, he had never seen such self-containment in one so young. Presence is given to very few, he was heard to remark some years later. It had been given to Richard Kane and had been passed on to his only son. On Thursday of that week William was six, but he didn't open any of his gifts.

The lists of survivors, arriving spasmodically from America, were checked and double-checked by Anne. Each confirmed that Richard Lowell Kane was still missing at sea, presumed drowned. After a further week even William had almost abandoned hope of his father's survival.

Anne found it painful to board the *Aquitania*, but William was strangely eager to put to sea. Hour after hour, he would sit on the observation deck, scanning the featureless water.

"Tomorrow I will find him," he promised his mother again and again, at first confidently and then in a voice that barely disguised his own disbelief.

"William, no one can survive for three weeks in the North Atlantic."

"Not even my father?"

"Not even your father."

When Anne returned to Boston, both grandmothers were waiting for her at the Red House, mindful of the duty that had been thrust upon them. The responsibility had been passed back to the grandmothers. Anne passively accepted their proprietary role. Life had little purpose left for her other than William, whose destiny they now seemed determined to control. William was polite but uncooperative. During the day he sat silently in his lessons with Mr. Munro and at night wept into the lap of his mother.

"What he needs is the company of other children," declared the grandmothers briskly, and they dismissed Mr. Munro and the nurse and sent William to Sayre Academy in the hope that an introduction to the real world and the constant company of other children might bring him back to his old self.

Richard had left the bulk of his estate to William, to remain in the family trust until his twenty-first birthday. There was a codicil to the will. Richard expected his son to become president and chairman of Kane and Cabot on merit. It was the only part of his father's testament that inspired William, for the rest was his by birthright. Anne received a capital sum of $500,000 and an income for life of $100,000 a year after taxes, which would cease at once if she remarried. She also received the house on Beacon Hill, the summer mansion on the North Shore, the home in Maine and a small island off Cape Cod, all of which were to pass to William on his mother's death. Both grandmothers received $250,000 and letters leaving them in no doubt about their responsibility if Richard died before them. The family trust was to be handled by the bank, with William's godparents acting as cotrustees. The income from the trust was to be reinvested each year in conservative enterprises.

It was a full year before the grandmothers came out of mourning, and although Anne was still only twenty-eight, she looked her age for the first time in her life.

The grandmothers, unlike Anne, concealed their grief from William until he finally reproached them for it.

"Don't you miss my father?" he asked, gazing at Grandmother Kane with the blue eyes that brought back memories of her own son.

"Yes, my child, but he would not have wished us to sit around and feel sorry for ourselves."

"But I want us to always remember him—always," said William, his voice cracking.

"William, I am going to speak to you for the first time as though you were quite grown up. We will always keep his memory hallowed between us, and you shall play your own part by living up to what your father would have expected of you. You are the head of the family now and the heir to a large fortune. You must, therefore, prepare yourself through work to be fit for that inheritance in the same spirit in which your father worked to increase the inheritance for you."

William made no reply. He was thus provided with the motive for life which he had lacked before and he acted upon his grandmother's advice. He learned to live with his sorrow without complaining, and from that moment on he threw himself steadfastly into his work at school, satisfied only if Grandmother Kane seemed impressed. At no subject did he fail to excel, and in mathematics he was not only top of his class but far ahead of his years. Anything his father had achieved, he was determined to better. He grew even closer to his mother and became suspicious of anyone who was not family, so that he was often thought of as a solitary child, a loner and, unfairly, a snob.

The grandmothers decided when William was in his seventh year that the time had come to instruct the boy in the value of money. They therefore allowed him pocket money of one dollar a week but insisted that he keep an inventory accounting for every cent he had spent. With this in mind, they presented him with a green leather-bound ledger, at a cost of 95 cents, which they deducted from his first week's allowance of one dollar. From the second week the grandmothers divided the dollar every Saturday morning. William invested 50 cents, spent 20 cents, gave 10 cents to any charity of his choice and kept 20 cents in reserve. At the end of each quarter the grandmothers would inspect the ledger and his written report on any transactions. When the first three months had passed, William was well ready to account for himself. He had given $1.30 to the newly founded Boy Scouts of America, and invested $5.55, which he had asked Grandmother Kane to place in a savings account at the bank of his godfather, J. P. Morgan. He had spent $2.60 for which he did not have to account, and had kept $2.60 in reserve. The ledger was a source of great satisfaction to the grandmothers: there was no doubt William was the son of Richard Kane.

At school, William still made few friends, partly because he was shy of mixing with anyone other than Cabots, Lowells or children from families wealthier than his own. This restricted his choice severely, so he became a somewhat broody child, which worried his mother, who wanted William to lead a more normal existence and did not in her heart approve of the ledger or the investment program. Anne would have preferred William to have a lot of young friends rather than old advisors, to get himself dirty and bruised rather than remain spotless, to collect toads and turtles rather than stocks and company reports—in short, to be like any other little boy. But she never had the courage to tell the grandmothers about her misgivings and in any case the grandmothers were not interested in any other little boy.

On his ninth birthday William presented the ledger to his grandmothers for the second annual inspection. The green leather book showed a saving during the two years of more than fifty dollars. He was particularly proud to point out to the grandmothers an old entry marked "B6," showing that he had taken his money out of J. P. Morgan's Bank immediately on hearing of the death of the great financier, because he had noted that his own father's bank's stock had fallen in value after his death had been announced. William had reinvested the same amount three months later before the public realized the company was bigger than any one man.

The grandmothers were suitably impressed and allowed William to trade in his old bicycle and purchase a new one, after which he still had a capital sum of over $100, which his Grandmother Kane invested for him in the Standard Oil Company of New Jersey. Oil, William said knowingly, could only become more expensive. He kept the ledger meticulously up to date until his twenty-first birthday. Had the grandmothers still been alive then, they would have been proud of the final entry in the right-hand column marked "Assets."

CHAPTER
SEVEN

Wladek was the only one of those left alive who knew the dungeons well. In his days of hide-and-seek with Leon he had spent many happy hours in the freedom of the small stone rooms, carefree in the knowledge that he could return to the castle whenever it suited him.

There were in all four dungeons, on two levels. Two of the rooms, a larger and a smaller one, were at ground level. The smaller one was adjacent to the castle wall, which afforded a thin filter of light through a grille set high in the stones. Down five steps there were two more stone rooms in perpetual darkness and with little air. Wladek led the Baron into the small upper dungeon, where he remained sitting in a corner, silent and motionless, staring fixedly into space; the boy then appointed Florentyna to be the Baron's personal servant.

As Wladek was the only person who dared to remain in the same room as the Baron, the servants never questioned his authority. Thus, at the age of nine, he took on the day-to-day responsibility for his fellow prisoners. The new occupants of the dungeons, their placidity rendered into miserable stupefaction by incarceration, found nothing strange in a situation that had put a nine-year-old in control of their lives. And in the dungeons he became their master. He split the remaining twenty-four servants into three groups of eight, trying to keep families together wherever possible. He moved them regularly in a shift system: the first eight hours in the upper dungeons for light, air, food and exercise, the second and most popular shift of eight hours working in the castle for their captors, and the final eight hours given over to sleep in one of the lower dungeons. No one except the Baron and Florentyna could be quite sure when Wladek slept, as he was always there at the end of every shift to supervise the servants as they moved on. Food was distributed every twelve hours. The guards would hand over a skin of goat's milk, black bread, millet and occasionally some nuts, all of which Wladek would divide by twenty-eight, always giving two portions to the Baron without ever letting him know.

Once Wladek had each shift organized, he would return to the Baron in the smaller dungeon. Initially he expected guidance from him, but the fixed gaze of his master was as implacable and comfortless in its own way as were the eyes of the constant succession of German guards. The Baron had never once spoken from the moment he had been thrust into captivity in his own castle. His beard had grown long and matted on his chest, and his strong frame was beginning to decline into frailty. The once proud look had been replaced with one of resignation. Wladek could scarcely remember the well-loved voice of his patron and accustomed himself to the thought that he would never hear it again. After a while he complied with the Baron's unspoken wishes by also remaining silent in his presence.

When he had lived in the safety of the castle, Wladek had never thought of the previous day with so much occupying him from hour to hour. Now he was unable to remember even the previous hour, because nothing ever changed. Hopeless minutes turned into hours, hours into days, and then months that he soon lost track of. Only the arrival of food, darkness or light indicated that another twelve hours had passed, while the intensity of that light, and its eventual giving way to storms, and then ice forming on the dungeon walls, melting only when a new sun appeared, heralded each season in a manner that Wladek could never have learned from a nature study lesson. During the long nights, Wladek became even more aware of the stench of death that permeated even the farthest corners of the four dungeons, alleviated occasionally by the morning sunshine, a cool breeze or the most blessed relief of all, the return of rain.

At the end of one day of unremitting storms, Wladek and Florentyna took advantage of the rain by washing themselves in a puddle of water which formed on the stone floor of the upper dungeon. Neither of them noticed that the Baron's eyes widened as Wladek removed his tattered shirt and rolled over in the relatively clean water, continuing to rub himself until white streaks appeared on his body. Suddenly, the Baron spoke.

"Wladek"—the word was barely audible—"I cannot see you clearly," he said, the voice cracking. "Come here."

Wladek was stupefied by the sound of his patron's voice after so long a silence and didn't even look in his direction. He was immediately sure that it presaged the madness that already held two of the older servants in its grip.

"Come here, boy."

Wladek obeyed fearfully and stood before the Baron, who narrowed his enfeebled eyes in a gesture of intense concentration as he groped toward the boy. He ran his finger over Wladek's chest and then peered at him incredulously.

"Wladek, can you explain this small deformity?"

"No, sir," said Wladek, embarrassed. "It has been with me since birth. My foster mother used to say it was the mark of God the Father upon me."

"Stupid woman. It is the mark of your own father," the Baron said softly, and relapsed into silence for some minutes. Wladek remained standing in front of him, not moving a muscle. When at last the Baron spoke again, his voice was brisk. "Sit down, boy."

Wladek obeyed immediately. As he sat down, he noticed once again the heavy band of silver, now hanging loosely around the Baron's wrist. A shaft of light through a crack in the wall made the magnificent engraving of the Rosnovski coat of arms glitter in the darkness of the dungeon.

"I do not know how long the Germans intend to keep us locked up here. I thought at first that this war would be over in a matter of weeks. I was wrong, and we must now consider the possibility that it will continue for a very long time. With that thought in mind, we must use our time more constructively, as I know my life is nearing an end."

"No, no," Wladek began to protest, but the Baron continued as if he had not heard him.

"Yours, my child, has yet to begin. I will, therefore, undertake the continuation of your education."

The Baron did not speak again that day. It was as if he was considering the implications of his pronouncement. Thus Wladek gained his new tutor, and as they possessed neither reading nor writing materials, he was made to repeat everything the Baron said. He was taught great tracts from the poems of Adam Mickiewicz and Jan Kochanowski and long passages from *The Aeneid*. In that austere classroom Wladek learned geography, mathematics and added to his command of four languages—Russian, German, French and English. But once again his happiest moments were when he was taught history. The history of his nation through a hundred years of partition, the disappointed hopes for a united Poland, the further anguish of the Poles at Napoleon's crushing loss to Russia in 1812. He learned of the brave tales of earlier and happier times, when King Jan Casimir had dedicated Poland to the Blessed Virgin after repulsing the Swedes at Czestochowa, and how the mighty Prince Radziwill, great landowner and lover of hunting, had held his court in the great castle near Warsaw. Wladek's final lesson each day was on the family history of the Rosnovskis. Again and again he was told—never tiring of the tale—how the Baron's illustrious ancestor who had served in 1794 under General Dabrowski and then in 1809 under Napoleon himself had been rewarded by the great Emperor with land and a barony. He also learned that the Baron's grandfather had sat on the Council of Warsaw and that his father had played his own part in building the new Poland. Wladek found such happiness when the Baron turned his little dungeon room into a classroom.

The guards at the dungeon door were changed every four hours and conversation between them and the prisoners was *strengst verboten.* In snatches and fragments Wladek learned of the progress of the war, of the actions of Hindenburg and Ludendorff, of the rise of revolution in Russia and of her subsequent withdrawal from the war by the Treaty of Brest-Litovsk.

Wladek began to believe that the only escape from the dungeons for the inmates was death. The doors to that filthy hellhole opened nine times during the next two years, and Wladek began to wonder if he was equipping himself with knowledge that would be useless if he never again knew freedom.

The Baron continued to tutor him despite his progressively failing sight and hearing. Wladek had to sit closer and closer to him each day.

Florentyna—his sister, mother and closest friend—engaged in a more physical struggle against the rankness of their predicament. Occasionally the guards would provide her with a fresh bucket of sand or straw to cover the soiled floor, and the stench became a little less oppressive for the next few days. Vermin scuttled around in the darkness for any dropped scraps of bread or potato and brought with them disease and still more filth. The sour smell of decomposed human and animal urine and excrement assaulted their nostrils and regularly brought Wladek to a state of sickness and nausea. He longed above all to be clean again and would sit for hours gazing at the dungeon ceiling, recalling the steaming tubs of hot water and the good, rough soap with which the *niania* had, so short a distance away and so long a time ago, washed the accretion of a mere day's fun from Leon and himself, with many a muttering and *tut-tut* for muddy knees or a dirty fingernail.

By the spring of 1918, only fifteen of the twenty-six captives incarcerated with Wladek were still alive. The Baron was always treated by everyone as the master, while Wladek had become his acknowledged steward. Wladek felt saddest for his beloved Florentyna, now twenty. She had long since despaired of life and was convinced that she was going to spend her remaining days in the dungeons. Wladek never admitted in her presence to giving up hope, but although he was only twelve, he too was beginning to wonder if he dared believe in any future.

One evening, early in the fall, Florentyna came to Wladek's side in the larger upper dungeon.

"The Baron is calling for you."

Wladek rose quickly, leaving the allocation of food to a senior servant, and went to the old man. The Baron was in severe pain, and Wladek saw with terrible clarity—as though for the first time—how illness had eroded whole areas of the Baron's flesh, leaving the green-mottled skin covering a now skeletal face. The Baron asked for water, and Florentyna brought it from the half-full mug that hung from a stick outside the stone grille. When the great man had finished drinking, he spoke slowly and with considerable difficulty.

"You have seen so much of death, Wladek, that one more will make little difference to you. I confess that I no longer fear escaping this world."

"No, no, it can't be!" cried Wladek, clinging to the old man for the first time in his life. "We have so nearly triumphed. Don't give up, Baron. The guards have assured me that the war is coming to an end and then we will soon be released."

"They have been promising us that for months, Wladek. We cannot believe them any longer, and in any case I fear I have no desire to live in the new world they are creating." He paused as he listened to the boy crying. The Baron's only thought was to collect the tears as drinking water, and then he remembered that tears were saline and he laughed to himself. "Call for my butler and first footman, Wladek."

Wladek obeyed immediately, not knowing why they should be required.

The two servants, awakened from a deep sleep, came and stood in front of the Baron. After three years' captivity sleep was the easiest commodity to come by. They still wore their embroidered uniforms, but one could no longer tell that they had once been the proud Rosnovski colors of green and gold. They stood silently waiting for their master to speak.

"Are they there, Wladek?" asked the Baron.

"Yes, sir. Can you not see them?" Wladek realized for the first time that the Baron was now completely blind.

"Bring them forward so that I might touch them."

Wladek brought the two men to him and the Baron touched their faces.

"Sit down," he commanded them. "Can you both hear me, Ludwik, Alfons?"

"Yes, sir."

"My name is Baron Rosnovski."

"We know, sir," the butler responded innocently.

"Do not interrupt me," said the Baron. "I am about to die."

Death had become so common that the two men made no protest.

"I am unable to make a new will as I have no paper, quill or ink. Therefore I make my testament in your presence and you can act as my two witnesses as recognized by the ancient law of Poland. Do you understand what I am saying?"

"Yes, sir," the two men replied in unison.

"My firstborn son, Leon, is dead"—the Baron paused—"and so I leave my entire estate and possessions to the boy known as Wladek Koskiewicz."

Wladek realized he had not heard his surname for many years and did not immediately comprehend the significance of the Baron's words.

"And as proof of my resolve," the Baron continued, "I give him the family band."

The old man slowly raised his right arm, removed the sil-

ver band from his wrist and held it forward to a speechless
Wladek, whom he clasped firmly, running his fingers over
the boy's chest as if to be sure that it was he. "My son," he
said as he placed the silver band on the boy's wrist.

Wladek wept, and lay in the arms of the Baron all night
until he could no longer hear his heart and could feel the fingers stiffening around him. In the morning the Baron's body
was removed by the guards and they allowed Wladek to bury
him by the side of his son, Leon, in the family churchyard,
up against the chapel. As the body was lowered into its shallow grave, dug by Wladek's bare hands, the Baron's tattered
shirt fell open. Wladek stared at the dead man's chest.

He had only one nipple.

Thus Wladek Koskiewicz, aged twelve, inherited 60,000
acres of land, one castle, two manor houses, twenty-seven
cottages and a valuable collection of paintings, furniture and
jewelry, while he lived in a small stone room under the earth.
From that day on, the remaining captives took him as their
rightful master; and his empire was four dungeons, his retinue thirteen broken servants, plus his only love, Florentyna.

He returned to what he felt was now an endless routine
until late in the winter of 1918. On a mild, dry day, there
burst upon the prisoners' ears a volley of shots and the sound
of a brief struggle. Wladek was sure that the Polish army had
come to rescue him and that he would now be able to lay
claim to his rightful inheritance. When the German guards
deserted the iron door of the dungeons, the inmates remained huddled in terrified silence in the lower rooms.
Wladek stood alone at the entrance, twisting the silver band
around his wrist, triumphant, waiting for his liberators.
Eventually those who had defeated the Germans arrived and
spoke in the coarse Slavic tongue, familiar from school
days, which he had learned to fear even more than German.
Wladek was dragged unceremoniously out into the passage
with his retinue. The prisoners waited, then were cursorily
inspected and thrown back into the dungeons. The new con-

querors were unaware that this twelve-year-old boy was the master of all their eyes beheld. They did not speak his tongue. Their orders were clear and not to be questioned: kill the enemy if they resist the agreement of Brest-Litovsk, which made this section of Poland theirs, and send those who do not resist to Camp 201 for the rest of their days. The Germans had left with only token resistance, to retreat behind their new border, while Wladek and his followers waited, hopeful of a new life, ignorant of their impending fate.

After spending two more nights in the dungeons, Wladek resigned himself to believing that they were to be incarcerated for another long spell. The new guards did not speak to him at all, a reminder of what life had been like three years before; he began to realize that hell had temporarily been lax under the Germans but once again was tight.

On the morning of the third day, much to Wladek's surprise, they were all dragged out on to the grass in front of the castle, fifteen thin, filthy bodies. Two of the servants collapsed in the unaccustomed sun. Wladek himself found the intense brightness his biggest problem and kept having to shield his eyes. The prisoners stood in silence on the grass and waited for the soldiers' next move. The guards made them all strip and ordered them down to the river to wash. Wladek hid the silver band in his clothes and ran down to the water's edge, his legs feeling weak even before he reached the river. He jumped in, gasping for breath at the coldness of the water, although it felt glorious on his skin. The rest of the prisoners joined him and tried vainly to remove three years of filth.

When Wladek came out of the river exhausted, he noticed that the guards were looking strangely at Florentyna as she washed herself in the water. They were laughing and pointing at her. The other women did not seem to arouse the same degree of interest. One of the guards, a large, ugly man whose eyes had never left Florentyna for a moment, grabbed her arm as she passed him on her way back up the riverbank and threw her to the ground and started to take his clothes off quickly, hungrily, while at the same time folding them neatly on the grass. Wladek stared in disbelief at the man's swollen, erect penis and flew at the soldier, who was now holding Florentyna down on the ground, and hit him in the middle of his stomach with his head with all the force he could muster. The man reeled back and a second soldier grabbed Wladek and held him helpless with his hands pinned behind his back. The commotion attracted the attention of the other guards and they strolled over to watch. Wladek's captor was now laughing, a loud belly laugh with no humor in it. The other soldiers' words only added to Wladek's anguish.

"Enter the great protector," said the first.

"Come to defend his nation's honor." The second one.

"Let's at least allow him a ringside view." The one who was holding him.

More laughter interspersed the remarks that Wladek couldn't always comprehend. He watched the naked soldier advance his hard, well-fed body slowly toward Florentyna, who started screaming. Once again Wladek struggled, trying desperately to free himself from the viselike grip, but he was helpless in the arms of the guard. The naked man fell clumsily on top of Florentyna and started kissing her and slapping her when she tried to fight or turn away; finally he lunged into her. She let out a scream such as Wladek had never heard before. The guards continued talking and laughing among themselves, some not even watching.

"Goddamn virgin," said the first soldier as he withdrew himself from her.

They all laughed.

"You've just made it a little easier for me," said the second guard.

More laughter. As Florentyna stared into Wladek's eyes, he began to retch. The soldier holding on to him showed little interest, other than to be sure that none of the boy's vomit soiled his uniform or boots. The first soldier, his penis now covered in blood, ran down to the stream, yelling as he hit the water. The second man undressed, while yet another held

Florentyna down. The second guard took a little longer over his pleasure and seemed to gain considerable satisfaction from hitting Florentyna; when he finally entered her, she screamed again but not quite so loud as before.

"Come on, Valdi, you've had enough."

With that the man came out of her suddenly and joined his companion-at-arms in the stream. Wladek made himself look at Florentyna. She was bruised and bleeding between the legs. The soldier holding him spoke again.

"Come and hold the little bastard, Boris. It's my turn."

The first soldier came out of the river and took hold of Wladek firmly. Again Wladek tried to hit out and this made the soldiers laugh again.

"Now we know the full might of the Polish army."

The unbearable laughter continued as yet another guard started undressing to take his turn with Florentyna, who now lay indifferent to his charms. When he had finished and had gone down to the river, the second soldier returned and started putting on his clothes.

"I think she's beginning to enjoy it," he said as he sat in the sun watching his companion. The fourth soldier began to advance on Florentyna. When he reached her, he turned her over, forced her legs as wide apart as possible, his large hands moving rapidly over her frail body. The scream when she was entered had now turned into a groan. Wladek counted sixteen soldiers who raped his sister. When the last soldier had finished with her, he swore and then added, "I think I've made love to a dead woman," and left her motionless on the grass.

They all laughed even more loudly, as the disgruntled soldier walked down to the river. At last Wladek's guard released him. He ran to Florentyna's side while the soldiers lay on the grass drinking wine and vodka taken from the Baron's cellar and eating the bread from the kitchens.

With the help of two of the servants, Wladek carried Florentyna to the edge of the river, and there he wept as he tried to wash away her blood and bruises. It was useless, for she was black and red all over, insensible to help and unable to speak. When Wladek had done the best he could, he covered her body with his jacket and held her in his arms. He kissed her gently on the mouth, the first woman he had ever kissed. She lay in his arms, but he knew she did not recognize him, and as the tears ran down his face onto her bruised body, he felt her go limp. He wept as he carried her dead body up the bank. The guards went silent as they watched him walk toward the chapel. He laid her down on the grass beside the Baron's grave and started digging with his bare hands. When the sinking sun had caused the castle to cast its long shadow over the graveyard, he had finished digging. He buried Florentyna next to Leon and made a little cross with two sticks which he placed at her head. Wladek collapsed on the ground between Leon and Florentyna, immediately falling asleep, caring not if he ever woke again.

CHAPTER
EIGHT

William returned to Sayre Academy in September more settled and willing to mix. He immediately began to look for
competition among those older than himself. Whatever he
took up, he was never satisfied unless he excelled at it, and
his contemporaries almost always proved too weak an opposition. William began to realize that most of those from
backgrounds as privileged as his own lacked any incentive to
compete, and that fiercer rivalry was to be found from boys
who had, compared with himself, relatively little.

In 1915 a craze for collecting matchbox labels hit Sayre
Academy. William observed this frenzy for a week with
great interest but did not join in. Within a few days, common
labels were changing hands at a dime, while rarities commanded as much as fifty cents. William considered the situation and decided to become not a collector but a dealer.

On the following Saturday he went to Leavitt and Peirce,
one of the largest tobacconists in Boston, and spent the afternoon taking down the names and addresses of major
match box manufacturers throughout the world, making a
special note of those nations that were not at war. He invested five dollars in notepaper, envelopes and stamps and
wrote to the chairman or president of every company he had
listed. His letter was simple despite having been rewritten
seven times.

Dear Mr. Chairman:

I am a dedicated collector of matchbox labels, but I cannot afford to buy all the matches. My pocket money is only one dollar a week, but I enclose a three-cent stamp for postage to prove that I am serious about my hobby. I am sorry to bother you personally, but yours was the only name I could find to write to.

Your friend,
William Kane (aged 9)

P.S. Yours are one of my favorites.

Within two weeks, William had a 55 percent reply, which yielded 78 different labels. Nearly all his correspondents also returned the three-cent stamp, as William had anticipated they would.

During the next seven days, William set up a market in labels within the school, always checking what he could sell even before he had made a purchase. He noticed that some boys showed no interest in the rarity of the matchbox label, only in its looks, and with them he made quick exchanges to obtain rare trophies for the more discerning collectors. After a further two weeks of buying and selling he sensed that the market was reaching its zenith and that if he was not careful, with the holidays fast approaching, interest might begin to die off. With much trumpeted advance publicity in the form of a printed handout, which cost him a half-cent a sheet, placed on every boy's desk, William announced that he would be holding an auction of all his matchbox labels, all 211 of them. The auction took place in the school washroom during the lunch hour and was better attended than most school hockey games.

The result was that William grossed $57.32, a net profit of $51.32 on his original investment. William put $25.00 on deposit with the bank at 2.5 percent, bought himself a camera for $10, gave $5 to the Young Men's Christian Association, which had broadened its activities to helping the new flood of immigrants, bought his mother some flowers and put the remaining few dollars into his pocket. The market in matchbox labels collapsed even before the school term ended. It was to be the first of many such occasions on which William got out at the top of the market. The grand-mothers were proud of him when they were informed of the details; it was not unlike the way their husbands had made their fortunes in the panic of 1873.

When the holidays came, William could not resist finding out if it was possible to obtain a better return on his invested capital than the 2.5 percent yielded by his savings account. For the next three months he invested—again through Grandmother Kane—in stocks highly recommended by *The Wall Street Journal*. During the next term at school he lost more than half the money he had made on the matchbox la-bels. It was the only time in his life that he relied solely on the expertise of *The Wall Street Journal*, or on any informa-tion available on any street corner.

Angry with his loss of more than $20, William decided that it must be recouped during the Easter holidays. He worked out which parties and other functions his mother would expect him to attend and found he was left with only fourteen free days, just enough time for his new venture. He sold all his remaining *Wall Street Journal* shares, which net-ted him only $12. With this money he bought himself a flat piece of wood, two sets of wheels, axles and a piece of rope, at a cost, after some bargaining, of $5. He then put on a flat cloth cap and an old suit he had outgrown and went off to the local railroad station. He stood outside the exit, looking hun-gry and tired, informing selected travelers that the main ho-tels in Boston were near the railroad station, so that there was no need to take a taxi or the occasional surviving han-som carriage as he, William, could carry their luggage on his moving board for 20 percent of what the taxis charged; he added that the walk would also do them good. Working six hours a day, he found he could make roughly $4.

Five days before the new school term was due to start, he

had made back all his original losses and chalked up a further $10 profit. He then hit a problem. The taxi drivers were starting to get annoyed with him. William assured them that he would retire, aged nine, if each one of them would give him 50 cents to cover the cost of his homemade dolly; they agreed and he made another $8.50. On the way home to Beacon Hill, William sold his dolly for $2 to a school friend two years his senior, promising he would not return to his beat. The friend was soon to discover that the taxi drivers were waiting for him; moreover, it rained the rest of the week.

On the day he returned to school, William put his money back on deposit in the bank, at 2.5 percent. During the following year this decision caused him no anxiety as he watched his savings rise steadily. The sinking of the *Lusitania* in May of 1915 and Wilson's declaration of war against Germany in April of 1917 didn't concern William. Nothing and no one could ever beat America, he assured his mother. William even invested $10 in Liberty Bonds to back his judgment.

By William's eleventh birthday the credit column of his ledger showed a profit of $412. He had given his mother a fountain pen and his two grandmothers brooches from a local jewelry shop. The fountain pen was a Parker and the jewelry arrived at his grandmothers' homes in Shreve, Crump and Low boxes, which he had found after much searching in the trash cans behind the famous store. To do the boy justice, he had not wanted to cheat his grandmothers, but he had already learned from his matchbox-label experience that good packaging sells products. The grandmothers, who noted the lack of the Shreve, Crump and Low hallmark, still wore their brooches with considerable pride.

They continued to follow William's every move and had decided that he would proceed as planned to the first form at St. Paul's, in Concord, New Hampshire, the following September. For good measure the boy rewarded them with the top mathematics scholarship, unnecessarily saving the family some $300 a year. William accepted the scholarship and the grandmothers returned the money for, as they expressed it, "a less fortunate child." Anne hated the thought that William was leaving her to go away to boarding school, but the grandmothers insisted, and more important, she knew it was what Richard had wanted. She sewed on William's name tapes, marked his boots, checked his clothes and finally packed his trunk, refusing any help from the servants. When the time came for William to go, his mother asked him how much pocket money he would like for the term ahead of him.

"None," he replied without further comment.

William kissed his mother on the cheek; he had no idea how much she was going to miss him. He marched off down the path in his first pair of long pants, his hair cut very short, carrying a small suitcase, toward Roberts, the chauffeur. He climbed into the back of the Rolls-Royce and it drove him away. He didn't look back. His mother waved and waved and later cried. William wanted to cry, too, but he knew his father would not have approved.

The first thing that struck William Kane as strange about his new prep school was that the other boys did not care who he was. The looks of admiration, the silent acknowledgment of his presence, were no longer there. One older boy actually asked his name, and what was worse, when told, was not manifestly impressed. Some even called him Bill, which he soon corrected with the explanation that no one had ever referred to his father as Dick.

William's new domain was a small room with wooden bookshelves, two tables, two chairs, two beds and a comfortably shabby leather settee. The other chair, table and bed were occupied by a boy from New York named Matthew Lester, whose father was chairman of Lester and Company of New York, another old family bank.

William soon became used to the school routine. Up at seven-thirty, wash, breakfast in the main dining room with the whole school—220 boys munching their way through eggs, bacon and porridge. After breakfast, chapel, three 50-minute classes before lunch and two after it, followed by a music lesson, which William detested because he could not sing a note in tune and he had even less desire to learn to play any musical instrument. Football in the fall, hockey and squash in the winter, and rowing and tennis in the spring left him with very little free time. As a mathematics scholar, William had special tutorials in the subject three times a week from his housemaster, G. Raglan, Esq., known to the boys as Grumpy.

During his first year, William proved to be well worthy of his scholarship, always among the top few boys in almost every subject and in a class of his own in mathematics. Only his new friend, Matthew Lester, was any real competition for him, and that was almost certainly because they shared the same room. While establishing himself academically, William also acquired a reputation as a financier. Although his first investment in the market had proved disastrous, he did not abandon his belief that to make a significant amount of money, sizable capital gains on the stock market were essential. He kept a wary eye on *The Wall Street Journal*, company reports and, while still aged twelve, started to experiment with a ghost portfolio of investments. He recorded every one of his ghost purchases and sales, the good and the not-so-good, in a newly acquired, different-colored ledger and compared his performance at the end of each month against the rest of the market. He did not bother with any of the leading stocks listed, concentrating instead on the more obscure companies, some of which traded only over the counter, so that it was impossible to buy more than a few shares in them at any one time. William expected four things from his investments: a low multiple of earnings, a high growth rate, strong asset backing and a favorable trading outlook. He found few shares that fulfilled all these rigorous criteria, but when he did, they almost invariably showed him a profit.

The moment he could prove that he was regularly beating the Dow Jones Index with his ghost investment program,

William knew he was ready to invest his own money once again. He started with $100 and never stopped refining his method. He would always follow profits and cut losses. Once a stock had doubled, he would sell half his holding but keep the remaining half intact, trading the stock he still held as a bonus. Some of his early finds, such as Eastman Kodak and I.B.M., went on to become national leaders. He also backed Sears, a large mail-order company, convinced it was a trend that would catch on more and more.

By the end of his first year he was advising half the school staff and some of the parents. William Kane was happy at school.

Anne Kane had been unhappy and lonely at home with William away at St. Paul's and with a family circle consisting only of herself and the two grandmothers, now approaching old age. She was miserably conscious that she was past thirty and that her smooth and youthful prettiness had disappeared without leaving much in its place. She started picking up the threads, severed by Richard's death, with some of her old friends. John and Milly Preston, William's godmother, whom she had known all her life, began inviting her to dinners and the theater, always including an extra man, trying to make a match for Anne. The Prestons' choices were almost always atrocious, and Anne used to laugh privately at their attempts at matchmaking until one day in January 1919, just after William had returned to school for the winter term, Anne was invited to yet another dinner for four. Milly confessed she had never met her other guest, Henry Osborne, but that they thought he had been at Harvard at the same time as John.

"Actually," confessed Milly over the phone, "John doesn't know much about him, darling, except that he is rather good-looking."

On that score, John's opinion was verified by Anne and Milly. Henry Osborne was warming himself by the fire when Anne arrived and he rose immediately to allow Milly to introduce them. A shade over six feet, with dark eyes, almost black, and straight black hair, he was slim and athletic-looking. Anne felt a quick flash of pleasure that she was paired for the evening with this energetic and youthful man, while Milly had to content herself with a husband who was fading into middle age by comparison with his dashing college contemporary. Henry Osborne's arm was in a sling, almost completely covering his Harvard tie.

"A war wound?" Anne asked sympathetically.

"No, I fell down the stairs the week after I got back from the western front," he said, laughing.

It was one of those dinners, lately so rare for Anne, at which the time at the table slipped by happily and unaccountably. Henry Osborne answered all Anne's inquisitive questions. After leaving Harvard, he had worked for a real estate management firm in Chicago, his hometown, but when the war came he couldn't resist having a go at the Germans. He had a fund of splendid stories about Europe and the life he had led there as a young lieutenant preserving the honor of America on the Marne. Milly and John had not seen Anne laugh so much since Richard's death and smiled at each other knowingly when Henry asked if he might drive her home.

"What are you going to do now that you've come back to a land fit for heroes?" asked Anne as Henry Osborne eased his Stutz out onto Charles Street.

"Haven't really decided," he replied. "Luckily, I have a little money of my own, so I don't have to rush into anything. Might even start my own real estate firm right here in Boston. I've always felt at home in the city since my days at Harvard."

"You won't be returning to Chicago, then?"

"No, there's nothing to take me back. My parents are both dead and I was an only child, so I can start fresh anywhere I choose. Where do I turn?"

"Oh, first on the right," said Anne.

"You live on Beacon Hill?"

"Yes. About a hundred and fifty yards on the right-hand

side up Chestnut and it's the red house on the corner of Louisburg Square."

Henry Osborne parked the car and accompanied Anne to the front door of her home. After saying good night, he was gone almost before she had time to thank him. She watched his car glide slowly back down Beacon Hill, knowing that she wanted to see him again. She was delighted, though not entirely surprised, when he telephoned her the following morning.

"Boston Symphony Orchestra, Mozart and that flamboyant new hero, Mahler, next Monday—can I persuade you?"

Anne was a little taken aback by the extent to which she looked forward to Monday. It seemed so long since a man whom she found attractive had pursued her. Henry Osborne arrived punctually for the outing, they shook hands rather awkwardly, and he accepted a Scotch highball.

"It must be pleasant to live on Louisburg Square. You're a lucky girl."

"Yes, I suppose so—I've never really given it much thought. I was born and raised on Commonwealth Avenue. If anything, I find this slightly cramped."

"I think I might buy a house on the Hill myself if I do decide to settle in Boston."

"They don't come on the market all that often," said Anne, "but you may be lucky. Hadn't we better be going? I hate being late for a concert and having to tread on other people's toes to reach my seat."

Henry glanced at his watch. "Yes, I agree—wouldn't do to miss the conductor's entrance. But you don't have to worry about anyone's feet except mine. We're on the aisle."

The cascades of sumptuous music made it natural for Henry to take Anne's arm as they walked to the Ritz. The only other person who had done that since Richard's death had been William, and only after considerable persuasion, because he considered it sissy. Once again the hours slipped by for Anne: was it the excellent food or was it Henry's company? This time he made her laugh with his stories of Harvard and cry with recollections of the war. Although she was well aware that he looked younger than herself, he had done so much with his life that she always felt deliciously youthful and inexperienced in his company. She told him about her husband's death and cried a little more. He took her hand and she spoke of her son with glowing pride and affection. He said he had always wanted a son. Henry scarcely mentioned Chicago or his own home life, but Anne felt sure that he must miss his family. When he took her home that night, he stayed for a quick drink and kissed her gently on the cheek as he left. Anne went back over the evening minute by minute before she fell asleep.

They went to the theater on Tuesday, visited Anne's summer mansion on the North Shore on Wednesday, drove deep into the snow-covered Massachusetts countryside on Thursday, shopped for antiques on Friday and made love on Saturday. After Sunday, they were rarely apart. Milly and John Preston were "absolutely delighted" that their matchmaking had at last proved so successful. Milly went around Boston telling everyone that she had been responsible for putting the two of them together.

The announcement during that summer of the engagement came as no surprise to anyone except William. He had disliked Henry intensely from the day that Anne, with a well-founded sense of misgiving, introduced them to each other. Their first conversation took the form of long questions from Henry, trying to prove he wanted to be a friend, and monosyllabic answers from William, showing that he didn't. And he never changed his mind. Anne ascribed her son's resentment to an understandable feeling of jealousy; William had been the center of her life since Richard's death. Moreover, it was perfectly proper that, in William's estimation, no one could possibly take the place of his own father. Anne convinced Henry that, given time, William would get over his sense of outrage.

Anne Kane became Mrs. Henry Osborne in October of that year at St. Paul's Episcopal Cathedral just as the golden and red leaves were beginning to fall, a little over nine months after they had met. William feigned illness in order not to attend the wedding and remained firmly at school. The grandmothers did attend but were unable to hide their disapproval of Anne's remarriage, particularly to someone who appeared to be so much younger than she. "It can only end in disaster," said Grandmother Kane.

The newlyweds sailed for Greece the following day and did not return to the Red House on the Hill until the second week of December, just in time to welcome William home for the Christmas holidays. William was shocked to find that the house had been redecorated, leaving almost no trace of his father. Over Christmas, William's attitude to his stepfather showed no sign of softening despite the present, as Henry saw it—bribe, as William construed it—of a new bicycle. Henry Osborne accepted this rebuff with surly resignation. It saddened Anne that her splendid new husband made little effort to win over her son's affection.

William felt ill at ease in his invaded home and would often disappear for long periods during the day. Whenever Anne inquired where he was going, she received little or no response: it certainly was not to either grandmother, both of whom also were missing him. When the Christmas holidays came to an end, William was only too happy to return to school, and Henry was not sad to see him go.

Anne, however, was uneasy about both the men in her life.

CHAPTER
NINE

"Up, boy! Up, boy!"

One of the soldiers was digging his rifle butt into Wladek's ribs. He sat up with a start and looked at the grave of his sister and those of Leon and of the Baron, and he did not shed a single tear as he turned toward the soldier.

"I will live, you will not kill me," he said in Polish. "This is my home and you are on my land."

The soldier spat on Wladek and pushed him back to the lawn where the servants were waiting, all dressed in what looked like gray pajamas with numbers on their backs. Wladek was shocked at the sight of them, realizing what was about to happen to him. He was taken by the soldier to the north side of the castle and made to kneel on the ground. He felt a knife scrape across his head as his thick black hair fell onto the grass. With ten bloody strokes, like the shearing of a sheep, the job was completed. Head shaven, he was ordered to put on his new uniform, a gray rubaskew shirt and trousers. Wladek managed to keep the silver band well hidden and rejoined his servants at the front of the castle.

While they all stood waiting on the grass—numbers, now, not names—Wladek became conscious of a noise in the distance which he had never heard before. His eyes turned toward the menacing sound. Through the great iron gates came a vehicle moving on four wheels but not drawn by horses or oxen. All the prisoners stared at the moving object in disbelief. When it had come to a halt, the soldiers dragged the reluctant prisoners toward it and made them climb aboard. Then the horseless wagon turned around, moved back down the path and through the iron gates. Nobody dared to speak. Wladek sat at the rear of the truck and stared at his castle until he could no longer see the Gothic turrets.

The horseless wagon somehow drove itself toward the village of Slonim. Wladek would have worried about how the vehicle worked if he had not been even more worried about where it was taking them. He began to recognize the roads from his days at school, but his memory had been dulled by three years in the dungeons, and he could not recall where the road finally led. After only a few miles the truck came to a stop and they were all pushed out. It was the local railway station. Wladek had seen it only once before in his life, when he and Leon had gone there to welcome the Baron home from his trip to Warsaw. He remembered that the guard had saluted them when they first walked onto the platform. This time there was no one saluting and the prisoners were fed on goat's milk, cabbage soup and black bread, Wladek again taking charge, dividing the portions carefully among the remaining thirteen others and himself. He sat on a wooden bench, assuming that they were waiting for a train. That night they slept on the ground below the stars, paradise compared with the dungeons. He thanked God that the winter was mild.

Morning came and still they waited. Wladek led the servants in some exercises, but most collapsed after only a few minutes. He began to make a mental note of the names of those who had survived thus far. Twelve of the men and two of the women, spared from the original twenty-seven in the dungeons. They spent the rest of the day waiting for a train that never came. Once a train did arrive, from which more soldiers disembarked, speaking their hateful tongue, but it departed without Wladek's pitiful army. They slept yet another night on the ground.

Wladek lay awake below the stars considering how he

might escape, but during the night one of his thirteen made a run for it across the railway track and was shot down by a guard even before he had reached the other side. Wladek gazed at the spot where his compatriot had fallen, frightened to go to his aid for fear he would meet the same fate. The guards left the body on the track in the morning as a warning to those who might consider a similar course of action.

No one spoke of the incident that day although Wladek's eyes rarely left the body of the dead man. It was the Baron's butler, Ludwik—one of the witnesses to the Baron's will— and Wladek's heritage—dead.

On the evening of the third day another train chugged into the station, a great steam locomotive hauling open freight cars and roofed passenger cars, the floors of the former strewn with straw and the word *Cattle* painted on the sides. Several open cars were already full of prisoners, but from where Wladek could not judge, so hideously did their appearance resemble his own. He and his small group were thrown together into one of the open cars to begin the journey. After a wait of several more hours the train started to move out of the station, in a direction that Wladek judged, from the setting sun, to be eastward.

Every three open cars there was a guard sitting cross-legged on a roofed car. Throughout the interminable journey an occasional flurry of bullet shots from above demonstrated to Wladek the futility of any further thoughts of escape.

When the train stopped at Minsk, they were given their first proper meal—black bread, water, nuts and millet—and then the journey continued. Sometimes they went for three days without seeing another station. Many of the reluctant travelers died of starvation and were thrown overboard from the moving train. And when the train did stop, they would often wait for two days to allow another train going west the use of the track. These trains that delayed their progress were inevitably full of soldiers and it became obvious to Wladek that the troop trains had priority over all other transport. Escape was always uppermost in Wladek's mind, but two things prevented him from advancing that ambition.

First, there was nothing but miles of wilderness on both sides of the track; and second, those who had survived the dungeons were now totally dependent on him. It was Wladek who organized their food and drink and tried to sustain their will to live. He was the youngest and the last one still to believe in life.

At night it was now bitterly cold, often 30 degrees below zero, and they would lie up against one another in a line on the car floor so that each body would keep the next body warm. Wladek would recite *The Aeneid* to himself while he tried to snatch some sleep. It was impossible to turn over unless everyone agreed, so Wladek would lie at the end and each hour, as closely as he could judge by the changing of the guards, he would slap the side of the car, and they would all roll over and face the other way. One after the other, the bodies would turn like falling dominoes. One night a body, one of the women in his group, did not move—because it no longer could—and Wladek was informed. He, in turn, informed the guard, and four of them picked up the body and threw it over the side of the moving train. The guards then pumped bullets into it to be sure it was not someone hoping to escape.

Two hundred miles beyond Minsk, they arrived in the town of Smolensk, where they received more warm cabbage soup and black bread. Wladek was joined in his car by some new prisoners who spoke the same tongue as the guards. Their leader seemed to be about the same age as Wladek. Wladek and his eleven remaining companions, ten men and one woman, were immediately suspicious of the new arrivals, and they divided the car in half, with the two groups remaining apart for several days.

One night, while Wladek lay awake staring at the stars, trying to get warm, he saw the leader of the Smolenskis crawl toward the end man of his own line with a small piece of rope in his hand. He watched him slip it around the neck of Alfons, the Baron's first footman, who was sleeping. Wladek knew that if he moved too quickly, the boy would hear him and escape back to his own half of the carriage and the protection of his comrades, so he crawled slowly on his belly down the line of Polish bodies. Eyes stared at him as he passed, but nobody spoke. When he reached the end of the line, he leaped forward upon the aggressor, immediately waking everyone in the car. Each faction shrank back to its own end of the car, with the exception of Alfons, who lay motionless in front of them.

The Smolenski leader was taller and more agile than Wladek, but it made little difference while the two were fighting on the floor. The struggle lasted for several minutes, which attracted the guards who laughed and took bets as they watched the two gladiators. One guard, who was getting bored by the lack of blood, threw a bayonet into the middle of the car. Both boys scrambled for the shining blade, with the Smolenski leader grabbing it first. The Smolenski band cheered their hero as he thrust the bayonet into the side of Wladek's leg, pulled the blood-covered steel back out and lunged again. On the second thrust the blade lodged firmly in the wooden floor of the jolting car next to Wladek's ear. As the Smolenski leader tried to wrench it free, Wladek kicked him in the crotch with every ounce of energy he had left, and in throwing his adversary backward, released the bayonet. With a leap, Wladek grabbed the handle and jumped on top of the Smolenski, running the blade right into his mouth. The boy gave out a shriek of agony that awoke the entire train. Wladek pulled the blade out, twisting it as he did so, and thrust it back into the Smolenski again and again, long after he had ceased to move. Wladek knelt over him, breathing heavily, and then picked up the body and threw it out of the carriage. He heard the *thud* as it hit the bank, and the shots that the guards pointlessly aimed after it.

Wladek limped toward Alfons, still lying motionless on the wooden boards, and knelt by his side, shaking his lifeless body: his second witness dead. Who would now believe that he, Wladek, was the chosen heir to the Baron's fortune? Was there any purpose left in life? He collapsed to his knees. He picked up the bayonet with both hands, pointing the blade toward his stomach. Immediately a guard jumped down into the car and wrestled the weapon away from him.

"Oh no, you don't," he grunted. "We need the lively ones like you for the camps. You can't expect us to do all the work."

Wladek buried his head in his hands, aware for the first time of a cold aching pain in his bayoneted leg. He had lost his inheritance, to become the leader of a band of penniless Smolenskis. The whole car once again was his domain and he now had twenty prisoners to care for. He immediately split them up so that a Pole would always sleep next to a Smolenski, making impossible any further warfare between the two groups.

Wladek spent a considerable part of his time learning their strange tongue, not realizing for several days that it was actually Russian, so greatly did it differ from the classical Russian language taught him by the Baron, and then the real significance of this discovery dawned on him for the first time when he realized where the train was heading.

During the day Wladek used to take on two Smolenskis at a time to tutor him, and as soon as they were tired, he would take on two more, and so on until they were all exhausted.

Gradually he became able to converse easily with his new dependents. Some of them he discovered were Russian soldiers, exiled after repatriation for the crime of having been captured by the Germans. The rest consisted of White Russians—farmers, miners, laborers—all bitterly hostile to the Revolution.

The train jolted on past terrain more barren than Wladek had ever seen before, and through towns of which he had never heard—Omsk, Novosibirsk, Krasnoyarsk—the names rang ominously in his ears. Finally, after two months and more than three thousand miles, they reached Irkutsk, where the railway track came to an abrupt end.

They were hustled off the train, fed and issued felt boots, jackets and heavy coats, and although fights broke out for the warmest clothing, they still provided little protection from the ever intensifying cold.

Horseless wagons appeared not unlike the one that had borne Wladek away from his castle, and long chains were thrown out. Then, to Wladek's disbelief and horror, the prisoners were cuffed to the chain by one hand, twenty-five pairs side by side on each chain. The wagons pulled the mass of prisoners along while the guards rode on the back. They marched like that for twelve hours, before being given a two-hour rest, and then they marched again. After three days, Wladek thought he would die of cold and exhaustion, but once clear of populated areas they traveled only during the day and rested at night. A mobile field kitchen run by prisoners from the camp supplied turnip soup and bread at first light and then again at night. Wladek learned from these prisoners that conditions at the camp were even worse.

For the first week, they were never unshackled from their chains, but later, when there could be no thought of escape, they were released at night to sleep, digging holes in the snow for warmth. Sometimes on good days they found a forest in which to bed down: luxury began to take strange forms. On and on they marched, past enormous lakes and across frozen rivers, ever northward, into the face of viciously cold winds and deeper falls of snow. Wladek's wounded leg gave him a constant dull pain, soon surpassed in intensity by the agony of frostbitten fingers and ears. There was no sign of life or food in all the expanse of whiteness, and Wladek knew that to attempt an escape at night could only mean slow death by starvation. The old and the sick were dying, quietly at night if they were lucky. The unlucky ones, unable to keep up the pace, were uncuffed from the chains and cast off to be left alone in the endless snow. Those who survived in the chains walked on and on, always toward the north, until Wladek lost all sense of time and was simply conscious of the inexorable tug of the chain, not even sure when he dug his hole in the snow to sleep in at night that he would waken the next morning. Those who didn't had dug their own grave.

After a trek of nine hundred miles, those who had survived were met by Ostyaks, nomads of the Russian steppes, in reindeer-drawn sleds. The prisoners, now chained to the sleds, were led on. A great blizzard forced them to halt for the greater part of two days and Wladek seized the opportunity to communicate with the young Ostyak to whose sled he was chained. Using classical Russian, with a Polish accent, he was understood only very imperfectly, but he did discover that the Ostyaks hated the Russians of the south, who treated them almost as badly as they treated their captives. The Ostyaks were not unsympathetic to the sad prisoners with no future, the "unfortunates," as they called them.

Nine days later, in the half-light of the early Arctic winter night, they reached Camp 201. Wladek would never have believed he could be glad to see such a place: row upon row of wooden huts in stark open space. The huts, like the prisoners, were numbered. Wladek's hut was 33. There was a small black stove in the middle of the room, and projecting from the walls were tiered wooden bunks on which were hard straw mattresses and one thin blanket. Few of the prisoners managed to sleep at all that first night, and the groans and cries that came from Hut 33 were often louder than the howls of the wolves outside.

The next morning before the sun rose, they were awakened by the sound of a hammer against an iron triangle. There was thick frost on both sides of the window, and Wladek thought that he must surely die of the cold. Breakfast in a freezing communal hall lasted for ten minutes and consisted of a bowl of lukewarm gruel with pieces of rotten fish and a leaf of cabbage floating in it. The newcomers spat the fish bones out onto the table, while the more seasoned prisoners ate the bones and even the fishes' eyes.

After breakfast, they were allocated tasks. Wladek became a wood chopper. He was taken seven miles through the featureless steppes into a forest and ordered to cut a certain number of trees each day. The guard would leave him and his little group of six to themselves with their food ration, tasteless yellow magara porridge and bread. The guards had no fear that the prisoners would attempt escape, for it was more than a thousand miles to the nearest town—even if one knew in which direction to head.

At the end of each day the guard would return and count the number of logs they had chopped; he had informed the prisoners that if their group failed to reach the required number, he would hold back its food for the following day. But when he returned at seven in the evening to collect the reluctant woodsmen, it was already dark, and he could not always see exactly how many new logs they had cut. Wladek taught the others in his team to spend the last part of the afternoon clearing the snow off the wood cut the previous day and lining it up with what they had chopped that day. It was a plan that always worked and Wladek's group never lost a day's food. Sometimes they managed to return to the camp with a small piece of wood, tied to the inside of a leg, to put in the coal stove at night. Caution was required, as at least one of them was searched every time they left and entered the camp, often having to remove one or both boots and to stand there in the numbing snow. If they were caught with anything on their person, the punishment was three days without food.

As the weeks went by, Wladek's leg became very stiff and painful. He longed for the coldest days, for when the temperature went down to 40 below zero, outside work was called off even though the lost day would have to be made up on a free Sunday, when they were normally allowed to lie on their bunks all day.

One evening when Wladek had been hauling logs across the waste, his leg began to throb unmercifully. When he looked at the scar caused by the Smolenski, he found that it had become puffy and shiny. That night he showed the wound to a guard, who ordered him to report to the camp doctor before first light in the morning. Wladek sat up all night with his leg nearly touching the stove, surrounded by wet boots, but the heat was so feeble that it couldn't ease the pain.

The next morning Wladek rose an hour earlier than usual.

If you had not seen the doctor before work was due to start, then you missed him until the next day. Wladek couldn't face another day of such intense pain. He reported to the doctor, giving his name and number. Pierre Dubien turned out to be a sympathetic old man, bald-headed, with a pronounced stoop—Wladek thought he looked even older than the Baron had in his final days. He inspected Wladek's leg without speaking.

"Will the wound be all right, Doctor?" asked Wladek.

"You speak Russian?"

"Yes, sir."

"Although you will always limp, young man, your leg will be good again, but good for what? A life here chopping wood."

"No, Doctor, I intend to escape and get back to Poland," said Wladek.

The doctor looked sharply at him. "Keep your voice down, stupid boy. . . . You must know by now that escape is impossible. I have been in captivity fifteen years and not a day has passed that I have not thought of escaping. There is no way; no one has ever escaped and lived, and even to talk of it means ten days in the punishment cell, and there they feed you every third day and light the stove only to melt the ice off the walls. If you come out of that place alive, you can consider yourself lucky."

"I will escape, I will, I will," said Wladek, staring at the old man.

The doctor looked into Wladek's eyes and smiled. "My friend, never mention escape again or they may kill you. Go back to work, keep your leg exercised and report to me first thing every morning."

Wladek returned to the forest and to the chopping of wood but found that he could not drag the logs more than a few feet and that the pain was so intense he believed his leg might fall off. When he returned the next morning, the doctor examined the leg more carefully.

"Worse, if anything," he said. "How old are you, boy?"

"I think I am thirteen," said Wladek. "What year is it?"

"Nineteen hundred and nineteen," replied the doctor.

"Yes, thirteen. How old are you?" asked Wladek.

The man looked down into the young boy's blue eyes, surprised by the question.

"Thirty-eight," he said quietly.

"God help me," said Wladek.

"You will look like this when you have been a prisoner for fifteen years, my boy," the doctor said matter-of-factly.

"Why are you here at all?" said Wladek. "Why haven't they let you go after all this time?"

"I was taken prisoner in Moscow in 1904, soon after I had qualified as a doctor. I was working in the French embassy there, and they said I was a spy and put me in a Moscow jail. I thought that was bad until after the Revolution, when they sent me to this hellhole. Even the French have now forgotten that I exist. The rest of the world wouldn't believe there is such a place. No one has ever completed a sentence at Camp Two-O-One, so I must die here, like everyone else, and it can't be too soon."

"No, you must not give up hope, Doctor."

"Hope? I gave up hope for myself a long time ago. Perhaps I shall not give it up for you, but always remember never to mention that hope to anyone; there are prisoners here who trade in loose tongues when their reward can be nothing more than an extra piece of bread or perhaps a blanket. Now Wladek, I am going to put you on kitchen duty for a month and you must continue to report to me every morning. It is the only chance you have of not losing that leg and I do not relish being the man who has to cut it off. We don't exactly have the latest surgical instruments here," he added, glancing at a large carving knife.

Wladek shuddered.

Dr. Dubien wrote Wladek's name on a slip of paper. Next morning, Wladek reported to the kitchens, where he cleaned the plates in freezing water and helped to prepare food that required no refrigeration. After chopping logs all day, he found it a welcome change: extra fish soup, thick black bread with shredded nettles, and the chance to stay inside and keep warm. On one occasion he even shared half an egg with the cook, although neither of them could be sure what fowl had laid it. Wladek's leg mended slowly, leaving him with a pronounced limp. There was little Dr. Dubien could do in the absence of any real medical supplies except to keep an eye on Wladek's progress. As the days went by, the doctor began to befriend Wladek and even to believe in his youthful hope for the future. They would converse in a different language each morning, but his new friend most enjoyed speaking in French, his native tongue.

"In seven days' time, Wladek, you will have to return to forest duty; the guards will inspect your leg and I will not be able to keep you in the kitchen any longer. So listen carefully, for I have decided upon a plan for your escape."

"Together, Doctor," said Wladek. "Together."

"No, only you. I am too old for such a long journey, and although I have dreamed about escape for over fifteen years, I would only hold you up. It will be enough for me to know someone else has achieved it, and you are the first person I've ever met who has convinced me that he might succeed."

Wladek sat on the floor in silence, listening to the doctor's plan.

"I have, over the last fifteen years, saved two hundred rubles—you don't exactly get overtime as a Russian prisoner." Wladek tried to laugh at the camp's oldest joke. "I keep the money hidden in a drug bottle, four fifty-ruble notes. When the time comes for you to leave, the money must be sewn into your clothes. I will have already done this for you."

"What clothes?" asked Wladek.

"I have a suit and a shirt I bribed from a guard twelve years ago when I still believed in escape. Not exactly the latest fashion, but they will serve your purpose."

Fifteen years to scrape together two hundred rubles, a shirt and a suit, and the doctor was willing to sacrifice them to Wladek in a moment. Wladek never again in his life experienced such an act of selflessness.

"Next Thursday will be your only chance," the doctor

continued. "New prisoners arrive by train at Irkutsk, and the guards always take four people from the kitchen to organize the food trucks for the new arrivals. I have already arranged with the senior 'cook' "—he laughed at the word—"that in exchange for some drugs you will find yourself on the kitchen truck. It was not too hard. No one exactly wants to make the trip there and back—but you will only be making the journey there."

Wladek was still listening intently.

"When you reach the station, wait until the prisoners' train arrives. Once they are all on the platform, cross the line and get yourself onto the train going to Moscow, which cannot leave until the prisoners' train comes in, as there is only one track outside the station. You must pray that with hundreds of new prisoners milling around, the guards will not notice your disappearance. From then on you're on your own. Remember, if they do spot you, they will shoot you on sight without a second thought. There is only one thing I can do for you. Fifteen years ago when I was brought here, I drew a map from memory of the route from Moscow to Turkey. It may not be totally accurate any longer, but it should be adequate for your purpose. Be sure to check that the Russians haven't taken over Turkey as well. God knows what they have been up to recently. They may even control France, for all I know."

The doctor walked over to the drug cabinet and took out a large bottle that looked as if it were full of a brown substance. He unscrewed the top and removed an old piece of parchment. The black ink had faded over the years. It was marked "October 1904." It showed a route from Moscow to Odessa, and from Odessa to Turkey, 1,500 miles to freedom.

"Come to me every morning this week and we will go over the plan again and again. If you fail, it must not be from lack of preparation."

Wladek stayed awake each night, gazing at the wolves' sun through the window, rehearsing what he would do in any given situation, preparing himself for every eventuality. In the morning he would go over the plan again and again with the doctor. On the Wednesday evening before Wladek was to try the escape, the doctor folded the map into eight, placed it with the four 50-ruble notes in a small package and pinned the package into a sleeve of the suit. Wladek took off his clothes, put on the shirt suit and then replaced the prison uniform on top of them. As he put on the uniform again, the doctor's eye caught the Baron's silver band, which Wladek, ever since he had been issued his prison uniform, had always kept above his elbow for fear the guards would spot his only treasure and steal it.

"What's that?" he asked. "It's quite magnificent."

"A gift from my father," said Wladek. "May I give it to you to show my thanks?" He slipped the band off his wrist and handed it to the doctor.

The doctor stared at the silver band for several moments and bowed his head. "Never," he said. "This can only belong to one person." He stared silently at the boy. "Your father must have been a great man."

The doctor placed the band back on Wladek's wrist and shook him warmly by the hand.

"Good luck, Wladek. I hope we never meet again."

They embraced and Wladek parted for what he prayed was his last night in the prison hut. He was unable to sleep at all that night in fear that one of the guards would discover the suit under his prison clothes. When the morning bell sounded, he was already dressed and he made sure that he was not late reporting to the kitchen. The senior prisoner in the kitchen pushed Wladek forward when the guards came for the truck detail. The team chosen were four in all. Wladek was by far the youngest.

"Why this one?" asked a guard, pointing to Wladek.

Wladek's heart stopped and he went cold all over. The doctor's plan was going to fail and there would not be another batch of prisoners coming to the camp for at least three months. By then he would no longer be in the kitchen.

"He's an excellent cook," said the senior prisoner, "trained in the castle of a baron. Only the best for the guards."

"Ah," said the guard, greed overcoming suspicion. "Hurry up, then."

The four of them ran to the truck, and the convoy started. The journey was again slow and arduous, but at least he was not walking this time, nor, it now being summer, was it unbearably cold. Wladek worked hard on preparing the food and, as he had no desire to be noticed, barely spoke to anyone for the entire journey other than Stanislaw, the chief cook.

When they eventually arrived at Irkutsk, the drive had taken nearly sixteen days. The train waiting to go to Moscow was already standing in the station. It had already been there for several hours but was unable to begin its return journey to Moscow until the train bringing the new prisoners had arrived. Wladek sat on the edge of the platform with the others from the field kitchen, three of them with no interest or purpose in anything around them, dulled by their experiences, but one of them intent on every move, carefully studying the train on the other side of the platform. There were several open entrances on the train and Wladek quickly selected the one he would use when his moment came.

"Are you going to try to escape?" Stanislaw asked suddenly.

Wladek began to sweat but did not answer.

Stanislaw stared at him. "You are."

Still Wladek said nothing.

The old cook continued to stare at the thirteen-year-old boy; then he nodded in agreement. If he had had a tail, it would have wagged.

"Good luck. I'll make sure they don't realize you're missing for as long as I can."

Stanislaw touched his arm, and Wladek caught sight of the prisoners' train in the distance, slowly inching its way toward them. He tensed in anticipation, his heart pounding, his eyes following the movement of every soldier. He waited for the incoming train to come to a halt and watched the tired prisoners pile out onto the platform, hundreds of them, anonymous men with only a past. When the station was a chaos of people and the guards were fully occupied, Wladek ran under the prisoner train and jumped onto the one bound for Moscow. No one aboard showed any interest as he went into a lavatory at the end of the carriage. He locked himself in and waited and prayed, every moment expecting someone to knock on the door. It seemed a lifetime to Wladek before the train began to move out of the station. It was, in fact, seventeen minutes.

"At last, at last," he said out loud. He looked through the little window of the lavatory and watched the station growing smaller and smaller in the distance, a mass of new prisoners being hitched up to the chains, ready for the journey to Camp 201, the guards laughing as they locked them in. How many would reach the camp alive? How many would be fed to the wolves? How long before they missed him?

Wladek sat in the lavatory for several more minutes, terrified to move, not sure what he ought to do next. Suddenly there was a banging on the door. Wladek thought quickly— the guard, the ticket collector, a soldier?—a succession of images flashed through his mind, each one more frightening than the last. He needed to use the lavatory for the first time. The banging persisted.

"Come on, come on," said a deep voice in coarse Russian.

Wladek had little choice. If it was a soldier, there was no way out—a dwarf could not have squeezed through the little window. If it wasn't a soldier, he would only draw attention to himself by staying in the lavatory. He took off his prison clothes, made them into as small a bundle as possible and threw them out of the window. Then he removed a soft hat from the pocket of his suit to cover his shaved head and opened the door. An agitated man pushed in, pulling down his trousers even before Wladek had left.

Once in the corridor, Wladek felt isolated and terrifyingly conspicuous in his out-of-date suit, an apple placed on a pile of oranges. He immediately went in search of another lavatory. When he found one that was unoccupied, he locked himself in and quickly unpinned the 50-ruble notes in his sleeve. He replaced three of them and returned to the corridor. He looked for the most crowded car he could find and crushed himself into a corner. Some men in the middle of the car were playing pitch-and-toss for a few rubles. Wladek had often beaten Leon when they had played in the castle and he would have liked to join the contestants, but he feared winning and drawing attention to himself. The game went on for a long time and Wladek began to remember the skills required. The temptation to risk his 200 rubles was almost irresistible.

One of the gamblers, who had parted with a considerable amount of his money, retired in disgust and sat down by Wladek, swearing.

"The luck wasn't with you," said Wladek, wanting to hear the sound of his own voice.

"Ah, it's not luck," the gambler said. "Most days I could beat that lot of peasants, but I have run out of rubles."

"Do you want to sell your coat?" asked Wladek.

The gambler was one of the few passengers in the car wearing a good, old, thick sheepskin coat. He stared at the youth.

"You couldn't afford it, boy." Wladek could tell from the man's voice that he hoped he could. "I would want seventy-five rubles."

"I'll give you forty," said Wladek.

"Sixty," said the gambler.

"Fifty," said Wladek.

"No. Sixty is the least I'd let it go for; it cost over a hundred," said the gambler.

"A long time ago," said Wladek as he considered the implications of taking money from inside the lining of his sleeve in order to get at the full amount needed. He decided against doing so lest it draw attention to himself; he would have to wait for another opportunity. Wladek was not willing to show he could not afford the coat, and he touched the collar of the garment and said, with considerable disdain, "You paid too much for it, my friend. Fifty rubles, not a kopeck more." Wladek rose as if to leave.

"Wait, wait," said the gambler. "I'll let you have it for fifty."

Wladek took the fifty rubles out of his pocket and the gambler took off the coat and exchanged it for the grimy red note. The coat was far too big for Wladek, nearly touching the ground, but it was exactly what he needed to cover his conspicuous suit. For a few moments he watched the gambler, back in the game, once again losing. From the new tutor he had learned two things: never to gamble unless the odds are tipped in your favor by your own superior knowledge or skill, and always be willing to walk away from a deal when you have reached your limit.

Wladek left the car, feeling a little safer under his new-old coat. He started to examine the makeup of the train with a little more confidence. The cars seemed to be in two classes, general ones in which passengers stood or sat on the wooden boards and special ones in which they sat on upholstered seats. Wladek found that all the cars were packed except one of the special ones, in which, strangely, there sat a solitary woman. She was middle-aged, as far as Wladek could tell, and dressed a little more smartly than most of the other passengers on the train. She wore a dark blue dress, and a scarf was drawn over her head. As Wladek stood staring at her hesitantly, she smiled at him, giving him the confidence to enter the compartment.

"May I sit down?"

"Please do," said the woman, looking at him carefully.

Wladek did not speak again, but when he could he studied the woman and her belongings. She had a sallow skin covered with tired lines, a little overweight—the little bit one could be on Russian food. Her short black hair and brown eyes suggested that she once might have been attractive. She had two large cloth bags on the overhead rack and a small valise by her side. Despite the danger of his position, Wladek was suddenly aware of feeling desperately tired. He was wondering if he dared to sleep, when the woman spoke.

"Where are you traveling?"

The question took Wladek by surprise. "Moscow," he said, holding his breath.

"So am I," she said.

Wladek was already regretting the isolation of the car and the information he had given, meager though it was. "Don't talk to anyone," the doctor had warned him. "Remember, trust nobody."

To Wladek's relief the woman asked no more questions. As he began to regain his lost confidence, the ticket collector arrived. Wladek started to sweat, despite the temperature of minus 20 degrees. The collector took the woman's ticket, tore it, gave it back to her and then turned to Wladek.

"Ticket, comrade" was all he said in a slow, monotonous tone.

Wladek was speechless and started thumbing around in his coat pocket for some money.

"He's my son," said the woman firmly.

The ticket collector looked back at her, once more at Wladek, and then bowed to the woman and left without another word.

Wladek stared at her. "Thank you," he breathed, not quite sure what else he could say.

"I watched you come from under the prisoners' train," the woman remarked quietly. Wladek felt sick. "But I shall not give you away. I have a young cousin in one of those terrible camps and all of us who know about them fear that one day we might end up there. What do you have on under your coat?"

Wladek weighed the relative merits of dashing out of the carriage and of unfastening his coat. If he dashed out, there was no place on the train where he could hide. He unfastened his coat.

"Not as bad as I had feared," she said. "What did you do with your prison uniform?"

"Threw it out of the window."

"Let's hope they don't find it before you reach Moscow."

Wladek said nothing.

"Do you have anywhere to stay in Moscow?"

He thought again of the doctor's advice to trust nobody, but he had to trust her.

"I have nowhere to go."

"Then you can stay with me until you find somewhere to live. My husband is the stationmaster in Moscow, and this carriage is for government officials only," she explained. "If you ever make that mistake again, you will be taking the train back to Irkutsk."

Wladek swallowed. "Should I leave now?"

"No, not now that the ticket collector has seen you. You will be safe with me for the time being. Do you have any identity papers?"

"No. What are they?"

"Since the Revolution every Russian citizen must have identity papers to show who he is, where he lives and where he works; otherwise he ends up in jail until he can produce them. And as he can never produce them once in jail, he stays there forever," she added matter-of-factly. "You will have to stay close to me once we reach Moscow, and be sure you don't open your mouth."

"You are being very kind to me," Wladek said suspiciously.

"Now the Tsar is dead, none of us is safe. I was lucky to be married to the right man," she added, "but there is not a citizen in Russia, including government officials, who does not live in constant fear of arrest and the camps. What is your name?"

"Wladek."

"Good. Now you sleep, Wladek, because you look exhausted and the journey is long and you are not safe yet."

Wladek slept.

When he awoke, several hours had passed and it was already dark outside. He stared at his protectress and she smiled. Wladek returned her smile, praying that she could be trusted not to tell the officials who he was—or had she already done so? She produced some food from one of her bundles and Wladek ate the offering silently. When they reached the next station, nearly all the passengers got out, some of them permanently and some to stretch stiff limbs, but most to seek what little refreshment was available.

The middle-aged woman rose and looked at Wladek. "Follow me," she said.

He stood up and followed her onto the platform. Was he about to be turned in? She put out her hand and he took it as any thirteen-year-old child accompanying his mother would do. She walked toward a lavatory marked for women. Wladek hesitated. She insisted and once inside she told Wladek to take off his clothes. He obeyed her unquestioningly, as he hadn't anyone since the death of the Báron. While he undressed she turned on the solitary tap, which with reluctance yielded a trickle of cold brownish water. She was disgusted. But to Wladek it was a vast improvement on the camp water. The woman started to bathe his wounds with a wet rag and attempted hopelessly to wash him. She winced when she saw the vicious wound on his leg. Wladek didn't murmur from the pain that came with each touch, gentle as she tried to be.

"When we get you home, I'll make a better job of those wounds," she said, "but this will have to do for now."

Then she saw the silver band, studied the inscription and looked carefully at Wladek. "Is that yours?" she asked. "Who did you steal it from?"

Wladek looked offended. "I didn't steal it. My father gave it to me before he died."

She stared at him again and a different look came into her eyes. Was it fear or respect? She bowed her head. "Be careful, Wladek. Men would kill for such a valuable prize."

He nodded his agreement and started to dress quickly. They returned to their carriage. A delay of an hour at a station was not unusual and when the train started lurching forward, Wladek was glad to feel the wheels clattering underneath him once again. The train took twelve and a half days to reach Moscow. Whenever a new ticket collector appeared, Wladek and the woman went through the same routine, he unconvincingly trying for the first time in his life to look innocent and young; she a convincing mother. The ticket collectors always bowed respectfully to the middle-aged lady and Wladek began to think that stationmasters must be very important in Russia.

By the time they had completed the one-thousand-mile journey to Moscow, Wladek had put his trust completely in the woman and was looking forward to seeing her house. It was early afternoon when the train came to its final halt, and despite everything Wladek had been through, he was terrified, once again tasting the fear of the unknown. He had never visited a big city, let alone the capital of all the Russias; he had never seen so many people, all of them rushing around. The woman sensed his apprehension.

"Follow me, do not speak and don't take your cap off."

Wladek took her bags down from the rack, pulled his cap over his head—now covered in a black stubble—and down to his ears and followed her out onto the platform. A throng of people at the barrier were waiting to go through a tiny exit, the holdup created because everyone had to show identification papers to the guard. As he and the lady approached the barrier, Wladek could hear his heart beating like a soldier's drum, but when their turn came the fear was over in a moment. The guard only glanced at the woman's documents.

"Comrade," he said, and saluted. He looked at Wladek.

"My son," she explained.

"Of course, comrade." He saluted again.

Wladek was in Moscow.

Despite the trust he had placed in his newfound companion, Wladek's first instinct was to run, but because 150 rubles were hardly enough to live on, he decided to bide his time—he could always run at some later opportunity. A horse and cart were waiting for them at the station and took the woman and her new son home. The stationmaster was not there when they arrived, so the woman immediately set about making up the spare bed for Wladek. Then she poured water, heated on a stove, into a large tin tub and told him to get in. It was the first bath he had had in more than four years, unless he counted the dip in the stream. She heated some more water and reintroduced him to soap, scrubbing his back. The water began to change color and after twenty minutes it was black. Once Wladek was dry, the woman put some ointment on his arms and legs and bandaged the parts of his body that looked particularly fierce. She stared at his one nipple. He dressed quickly and then joined her in the kitchen. She had already prepared a bowl of hot soup and some beans. Wladek ate the veritable feast hungrily. Neither of them spoke. When he had finished the meal, she suggested that it might be wise for him to go to bed and rest.

"I do not want my husband to see you before I have told him why you are here," she explained. "Would you like to stay with us, Wladek, if my husband agrees?"

Wladek nodded thankfully.

"Then off you go to bed," she said.

Wladek obeyed and prayed that the lady's husband would allow him to live with them. He undressed slowly and climbed onto the bed. He was too clean, the sheets were too clean, the mattress was too soft and he threw the pillow onto the floor, but he was so tired that he slept despite the comfort of the bed. He was awakened from a deep sleep some hours later by the sound of raised voices coming from the kitchen. He could not tell how long he had slept. It was already dark outside as he crept off the bed, walked to the door, eased it open and listened to the conversation taking place in the kitchen below.

"You stupid woman," Wladek heard a piping voice. "Do you not understand what would have happened if you had been caught? It would have been you who would have been sent to the camps."

"But if you had seen him, Piotr, like a hunted animal."

"So you decided to turn us into hunted animals," said the male voice. "Has anyone else seen him?"

"No," said the woman, "I don't think so."

"Thank God for that. He must go immediately before anyone knows he's here—it's our only hope."

"But go where, Piotr? He is lost and has no one," Wladek's protectress pleaded. "And I have always wanted a son."

"I do not care what you want or where he goes, he is not our responsibility and we must be quickly rid of him."

"But Piotr, I think he is royal; I think his father was a baron. He wears a silver band around his wrist and inscribed on it are the words—"

"That only makes it worse. You know what our new leaders have decreed. No tsars, no royalty, no privileges. We would not even have to bother to go to the camp—the authorities would just shoot us."

"We have always wanted a son, Piotr. Can we not take this one risk in our lives?"

"In your life, perhaps, but not in mine. I say he must go and go now."

Wladek did not need to listen to any more of their conversation. Deciding that the only way he could help his benefactress would be to disappear without trace into the night, he dressed quickly and stared at the slept-in bed, hoping it would not be four more years before he saw another one. He was unlatching the window when the door was flung open and into the room came the stationmaster, a tiny man, no taller than Wladek, with a large stomach and a bald head except for a few gray strands vainly combed but leaving the impression of a wig. He wore rimless spectacles, which had produced little red semicircles under each eye. The man carried a paraffin lamp. He stood staring at Wladek. Wladek stared defiantly back.

"Come downstairs," the man commanded.

Wladek followed him reluctantly to the kitchen. The woman was sitting at the table crying.

"Now listen, boy," the man said.

"His name is Wladek," the woman interjected.

"Now listen, boy," the man repeated. "You are trouble and I want you out of here and as far away as possible. I'll tell you what I am going to do to help you."

Help? Wladek gazed at him stonily.

"I am going to give you a train ticket. Where do you want to go?"

"Odessa," said Wladek, ignorant of where it was or how

much it would cost, knowing only that it was the next city on the doctor's map to freedom.

"Odessa, the mother of crime—an appropriate destination," sneered the stationmaster. "You can only be among your own kind and come to harm there."

"Then let him stay with us, Piotr. I will take care of him, I will——"

"No, never. I would rather pay the bastard."

"But how can he hope to get past the authorities?" the woman pleaded.

"I will have to issue him with a ticket and a working pass for Odessa." He turned his head toward Wladek. "Once you are on that train, boy, if I see or hear of you again in Moscow, I will have you arrested on sight and thrown into the nearest jail. You will then be back in that prison camp as fast as the train can get you there—if they don't shoot you first."

He stared at the clock on the kitchen mantelpiece: five after eleven. He turned to his wife. "There is a train that leaves for Odessa at midnight. I will take him to the station myself. I want to be sure he leaves Moscow. Have you any baggage, boy?"

Wladek was about to say no, when the woman said, "Yes, I will go and fetch it."

Wladek and the stationmaster stared at each other with mutual contempt. The woman was gone for a long time. The grandfather clock struck once in her absence. Still neither spoke and the stationmaster's eyes never left Wladek. When his wife returned, she was carrying a large brown paper parcel tied with string. Wladek stared at it and began to protest, but as their eyes met, he saw such fear in hers that he only just got out the words "Thank you."

"Eat this," she said, thrusting her bowl of cold soup toward him.

He obeyed, although his shrunken stomach was now overfull, gulping down the soup as quickly as possible, not wanting her to be in any more trouble.

"Animal," the man said.

Wladek looked at him, hatred in his eyes. He felt pity for the woman, bound to such a man for life.

"Come, boy, it's time to leave," the stationmaster said. "We don't want you to miss your train, do we?"

Wladek followed the man out of the kitchen, hesitating as he passed the woman. He touched her hand, feeling the response. Nothing was said; words would have been inadequate. The stationmaster and the refugee crept through the streets of Moscow, hiding in the shadows, until they reached the station. The stationmaster obtained a one-way ticket to Odessa and gave the little red slip of paper to Wladek.

"My pass?" Wladek said defiantly.

From his inside pocket the man drew out an official-looking form, signed it hurriedly and furtively handed it over to Wladek. The stationmaster's eyes kept looking all around him for any possible danger. Wladek had seen those eyes so many times during the past four years: the eyes of a coward.

"Never let me see or hear of you again," the stationmaster said: the voice of a bully. Wladek had heard that voice many times in the last four years.

He looked up, wanting to say something, but the stationmaster had already retreated into the shadows of the night, where he belonged. Wladek looked at the eyes of the people who hurried past him. The same eyes, the same fear; was anyone in the world free? Wladek gathered the brown paper parcel under his arm, adjusted his hat and walked toward the barrier. This time he felt more confident. He showed his pass to the guard and was ushered through without comment. He climbed on board the train. It had been a short visit to Moscow and he would never see the city again in his life, though he would always remember the kindness of the woman, the stationmaster's wife, comrade. . . . He didn't even know her name.

Wladek stayed in the general-class car for his journey. Odessa was much less distant from Moscow than Irkutsk, about a thumb's length on the doctor's sketch, 800 miles in reality. While Wladek was studying his rudimentary map, he became distracted by another game of pitch-and-toss which was taking place in the car. He folded the parchment, replaced it safely in the lining of his suit and began taking a closer interest in the game. He noticed that one of the gamblers was winning consistently, even when the odds were stacked against him. Wladek watched the man more carefully and soon realized that he was cheating.

He moved to the other side of the car to make sure he could still see the man cheating when facing him, but he couldn't. He edged forward and made a place for himself in the circle of gamblers. Every time the cheat had lost twice in a row, Wladek backed him with one ruble, doubling his stake until he won. The cheat was either flattered or aware he would be wise to remain silent about Wladek's luck, because he never once even glanced in his direction. By the time they reached the next station, Wladek had won fourteen rubles, two of which he used to buy himself an apple and a cup of hot soup. He had won enough to last the entire journey to Odessa, and pleased with the thought that he could win even more rubles with his new safe system, he silently thanked the unknown gambler and climbed back into the train, ready to pursue this strategy. As his foot touched the top step, he was knocked flying into a corner. His arm was jerked painfully behind his back, and his face was pushed hard against the car wall. His nose began to bleed and he could feel the point of a knife touching the lobe of his ear.

"Do you hear me, boy?"

"Yes," said Wladek, petrified.

"If you go back to my car again, I take this ear right off. Then you won't be able to hear me, will you?"

"No, sir," said Wladek.

Wladek felt the point of the knife breaking the surface of the skin behind his ear and blood began trickling down his neck.

"Let that be a warning to you, boy."

A knee suddenly came up into his kidneys with as much force as the gambler could muster. Wladek collapsed to the floor. A hand rummaged into his coat pockets and the recently acquired rubles were removed.

"Mine, I think," the voice said.

Blood was still coming out of Wladek's nose and from behind his ear. When he summoned the courage to look up, he was alone; there was no sign of the gambler. He tried to get to his feet, but his body refused to obey the order from his brain, so he remained slumped in the corner for several minutes. Eventually, when he was able to rise, he walked slowly to the other end of the train, as far away from the gambler's car as possible, his limp grotesquely exaggerated. He hid in a car occupied mostly by women and children and fell into a deep sleep.

At the next stop, Wladek didn't leave the train. He undid his little parcel and started to investigate. Apples, bread, nuts, a shirt, a pair of trousers and even shoes were contained in that brown-papered treasure trove. He changed into his new clothes. What a woman, what a husband.

He ate, he slept, he dreamed. And finally, after five nights and four days, the train chugged into the terminal at Odessa. The same check at the ticket barrier, but his papers were all in order and the guard barely gave Wladek a second look. Now he was on his own. He still had 150 rubles in the lining of his sleeve, and no intention of wasting any of them.

Wladek spent the rest of the day walking around the town trying to familiarize himself with its geography, but he found he was continually distracted by sights he had never seen before: big town houses, shops with windows, hawkers selling their colorful trinkets on the street, gaslights, and even a monkey on a stick. Wladek walked on until he reached the harbor and the open sea beyond it. Yes, there it was—what the Baron had called a sea. Wladek gazed longingly into the blue expanse: that way lay freedom and escape from Russia. The city must have seen its fair share of fighting: burned-out houses and squalor were all too evident, grotesque in the mild, flower-scented sea air. Wladek wondered whether the city was still at war. There was no one he could ask. As the sun disappeared behind the high buildings, he began to look for somewhere to spend the night. Wladek took a side road and kept walking; he must have seemed a strange sight with his sheepskin coat practically dragging along the ground and the brown paper parcel under his arm. Nothing looked safe to him until he came across a railway siding in which a solitary old railroad car stood in isolation. He stared into it cautiously: darkness and silence; no one was there. He threw his paper parcel into the carriage, raised his tired body up onto the boards, crawled into a corner and lay down to sleep. As his head touched the wooden floor, a body leaped on top of him and two hands were quickly around his throat. He could barely breathe.

"Who are you?" growled the voice of a boy who, in the darkness, sounded no older than himself.

"Wladek Koskiewicz."

"Where do you come from?"

"Moscow." Slonim had been on the tip of Wladek's tongue.

"Well, you're not sleeping in my carriage, Muscovite," said the voice.

"Sorry," said Wladek. "I didn't know."

"Got any money?" His thumbs pressed into Wladek's throat.

"A little," said Wladek.

"How much?"

"Seven rubles."

"Hand it over."

Wladek rummaged in the pocket of his overcoat, while the boy also pushed one hand firmly into it, releasing the pressure on Wladek's throat.

In one moment, Wladek brought his knee into the boy's crotch with every ounce of force he could muster. His attacker flew back in agony, clutching his groin. Wladek leaped on him, hitting out at him fiercely. The advantage had suddenly changed. He was no competition for Wladek; sleeping in a derelict railroad car was five-star luxury compared to living in the dungeons and a Russian labor camp.

Wladek stopped only when his adversary was pinned to the car floor, helpless. The boy pleaded with Wladek.

"Go to the far end of the car and stay there," said Wladek. "If you so much as move a muscle, I'll kill you."

"Yes, yes," said the boy, scrambling away.

Wladek heard him hit the far end of the car. He sat still and listened for a few moments—no movement—then he lowered his head once more to the floor and in moments he was sleeping soundly.

When he awoke, the sun was already shining through between the boards of the car. He turned over and glanced at his adversary of the previous night for the first time. He was lying in a fetal position, still asleep at the other end of the car.

"Come here," commanded Wladek.

The boy awakened slowly.

"Come here," repeated Wladek, a little more loudly.

The boy obeyed immediately. It was the first chance Wladek had had to look at him properly. They were about the same age, but the boy was a clear foot taller, with a younger-looking face and fair scruffy hair.

"First things first," said Wladek. "How does one get something to eat?"

"Follow me," said the boy, and he leaped out of the car. Wladek limped after him, following him up the hill into the town, where the morning market was being set up. He had not seen so much wholesome food since those magnificent dinners with the Baron. Row upon row of stalls with fruit, vegetables, greens and even his favorite nuts. The boy could see that Wladek was overwhelmed by the sight.

"Now I'll tell you what we do," the boy said, sounding confident for the first time. "I will go over to the corner stall and steal an orange and then make a run for it. You will shout at the top of your voice 'Stop thief!' The stallkeeper will chase me and when he does, you move in and fill your pockets. Don't be greedy; enough for one meal. Then you return here. Got it?"

"Yes, I think so," said Wladek.

"Let's see if you're up to it, Muscovite." The boy looked at him, snarled and was gone. Wladek watched him in admiration as he swaggered to the corner of the first market stall, removed an orange from the top of a pyramid, made a short unheard remark to the stallkeeper and started to run slowly. He glanced back at Wladek, who had entirely forgotten to shout "Stop thief," but then the stall owner looked up and began to chase the boy. While everyone's eyes were on Wladek's accomplice, he moved in quickly and managed to take three oranges, an apple and a potato and put them in the large pockets of his overcoat. When the stallkeeper looked as if he was about to catch Wladek's accomplice, the boy lobbed the orange back at him. The man stopped to pick it up and swore at him, waving his fist, complaining vociferously to the other merchants as he returned to his stall.

Wladek was shaking with mirth as he took in the scene when a hand was placed firmly on his shoulder. He turned around in the horror of having been caught.

"Did you get anything, Muscovite, or are you only here as a sightseer?"

Wladek burst out laughing with relief and produced the three oranges, the apple and the potato. The boy joined in the laughter.

"What's your name?" said Wladek.

"Stefan."

"Let's do it again, Stefan."

"Hold on, Muscovite; don't you start getting too clever. If we do it again, we'll have to go to the other end of the market and wait for at least an hour. You're working with a professional, but don't imagine you won't get caught occasionally."

The two boys went quietly through to the other end of the market, Stefan walking with a swagger for which Wladek would have traded the three oranges, the apple, the potato and the 150 rubles. They mingled with the morning shoppers and when Stefan decided the time was right, they repeated the trick twice. Satisfied with the results, they returned to the railway car to enjoy their captured spoils: six oranges, five apples, three potatoes, a pear, several varieties of nuts and the special prize, a melon. In the past, Stefan had never had pockets big enough to hold a melon. Wladek's greatcoat took care of that.

"Not bad," said Wladek as he dug his teeth into a potato.

"Do you eat the skins as well?" asked Stefan, horrified.

"I've been places where the skins are a luxury," replied Wladek.

Stefan looked at him with admiration.

"Next problem is, How do we get some money?" said Wladek.

"You want everything in one day, don't you, oh master?" said Stefan. "Chain gang on the waterfront is the best bet, if you think you're up to some real work, Muscovite."

"Show me," said Wladek.

After they had eaten half the fruit and hidden the rest under the straw in the corner of the railway car, Stefan took Wladek down the steps to the harbor and showed him the many ships. Wladek couldn't believe his eyes. He had been told by the Baron of the great ships that crossed the high seas delivering their cargoes to foreign lands, but these were so much bigger than he had ever imagined, and they stood in a line as far as the eye could see.

Stefan interrupted his thoughts. "See that one over there, the big green one? Well, what you have to do is pick up a basket at the bottom of the gangplank, fill it with grain, climb up the ladder and then drop your load in the hold. You get a ruble for every four trips you make. Be sure you can count, Muscovite, because the bastard in charge of the gang will swindle you as soon as look at you and pocket the money for himself."

Stefan and Wladek spent the rest of the afternoon carrying grain up the ladder. They made twenty-six rubles between them. After a dinner of stolen nuts, bread and an onion they hadn't intended to take, they slept happily in their railroad car.

Wladek was the first to wake the next morning and Stefan found him studying his map.

"What's that?" asked Stefan.

"This is a route showing me how to get out of Russia."

"What do you want to leave Russia for when you can stay here and team up with me?" said Stefan. "We could be partners."

"No, I must get to Turkey; there I will be a free man for the first time. Why don't you come with me, Stefan?"

"I could never leave Odessa. This is my home, the railway is where I live and these are the people I have known all my life. It's not good, but it might be worse in Turkey. But if that's what you want, I will help you."

"How do I discover which ship is going to Turkey?" asked Wladek.

"Easy—because I know how to find out where every ship is going. We'll get the information from One Tooth Joe at the end of the pier. You'll have to give him a ruble."

"I'll bet he splits the money with you."

"Fifty-fifty," said Stefan. "You're learning fast, Muscovite." And with that he again leaped out of the car.

Wladek followed him as he ran between other railroad cars, again conscious of how easily other boys moved and how he limped. When they reached the end of the pier, Stefan took him into a small room full of dust-covered books and old timetables. Wladek couldn't see anyone there, but then he heard a voice from behind a large pile of books saying, "What do you want, urchin? I do not have time to waste on you."

"Some information for my traveling companion, Joe. When is the next luxury cruise to Turkey?"

"Money up front," said an old man whose head appeared from behind the books, a lined, weather-beaten face below a seaman's cap. His black eyes were taking in Wladek.

"Used to be a great sea dog," said Stefan in a whisper loud enough for Joe to hear.

"None of your cheek, boy. Where is the ruble?"

"My friend carries my purse," said Stefan. "Show him the ruble, Wladek."

Wladek pulled out a coin. Joe bit it with his one remaining tooth, shuffled over to the bookcase and pulled out a large green timetable. Dust flew everywhere. He started coughing as he thumbed through the dirty pages, moving his short, stubby, rope-worn finger down the long columns of names.

"Next Thursday the *Renaska* is coming in to pick up coal—probably will leave on Saturday. If the ship can load quickly enough, she may sail on the Friday night and save the berthing tariffs. She'll dock at Berth Seventeen."

"Thanks, One Tooth," said Stefan. "I'll see if I can bring in some more of my wealthy associates in the future."

One Tooth Joe raised his fist, cursing, as Stefan and Wladek ran out onto the wharf.

For the next three days the two boys stole food, loaded grain and slept. By the time the Turkish ship arrived on the following Thursday, Stefan had almost convinced Wladek that he should remain in Odessa. But Wladek's fear of the Russians outweighed the attraction of his new life with Stefan.

They stood on the quayside, staring at the new arrival docking at Berth 17.

"How will I get on the ship?" asked Wladek.

"Simple," said Stefan. "We can join the chain gang tomorrow morning. I'll take the place behind you, and when the coal hold is nearly full, you can jump in and hide while I pick up your basket and walk on down the other side."

"And collect my share of the money, no doubt," said Wladek.

"Naturally," said Stefan. "There must be some financial reward for my superior intelligence or how could a man hope to sustain his belief in free enterprise?"

They joined the chain gang first thing the next morning and hauled coal up and down the gangplank until they were both ready to drop, but it still wasn't enough. The hold wasn't half full by nightfall. The two boys slept soundly that night. The following morning, they started again, and mid-afternoon, when the hold was nearly full, Stefan kicked Wladek's ankle.

"Next time, Muscovite," he said.

When they reached the top of the gangway, Wladek threw his coal in, dropped the basket on the deck, jumped over the side of the hold and landed on the coal, while Stefan picked up Wladek's basket and continued down the other side of the gangplank whistling.

"Good-bye, my friend," he said, "and good luck with the infidel Turks."

Wladek pressed himself in a corner of the hold and watched the coal come pouring in beside him. The dust was everywhere, in his nose and mouth, in his lungs and eyes. With painful effort he avoided coughing for fear of being heard by one of the ship's crew. Just as he thought that he could no longer bear the air of the hold and that he would return to Stefan and find some other way of escaping, he saw the doors close above him. He coughed luxuriously.

After a few moments he felt something take a bite at his ankle. His blood went cold as he realized what it had to be. He looked down, trying to work out where it had come from. No sooner had he thrown a piece of coal at the monster and sent him scurrying away than another one came at him, then another and another. The braver ones went for his legs. They seemed to appear from nowhere. Black, large and hungry. He stared down, searching for them. It was the first time in his life that Wladek realized that rats had red eyes. He clambered desperately to the top of the pile of coal and pushed open the hatch. The sunlight came flooding through and the rats disappeared back into their tunnels in the coal. He started to climb out, but the ship was already well clear of the quayside. He fell back into the hold, terrified. If the ship were forced to return and to hand Wladek over, he knew it would mean a one-way journey back to Camp 201 and the White Russians. He chose to stay with the black rats. As soon as Wladek closed the hatch, they came at him again. As fast as he could throw lumps of coal at the verminous creatures, a new one would appear in some spot. Every few moments Wladek had to open the hatch to let some light in, for light seemed to be the only ally that would frighten the rodents away.

For two days and three nights Wladek waged a running battle with the rats without ever catching a moment of quiet sleep. When the ship finally reached the port of Constantinople and a deckhand opened the hold, Wladek was black from his head to his knees with dirt, and red from his knees to his toes with blood. The deckhand dragged him out. Wladek tried to stand up but collapsed in a heap on the deck.

When Wladek came to—he knew not where or how much later—he found himself on a bed in a small room with three men in long white coats who were studying him carefully, speaking a tongue he had never heard before. How many languages were there in the world? He looked at himself, still red and black, and when he tried to sit up, one of the white-coated men, the oldest of the three, with a thin, lined face and a goatee, pushed him firmly back down. He addressed Wladek in the strange tongue. Wladek shook his head. The man then tried Russian. Wladek again shook his head—that would be the quickest way back to where he had come from. The next language the doctor tried was German, and Wladek realized that his command of that language was greater than his inquisitor's.

"You speak German?"

"Yes."

"Ah, so you're not Russian then?"

"No."

"What were you doing in Russia?"

"Trying to escape."

"Ah." The man then turned to his companions and seemed to report the conversation in his own tongue. The three left the room.

A nurse came in and scrubbed Wladek clean, taking little notice of his cries of anguish. She covered his legs in a thick brown ointment and left him to sleep again. When Wladek awoke for the second time, he was quite alone. He lay staring at the white ceiling, considering his next move.

Still not sure of which country he was in, he climbed onto the windowsill and stared out of the window. He could see a marketplace, not unlike the one in Odessa, except that the men wore long white robes and had darker skin. They also wore colorful hats that looked like small flowerpots upside down and sandals on their feet. The women were all in black; even their faces were covered except for their black eyes. Wladek watched the bustle in the marketplace as the women bargained for their daily food; that was one thing at least that seemed to be international.

It was several minutes before he noticed that running down by the side of the building window was a red iron ladder stretching all the way to the ground. He climbed down from the windowsill, walked cautiously to the door, opened it and peered into the corridor. Men and women were walking up and down, but none of them showed any interest in him. He closed the door gently, found his belongings in a closet in the corner of his room and dressed quickly. His clothes were still black with coal dust and felt gritty to his clean skin. Back to the windowsill. The window opened easily. He gripped the fire escape, swung out of the window and started to climb down toward freedom. The first thing that hit him was the heat. He wished he were no longer wearing the heavy overcoat.

Once he touched the ground Wladek tried to run, but his legs were so weak and painful that he could only walk slowly. How he wished he could rid himself of that limp. He did not look back at the hospital until he was lost in the throng in the marketplace.

Wladek stared at the tempting food at the stalls and decided to buy an orange and some nuts. He went to the lining in his suit; surely the money had been in his sleeve. Yes it had, but it was no longer there, and far worse, the silver band was also gone. The men in the white coats had stolen his possessions. He considered going back to the hospital to retrieve the lost heirloom but decided against returning until he had had something to eat. Perhaps there was still some money in his pockets. He searched around in the large overcoat pocket and immediately found the three notes and some coins. They were all together with the doctor's map and the silver band. Wladek was overjoyed at the discovery. He slipped the silver band on and pushed it above his elbow.

Wladek chose the largest orange he could see and a handful of nuts. The stallkeeper said something to him that he could not understand. Wladek felt the easiest way out of the language barrier was to hand over a 50-ruble note. The stallkeeper looked at it, laughed and threw his arms in the sky.

"Allah!" he cried, snatching the nuts and the orange from Wladek and waving him away with his forefinger. Wladek walked off in despair; a different language means different money, he supposed. In Russia he had been poor; here he was penniless. He would have to steal an orange; if he was about to be caught, he would throw it back to the stallkeeper. Wladek walked to the other end of the marketplace in the same way as Stefan had, but he couldn't imitate the swagger and he didn't feel the same confidence. He chose the end stall and when he was sure no one was watching, he picked up an orange and started to run. Suddenly there was an uproar. It seemed as if half the city were chasing him.

A big man jumped on the limping Wladek and threw him to the ground. Six or seven people seized hold of different parts of his body while a larger group thronged around as he was dragged back to the stall. A policeman awaited them. Notes were taken, and there was a shouted exchange between the stall owner and the policeman, each man's voice rising with each statement. The policeman then turned to Wladek and shouted at him too, but Wladek could not understand a word. The policeman shrugged his shoulders and marched Wladek off by the ear. People continued to bawl at him. Some of them spat on him. When Wladek reached the police station he was taken underground and thrown into a tiny cell, already occupied by twenty or thirty criminals—thugs, thieves or he knew not what. Wladek did not speak to them and they showed no desire to talk to him. He remained

with his back to a wall, cowering, quiet, terrified. For a day
and a night he was left there with no food. The smell of exc-
reta made him vomit until there was nothing left in him. He
never thought the day would come when the dungeons in
Slonim would seem uncrowded and peaceful.   .

The next morning Wladek was dragged from the basement by two guards and marched to a hall, where he was
lined up with several other prisoners. They were all roped to
each other around the waist and led from the jail in a long
line down into the street. Another large crowd had gathered
outside, and their loud cheer of welcome made Wladek feel
that they had been waiting some time for the prisoners to appear. The crowd followed them all the way to the marketplace—screaming, clapping and shouting—for what reason,
Wladek feared even to contemplate. The line came to a halt
when they reached the market square. The first prisoner was
unleashed from his rope and taken into the center of the
square, which was already crammed with hundreds of people, all shouting at the top of their voices.

Wladek watched the scene in disbelief. When the first
prisoner reached the middle of the square, he was knocked
to his knees by the guard and then his right hand was
strapped to a wooden block by a giant of a man who raised a
large sword above his head and brought it down with terrible
force, aiming at the prisoner's wrist. He managed to catch
only the tips of the fingers. The prisoner screamed with pain
as the sword was raised again. This time the sword hit the
wrist but still did not finish the job properly, and the wrist
dangled from the prisoner's arm, blood pouring out onto the
sand. The sword was raised for a third time and for the third
time it came down. The prisoner's hand at last fell to the
ground. The crowd roared its approval. The prisoner was at
last released and he slumped in a heap, unconscious. He was
dragged off by a disinterested guard and left on the edge of
the crowd. A weeping woman—his wife, Wladek presumed—hurriedly tied a tourniquet of dirty cloth around the
bloody stump. The second prisoner died of shock before the
fourth blow was struck. The giant executioner was not inter-

ested in death, so he hurriedly continued his task; he was paid to remove hands.

Wladek looked around in terror and retched; he would have vomited if there had been anything left in his stomach. He searched in every direction for help or some means of escape; no one had told him that under Islamic law the punishment for trying to escape would be the loss of a foot. His eyes darted around the mass of faces until he saw a man in the crowd dressed like a European, wearing a dark suit. The man was standing about twenty yards away from Wladek and was watching the spectacle with obvious disgust. But he did not once look in Wladek's direction, nor could he hear the boy's shouts for help in the uproar every time the sword was brought down. Was he French, German, English or even Polish? Wladek could not tell, but for some reason he was witnessing this macabre spectacle. Wladek stared at him, willing him to look his way. But he did not. Wladek waved his free arm but still could not gain the European's attention. They untied the man two in front of Wladek and dragged him along the ground toward the block. When the sword went up again and the crowd cheered, the man in the dark suit turned his eyes away in disgust and Wladek waved frantically at him again.

The man stared at Wladek and then turned to talk to a companion, whom Wladek had not noticed. The guard was now struggling with the prisoner immediately in front of Wladek. He placed the prisoner's hand under the strap; the sword went up and removed the hand in one blow. The crowd seemed disappointed. Wladek stared again at the Europeans. They were now both looking at him. He willed them to move, but they only continued to stare.

The guard came over, threw Wladek's 50-ruble overcoat to the ground, undid his cuff and rolled up his sleeve. Wladek struggled futilely as he was dragged across the square. He was no match for the guard. When he reached the block, he was kicked in the back of his knees and collapsed to the ground. The strap was fastened over his right wrist, and there was nothing left for him to do but close his eyes as

the sword was raised above the executioner's head. He
waited in agony for the terrible blow and then there was a
sudden hush in the crowd as the Baron's silver band fell
from Wladek's elbow down to his wrist and onto the block.
An eerie silence came over the crowd as the heirloom shone
brightly in the sunlight. The executioner stopped and put
down his sword and studied the silver band. Wladek opened
his eyes. The guard tried to pull the band over Wladek's
wrist, but he couldn't get it past the leather strap. A man in
uniform ran quickly forward and joined the executioner. He
too studied the band and the inscription and then ran to another man, who must have been of higher authority, because
as he now walked toward Wladek he walked slowly. The
sword was resting on the ground, and the crowd was now beginning to jeer and hoot. The second officer also tried to pull
the silver band off but could not get it over the block and he
seemed unwilling to undo the strap. He shouted words at
Wladek, who did not understand what he was saying and
replied in Polish, "I do not speak your language."

The officer looked surprised and threw his hands in the
air shouting "Allah!" That must be the same as "Holy God,"
thought Wladek. The officer walked slowly toward the two
men in the crowd wearing Western suits, arms going in
every direction like a disorganized windmill. Wladek prayed
to God—in such situations any man prays to any god, be it
Allah or the Virgin Mary. The Europeans were still staring at
Wladek and Wladek was nodding frantically. One of the two
men joined the Turkish officer as he walked back toward the
block. The former knelt on one knee by Wladek's side, studied the silver band and then looked carefully at him. Wladek
waited. He could converse in five languages and prayed that
the gentleman would speak one of them. His heart sank
when the European turned to the officer and addressed him
in his own tongue. The crowd was now hissing and throwing
rotten fruit at the block. The officer was nodding his agreement while the gentleman stared intently at Wladek.

"Do you speak English?"

Wladek heaved a sigh of relief. "Yes, sir, not bad. I am Polish citizen."

"How did you come into possession of that silver band?"

"It belong my father, sir. He die in prison by the Germans in Poland and I captured and sent to a prison camp in Russia. I escape and come here by ship. I have no eat for days. When stallkeeper no accept my rubles for orange, I take one because I much, much hungry."

The Englishman rose slowly from his knee, turned to the officer and spoke to him very firmly. The latter, in turn, addressed the executioner, who looked doubtful, but when the officer repeated the order a little louder, he bent down and reluctantly undid the leather strap. Wladek retched again.

"Come with me," said the Englishman. "And quickly, before they change their minds."

Still in a daze, Wladek grabbed his coat and followed him. The crowd booed and jeered, throwing things at him as he departed, and the swordsman quickly put the next prisoner's hand on the block and with his first blow managed to remove only a thumb. This seemed to pacify the mob.

The Englishman moved swiftly through the hustling crowd out of the square, where he was joined by his companion.

"What's happening, Edward?"

"The boy says he is a Pole and that he escaped from Russia. I told the official in charge that he was English, so now he is our responsibility. Let's get him to the embassy and find out if the boy's story bears any resemblance to the truth."

Wladek ran between the two men as they hurried on through the bazaar and into the Street of Seven Kings. He could still faintly hear the mob behind him, screaming their approval every time the executioner brought down his sword.

The two Englishmen walked through an archway over a pebbled courtyard toward a large gray building and beckoned Wladek to follow them. On the door were the welcoming words BRITISH EMBASSY. Once inside the building, Wladek began to feel safe for the first time. He walked a pace behind the two men down a long hall with walls covered with paintings of strangely clad soldiers and sailors. At the far end was a magnificent portrait of an old man in a blue naval uniform liberally adorned with medals. His fine beard reminded Wladek of the Baron. A soldier appeared from nowhere and saluted.

"Take this boy, Corporal Smithers, and see that he gets a bath. Then feed him in the kitchen. When he has eaten and smells a little less like a walking pigsty, find him some new clothes and bring him to my office."

"Yes, sir," the corporal said, and saluted.

"Come with me, my lad." The soldier marched away. Wladek followed him obediently, having to run to keep up with his walking pace. He was taken to the basement of the embassy and left in a little room; it had a tiny window. The corporal told him to get undressed and then left him on his own. He returned a few minutes later with some clothes, only to find Wladek still sitting on the edge of the bed fully dressed, dazedly twisting the silver band around and around his wrist.

"Hurry up, lad. You're not on a rest cure."

"Sorry, sir," Wladek said.

"Don't call me sir, lad. I am Corporal Smithers. You call me Corporal."

"I am Wladek Koskiewicz. You call me Wladek."

"Don't be funny with me, lad. We've got enough funny people in the British army without you wishing to join the ranks."

Wladek did not understand what the soldier meant. He undressed quickly.

"Follow me at the double."

Another marvelous bath with hot water and soap. Wladek thought of his Russian protectress, and of the son he might have become to her but for her husband. A new set of clothes, strange but clean and fresh-smelling. Whose son had they belonged to? The soldier was back at the door.

Corporal Smithers took Wladek to the kitchen and left him with a plump, pink-faced cook, with the warmest face Wladek had seen since leaving Poland. She reminded him of Niania. Wladek could not help wondering what would happen to her waistline after a few weeks in Camp 201.

"Hello," she said with a beaming smile. "What's your name then?"

Wladek told her.

"Well, laddie, it looks as though you could do with a good British meal inside of you—none of this Turkish muck will suffice. We'll start with some hot soup and beef. You'll need something substantial if you're to face Mr. Prendergast." She laughed. "Just remember his bite's not as bad as his bark. Although he is an Englishman, his heart's in the right place."

"You are an English, Mrs. Cook?" asked Wladek, surprised.

"Good Lord no, laddie, I'm Scottish. There's a world of difference. We hate the English more than the Germans do," she said, laughing. She set a dish of steaming soup, thick with meat and vegetables, in front of Wladek. He had entirely forgotten that food could smell and taste so good. He ate the meal slowly, fearing that something like it might not happen again for a very long time.

The corporal reappeared. "Have you had enough to eat, my lad?"

"Yes, thank you, Mr. Corporal."

The corporal gave Wladek a suspicious look, but he saw no trace of cheek in the boy's expression. "Good. Then let's be moving. Can't be late on parade for Mr. Prendergast."

The corporal disappeared through the kitchen door and Wladek stared at the cook. He always hated saying goodbye to someone he had just met, especially when the person had been kind.

"Off you go, laddie, if you know what's good for you."

"Thank you, Mrs. Cook," said Wladek. "Your food is best I can ever remember."

The cook smiled at him. He again had to limp hard to

catch up with the corporal, whose marching pace still kept
Wladek trotting. The soldier came to a brisk halt outside a
door that Wladek nearly ran into.

"Look where you're going, my lad, look where you're
going."

The corporal gave a short *rap-rap* on the door.

"Come," said a voice.

The corporal opened the door and saluted. "The Polish
boy, sir, as you requested, scrubbed and fed."

"Thank you, Corporal. Perhaps you would be kind
enough to ask Mr. Grant to join us."

Edward Prendergast looked up from his desk. He waved
Wladek to a seat without speaking and continued to work at
some papers. Wladek sat looking at him and then at the portraits on the wall. More generals and admirals and that old
bearded gentleman again, this time in khaki army uniform.
A few minutes later the other Englishman he remembered
from the market square came in.

"Thank you for joining us, Harry. Do have a seat, old
boy." Mr. Prendergast turned to Wladek. "Now, my lad, let's
hear your story from the beginning, with no exaggerations,
only the truth. Do you understand?"

"Yes, sir."

Wladek started his story with his days in Poland. It took
him some time to find the right English words. It was apparent from the looks on the faces of the two Englishmen that
they were at first incredulous. They occasionally stopped
him and asked questions, nodding to each other at his answers. After an hour of talking, Wladek's life history had
reached the point where he was in the office of His Britannic
Majesty's Second Consul to Turkey.

"I think, Harry," said the Second Consul, "it is our duty to
inform the Polish delegation immediately and then hand
young Koskiewicz over to them. I feel in the circumstances
he is undoubtedly their responsibility."

"Agreed," said the man called Harry. "You know, my boy,
you had a narrow escape in the market today. The Sher—

that is, the old Islamic religious law—which provides for cutting off a hand for theft was officially abandoned in theory years ago. In fact, it is a crime under the Ottoman Penal Code to still inflict such a punishment. Nevertheless, in practice the barbarians still continue to carry it out." He shrugged.

"Why not my hand?" asked Wladek, holding onto his wrist.

"I told them they could cut off all the Moslem hands they wanted, but not an Englishman's," Edward Prendergast interjected.

"Thank God," Wladek said faintly.

"Edward Prendergast, actually," the Second Consul said, smiling for the first time. "You can spend the night here and we will take you to your own delegation tomorrow. The Poles do not actually have an embassy in Constantinople," he said, slightly disdainfully, "but my opposite number is a good fellow considering he's a foreigner." He pressed a button, and the corporal reappeared immediately.

"Sir."

"Corporal, take young Koskiewicz to his room and in the morning see he is given breakfast and is brought to me at nine sharp."

"Sir. This way, boy, at the double."

Wladek was led away by the corporal. He had not even had enough time to thank the two Englishmen who had saved his hand—and perhaps his life. Back in the clean little room, with its clean bed neatly turned down as if he were an honored guest, he undressed, threw his pillow on the floor and slept soundly in the bed until the morning light shone through the tiny window.

"Rise and shine, lad, sharpish."

It was the corporal, his uniform immaculately smart and knife-edge pressed, looking as though he had never been to bed. For an instant Wladek, surfacing from sleep, thought himself back in Camp 201, for the corporal's banging on the end of the metal bed frame with his cane resembled the noise of the banging on the triangle that Wladek had grown so accustomed to. He slid out of bed and reached for his clothes.

"Wash first, my lad, wash first. We don't want your horrible smells worrying Mr. Prendergast so early in the morning, do we?"

Wladek was unsure which part of himself to wash, so unusually clean did he feel himself to be. The corporal was staring at him.

"What's wrong with your leg, lad?"

"Nothing, nothing," said Wladek, turning away from the staring eyes.

"Right. I'll be back in three minutes. Three minutes, do you hear, my lad? Be sure you're ready."

Wladek washed his hands and face quickly and then dressed. He was waiting at the end of the bed, holding his long sheepskin coat, when the corporal returned to take him to the Second Consul. Mr. Prendergast welcomed him and seemed to have softened considerably since their first meeting.

"Good morning, Koskiewicz."

"Good morning, sir."

"Did you enjoy your breakfast?"

"I no had breakfast, sir."

"Why not?" said the Second Consul, looking toward the corporal.

"Overslept, I'm afraid, sir. He would have been late for you."

"Well, we must see what we can do about that. Corporal, will you ask Mrs. Henderson to rustle up an apple or something?"

"Yes, sir."

Wladek and the Second Consul walked slowly along the corridor toward the front door of the embassy and across the pebbled courtyard to a waiting car, an Austin, one of the few engine-driven vehicles in Turkey and Wladek's first journey in a private car. He was sorry to be leaving the British embassy. It was the first place in which he had felt safe for years. He wondered if he was ever going to sleep more than one night in the same bed for the rest of his life. The corporal ran down the steps and took the driver's seat. He passed Wladek an apple and some warm fresh bread.

"See there are no crumbs left in the car, lad. The cook sends her compliments."

The drive through the hot, busy streets was conducted at walking pace as the Turks did not believe anything could go faster than a camel and made no attempt to clear a path for the little Austin. Even with all the windows open Wladek was sweating from the oppressive heat while Mr. Prendergast remained quite cool and unperturbed. Wladek tried to hide himself in the back of the car for fear that someone who had witnessed the previous day's events might recognize him and stir the mob to anger again. When the little black Austin came to a halt outside a small, decaying building marked KONSULAT POLSKI, Wladek felt a twinge of excitement mingled with disappointment.

The three of them climbed out.

"Where's the apple core, boy?" demanded the corporal.

"I eat him."

The corporal laughed and knocked on the door. A friendly-looking little man, with dark hair and a firm jaw, opened it. He was in shirt sleeves and deeply tanned, obviously by the Turkish sun. He addressed them in Polish. His words were the first Wladek had heard in his native tongue since leaving the labor camp. Wladek answered quickly, explaining his presence. His fellow countryman turned to the British Second Consul.

"This way, Mr. Prendergast," he said in perfect English. "It was good of you to bring the boy over personally."

A few diplomatic niceties were exchanged before Prendergast and the corporal took their leave. Wladek gazed at them, fumbling for an English expression more adequate than "Thank you."

Prendergast patted Wladek on the head as he might a

cocker spaniel. And as the corporal closed the door, he winked at Wladek. "Good luck, my lad. God knows you deserve it."

The Polish Consul introduced himself to Wladek as Pawel Zaleski. Again Wladek was required to recount the story of his life, finding it easier in Polish than he had in English. Pawel Zaleski heard him out in silence, shaking his head sorrowfully.

"My poor child," he said heavily. "You have borne more than your share of our country's suffering for one so young. And now what are we to do with you?"

"I must return to Poland and reclaim my castle," said Wladek.

"Poland," said Pawel Zaleski. "Where's that? The area of land where you lived remains in dispute and there is still heavy fighting going on between the Poles and the Russians. General Pilsudski is doing all he can to protect the territorial integrity of our fatherland. But it would be foolish for any of us to be optimistic. There is little left for you now in Poland. No, your best plan would be to start a new life in England or America."

"But I don't want to go to England or America. I am Polish."

"You will always be Polish, Wladek—no one can take that away from you wherever you decide to settle. But you must be realistic about your life—which has hardly even begun."

Wladek lowered his head in despair. Had he gone through all this only to be told he could never return to his native land? He fought back the tears.

Pawel Zaleski put his arm around the boy's shoulders. "Never forget that you are one of the lucky ones who escaped, who came out alive. You only have to remember your friend Dr. Dubien to be aware of what life might have been like."

Wladek didn't speak.

"Now you must put all thoughts of the past behind you and think only of the future, Wladek, and perhaps in your lifetime you will see Poland rise again, which is more than I dare hope for."

Wladek remained silent.

"Well, there's no need to make an immediate decision," the Consul said kindly. "You can stay here for as long as it takes to decide on your future."

CHAPTER
TEN

The future was something that was worrying Anne. The first few months of her marriage were happy, marred only by her anxiety over William's increasing dislike of Henry, and her new husband's seeming inability to start working. Henry was a little touchy on the point, explaining to Anne that he was still disoriented by the war and that he wasn't willing to rush into something he might well be stuck with for the rest of his life. She found this hard to swallow and finally the matter brought on their first row.

"I don't understand why you haven't opened that real estate business you used to be so keen on, Henry."

"I can't. The time isn't quite right. The realty market doesn't look that promising at the moment."

"You've been saying that now for nearly a year. I wonder if it will ever be promising enough for you."

"Sure it will. Truth is, I need a little more capital to get myself started. Now, if you would let me have some of your money, I could get cracking tomorrow."

"That's impossible, Henry. You know the terms of Richard's will. My allowance was stopped the day we were married and now I have only the capital left."

"A little of that would help me to get going, and don't forget that precious boy of yours has well over twenty million in the family trust."

"You seem to know a lot about William's trust," Anne said suspiciously.

"Oh, come on, Anne, give me a chance to be your husband. Don't make me feel like a guest in my own home."

"What's happened to your money, Henry? You always led me to believe you had enough to start your own business."

"You've always known I was not in Richard's class financially, and there was a time, Anne, when you claimed it didn't matter. 'I'd marry you, Henry, if you were penniless,' " he mocked.

Anne burst into tears, and Henry tried to console her. She spent the rest of the evening in his arms talking the problem over. Anne managed to convince herself she was being unwifely and ungenerous. She had more money than she could possibly need; couldn't she entrust a little of it to the man to whom she was so willing to entrust the rest of her life?

Acting upon these thoughts, she agreed to let Henry have $100,000 to set up his own real estate firm in Boston. Within a month Henry had found a smart new office in a fashionable part of town, appointed a staff and started work. Soon he was mixing with the important city politicians and real estate men in Boston. They talked of the boom in farmland and they flattered Henry. Anne didn't care very much for them as social company, but Henry was happy and appeared to be successful at his work.

When William was fifteen he was in his third year at St. Paul's, sixth in his class overall and first in mathematics. He had also become a rising figure in the Debating Society. He wrote to his mother once a week, reporting his progress, always addressing his letters to Mrs. Richard Kane, refusing to acknowledge that Henry Osborne even existed. Anne wasn't sure whether she should talk to him about it, and each Monday she would carefully extract William's letter from the box to be certain that Henry never saw the envelope. She continued to hope that in time William would come around to liking Henry, but it became clear that that hope was unrealistic when, in one particular letter to his mother, William sought her permission to spend the summer holidays with his friend Matthew Lester, first at a summer camp in Vermont, then with the Lester family in New York. The request came as a painful blow to Anne, but she took the easy way out and fell in with William's plans, which Henry also seemed to favor.

William hated Henry Osborne and nursed the hatred passionately, not sure what he could actually do about it. He was grateful that Henry never visited him at school; he could not have tolerated having the other boys see his mother with that man. It was bad enough that he had to live with Henry in Boston.

For the first time since his mother's marriage, William was anxious for the holidays to come.

The Lesters' Packard chauffeured William and Matthew noiselessly to the camp in Vermont. On the journey Matthew casually asked William what he intended to do when the time came for him to leave St. Paul's.

"When I leave I will be top of the class, class president, and I will have won the Hamilton Memorial Mathematics Scholarship to Harvard," replied William without hesitation.

"Why is all that so important?" Matthew asked innocently.

"My father did all three."

"When you've finished beating your father, I will introduce you to mine."

William smiled.

The two boys had an energetic and enjoyable six weeks in Vermont, playing every game from chess to football. When the time came to an end, they traveled to New York to spend the last month of the holiday with the Lester family.

They were greeted at the door by a butler, who addressed Matthew as "Sir," and a twelve-year-old girl covered in freckles who called him "Fatty." It made William laugh, because his friend was so thin, and it was she who was fat. The girl smiled and revealed teeth almost totally hidden behind braces.

"You would never believe Susan was my sister, would you?" said Matthew disdainfully.

"No, I suppose not," said William, smiling at Susan. "She is so much better-looking than you."

She adored William from that moment on.

William adored Matthew's father the moment they met; he reminded him in so many ways of his own father and he begged Charles Lester to let him see the great bank of which he was chairman. Charles Lester thought carefully about the request. No child had been allowed to enter the orderly precincts of 17 Broad Street before, not even his own son. He compromised, as bankers often do, and showed the boy around the Wall Street building on a Sunday afternoon.

William was fascinated by the different offices, the vaults, the foreign exchange dealing room, the boardroom and the chairman's office. The Lester bank's activities were considerably more extensive than were Kane and Cabot's, and William knew from his own small personal investment account, which provided him with a copy of the annual general report, that Lester's had a far larger capital base than Kane and Cabot. William was silent, pensive, as they were driven home in the car.

"Well, William, did you enjoy seeing the bank?" Charles Lester asked genially.

"Oh yes, sir," replied William. "I certainly did." William paused for a moment and then added: "I intend to be chairman of your bank one day, Mr. Lester."

Charles Lester laughed. He would tell his dinner guests that night about young William Kane's reaction to Lester and Company, which would make them laugh, too.

Only William had not meant the remark as a joke.

Anne was shocked when Henry came back to her for more money.

"It's as safe as a house," he assured her. "Ask Alan Lloyd. As chairman of the bank he can only have your best interests at heart."

"But two hundred and fifty thousand?" Anne queried.

"A superb opportunity, my dear. Look upon it as an investment that will be worth double that amount within two years."

After another, prolonged row, Anne gave in once again and life returned to the same smooth routine. When she checked her investment portfolio with the bank, Anne found her capital down to $150,000, but Henry seemed to be seeing all the right people and clinching all the right deals. She considered discussing the whole problem with Alan Lloyd at Kane and Cabot but in the end dismissed the idea; it would have meant displaying distrust in the husband whom she wished the world to respect, and surely Henry would not have made the suggestion at all had he not been sure the loan would meet with Alan's approval.

Anne also started seeing Dr. MacKenzie again to find out if there was any hope of her having another baby, but he still advised against the idea. With the high blood pressure that had caused her earlier miscarriage, Andrew MacKenzie did not consider thirty-five a good age for Anne to start thinking about being a mother again. Anne raised the idea with the grandmothers, but they agreed wholeheartedly with the views of the good doctor. Neither of them cared for Henry very much, and they cared even less for the thought of an Osborne offspring making claims on the Kane family fortune after they were gone. Anne began to resign herself to being the mother of only one child. Henry became very angry about what he described as her betrayal and told Anne that if Richard were still alive, she would have tried again. How different the two men were, she thought, and couldn't account for her love of them both. She tried to soothe Henry, praying that his business projects would work out well and keep him fully occupied. He certainly had taken to working very late at the office.

It was on a Monday in October, the weekend after they

had celebrated their second wedding anniversary, that Anne started receiving the letters from an unsigned "friend," informing her that Henry could be seen escorting other women around Boston, and one lady in particular, whom the writer didn't care to name. To begin with, Anne burned the letters immediately and although they worried her, she never discussed them with Henry, praying that each letter would be the last. She couldn't even summon up the courage to raise the matter with Henry when he asked her for her last $150,000.

"I am going to lose the whole deal if I don't have that money right now, Anne."

"But it's all I have, Henry. If I give you any more money, I'll be left with nothing."

"This house alone must be worth over two hundred thousand. You could mortgage it tomorrow."

"The house belongs to William."

"William, William, William. It's always William who gets in the way of my success," shouted Henry as he stormed out.

He returned home after midnight, contrite, and told her he would rather she kept her money and that he went under, for at least they would still love each other. Anne was comforted by his words and later they made love. She signed a check for $150,000 the next morning, trying to forget that it would leave her penniless until Henry pulled off the deal he was pursuing. She couldn't help wondering if it was more than a coincidence that Henry had asked for the exact amount that remained of her inheritance.

The next month Anne missed her period.

Dr. MacKenzie was anxious but tried not to show it; the grandmothers were horrified and did; while Henry was delighted and assured Anne that it was the most wonderful thing that had happened to him in his whole life. He even agreed to build a new children's wing for the hospital, which Richard had planned before he died.

When William heard the news by letter from his mother, he sat deep in thought all evening, unable to tell even

Matthew what was preoccupying him. The following Saturday morning, having been granted special permission by his housemaster, Grumpy Raglan, he boarded a train to Boston and on arrival withdrew one hundred dollars from his savings account. He then proceeded to the law offices of Cohen, Cohen and Yablons on Jefferson Street. Mr. Thomas Cohen, the senior partner, a tall, angular man with dark jowls, was somewhat surprised when William was ushered into his office.

"I have never been retained by a sixteen-year-old before," Mr. Cohen began. "It will be quite a novelty for me"—he hesitated—"Mr. Kane." He found that "Mr. Kane" did not run off his tongue easily. "Especially as your father was not exactly—how shall I put it?—known for his sympathy for my coreligionists."

"My father," replied William, "was a great admirer of the achievements of the Hebrew race and in particular had considerable respect for your firm when you acted on behalf of rivals. I heard him and Mr. Lloyd mention your name on several occasions. That's why I have chosen you, Mr. Cohen, not you me. That should be reassurance enough."

Mr. Cohen quickly put aside the matter of William's age. "Indeed, indeed. I feel I can make an exception for the son of Richard Kane. Now, what can we do for you?"

"I wish you to answer three questions for me, Mr. Cohen. One, I want to know whether if my mother, Mrs. Henry Osborne, were to give birth to a child, son or daughter, that child would have any legal rights to the Kane family trust. Two, do I have any legal obligations to Mr. Henry Osborne because he is married to my mother? And three, at what age can I insist that Mr. Henry Osborne leave my house on Louisburg Square in Boston?"

Thomas Cohen's pen sped furiously across the paper in front of him, spattering little blue spots on an already ink-stained desk top.

William placed one hundred dollars on the desk. The lawyer was taken aback but picked the bills up and counted them.

"Use the money prudently, Mr. Cohen. I will need a good lawyer when I leave Harvard."

"You have already been accepted at Harvard, Mr. Kane? My congratulations. I am hoping my son will go there, too."

"No, I have not, but I shall have done so in two years' time. I will return to Boston to see you in one week, Mr. Cohen. If I ever hear in my lifetime from anyone other than yourself on this subject, you may consider our relationship at an end. Good day, sir."

Thomas Cohen would have also said good day—if he could have spluttered the words out before William closed the door behind him.

William returned to the offices of Cohen, Cohen and Yablons seven days later.

"Ah, Mr. Kane," said Thomas Cohen, "how nice to see you again. Would you care for some coffee?"

"No, thank you."

"Shall I send someone out for a Coca-Cola?"

William's face was expressionless.

"To business, to business," said Mr. Cohen, slightly embarrassed. "We have dug around a little on your behalf, Mr. Kane, with the help of a very respectable firm of private investigators to assist us with the questions you asked that were not purely academic. I think I can safely say we have the answers to all your questions. You asked if Mr. Osborne's offspring by your mother, were there to be any, would have a claim on the Kane estate, or in particular on the trust left to you by your father. No is the simple answer, but of course Mrs. Osborne can leave any part of the five hundred thousand dollars bequeathed to her by your father to whom she pleases."

Mr. Cohen looked up.

"However, it may interest you to know, Mr. Kane, that your mother has drawn out the entire five hundred thousand from her private account at Kane and Cabot during the last eighteen months, but we have been unable to trace how the money has been used. It is possible she might have decided to deposit the amount in another bank."

William looked shocked, the first sign of any lack of the self-control, which Thomas Cohen noted.

"There would be no reason for her to do that," William said. "The money can only have gone to one person."

The lawyer remained silent, expecting to hear more, but William steadied himself and added nothing, so Mr. Cohen continued.

"The answer to your second question is that you have no personal or legal obligations to Mr. Henry Osborne at all. Under the terms of your father's will, your mother is a trustee of the estate along with a Mr. Alan Lloyd and a Mrs. John Preston, your surviving godparents, until you come of age at twenty-one."

Thomas Cohen looked up again. William's face showed no expression at all. Cohen had already learned that that meant he should continue.

"And thirdly, Mr. Kane, you can never remove Mr. Osborne from Beacon Hill as long as he remains married to your mother and continues to reside with her. The property comes into your possession by natural right on her death. Were he still alive then, you could require him to leave. I think you will find that covers all your questions, Mr. Kane."

"Thank you, Mr. Cohen," said William. "I am obliged for your efficiency and discretion in this matter. Now, perhaps you could let me know your professional charges?"

"One hundred dollars doesn't quite cover the work, Mr. Kane, but we have faith in your future and——"

"I do not wish to be beholden to anyone, Mr. Cohen. You must treat me as someone with whom you might never deal again. With that in mind, how much do I owe you?"

Mr. Cohen considered the matter for a moment. "In those circumstances, we would have charged you two hundred and twenty dollars, Mr. Kane."

William took six $20 bills from his inside pocket and handed them over to Cohen. This time, the lawyer did not count them.

"I am grateful to you for your assistance, Mr. Cohen. I am sure we shall meet again. Good day, sir."

"Good day, Mr. Kane. May I be permitted to say that I never had the privilege of meeting your distinguished father, but having dealt with you, I wish that I had."

William smiled and softened. "Thank you, sir."

Preparing for the baby kept Anne fully occupied; she found herself easily tired and resting a good deal. Whenever she inquired of Henry how business was going, he always had some answer plausible enough to reassure her that all was well without supplying her any actual details.

Then one morning the anonymous letters started coming again. This time they gave more details—the names of the women involved and the places they could be seen with Henry. Anne burned them even before she could commit the names or places to memory. She didn't want to believe that her husband could be unfaithful while she was carrying his child. Someone was jealous and had it in for Henry and he or she had to be lying.

The letters kept coming, sometimes with new names. Anne still continued to destroy them, but they were now beginning to prey on her mind. She wanted to discuss the whole problem with someone but couldn't think of anybody in whom she could confide. The grandmothers would have been appalled and were, in any case, already prejudiced against Henry. Alan Lloyd at the bank could not be expected to understand, as he had never married, and William was far too young. No one seemed suitable. Anne considered consulting a psychiatrist after listening to a lecture given by Sigmund Freud, but a Cabot could never discuss a family problem with a complete stranger.

The matter finally came to a head in a way that even Anne had not been prepared for. One Monday morning she received three letters, the usual one from William addressed to Mrs. Richard Kane, asking if he could once again spend his summer vacation with his friend Matthew Lester. Another anonymous letter alleging that Henry was having an affair with, with . . . Milly Preston; and the third from Alan Lloyd, as chairman of the bank, asking if she would be kind enough to telephone and make an appointment to see him. Anne sat down heavily, feeling breathless and unwell, and forced herself to reread all three letters. William's letter stung her by its detachment. She hated knowing that he preferred to spend his summer with Matthew Lester. They had been steadily growing further apart since her marriage to Henry. The anonymous letter suggesting that Henry was having an affair with her closest friend was impossible to ignore. Anne couldn't help remembering that it had been Milly who had introduced her to Henry in the first place, and that she was William's godmother. The third letter, from Alan Lloyd, who had become chairman of Kane and Cabot after Richard's death, somehow filled her with even more apprehension. The only other letter she had ever received from Alan was one of condolence on the death of Richard. She feared that this one could only mean more bad news.

She called the bank. The operator put her straight through.

"Alan, you wanted to see me?"

"Yes, my dear, I would like to have a chat sometime. When would suit you?"

"Is it bad news?" asked Anne.

"Not exactly, but I would rather not say anything over the phone. There's nothing for you to worry about. Are you free for lunch by any chance?"

"Yes I am, Alan."

"Well, let's meet at the Ritz at one o'clock. I look forward to seeing you then, Anne."

One o'clock, only three hours away. Her mind switched from Alan to William to Henry but settled on Milly Preston. Could it be true? Anne decided to take a long warm bath and put on a new dress. It didn't help. She felt, and was beginning to look, bloated. Her ankles and calves, which had always been so elegant and so slim, were becoming mottled and puffy. It was a little frightening to conjecture how much worse things might become before the baby was born. She sighed at herself in the mirror and did the best she could with her outward appearance.

"You look very smart, Anne. If I weren't an old bachelor considered well past it, I'd flirt with you shamelessly," said the silver-haired banker, greeting her with a kiss on both cheeks as though he were a French general. He guided her to his table.

It was an unspoken tradition that the table in the corner was always occupied by the chairman of Kane and Cabot if he was not lunching at the bank. Richard had done so and now it was the turn of Alan Lloyd. It was the first time Anne had sat at the table with anyone. Waiters fluttered around them like starlings, seeming to know exactly when to disappear and reappear without interrupting a private conversation.

"When's the baby due, Anne?"

"Oh, not for another three months."

"No complications, I hope. I seem to remember—"

"Well," admitted Anne, "the doctor sees me once a week and pulls long faces about my blood pressure, but I'm not too worried."

"I'm so glad, my dear," he said, and touched her hand gently as an uncle might. "You do look rather tired—I hope you're not overdoing things."

Alan Lloyd raised his hand slightly. A waiter materialized at his side and they both ordered.

"Anne, I want to seek some advice from you."

Anne was painfully aware of Alan Lloyd's gift for diplomacy. He wasn't having lunch with her for advice. There was no doubt in her mind that he had come to dispense it—kindly.

"Do you have any idea how well Henry's real estate projects are going?"

"No, I don't," said Anne. "I never involve myself with Henry's business activities. You'll remember I didn't with Richard's either. Why? Is there any cause for concern?"

"No, no, none of which we at the bank are aware. On the contrary, we know Henry is bidding for a large city contract to build the new hospital complex. I was only inquiring because he has come to the bank for a loan of five hundred thousand dollars."

Anne was stunned.

"I see that surprises you," he said. "Now, we know from your stock account that you have a little under twenty thousand dollars in reserve, while running a small overdraft of seventeen thousand dollars on your personal account."

Anne put down her soup spoon, horrified. She had not realized that she was so badly overdrawn. Alan could see her distress.

"That's not what this lunch is about, Anne," he added quickly. "The bank is quite happy to lose money on the personal account for the rest of your life. William is making over a million dollars a year on the interest from his trust, so your overdraft is hardly significant; nor indeed is the five hundred thousand Henry is requesting, if it were to receive your backing as William's legal guardian."

"I didn't realize I had any authority over William's trust money," said Anne.

"You don't on the capital sum, but legally the interest earned from his trust can be invested in any project thought to benefit William and is under the guardianship of yourself and of myself and Milly Preston as godparents until William is twenty-one. Now, as chairman of William's trust I can put up that five hundred thousand with your approval. Milly has already informed me that she would be quite happy to give her approval, so that would give you two votes, and my opinion would therefore be invalid."

"Milly Preston has already given her approval, Alan?"

"Yes. Hasn't she mentioned the matter to you?"

Anne did not reply immediately.

"What *is your* opinion?" Anne asked finally.

"Well, I haven't seen Henry's accounts, because he only started his company eighteen months ago and he doesn't bank with us, so I have no idea what expenditure is over income for the current year and what return he is predicting for 1923. I do know he has made an application for the new hospital contract and rumor suggests he has been taken seriously."

"You realize that during the last eighteen months I've given Henry five hundred thousand of my own money?" said Anne.

"My chief teller informs me any time a large amount of cash is withdrawn from any account. I didn't know that was what you were using the money for, and it was none of my business, Anne. That money was left to you by Richard and is yours to spend as you see fit.

"Now, in the case of the interest from the family trust, that is a different matter. If you did decide to withdraw five hundred thousand dollars to invest in Henry's firm, then the bank will have to inspect Henry's books, because the money would be considered as another investment in William's portfolio. Richard did not give the trustees the authority to make loans, only to invest on William's behalf. I have already explained this situation to Henry, and if we were to go ahead and make this investment, the trustees would have to decide what percentage of Henry's company would be an appropriate exchange for the five hundred thousand. William, of course, is always aware what we are doing with his trust income, because we saw no reason not to comply with his request that he receive a quarterly investment program statement from the bank in the same way as all the trustees do. I have no doubt in my own mind that he will have his own ideas on the subject, which he will be fully aware of after he receives the next quarterly report.

"It may amuse you to know that since the beginning of his sixteenth year William has been sending me back his own opinions on every investment we make. To begin with,

I looked on them with the passing interest of a benevolent guardian. Of late, I have been studying them with considerable respect. When William takes his place on the board of Kane and Cabot, this bank may well turn out to be too small for him."

"I've never been asked for advice on William's trust before," Anne said forlornly.

"Well, my dear, you do see the reports that the bank sends you on the first day of every quarter, and it has always been in your power as a trustee to query any of the investments we make on William's behalf."

Alan Lloyd took a slip of paper from his pocket and remained silent until the sommelier had finished pouring the Nuits-St.-Georges. Once he was out of earshot, Alan continued.

"William has a little over twenty-one million invested by the bank at four and a half percent until his twenty-first birthday. We reinvest the interest for him each quarter in stocks and bonds. We have never in the past invested in a private company. It may surprise you to hear, Anne, that we now carry out this reinvestment on a fifty-fifty basis: fifty percent following the bank's advice and fifty percent following the suggestions put forward by William. At the moment we are a little ahead of him, much to the satisfaction of Tony Simmons, our investment director, whom William has promised a Rolls-Royce in any year that he can beat the boy by over ten percent."

"But where would William get hold of the ten thousand dollars for a Rolls-Royce if he lost the bet—if he's not allowed to touch the money in his trust until he is twenty-one?"

"I do not know the answer to that, Anne. What I do know is he would be far too proud to come to us direct and I am certain he would not have made the wager if he could not honor it. Have you by any chance seen his famous ledger lately?"

"The one given to him by his grandmothers?"

Alan Lloyd nodded.

"No, I haven't seen it since he went away to school. I didn't know it still existed."

"It still exists," said the banker, "and I would give a month's wages to know what the credit column now stands at. I suppose you are aware that he now banks his money with Lester's in New York and not with us? They don't take on private accounts at under ten thousand dollars. I'm also fairly certain they wouldn't make an exception, even for the son of Richard Kane."

"The son of Richard Kane," said Anne.

"I'm sorry, I didn't mean to sound rude, Anne."

"No, no, there is no doubt he is the son of Richard Kane. Do you know he has never asked me for a penny since his twelfth birthday?" She paused. "I think I should warn you, Alan, that he won't take kindly to being told he has to invest five hundred thousand dollars of his trust money in Henry's company."

"They don't get on well?" inquired Alan, his eyebrows rising.

"I'm afraid not," said Anne.

"I'm sorry to hear that. It certainly would make the transaction more complicated if William really stood against the whole scheme. Although he has no authority over the trust until he is twenty-one, we have already discovered through sources of our own that he is not beyond going to an independent lawyer to find out his legal position."

"Good God," said Anne, "you can't be serious."

"Oh, yes, quite serious, but there's nothing for you to worry about. To be frank, we at the bank were all rather impressed, and once we realized where the inquiry was coming from, we released information we would normally have kept very much to ourselves. For some private reason he obviously didn't want to approach us directly."

"Good heavens," said Anne, "what will he be like when he's thirty?"

"That will depend," said Alan, "on whether he is lucky enough to fall in love with someone as lovely as you. That was always Richard's strength."

"You are an old flatterer, Alan. Can we leave the problem of the five hundred thousand until I have had a chance to discuss it with Henry?"

"Of course, my dear. I told you I had come to seek your advice."

Alan ordered coffee and took Anne's hand gently in his. "And do remember to take care of yourself, Anne. You are far more important than the fate of a few thousand dollars."

When Anne returned home from lunch she immediately started to worry about the other two letters she had received that morning. Of one thing she was now certain after all she had learned about her own son from Alan Lloyd: she would be wise to give in gracefully and let William spend the forthcoming vacation with Matthew Lester.

The possibility that Henry and Milly were having an affair raised a problem to which she was unable to compose so simple a solution. She sat in the maroon leather chair, Richard's favorite, looking out through the bay window onto a beautiful bed of red and white roses, seeing nothing, only thinking. Anne always took a long time to make a decision, but once she had, she seldom reversed it.

Henry came home earlier than usual that evening and she couldn't help wondering why. She soon found out.

"I hear you had lunch with Alan Lloyd today," he said as he entered the room.

"Who told you that, Henry?"

"I have spies everywhere," he said, laughing.

"Yes, Alan invited me to lunch. He wanted to know how I felt about permitting the bank to invest five hundred thousand dollars of William's trust money in your company."

"What did you say?" asked Henry, trying not to sound anxious.

"I told him I wanted to discuss the matter with you first, but why in heaven's name didn't you let me know earlier that you had approached the bank, Henry? I felt such a fool hearing the whole thing from Alan for the first time."

"I didn't think you took any interest in business, my dear, and I only found out by sheer accident that you, Alan Lloyd and Milly Preston are all trustees and each has a vote on William's investment income."

"How did you find out," asked Anne, "when I wasn't aware of the situation myself?"

"You don't read the small print, my darling. As a matter of fact, I didn't myself until recently. Quite by chance, Milly Preston told me the details of the trust. Not only is she William's godmother, it seems she is also a trustee—it came as quite a surprise to her when she was first told. Now let's see if we can turn the position to our advantage. Milly says she will back me if you agree."

The mere sound of Milly's name made Anne feel uneasy.

"I don't think we ought to touch William's money," she said. "I've never looked upon the trust as having anything to do with me. I'd be much happier leaving well enough alone and just continue letting the bank reinvest the interest as it's always done in the past."

"Why be satisfied with the bank's investment program when I'm on to such a good thing with this city hospital contract? William would make a lot more money out of my company. Surely Alan went along with that?"

"I'm not certain how he felt. He was his usual discreet self, though he certainly said the contract would be an excellent one to win and that you had a good chance of being awarded it."

"Exactly."

"But he did want to see your books before he came to any firm conclusions, and he also wondered what had happened to my five hundred thousand."

"Our five hundred thousand, my darling, is doing very well, as you will soon discover. I'll send the books around to Alan tomorrow morning so that he can inspect them for himself. I can assure you he'll be very impressed."

"I hope so, Henry, for both our sakes," said Anne. "Now let's wait and see what his opinion is—you know how much I've always trusted Alan."

"But not me," said Henry.

"Oh, no, Henry, I didn't mean——"

"I was only teasing. I assumed you would trust your own husband."

Anne felt welling up within her the tearfulness she had always suppressed in front of Richard. With Henry she didn't even try to hold it back.

"I hope I can. I've never had to worry about money before and it's all too much to cope with just now. The baby always makes me feel so tired and depressed."

Henry's manner changed quickly to one of solicitude. "I know, my darling, and I don't want you ever to have to bother your head with business matters—I can always handle that side of things. Look, why don't you go to bed early and I'll bring you some supper on a tray? That will give me a chance to go back to the office and pick up the files I need to show Alan in the morning."

Anne complied, but once Henry had left, she made no attempt to sleep, tired as she was, but sat up in bed reading Sinclair Lewis. She knew it would take Henry about fifteen minutes to reach his office, so she waited a full twenty and then called his number. The ringing tone continued for almost a minute.

Anne tried a second time twenty minutes later; still no one answered. She kept trying every twenty minutes, but no one ever came on the line. Henry's remark about trust began to echo bitterly in her head.

When Henry eventually returned home after midnight, he appeared apprehensive upon finding Anne sitting up in bed. She was still reading Sinclair Lewis.

"You shouldn't have stayed awake for me."

He gave her a warm kiss. Anne thought she could smell perfume—or was she becoming overly suspicious?

"I had to stay on a little later than I expected—at first I couldn't find all the papers Alan will need. Damn silly secretary filed some of them under the wrong headings."

"It must be lonely sitting there in the office all on your own in the middle of the night," said Anne.

"Oh, it's not that bad if you have a worthwhile job to do," said Henry, climbing into bed and settling against Anne's back. "At least there's one thing to be said for it: you can get a lot more done when the phone isn't continually interrupting you."

He was asleep in minutes. Anne lay awake, now resolved to carry through the decision she had made that afternoon.

When Henry had left for work after breakfast the next morning—not that Anne was any longer sure where Henry went—she studied the *Boston Globe* and did a little research among the small advertisements. Then she picked up the phone and made an appointment that took her to the south side of Boston a few minutes before midday. Anne was shocked by the dinginess of the buildings. She had never previously visited the southern district of the city, and in normal circumstances she could have gone through her entire life without even knowing such places existed.

A small wooden staircase littered with matches, cigarette butts and other rubbish created its own paper chase to a door with a frosted window on which appeared large black letters: GLEN RICARDO and, underneath, PRIVATE DETECTIVE (REGISTERED IN THE COMMONWEALTH OF MASSACHUSETTS). Anne knocked softly.

"Come right in, the door's open," shouted a deep, hoarse voice.

Anne entered. The man seated behind the desk, his legs stretched over its surface, glanced up from what might have been a girly magazine. His cigar stub nearly fell out of his mouth when he caught sight of Anne. It was the first time a mink coat had ever walked into his office.

"Good morning," he said, rising quickly. "My name is Glen Ricardo." He leaned across the desk and offered a hairy, nicotine-stained hand to Anne. She took it, glad that she was wearing gloves. "Do you have an appointment?" Ricardo asked, not that he cared whether she did or not. He was always available for a consultation with a mink coat.

"Yes, I do."

"Ah, then you must be Mrs. Osborne. Can I take your coat?"

"I prefer to keep it on," said Anne, unable to see any place where Ricardo could hang it except on the floor.

"Of course, of course."

Anne eyed Ricardo covertly as he sat back in his seat and lit a new cigar. She did not care for his light green suit, the motley tie or his thickly greased hair. It was only her doubt that it would be better anywhere else that kept her seated.

"Now, what's the problem?" said Ricardo, who was sharpening an already short pencil with a blunt knife. The wooden shavings dropped everywhere except into the wastepaper basket. "Have you lost your dog, your jewelry or your husband?"

"First, Mr. Ricardo, I want to be assured of your complete discretion," Anne began.

"Of course, of course, it goes without saying," said Ricardo, not looking up from his disappearing pencil.

"Nevertheless, I am saying it," said Anne.

"Of course, of course."

Anne thought that if the man said "of course" once more, she would scream. She drew a deep breath. "I have been receiving anonymous letters which allege that my husband has been having an affair with a close friend. I want to know who is sending the letters and if there is any truth in the accusations."

Anne felt an immense sense of relief at having voiced her fears for the first time. Ricardo looked at her impassively, as if it was not the first time he had heard such fears expressed. He put his hand through his long black hair, which, Anne noticed for the first time, matched his fingernails.

"Right," he began. "The husband will be easy. Who's responsible for sending the letters will be a lot harder. You've kept the letters, of course?"

"Only the last one," said Anne.

Glen Ricardo sighed and stretched his hand across the

table wearily. Anne reluctantly took the letter out of her bag and then hesitated for a moment.

"I know how you feel, Mrs. Osborne, but I can't do the job with one hand tied behind my back."

"Of course, Mr. Ricardo, I'm sorry."

Anne couldn't believe she had said "of course."

Ricardo read the letter through two or three times before speaking. "Have they all been typed on this sort of paper and sent in this sort of envelope?"

"Yes, I think so," said Anne. "As far as I can remember."

"Well, when the next one comes, be sure to——"

"Can you be so certain there will be another one?" interrupted Anne.

"Of course. So be sure to keep it. Now, give me all the details about your husband. Do you have a photograph?"

"Yes." Once again she hesitated.

"I only want to look at the face. Don't want to waste my time chasing the wrong man, do I?" said Ricardo.

Anne opened her bag again and passed him a worn-edged photograph of Henry in a lieutenant's uniform.

"Good-looking man, Mr. Osborne," said the detective. "When was this photograph taken?"

"About five years ago, I think," said Anne. "I didn't know him when he was in the Army."

Ricardo questioned Anne for several minutes on Henry's daily movements. She was surprised to find how little she really knew of Henry's habits, or past.

"Not a lot to go on, Mrs. Osborne, but I'll do the best I can. Now, my charges are ten dollars a day plus expenses. I will make a written report for you approximately once a week. Two weeks' payment in advance, please." His hand came across the desk again, more eagerly than before.

Anne opened her handbag once more, took out two crisp $100 bills and passed them across to Ricardo. He studied the bills carefully, as if he couldn't remember which distinguished American should be engraved on them. Benjamin Franklin gazed imperturbably at Ricardo, who obviously

had not seen the great man for some time. Ricardo handed
Anne $60 in grubby fives.

"I see you work on Sundays, Mr. Ricardo," said Anne,
pleased with her mental arithmetic.

"Of course," he said. "Will the same time a week from
Thursday suit you, Mrs. Osborne?"

"Of course," said Anne, and she left quickly to avoid having to shake hands with the man behind the desk.

When William read in his quarterly trust report from Kane
and Cabot that Henry Osborne ("Henry Osborne"—he repeated the name out loud to be sure he could believe it) was
requesting $500,000 for a personal investment, he had a bad
day. For the first time in four years at St. Paul's he came in
second on a math test. Matthew Lester, who beat him, asked
if he was feeling well.

That evening, William called Alan Lloyd at home. The
chairman of Kane and Cabot was not altogether surprised to
hear from him after Anne's disclosure of the unhappy relationship between her son and Henry.

"William, dear boy, how are you and how are things at St.
Paul's?"

"All is well at this end, thank you, sir, but that's not why I
telephoned."

The tact of an advancing Mack truck, thought Alan. "No,
I didn't imagine it was," he said dryly. "What can I do for
you?"

"I'd like to see you tomorrow afternoon."

"On a Sunday, William?"

"Yes, it's the only day I can get away from school. I'll
come to you anytime anyplace." William made the statement
sound as though it were a concession on his part. "And under
no condition is my mother to know of our meeting."

"Well, William——" Alan Lloyd began.

William's voice grew firmer. "I don't have to remind you,
sir, that the investment of trust money in my stepfather's per-

sonal venture, while not actually illegal, would undoubtedly be considered as unethical."

Alan Lloyd was silent for a few moments, wondering if he should try to placate the boy over the telephone. The boy. He also thought about remonstrating with him, but the time for that had now passed.

"Fine, William. Why don't you join me for a spot of lunch at the Hunt Club, say one o'clock?"

"I'll look forward to seeing you then, sir." The telephone clicked.

At least the confrontation is to be on my home ground, thought Alan Lloyd with some relief as he replaced the mouthpiece, cursing Mr. Bell for inventing the damn machine.

Alan had chosen the Hunt Club because he did not want the meeting to be too private. The first thing William asked when he arrived at the clubhouse was that he should be allowed a round of golf after lunch.

"Delighted, my boy," said Alan, and reserved the first tee for three o'clock.

He was surprised when William did not discuss Henry Osborne's proposal at all during lunch. Far from it, the boy talked knowledgeably about President Harding's views on tariff reform and the incompetence of Charles G. Dawes as the President's Director of the Budget. Alan began to wonder whether William, having slept on it, had changed his mind about discussing Henry Osborne's loan and was going through with the meeting not wishing to admit a change of heart. Well, if that's the way the boy wants to play it, thought Alan, that's fine by me. He looked forward to a quiet afternoon of golf. After an agreeable lunch and the better part of a bottle of wine—William limited himself to one glass—they changed in the clubhouse and walked to the first tee.

"Do you still have a nine handicap, sir?" asked William.

"Thereabouts, my boy. Why?"

"Will ten dollars a hole suit you?"

Alan Lloyd hesitated, remembering that golf was the one game that William played competently. "Yes, fine."

Nothing was said at the first hole, which Alan managed in four while William took a five. Alan also won the second and the third quite comfortably and began to relax a little, rather pleased with his game. By the time they had reached the fourth, they were over half a mile from the clubhouse. William waited for Alan to raise his club.

"There are no conditions under which you will loan five hundred thousand dollars of my trust money to any company or person associated with Henry Osborne."

Alan hit a bad tee shot that went wild into the rough. Its only virtue was that it put him far enough away from William, who had made a good drive, to give him a few minutes to think about how to address both William and the ball. After Alan Lloyd had played three more shots, they eventually met on the green. Alan conceded the hole.

"William, you know I only have one vote out of three as a trustee and you must also be aware that you have no authority over trust decisions, as you will not control the money in your own right until your twenty-first birthday. You must also realize that we ought not to be discussing this subject at all."

"I am fully aware of the legal implications, sir, but as both the other trustees were sleeping with Henry Osborne—"

Alan Lloyd looked shocked.

"Don't tell me you are the only person in Boston who doesn't know that Milly Preston is having an affair with my stepfather?"

Alan Lloyd said nothing.

William continued: "I want to be certain that I have your vote and that you intend to do everything in your power to influence my mother against this loan, even if it means going to the extreme of telling her the truth about Milly Preston."

Alan hit an even worse tee shot. William's went right down the middle of the fairway. Alan chopped the next shot into a bush he had never even realized existed before and said "Shit!" out loud for the first time in forty-three years. (He had got a hiding on that occasion as well.)

"That's asking a little too much," said Alan as he joined up with William on the fifth green.

"It's nothing compared with what I'd do if I couldn't be sure of your support, sir."

"I don't think your father would have approved of threats, William," said Alan as he watched William's ball sink from fourteen feet.

"The only thing of which my father would not have approved is Osborne," retorted William. Alan Lloyd two-putted four feet from the hole.

"In any case, sir, you must be well aware that my father had a clause inserted in the trust deed that money invested by the trust was a private affair and the benefactor should never know that the Kane family was personally involved. It was a rule he never broke in his life as a banker. That way he could always be certain there was no conflict of interest between the bank's investments and those of the family trust."

"Well, your mother perhaps feels that the rule can be broken for a member of the family."

"Henry Osborne is not a member of my family and when I control the trust it will be a rule I, like my father, will never break."

"You may live to regret taking such a rigid stance, William."

"I think not, sir."

"Well, try to consider for a moment the effect that finding out about Milly might have on your mother," added Alan.

"My mother has already lost five hundred thousand dollars of her own money, sir. Isn't that enough for one husband? Why do I have to lose five hundred thousand of mine as well?"

"We don't know that to be the case, William. The investment may still yield an excellent return; I haven't had a chance yet to look carefully into Henry's books."

William winced when Alan Lloyd called him Henry.

"I can assure you, sir, he's blown nearly every penny of my mother's money. To be exact, he has thirty-three thousand four hundred and twelve dollars left. I suggest you take very little notice of Osborne's books and check a little more thoroughly into his background, past business record and associates. Not to mention the fact that he gambles—heavily."

From the eighth tee Alan hit his ball into a lake directly in front of them, a lake even novice women players managed to clear. He conceded the hole.

"How did you come by your information on Henry?" asked Alan, fairly certain it had been through Thomas Cohen's office.

"I prefer not to say, sir."

Alan kept his own counsel; he thought he might need that particular ace up his sleeve to play a little later in William's life.

"If all you claim turned out to be accurate, William, naturally I would have to advise your mother against any investment in Henry's firm, and it would be my duty to have the whole thing out in the open with Henry as well."

"So be it, sir."

Alan hit a better shot but felt he wasn't winning.

William continued. "It may also interest you to know that Osborne needs the five hundred thousand from my trust not for the hospital contract but to clear a long-standing debt in Chicago. I take it that you were not aware of that, sir?"

Alan said nothing; he certainly had not been aware of it. William won the hole.

When they reached the eighteenth, Alan was eight holes down and was about to complete the worst round he cared to remember. He had a five-foot putt that would at least enable him to halve the final hole with William.

"Do you have any more bombshells for me?" asked Alan.

"Before or after your putt, sir?"

Alan laughed and decided to call his bluff. "Before the putt, William," he said, leaning on his club.

"Osborne will not be awarded the hospital contract. It is thought by those who matter that he's been bribing junior officials in the city government. Nothing will be brought out into the open, but to be sure of no repercussions later, his company has been removed from the final list. The contract will actually be awarded to Kirkbride and Carter. That last piece of information, sir, is confidential. Even Kirkbride and Carter will not be informed until a week from Thursday, so I'd be obliged if you would keep it to yourself."

Alan missed his putt. William holed his, walked over to the Chairman and shook him warmly by the hand.

"Thank you for the game, sir. I think you'll find you owe me ninety dollars."

Alan took out his wallet and handed over a hundred-dollar bill. "William, I think the time has come for you to stop calling me 'sir.' My name, as you well know, is Alan."

"Thank you, Alan." William handed him ten dollars.

Alan Lloyd arrived at the bank on Monday morning with a little more to do than he had anticipated before his meeting with William. He put five departmental managers to work immediately on checking out the accuracy of William's allegations. He feared that he already knew what their inquiries would reveal, and because of Anne's position at the bank, he made certain that no one department was aware of what the others were up to. His instructions to each manager were clear: All reports were to be strictly confidential and for the chairman's eyes only. By Wednesday of the same week he had five preliminary reports on his desk. They all seemed to be in agreement with William's judgment, although each manager had asked for more time to verify some details. Alan decided against worrying Anne until he had some more concrete evidence to go on. The best he felt he could do for the time being was to take advantage of a buffet supper the Osbornes were giving that evening; he could advise Anne then against any immediate decision on the loan.

When Alan arrived at the party, he was shocked to see how tired and drawn Anne looked, which predisposed him to soften his approach even more. When he managed to catch her alone, they had only a few moments together. If only she were not having a baby just at the time all this was happening, he thought.

Anne turned and smiled at him. "How kind of you to come, Alan, when you must be so busy at the bank."

"I couldn't afford to miss out on one of your parties, my dear. They're still the toast of Boston."

She smiled. "I wonder if you ever say the wrong thing."

"All too frequently. Anne, have you had time to give any more thought to the loan?" He tried to sound casual.

"No, I am afraid I haven't. I've been up to my ears with other things, Alan. How did Henry's accounts look?"

"Fine, but we only have one year's figures to go on, so I think we ought to bring in our own accountants to check them over. It's normal banking policy to do that with anyone who has been operating for less than three years. I'm sure Henry would understand our position and agree."

"Anne, darling, lovely party," said a loud voice over Alan's shoulder. He did not recognize the face; presumably one of Henry's politician friends. "How's the little mother-to-be?" continued the effusive voice.

Alan slipped away, hoping that he had bought some time for the bank. There were a lot of politicians at the party, from City Hall and even a couple from Congress, which made him wonder if William would turn out to be wrong about the big contract. Not that the bank would have to investigate that: the official announcement from City Hall was due the following week. He said good-bye to his host and hostess, picked up his black overcoat from the cloakroom and left.

"This time next week," he said aloud, as if to reassure himself as he walked back down Chestnut Street to his own house. . . .

During the party, Anne found time to watch Henry whenever he was near Milly Preston. There was certainly no outward sign of anything between them; in fact, Henry spent more of his time with John Preston. Anne began to wonder if she had not misjudged her husband and thought about canceling her appointment with Glen Ricardo the next day. The party came to an end two hours later than Anne had anticipated; she hoped it meant that the guests had all enjoyed themselves.

"Great party, Anne, thanks for inviting us." It was the loud voice again, leaving last. Anne couldn't remember his name, something to do with City Hall. He disappeared down the drive.

Anne stumbled upstairs, undoing her dress even before she had reached the bedroom, promising herself that she would give no more parties before having the baby in ten weeks' time.

Henry was already undressing. "Did you get a chance to have a word with Alan, darling?"

"Yes, I did," replied Anne. "He said the books look fine, but as the company can only show one year's figures, he must bring his own accountants in to double-check. Apparently that's normal banking policy."

" 'Normal banking policy' be damned. Can't you sense William's presence behind all this? He's trying to hold up the loan, Anne."

"How can you say that? Alan said nothing about William."

"Didn't he?" said Henry, his voice rising. "He didn't bother to mention that William had lunch with him Sunday at the golf club while we sat here at home alone?"

"What?" said Anne. "I don't believe it. William would never come to Boston without seeing me. You must be mistaken, Henry."

"My dear, half the city was there, and I don't imagine that William traveled some fifty miles just for a round of golf with Alan Lloyd. Listen, Anne, I need that loan or I'm going to fail to qualify as a bidder for the city contract. Some time—and very soon now—you are going to have to decide whether you trust William or me. I must have the money by a week from tomorrow, only eight days from now, because if I can't show City Hall I'm good for that amount, I'll be disqualified. Disqualified because William didn't approve of

your wanting to marry me. Please, Anne, will you call Alan
tomorrow and tell him to transfer the money?"

His angry voice boomed in Anne's head, making her feel
faint and dizzy.

"No, not tomorrow, Henry. Can it wait until Friday? I
have a heavy day tomorrow."

Henry collected himself with an effort and came over to
her as she stood naked, looking at herself in the mirror. He
ran his hand over her bulging stomach. "I want this little fellow to be given as good a chance as William."

The next day Anne told herself a hundred times that she
would not go to see Glen Ricardo, but a little before noon
she found herself riding in a cab. She climbed the creaky
wooden stairs, apprehensive of what she might learn. She
could still turn back. She hesitated, then knocked on the
door.

"Come in."

She opened the door.

"Ah, Mrs. Osborne, how nice to see you again. Do have a
seat."

Anne sat and they stared at each other.

"The news, I am afraid, is not good," said Glen Ricardo,
pushing his hand through his long, dark hair.

Anne's heart sank. She felt sick.

"Mr. Osborne has not been seen with Mrs. Preston or any
other woman during the past seven days."

"But you said the news wasn't good," said Anne.

"Of course, Mrs. Osborne, I assumed you were looking
for grounds for divorce. Angry wives don't normally come
to me hoping I'll prove their husbands are innocent."

"No, no," said Anne, suffused with relief. "It's the best
piece of news I've had in weeks."

"Oh, good," said Mr. Ricardo, slightly taken aback. "Let
us hope the second week reveals nothing as well."

"Oh, you can stop the investigation now, Mr. Ricardo. I

am sure you will not find anything of any consequence next week."

"I don't think that would be wise, Mrs. Osborne. To make a final judgment on only one week's observation would be, to say the least, premature."

"All right, if you believe it will prove the point, but I still feel confident that you won't uncover anything new next week."

"In any case," continued Glen Ricardo, puffing away at his cigar, which looked bigger and smelled better to Anne than it had the previous week, "you have already paid for the two weeks."

"What about the letters?" asked Anne, suddenly remembering them. "I suppose they must have come from someone jealous of my husband's achievements."

"Well, as I pointed out to you last week, Mrs. Osborne, tracing the sender of anonymous letters is never easy. However, we have been able to locate the shop where the stationery was bought, as the brand was fairly unusual, but for the moment I have nothing further to report on that front. Again, I may have a lead by this time next week. Did you get any more letters in the past few days?"

"No, I didn't."

"Good. Then it all seems to be working out for the best. Let us hope, for your sake, that next week's meeting, on Thursday, will be our last."

"Yes," said Anne happily, "let us hope so. Can I settle your expenses next week?"

"Of course, of course."

Anne had nearly forgotten the phrase, but this time it only made her laugh. She decided as she was driven home that Henry must have the $500,000 and the chance to prove William and Alan wrong. She had still not recovered from the knowledge that William had come to Boston without letting her know; perhaps Henry had been right in his suggestion that William was trying to work behind their backs.

. . .

Henry was delighted when Anne told him that night of her decision on the loan and he produced the legal documents the following morning for her signature. Anne couldn't help thinking that he must have had the papers prepared for some time, especially as Milly Preston's signature was already on them, or was she being overly suspicious again? She dismissed the idea and signed quickly.

She was fully prepared for Alan Lloyd when he telephoned the following Monday morning.

"Anne, let me at least hold things up until Thursday. Then we'll know who has been awarded the hospital contract."

"No, Alan, the decision has been made. Henry needs the money now. He has to prove to City Hall that he's financially strong enough to fulfill the contract, and you already have the signatures of two trustees so the responsibility is no longer yours."

"The bank could always guarantee Henry's position without actually passing over the money. I'm sure City Hall would find that acceptable. In any case, I haven't had enough time to check over his company's accounts."

"But you did find enough time to have lunch with William a week ago Sunday without bothering to inform me."

There was a momentary silence on the other end of the line.

"Anne, I——"

"Don't say you didn't have the opportunity. You came to our party on Wednesday and you could easily have mentioned it to me then. You chose not to, but you did find the time to advise me to postpone judgment on the loan to Henry."

"Anne, I am sorry. I can understand how that might look and why you are upset, but there really was a reason, believe me. May I come around and explain everything to you?"

"No, Alan, you can't. You're all ganging up against my

husband. None of you wants to give him a chance to prove himself. Well, I am going to give him that chance."

Anne put the telephone down, pleased with herself, feeling she had been loyal to Henry in a way that fully atoned for her ever having doubted him in the first place.

Alan Lloyd rang back, but Anne instructed the maid to say she was out for the rest of the day. When Henry returned home that night, he was delighted to hear how Anne had dealt with Alan.

"It will all turn out for the best, my love, you'll see. On Thursday morning I will be awarded the contract and you can kiss and make up with Alan; still, you had better keep out of his way until then. In fact, if you like we can have a celebration lunch on Thursday at the Ritz and wave at him from the other side of the room."

Anne smiled and agreed. She could not help remembering that she was meant to be seeing Ricardo for the last time at twelve o'clock that day. Still, that would be early enough for her to be at the Ritz by one, and she could celebrate both triumphs at once.

Alan tried repeatedly to reach Anne, but the maid always had a ready excuse. Since the document had been signed by two trustees, he could not hold up payment for more than twenty-four hours. The wording was typical of a legal agreement drawn up by Richard Kane; there were no loopholes to crawl through. When the check for $500,000 left the bank by special messenger on Tuesday afternoon, Alan wrote a long letter to William, setting down the events that had culminated in the transfer of the money, withholding only the unconfirmed findings of his departmental reports. He sent a copy of the letter to each director of the bank, conscious that although he had behaved with the utmost propriety, he had laid himself open to accusations of concealment.

William received Alan Lloyd's letter at St. Paul's on the Thursday morning while having breakfast with Matthew.

Breakfast on Thursday morning at Beacon Hill was the usual eggs and bacon, hot toast, cold oatmeal and a pot of steaming coffee. Henry was simultaneously tense and jaunty, snapping at the maid, joking with a junior city official who telephoned to say the name of the company that had been awarded the hospital contract would be posted on the notice board at City Hall around ten o'clock. Anne was almost looking forward to her last meeting with Glen Ricardo. She flicked through *Vogue*, trying not to notice that Henry's hands, clutching the *Boston Globe*, were trembling.

"What are you going to do this morning?" Henry asked, trying to make conversation.

"Oh, nothing much before we have our celebration lunch. Will you be able to name the children's wing in memory of Richard?" Anne asked.

"Not in memory of Richard, my darling. This will be my achievement, so let it be in your honor. The Mrs. Henry Osborne wing," he added grandly.

"What a nice idea," Anne said as she put her magazine down and smiled at him. "You mustn't let me drink too much champagne at lunch as I have a full checkup with Dr. MacKenzie this afternoon, and I don't think he would approve if I was drunk only nine weeks before the baby is due. When will you know for certain that the contract is yours?"

"I know now," Henry said. "The clerk I just spoke to was one hundred percent confident, but it will be official at ten o'clock."

"The first thing you must do then, Henry, is to phone Alan and tell him the good news. I'm beginning to feel quite guilty about the way I treated him last week."

"No need for you to feel any guilt; he didn't bother to keep you informed of William's actions."

"No, but he tried to explain later, Henry, and I didn't give him a chance to tell me his side of the story."

"All right, all right, anything you say. If it'll make you happy I'll phone him at five past ten and then you can tell William I've made him another million." He looked at his watch. "I'd better be going. Wish me luck."

"I thought you didn't need any luck," said Anne.

"I don't, I don't, it's only an expression. See you at the Ritz at one o'clock." He kissed her on the forehead. "By tonight you'll be able to laugh about Alan, William and contracts and treat them all as problems of the past, believe me. Good-bye, darling."

"I hope so, Henry."

An uneaten breakfast was laid out in front of Alan Lloyd. He was reading the financial pages of the *Boston Globe*, noting a small paragraph in a right-hand column reporting that at ten o'clock that morning the city would announce which company had been awarded the $5 million hospital contract.

Alan Lloyd had already decided what course of action he must take if Henry failed to secure the contract and everything that William had claimed turned out to be accurate. He would do exactly what Richard would have done faced with the same predicament: act only in the best interests of the bank. The latest departmental reports on Henry's personal finances disturbed Alan Lloyd greatly. Osborne was indeed a heavy gambler, and no trace could be found that the trust's $500,000 had gone into Henry's company. Alan Lloyd sipped his orange juice and left the rest of his breakfast untouched, apologized to his housekeeper and walked to the bank. It was a pleasant day.

"William, are you up to a game of tennis this afternoon?"

They were at breakfast, and Matthew Lester was standing over William as he read the letter from Alan Lloyd for a second time.

"What did you say?"

"Are you going deaf or developing into a senile adolescent? Do you want me to beat you black and blue on the tennis court this afternoon?"

"No, I won't be here this afternoon, Matthew. I have more important things to attend to."

"Naturally, old buddy, I forgot that you're off on another of your mysterious trips to the White House. I know President Harding is looking for someone to be his new fiscal advisor, and you're exactly the right man to take the place of that posturing fool Charles G. Dawes. Tell him you'll accept, subject to his inviting Matthew Lester to be the Administration's next Attorney General."

There was no response from William.

"I know the joke was pretty weak, but I thought it worthy of some comment," said Matthew as he sat down beside William and looked more carefully at his friend. "It's the eggs, isn't it? Taste as though they've come out of a Russian prisoner-of-war camp."

"Matthew, I need your help," began William as he put Alan's letter back into its envelope.

"You've had a letter from my sister and she thinks you'll do as a replacement for Rudolph Valentino."

William stood up. "Quit kidding, Matthew. If your father's bank were being robbed, would you sit around making jokes about it?"

The expression on William's face was unmistakably serious. Matthew's tone changed. "No, I wouldn't."

"Right. Then let's get out of here and I'll explain everything."

Anne left Beacon Hill a little after ten to do some shopping before going on to her final meeting with Glen Ricardo. The telephone started to ring as she disappeared down Chestnut Street. The maid answered it, looked out the window and decided that her mistress was too far away to be pursued. If Anne had returned to take the call she would have been informed of City Hall's decision on the hospital contract; instead she bought some silk stockings and tried out a new perfume. She arrived at Glen Ricardo's office a little after twelve, hoping the new perfume might counter the smell of cigar smoke.

"I hope I'm not late, Mr. Ricardo," she began briskly.

"Have a seat, Mrs. Osborne." Ricardo did not look particularly cheerful, but, thought Anne to herself, he never does. Then she noticed that he was not smoking his usual cigar.

Glen Ricardo opened a smart brown file, the only new thing Anne could see in the office, and unclipped some papers.

"Let's start with the anonymous letters, shall we, Mrs. Osborne?"

Anne did not like the tone of his voice at all. "Yes, all right," she managed to get out.

"They are being sent by a Mrs. Ruby Flowers."

"Who? Why?" said Anne, impatient for an answer she did not want to hear.

"I suspect one of the reasons is that Mrs. Flowers is at present suing your husband."

"Well, that explains the whole mystery," said Anne. "She must want revenge. How much does she claim Henry owes her?"

"She is not suggesting debt, Mrs. Osborne."

"Well, what is she suggesting then?"

Glen Ricardo pushed himself up from the chair, as if the movement required the full strength of both his arms to raise his tired frame. He walked to the window and looked out over the crowded Boston harbor.

"She is suing for a breach of promise, Mrs. Osborne."

"Oh, no," said Anne.

"It appears that they were engaged to be married at the time that Mr. Osborne met you, when the engagement was suddenly terminated for no apparent reason."

"Gold digger. She must have wanted Henry's money."

"No, I don't think so. You see, Mrs. Flowers is already well off. Not in your class, of course, but well off all the same. Her late husband owned a soft-drink-bottling company and left her financially secure."

"Her late husband—how old is she?"

The detective walked back to the table and flicked over a page or two of his file before his thumb started moving down the page. The black nail came to a halt.

"She'll be fifty-three on her next birthday."

"Oh, my God!" said Anne. "The poor woman. She must hate me."

"I dare say she does, Mrs. Osborne, but that will not help us. Now I must turn to your husband's other activities."

The nicotine-stained finger turned over some more pages.

Anne began to feel sick. Why had she come, why hadn't she left well enough alone last week? She didn't have to know. She didn't want to know. Why didn't she get up and walk away? How she wished Richard were by her side. He would have known exactly how to deal with the whole situation. She found herself unable to move, transfixed by Glen Ricardo and the contents of his smart new file.

"On two occasions last week Mr. Osborne spent over three hours alone with Mrs. Preston."

"But that doesn't prove anything," began Anne desperately. "I know they were discussing a very important financial document."

"In a small hotel on La Salle Street."

Anne didn't interrupt the detective again.

"On both occasions they were seen walking into the hotel, holding hands, whispering and laughing. It's not conclusive, of course, but we have photographs of them together entering and leaving the hotel."

"Destroy them," Anne said quietly.

Glen Ricardo blinked. "As you wish, Mrs. Osborne. I'm afraid there is more. Further inquiries show that Mr. Osborne was never at Harvard, nor was he an officer in the American Armed Forces. There was a Henry Osborne at Harvard who was five foot five, sandy-haired and came from Alabama. He was killed on the *Maine* in 1917. We also know that your husband is considerably younger than he claims to be and that his real name is Vittorio Togna, and he has served——"

"I don't want to hear any more," said Anne, tears flooding down her cheeks. "I don't want to hear any more."

"Of course, Mrs. Osborne, I understand. I am only sorry that my news is so distressing. In my job sometimes——"

Anne fought for a measure of self-control. "Thank you, Mr. Ricardo, I appreciate all you have done. How much do I owe you?"

"Well, you have already paid for the two weeks in advance. There are two additional days and my expenses came to seventy-three dollars."

Anne passed him a hundred-dollar bill and rose from her chair.

"Don't forget your change, Mrs. Osborne."

She shook her head and waved a disinterested hand.

"Are you feeling all right, Mrs. Osborne? You look a little pale. Can I get you a glass of water or something?"

"I'm fine," lied Anne.

"Perhaps you would allow me to drive you home?"

"No, thank you, Mr. Ricardo, I'll be able to get myself home." She turned and smiled at him. "It is kind of you to offer."

Glen Ricardo closed the door quietly behind his client, walked slowly to the window, bit the end off his last big cigar, spat it out and cursed his job.

Anne paused at the top of the littered stairs, clinging to the banister, almost fainting. The baby kicked inside her, making her feel nauseous. She found a cab on the corner of the block and huddled into the back; she was unable to stop herself from sobbing, to think what to do next. As soon as she was dropped back at the Red House, she went to her bedroom before any of the staff could see her distress. The telephone was ringing as she entered the room and she picked it up, more out of habit than from any curiosity about who it might be.

"Could I speak to Mrs. Kane, please?"

She recognized Alan's clipped tone at once. Another tired, unhappy voice.

"Hello, Alan. This *is* Anne."

"Anne, my dear, I was sorry to learn about this morning's news."

"How do you know about it, Alan? How can you possibly know? Who told you?"

"City Hall phoned me and gave me the details soon after ten this morning. I tried to call you then, but your maid said you had already left to do some shopping."

"Oh, my God," said Anne, "I had quite forgotten about the contract." She sat down heavily, unable to breathe freely.

"Are you all right, Anne?"

"Yes, I'm just fine," she said, trying unsuccessfully to hide the sobbing in her voice. "What did City Hall have to say?"

"The hospital contract was awarded to a firm called Kirkbride and Carter. Apparently Henry wasn't even placed in the top three. I've been trying to reach him all morning, but it seems he left his office soon after ten and he hasn't been back since. I don't suppose you know where he is, Anne?"

"No, I haven't any idea."

"Do you want me to come around, my dear?" he said. "I could be with you in a few minutes."

"No, thank you, Alan." Anne paused to draw a shaky breath. "Please forgive me for the way I have been treating you these past few days. If Richard were still alive, he would never forgive me."

"Don't be silly, Anne. Our friendship has lasted for far too many years for an incident like that to be of any significance."

The kindness of his voice triggered off a fresh burst of weeping. Anne staggered to her feet.

"I must go, Alan. I can hear someone at the front door—it may be Henry."

"Take care, Anne, and don't worry about today. As long as I'm chairman, the bank will always support you. Don't hesitate to call if you need me."

Anne put the telephone down, the noise thudding in her ears. The effort of breathing was stupendous. She sank to the floor and as she did so, the long-forgotten sensation of a vigorous contraction overwhelmed her.

A few moments later the maid knocked quietly on the door. She looked in; William was at her shoulder. He had not entered his mother's bedroom since her marriage to Henry Osborne. The two rushed to Anne's side. She was shaking convulsively, unaware of their presence. Little flecks of foam spattered her upper lip. In a few seconds the attack passed and she lay moaning quietly.

"Mother," William said urgently, "what's the matter?"

Anne opened her eyes and stared wildly at her son. "Richard. Thank God you've come. I need you."

"It's William, Mother."

Her gaze faltered. "I have no more strength left, Richard. I must pay for my mistake. Forgive—"

Her voice trailed off to a groan as another powerful contraction started.

"What's happening?" said William helplessly.

"I think it must be the baby coming," the maid said. "Though it isn't due for several weeks."

"Get Dr. MacKenzie on the phone immediately," said William to the maid as he ran to the bedroom door. "Matthew!" he shouted. "Come up quickly."

Matthew bounded up the stairs and joined William in the bedroom.

"Help me get my mother down to the car."

Matthew knelt down. The two boys picked Anne up and carried her gently downstairs and out to the car. She was panting and groaning and obviously still in immense pain. William ran back to the house and grabbed the phone from the maid while Matthew waited in the car.

"Dr. MacKenzie."

"Yes, who's this?"

"My name is William Kane—you won't know me, sir."

"Don't know you, young man? I delivered you. What can I do for you now?"

"I think my mother is in labor. I am bringing her to the hospital immediately. I should be there in a few minutes' time."

Dr. MacKenzie's tone changed. "All right, William, don't worry. I'll be here waiting for you and everything will be under control by the time you arrive."

"Thank you, sir." William hesitated. "She seemed to have some sort of a fit. Is that normal?"

William's words chilled the doctor. He too hesitated.

"Well, not quite normal. But she'll be all right once she's had the baby. Get here as quickly as you can."

William put down the phone, ran out of the house and jumped into the Rolls-Royce.

Matthew drove the car in fits and starts, never once getting out of first gear and never stopping for anything until they had reached the hospital. The two boys carried Anne, and a nurse with a stretcher quickly guided them through to the maternity section. Dr. MacKenzie was standing at the entrance of an operating room, waiting. He took over and asked them both to remain outside.

William and Matthew sat in silence on the small bench and waited. Frightening cries and screams, unlike any sound they had ever heard anyone make, came from the delivery room—to be succeeded by an even more frightening silence. For the first time in his life William felt totally helpless. The two boys sat on the bench for over an hour, no word passing between them. Eventually a tired Dr. MacKenzie emerged. The two boys rose and the doctor looked at Matthew Lester.

"William?" he asked.

"No, sir, I am Matthew Lester. This is William."

The doctor turned and put a hand on William's shoulder. "William, I'm so sorry. Your mother died a few minutes ago. . . . and the child, a little girl, was stillborn."

William's legs gave way as he sank onto the bench.

"We did everything in our power to save them, but it was too late." He shook his head wearily. "She wouldn't listen to me—she insisted on having the baby. It should never have happened."

William sat first in silence, stunned by the whiplash sound of the words. Then he whispered, "How *could* she die? How could you *let* her die?"

The doctor sat down on the bench between the boys. "She wouldn't listen," he repeated slowly. "I warned her repeatedly after her miscarriage not to have another child, but when she married again, she and your stepfather never took my warnings seriously. She had high blood pressure during her last pregnancy. It was worrying me during this one, but it was never near danger level. But when you brought her in today, for no apparent reason it had soared to the level where eclampsia ensues."

"Eclampsia?"

"Convulsions. Sometimes patients can survive several attacks. Sometimes they simply—stop breathing."

William drew a shuddering breath and let his head fall into his hands. Matthew Lester guided his friend gently along the corridor. The doctor followed them. When they reached the elevator, he looked at William.

"Her blood pressure went up so suddenly. It's very unusual and she didn't put up a real fight, almost as if she didn't care. Strange—had something been troubling her lately?"

William raised his tear-streaked face. "Not *something*," he said with hatred. "Some*one*."

Alan Lloyd was sitting in a corner of the drawing room when the two boys arrived back at the Red House. He rose as they entered.

"William," he said immediately. "I blame myself for authorizing the loan."

William stared at him, not taking in what he was saying.

Matthew Lester stepped into the silence. "I don't think that's important any longer, sir," he said quietly. "William's mother has just died in childbirth."

Alan Lloyd turned ashen, steadied himself by grasping the mantelpiece and turned away. It was the first time that either of them had seen a grown man weep.

"It's my fault," said the banker. "I'll never forgive myself. I didn't tell her everything I knew. I loved her so much that I never wanted her to be distressed."

His anguish enabled William to be calm.

"It certainly was not your fault, Alan," he said firmly. "You did everything you could, I know that, and now it's I who am going to need your help."

Alan Lloyd braced himself. "Has Osborne been informed about your mother's death?"

"I neither know nor care."

"I've been trying to reach him all day about the investment. He left his office soon after ten this morning and he hasn't been seen since."

"He'll turn up here sooner or later," William said grimly.

After Alan Lloyd had left, William and Matthew sat alone in the front room for most of the night, dozing off and on. At four o'clock in the morning, as William counted the chimes of the grandfather clock, he thought he heard a noise in the street. Matthew was staring out of the window down the drive. William walked stiffly over to join him. They both watched Henry Osborne stagger across Louisburg Square, a bottle in his hand. He fumbled with some keys for some time and finally appeared in the doorway to the front room, blinking dazedly at the two boys.

"I want Anne, not you. Why aren't you at school? I don't want you," he said, his voice thick and slurred, as he tried to push William aside. "Where's Anne?"

"My mother is dead," said William quietly.

Henry Osborne looked at him stupidly for a few seconds. The incomprehension of his gaze snapped William's self-control.

"Where were you when she needed a husband?" he shouted.

Still Osborne stood, swaying slightly. "What about the baby?"

"Stillborn, a little girl."

Henry Osborne slumped into a chair, drunken tears starting to run down his face. "She lost my little baby?"

William was nearly incoherent with rage and grief. "Your

baby? Stop thinking about yourself for once," he shouted. "You know Dr. MacKenzie advised her against becoming pregnant again."

"Expert in that as well, are we, like everything else? If you had minded your own fucking business, I could have taken care of my own wife without your interference."

"And her money, it seems."

"Money. You tightfisted little bastard, I bet losing that hurts you more than anything else."

"Get up!" William said between his teeth.

Henry Osborne pushed himself up and smashed the bottle across the corner of the chair. Whiskey splashed over the carpet. He swayed toward William, the broken bottle in his raised hand. William stood his ground while Matthew came between them and easily removed the bottle from the drunken man's grasp.

William pushed his friend aside and advanced until his face was only inches away from Henry Osborne's.

"Now, you listen to me and listen carefully. I want you out of this house in one hour. If I ever hear from you again in my life, I shall instigate a full legal investigation into what has happened to my mother's half-million-dollar investment in your firm, and I shall reopen my research into who you really are and your past in Chicago. If on the other hand, I do not hear from you again, ever, I shall consider the ledger balanced and the matter closed. Now get out before I kill you."

The two boys watched him leave, sobbing, incoherent and furious.

The next morning William paid a visit to the bank. He was shown immediately into the chairman's office. Alan Lloyd was packing some documents into a briefcase. He looked up and handed a piece of paper to William without speaking. It was a short letter to all board members tendering his resignation as chairman of the bank.

"Could you ask your secretary to come in?" said William quietly.

"As you wish."

Alan Lloyd pressed a button on the side of his desk, and a middle-aged, conservatively dressed woman entered the room from a side door.

"Good morning, Mr. Kane," she said when she saw William. "I was so sorry to learn about your mother."

"Thank you," said William. "Has anyone else seen this letter?"

"No sir," said the secretary. "I was about to type twelve copies for Mr. Lloyd to sign."

"Well, don't type them, and please forget that this draft ever existed. Never mention its existence to anyone, do you understand?"

She stared into the blue eyes of the sixteen-year-old boy. So like his father, she thought. "Yes, Mr. Kane." She left quietly, closing the door. Alan Lloyd looked up.

"Kane and Cabot doesn't need a new chairman at the moment, Alan," said William. "You did nothing my father would not have done in the same circumstances."

"It's not as easy as that," Alan said.

"It's as easy as that," said William. "We can discuss this again when I am twenty-one and not before. Until then I would be obliged if you would run my bank in your usual diplomatic and conservative manner. I want nothing of what has happened to be discussed outside this office. You will destroy any information you have on Henry Osborne and consider the matter closed."

William tore up the letter of resignation and dropped the pieces of paper into the fire. He put his arm around Alan's shoulders.

"I have no family now, Alan, only you. For God's sake, don't desert me."

William was driven back to Beacon Hill. Grandmother Kane and Grandmother Cabot were sitting in silence in the drawing room. They both rose as he entered the room. It was the first time that William realized he was now the head of the Kane family.

The funeral took place quietly two days later at St. Paul's Episcopal Cathedral. None but the family and close friends was invited; the only notable absentee was Henry Osborne. As the mourners departed, they paid their respects to William. The grandmothers stood one pace behind him, like sentinels, watching, approving the calm and dignified way in which he conducted himself. When everyone had left, William accompanied Alan Lloyd to his car.

The Chairman was delighted by William's request of him.

"As you know, Alan, my mother had always intended to build a children's wing for Mass. General, in memory of my father. I would like her wishes carried out."

CHAPTER
ELEVEN

Wladek stayed at the Polish consulate in Constantinople for a year and not the few days he had originally expected, working day and night for Pawel Zaleski, becoming an indispensable aide and close friend. Nothing was too much trouble for him, and Zaleski soon began to wonder how he had managed before Wladek arrived. The boy visited the British embassy once a week to eat in the kitchen with Mrs. Henderson, the Scottish cook, and, on one occasion, with His Britannic Majesty's Second Consul himself.

Around them the old Islamic way of life was dissolving and the Ottoman Empire was beginning to totter. Mustafa Kemal was the name on everyone's lips. The sense of impending change made Wladek restless. His mind returned incessantly to the Baron and all whom he had loved in the castle. The necessity of surviving from day to day in Russia had kept them from his mind's eye, but in Turkey they rose up before him, a silent and slow procession. Sometimes he could see them strong and happy—Leon swimming in the river, Florentyna playing cat's cradle in his bedroom, the Baron's face strong and proud in the evening candlelight—but always the well-remembered, well-loved faces would waver and, try as Wladek would to hold them firm, they would change horribly to that last dreadful aspect—Leon dead on top of him, Florentyna bleeding in agony, and the Baron almost blind and broken.

Wladek began to realize that he could never return to a land peopled by such ghosts until he had made something worthwhile of his life. With that single thought in mind he set his heart on going to America, as his countryman Tadeusz Kosciusko, of whom the Baron had told so many enthralling tales, had so long before him. The United States, described by Pawel Zaleski as the "New World." The epithet inspired Wladek with a hope for the future and a chance to return one day to Poland in triumph.

It was Pawel Zaleski who put up the money to purchase an immigrant passage for Wladek to the United States. They were difficult to come by, for they were always booked at least a year in advance. It seemed to Wladek as though the whole of Eastern Europe were trying to escape and start afresh in the New World.

In the spring of 1921, Wladek Koskiewicz finally left Constantinople and boarded the S.S. *Black Arrow*, bound for Ellis Island, New York. He possessed one suitcase, containing all his belongings, and a set of papers issued by Pawel Zaleski.

The Polish Consul accompanied him to the wharf and embraced him affectionately. "Go with God, my boy."

The traditional Polish response came naturally from the depths of Wladek's early childhood. "Remain with God," he replied.

As he reached the top of the gangplank, Wladek recalled his terrifying journey from Odessa to Constantinople. This time there was no coal in sight, only people, people everywhere—Poles, Lithuanians, Estonians, Ukrainians and others of many racial types unfamiliar to Wladek. He clutched his few belongings and waited in the line, the first of many long waits with which he later associated his entry into the United States.

His papers were sternly scrutinized by a deck officer who was clearly predisposed to the suspicion that Wladek was trying to avoid military service in Turkey, but Pawel Zaleski's documents were impeccable; Wladek invoked a silent blessing on his fellow countryman's head as he watched others being turned back.

Next came a vaccination and a cursory medical examination, which, had he not had a year of good food and the chance to recover his health in Constantinople, Wladek would certainly have failed. At last, with all the checks over, he was allowed belowdecks into the steerage quarters. There were separate compartments for males, females and married couples. Wladek quickly made his way to the male quarters and found the Polish group occupying a large block of iron berths, each containing four two-tiered bunk beds. Each bunk had a thin straw mattress, a light blanket and no pillow. Having no pillow didn't worry Wladek, who had never been able to sleep on one since leaving Russia.

Wladek selected a bunk below a boy of roughly his own age and introduced himself.

"I'm Wladek Koskiewicz."

"I'm Jerzy Nowak from Warsaw," volunteered the boy in his native Polish, "and I'm going to make my fortune in America."

The boy thrust forward his hand.

Wladek and Jerzy spent the time before the ship sailed telling each other of their experiences, both pleased to have someone to share their loneliness with, neither willing to admit his total ignorance of America. Jerzy, it turned out, had lost both his parents in the war but had few other claims to attention. He was entranced by Wladek's stories: the son of a baron, brought up in a trapper's cottage, imprisoned by the Germans and the Russians, escaped from Siberia and then from a Turkish executioner thanks to the heavy silver band that Jerzy couldn't take his eyes off. Wladek had packed more into his fifteen years than Jerzy thought he himself would manage in a lifetime. Wladek talked all night of the past while Jerzy listened intently, neither wanting to sleep and neither wanting to admit his apprehension of the future.

The following morning the *Black Arrow* sailed. Wladek and Jerzy stood at the rail and watched Constantinople slip away in the blue distance of the Bosphorus. After the calm of the Sea of Marmara, the choppiness of the Aegean afflicted them and most of the other passengers with a horrible abruptness. The two washrooms for steerage passengers, with ten basins apiece, six toilets and cold saltwater faucets were wholly inadequate. After a couple of days the stench of their quarters was oppressive.

Food was served on long tables in a large, filthy dining hall: warm soup, potatoes, fish, boiled beef and cabbage, brown or black bread. Wladek had tasted worse food but not since Russia and was glad of the provisions Mrs. Henderson had packed for him: sausages, nuts and a little brandy. He and Jerzy shared them huddled in the corner of their berth. It was an unspoken understanding. They ate together, explored the ship together and, at night, slept one above the other.

On the third day at sea Jerzy brought a Polish girl to their table for supper. Her name, he informed Wladek casually, was Zaphia. It was the first time in his life that Wladek had ever looked at a girl twice, but he couldn't stop looking at Zaphia. She rekindled memories of Florentyna. The warm gray eyes, the long fair hair that fell onto her shoulders, and the soft voice. Wladek found he wanted to touch her. The girl occasionally smiled across at Wladek, who was miserably aware of how much better-looking Jerzy was than he. He tagged along as Jerzy escorted Zaphia back to the women's quarters.

Jerzy turned to him afterward, mildly irritated. "Can't you find a girl of your own? This one's mine."

Wladek was not prepared to admit that he had no idea how to set about finding a girl of his own.

"There will be enough time for girls when we reach America," he said scornfully.

"Why wait for America? I intend to have as many on this ship as possible."

"How will you go about that?" asked Wladek, intent on the acquisition of knowledge without admitting to his own ignorance.

"We have twelve more days in this awful tub and I am going to have twelve women," boasted Jerzy.

"What can you do with twelve women?" asked Wladek.

"Fuck them, what else?"

Wladek looked perplexed.

"Good God," said Jerzy. "Don't tell me the man who survived the Germans and escaped from the Russians, killed a man at the age of twelve and narrowly missed having his hand chopped off by a bunch of savage Turks has never had a woman?"

He laughed and a multilingual chorus from the surrounding bunks told him to shut up.

"Well," Jerzy continued in a whisper, "the time has come to broaden your education, because at last I've found something I can teach you." He peered over the side of his bunk even though he could not see Wladek's face in the dark. "Zaphia's an understanding girl. I daresay she could be persuaded to expand your education a little. I shall arrange it."

Wladek didn't reply.

No more was said on the subject, but the next day Zaphia started to pay attention to Wladek. She sat next to him at meals and they talked for hours of their experiences and hopes. She was an orphan from Poznan, on her way to join cousins in Chicago. Wladek told Zaphia that he was going to New York and would probably live with Jerzy.

"I hope New York is very near Chicago," said Zaphia.

"Then you can come and see me when I am the mayor," said Jerzy expansively.

She sniffed disparagingly. "You're too Polish, Jerzy. You can't even speak nice English like Wladek."

"I'll learn," Jerzy said confidently, "and I'll start by making my name American. From today I shall be George Novak. Then I'll have no trouble at all. Everyone in the United States will think I'm American. What about you, Wladek Koskiewicz? Nothing much you can do with that name, is there?"

Wladek looked at the newly christened George in silent resentment of his own name. Unable to adopt the title to which he felt himself the rightful heir, he hated the name Koskiewicz and the continual reminder of his illegitimacy.

"I'll manage," he said. "I'll even help you with your English if you like."

"And I'll help you find a girl."

Zaphia giggled. "You needn't bother, he's found one."

Jerzy, or George, as he now insisted they call him, retreated after supper each night into one of the tarpaulin-covered lifeboats with a different girl. Wladek longed to know what he did there, even though some of the ladies of George's choice were not merely filthy, but would clearly have been unattractive even when scrubbed clean.

One night after supper, when George had disappeared again, Wladek and Zaphia sat out on deck and she put her arms around him and asked him to kiss her. He pressed his mouth stiffly against hers; he felt horribly unfamiliar with what he was meant to do. To his surprise and embarrassment, her tongue parted his lips. After a few moments of apprehension, Wladek found her open mouth intensely exciting and was alarmed to find his penis stiffening. He tried to draw away from her, ashamed, but she did not seem to mind in the least. On the contrary, she began to press her body gently and rhythmically against him and drew his hands down to her buttocks. His swollen penis throbbed against her, giving him almost unbearable pleasure. She disengaged her mouth and whispered in his ear.

"Do you want me to take my clothes off, Wladek?"

He could not bring himself to reply.

She detached herself from him, laughing. "Well, maybe tomorrow," she said, getting up from the deck and leaving him.

He stumbled back to his bunk in a daze, determined that the next day he would finish the job Zaphia had started. No sooner had he settled in his berth, thinking of how he would go about the task, than a large hand grabbed him by the hair and pulled him down from his bunk onto the floor. In an instant his sexual excitement vanished. Two men whom he had never seen before were towering above him. They dragged him to a far corner and threw him up against the wall. A large hand was now clamped firmly on Wladek's mouth while a knife touched his throat.

"Don't breathe," whispered the man holding the knife, pushing the blade against the skin. "All we want is the silver band around your wrist."

The sudden realization that his treasure might be stolen from him was almost as horrifying to Wladek as had been the thought of losing his hand. Before he could think of anything to do, one of the men jerked the band off his wrist. He couldn't see their faces in the dark and he feared he must have lost the band forever, when someone leaped onto the back of the man holding the knife. This action gave Wladek the chance to punch the one who was holding him pinned to the wall. The sleepy immigrants around them began to wake and take an interest in what was happening. The two men escaped as quickly as they could but not before George had managed to stick the knife in the side of one of the assailants.

"Go to the cholera," shouted Wladek at his retreating back.

"It looks as if I got here just in time," said George. "I don't think they'll be back in a hurry." He stared down at the silver band, lying in the trampled sawdust on the floor. "It's magnificent," he said almost solemnly. "There will always be men who want to steal such a prize from you."

Wladek picked the band up and slipped it back onto his wrist.

"Well, you nearly lost the damn thing for good that time," said George. "Lucky for you I was a little late getting back tonight."

"Why were you a little late getting back?" asked Wladek.

"My reputation," said George boastfully, "now goes before me. In fact, I found some other idiot in my lifeboat tonight, already with his pants down. I soon got rid of him, though, when I told him he was with a girl I would have had last week but I couldn't be sure she hadn't got the pox. I've never seen anyone get dressed so quickly."

"What do you do in the boat?" asked Wladek.

"Fuck them silly, you ass—what do you think?" And with that George rolled over and went to sleep.

Wladek stared at the ceiling and, touching the silver

band, thought about what George had said, wondering what it would be like to "fuck" Zaphia.

The next morning they hit a storm, and all the passengers were confined belowdecks. The stench, intensified by the ship's heating system, seemed to permeate Wladek's very marrow.

"And the worst of it is," groaned George, "I won't make a round dozen now."

When the storm abated, nearly all the passengers escaped to the deck. Wladek and George fought their way around the crowded gangways, thankful for the fresh air. Many of the girls smiled at George, but it seemed to Wladek that they didn't notice him at all. A dark-haired girl, her cheeks made pink by the wind, passed George and smiled at him. He turned to Wladek.

"I'll have her tonight."

Wladek stared at the girl and studied the way she looked at George.

"Tonight," said George as she passed within earshot. She pretended not to hear him and walked away, a little too quickly.

"Turn round, Wladek, and see if she is looking back at me."

Wladek turned around. "Yes, she is," he said, surprised.

"She's mine tonight," said George. "Have you had Zaphia yet?"

"No," said Wladek. "Tonight."

"About time, isn't it? You'll never see the girl again once we've reached New York."

Sure enough, George arrived at supper that night with the dark-haired girl. Without a word being said, Wladek and Zaphia left them, arms around each other's waist, and went on to the deck and strolled around the ship several times. Wladek looked sideways at her pretty young profile. It was going to be now or never, he decided. He led her to a shadowy corner and started to kiss her as she had kissed him, openmouthed. She moved backward a little until her shoulders were resting against a bulwark, and Wladek moved with her. She drew his hands slowly down to her breasts. He touched them tentatively, surprised by their softness. She undid a couple of buttons on her blouse and slipped his hand inside. The first feel of the naked flesh was delicious.

"Christ, your hand is cold!" Zaphia said.

Wladek crushed himself against her, his mouth dry, his breath heavy. She parted her legs a little and Wladek thrust clumsily against her through several intervening layers of cloth. She moved in sympathy with him for a couple of minutes and then pushed him away.

"Not here on the deck," she said. "Let's find a boat."

The first three boats they looked into were occupied, but they finally found an empty one and wriggled under the tarpaulin. In the constricted darkness Zaphia made some adjustments to her clothing that Wladek could not figure out and pulled him gently on top of her. It took her very little time to bring Wladek to his earlier pitch of excitement through the few remaining layers of cloth between them. He thrust himself between her legs and was on the point of orgasm when she again drew her mouth away.

"Undo your trousers," she whispered.

He felt like an idiot but hurriedly undid them and thrust himself into the yielding softness, coming immediately, feeling the sticky wetness running down the inside of her thigh. He lay dazed, amazed by the abruptness of the act, suddenly aware that the wooden notches of the lifeboat were digging uncomfortably into his elbows and knees.

"Was that the first time you've made love to a girl?" asked Zaphia, wishing he would move over.

"No, of course not," said Wladek.

"Do you love me, Wladek?"

"Yes, I do," he said, "and as soon as I've settled in New York, I'll come and find you in Chicago."

"I'd like that, Wladek," she said as she buttoned up her dress. "I love you, too."

"Did you fuck her?" was George's immediate question on Wladek's return.

"Yes."

"Was it good?"

"Yes," said Wladek, uncertainly, and then fell asleep.

In the morning, they were awakened by the excitement of the other passengers, happy in the knowledge that this was their last day on board the *Black Arrow*. Some of them had been up on deck before sunrise, hoping to catch the first sign of land. Wladek packed his few belongings in his new suitcase, put on his only suit and his cap and then joined Zaphia and George on deck. The three of them stared into the mist that hung over the sea, waiting in silence for their first sight of the United States of America.

"There it is!" shouted a passenger on a deck above them, and cheering went up at the sight of the gray strip of Long Island approaching through the spring morning.

Little tugs bustled up to the side of the *Black Arrow* and guided her between Brooklyn and Staten Island into New York Harbor. The colossal Statue of Liberty seemed to regard them austerely as they gazed in awe at the emerging skyline of Manhattan, her lamp lifted high into the early morning sky.

Finally they moored near the turreted and spired red brick buildings of Ellis Island. The passengers who had private cabins left the ship first. Wladek hadn't noticed them until that day. They must have been on a separate deck with their own dining hall. Their bags were carried for them by porters and they were greeted by smiling faces at the dockside. Wladek knew that wasn't going to happen to him.

After the favored few had disembarked, the captain announced over the loudspeaker to the rest of the passengers that they would not be leaving the ship for several hours. A groan of disappointment went up and Zaphia sat down on the deck and burst into tears. Wladek tried to comfort her. Eventually an official came around with coffee, a second with numbered labels, which were hung around the passengers' necks. Wladek's was B.127; it reminded him of the last time he was a number. What had he let himself in for? Was America like the Russian camps?

In the middle of the afternoon—they had been given no food nor further information—they were brought dockside to Ellis Island. There the men were separated from the women and sent off to different sheds. Wladek kissed Zaphia and wouldn't let her go, holding up the line. A passing official parted them.

"All right, let's get moving," he said. "Keep that up and we'll have you two married in no time."

Wladek lost sight of Zaphia as he and George were pushed forward. They spent the night in an old, damp shed, unable to sleep as interpreters moved among the crowded rows of bunks, offering curt, but not unkind, assistance to the bewildered immigrants.

In the morning they were sent for medical examinations. The first hurdle was the hardest: Wladek was told to climb a steep flight of stairs. The blue-uniformed doctor made him do it twice, watching his gait carefully. Wladek tried very hard to minimize his limp and finally the doctor was satisfied. Wladek was then made to remove his hat and stiff collar so that his face, eyes, hair, hands and neck could be examined carefully. The man directly behind Wladek had a harelip; the doctor stopped him immediately, put a chalk cross on his right shoulder and sent him to the other end of the shed. After the physical was over, Wladek joined up with George again in another long line outside the Public Examination room, where each person's interview seemed to be taking about five minutes. Three hours later when George was ushered into the room, Wladek wondered what they would ask him.

When George eventually came out, he grinned at Wladek. "Easy, you'll walk right through it," he said. Wladek could feel the palms of his hands sweating as he stepped forward.

He followed the official into a small, undecorated room. There were two examiners seated and writing furiously on what looked like official papers.

"Do you speak English?" asked the first.

"Yes, sir, I do quite good," replied Wladek, wishing he had spoken more English on the voyage.

"What is your name?"

"Wladek Koskiewicz, sir."

The men passed him a big black book. "Do you know what this is?"

"Yes, sir, the Bible."

"Do you believe in God?"

"Yes, sir, I do."

"Put your hand on the Bible and swear that you will answer our questions truthfully."

Wladek took the Bible in his left hand, placed his right hand on it and said, "I promise I tell the truth."

"What is your nationality?"

"Polish."

"Who paid for your passage here?"

"I paid from my money that I earn in Polish consulate in Constantinople."

One of the officials studied Wladek's papers, nodded and then asked, "Do you have a home to go to?"

"Yes, sir. I go stay at Mr. Peter Novak. He my friend's uncle. He live in New York."

"Good. Do you have work to go to?"

"Yes, sir. I go work in bakery of Mr. Novak."

"Have you ever been arrested?"

Russia flashed through Wladek's mind. That couldn't count. Turkey—he wasn't going to mention that.

"No, sir, never."

"Are you an anarchist?"

"No, sir. I hate Communists—they kill my sister."

"Are you willing to abide by the laws of the United States of America?"

"Yes, sir."

"Have you any money?"

"Yes, sir."

"May we see it?"

"Yes, sir." Wladek placed on the table a bundle of bills and a few coins.

"Thank you," said the examiner. "You may put the money back in your pocket."

The second examiner looked at Wladek. "What is twenty-one plus twenty-four?"

"Forty-five," said Wladek without hesitation.

"How many legs does a cow have?"

Wladek could not believe his ears. "Four, sir," he said, wondering if the question were a trick.

"And a horse?"

"Four, sir," said Wladek, still in disbelief.

"Which would you throw overboard if you were out at sea in a small boat which needed to be lightened, bread or money?"

"The money, sir," said Wladek.

"Good." The examiner picked up a card marked "Admitted" and handed it over to Wladek. "After you have changed your money, show this card to the Immigration Officer. Tell him your full name and he will give you a registration card. You will then be given an entry certificate. If you do not commit a crime for five years and pass a simple reading and writing examination in English and agree to support the Constitution, you will be permitted to apply for full United States citizenship. Good luck, Wladek."

"Thank you, sir."

At the money-exchange counter Wladek handed in eighteen months of Turkish savings and the three 50-ruble notes. He was handed $47.20 in exchange for the Turkish money but was told the rubles were worthless. He could only think of Dr. Dubien and his fifteen years of diligent saving.

The final step was to see the Immigration Officer, who was seated behind a counter at the exit barrier directly under a picture of President Harding. Wladek and George went over to him.

"Full name?" the officer asked George.

"George Novak" was the firm reply. The officer wrote the name on a card.

"And your address?" he asked.

"286 Broome Street, New York, New York."

The officer passed George the card. "This is your Immigration Certificate, 21871—George Novak. Welcome to the

United States, George. I'm Polish, too. You'll like it here. Many congratulations and good luck."

George smiled and shook hands with the officer, stood to one side and waited for Wladek. The officer stared at Wladek. Wladek passed him the card marked "Admitted."

"Full name?" asked the officer.

Wladek hesitated.

"What's your name?" repeated the man, a little louder, slightly impatient.

Wladek couldn't get the words out. How he hated that peasant name.

"For the last time, what's your name?"

George was staring at Wladek. So were others who had joined the queue for the immigration officer. Wladek still didn't speak. The officer suddenly grabbed his wrist, stared closely at the inscription on the silver band, wrote on a card and passed it to Wladek.

"21872—Baron Abel Rosnovski. Welcome to the United States. Many congratulations and good luck, Abel."

PART TWO
1923–1928

CHAPTER
TWELVE

William returned to start his last year at St. Paul's in September 1923 and was elected president of the senior class, exactly thirty-three years after his father had held the same office. William did not win the election in the usual fashion, by virtue of being the finest athlete or the most popular boy in the school. Matthew Lester, his closest friend, would undoubtedly have won any contest based on those criteria. It was simply that William was the most impressive boy in the school, and for that reason Matthew Lester could not be prevailed upon to run against him. St. Paul's entered William's name as its candidate for the Hamilton Memorial Mathematics Scholarship at Harvard, and William worked single-mindedly toward that goal during this fall term.

When William returned to the Red House for Christmas, he was looking forward to an uninterrupted period in which to get to grips with *Principia Mathematica*. But it was not to be, for there were several invitations to parties and balls awaiting his arrival. To most of them he felt able to return a tactful regret, but one was absolutely inescapable. The grandmothers had arranged a ball, to be held at the Red House on Louisburg Square. William wondered at what age he would find it possible to defend his home against invasion by the two great ladies and decided the time had not yet come, and at least it would give the servants something to do. He had few close friends in Boston, but this did not in-

hibit the grandmothers in their compilation of a formidable
guest list.

To mark the occasion they presented William with his
first dinner jacket in the latest double-breasted style; he received the gift with some pretense at indifference but later
swaggered around his bedroom in the suit, often stopping to
stare at himself in the mirror. The next day he put through a
long-distance call to New York and asked Matthew Lester to
join him for the fateful affair. Matthew's sister wanted to
come as well, but her mother didn't think it would be "suitable."

William was there to meet him at the train.

"Come to think of it," said Matthew as the chauffeur
drove them to Beacon Hill, "isn't it time you got yourself
laid, William? There must be some girls in Boston with absolutely no taste."

"Why, have you had a girl, Matthew?"

"Sure, last winter in New York."

"What was I doing at the time?"

"Probably touching up Bertrand Russell."   ,

"You never told me about it."

"Nothing much to tell. In any case, you seemed more involved in my father's bank than my budding love life. It all
happened at a staff party my father gave to celebrate Washington's Birthday. Another first for old wooden teeth. Actually, to put the incident in its proper perspective, I was raped
by one of the directors' secretaries, a large lady called Cynthia with even larger breasts that wobbled when—"

"Did you enjoy it?"

"Yes, but I can't believe for one moment that Cynthia did.
She was far too drunk to realize I was there at the time. Still,
you have to begin somewhere and she was willing to give
the boss's son a helping hand."

A vision of Alan Lloyd's prim, middle-aged secretary
flashed across William's mind.

"I don't think my chances of initiation by the chairman's
secretary are very good," he mused.

"You'd be surprised," said Matthew knowingly. "The

ones that go around with their legs so firmly together are often the ones who can't wait to get them apart. I now accept most invitations formal or informal, not that dress matters much on these occasions."

The chauffeur put the car in the garage while the two young men walked up the steps into William's house.

"You've certainly made some changes since I was last here," said Matthew, admiring the modern cane furniture and new paisley wallpaper. Only the crimson leather chair remained firmly rooted in its usual spot.

"The place needed brightening up a little," William offered. "It was like living in the Stone Age. Besides, I didn't want to be reminded of . . . Come on, this is no time to hang around discussing interior decoration."

"When is everybody arriving for this party?"

"Ball, Matthew—the grandmothers insist on calling it a ball."

"There is only one thing that can be described as a ball on these occasions."

"Matthew, one director's secretary does not entitle you to consider yourself a national authority on sex education."

"Oh, such jealousy, and from one's dearest friend." Matthew sighed mockingly.

William laughed and looked at his watch. "The first guest should arrive in a couple of hours. Time for a shower and to change. Did you remember to bring a tuxedo?"

"Yes, but if I didn't I could always wear my pajamas. I usually leave one or the other behind, but I've never yet managed to forget both. In fact, it might start a whole new craze if I went to the ball in my pajamas."

"I can't see my grandmothers enjoying the joke," said William.

The caterers arrived at six o'clock, twenty-three of them in all, and the grandmothers at seven, regal in long black lace that swept along the floor. William and Matthew joined them in the front room a few minutes before eight.

William was about to remove an inviting red cherry from the top of a magnificent iced cake when he heard Grandmother Kane's voice from behind him.

"Don't touch the food, William, it's not for you."

He swung around. "Then who is it for?" he asked as he kissed her on the cheek.

"Don't be fresh, William. Just because you're over six feet doesn't mean I wouldn't spank you."

Matthew Lester laughed.

"Grandmother, may I introduce my closest friend, Matthew Lester?"

Grandmother Kane subjected him to a careful appraisal through her pince-nez before venturing: "How do you do, young man?"

"It's an honor to meet you, Mrs. Kane. I believe you knew my grandfather."

"Knew your grandfather? Caleb Longworth Lester? He proposed marriage to me once, over fifty years ago. I turned him down. I told him he drank too much and that it would lead him to an early grave. I was right, so don't you drink, either of you. Remember, alcohol dulls the brain."

"We hardly get much chance with Prohibition," remarked Matthew innocently.

"That will end soon enough, I'm afraid," said Grandmother Kane, sniffing. "President Coolidge is forgetting his upbringing. He would never have become President if that idiot Harding hadn't foolishly died."

William laughed. "Really, Grandmother, your memory is getting selective. You wouldn't hear a word against him during the police strike."

Mrs. Kane did not respond.

The guests began to appear, many of them complete strangers to their host, who was delighted to see Alan Lloyd among the early arrivals.

"You're looking well, my boy," Alan said, finding himself looking up at William for the first time in his life.

"You too, sir. It was kind of you to come."

"Kind? Have you forgotten that the invitation came from

your grandmothers? I am possibly brave enough to refuse
one of them, but both——"

"You too, Alan?" William laughed. "Can you spare a moment for a private word?" He guided his guest toward a quiet
corner. "I want to change my investment plan slightly and
start buying Lester's bank stock whenever it comes onto the
market. I'd like to be holding about five percent of their
stock by the time I'm twenty-one."

"It's not that easy," said Alan. "Lester's stock doesn't
come on the market all that often, because it is all in private
hands, but I'll see what can be done. What is going on in that
mind of yours, William?"

"Well, my real aim is——"

"William." Grandmother Cabot was bearing down on
them at speed. "Here you are conspiring in a corner with Mr.
Lloyd and I haven't seen you dance with one young lady yet.
What do you imagine we organized this ball for?"

"Quite right," said Alan Lloyd, rising. "You come and sit
down with me, Mrs. Cabot, and I'll kick the boy out into
the world. We can rest, watch him dance and listen to the
music."

"Music? That's not music, Alan. It's nothing more than a
loud cacophony of sound with no suggestion of melody."

"My dear grandmother," said William, "that is 'Yes, We
Have No Bananas,' the latest hit song."

"Then the time has come for me to depart this world,"
said Grandmother Cabot, wincing.

"Never," Alan Lloyd said gallantly.

William danced with a couple of girls whom he had a
vague recollection of knowing, but he had to be reminded of
their names, and when he spotted Matthew sitting in a corner, he was glad of the excuse to escape the dance floor. He
had not noticed the girl sitting next to Matthew until he was
right on top of them. When she looked up into William's
eyes, he felt his knees give way.

"Do you know Abby Blount?" asked Matthew casually.

"No," said William, barely restraining himself from
straightening his tie.

"This is your host, Mr. William Lowell Kane."

The young lady cast her eyes demurely downward as William took the seat on the other side of her. Matthew had noted the look William had given Abby and went off in search of some punch.

"How is it I've lived in Boston all my life and we've never met?" William said.

"We did meet once before. On that occasion you pushed me into the pond on the Common; we were both three at the time. It's taken me fourteen years to recover."

"I am sorry," said William after a pause during which he searched in vain for more telling repartee.

"What a lovely house you have, William."

There was a second busy pause. "Thank you," said William weakly. He glanced sideways at Abby, trying to look as though he were not studying her. She was slim—oh, so slim—with huge brown eyes, long eyelashes and a profile that captivated William. Abby had bobbed her auburn hair in a style William had hated until that moment.

"Matthew tells me you are going to Harvard next year," she tried again.

"Yes, I am. I mean, would you like to dance?"

"Thank you," she said.

The steps that had come so easily a few minutes before seemed now to forsake him. He trod on her toes and continually propelled her into other dancers. He apologized, she smiled. He held her a little more closely and they danced on.

"Do we know that young lady who seems to have been monopolizing William for the last hour?" Grandmother Cabot said suspiciously.

Grandmother Kane picked up her pince-nez and studied the girl accompanying William as he strolled through the open bay windows out onto the lawn.

"Abby Blount," Grandmother Kane declared.

"Admiral Blount's granddaughter?" inquired Grandmother Cabot.

"Yes."

Grandmother Cabot nodded a degree of approval.

William guided Abby Blount toward the far end of the garden and stopped by a large chestnut tree that he had used in the past only for climbing.

"Do you always try to kiss a girl the first time you meet her?" asked Abby.

"To be honest," said William, "I've never kissed a girl before."

Abby laughed. "I'm very flattered."

She offered first her pink cheek and then her rosy, pursed lips and then insisted upon returning indoors. The grandmothers observed their early reentry with some relief.

Later, in William's bedroom, the two boys discussed the evening.

"Not a bad party," said Matthew. "Almost worth the trip from New York out here to the provinces, despite your stealing my girl."

"Do you think she'll help me lose my virginity?" asked William, ignoring Matthew's mock accusation.

"Well, you have three weeks to find out, but I fear you'll discover she hasn't lost hers yet," said Matthew. "Such is my expertise in these matters that I'm willing to bet you five dollars she doesn't succumb even to the charms of William Lowell Kane."

William planned a careful stratagem. Virginity was one thing, but losing five dollars to Matthew was quite another. He saw Abby Blount nearly every day after the ball, taking advantage for the first time of owning his own house and car at seventeen. He began to feel he would do better without the discreet but persistent chaperonage of Abby's parents, who seemed always to be in the middle distance, and he was not perceptibly nearer his goal when the last day of the holidays dawned.

Determined to win his five dollars, William sent Abby a dozen roses early in the day, took her out to an expensive dinner at Joseph's that evening and finally succeeded in coaxing her back into his front room.

"How did you get hold of a bottle of whiskey?" asked Abby. "It's Prohibition."

"Oh, it's not so hard," William boasted.

The truth was that he had hidden a bottle of Henry Osborne's bourbon in his bedroom soon after he had left and was now glad he had not poured it down the drain as had been his original intention.

William poured drinks that made him gasp and brought tears to Abby's eyes.

He sat down beside her and put his arm confidently around her shoulder. She settled into it.

"Abby, I think you're terribly pretty," he murmured in a preliminary way at her auburn curls.

She gazed at him earnestly, her brown eyes wide. "Oh, William," she breathed. "And I think you're just wonderful."

Her doll-like face was irresistible. She allowed herself to be kissed. Thus emboldened, William slipped a tentative hand from her wrist onto her breast and left it there like a traffic cop halting an advancing stream of automobiles. She became pinkly indignant and pushed his arm down to allow the traffic to move on.

"William, you mustn't do that."

"Why not?" said William, struggling vainly to retain his grasp of her.

"Because you can't tell where it might end."

"I've got a fair idea."

Before he could renew his advances, Abby pushed him away and rose hastily, smoothing her dress.

"I think I ought to be getting home now, William."

"But you've only just arrived."

"Mother will want to know what I've been doing."

"You'll be able to tell her—nothing."

"And I think it's best it stays that way," she added.

"But I'm going back tomorrow." He avoided saying "to school."

"Well, you can write to me, William."

Unlike Valentino, William knew when he was beaten. He

rose, straightened his tie, took Abby by the hand and drove her home.

The following day, back at school, Matthew Lester accepted the proffered five-dollar bill with eyebrows raised in mock astonishment.

"Just say one word, Matthew, and I'll chase you right around St. Paul's with a baseball bat."

"I can't think of any words that would truly express my deep feeling of sympathy."

"Matthew, right around St. Paul's."

William began to be aware of his housemaster's wife during his last semester at St. Paul's. She was a good-looking woman, a little slack around the stomach and hips perhaps, but she carried her splendid bosom well and the luxuriant dark hair piled on top of her head was no more streaked with gray than was becoming. One Saturday when William had sprained his wrist on the hockey field, Mrs. Raglan bandaged it for him in a cool compress, standing a little closer than was necessary, allowing William's arm to brush against her breast. He enjoyed the sensation. Then on another occasion when he had a fever and was confined to the infirmary for a few days, she brought him all his meals herself and sat on his bed, her body touching his legs through the thin covering while he ate. He enjoyed that too.

She was rumored to be Grumpy Raglan's second wife. No one in the house could imagine how Grumpy had managed to secure even one spouse. Mrs. Raglan occasionally indicated by the subtlest of sighs and silences that she shared something of their incredulity at her fate.

As part of his duties as house captain William was required to report to Grumpy Raglan every night at ten-thirty when he had completed the lights-out round and was about to go to bed himself. One Monday evening when he knocked on Grumpy's door as usual, he was surprised to hear Mrs. Raglan's voice bidding him to enter. She was lying on the chaise longue dressed in a loose silk robe of faintly Japanese appearance.

William kept a firm grasp on the cold doorknob. "All the lights are out and I've locked the front door, Mrs. Raglan. Good night."

She swung her legs onto the ground, a pale flash of thigh appearing momentarily from under the draped silk.

"You're always in such a hurry, William. You can't wait for your life to start, can you?" She walked over to a side table. "Why don't you stay and have some hot chocolate? Silly me, I made enough for two—I quite forgot that Mr. Raglan won't be back until Saturday."

There was a definite emphasis on the word "Saturday." She carried a steaming cup over to William and looked up at him to see whether the significance of her remarks had registered on him. Satisfied, she passed him the cup, letting her hand touch his. He stirred the hot chocolate assiduously.

"Gerald has gone to a conference," she continued explaining. It was the first time he had ever heard Grumpy Raglan's first name. "Do shut the door, William, and come and sit down."

William hesitated; he shut the door, but he did not want to take Grumpy's chair, nor did he want to sit next to Mrs. Raglan. He decided Grumpy's chair was the lesser of two evils and moved toward it.

"No, no," she said as she patted the seat next to her.

William shuffled over and sat down nervously by her side, staring into his cup for inspiration. Finding none, he gulped the contents down, burning his tongue. He was relieved to see that Mrs. Raglan was getting up. She refilled his cup, ignoring his murmured refusal, and then moved silently across the room, wound up the Victrola and placed the needle on the record. He was still looking at the floor when she returned.

"You wouldn't let a lady dance by herself, would you, William?"

He looked up. Mrs. Raglan was swaying slightly in time to the music. William stood up and put his arm formally around her. Grumpy could have fitted in between them without any trouble. After a few bars she moved closer to William, and he stared over her right shoulder fixedly to indicate to her that he had not noticed that her left hand had slipped from his shoulder to the small of his back. When the record stopped, William thought he would have a chance to return to the safety of his hot chocolate, but she had turned the disc over and was back in his arms before he could move.

"Mrs. Raglan, I think I ought to——"

"Relax a little, William."

At last he found the courage to look her in the eyes. He tried to reply, but he couldn't speak. Her hand was now exploring his back and he felt her thigh move gently into his groin. He tightened his hold around her waist.

"That's better," she said.

They slowly circled the room, closely entwined, slower and slower, keeping time with the music as the record gently ran down. When she slipped away and turned out the light, William wanted her to return quickly. He stood in the dark, not moving, hearing the rustle of silk, and able to see only a silhouette discarding clothes.

The crooner had completed his song, and the needle was scratching at the end of the record by the time she had helped William out of his clothes and led him back to the chaise longue. He groped for her in the dark, and his shy novice's fingers encountered several parts of her body that did not feel at all as he had imagined they would. He withdrew them hastily to the comparatively familiar territory of her breast. Her fingers exhibited no such reticence and he began to feel sensations he had never dreamed possible. He wanted to moan out loud but checked himself, fearing it would sound stupid. Her hands were on his back, pulling him gently on top of her.

William moved around, wondering how he would ever enter her without showing his total lack of experience. It was not as easy as he had expected and he began to get more desperate by the second. Then once again her fingers moved across his stomach and guided him expertly. With her help he entered her easily and had an immediate orgasm.

"I'm sorry," said William, not sure what to do next. He lay silently on top of her for some time before she spoke.

"It will be better tomorrow."

The sound of the scratching record returned to his ears.

Mrs. Raglan remained in William's mind all the endless next day. That night, she sighed. On Wednesday she panted. On Thursday she moaned. On Friday she cried out.

On Saturday, Grumpy Raglan returned from his conference, by which time William's education was complete.

At the end of the Easter vacation, on Ascension Day, to be exact, Abby Blount finally succumbed to William's charms. It cost Matthew five dollars and Abby her virginity. She was, after Mrs. Raglan, something of an anticlimax. It was the only event of note that happened during the entire vacation, because Abby went off to Palm Beach with her parents, and William spent most of his time shut away indoors with his books, at home to no one other than the grandmothers and Alan Lloyd. His final examinations were soon only a matter of weeks away and as Grumpy Raglan went to no further conferences, William had no other outside activities.

During their last term, he and Matthew would sit in their study at St. Paul's for hours, never speaking unless Matthew had some mathematical problem he was quite unable to solve. When the long-awaited examinations finally came, they lasted for only one brutal week. The moment they were over, both boys were sanguine about their results, but as the days went by and they waited and waited, their confidence began to diminish. The Hamilton Memorial Mathematics Scholarship to Harvard for mathematics was awarded on a strictly competitive basis and it was open to every schoolboy in America. William had no way of judging how tough his opposition might be. As more time went by and still he heard nothing, William began to assume the worst.

When the telegram arrived, delivered by a second-former,

William was out playing baseball with some other sixth-
formers, killing the last few days of the term before leaving
school, those warm summer days when boys are most likely
to be expelled for drunkenness, breaking windows or trying
to get into bed with one of the masters' daughters, if not their
wives.

William was declaring in a loud voice to those who cared
to listen that he was about to hit his first home run ever. The
Babe Ruth of St. Paul's, declared Matthew. Much laughter
greeted this exaggerated claim. When the telegram was
handed to him, home runs were suddenly forgotten. He
dropped his bat and tore open the little yellow envelope. The
pitcher waited, impatient, as did the outfielders as he read
the communication slowly.

"They want you to turn professional," someone shouted
from first base, the arrival of a telegram being an uncommon
occurrence during a baseball game. Matthew walked in from
the outfield to join William, trying to make out from his
friend's face if the news was good or bad. Without changing
his expression, William passed the telegram to Matthew,
who read it, leaped high into the air with delight and
dropped the piece of paper to the ground to accompany
William, racing around the bases even though no one had
actually hit the ball. The pitcher strode to the telegram,
picked it up, read it and with gusto threw his ball into the
bleachers. The little piece of yellow paper was then passed
eagerly from player to player. The last to read it was the
second-former, who, having caused so much happiness but
receiving no thanks, decided the least he deserved was to
know the cause of so much excitement.

The telegram was addressed to Mr. William Lowell Kane,
whom the boy assumed to be the incompetent hitter. It read:
"Congratulations on winning the Hamilton Memorial Mathematics Scholarship to Harvard, full details to follow. Abbot
Lawrence Lowell, President." William never did get his
home run and he was heavily set upon by several fielders before he reached home plate.

Matthew looked on with delight at the success of his

closest friend, but he was sad to think that it meant they might now be parted. William felt it, too, but said nothing; the two boys had to wait another nine days to learn that Matthew had also been accepted at Harvard.

Upon the heels of that news, another telegram arrived, this one from Charles Lester, congratulating his son and inviting the boys to tea at the Plaza Hotel in New York. Both grandmothers sent congratulations to William, but as Grandmother Kane informed Alan Lloyd, somewhat testily, "The boy has done no less than was expected of him and no more than his father did before him."

The two young men sauntered down Fifth Avenue on the appointed day with considerable pride. Girls' eyes were drawn to the handsome pair, who affected not to notice. They removed their straw boaters as they entered the front door of the Plaza at three fifty-nine and strolled nonchalantly to the Palm Court, where they observed the family group awaiting them. There, upright in the comfortable chairs, sat both grandmothers, Kane and Cabot, flanking another old lady, who, William assumed, was the Lester family's equivalent of Grandmother Kane. Mr. and Mrs. Charles Lester, their daughter Susan (whose eyes never left William) and Alan Lloyd completed the circle, leaving two vacant chairs for William and Matthew.

Grandmother Kane summoned the nearest waiter with an imperious eyebrow. "A fresh pot of tea and more cakes, please."

The waiter made haste to the kitchens. "A pot of tea and cream cakes, madam," he said on his return.

"Your father would have been proud of you today, William," the older man was saying to the taller of the two youths.

The waiter wondered what it was that the good-looking young man had achieved to elicit such a comment.

William would not have noticed the waiter at all but for the silver band around his wrist. The piece so easily might have come from Tiffany's; the incongruity of it puzzled him.

"William," said Grandmother Kane. "Two cakes are

quite sufficient; this is not your last meal before you go to Harvard."

He looked at the old lady with affection and quite forgot the silver band.

CHAPTER
THIRTEEN

That night as Abel lay awake in his small room at the Plaza Hotel, thinking about the boy, William, whose father would have been proud of him, he realized for the first time in his life exactly what he wanted to achieve. He wanted to be thought of as an equal by the Williams of this world.

Abel had had quite a struggle on his arrival in New York. He had occupied a room that contained only two beds, which he was obliged to share with George and two of his cousins. As a result, Abel slept only when one of the beds was free. George's uncle had been unable to offer Abel a job, and after a few anxious weeks during which most of his savings had to be spent on staying alive while he searched from Brooklyn to Queens, he finally found work in a butcher's shop. It paid nine dollars for a six-and-a-half-day week and allowed him to sleep above the premises. The shop was in the heart of an almost self-sufficient little Polish community on the Lower East Side, and Abel rapidly became impatient with the insularity of his fellow countrymen, many of whom made no effort even to learn to speak English.

Abel still saw George and his constant succession of girl-friends regularly on weekends, but he spent most of his free evenings during the week at night school improving his ability to read and write English. He was not ashamed of his slow progress, for he had had little opportunity to write English at all since the age of eight, but within two years he had made himself fluent in his new tongue, showing only the slightest trace of an accent. He now felt ready to move out of the butcher's shop—but to what, and how? Then while dressing a leg of lamb one morning he overheard one of the shop's biggest customers, the catering manager of the Plaza Hotel, grumbling to the butcher that he had had to fire a junior waiter for petty theft. "How can I find a replacement at such short notice," the manager complained. The butcher had no solution to offer. Abel did. He put on his only suit, walked forty-seven blocks uptown and five across and got the job.

Once he had settled in at the Plaza, he enrolled in a night course in advanced English at Columbia University. He worked steadily every night, dictionary open in one hand, pen scratching away in the other. During the mornings, between serving breakfast and setting up for lunch, he would copy out the editorials from *The New York Times*, looking up in his secondhand *Webster's* any word he was uncertain of.

For the next three years, Abel worked his way through the ranks of the Plaza until he was promoted and became a waiter in the Oak Room, making about twenty-five dollars a week with tips. In his own world, he lacked for nothing.

Abel's instructor was so impressed by his diligent progress that he advised Abel to enroll in a further night course, which was to be his first step toward a Bachelor of Arts degree. He switched his spare-time reading from linguistics to economics and started copying out the editorials in *The Wall Street Journal* instead of those in *The Times*. His new world totally absorbed him and, with the exception of George, he lost touch with his Polish friends of the early days.

When Abel served at table in the Plaza he would always study the famous among the guests carefully—the Bakers, Loebs, Whitneys, Morgans and Phelps—and try to work out why the rich were different. He read H. L. Mencken, *The American Mercury*, Scott Fitzgerald, Sinclair Lewis and Theodore Dreiser in an endless quest for knowledge. He studied *The New York Times* while the other waiters flipped through the *Mirror*, and he read *The Wall Street Journal* in his hour's break while they dozed. He was not sure where his newly acquired knowledge would lead him, but he never doubted the Baron's maxim that there was no true substitute for a good education.

One Thursday in August 1926—he remembered the occasion well because it was the day that Rudolph Valentino died and many of the ladies shopping on Fifth Avenue wore black—Abel was serving as usual at one of the corner tables. The corner tables were always reserved for top businessmen who wished to lunch in privacy without worrying about prying ears. He enjoyed serving at this particular table, for this was the era of expanding business and he often picked up some inside information from the tidbits of conversation. After the meal was over, if the host had been from a bank or large holding company, Abel would check the stock prices of the companies of the luncheon guests, and if the tone of the conversation had been optimistic and a small and a large company had been involved, he would invest one hundred dollars in the small company, in the hope that it would be a line for a takeover or expansion with the help of the larger company. If the host had ordered cigars at the end of the meal, Abel would increase his investment to two hundred dollars. Seven times out of ten, the value of the stock he had selected in this way doubled within six months, the period Abel would allow himself to hold onto the stock. Using this system, he lost money only three times during the four years he worked at the Plaza.

What made waiting on the corner table unusual on this particular day was that the guests had ordered cigars even before the meal had started. Later they were joined by more guests, who ordered more cigars. Abel looked up the name of the host in the maître d's reservation book. Woolworth. Abel had seen the name in the financial columns quite recently, but he could not immediately place it. The other guest was Charles Lester, a regular patron of the Plaza, one Abel knew to be a distinguished New York banker. He listened to as much of the conversation as he could while serving the meal. The guests showed absolutely no interest in the attentive waiter. Abel could not discover any specific details of importance, but he gathered that some sort of deal had been closed that morning and would be announced to an unsuspecting public later in the day. Then he remembered. He had seen the name in *The Wall Street Journal*. Woolworth was the man whose father had started the first five-and-ten-cents store; now the son was trying to raise money to expand. While the guests were enjoying their dessert course—most of them had chosen the strawberry cheese cake (Abel's recommendation)—he took the opportunity to leave the dining room for a few moments to call his broker on Wall Street.

"What is Woolworth trading at?" he asked.

There was a pause from the other end of the line. "Two and one-eighth. Quite a lot of movement lately; don't know why, though" came the reply.

"Buy up to the limit of my account until you hear an announcement from the company later today."

"What will the announcement say?" asked the puzzled broker.

"I am not at liberty to reveal that," replied Abel.

The broker was suitably impressed: Abel's record in the past had led him not to inquire too closely into the source of his client's information. Abel hurried back to the Oak Room in time to serve the guests' coffee. They lingered over it for some time and Abel returned to the table only as they were preparing to leave. The man who picked up the check thanked Abel for his attentive service and, turning so that his friends could hear him, said, "Do you want a tip, young man?"

"Thank you, sir," said Abel.

"Buy Woolworth stock."

The guests all laughed. Abel laughed as well, took the $5 the man held out and thanked him. He took a further $2,412 profit on Woolworth stock during the next six weeks.

. . .

When Abel was granted full citizenship in the United States, a few days after his twenty-first birthday, he decided the occasion ought to be celebrated. He invited George and Monika, George's latest love, and a girl called Clara, an ex-love of George's, to the movies to see John Barrymore in *Don Juan* and then on to Bigo's for dinner. George was still an apprentice in his uncle's bakery at eight dollars a week, and although Abel still looked upon him as his closest friend, he was aware of the growing difference between the penniless George and himself, who now had over eight thousand dollars in the bank and was now in his last year at Columbia University studying for his B.A. in economics. Abel knew exactly where he was going, whereas George had stopped telling everyone he would be the mayor of New York.

The four of them had a memorable evening, mainly because Abel knew exactly what to expect from a good restaurant. His three guests all had a great deal too much to eat, and when the check was presented, George was aghast to see that it came to more than he earned in a month. Abel paid the bill without a second glance. If you have to pay a check, make it look as if the amount is of no consequence. If it is, don't go to the restaurant again, but whatever you do, don't comment or look surprised—something else the rich had taught him.

When the party broke up at about two in the morning, George and Monika returned to the Lower East Side, while Abel felt he had earned Clara. He smuggled her through the service entrance of the Plaza to a laundry elevator and then up to his room. She did not require much enticement into bed and Abel set about her with haste, mindful that he had some serious sleeping to do before reporting for breakfast duty. To his satisfaction, he had completed his task by two-thirty and he sank into an uninterrupted sleep until his alarm rang at 6 A.M. This left him just time enough to have Clara once again before he had to get dressed.

Clara sat up in his bed and regarded Abel sullenly as he tied his white bow tie, then kissed her a perfunctory good-bye.

"Be sure you leave the way you came or you'll get me into a load of trouble," said Abel. "When will I see you again?"

"You won't," said Clara stonily.

"Why not?" asked Abel, surprised. "Something I did?"

"No, something you didn't do." She jumped out of bed and started to dress hastily.

"What didn't I do?" asked Abel, aggrieved. "You wanted to go to bed with me, didn't you?"

She turned around and faced him. "I thought I did until I realized you have only one thing in common with Valentino—you're both dead. You may be the greatest thing the Plaza has seen in a bad year, but in bed, I can tell you, you are nothing." Fully dressed now, she paused with her hand on the doorknob, composing her parting thrust. "Tell me, have you ever persuaded any girl to go to bed with you more than once?"

Stunned, Abel stared at the slammed door and spent the rest of the day worrying about Clara's accusation. He could think of no one with whom he could discuss the problem. George would only have laughed at him, and the staff at the Plaza all thought he knew everything. He decided that this problem, like all the others he had encountered in his life, must be one he could surmount with knowledge or experience.

After lunch, on his half-day, he went to Scribner's bookshop on Fifth Avenue. The store had in the past solved all his economics and linguistic problems, but he couldn't find anything there that looked as if it might even begin to help his sexual ones. Their special book on etiquette was useless and *The Moral Dilemma* turned out to be utterly inappropriate.

Abel left the book shop without making a purchase and spent the rest of the afternoon in a dingy Broadway movie theater, not watching the movie but thinking only about what Clara had said. The film, a love story with Greta Garbo

that did not reach the kissing stage until the last reel, provided no more assistance than Scribner's had.

When Abel left the movie house the sky was already dark
and there was a cool breeze blowing down Broadway. It still
surprised Abel that any city could be almost as noisy and
light by night as it was by day. He started walking uptown
toward Fifty-ninth Street, hoping the fresh air would clear
his mind. He stopped on the corner of Fifty-second Street to
buy an evening paper.

"Looking for a girl?" said a voice from the corner by the
newsstand.

Abel stared at the voice. She was about thirty-five and
heavily made up, wearing the new, fashionable shade of lipstick. Her white silk blouse had a button undone and she
wore a long black skirt with black stockings and black
shoes.

"Only five dollars, worth every penny," she said, pushing
her hip out at an angle, allowing the slit in her skirt to part
and reveal the top of her stockings.

"Where?" said Abel.

"I have a little place of my own in the next block."

She turned her head, indicating to Abel which direction
she meant, and he could, for the first time, see her face
clearly under the streetlight. She was not unattractive. Abel
nodded his agreement and she took his arm and they started
walking.

"If the police stop us," she said, "you're an old friend and
my name's Joyce."

They walked to the next block and into a squalid little
apartment building. Abel was horrified by the dingy room
she lived in, with its single bare lightbulb, one chair, a wash
basin and a crumpled double bed, which had obviously already been used several times that day.

"You live here?" he said incredulously.

"Good God, no. I only use this place for my work."

"Why do you do this?" asked Abel, wondering if he now
wanted to go through with his plan.

"I have two children to bring up and no husband. Can you think of a better reason? Now, do you want me or not?"

"Yes, but not the way you think," said Abel.

She eyed him warily. "Not another of those wacky ones, a follower of the Marquis de Sade, are you?"

"Certainly not," said Abel.

"You're not gonna burn me with cigarettes?"

"No, nothing like that," said Abel, startled. "I want to be taught properly. I want lessons."

"Lessons? Are you joking? What do you think this is, darling, a fucking night school?"

"Something like that," said Abel, and he sat down on the corner of the bed and explained to her how Clara had reacted the night before. "Do you think you can help?"

The lady of the night studied Abel carefully, wondering if it were April the First.

"Sure," she said finally, "but it's going to cost you five dollars a time for a thirty-minute session."

"More expensive than a B.A. from Columbia," said Abel. "How many lessons will I need?"

"Depends how quick a learner you are, doesn't it?" she said.

"Well, let's start right now," said Abel, taking five dollars out of his inside pocket. He handed the money over to her. She put the bill in the top of her stocking, a sure sign she never took them off.

"Clothes off, darling," she said. "You won't learn much fully dressed."

When he was stripped, she looked at him critically. "You're not exactly Douglas Fairbanks, are you? Don't worry about it—it doesn't matter what you look like once the lights are out; it only matters what you can do."

Abel sat on the edge of the bed while she started telling him about how to treat a lady. She was surprised that Abel really did not want her and was even more surprised when he continued to turn up every day for the next two weeks.

"When will I know I've made it?" Abel inquired.

"You'll know, baby," replied Joyce. "If you can make me come, you can make an Egyptian mummy come."

She taught him first what the sensitive parts of a woman's body were and then to be patient in his lovemaking—and the signs by which he might know that what he was doing was pleasing. How to use his tongue and lips on every place other than a woman's mouth.

Abel listened carefully to all she said and followed her instructions scrupulously and, to begin with, a little bit too mechanically. Despite her assurance that he was improving out of all recognition, he had no real idea if she was telling him the truth, until about three weeks and $110 later, when to his surprise and delight, Joyce suddenly came alive in his arms for the first time. She held his head close to her as he gently licked her nipples. As he stroked her gently between the legs, he found she was wet—for the first time—and after he had entered her she moaned, a sound Abel had never heard before and found intensely pleasing. She clawed at his back, commanding him not to stop. The moaning continued, sometimes loud, sometimes soft. Finally she cried out sharply and the hands that had clutched him to her so fiercely relaxed.

When she had caught her breath, she said, "Baby, you just graduated top of the class."

Abel hadn't even come.

Abel celebrated the awarding of both his degrees by paying scalper's prices for ringside seats and taking George, Monika and a reluctant Clara to watch Gene Tunney fight Jack Dempsey for the heavyweight championship of the world. That night after the fight, Clara felt it was nothing less than her duty to go to bed with Abel—he had spent so much money on her. By the morning she was begging him not to leave her.

Abel never asked her out again.

After he had graduated from Columbia, Abel became dissatisfied with his life at the Plaza Hotel but could not figure out how to advance himself further. Although he served some of the wealthiest and most successful men in America, he was unable to approach any of them directly, knowing that to do so might well cost him his job. And in any case, the customers would not take seriously the aspirations of a waiter. Abel decided that he wanted to be a headwaiter.

One day Mr. and Mrs. Ellsworth Statler came to lunch at the Plaza's Edwardian Room, where Abel had been on relief duty for a week. He thought his chance had come. He did everything he could think of to impress the famous hotelier, and the meal went splendidly. As he left, Statler thanked Abel warmly and gave him ten dollars, but that was the end of their association. Abel watched him disappear through the revolving doors of the Plaza, wondering if he was ever going to get a break.

Sammy, the headwaiter, tapped him on the shoulder. "What did you get from Mr. Statler?"

"Nothing," said Abel.

"He didn't tip you?" queried Sammy in a disbelieving tone.

"Oh, yes, sure," said Abel. "Ten dollars." He handed the money over to Sammy.

"That's more like it," said Sammy. "I was beginning to think you was double-dealing me, Abel. Ten dollars, that's good even for Mr. Statler. You must have impressed him."

"No, I didn't."

"What do you mean?" asked Sammy.

"It doesn't matter," said Abel as he started walking away.

"Wait a moment, Abel, I have a note here for you. The gentleman at table seventeen, a Mr. Leroy, wants to speak to you personally."

"What's it about, Sammy?"

"How should I know? Probably likes your blue eyes."

Abel glanced over to number 17, strictly for the meek and the unknown, because the table was so badly placed near a swinging door into the kitchen. Abel usually tried to avoid serving any of the tables at that end of the room.

"Who is he?" asked Abel. "What does he want?"

"I don't know," said Sammy, not bothering to look up.
"I'm not in touch with the life history of the customers the
way you are. Give them a good meal, make sure you get
yourself a big tip and hope they come again. You may feel
it's a simple philosophy, but it's sure good enough for me.
Maybe they forgot to teach you the basics at Columbia. Now
get your butt over there, Abel, and if it's a tip be certain you
bring the money straight back to me."

Abel smiled at Sammy's bald head and went over to 17.
There were two people seated at the table—a man in a colorful checked jacket, of which Abel did not approve, and an
attractive young woman with a mop of blond, curly hair,
which momentarily distracted Abel, who uncharitably assumed she was the checked jacket's New York girlfriend.
Abel put on his "sorry smile," betting himself a silver dollar
that the man was going to make a big fuss about the swinging doors and try to get his table changed to impress the stunning blonde. No one liked being near the smell of the kitchen
and the continual banging of waiters through the doors. But
it was impossible to avoid using the table when the hotel was
packed with residents and many New Yorkers who used the
restaurant as their regular eating place and looked upon visitors as nothing more than intruders. Why did Sammy always leave the tricky customers for him to deal with? Abel
approached the checked jacket cautiously.

"You asked to speak to me, sir?"

"Sure did," said a southern accent. "My name is Davis
Leroy and this is my daughter, Melanie."

Abel's eyes left Mr. Leroy momentarily and encountered
a pair of eyes as green as any he had ever seen.

"I have been watching you, Abel, for the last five days,"
Mr. Leroy was saying in his southern drawl.

If pressed, Abel would have had to admit that he had not
taken a great deal of notice of Mr. Leroy until the last five
minutes.

"I have been very impressed by what I have seen, Abel,
because you got class, real class, and I am always on the

looking-out for that. Ellsworth Statler was a fool not to pick you up."

Abel began to take a closer look at Mr. Leroy. His purple cheeks and double chin left Abel in no doubt that he had not been told of Prohibition, and the empty plates in front of him accounted for his basketball belly, but neither the name nor the face meant anything to him. At a normal lunchtime, Abel was familiar with the background of anyone sitting at 37 of the 39 tables in the Edwardian Room. That day Mr. Leroy's table was one of the unknown two.

The southerner was still talking. "Now, I'm not one of those multimillionaires who have to sit at your corner tables when they stay at the Plaza."

Abel was impressed. The average customer wasn't supposed to appreciate the relative merits of the various tables.

"But I'm not doing so badly for myself. In fact, my best hotel may well grow to be as impressive as this one some-day, Abel."

"I am sure it will be, sir," said Abel, playing for time.

Leroy, Leroy, Leroy. The name didn't mean a thing.

"Lemme git to the point, son. The number one hotel in my group needs a new assistant manager in charge of the restaurants. If you're interested, join me in my room when you get off duty."

He handed Abel a large embossed card.

"Thank you, sir," said Abel, looking at it: "Davis Leroy. The Richmond Group of Hotels, Dallas." Underneath was inscribed the motto: "One day a hotel in every state." The name still meant nothing to Abel.

"I look forward to seeing you," said the friendly check-coated Texan.

"Thank you, sir," said Abel. He smiled at Melanie, whose eyes were as coolly green as before, and returned to Sammy, still head down, counting his takings.

"Ever heard of the Richmond Group of Hotels, Sammy?"

"Yes, sure, my brother was a junior waiter in one once. Must be about eight or nine of them, all over the South, run by a mad Texan, but I can't remember the guy's name. Why you asking?" said Sammy, looking up suspiciously.

"No particular reason," said Abel.

"There's always a reason with you. What did table seventeen want?" said Sammy.

"Grumbling about the noise from the kitchen. Can't say I blame him."

"What does he expect me to do, put him out on the veranda? Who does the guy think he is, John D. Rockefeller?"

Abel left Sammy to his counting and grumbling and cleared his own tables as quickly as possible. Then he went to his room and started to check out the Richmond Group. A few calls and he'd learned enough to satisfy his curiosity. The group turned out to be a private company, with eleven hotels in all, the most impressive one a 342-room deluxe establishment, in Chicago, the Richmond Continental. Abel decided he had nothing to lose by paying a call on Mr. Leroy and Melanie. He checked Mr. Leroy's room number—85—one of the better smaller rooms. He arrived a little before four o'clock and was disappointed to discover that Melanie was not there.

"Glad you could drop by, Abel. Take a seat."

It was the first time Abel had sat down as a guest in the more than four years he had worked at the Plaza.

"What are you paid?" said Mr. Leroy.

The suddenness of the question took Abel by surprise.

"I take in around twenty-five dollars a week with tips."

"I'll start you at thirty-five a week."

"Which hotel are you referring to?" asked Abel.

"If I'm a judge of character, Abel, you got off table duty about three-thirty and took the next thirty minutes finding out which hotel, am I right?"

Abel was beginning to like the man. "The Richmond Continental in Chicago?" he ventured.

Davis Leroy laughed. "I was right—and right about you."

Abel's mind was working fast. "How many people are over the assistant manager?"

"Only the manager and me. The manager is slow, gentle, and near retirement and as I have ten other hotels to worry about, I don't think you'll have too much trouble. Although I must confess Chicago is my favorite, my first hotel in the North, and with Melanie at school there, I find I spend more time in the Windy City than I ought to. Don't ever make the mistake New Yorkers do of underestimating Chicago. They think Chicago is only a postage stamp on a very large envelope, and they are the envelope."

Abel smiled.

"The hotel is a little run-down at the moment," Mr. Leroy continued, "as the last assistant manager walked out on me suddenly, so I need a good man to take his place and realize its full potential. Now listen, Abel, I've watched you carefully for the last five days and I know you're that man. Do you think you would be interested in coming to Chicago?"

"Forty dollars and ten percent of any increased profits and I'll take the job."

"What?" said Davis Leroy, flabbergasted. "None of my managers are paid on a profit basis. The others would raise hell if they ever found out."

"I'm not going to tell them if you don't," said Abel.

"Now I know I chose the right man, even if he bargains a damn sight better than a Yankee with six daughters." He slapped the side of his chair. "I agree to your terms, Abel."

"Will you be requiring references, Mr. Leroy?"

"References? I know your background and history since you left Europe right through to getting a degree in economics at Columbia. What do you think I've been doing the last few days? I wouldn't put someone who needed references in as number two in my best hotel. When can you start?"

"A month from today."

"Good. I look forward to seeing you then, Abel."

Abel rose from the hotel chair; he felt even happier standing. He shook hands with Mr. Davis Leroy, the man from table 17—the one that was strictly for unknowns.

Leaving New York City and the Plaza Hotel, his first real home since the castle near Slonim, turned out to be more of a wrench than Abel had anticipated. Good-byes to George, Monika and his few Columbia friends were unexpectedly hard. Sammy and the other waiters threw a farewell party for him.

"We haven't heard the last of you, Abel Rosnovski," Sammy said, and they all agreed.

The Richmond Continental in Chicago was well placed on Michigan Avenue, in the heart of one of the fastest-growing cities in America. This pleased Abel, who was familiar with Ellsworth Statler's maxim that just three things about a hotel really mattered: position, position and position. Abel soon discovered that position was about the only good thing the Richmond had. Davis Leroy had understated the case when he said that the hotel was a little run-down. Desmond Pacey, the manager, wasn't slow and quiet as Davis Leroy had suggested; he was plain lazy and didn't endear himself to Abel when he put his new assistant in a tiny room in the staff annex across the street and not in the main hotel. A quick check on the Richmond's books revealed that the daily occupancy rate was running at less than 40 percent and that the restaurant was never more than half full, not least of all because the food was appalling. The staff spoke three or four languages among them, none of which seemed to be English, and they were certainly not showing any signs of welcome to the stupid Polack from New York. It was not hard to see why the last assistant manager had left in such a hurry. If the Richmond was Davis Leroy's favorite hotel, Abel feared for the other ten in the group even though his new employer seemed to have a bottomless pot of gold at the end of his Texas rainbow.

The best news that Abel learned during his first days in Chicago was that Melanie Leroy was an only child.

CHAPTER
FOURTEEN

William and Matthew started their freshman year at Harvard in the fall of 1924. Despite his grandmothers' disapproval, William accepted the Hamilton Memorial Mathematics Scholarship and at a cost of $290, treated himself to "Daisy," the latest Model T Ford and the first real love of William's life. He painted Daisy bright yellow, which halved her value and doubled the number of his girlfriends. Calvin Coolidge won a landslide election to return to the White House and the volume on the New York Stock Exchange reached a five-year record of 2,336,160 shares.

Both young men ("We can no longer refer to them as children," pronounced Grandmother Cabot) had been looking forward to college. After an energetic summer of tennis and golf, they were ready to get down to more serious pursuits. William started work on the day he arrived in their new room on the "Gold Coast," a considerable improvement on their small room at St. Paul's, while Matthew went in search of the university rowing club. Matthew was elected to captain the freshmen crew, and William left his books every Sunday afternoon to watch his friend from the banks of the Charles River. He covertly enjoyed Matthew's success but was outwardly scathing.

"Life is not about eight big men pulling unwieldy pieces of misshapen wood through choppy water while one smaller man shouts at them," declared William haughtily.

"Tell Yale that," said Matthew.

William, meanwhile, quickly demonstrated to his mathematics professors that he was what Matthew was—a mile ahead of the field. William also became chairman of the freshman Debating Society and talked his great-uncle, President Lowell, into the first university insurance plan, whereby students graduating from Harvard would take out a life policy for $1,000 each, naming the university as the beneficiary. William estimated that the cost to each participant would be less than a dollar per week and that if 40 percent of the alumni joined the scheme, Harvard would have a guaranteed income of about $3 million a year from 1950 onward. The President was impressed and gave the scheme his full support and a year later he invited William to join the board of the University Fund Raising Committee. William accepted with pride, not realizing that the appointment was for life. President Lowell informed Grandmother Kane that he had captured one of the best financial brains of his generation free of charge. Grandmother Kane testily told her cousin that "everything had its purpose and that would teach William to read the fine print."

Almost as soon as the sophomore year began, it became time to choose (or to be chosen for) one of the Finals Clubs that dominated the social landscape of the well-to-do at Harvard. William was "punched" for the Porcellian, the oldest, richest, most exclusive and least ostentatious of such clubs. In the clubhouse on Massachusetts Avenue, which was incongruously situated over a cheap Hayes-Bickford cafeteria, he would sit in a comfortable armchair, considering the four-color-map problem, discussing the repercussions of the Loeb-Leopold trial and idly watching the street below through the conveniently angled mirror while listening to the large, newfangled radio.

When the Christmas vacation came, William was persuaded to ski with Matthew in Vermont and spent a week panting uphill in the footsteps of his fitter friend.

"Tell me, Matthew, what is the point of spending one hour climbing up a hill only to come back down the same hill in a few seconds at considerable risk to life and limb?"

Matthew grunted. "Sure gives me a bigger kick than graph theory, William. Why don't you admit you're not very good either at the going up or the coming down?"

They both did enough work in their sophomore year to get by, although their interpretations of "getting by" were wildly different. For the first two months of the summer vacation, they worked as junior management assistants in Charles Lester's bank in New York, Matthew's father having long since given up the battle of trying to keep William away. When the dog days of August arrived, they spent most of their time dashing about the New England countryside in "Daisy," sailing on the Charles River with as many different girls as possible and attending any house party to which they could get themselves invited. In no time they were among the accredited personalities of the university, known to the *cognoscenti* as the Scholar and the Sweat. It was perfectly understood in Boston society that the girl who married William Kane or Matthew Lester would have no fears for her future, but as fast as hopeful mothers appeared with their fresh-faced daughters, Grandmother Kane and Grandmother Cabot unceremoniously dispatched them.

On April 18, 1927, William celebrated his twenty-first birthday by attending the final meeting of the trustees of his estate. Alan Lloyd and Tony Simmons had prepared all the documents for signature.

"Well, William dear," said Milly Preston as if a great responsibility had been lifted from her shoulders, "I'm sure you'll be able to do every bit as well as we did."

"I hope so, Mrs. Preston, but if ever I need to lose half a million overnight, I'll know just who to call."

Milly Preston went bright red but made no attempt to respond.

The trust now stood at over $32 million and William had

definite plans for nurturing that money, but he had also set himself the task of making a million dollars in his own right before he left Harvard. It was not a large sum compared with the amount in his trust, but his inherited wealth meant far less to him than the balance in his account at Lester's.

That summer, the grandmothers, fearing a fresh outbreak of predatory girls, dispatched William and Matthew on the grand tour of Europe, which turned out to be a great success for both of them. Matthew, surmounting all language barriers, found a beautiful girl in every major European capital—love, he assured William, was an international commodity. William secured introductions to a director of most of the major European banks—money, he assured Matthew, was also an international commodity. From London to Berlin to Rome, the two young men left a trail of broken hearts and suitably impressed bankers. When they returned to Harvard in September, they were both ready to hit the books for their final year.

In the bitter winter of 1927, Grandmother Kane died, aged eighty-five, and William wept for the first time since his mother's death.

"Come on," said Matthew after bearing with William's depression for several days. "She had a good life and waited a long time to find out whether God was a Cabot or a Lowell."

William missed the shrewd words he had so little appreciated in his grandmother's lifetime and he had arranged a funeral she would have been proud to attend. Although the great lady had arrived at the cemetery in a black Packard hearse ("One of those outrageous contraptions—over my dead body," but—as it turned out—under it), her only criticism of William's orchestration of her departure would have concerned this unsound mode of transport. Her death drove William to work with even more purpose during that final year at Harvard. He dedicated himself to winning the university's top mathematics prize in her memory. Grandmother

Cabot died some six months after Grandmother Kane—probably, said William, because there was no one left for her to talk to.

In February 1928, William received a visit from the captain of the Debating Team. There was to be a full-dress debate the following month on the motion "Socialism or Capitalism for America's Future" and William was, naturally, asked to represent capitalism.

"And what if I told you I was only willing to speak on behalf of the downtrodden masses?" William inquired of the surprised captain, slightly nettled by the thought that his intellectual views were simply assumed by outsiders because he had inherited a famous name and a prosperous bank.

"Well, I must say, William, we did imagine your own preference would be for, er—"

"It is. I accept your invitation. I take it that I am at liberty to select my partner?"

"Naturally."

"Good. Then I choose Matthew Lester. May I know who our opponents will be?"

"You will not be informed until the day before, when the posters go up in the Yard."

For the next month Matthew and William turned their breakfast critiques of the newspapers of the Left and Right, and their nightly discussions about the Meaning of Life, into strategy sessions for what the campus was beginning to call "The Great Debate." William decided that Matthew should lead off.

As the fateful day approached, it became clear that most of the politically aware students, professors and even some Boston and Cambridge notables would be attending. On the morning before the two friends walked over to the Yard to discover who their opposition would be.

"Leland Crosby and Thaddeus Cohen. Either name ring a bell with you, William? Crosby must be one of the Philadelphia Crosbys, I suppose."

"Of course he is. 'The Red Maniac of Rittenhouse Square,' as his own aunt once described him. Accurately. He's the most convincing revolutionary on campus. He's loaded and he spends all his money on the popular radical causes. I can hear his opening now."

William parodied Crosby's grating tone. " 'I know at first hand the rapacity and the utter lack of social conscience of the American monied class.' If everyone in the audience hasn't already heard that fifty times, I'd say he'll make a formidable opponent."

"And Thaddeus Cohen?"

"Never heard of him."

The following evening, refusing to admit to stage fright, they made their way through the snow and cold wind, heavy overcoats flapping behind them, past the gleaming columns of the Widener Library—like William's father, the donor's son had gone down on the *Titanic*—to Boylston Hall.

"With weather like this, at least if we take a beating, there won't be many to tell the tale," said Matthew hopefully.

But as they rounded the side of the library, they could see a steady stream of stamping, huffing figures ascending the stairs and filing into the hall. Inside, they were shown to chairs on the podium. William sat still, but his eyes picked out the people he knew in the audience: President Lowell, sitting discreetly in a middle row; ancient Newbury St. John, professor of botany; a pair of Brattle Street bluestockings he recognized from Red House parties; and, to his right, a group of Bohemian-looking young men and women, some not even wearing ties, who turned and started to clap as their spokesmen—Crosby and Cohen—walked onto the stage.

Crosby was the more striking of the two, tall and thin almost to the point of caricature, dressed absentmindedly—or very carefully—in a shaggy tweed suit but with a stiffly pressed shirt, and dangling a pipe with no apparent connection to his body except at his lower lip. Thaddeus Cohen was shorter and wore rimless glasses and an almost too perfectly cut dark worsted suit.

The four speakers shook hands cautiously as the last-minute arrangements were made. The bells of Memorial Church, only a hundred feet away, sounded vague and distant as they rang out seven times.

"Mr. Leland Crosby, Junior," said the captain.

Crosby's speech gave William cause for self-congratulation. He had anticipated everything—the strident tone Crosby would take, the overstressed, nearly hysterical points he would make. He recited the incantations of American radicalism—Haymarket, Money Trust, Standard Oil, even Cross of Gold. William didn't think Crosby had made more than an exhibition of himself although he garnered the expected applause from his claque on William's right. When Crosby sat down, he had clearly won no new supporters and it looked as though he might have lost a few old ones. The comparison with William and Matthew—equally rich, equally socially distinguished but selfishly refusing martyrdom for the cause of the advancement of social justice—just might be devastating.

Matthew spoke well and to the point, soothing his listeners, the incarnation of liberal toleration. William pumped his friend's hand warmly when he returned to his chair to loud applause.

"It's all over but the shouting, I think," he whispered.

But Thaddeus Cohen surprised virtually everyone. He had a pleasant, diffident manner and a sympathetic style. His references and quotations were catholic, pointed and illuminating. Without conveying to the audience the feeling that it was being deliberately impressed, he exuded a moral earnestness that made anything less seem a failure to a rational human being. He was willing to admit the excesses of his own side and the inadequacy of its leaders, but he left the impression that, in spite of its dangers, there was no alternative to socialism if the lot of mankind was ever to be improved.

William was flustered. A surgically logical attack on the political platform of his adversaries would be useless against Cohen's gentle and persuasive presentation. Yet to outdo him as a spokesman of hope and faith in the human spirit would be impossible. William concentrated first on refuting some of Crosby's charges and then countered Cohen's arguments with a declaration of his own faith in the ability of the American system to produce the best results through competition, intellectual and economic. He felt he had played a good defensive game, but no more, and sat down supposing that he had been well beaten by Cohen.

Crosby was his opponents' rebuttal speaker. He began ferociously, sounding as if he now needed to beat Cohen as much as William and Matthew, asking the audience if they could identify an "enemy of the people" among themselves that night. He glared around the room for several long seconds as members of the audience squirmed in embarrassed silence and his dedicated supporters studied their shoes. Then he learned forward and roared:

"He stands before you. He has just spoken in your midst. His name is William Lowell Kane." Gesturing with one hand toward William—but without looking at him—he thundered: "His bank owns mines in which the workers die to give its owners an extra million a year in dividends. His bank supports the bloody, corrupt dictatorships of Latin America. Through his bank, the American Congress is bribed into crushing the small farmer. His bank . . ."

The tirade went on for several minutes. William sat in stony silence, occasionally jotting down a comment on his yellow legal pad. A few members of the audience had begun shouting "No." Crosby's supporters shouted loyally back. The officials began to look nervous.

Crosby's allotted time was about up. He raised his fist and said, "Gentlemen, I submit that not more than two hundred yards from this very room we have the answer to the plight of America. There stands the Widener Library, the greatest private library in the world. Here poor and immigrant scholars come, along with the best-educated Americans, to increase the knowledge and prosperity of the world. Why does it exist? Because one rich playboy had the misfortune to set sail sixteen years ago on a pleasure boat called the *Titanic*. I suggest, ladies and gentlemen, that not until the people of America hand each and every member of the ruling class a ticket for his own private cabin on the *Titanic* of capitalism, will the hoarded wealth of this great continent be freed and devoted to the service of liberty, equality and progress."

As Matthew listened to Crosby's speech, his sentiments changed from exultation that, by this blunder, the victory had been secured for his side, through embarrassment at the behavior of his adversary, to rage at the reference to the *Titanic*. He had no idea how William would respond to such provocation.

When some measure of silence had been restored, the captain walked to the lectern and said, "Mr. William Lowell Kane."

William strode to the platform and looked out over the audience. An expectant hush filled the room.

"It is my opinion that the views expressed by Mr. Crosby do not merit a response."

He sat down. There was a moment of surprised silence— and then loud applause.

The captain returned to the platform but appeared uncertain what to do. A voice from behind him broke the tension.

"If I may, Mr. Chairman, I would like to ask Mr. Kane if I might use his rebuttal time." It was Thaddeus Cohen.

William nodded his agreement to the captain.

Cohen walked to the lectern and blinked at the audience disarmingly. "It has long been true," he began, "that the greatest obstacle to the success of democratic socialism in the United States has been the extremism of some of its allies. Nothing could have exemplified this unfortunate fact more clearly than my colleague's speech tonight. The propensity to damage the progressive cause by calling for the physical extermination of those who oppose it might be understandable in a battle-hardened immigrant, a veteran of foreign struggles fiercer than our own. In America it is pathetic and inexcusable. Speaking for myself, I extend my sincere apologies to Mr. Kane."

This time the applause was instantaneous. Virtually the entire audience rose to its feet clapping continuously.

William walked over to shake hands with Thaddeus Cohen. It was no surprise to either of them that William and Matthew won the vote by a margin of more than 150 votes. The evening was over and the audience filed out into the silent, snow-covered paths, walking in the middle of the street, talking animatedly at the tops of their voices.

William insisted that Thaddeus Cohen join him and Matthew for a drink. They set off together across Massachusetts Avenue, barely able to see where they were going in the drifting snow, and came to a halt outside a big black door almost directly opposite Boylston Hall. William opened it with his key and the three entered the vestibule.

Before the door shut behind him, Thaddeus Cohen spoke. "I'm afraid I won't be welcome here."

William looked startled for a second. "Nonsense. You're with me."

Matthew gave his friend a cautionary glance but saw that William was determined.

They went up the stairs and into a large room, comfortably but not luxuriously furnished, in which there were about a dozen young men sitting in armchairs or standing in knots of two or three. As soon as William appeared in the doorway, the congratulations started.

"You were marvelous, William. That's exactly the way to treat those sort of people."

"Enter in triumph, Bolski slayer."

Thaddeus Cohen hung back, still half-shadowed by the doorway, but William had not forgotten him.

"And gentlemen, may I present my worthy adversary, Mr. Thaddeus Cohen."

Cohen stepped forward hesitantly.

All noise ceased. A number of heads were averted, as if they were looking at the elm trees in the Yard, their branches weighed down with new snow.

Finally there was the crack of a floorboard as one young

man left the room by another door. Then there was another departure. Without haste, without apparent agreement, the entire group filed out. The last to leave gave William a long look, then turned on his heel and disappeared.

Matthew gazed at his companions in dismay. Thaddeus Cohen had turned a dull red and stood with his head bowed. William's lips were drawn together in the same tight, cold fury that had been apparent when Crosby had made his reference to the *Titanic*.

Matthew touched his friend's arm. "We'd better go."

The three trudged off to William's rooms and silently drank some indifferent brandy.

When William woke in the morning, there was an envelope under his door. Inside, there was a short note, from the chairman of the Porcellian Club, informing him that he hoped "there would never be a recurrence of last night's best-forgotten incident."

By lunchtime the chairman had received two letters of resignation.

After months of long, studious days, William and Matthew were almost ready—no one ever thinks he is quite ready— for their final examinations. For six days they answered questions and filled up sheets and sheets of the little blue books and then they waited, not in vain, for they both graduated as expected from Harvard in June of 1928.

A week after the exams it was announced that William had won the President's Mathematics Prize. He wished his father had been alive to witness the presentation ceremony on graduation day. Matthew had managed a "gentleman's C," which came as a relief to him and no great surprise to anyone else. Neither had any interest in further education, both having elected to join the "real" world as quickly as possible.

William's bank account in New York edged over the million-dollar mark eight days before he left Harvard. It was then that he discussed in greater detail with Matthew his long-term plan to gain control of Lester's Bank by merging it with Kane and Cabot.

Matthew was enthusiastic about the idea and confessed, "That's about the only way I'll ever improve on what my old man will undoubtedly leave me when he dies."

On graduation day, Alan Lloyd, now in his sixtieth year, came to Harvard. After the graduation ceremony William took his guest for tea on the square. Alan eyed the tall young man affectionately.

"And what do you intend to do now that you have put Harvard behind you?"

"I'm going to join Charles Lester's bank in New York. I want some experience before I come to Kane and Cabot a few years from now."

"But you've been living in Lester's bank since you were twelve years old, William. Why don't you come straight to us now? We would appoint you a director immediately."

Alan Lloyd waited for his reply. It was not forthcoming.

"Well, I must say, William, it's most unlike you to be rendered speechless by anything."

"But I never imagined you would invite me to join the board before my twenty-fifth birthday, when my father . . ."

"It's true your father was elected when he was twenty-five. However, that's no reason to prevent you from joining the board before then if the other directors support the idea, and I know that they do. In any case, there are personal reasons why I'd like to see you a director as soon as possible. When I retire from the bank in five years, we must be sure of electing the right chairman. You will be in a stronger position to influence that decision if you have been working for Kane and Cabot during those five years rather than as a grand functionary at Lester's. Well, my boy, will you join the board?"

It was the second time that day that William wished his father were still alive.

"I should be delighted to accept, sir," he said.

Alan looked up at William. "That's the first time you've called me 'sir' since we played golf together. I shall have to watch you very carefully."

William smiled.

"Good," said Alan Lloyd, "that's settled, then. You'll be a junior director in charge of investments, working directly under Tony Simmons."

"Can I appoint my own assistant?" asked William.

Alan Lloyd looked at him quizzically. "Matthew Lester, no doubt?"

"Yes."

"No. I don't want him doing in our bank what you intended to do in theirs. Thomas Cohen should have taught you that." William said nothing but never underestimated Alan again.

Charles Lester laughed when William repeated the conversation word for word to him.

"I'm sorry to hear you won't be coming to us, even as a spy," he said genially, "but I have no doubt you'll end up here someday—in one capacity or another."

PART THREE
1928–1932

CHAPTER
FIFTEEN

When William started work as a junior director of Kane and Cabot in September 1928, he felt for the first time in his life that he was doing something really worthwhile. He began his career in a small office next to Tony Simmons, the bank's Investment Director. From the week that William arrived, he knew, even though nothing had been said, that Tony Simmons was hoping to succeed Alan Lloyd as chairman of the bank.

The bank's entire investment program was Simmons's responsibility. He quickly delegated to William some aspects of his work, in particular, private investment in small businesses, land and any other outside entrepreneurial activities in which the bank was involved. Among William's official duties was a monthly report on the investments he wished to recommend, at a full meeting of the board. The 17 board members met once a month in a larger oak-paneled room, dominated at both ends by portraits, one of William's father, the other of his grandfather. William had never known his grandfather but had always thought he must have been a "hell of a man" to have married Grandmother Kane. There was ample room left on the walls for his own portrait.

William conducted himself during those early days at the bank with caution and his fellow board members soon came to respect his judgment and follow his recommendations with rare exceptions. As it turned out, the advice they re-

jected was among the best that William ever gave. On the
first occasion, a Mr. Mayer sought a loan from the bank to
invest in "talking pictures," but the board refused to see that
the notion had any merit or future. Another time, a Mr. Paley
came to William with an ambitious plan for United, the radio network. Alan Lloyd, who had about as much respect for
telegraphy as for telepathy, would have nothing to do with
the scheme. The board supported Alan's view, and Louis B.
Mayer later headed MGM; and William Paley, the company
that became CBS. William believed in his own judgment
and had backed both men with money from his trust and,
like his father, never informed the recipients of his support.

One of the more unpleasant aspects of William's day-to-
day work was the handling of the liquidations and bankruptcies of clients who had borrowed large sums from the bank
and had subsequently found themselves unable to repay
their loans. William was not by nature a soft person, as
Henry Osborne had learned to his cost, but insisting that old
and respected clients liquidate their stocks and even sell
their homes did not make for easy sleeping at nights.
William soon learned that these clients fell into two distinct
categories—those who looked upon bankruptcy as a part of
everyday business and those who were appalled by the very
word and who would spend the rest of their lives trying to
repay every penny they had borrowed. William found it natural to be tough with the first category but was almost always far more lenient with the second, with the grudging
approval of Tony Simmons.

It was during such a case that William broke one of the
bank's golden rules and became personally involved with a
client. Her name was Katherine Brookes, and her husband,
Max Brookes, had borrowed more than a million dollars
from Kane and Cabot to invest in the Florida land boom of
1925, an investment William would never have backed had
he then been working at the bank. Max Brookes had, however, been something of a hero in Massachusetts as one of
the new intrepid breed of balloonists and flyers and a close

friend of Charles Lindbergh in the bargain. Brookes's tragic
death when the small plane he was piloting, at a height of all
of ten feet above the ground, hit a tree only a hundred yards
after takeoff was reported in the press across the length and
breadth of America as a national loss.

William, acting for the bank, immediately took over the
Brookes estate, which was already insolvent, dissolved it
and tried to cut the bank's losses by selling all the land held
in Florida except for two acres on which the family home
stood. The bank's loss still turned out to be over $300,000.
Some directors were slightly critical of William's snap decision to sell off the land, a decision with which Tony Simmons had not agreed. William had Simmons's disapproval
of his actions entered on the minutes and was in a position to
point out some months later that if they had held onto the
land, the bank would have lost most of its original investment of more than $1 million. This demonstration of fore-
sight did not endear him to Tony Simmons although it made
the rest of the board conscious of William's uncommon perspicacity.

When William had liquidated everything the bank held in
Max Brookes's name, he turned his attention to Mrs.
Brookes, who was still under a personal guarantee for her
late husband's debts. Although William always tried to secure such a guarantee on any loans granted by the bank, the
undertaking of such an obligation was not a course that he
ever recommended to friends, however confident they might
feel about the venture, as failure almost invariably caused
great distress to the guarantor.

William wrote a formal letter to Mrs. Brookes, suggesting that she make an appointment to discuss the position. He
had read the Brookes file conscientiously and knew that she
was only twenty-two years old, a daughter of Andrew Higginson, a member of an old and distinguished Boston family
and great-niece of Henry Lee Higginson, founder of the
Boston Symphony. He also noted that she had substantial assets of her own. He did not relish the thought of requiring

her to make them over to the bank, but he and Tony Simmons were, for once, in agreement on the line to be taken, so he steeled himself for an unpleasant encounter.

What William had not bargained for was Katherine Brookes herself. In later life he could always recall in great detail the events of that morning. He had had some harsh words with Tony Simmons about a substantial investment in copper and tin that he wished to recommend to the board. Industrial demand for the two metals was rising steadily and William was confident that a world shortage was certain to follow. Tony Simmons could not agree with him, feeling they should invest more cash in the stock market, and the matter was still uppermost in William's mind when his secretary ushered Mrs. Brookes into his office. With one tentative smile, she removed copper, tin and all other world shortages from his mind. Before she could sit down, he was around on the other side of his desk, settling her into a chair, simply to assure himself that she would not vanish like a mirage on closer inspection. Never had William encountered a woman he considered half as lovely as Katherine Brookes. Her long fair hair fell in loose and wayward curls to her shoulders, and little wisps escaped enchantingly from her hat and clung around her temples. The fact that she was in mourning in no way detracted from the beauty of her slim figure, and the fine bone structure ensured that she was a woman who was going to look lovely at any age. Her brown eyes were enormous. They were also, unmistakably, apprehensive of him and what he was about to say.

William strove for his business tone of voice. "Mrs. Brookes, may I say how sorry I was to learn of your husband's death and how much I regret the necessity of asking you to come here today."

Two lies in a single sentence which would have been true five minutes before. He waited to hear her speak.

"Thank you, Mr. Kane." Her voice was soft and had a gentle, low pitch. "I am aware of my obligations to your bank and I assure you I will do everything in my power to meet them."

William said nothing, hoping she would go on speaking. She did not, so he outlined the disposition of Max Brookes's estate. She listened with downcast eyes.

"Now, Mrs. Brookes, you acted as guarantor for your husband's loan and that brings us to the question of your personal assets." He consulted his file. "You have some eighty thousand dollars in investments—your own family money, I believe—and seventeen thousand four hundred and fifty-six dollars in your personal account."

She looked up. "Your knowledge of my financial position is commendable, Mr. Kane. You should add, however, Buckhurst Park, our house in Florida, which was in Max's name, and some quite valuable jewelry of my own. I estimate that altogether I'm worth the three hundred thousand dollars you still require, and I've made arrangements to realize the full amount for you as soon as possible."

There was only the slightest tremor in her voice. William gazed at her in admiration.

"Mrs. Brookes, the bank has no intention of relieving you of your every last possession. With your agreement we would like to sell your stocks and bonds. Everything else you mentioned, including the house, we believe should remain in your possession."

She hesitated. "I appreciate your generosity, Mr. Kane. However, I have no wish to remain under any obligation to your bank or leave my husband's name under a cloud." The little tremor again, but quickly suppressed. "Anyway, I have decided to sell the house in Florida and return to my parents' home as soon as possible."

William's pulse quickened to hear that she would be coming back to Boston. "In that case, perhaps we can reach some agreement about the proceeds of the sale," he said.

"We can do that now," she said flatly. "You must have the entire amount."

William played for another meeting. "Don't let's make too hasty a decision. I think it might be wise to consult my colleagues and discuss this with you again."

She shrugged slightly. "As you wish. I don't really care

about the money either way and I wouldn't want to put you to any more inconvenience."

William blinked. "Mrs. Brookes, I must confess to have been surprised by your magnanimous attitude. At least allow me the pleasure of taking you to lunch."

She smiled for the first time, revealing an unsuspected dimple in her right cheek. William gazed at it in delight and did his utmost to provoke its reappearance over a long lunch at the Ritz. By the time he returned to his desk, it was well past three o'clock.

"Long lunch, William," commented Tony Simmons.

"Yes, the Brookes problem turned out to be trickier than I had expected."

"It looked fairly straightforward to me when I went over the papers," said Simmons. "She isn't complaining about our offer, is she? I thought we were being rather generous in the circumstances."

"Yes, she thought so, too. I had to talk her out of divesting herself of her last dollar to swell our reserves."

Tony Simmons stared. "That doesn't sound like the William Kane we all know and love so well. Still, there has never been a better time for the bank to be magnanimous."

William grimaced. Since the day of his arrival, he and Tony Simmons had been in growing disagreement about where the stock market was heading. The market had been moving steadily upward since Herbert Hoover's election to the White House in November 1928. In fact, only ten days later, the New York Stock Exchange posted a record volume of over six million shares in one day. But William was convinced that the upward trend, fueled by the large influx of money from the automobile industry, would result in an inflation of prices to the point of instability. Tony Simmons, on the other hand, was confident that the boom would continue, so when William advocated caution at board meetings he was invariably overruled. However, with his trust money, he was free to follow his own intuition and started investing in land, gold, commodities and even in some carefully selected

Kane & Abel   *241*

impressionist paintings, leaving only 50 percent of his assets in stocks.

When the Federal Reserve Bank of New York put out an edict declaring that it would not rediscount loans to those banks that were releasing money to their customers for the sole purpose of speculation, William considered that the first nail had been driven into the speculator's coffin. He immediately reviewed the bank's lending program and estimated that Kane and Cabot had more than $26 million out on such loans. He begged Tony Simmons to call in these amounts, certain that, with such a government regulation in operation, stock prices would inevitably fall in the long term. They nearly had a stand-up fight at the monthly board meeting and William was voted down by 12 to 2.

On March 21, 1929, Blair and Company announced its consolidation with the Bank of America, the third in a series of bank mergers that seemed to point to a brighter tomorrow, and on March 25, Tony Simmons sent William a note pointing out to him that the market had broken through to yet another all-time record, and proceeded to put more of the bank's money into stocks. By then, William had rearranged his capital so that only 25 percent was in the stock market, a move that had already cost him more than $2 million—and a troubled reprimand from Alan Lloyd.

"I hope to goodness you know what you're doing, William."

"Alan, I've been beating the stock market since I was fourteen and I've always done it by bucking the trend."

But as the market continued to climb through the summer of 1929, even William stopped selling, wondering if Tony Simmons's judgment was, in fact, correct.

As the time for Alan Lloyd's retirement drew nearer, Tony Simmons's clear intent to succeed him as chairman began to take on the look of a *fait accompli*. The prospect troubled William, who considered Simmons's thinking far too conventional. He was always a yard behind the rest of the market, which is fine during boom years when investments are going well, but can be dangerous for a bank in leaner, more competitive times. A shrewd investor, in William's eyes, did not invariably run with the herd, thundering or otherwise, but worked out in advance in which direction the herd would be turning next. William still felt that future investment in the stock market looked risky, while Tony Simmons was convinced that America was entering a golden era.

William's other problem was simply that Tony Simmons was only thirty-nine years old, which meant that William could not hope to become chairman of Kane and Cabot for at least another twenty-six years. That hardly fitted what at Harvard had been called "one's career pattern."

Meanwhile, the image of Katherine Brookes remained clear in William's mind. He wrote to her as often as he could about the sale of her stocks and bonds: formal typewritten letters that elicited no more than formal handwritten responses. She must have thought he was the most conscientious banker in the world. Then early in the fall she wrote to say she had found a firm buyer for the Florida estate. William wrote to request that she allow him to negotiate the terms of the sale on the bank's behalf and she agreed.

He traveled down to Florida in early September 1929. Mrs. Brookes met him at the railroad station and he was overwhelmed by how much more beautiful she appeared in person than in his memory. The slight wind blew her black dress against her body as she stood waiting on the platform, leaving a profile that ensured that every man except William would look at her a second time. William's eyes never left her.

She was still in mourning and her manner toward him was so reserved and correct that William initially despaired of making any impression on her. He spun out the negotiations with the farmer who was purchasing Buckhurst Park for as long as he could and persuaded Katherine Brookes to accept one-third of the agreed sale price while the bank kept two-thirds. Finally, after the legal papers were signed, he could find no more excuses for not returning to Boston. He invited her to dinner at his hotel, resolved to reveal something of his feelings for her. Not for the first time she took him by surprise. Before he had broached the subject, she asked him, twirling her glass to avoid looking at him, if he would like to stay over at Buckhurst Park for a few days.

"A sort of vacation for us both." She blushed; William remained silent.

Finally she found the courage to continue. "I know this is mad, but you must realize I've been very lonely. The extraordinary thing is that I seem to have enjoyed the last few days with you more than any time I can remember." She blushed again. "I've expressed that badly and you'll think the worst of me."

William's pulse leaped. "Kate, I have wanted to say something at least as bad as that for the last nine months."

"Then you'll stay for a few days, William?"

"Yes, Kate, I will."

That night she installed him in the main guest bedroom at Buckhurst Park. In later life William always looked back on these few days as a golden interlude in his life. He rode with Kate and she outjumped him. He swam with her and she out-distanced him. He walked with her and always turned back first, and so finally he resorted to playing poker with her and won $3.5 million in 3.5 hours of playing.

"Will you take a check?" she said grandly.

"You forget I know what you're worth, Mrs. Brookes, but I'll make a deal with you. We'll go on playing until you've won it back."

"It may take a few years," said Kate.

"I'll wait," said William.

He found himself telling her of long-buried incidents in his past, things he had barely discussed even with Matthew—his respect for his father, his love for his mother, his blind hatred of Henry Osborne, his ambitions for Kane and Cabot. She, in turn, told him of her childhood in Boston, her school days in Virginia and her early marriage to Max Brookes.

Seven days later when she said good-bye to him at the station, he kissed her for the first time.

"Kate, I'm going to say something very presumptuous. I hope one day you'll feel more for me than you felt for Max."

"I'm beginning to feel that way already," she said quietly.

William looked at her steadily. "Don't stay out of my life for another nine months."

"I can't—you've sold my house."

On the way back to Boston, feeling happier and more settled than at any other time since before his father's death, William drafted a report on the sale of Buckhurst Park, his mind returning continually to Kate and the past five days. Just before the train drew into the South Station, he scribbled a quick note in his neat but illegible handwriting.

> *Kate,*
>
> *I find I am missing you already. And it's only a few hours. Please write and let me know when you will be coming to Boston. Meanwhile I shall be getting back to the bank's business and find I can put you out of my mind for quite long periods (i.e. 10 ± 5 minutes) at a stretch.*
>
> *Love,*
> *William*

He had just dropped the envelope into the mailbox on Charles Street when all thoughts of Kate were driven from his mind by the cry of a newsboy.

" 'Wall Street Collapse!' "

William seized a copy of the paper and rapidly skimmed the lead story. The market had plummeted overnight; some financiers viewed it as nothing more than a readjustment; William saw it as the beginning of the landslide he had been predicting for months. He hurried to the bank and went straight to the chairman's office.

"I feel the market will steady up in the long run," Alan Lloyd said soothingly.

"Never," said William. "The market is overloaded. Overloaded with small investors who thought they were in for a quick profit and are certain to run for their lives now. Don't you see the balloon is about to burst? I'm going to sell everything. By the end of the year the bottom will have dropped out of this market, and I did warn you in February, Alan."

"I still don't agree with you, William, but I'll call a full board meeting for tomorrow, so that we can discuss your views in more detail."

"Thank you," said William. He returned to his office and picked up the interoffice phone.

"Alan, I forgot to tell you. I've met the girl I'm going to marry."

"Does she know yet?" asked Alan.

"No," said William.

"I see," said Alan. "Then your marriage will closely resemble your banking career, William. Anyone directly involved will be informed after you've made your decisions."

William laughed, picked up the other phone, put his own major holdings on the market and went into cash. Tony Simmons had just come in. Standing at the open door, he watched William, thinking he had gone quite mad.

"You could lose your shirt overnight dumping all those stocks with the market in its present state."

"I'll lose a lot more if I hold on to them," replied William.

The loss he was to suffer in the following week, over $1 million, would have staggered a less confident man.

At the board meeting the next day, he also lost—by 8 votes to 6—his proposal to liquidate the bank's stocks; Tony Simmons convinced the board that it would be irresponsible not to hold out a little longer. The only small victory William notched up was persuading his fellow directors that the bank should no longer be a buyer.

The market rose a little that day, which gave William the opportunity to sell some more of his own stock. By the end of the week, when the index had risen steadily for four days in a row, William began to wonder if he had been overreacting, but all his past training and instinct told him he had made the right decision. Alan Lloyd said nothing; the money William was losing was not his and he was looking forward to a quiet retirement.

On October 22 the market suffered further heavy losses and William again begged Alan Lloyd to get out while there was still a chance. This time Alan listened and allowed William to place a sell order on some of the bank's major stocks. The following day the market fell again in an avalanche of selling, and it mattered little what issues the bank tried to dispose of, because there were no longer any buyers. The dumping of stock turned into a stampede as every small investor in America put in a sell bid to try to get out from under. Such was the panic that the ticker tape could not keep pace with the transactions. Only when the Exchange opened in the morning, after the clerks had worked all night, did traders know for a fact how much they had lost the day before.

Alan Lloyd had a phone conversation with the Morgan bank and agreed that Kane and Cabot should join a group of banks who would try to shore up the national collapse in major stocks. William did not disapprove of this policy, on the ground that if there had to be a group effort, Kane and Cabot should be responsibly involved in the action. And, of course, if it worked, all the banks would be better off. Richard Whitney, the vice president of the New York Stock Exchange and the representative of the group Morgan had put together, went on the floor of the Exchange the next day and invested $30 million in blue chip stocks. The market began to hold. That day 12,894,650 shares were traded and for the next two days the market held steady. Everyone, from President

Hoover to the runners in the brokerage houses, believed that the worst was behind them.

William had sold nearly all his private stocks, and his personal loss was proportionately far smaller than the bank's, which had lost over $3 million in four days; even Tony Simmons had taken to following all of William's suggestions. On October 29, Black Tuesday, as the day came to be known, the market fell again. Sixteen million six hundred and ten thousand and thirty shares were traded. Banks all over the country knew that the truth was that they were now insolvent. If every one of their customers demanded cash— or if they in turn tried to call in all their loans—the whole banking system would collapse around their ears.

A board meeting held on November 9 opened with one minute's silence in memory of John J. Riordan, president of the County Trust and a director of Kane and Cabot, who had shot himself to death in his home. It was the eleventh suicide in Boston banking circles in two weeks; the dead man had been a close personal friend of Alan Lloyd's. The chairman went on to announce that Kane and Cabot had themselves now lost nearly $4 million, the Morgan Group had failed in its effort at unification, and it was now expected that every bank should act in its own best interests. Nearly all the bank's small investors had gone under and most of the larger ones were having impossible cash problems. Angry mobs had already gathered outside banks in New York, and the elderly guards had had to be supplemented with Pinkertons. Another week like this, said Alan, and every one of us will be wiped out. He offered his resignation, but the directors would not hear of it. His position was no different from that of any other chairman of any major American bank. Tony Simmons also offered his resignation, but his fellow directors once again would not hear of it. Tony looked as if he were no longer destined to take Alan Lloyd's place, so William kept a magnanimous silence.

As a compromise, Simmons was sent to London to take charge of overseas investments. Out of harm's way, thought William, who now found himself appointed Investment Director, in charge of all the bank's investments. He immediately invited Matthew Lester to join him as his number two. This time Alan Lloyd didn't even raise an eyebrow.

Matthew agreed to join William early in the spring, which was the soonest his father could release him. Lester's hadn't been without its own troubles. William, therefore, ran the investment department on his own until Matthew's arrival. The winter of 1929 turned out to be an upsetting period for him as he watched small firms and large firms alike, run by Bostonians he had known all his life, go under. For some time he even wondered if Kane and Cabot itself could survive.

At Christmas, William spent a glorious week in Florida with Kate, helping her pack her belongings in tea chests for her return to Boston (the ones Kane and Cabot let me keep, she teased). William's Christmas presents filled another tea chest, and Kate felt quite guilty about his generosity.

"What can a penniless widow hope to give you in return?" she mocked.

William responded by bundling her into the remaining tea chest and labeling it "William's Present."

He returned to Boston in high spirits, hoping his time with Kate augured the start of a better year. He settled down in Tony Simmons's old office to read the morning mail, knowing he would have to preside over the usual two or three liquidation meetings scheduled for that week. He asked his secretary whom he was to see first.

"I'm afraid it's another bankruptcy, Mr. Kane."

"Oh, yes, I remember the case," said William. The name had meant nothing to him. "I read over the file last night. A most unfortunate affair. What time is he due?"

"At ten o'clock, but the gentleman is already in the lobby waiting for you, sir."

"Right," said William, "please send him in. Let's get it over with."

William opened his file again to remind himself quickly of the salient facts. There was a line drawn through the name of the original client, a Davis Leroy. It had been replaced by that of the morning's visitor, Abel Rosnovski.

William vividly remembered the last conversation he had had with Mr. Rosnovski and was already regretting it.

CHAPTER
SIXTEEN

It took Abel about three months to appreciate the full extent of the problems facing the Richmond Continental and why the hotel was losing so much money. The simple conclusion he came to after 12 weeks of keeping his eyes wide open, while at the same time allowing the rest of the staff to believe he was half-asleep, was that the hotel's profits were being stolen. The Richmond staff was working a collusive system on a scale that even Abel had not previously come across. The system did not, however, take into account a new assistant manager who had had to steal bread from the Russians to stay alive. Abel's first problem now was not to let anybody know the extent of his discovery until he had had a chance to look into every department of the hotel. It didn't take him long to figure out that each department had perfected its own system for stealing.

Deception started at the front desk, where the clerks were registering only eight out of every ten guests and pocketing the cash payments from the remaining two. The routine they were using was a simple one; anyone who had tried it at the Plaza in New York would have been found out in a few minutes and fired. The head desk clerk would choose an elderly couple who had booked in from another state for only one night. He would then discreetly make sure they had no business connections in the city and simply fail to register them. If they paid cash the following morning, the money was pocketed, and provided they had not signed the register, there was no record that the guests had ever been in the hotel. Abel had long thought that all hotels should be required to register every guest. The Plaza was already doing so.

In the dining room the system had been refined. Of course, the cash payments of any nonresident guests of a check for lunch or dinner were already being taken. Abel had expected this, but it took him a little longer to check through the restaurant bills and establish that the front desk was working with the dining-room staff to ensure that there were no restaurant bills for those guests whom they had already chosen not to register. Over and above this, there was a steady trail of fictitious breakages and repairs, missing equipment, disappearing food, lost bed linen and even an occasional mattress gone astray. After checking every department thoroughly, Abel concluded that more than half of the Richmond's staff were involved in the conspiracy and that no one department had a completely clean record.

When he had first come to the Richmond, Abel had wondered why the manager, Desmond Pacey, hadn't noticed what had been going on under his nose for a long time. He wrongly assumed the reason was that the man was lazy and could not be bothered to follow up complaints. Even Abel was slow to realize that the lazy manager was the mastermind behind the entire operation, and the reason it worked so well. Pacey had worked for the Richmond group for more than thirty years. There was not a single hotel in the group in which he had not held a senior position at one time or another, which made Abel fearful for the solvency of the entire chain. Moreover, Desmond Pacey was a personal friend of Davis Leroy. The Chicago Richmond was losing more than $30,000 a year, a situation Abel knew could be remedied overnight by firing a large portion of the staff, starting with Desmond Pacey. This posed a problem, because in thirty years Davis Leroy had rarely fired anyone. He simply tolerated the problems, hoping that in time they would go away. As far as Abel could determine, Richmond hotel staff went on stealing the hotel blind until they reluctantly retired.

Abel knew that the only way he could reverse the hotel's fortunes was to have a showdown with Davis Leroy, and to that end, early in 1928, he boarded the Great Express from Illinois Central to St. Louis and on, via the Missouri Pacific, to Dallas. Under his arm was a 200-page report he had taken three months to compile in his small room in the hotel annex. When Davis Leroy had finished reading through the mass of evidence, he sat staring at Abel in dismay.

"These people are my friends" were his first words as he closed the dossier. "Some of them have been with me for thirty years. Hell—there's always been a little fiddling around in this business, but now you tell me they've been robbing me behind my back?"

"Some of them, I should think, for all of those thirty years," said Abel.

"What in hell's name am I going to do about it?" said Leroy.

"I can stop the rot if you remove Desmond Pacey and give me carte blanche to sack anyone immediately who has been involved in the thefts."

"Well now, Abel, I wish the problem was as simple as that."

"The problem is just that simple," said Abel. "And if you won't let me deal with the culprits, you can have my resignation as of this minute, because I have no interest in being a part of the most corruptly run hotel in America."

"Couldn't we just demote Desmond Pacey to assistant manager? Then I could make you manager and the problem would come under your control."

"Never," replied Abel. "Pacey has over two years to go— he has a firm hold over the entire Richmond staff. By the time I could get him in line you'd be dead or bankrupt or both—I suspect all your other hotels are being run in the same crooked way. If you want the trend reversed in Chicago, you'll have to make a firm decision about Pacey right now or you can go to the wall on your own. Take it or leave it."

"Us Texans have a reputation for speaking our mind,

Abel, but we're sure not in your class. Okay, okay, I'll give you the authority as of this minute. Congratulations. You're the new manager of the Chicago Richmond. Congratulations. Wait till Al Capone hears you've arrived in Chicago; he'll join me down here in the peace and quiet of the great Southwest. Abel, my boy," continued Leroy, standing up and slapping his new manager on the shoulder, "don't think I'm ungrateful. You've done a great job in Chicago and from now on I shall look upon you as my right-hand man. To be honest with you, Abel, I have been doing so well on the Stock Exchange I haven't even noticed the losses, so thank God I have one honest friend. Why don't you stay overnight and have a bite to eat."

"I'd be delighted to join you for dinner, Mr. Leroy, but I want to spend the night at the Dallas Richmond for personal reasons."

"You're not going to let anyone off the hook, are you, Abel?"

"Not if I can help it."

That evening Davis Leroy gave Abel a sumptuous meal and a little too much whiskey, which he insisted was no more than down-home hospitality. He also admitted to Abel that he was considering having someone else run the Richmond Group so that he could take life a little easier.

"Are you sure you want a dumb Polack?" slurred Abel, feeling his one-too-many drinks.

"Abel, it's me who's been dumb. If you hadn't proved to be so reliable in smoking out those thieves, I might have gone under. But now that I know the truth, we'll lick them together, and I'm going to give you the chance to put the Richmond Group back on the map."

Abel shakily raised his glass. "I'll drink to that—and to a long and successful partnership."

"Go get 'em, boy."

Abel spent the night at the Dallas Richmond, giving a false name and pointedly telling the desk clerk that he would be staying only one night. In the morning when he watched as the hotel's only copy of the receipt for his cash payment

disappeared into the wastepaper basket, Abel's suspicions
were confirmed. The problem was not Chicago's alone. He
decided he would have to get Chicago straightened out first;
the rest of the group's finaglings would have to wait until
later. He made one call to Davis Leroy, to tell him that he
had proved that the disease had spread to more than one
member of the group.

Abel traveled back the way he had come. The Mississippi
Valley lay sullen outside the train windows, devastated by
the floods of the previous year. Abel thought about the devastation he was going to cause when he returned to the
Chicago Richmond.

When he arrived, there was no night porter on duty and
only one clerk could be found. Abel decided to let them all
have a good night's rest before he bid them farewell. A
young bellboy opened the front door for him as he made his
way back to the annex.

"Have a good trip, Mr. Rosnovski?" he asked.

"Yes, thank you. How have things been here?"

"Oh, very quiet."

You may find it even quieter this time tomorrow, thought
Abel, when you're the only member of the staff left.

Abel unpacked and called room service to order a light
meal; it arrived in something more than an hour. When he
had finished his coffee, Abel undressed and stood in a cold
shower, going over his plan for the following day. He had
picked a good time of year for his massacre. It was early
February and the hotel had only about a 25 percent occupancy, and Abel was confident that he could run the Richmond with about half its present staff. He climbed into bed,
threw the pillow on the floor and slept, like his unsuspecting
staff, soundly.

Desmond Pacey, known to everyone at the Richmond as
Lazy Pacey, was sixty-three years old. He was considerably
overweight and rather slow of movement on his short legs.
Desmond Pacey had seen seven assistant managers come
and go in the Richmond. Some had been greedy and had
wanted more of the "take"; some couldn't seem to under-

stand how the system worked. The Polack, he decided, wasn't turning out to be any brighter than the others. Pacey hummed to himself as he walked slowly toward Abel's office for their daily ten o'clock meeting. It was seventeen minutes past ten.

"Sorry to have kept you waiting," said the manager, not sounding sorry at all.

Abel made no comment.

"I was held up with something at the front desk—you know how it is."

Abel knew exactly how it was at the front desk. He slowly opened the drawer of the desk in front of him and laid out forty crumpled hotel bills, some of them in four or five pieces, bills he had recovered from wastepaper baskets and ashtrays, bills for those guests who had paid cash and who had never been registered. He watched the fat little manager trying to work out what they were, upside down.

Desmond Pacey couldn't quite fathom it. Not that he cared that much. There was nothing for him to worry about. If the stupid Polack had caught on to the system, he could either take his cut or leave. Pacey was wondering what percentage he would have to give him. Perhaps a nice room in the hotel would keep him quiet for the time being.

"You're fired, Mr. Pacey, and I want you off the premises within the hour."

Desmond Pacey didn't actually take in the words, because he couldn't believe them.

"What was that you said? I don't think I heard you right."

"You did," said Abel. "You're fired."

"You can't fire me. I'm the manager and I've been with the Richmond Group for over thirty years. If there's any firing to be done, I'll do it. Who in God's name do you think you are?"

"I am the new manager."

"You're *what*?"

"The new manager," Abel repeated. "Mr. Leroy appointed me yesterday and I have just fired you, Mr. Pacey."

"What for?"

"For larceny on a grand scale." Abel turned the bills around so that the bespectacled man could see them all properly. "Every one of these guests paid their bill, but not one penny of the money reached the Richmond account. And they all have one thing in common—your signature is on them."

"You couldn't prove anything in a hundred years."

"I know," said Abel. "You've been running a good system. Well, you can go and run that system somewhere else, because your luck's run out here. There is an old Polish saying, Mr. Pacey: The pitcher carries water only until the handle breaks. The handle has just broken and you're fired."

"You don't have the authority to fire me," said Pacey. Sweat peppered out on his forehead. "Davis Leroy is a close personal friend of mine. He's the only man who can fire me. You only came out from New York three months ago. He wouldn't even listen to you if I had spoken to him. I could get you thrown out of this hotel with one phone call."

"Go ahead," said Abel. He picked up the telephone and asked the operator to get Davis Leroy in Dallas. The two men waited, staring at each other. The sweat had now trickled down to the tip of Pacey's nose. For a second, Abel wondered if his employer would remain firm.

"Good morning, Mr. Leroy, it's Abel Rosnovski calling from Chicago. I've just fired Desmond Pacey and he wants a word with you."

Shakily, Pacey took the telephone. He listened for only a few moments.

"But Davis, I . . . What could I do . . . ? I swear to you it isn't true. . . . There must be some mistake."

Abel heard the line click.

"One hour, Mr. Pacey," said Abel, "or I'll hand over these bills to the Chicago Police Department."

"Now wait a moment," Pacey said. "Don't act so hasty." His tone and attitude had changed abruptly. "We could bring you in on the whole operation, you could make a very steady little income if we ran this hotel together, and no one would be any the wiser. The money would be far more than you're making as assistant manager and we all know Davis can afford the losses——"

"I'm not the assistant manager any longer, Mr. Pacey. I'm the manager, so get out before I throw you out."

"You fucking Polack," said the ex-manager, realizing he had played his last card and lost. "You had better keep your eyes wide open, Polack, because I'm going to cut you down to size."

He left. By lunch he had been joined on the street by the headwaiter, head chef, senior housekeeper, chief desk clerk, head porter and 17 other members of the Richmond staff who Abel felt were past redemption. In the afternoon, he called a meeting of the remainder of the employees, explained to them in detail why he had done what he had done and assured them that their jobs were not in any danger.

"But if I can find *one*," said Abel, "I repeat, *one* dollar misplaced, the person involved will be fired without references there and then. Am I understood?"

No one spoke.

Several other members of the staff left the Richmond during the next few weeks when they realized that Abel did not intend to continue Desmond Pacey's system on his own behalf. They were quickly replaced.

By the end of March, Abel had invited four employees from the Plaza to join him at the Richmond. They had three things in common: they were young, ambitious and honest. Within six months, only 37 of the original staff of 110 were still employed at the Richmond. At the end of the first year, Abel cracked a large bottle of champagne with Davis Leroy to celebrate the year's figures for the Chicago Richmond. They had shown a profit of $3,468. Small, but the first profit the hotel had shown in the thirty years of its existence. Abel was projecting a profit of more than $25,000 in 1929.

Davis Leroy was mightily impressed. He visited Chicago once a month and began to rely heavily on Abel's judgment. He even came around to admitting that what had been true of the Chicago Richmond might well be true of the other hotels in the group. Abel wanted to see the Chicago hotel running smoothly as an honest, profitable enterprise before he considered tackling the others. Leroy agreed—then talked of a partnership for Abel if he could do for the rest of the group what he had done for Chicago.

They started going to baseball games and the races together whenever Davis was in Chicago. On one occasion, when Davis had lost $700 without coming close in any of the six races, he threw up his arms in disgust and said, "Why do I bother with horses, Abel? You're the best bet I've ever made."

Melanie Leroy always dined with her father on his visits. Cool, pretty, with a slim figure and long legs that attracted many a stare from the hotel guests, she treated Abel with a slight degree of hauteur that gave him no encouragement for the aspirations he had begun to formulate for her, nor did she invite him to substitute "Melanie" for "Miss Leroy" until she discovered he was the holder of an economics degree from Columbia and knew more about discounted cash flow than she did herself. After that, she had softened a little and from time to time came to dine with Abel alone in the hotel and seek assistance with the work she was doing for her Liberal Arts degree at the University of Chicago. Emboldened, he occasionally escorted her to concerts and the theater and began to feel a proprietorial jealousy whenever she brought other men to dine at the hotel, though she never came with the same escort twice.

So greatly had the cuisine improved under Abel's iron fist that people who had lived in Chicago for thirty years and scarcely realized the hotel existed were making dinner reservations every Saturday evening. Abel had the whole hotel redecorated—for the first time in twenty years—and dressed the staff in smart new green-and-gold uniforms. One guest, who had stayed at the Richmond for one week every year over a decade actually retreated out of the front door on arrival, thinking he had walked into the wrong establishment. When Al Capone booked a dinner party for sixteen in a private room to celebrate his thirtieth birthday, Abel knew he had arrived.

• • •

Abel's personal wealth grew during this period while the stock market flourished. He had left the Plaza with $8,000 eighteen months before; his brokerage account now stood at more than $30,000. He was confident that the market would continue to rise, and so he always reinvested his profits. His personal requirements were still fairly modest. He had acquired two new suits and his first pair of brown shoes. His rooms and food were provided by the hotel and he had few out-of-pocket expenses. There seemed to be nothing but a bright future for him. The Continental Trust had handled the Richmond account for more than thirty years, so Abel had transferred his own account to that bank when he first came to Chicago. Every day he would go to the bank and deposit the hotel's previous day's receipts. He was taken by surprise one Friday morning by a message that the manager was asking to see him. He knew his personal account was never overdrawn, so he presumed the meeting must have something to do with the Richmond. The bank could hardly be about to complain that the hotel's account was solvent for the first time in thirty years. A junior clerk guided Abel through a tangle of corridors until he reached a handsome wooden door. A gentle knock and he was ushered in to meet the manager.

"My name is Curtis Fenton," said the man behind the desk, offering Abel his hand before motioning him into a green leather button chair. He was a neat, rotund man who wore half-moon spectacles and an impeccable white collar and black tie to go with his three-piece banker's suit.

"Thank you," said Abel nervously. The circumstances brought back to him memories he associated only with the fear of being uncertain of what was going to happen next.

"I would have invited you to lunch, Mr. Rosnovski . . ."

Abel's heartbeat steadied a little. He was only too aware that bank managers do not dispense free meals when they have unpleasant messages to deliver.

". . . but something has arisen that requires immediate action and so I hope you won't mind if I discuss the problem with you without delay. I'll come straight to the point, Mr. Rosnovski. One of my most respected customers, an elderly lady, Miss Amy Leroy"—the name made Abel sit up instantly—"is in possession of twenty-five percent of the Richmond Group stock. She has offered this holding to her brother, Mr. Davis Leroy, several times in the past, but he has shown absolutely no interest in purchasing Miss Amy's shares. I can understand Mr. Leroy's reasoning. He already owns seventy-five percent of the company and I daresay he feels he has no need to worry about the other twenty-five percent, which, incidentally, was a legacy from their late father. However, Miss Amy Leroy is still keen on disposing of her stock, as it has never paid a dividend."

Abel was not surprised to hear this.

"Mr. Leroy has indicated that he has no objection to her selling the stock and she feels that at her age she would rather have a little cash to spend now than wait in the hope that the group may one day prove profitable. With that in mind, Mr. Rosnovski, I thought I would apprise you of the situation in case you might know of someone with an interest in the hotel trade and, therefore, interested in the purchase of my client's shares."

"How much is Miss Leroy hoping to realize from her stock?" asked Abel.

"Oh, I feel she'd be happy to let them go for as little as sixty-five thousand dollars."

"Sixty-five thousand dollars is rather high for a stock that has never paid a dividend," said Abel. "And has no hope of doing so for some years to come," he added.

"Ah," said Curtis Fenton, "but you must remember that the value of the eleven hotels should also be taken into consideration."

"But control of the company would still remain in the hands of Mr. Leroy, which makes Miss Leroy's twenty-five percent holding nothing but pieces of paper."

"Come, come, Mr. Rosnovski, twenty-five percent of

eleven hotels would be a very valuable holding for only sixty-five thousand dollars."

"Not while Davis Leroy has overall control. Offer Miss Leroy forty thousand dollars, Mr. Fenton, and I may be able to find you someone who is interested."

"You don't think that person might go a little higher, do you?" Mr. Fenton's eyebrows raised on the word *higher*.

"Not a penny more, Mr. Fenton."

The bank manager brought his fingertips delicately together, pleased with his appraisal of Abel.

"In the circumstances, I can only ask Miss Amy what her attitude would be to such an offer. I will contact you again as soon as she has instructed me."

After he left Curtis Fenton's office, Abel's heart was beating as rapidly as when he had entered. He hurried back to the hotel to double-check on his own personal holdings. His brokerage account stood at $33,112 and his personal checking account at $3,008. Abel then tried to carry out a normal day's work. He found it difficult to concentrate, wondering how Miss Amy Leroy would react to the bid and daydreaming about what he would do if he held a 25 percent interest in the Richmond Group.

He hesitated before informing Davis Leroy of his bid, fearful that the genial Texan might view his ambitions as a threat. But after a couple of days, during which he considered the matter carefully, he decided the fairest thing to do would be to call Davis and acquaint him with his intentions.

"I want you to know why I am doing this, Davis. I believe the Richmond Group has a great future and you can be sure that I shall work all the harder if I know my own money is also involved." He paused. "But if you want to take up that twenty-five percent yourself, I shall naturally understand."

To his surprise, the escape ladder was not grasped.

"Well, see here, Abel, if you have that much confidence in the group, go ahead, son, and buy Amy out. I'd be proud to have you for a partner. You've earned it. By the way, I'll be up next week for the Reds-Cubs game. See you then."

Abel was jubilant. "Thank you, Davis—you'll never have course to regret your decision."

"I'm sure I won't, pardner."

Abel returned to the bank a week later. This time it was he who asked to see the manager. Once again he sat in the green leather button chair and waited for Mr. Fenton to speak.

"I am surprised to find," began Curtis Fenton, not looking at all surprised, "that Miss Leroy will accept the bid of forty thousand dollars for her twenty-five percent holding in the Richmond Group." He paused before looking up at Abel. "As I have now secured her agreement, I must ask if you are in a position to disclose your buyer?"

"Yes," said Abel confidently. "I will be the principal."

"I see, Mr. Rosnovski"—again not showing any surprise. "May I ask how you propose to find the forty thousand dollars?"

"I shall liquidate my stock holdings and release the spare cash in my personal account, which will leave me a shortfall of about four thousand dollars. I hoped that you would be willing to loan me that sum—since you are so confident that the Richmond Group stock is undervalued. In any case, the four thousand dollars probably represents nothing more than the bank's commission on the deal."

Curtis Fenton blinked and frowned. Gentlemen did not make that sort of remark in his office; it stung all the more because Abel had the sum exactly right. "Will you give me a little more time to consider your proposal, Mr. Rosnovski, and then I will come back to you?"

"If you wait long enough, I won't need a loan," said Abel. "The way the market is moving at the moment, my other investments will soon be worth the full forty thousand."

Abel had to wait a further week to be told that Continental Trust was willing to back him. He immediately cleared both his accounts and borrowed a little under $4,000 to make up the shortfall on the 40 thousand.

· · ·

Within six months, Abel had paid off his $4,000 loan by careful buying and selling of stock from March to August 1929, some of the best days the stock market was ever to know.

By September both his accounts were slightly ahead again and he even had enough over to buy a new Buick as well as being the owner of 25 percent of the Richmond Group of Hotels. Abel was pleased to have acquired such a firm holding in Davis Leroy's empire. It gave him the confidence to pursue his daughter and the other 75 percent.

Early in October he invited Melanie to a program of Mozart at the Chicago Symphony Hall. Donning his smartest suit, which only emphasized that he was gaining some weight, and wearing his first silk tie, he felt certain as he glanced in the mirror that the evening would be a success. After the concert was over Abel avoided the Richmond, excellent though its food had become, and took Melanie to the Loop for dinner. He was particularly careful to talk only of economics and politics, two subjects about which she knew he was greatly the more knowledgeable. Finally, he asked her to his rooms for a drink. It was the first time she had seen them and she was both piqued and surprised by their smartness.

Abel poured the Coca-Cola she requested, dropped two cubes of ice into it and felt new confidence from the smile that rewarded him as he passed her the glass. He couldn't help staring briefly at her slim, crossed legs. He poured himself a bourbon.

"Thank you, Abel, for a wonderful evening."

He sat down beside her and reflectively swirled the drink in his glass. "For many years I heard no music. When I did, Mozart spoke to my heart as no other composer has done."

"How very middle-European you sound sometimes, Abel." She pulled free the edge of her silk dress, which Abel was sitting on. "Who would have thought a hotel manager would give a damn for Mozart?"

"One of my ancestors, the first Baron Rosnovski," said Abel, "once met the maestro and he became a close friend of the family, so I have always felt he was part of my life."

Melanie's smile was unfathomable. Abel leaned sideways and kissed her cheek above the ear, where her fair hair was drawn back from her face. She continued the conversation without giving the slightest indication that she had even been aware of his action.

"Frederick Stock captured the mood of the third movement to perfection, wouldn't you say?"

Abel tried a kiss again. This time she turned her face toward him and allowed herself to be kissed on the lips. Then she drew away.

"I think I ought to be getting back to the university."

"But you've only just arrived," said Abel, dismayed.

"Yes, I know, but I have to be up early in the morning. I have a heavy day ahead."

Abel kissed her again. She fell back on the couch and Abel tried to move his hand onto her breast. She broke quickly from the kiss and pushed him away.

"I must be going, Abel," she insisted.

"Oh, come on," he said, "you don't have to go yet," and once again he tried to kiss her.

This time she stopped him by pushing him away more firmly.

"Abel, what do you think you are doing? Because you give me an occasional meal and take me to a concert doesn't mean you have the right to maul me."

"But we've been going out together for months," said Abel. "I didn't think you would mind."

"We have not been going out together for months, Abel. I eat with you occasionally in my father's dining room, but you should not construe that to mean we have been going out together for months."

"I'm sorry," said Abel. "The last thing I wanted you to

think was that I was mauling you. I only wanted to touch you."

"I would never allow a man to touch me," she said, "unless I was going to marry him."

"But I want to marry you," said Abel quietly.

Melanie burst out laughing.

"What's so funny about that?" Abel asked, reddening.

"Don't be silly, Abel, I could never marry you."

"Why not?" demanded Abel, shocked by the vehemence in her voice.

"It would never do for a southern lady to marry a first-generation Polish immigrant," she replied, sitting up very straight and pushing her silk dress back into place.

"But I am a Baron," said Abel, a little haughtily.

Melanie burst out laughing again. "You don't think anybody believes that, do you, Abel? Don't you realize the whole staff laughs behind your back whenever you mention your title?"

He was stunned and felt sick, his face draining now of all color. "They all laugh at me behind my back?" His normally slight accent had become pronounced.

"Yes," she said. "Surely you know what your nickname in the hotel is: The Chicago Baron."

Abel was speechless.

"Now don't be silly and get all self-conscious about it, I think you've done a wonderful job for Daddy, and I know he admires you, but I could never marry you."

Abel sat quietly, *"I could never marry you,"* he repeated.

"Of course not. Daddy likes you, but he would never agree to have you as a son-in-law."

"I'm sorry to have offended you," said Abel.

"You haven't, Abel. I'm flattered. Now, let's forget you ever mentioned the subject. Perhaps you would be kind enough to take me home?"

She rose and strode toward the door while Abel remained seated, still stunned. Somehow he managed to push himself up slowly and help Melanie on with her cloak. He became

conscious of his limp as they walked along the corridor together. They went down in the elevator and as he took her
home in a cab neither spoke. While the taxi waited, he accompanied her to the front gate of her dormitory. He kissed
her hand.

"I do hope this doesn't mean we can't still be friends,"
said Melanie.

"Of course not," he managed.

"Thank you for taking me to the concert, Abel. I'm sure
you'll have no trouble in finding a nice Polish girl to marry
you. Good night."

"Good-bye," said Abel.

Abel did not think there would be any real trouble on the
New York stock market until one of his guests asked if he
might settle his hotel bill with stock. Abel held only a small
amount of stock himself, since nearly all his money was now
tied up in the Richmond Group, but he took his broker's advice and sold off his remaining shares at a small loss, relieved that the bulk of his assets was secure in bricks and
mortar. He had not taken as close an interest in the day-to-
day movement of the Dow Jones as he would have if most of
his capital had still been in the market.

The hotel did well in the first part of the year. Abel considered he was set fair to achieve his profit forecast of over
$25,000 for 1929 and he kept Davis Leroy informed of
progress.

But when the crash came in October the hotel was half-
empty. Abel placed a call through to Davis Leroy on Black
Tuesday. The usually genial Texan sounded depressed and
preoccupied and would not be drawn into making decisions
about the laying off of hotel staff, which Abel now considered urgent.

"Stick with it, Abel," he said. "I'll come up next week
and we'll sort it out together—or we'll try to."

Abel did not like the ring of the last phrase.

"What's the problem, Davis? Is it anything I can help with?"

"Not for the time being."

Abel remained puzzled. "Why don't you just give me the authority to get on with it and I can brief you when you come up next week?"

"It's not quite as easy as that, Abel. I didn't want to discuss my problems on the phone, but the bank is giving me a little trouble over my losses in the stock market and they're threatening to make me sell the hotels if I can't raise enough money to cover my debts."

Abel went cold.

"Nothing for you to worry about, my boy," continued Davis unconvincingly. "I will fill you in on the details when I come to Chicago next week. I'm sure I can fix up something by then."

Abel heard the phone click; his whole body was now sweating. His first reaction was to wonder how he could assist Davis. He put a call through to Curtis Fenton and pried out of him the name of the banker who controlled the Richmond Group, feeling if he could see him it might make things easier for his friend.

Abel called Davis several times during the next few days to tell him that the situation was going from bad to worse and that decisions must be made, but the older man sounded more and more preoccupied and was still unwilling to make any firm decisions. When matters started getting out of control, Abel made a decision. He asked his secretary to get the banker who controlled the Richmond Group on the phone.

"Whom are you calling, Mr. Rosnovski?" asked a prim-sounding lady.

Abel looked down at the name on the piece of paper in front of him and said it firmly.

"I'll put you through."

"Good morning," said an authoritative voice. "May I help you?"

"I hope so. My name is Abel Rosnovski," Abel began nervously. "I am the manager of the Richmond Chicago and wanted to make an appointment to see you and discuss the future of the Richmond Group."

"I have no authority to deal with anyone except Mr. Davis Leroy," said the clipped accent.

"But I own twenty-five percent of the Richmond Group," said Abel.

"Then no doubt someone will explain to you that until you own fifty-one percent you are in no position to deal with the bank unless you have the authority of Mr. Davis Leroy."

"But he's a close personal friend——"

"I am sure that is the case, Mr. Rosnovski."

". . . and I'm trying to help."

"Has Mr. Leroy given you the authority to represent him?"

"No, but——"

"Then I am sorry. It would be most unprofessional of me to continue this conversation."

"You couldn't be less helpful, could you?" asked Abel, immediately regretting his words.

"That is no doubt how you see it, Mr. Rosnovski. Good day, sir."

Oh, to hell with you, thought Abel, slamming down the phone, worried that he might have done more harm than good. What should he do next?

He didn't have long to find out.

The next evening Abel spotted Melanie in the restaurant, not displaying her usual well-groomed confidence but looking tired and anxious, and he nearly asked her if everything was all right but decided against approaching her. He left the dining room to go to his office and found Davis Leroy standing alone in the front hall. He had on the checked jacket he had been wearing the first day he talked to Abel at the Plaza.

"Is Melanie in the dining room?"

"Yes, she is," said Abel. "I didn't know you were coming into town today, Davis. I'll get the Presidential Suite ready for you immediately."

"Only for one night, Abel, and I'd like to see you in private later."

"Certainly."

Abel didn't like the sound of "in private." Had Melanie been complaining to her father? Was that why he had not found it possible to get a decision out of Davis during the last few days?

Davis Leroy hurried past him into the dining room while Abel went over to the reception desk to check on whether the suite on floor seventeen was available. Half the rooms in the hotel were unoccupied and it came as no surprise that the Presidential Suite was free. Abel booked his employer in and then waited by the reception desk for over an hour. He saw Melanie leave, her face blotched, as if she had been crying. Her father followed her from the dining room a few minutes later.

"Get yourself a bottle of bourbon, Abel—don't tell me we don't have one—and then join me in my suite."

Abel picked up two bottles of bourbon from his safe and joined Leroy in the suite on the seventeenth floor, still wondering if Melanie had said anything to her father.

"Open the bottle and pour yourself a very large one, Abel," Davis Leroy instructed.

Once again Abel felt the fear of the unknown. The palms of his hands began to sweat. Surely he was not going to be fired for wanting to marry the boss's daughter? He and Leroy had been friends for over a year now, close friends. He did not have to wait long to find out what the unknown was.

"Finish your bourbon."

Abel poured the drink down in one gulp and Davis Leroy swallowed his.

"Abel, I'm wiped out." Leroy paused and poured them both another drink. "So is half of America, come to think of it."

Abel did not speak, partly because he could not think of what to say. They sat staring at each other for several minutes; then, after another glass of bourbon, Abel managed, "But you still own eleven hotels."

"Used to own," said Davis Leroy. "Have to put it in the past tense now, Abel. I no longer own any of them; the bank took possession of them last Thursday."

"But they belong to you—they have been in your family for two generations," said Abel.

"They were. They aren't any longer. Now they belong to a bank. There's no reason why you shouldn't know the whole truth, Abel; the same thing's happening to almost everyone in America right now, big or small. About ten years ago I borrowed two million dollars using the hotels as collateral, and invested the money right across the board in stocks and bonds, fairly conservatively and in well-established companies. I built the capital up to nearly five million, which was one of the reasons the hotel losses never bothered me too much—they were always tax deductible against the profit I was making in the market. Today I couldn't give those shares away. We may as well use them as toilet paper in the eleven hotels. For the last three weeks I've been selling as fast as I can, but there are no buyers left. The bank foreclosed on my loan last Thursday." Abel couldn't help remembering that it was Thursday when he spoke to the banker. "Most people who are affected by the crash have only pieces of paper to cover their loans, but in my case the bank who backed me has the deeds on the eleven hotels as security against their original loan. So when the bottom dropped out, they immediately took possession of them. The bastards have let me know that they intend to sell the group as quickly as possible."

"That's madness. They'll get nothing for them right now, and if they supported us through this period, together we could show them a good return on their investment."

"I know *you* could, Abel, but they have my past record to throw back in my face. I went up to their main office to suggest just that. I explained about you and told them I would put all my time into the group if they would give us their backing, but they weren't interested. They fobbed me off with some smooth young puppy who had all the textbook answers about cash flows, no capital base and credit restrictions. By God, if I ever get back, I'll screw him personally and then his bank. Right now, the best thing we can do is get ourselves uproariously drunk, because I am finished, penniless, bankrupt."

"Then so am I," said Abel quietly.

"No, you have a great future ahead of you, son. Anyone who takes over this group couldn't make a move without you."

"You forget that I own twenty-five percent of the group."

Davis Leroy stared at him. It was obvious that that fact had slipped his mind.

"Oh my God, Abel! I hope you didn't put all your money into me." His voice was becoming thick.

"Every last cent," said Abel. "But I don't regret it, Davis. Better to lose with a wise man than win with a fool." He poured himself another bourbon.

The tears were standing in the corners of Davis Leroy's eyes. "You know, Abel, you're the best friend a man could ask for. You knock this hotel into shape, you invest your own money, I make you penniless and you don't even complain. And then for good measure my daughter refuses to marry you."

"You didn't mind my asking her?" said Abel, less incredulous than he would have been without the bourbon.

"Silly little bitch doesn't know a good thing when she sees one. She wants to marry some horse-breeding gentleman from the South with three Confederate generals in his family tree, or if she does marry a northerner, his great grandfather has to have come over on the *Mayflower*. If everyone who claims they had a relative on that boat were ever on board together, the whole damn thing would have sunk a thousand times before it reached America. Too bad I don't have another daughter for you, Abel. No one has served me more loyally than you have. I sure would have been proud to have you as a member of the family. You and I would have made a great team, but I still reckon you can beat them all by yourself. You're young—you still have everything ahead of you."

At twenty-three Abel suddenly felt very old.

"Thank you for your confidence, Davis," he said, "and who gives a damn for the stock market anyway? You know, you're the best friend I ever had." The drink was beginning to talk.

Abel poured himself yet another bourbon and threw it down. Between them they had finished both bottles by early morning. When Davis fell asleep in his chair, Abel managed to stagger down to the tenth floor, undress and collapse onto his own bed. He was awakened from a heavy sleep by a loud banging on the door. His head was going round and round, but the banging went on and on, louder and louder. Somehow he managed to get himself off the bed and grope his way to the door. It was a bellboy.

"Come quickly, Mr. Abel, come quickly," the boy said as he ran down the hall.

Abel threw on a dressing gown and slippers and staggered down the corridor to join the bellboy, who was holding back the elevator door for him.

"Quickly, Mr. Abel," the boy repeated.

"What's the hurry?" demanded Abel, his head still going around as the elevator moved slowly down. Then he recalled the evening's talk. Maybe the bank had come to take possession.

"Someone has jumped out the window."

Abel sobered up immediately. "A guest?"

"Yes, I think so," said the bellboy, "but I'm not sure."

The elevator came to a stop at the ground floor. Abel thrust back the iron gates and ran out into the street. The police were already there. He wouldn't have recognized the body if it had not been for the checked jacket. A policeman was taking down details. A man in plainclothes came over to Abel.

"You the manager?"

"Yes, I am."

"Do you have any idea who this man might be?"

"Yes," said Abel, slurring the word. "His name is Davis Leroy."

"Do you know where he's from or how we can contact his next of kin?"

Abel averted his eyes away from the broken body and answered automatically.

"He's from Dallas and a Miss Melanie Leroy, his daughter, is his next of kin. She's a student living out on the Chicago University campus."

"Right. We'll get someone right over to her."

"No, don't do that. I'll go and see her myself," said Abel.

"Thank you. It's always better if they don't hear the news from a stranger."

"What a terrible, unnecessary thing," said Abel, his eyes drawn back to the body of his friend.

"It's the seventh in Chicago today," said the officer flatly as he closed his little black notebook. "We'll be needing to check his room later. Don't rent it again until we give you an all clear."

"Whatever you say, officer."

The policeman strolled over toward the ambulance.

Abel watched the stretcher-bearers remove Davis Leroy's body from the sidewalk. He felt cold, sank to his knees and was violently sick in the gutter. Once again he had lost his closest friend. Perhaps if I had drunk less and *thought* more, I might have saved him. He picked himself up and returned to his room, took a long, cold shower and somehow managed to get himself dressed. He ordered some black coffee and then, reluctantly, went up to the Presidential Suite and unlocked the door. Other than a couple of empty bourbon bottles, there seemed to be no sign of the drama that had been enacted there a few minutes earlier. Then he saw the letters on the side table by a bed, which had not been slept in. The first was addressed to Melanie, the second to a lawyer in Dallas and the third to Abel. He tore his open but could barely read Davis Leroy's last words.

Dear Abel,

I'm taking the only way out after the bank's decision. There is nothing left for me to live for as I am far too old to start over. I want you to know I believe you're the one person who might make something good come out of this terrible mess.

I have made a new will in which I have left you the other 75 percent of the stock in the Richmond Group. I realize the stock is useless, but it will secure your position as the legal owner of the group. As you had the guts to buy 25 percent with your own money, you deserve the right to see if you can make some deal with the bank. I've left everything else I own, including the house, to Melanie. Please be the one who tells her. Don't let it be the police. I would have been proud to have you as a son-in-law, partner.

Your friend,
Davis

Abel read the letter again and again and then folded it neatly and placed it in his wallet.

He went over to the university campus later that morning and broke the news as gently as he could to Melanie. He sat nervously on the couch, unsure what he could add to the bland statement of death. She took it surprisingly well, almost as if she had known what was going to happen, although she was obviously moved. No tears in front of Abel—perhaps later when he wasn't there. He felt sorry for her for the first time in his life.

Abel returned to the hotel, decided not to have any lunch and asked a waiter to bring him a glass of tomato juice while he went over his mail. There was a letter from Curtis Fenton at the Continental Trust. It was obviously going to be a day for letters. Fenton had received the advice that a Boston bank called Kane and Cabot had taken over the financial responsibility of the Richmond Group. For the time being, business was to continue as usual, until meetings had been arranged with Mr. Davis Leroy to discuss the disposal of all the hotels in the Group. Abel sat staring at the words, and after a second glass of tomato juice, he drafted a letter to the chairman of Kane and Cabot, a Mr. Alan Lloyd. He received a reply some five days later asking Abel to attend a meeting in Boston on January 4 to discuss the liquidation of the group with the director in charge of bankruptcies. The interval would give the bank enough time to sort out the implications of Mr. Leroy's sudden and tragic death.

Sudden and tragic death? "And who caused that death?" said Abel aloud in a fury, remembering Davis Leroy's own words: *"They fobbed me off with some smooth young puppy. . . . By God, if I ever get back, I'll screw him personally and then his bank."*

"Don't worry, Davis, I'll do the job for you," Abel said out loud.

Abel ran the Richmond Continental during the last weeks of that year with rigid control of his staff and prices and just managed to keep his head above water. He couldn't help wondering what was happening to the other ten hotels in the group, but he didn't have the time to find out and it was not his responsibility anyway.

CHAPTER
SEVENTEEN

On January 4, 1930, Abel Rosnovski arrived in Boston. He took a taxi from the station to Kane and Cabot and was a few minutes early. He sat in the reception room, which was larger and more ornate than any bedroom in the Chicago Richmond. He started reading *The Wall Street Journal*. Nineteen thirty was going to be a better year, the paper was trying to assure him. He doubted it. A prim middle-aged woman entered the room.

"Mr. Kane will see you now, Mr. Rosnovski."

Abel rose and followed her down a long corridor into a small oak-paneled room with a large leather-topped desk, behind which sat a tall, good-looking man who must, Abel thought, have been about the same age as himself. His eyes were as blue as Abel's. There was a picture on the wall behind him of an older man, whom the young man behind the desk greatly resembled. I'll bet that's Dad, Abel thought bitterly. You can be sure he'll survive the collapse; banks always seem to win both ways.

"My name is William Kane," said the young man, rising and extending his hand. "Please have a seat, Mr. Rosnovski."

"Thank you," said Abel.

William stared at the little man in his ill-fitting suit but also noted the determined eyes. "Perhaps you will allow me to apprise you of the latest situation as I see it," continued the blue-eyed banker.

"Of course."

"Mr. Leroy's tragic and premature death . . ." William began, hating the pomposity of his words.

Caused by your callousness, thought Abel.

". . . seems to have left you with the immediate job of running the Richmond Group until the bank is in a position to find a buyer for the hotels. Although one hundred percent of the shares of the group are now in your name, the property, in the form of eleven hotels, which was held as collateral for the late Mr. Leroy's loan of two million dollars, is legally in our possession. This leaves you with no responsibility at all, and if you wish to disassociate yourself from the whole program, we will naturally understand."

An insulting thing to suggest, thought William, but it has to be said.

The sort of thing a banker would expect a man to do, walk away from something the moment any problem arose, thought Abel.

William Kane continued. "Until the two million debt to the bank is cleared I fear we must consider the estate of the late Mr. Leroy insolvent. We at the bank appreciate your personal involvement with the group and we have done nothing about disposing of the hotels until we had the opportunity to speak to you in person. We thought it possible you might know of a party interested in the purchase of the property, as the buildings, the land and the business are obviously a valuable asset."

"But not valuable enough for you to back me," said Abel. He ran his hand wearily through his thick, dark hair. "How long will you give me to find a buyer?"

William hesitated for a moment when he saw the silver band around Abel Rosnovski's wrist. He had seen that band somewhere before, but he couldn't think where. "Thirty days. You must understand that the bank is carrying the day-to-day losses on ten of the eleven hotels. Only the Chicago Richmond is making a small profit."

"If you would give me the time and backing, Mr. Kane, I could turn all the hotels into profitable concerns. I know I

could," said Abel. "Just give me the chance to prove I can do
it, sir." Abel found the last word sticking in his throat.

"So Mr. Leroy assured the bank when he came to see us
last fall," said William. "But these are hard times. There's no
telling if the hotel trade will pick up, and we are not hote-
liers, Mr. Rosnovski; we are bankers."

Abel was beginning to lose his temper with the smoothly
dressed "young puppy"; Davis had been right. "They'll be
hard times, all right, for my hotel staff," he said. "What will
they do if you sell off the roofs from over their heads? What
do you imagine will happen to them?"

"I am afraid they are not our responsibility, Mr. Rosnovski. I must act in the bank's best interests."

"In *your* own best interests, Mr. Kane?" said Abel hotly.

The other man flushed. "That is an unjust remark, Mr.
Rosnovski, and I would greatly resent it if I did not understand what you are going through."

"Too bad you didn't wheel out your understanding in
time for Davis Leroy," said Abel. "He could have used it.
You killed him, Mr. Kane, just as surely as if you had pushed
him out of that window yourself, you and your Simon-pure
colleagues, sitting here on your asses while we sweat our
guts out to be sure you can take a rake-off when times are
good and tread on people when times are bad."

William, too, was becoming angry. Unlike Abel Rosnovski, he did not show it. "This line of discussion is getting
us nowhere, Mr. Rosnovski. I must warn you that if you are
unable to find a purchaser for the group within thirty days, I
shall have no choice but to put the hotels up for auction on
the open market."

"You'll be advising me to ask another bank for a loan
next," said Abel sarcastically. "You *know* my record and you
won't back me, so where the hell do you expect me to go
from here?"

"I'm afraid I have no idea," replied William. "That's entirely up to you. My board's instructions are simply to wind
up the account as quickly as possible and that is what I intend to do. Perhaps you would be kind enough to contact

me no later than February fourth and let me know whether you have had any success in finding a buyer. Good day, Mr. Rosnovski."

William rose from behind the desk and again offered his hand. This time Abel ignored it and went to the door.

"I thought after our phone conversation, Mr. Kane, you might feel embarrassed enough to offer a helping hand. I was wrong. You're just a bastard through and through, so when you go to bed at night, Mr. Kane, be sure to think about me. When you wake up in the morning, think about me again, because I'll never cease thinking about my plans for you."

William stood frowning at the closed door. The silver band bothered him—where had he seen it before?

His secretary returned. "What a dreadful little man," she said.

"No, not really," said William. "He thinks we killed his business partner, and now we are disbanding his company without any thought for his employees, not to mention himself, when he has actually proved to be very capable. Mr. Rosnovski was remarkably polite given the circumstances and I must confess I was almost sorry the board felt unable to back him." William looked up at his secretary.

"Get Mr. Cohen on the phone."

CHAPTER
EIGHTEEN

Abel arrived back in Chicago on the morning of the following day, still preoccupied and furious with his treatment at the hands of William Kane. He didn't catch exactly what the boy was shouting at the corner newsstand as he hailed a cab and climbed into the back seat.

"The Richmond Hotel, please."

"Are you from the newspapers?" asked the cabdriver as he moved out onto State Street.

"No. What made you ask that?" said Abel.

"Oh, only because you asked for the Richmond. All the reporters are there today."

Abel couldn't remember any functions scheduled for the Richmond which would attract the press.

The driver continued: "If you're not a newspaperman, maybe I should take you to another hotel."

"Why?" asked Abel, even more puzzled.

"Well, you won't have a very good night's sleep if you're booked in there. The Richmond has been burned to the ground."

As the cab turned the corner of the block, Abel was faced head on with the smoldering shell of the Chicago Richmond. Police cars, fire engines, charred wood and water flooding the street. He stepped out of the cab and stared at the scorched remains of the flagship of Davis Leroy's group.

The Pole is wise when the damage is done, thought Abel

as he clenched his fist and started banging on his lame leg.
He felt no pain—there was nothing left to feel.

"You bastards!" he shouted aloud. "I've been lower than
this before, and I'll still beat every one of you. Germans,
Russians, Turks, that bastard Kane and now this. Everyone.
I'll beat you all. Nobody kills Abel Rosnovski."

The assistant manager saw Abel gesticulating by the cab
and ran over to him. Abel forced himself to be calm.

"Did everybody get out safely?" he asked.

"Yes, thank God. The hotel was nearly empty, so getting
everyone out was no great problem. There were one or two
minor injuries and burns—the people were taken to the hospital—but there's nothing for you to worry about."

"Good. At least that's a relief. Thank God the hotel was
well insured—over a million, if I remember. We may yet be
able to turn this disaster to our advantage."

"Not if what they're suggesting in this morning's papers
is true."

"What do you mean?" asked Abel.

"I'd rather you read it for yourself, boss," the assistant
manager replied.

Abel walked over to the nearby newsstand and paid the
boy two cents for the latest edition of the *Chicago Tribune*.
The banner headline told it all:

RICHMOND HOTEL BLAZE — ARSON SUSPECTED

Abel shook his head incredulously and reread the headline.

"Can anything else happen?" he muttered.

"Got yourself a problem?" the newsboy asked.

"A little one," said Abel, and returned to his assistant
manager.

"Who's in charge of the police inquiry?"

"That officer over there leaning on the police car," said
the assistant manager, pointing to a tall, spare man who was
going prematurely bald. "His name is Lieutenant O'Malley."

"It would be," said Abel. "Now, you get the staff into the

annex and I'll see them all there at ten o'clock tomorrow morning. If anybody wants me before then, I'll be staying at the Stevens until I get this thing sorted out."

"Will do, boss."

Abel walked over to Lieutenant O'Malley and introduced himself.

The tall, spare policeman stooped slightly to shake hands with Abel.

"Ah, the long-lost ex-manager has returned to his charred remains."

"I don't find that funny, officer," said Abel.

"I'm sorry," he said. "It isn't funny. It's been a long night. Let's go and have a drink."

The policeman took Abel by the elbow and guided him across Michigan Avenue to a diner on the corner. Lieutenant O'Malley ordered two milk shakes.

Abel laughed when the white, frothy mixture was put in front of him. Since he had never had a youth, it was his first milk shake.

"I know. It's funny, everybody in this city breaks the law drinking bourbon and beer," said the detective, "so someone has to play it straight. In any case, Prohibition isn't going to last forever, and then my troubles will begin, because the gangsters are going to discover I really do like milk shakes."

Abel laughed for a second time.

"Now to your problems, Mr. Rosnovski. First I have to tell you, I don't think you have a snowball's chance in hell of picking up the insurance on that hotel. The fire experts have been going over the remains of the building with a fine tooth comb and they found the place was soaked in kerosene. No attempt to even disguise it. There were traces of the stuff all over the basement. One match and the building must have gone up like a Roman candle."

"Do you have any idea who is responsible?" asked Abel.

"Let me ask the questions. Do you have any idea who might bear a grudge against the hotel or you personally?"

Abel grunted. "About fifty people, Lieutenant. I cleared

out a real can of worms when I first arrived here. I can give you a list, if you think it might help."

"I think it might, but the way people are talking out there, I may not need it," said the Lieutenant. "But if you pick up any definite information, let me know, Mr. Rosnovski. You let me know, because I warn you, you have enemies out there." He pointed into the milling street.

"What do you mean?" asked Abel.

"Someone is saying you did it because you lost everything in the crash and needed the insurance money."

Abel leaped off his stool.

"Calm down, calm down. I know you were in Boston all day and, more important, you have a reputation in Chicago for building hotels up, not burning them down. But someone did burn the Richmond down and you can bet your ass I'm going to find out who. So let's leave it at that for the moment." He swiveled off his own stool. "The milk shake's on me, Mr. Rosnovski. I'll expect a favor from you sometime in the future."

As the two men walked toward the door, the policeman smiled at the girl at the cash register, admiring her ankles and cursing the new fashion for long skirts. He handed her fifty cents. "Keep the change, honey."

"A big thank you," the girl said.

"Nobody appreciates me," said the lieutenant.

Abel laughed for a third time, which he would not have thought possible an hour before.

"By the way," the lieutenant continued as they reached the door. "The insurance people are looking for you. I can't remember the name of the guy, but I guess he'll find you. Don't hit him. If he feels you were involved, who can blame him? Keep in touch, Mr. Rosnovski—I'll be wanting to talk to you again."

Abel watched the lieutenant vanish into the crowd of spectators and then walked slowly over to the Stevens Hotel and booked himself in for the night. The desk clerk, who had already checked in most of the Richmond's guests, couldn't suppress a smile at the idea of booking the manager in, too.

Once in his room, Abel sat down and wrote a formal letter to Mr. William Kane, giving him whatever details of the fire he could supply and telling him that he intended to use his unexpected freedom to make a round of the other hotels in the group. Abel could see no point in hanging around in Chicago warming himself in the Richmond embers, in the vain hope that someone would come along and bail him out.

After a first-class breakfast at the Stevens the next morning—it always made Abel feel good to be in a well-run hotel—he walked over to see Curtis Fenton at the Continental Trust to apprise him of Kane and Cabot's attitude—or to be more accurate, of William Kane's attitude. Although Abel thought the request was pointless, he added that he was looking for a buyer for the Richmond group at $2 million.

"That fire isn't going to help us, but I'll see what I can do," said Fenton, sounding far more positive than Abel had expected. "At the time you bought the twenty-five percent from Miss Leroy I told you that I thought the hotels were a valuable asset and that you'd made a good deal. Despite the crash I see no reason to change my mind about that, Mr. Rosnovski. I've watched you running your hotel for nearly two years now, and I'd back you if the decision were left to me personally, but I fear my bank would never agree to support the Richmond Group. We've seen the financial situation for far too long to have any faith in the group's future, and that fire was the last straw. Nevertheless, I do have some outside contacts and I'll see if they can do anything to help. You probably have more admirers in this city than you realize, Mr. Rosnovski."

After Lieutenant O'Malley's comments, Abel had wondered if he had any friends left in Chicago at all. He thanked Curtis Fenton, returned to the teller's cage and withdrew $5,000 in cash from the hotel account. He spent the rest of the morning in the Richmond annex. He gave every member of his staff two weeks' wages and told them they could stay on at the annex for at least a month or until they had found new jobs. He then returned to the Stevens, packed the new clothes he'd had to buy as a result of the fire and prepared for a tour of the rest of the Richmond hotels.

He drove south in the Buick he'd bought just before the stock market crash and started with the St. Louis Richmond. The trip to all the hotels in the group took nearly four weeks and although they were run-down and, without exception, losing money, none of them was, in Abel's view, a hopeless case. They all had good locations; some were even the best-placed in the city. Old man Leroy must have been a shrewder man than his son, thought Abel. He checked every hotel insurance policy carefully; no problems there. When he finally reached the Dallas Richmond, he was certain of only one thing: that anyone who managed to buy the group for $2 million would be making himself a good deal. He wished he could be given the chance, because he knew exactly what had to be done to make the group profitable.

On his return to Chicago he again checked into the Stevens. There were several messages awaiting him. Lieutenant O'Malley wished to contact him. So did William Kane, Curtis Fenton and finally a Mr. Henry Osborne.

Abel started with the law, and after a short phone conversation with O'Malley, agreed to meet him at the diner on Michigan Avenue. Abel sat on a stool, with his back to the counter, staring at the charred shell of the Richmond Hotel while he waited for the lieutenant. O'Malley was a few minutes late, but he did not bother to apologize as he took the next stool and swiveled around to face Abel.

"Why do we keep meeting like this?" asked Abel.

"You owe me a favor," said the lieutenant, "and nobody in Chicago gets away with owing O'Malley a milk shake."

Abel ordered two, one giant, one regular.

"What did you find out?" asked Abel as he passed the detective two red-and-white-striped straws.

"The boys from the fire department were right—it was arson okay. We've arrested a guy called Desmond Pacey, who turns out to be the old manager at the Richmond. That was in your time, right?"

"I'm afraid it was," said Abel.

"Why do you say that?" asked the lieutenant.

"I had Pacey fired for embezzling hotel receipts. He said he'd get even with me if it was the last thing he did. I didn't pay any attention—I've had too many threats in my life, Lieutenant, to take any one of them that seriously, especially from a creature like Pacey."

"Well, I have to tell you we've taken him seriously, and so have the insurance people, because I'm told they're not paying out one penny until it's proved there was no collusion between you and Pacey over the fire."

"That's all I need at the moment," said Abel. "How can you be so certain it's Pacey?"

"We traced him to the casualty ward at the local hospital, the same day as the fire. A routine check asking the hospital to give us the names of everyone who had come in that day with severe burns. By chance—which is so often the case in police work since we're not all born to be Sherlock Holmes—a sergeant's wife heard the name. She had been a waitress at the Richmond and told us he used to be the manager. Even I can put those two and two's together. The guy came clean pretty quick—didn't seem that interested in not being caught, only in pulling off what he called his own St. Valentine's Day massacre. Until a few moments ago I wasn't sure what the object of that revenge was, but I sure know now—though I'm not too surprised. So that just about wraps the case up, Mr. Rosnovski."

The lieutenant sucked on his straw until a loud gurgle convinced him he had drained the last drop.

"Have another milk shake?" asked Abel.

"No, I'll pass it up. I've got a heavy day ahead of me." He stood up. "Good luck, Mr. Rosnovski. If you can prove to the insurance boys you had no involvement with Pacey, you'll get your money. I'll do everything I can to help if the case reaches court. Keep in touch."

Abel watched him disappear through the door. He gave the waitress a dollar and then, outside, stood on the sidewalk staring into space, a space where the Richmond Hotel had been less than a month ago. Then he turned and walked back to the Stevens.

There was another message from Henry Osborne, still leaving no clue as to who he was. There was only one way to find out. Abel called Osborne, who turned out to be a claims inspector with the Great Western Casualty Insurance Company, with which the hotel had its policy. Abel made an appointment to see Osborne at noon. He then called William Kane in Boston and gave him a report on the hotels he had visited in the group.

"And may I say again, Mr. Kane, that I could turn those hotels' losses into profits if your bank would give me the time and the backing. What I did in Chicago I know I can do for the rest of the group."

"Possibly you could, Mr. Rosnovski, but I fear it will not be with Kane and Cabot's money. May I remind you that you have only a few days left in which to find a backer. Good day, sir."

"Ivy League snob," said Abel into the deaf telephone. "I'm not classy enough for your money, am I? Someday, you bastard . . ."

The next item on Abel's agenda was the insurance man. Henry Osborne turned out to be a tall, good-looking man with dark eyes and a mop of dark hair just turning gray. Abel found his easy manner congenial. Osborne had little to add to Lieutenant O'Malley's story. The Great Western Casualty Insurance Company had no intention of paying any part of the claim while the police were pressing for a charge of arson against Desmond Pacey and until it was proved that Abel himself was in no way involved. Henry Osborne seemed to be very understanding about the whole problem.

"Has the Richmond Group enough money to rebuild the hotel?" asked Osborne.

"Not a red cent," said Abel. "The rest of the group is mortgaged up to the hilt and the bank is pressing me to sell."

"Why you?" said Osborne.

Abel explained how he had come to own the group's shares without actually owning the hotels. Henry Osborne seemed somewhat surprised.

"Surely the bank can see for themselves how well you ran this hotel? Every businessman in Chicago is aware that you were the first manager ever to make a profit for Davis Leroy. I realize the banks are going through hard times, but even they ought to know when to make an exception for their own good."

"Not this bank."

"Continental Trust?" said Osborne. "I've always found old Curtis Fenton a bit starchy but amenable enough."

"It's not Continental. The hotels are owned by a Boston bank called Kane and Cabot."

Henry Osborne went white and sank back in his chair.

"Are you all right?" asked Abel.

"Yes, I'm fine."

"You don't by any chance know Kane and Cabot?"

"Off the record?" said Henry Osborne.

"Sure."

"Yes, my company had to deal with them once before in the past." He seemed to be hesitating. "And we ended up having to take them to court."

"Why?"

"I can't reveal the details. A messy business—let's just say one of the directors was not totally honest and open with us."

"Which one?" asked Abel.

"Which one did you have to deal with?" Osborne inquired.

"A man named William Kane."

Osborne seemed to hesitate again. "Be careful," he said. "He's the world's meanest son of a bitch. I can give you the lowdown on him if you want it, but that would be strictly between us."

"I certainly owe him no favors," said Abel. "I may well be in touch with you, Mr. Osborne. I have a score to settle with young Mr. Kane for his treatment of Davis Leroy."

"Well, you can count on me to help in any way I can if William Kane is involved," said Henry Osborne, rising from behind his desk, "but that must be strictly between us. And if the court shows that Desmond Pacey burned the Richmond and no one else was involved, the company will pay up the same day. Then perhaps we can do additional business with your other hotels."

"Perhaps," said Abel.

He walked back to the Stevens and decided to have lunch and find out for himself how well the main dining room was run. There was another message at the desk for him. A Mr. David Maxton wondered if Abel was free to join him for lunch at one.

"David Maxton," Abel said out loud, and the receptionist looked up. "Why do I know that name?" he asked the staring girl.

"He owns this hotel, Mr. Rosnovski."

"Ah, yes. Please let Mr. Maxton know that I shall be delighted to have lunch with him." Abel glanced at his watch. "And would you tell him that I may be a few minutes late?"

"Certainly, sir," said the girl.

Abel went quickly up to his room and changed into a new white shirt while wondering what David Maxton could possibly want.

The dining room was already packed when Abel arrived. The headwaiter showed him to a private table in an alcove where the owner of the Stevens was sitting alone. He rose to greet Abel.

"Abel Rosnovski, sir."

"Yes, I know you," said Maxton, "or, to be more accurate, I know you by reputation. Do sit down and let's order lunch."

Abel was compelled to admire the Stevens. The food and the service were every bit as good as the Plaza. If he was to have the best hotel in Chicago, he knew it would have to be better than this one.

The headwaiter reappeared with menus. Abel studied his carefully, politely declined a first course and selected the beef, the quickest way to tell if a restaurant is dealing with the right butcher. David Maxton did not look at his menu and simply ordered the salmon. The headwaiter hurried away.

"You must be wondering why I invited you to join me for lunch, Mr. Rosnovski."

"I assumed," said Abel, laughing, "you were going to ask me to take over the Stevens for you."

"You're absolutely right, Mr. Rosnovski."

Abel was speechless. It was Maxton's turn to laugh. Even the arrival of their waiter wheeling a trolly of the finest beef did not help. The carver waited. Maxton squeezed lemon over his salmon and continued.

"My manager is due to retire in five months after twenty-two years of loyal service and the assistant manager is also due for retirement very soon afterwards, so I'm looking for a new broom."

"Place looks pretty clean to me," said Abel.

"I'm always willing to improve, Mr. Rosnovski. Never be satisfied with standing still," said Maxton. "I've been watching your activities carefully. It wasn't until you took the Richmond over that it could even be classified as a hotel. It was a huge flophouse before that. In another two or three years, you would have been a rival to the Stevens if some fool hadn't burned the place down before you were given the chance."

"Potatoes, sir?"

Abel looked up at a very attractive junior waitress. She smiled at him.

"No, thank you," he said to her. "Well, I'm very flattered, Mr. Maxton, both by your comments and the offer."

"I think you'd be happy here, Mr. Rosnovski. The Stevens is a well-run hotel and I would be willing to start you off at fifty dollars a week and two percent of the profits. You could start as soon as you like."

"I'll need a few days to think over your generous offer, Mr. Maxton," said Abel, "but I confess I am very tempted.

Nevertheless, I still have a few problems left over from the Richmond."

"String beans, sir?" The same waitress, and the same smile.

The face looked familiar. Abel felt sure he had seen her somewhere before. Perhaps she had once worked at the Richmond.

"Yes, please."

He watched her walk away. There was something about her.

"Why don't you stay on at the hotel as my guest for a few days," Maxton asked, "and see how we run the place? It may help you make your decision."

"That won't be necessary, Mr. Maxton. After only one day as a guest here I knew how well the hotel is run. My problem is that I own the Richmond Group."

David Maxton's face registered surprise. "I had no idea," he said. "I assumed old Davis Leroy's daughter would now be the owner."

"It's a long story," said Abel, and he explained to Maxton how he had come into the ownership of the group's stock.

"The problem is a simple one, Mr. Maxton. What I really want to do is find the two million dollars myself and build that group up into something worthwhile. Something that would even give you a good run for your money."

"I see," said Maxton, looking quizzically at his empty plate. A waiter removed it.

"Would you like some coffee?" The same waitress. The same familiar look. It was beginning to worry Abel.

"And you say Curtis Fenton of Continental Trust is looking for a buyer on your behalf?"

"Yes. He has been for nearly a month," said Abel. "In fact, I'll know later this afternoon if they've had any success, but I'm not optimistic."

"Well, that's most interesting. I had no idea the Richmond Group was looking for a buyer. Will you please keep me informed either way?"

"Certainly," said Abel.

"How much more time is the Boston bank giving you to find the two million?"

"Only a few more days, so it won't be long before I can let you know my decision."

"Thank you," said Maxton. "It's been a pleasure to meet you, Mr. Rosnovski. I feel sure I'd enjoy working with you." He shook Abel's hand warmly.

The waitress smiled at Abel again as he passed her on his way out of the dining room. When Abel reached the head-waiter, he stopped and asked what her name was.

"I'm sorry, sir, we're not allowed to give the names of any of our staff to our customers—it's strictly against company policy. If you have a complaint, perhaps you'd be kind enough to make it to me, sir."

"No complaint," said Abel. "On the contrary, an excellent lunch."

With a job offer under his belt, Abel felt more confident about facing Curtis Fenton. He was certain the banker would not have found a buyer, but nonetheless, he strolled over to the Continental Trust with a spring in his heels. He liked the idea of being the manager of the best hotel in Chicago. Perhaps he could make it the best hotel in America. As soon as he arrived at the bank, he was ushered directly into Curtis Fenton's office. The tall, thin banker—did he wear the same suit every day or did he have three identical ones?—offered Abel a seat, a large smile appearing across his usually solemn face.

"Mr. Rosnovski, how good to see you again. If you had come this morning, I would have had no news to give you, but only a few moments ago I received a call from an interested party."

Abel's heart leaped with surprise and pleasure. He was silent for a few moments and then he said, "Can you tell me who it is?"

"I'm afraid not. The party concerned has given me strict instructions that he must remain anonymous, as the transaction would be a private investment in some potential conflict with his own business."

"David Maxton," Abel murmured. "God bless him."

Curtis Fenton did not respond and continued: "Well, as I said, Mr. Rosnovski, I'm not in a position——"

"Quite, quite," said Abel. "How long do you think it will be before you're in a position to let me know the gentleman's decision one way or the other?"

"I can't be sure at the moment, but I may have more news for you by Monday, so if you happen to be passing by——"

"Happen to be passing by?" said Abel. "You're discussing my whole life."

"Then perhaps we should make a firm appointment for Monday morning."

Abel hummed "Stardust" as he walked down Michigan Avenue on his way back to the Stevens. He took the elevator up to his room and called William Kane to ask for an extension until the following Monday, telling him he thought he might have found a buyer. Kane seemed reluctant but eventually agreed.

"Bastard," Abel repeated several times as he put the phone back on the hook. "Just give me a little time, Kane. You'll live to regret killing Davis Leroy."

Abel sat on the end of his bed, his fingers tapping on the footboard, wondering how he could pass the time waiting for Monday. He wandered down into the hotel lobby. There she was again, the waitress who had served him at lunch, now on tea duty in the Tropical Garden. Abel's curiosity got the better of him and he walked over and took a seat at the far side of the room. She came up.

"Good afternoon, sir," she said. "Would you like some tea?" The same familiar smile again.

"We know each other, don't we?" said Abel.

"Yes, we do, Wladek."

Abel cringed at the sound of the name and reddened slightly, remembering how the short, fair hair had been long and smooth and the veiled eyes had been so inviting. "Zaphia, we *came* to America on the same ship—the *Black Arrow*. Of course, you went to Chicago. What are you doing here?"

"I work here, as you can see. Would you like some tea, sir?" Her Polish accent warmed Abel.

"Have dinner with me tonight," he said.

"I can't, Wladek. We're not allowed to go out with the customers. If we do, we automatically lose our jobs."

"I'm not a customer," said Abel. "I'm an old friend."

". . . who was going to come and visit me in Chicago as soon as he had settled down," said Zaphia. "And when he did come, he didn't even remember I was here."

"I know, I know. Forgive me. Zaphia, have dinner with me tonight. Just this once," said Abel.

"Just this once," she repeated.

"Meet me at Brundage's at seven o'clock. Would that suit you?"

Zaphia flushed at the name. It was probably the most expensive restaurant in Chicago and she would have been nervous to be there as a waitress, let alone as a customer.

"No, let's go somewhere less grand, Wladek."

"Where?" said Abel.

"Do you know The Sausage on the corner of Forty-third?"

"No, I don't," he admitted, "but I'll find it. Seven o'clock."

"Seven o'clock, Wladek. That will be lovely. By the way, do you want any tea?"

"No, I think I'll skip it," said Abel.

She smiled and walked away. He sat watching her serve tea for several minutes. She was much prettier than he had remembered. Perhaps killing time until Monday wasn't going to be so difficult after all.

The Sausage brought back all of Abel's worst memories of his first days in America. He sipped a cold ginger beer while he waited for Zaphia and watched with professional disapproval as the waiters slapped the food around. He was unable to decide which was worse—the service or the food. Zaphia was nearly twenty minutes late by the time she appeared in the doorway, as smart as a bandbox in a crisp yellow dress that had probably been recently let down a few inches to conform with the latest fashion but still revealed how appealing her formerly slight body had filled out. Her gray eyes searched the tables for Wladek, and her pink cheeks reddened as she became conscious that the eyes of many were upon her.

"Good evening, Wladek," she said in Polish as she reached Abel's side.

Abel rose and offered her his chair, which was near an open fire. "I am so glad you could make it," he said in English.

She looked perplexed for a moment, then, in English, she said, "I'm sorry I'm late."

"Oh, I hadn't noticed. Would you like something to drink, Zaphia?"

"No, thank you."

Neither of them spoke for a moment, and then they both tried to talk at once.

"I'd forgotten how pretty . . . ," said Abel.

"How have you . . . ?" said Zaphia.

She smiled shyly and Abel wanted to touch her. He remembered so well experiencing the same reaction the first time he had ever seen her, more than eight years before.

"How's George?" she asked.

"I haven't seen him for over two years," replied Abel, suddenly feeling guilty. "I've been working in a hotel here in Chicago, and then——"

"I know," said Zaphia. "Somebody burned it down."

"Why didn't you ever come over and say hello?" asked Abel.

"I didn't think you'd remember, Wladek, and I was right."

"Then, how did you ever recognize me?" said Abel. "I've put on so much weight."

"Your silver band," she said simply.

Abel looked down at his wrist and laughed. "I have a lot to thank my band for and now I can add that it has brought us back together."

She avoided his eyes. "What are you doing now that you no longer have a hotel to run?"

"I'm looking for a job," said Abel, not wanting to intimidate her with the fact that he'd been offered the chance to manage the Stevens.

"There's a big job coming up at the Stevens. My boyfriend told me."

"Your boyfriend told you?" said Abel, repeating each painful word.

"Yes," she said. "The hotel will soon be looking for a new assistant manager. Why don't you apply for the job? I'm sure you'd have a good chance of getting it, Wladek. I always knew you would be a success in America."

"I might well apply," Abel said. "It was kind of you to think of me. Why doesn't your boyfriend apply?"

"Oh, no, he's far too junior to be considered—he's only a waiter in the dining room with me."

Suddenly Abel wanted to change places with him.

"Shall we have dinner?" he said.

"I'm not used to eating out," Zaphia said. She gazed at the menu. Abel, suddenly aware she still couldn't read English, ordered for them both.

She ate with relish and was full of praise for the indifferent food. Abel found her uncritical enthusiasm a tonic after the bored sophistication of Melanie. They exchanged the history of their lives in America. Zaphia had started in domestic service and progressed to being a waitress at the Stevens, where she had now been for six years. Abel talked of many of his experiences until finally she glanced at his watch.

"Look at the time, Wladek," she said. "It's past eleven and I'm on first breakfast call at six tomorrow."

Abel had not noticed the four hours pass. He would have

happily sat there talking to Zaphia for the rest of the night, soothed by her admiration, which she confessed so artlessly.

"May I see you again, Zaphia?" he asked as they walked back to the Stevens arm in arm.

"If you want to, Wladek."

They stopped at the servants' entrance at the back of the hotel.

"This is where I go in," she said. "If you were to become the assistant manager, Wladek, you'd be allowed to go in by the front entrance."

"Would you mind calling me Abel?" he asked her.

"Abel?" she said as if she were trying the name on like a new glove. "But your name is Wladek."

"It was, but it isn't any longer. My name is Abel Rosnovski."

"Abel's a funny name, but it suits you," she said. "Thank you for dinner, Abel. It was lovely to see you again. Good night."

"Good night, Zaphia," he said, and she was gone.

He watched her disappear through the servants' entrance; then he walked slowly around the block and into the hotel by the front entrance. Suddenly—and not for the first time in his life—he felt very lonely.

Abel spent the weekend thinking about Zaphia and the images associated with her—the stench of the steerage quarters, the confused queues of immigrants on Ellis Island and, above all, their brief but passionate encounter in the lifeboat. He took all his meals in the hotel dining room to be near her and to study the boyfriend, who, Abel had concluded, must be the young, pimply one. He thought he had pimples, he hoped he had pimples—yes, he did have pimples. He was, regrettably, the best-looking boy among the waiters, pimples notwithstanding.

Abel wanted to take Zaphia out on Saturday, but she was working all day. Nevertheless, he managed to accompany her to church on Sunday morning and listened with mingled nostalgia and exasperation to the Polish priest intoning the unforgotten words of the Mass. It was the first time Abel had been in a church since his days at the castle in Poland. At that time he had yet to see or endure the cruelty that now made it impossible for him to believe in any benevolent deity. His reward for attending church came when Zaphia allowed him to hold her hand as they walked back toward the hotel together.

"Have you thought any more about the position at the Stevens?" she inquired.

"I'll know first thing tomorrow morning what their final decision is."

"Oh, I'm so glad, Abel. I'm sure you would make a very good assistant manager."

"Thank you," said Abel, realizing they had been talking about different things.

"Would you like to have supper with my cousins tonight?" Zaphia asked. "I always spend Sunday evening with them."

"Yes, I'd like that very much."

Zaphia's cousins lived right near The Sausage in the heart of the city. Her cousins were very impressed when she arrived with a Polish friend who drove a new Buick. The family, as Zaphia called them, consisted of two sisters, Katya and Janina, and Katya's husband, Janek. Abel presented the sisters with a bunch of roses and then sat down and answered, in fluent Polish, all their questions about his future prospects. Zaphia was obviously embarrassed, but Abel knew the same would be required of any boyfriend in any Polish-American household. Aware that Janek's envious eyes never left him, he made an effort to play down his progress since his early days in the butcher shop. Katya served a simple Polish meal of *pierogi* and *bigos,* which Abel would have eaten with a good deal more relish fifteen years earlier. He gave Janek up as a bad job and concentrated on making the sisters approve of him. It looked as though they did. Perhaps they also approved of the pimply youth. No, they couldn't; he wasn't even Polish—or maybe he was. Abel didn't know his name and had never heard him speak.

On the way back to the Stevens, Zaphia asked, with a flash of the coquettishness he remembered, if it was considered safe to drive a motor car and hold a lady's hand at the same time. Abel laughed and put his hand back on the steering wheel for the rest of the drive back to the hotel.

"Will you have time to see me tomorrow?" he asked.

"I hope so, Abel," she said. "Perhaps by then you'll be my boss. Good luck anyway."

He smiled to himself as he watched her go through the back door, wondering how she would feel if she knew the real consequences of the next day's outcome. He did not move until she had disappeared through the service entrance.

"Assistant manager, indeed," he said, laughing out loud as he climbed into bed, wondering what Curtis Fenton's news would bring in the morning, trying to put Zaphia out of his mind as he threw his pillow onto the floor.

He woke a few minutes before five the next day. The room was still dark when he called for the early edition of the *Tribune*. He went through the motions of reading the financial section and was dressed and ready for breakfast when the restaurant opened at seven o'clock. Zaphia was not serving in the main dining room this morning, but the pimply boyfriend was, which Abel took to be a bad omen. After breakfast he returned to his room; had he but known, only five minutes before Zaphia came on duty. He checked his tie in the mirror for the twentieth time and once again looked at his watch. He estimated that if he walked very slowly, he would arrive at the bank as the doors were opening. In fact, he arrived five minutes early and walked once around the block, staring aimlessly into store windows at expensive jewelry and radios and hand-tailored suits. Would he ever be able to afford clothes like that? he wondered. He arrived back at the bank at four minutes past nine.

"Mr. Fenton is not free at the moment. Can you come

back in half an hour or would you prefer to wait?" the secretary asked.

"I'll come back," said Abel, not wishing to appear over-anxious.

It was the longest thirty minutes he could remember since he had come to Chicago. He studied every shop window on La Salle Street, even the women's clothes, which made him think happily of Zaphia.

On his return to the Continental Trust the secretary informed him that Fenton would see him now.

Abel, his hands sweating, walked into the bank manager's office.

"Good morning, Mr. Rosnovski. Do have a seat."

Curtis Fenton took a file out of his desk. Abel could see "Confidential" written across the cover.

"Now," the older man began, "I hope you will find my news is to your liking. The principal concerned is willing to go ahead with the purchase of the hotels on what I can only describe as favorable terms."

"God Almighty!" said Abel.

Curtis Fenton pretended not to hear him and continued: "In fact, most favorable terms. He will be responsible for putting up the full two million required to clear Mr. Leroy's debt, while at the same time he will form a new company with you in which the shares will be split sixty percent to him and forty percent to you. Your forty percent is therefore valued at eight hundred thousand dollars, which will be treated as a loan to you by the new company, a loan that will be made for a term not to exceed ten years, at four percent, which can be paid off from the company profits at the same rate. That is to say, if the company was to make in any one year a profit of one hundred thousand dollars, forty thousand of that profit would be set against your eight hundred thousand debt, plus the four percent interest. If you clear the loan of eight hundred thousand in under ten years you will be given the one-time option of buying the remaining sixty percent of the company for a further three million dollars. This would give my client a first-class return on his investment and you the opportunity to own the Richmond Group outright.

"In addition to this, you will receive a salary of five thousand dollars per annum, and your position as president of the group will give you complete day-to-day control of the hotels. You will be asked to refer to me only on matters concerning finance. I have been entrusted with the task of reporting directly to your principal and he has asked me to represent his interests on the board of the new Richmond Group. I have been happy to comply with this stipulation. My client does not wish to be involved personally. As I have said before, there might be a conflict of professional interests for him in this transaction, which I am sure you will thoroughly understand. He also insists that you will at no time make any attempt to discover his identity. He will give you fourteen days to consider his terms, on which there can be no negotiation, as he considers—and I must agree with him—that he is striking a more than fair bargain."

Abel could not speak.

"Pray do say something, Mr. Rosnovski."

"I don't need fourteen days to make a decision," said Abel finally. "I accept your client's terms. Please thank him and tell him I will certainly respect his request for anonymity."

"That's splendid," said Curtis Fenton, permitting himself a wry smile. "Now, a few small points. The accounts for all the hotels in the group will be placed with Continental Trust affiliates and the main account will be here in this office under my direct control. I will, in turn, receive one thousand dollars a year as a director of the new company."

"I'm glad you're going to get something out of the deal," said Abel.

"I beg your pardon?" said the banker.

"I'll be pleased to be working with you, Mr. Fenton."

"Your principal has also placed two hundred and fifty thousand dollars on deposit with the bank to be used as the day-to-day finance for the running of the hotels during the next few months. This will also be regarded as a loan at four percent. You are to advise me if this amount turns out to be insufficient for your needs. I consider it would enhance your reputation with my client if you found the two hundred and fifty thousand to be sufficient."

"I shall bear that in mind," said Abel, solemnly trying to imitate the banker's locution.

Curtis Fenton opened a desk drawer and produced a large Cuban cigar.

"Do you smoke?"

"Yes," said Abel, who had never smoked a cigar before in his life.

He coughed himself down La Salle Street all the way back to the Stevens. David Maxton was standing proprietarily in the foyer of the hotel as Abel arrived. Abel stubbed out his half-finished cigar with some relief and walked over to him.

"Mr. Rosnovski, you look a happy man this morning."

"I am, sir, and I am only sorry that I will not be working for you as the manager of this hotel."

"Then so am I, Mr. Rosnovski, but frankly the news doesn't surprise me."

"Thank you for everything," said Abel, injecting as much feeling as he could into the little phrase and the look with which he accompanied it.

He left David Maxton and went into the dining room in search of Zaphia, but she had already gone off duty. Abel took the elevator to his room, relit the cigar, took a cautious puff and called Kane and Cabot. A secretary put him through to William Kane.

"Mr. Kane, I have found it possible to raise the money required for me to take over ownership of the Richmond Group. A Mr. Curtis Fenton of Continental Trust will be in touch with you later today to provide you with the details. There will therefore be no necessity to place the hotels for sale on the open market."

There was a short pause. Abel thought with satisfaction how galling his news must be to William Kane.

"Thank you for keeping me informed, Mr. Rosnovski.

May I say how delighted I am that you found someone to back you. I wish you every success for the future."

"Which is more than I wish you, Mr. Kane."

Abel put the phone down, lay on his bed and thought about the future.

"One day," he promised the ceiling, "I am going to buy your goddamn bank and make you want to jump out of a hotel bedroom on the seventeenth floor." He picked up the phone again and asked the girl on the switchboard to get him Mr. Henry Osborne at Great Western Casualty.

CHAPTER
NINETEEN

William put the telephone back on the hook, more amused than annoyed by Abel Rosnovski's pugnacious approach. He was sorry that he had been unable to persuade the bank to support the little Pole who believed so strongly that he could pull the Richmond Group through. He fulfilled his remaining responsibilities by informing the Financial Committee that Abel Rosnovski had found a backer, preparing the legal documents for the takeover of the hotels and then finally closing the bank's file on the Richmond Group.

William was delighted when Matthew arrived in Boston a few days later to take up his position as manager of the bank's investment department. Charles Lester had made no secret that he considered any professional expertise gained in a rival establishment a valuable part of Matthew's long-term preparation to be chairman of Lester's. William's work load was instantly halved, but his time became even more fully occupied. He found himself dragged, protesting in mock horror, onto tennis courts and into swimming pools at every available free moment; only Matthew's suggestion of a ski trip to Vermont brought a determined "No" from William, but the sudden activity at least served to somewhat alleviate his loneliness and impatience to be with Kate.

Matthew was frankly incredulous. "I must meet the woman who can make William Kane daydream at a board meeting that's discussing whether the bank should buy more gold."

"Wait till you see her, Matthew. I think you'll agree she's a better investment than gold."

"I believe you. I just don't want to be the one to tell Susan. She still thinks you're the only man for her in the world."

William laughed. It had never crossed his mind.

The little pile of letters from Kate, which had been growing weekly, lay in the locked drawer of William's bureau in the Red House. He read them over again and again and soon knew them all virtually by heart. At last the one he had been waiting for came, appropriately dated.

> *Buckhurst Park*
> *14 February 1930*
>
> *Dearest William,*
>
> *Finally I have packed up, sold off, given away or otherwise disposed of everything left here and I shall be coming up to Boston on the nineteenth. I am almost frightened at the thought of seeing you again. What if this whole marvelous enchantment bursts like a bubble in the cold of a winter on the Eastern Seaboard? Dear God, I hope not. I can't be sure how I would have gotten through these lonely months but for you.*
>
> *With love,*
> *Kate*

The night before Kate was due to arrive, William promised himself that he would not rush her into anything that either of them might later regret. It was impossible for him to assess the extent to which her feelings might have developed while she was in a transient state of mind engendered by her husband's death, as he told Matthew.

"Stop being so pathetic," said Matthew. "You're in love and you may as well face that fact."

When he first spotted Kate at the station, William almost abandoned his cautious intentions there and then in the joy of watching that simple smile light up her face. He pushed toward her through the throng of travelers and clasped her so firmly in his arms that she could barely breathe.

"Welcome home, Kate."

William was about to kiss her when she drew away. He was a little surprised.

"William, I don't think you've met my parents."

That night William dined with Kate's family and then saw her every day that he could escape from the bank's problems and Matthew's tennis racket, even if only for a couple of hours. After Matthew had met Kate for the first time, he offered William all his gold shares in exchange for one Kate.

"I never undersell," replied William, "and unlike you, Matthew, I have never been interested in quantity—only quality."

"Then I insist you tell me," demanded Matthew, "where you find someone as valuable as Kate?"

"In the liquidation department, where else?" replied William.

"Turn her into a personal asset, William, quickly, because if you don't, you can be sure I will."

Kane and Cabot's net loss from the 1929 crash came out at over $7 million, which turned out to be about average for a bank its size. Many not much smaller banks had gone under, and William found himself conducting a sustained holding operation throughout 1930, which kept him under constant pressure.

When Franklin D. Roosevelt was elected President of the United States on a ticket of relief, recovery and reform,

William feared that the New Deal would have little to offer Kane and Cabot. Business picked up very slowly and William found himself planning tentatively for expansion.

Meanwhile Tony Simmons, still running the London office, had broadened the scope of its activities and had made a respectable profit for Kane and Cabot during his first two years. His achievements looked all the better against those of William, who had barely been able to break even during the same period.

Late in 1932, Alan Lloyd recalled Tony Simmons to Boston to make a full report to the board on the bank's activities in London. No sooner had Simmons reappeared than he announced his intention of running for the chairmanship when Alan Lloyd retired in fifteen months' time. William was completely taken by surprise, for he had dismissed Simmons's chances when he had disappeared to London under a small cloud. It seemed to William unfair that that cloud had been dispelled, not by Simmons's acuity but simply because the British economy had been a little less paralyzed than American business during the same period.

Tony Simmons returned to London for a further successful year and addressed the first board meeting, after his return, in a blaze of glory, with the announcement that the final third year's figures for the London office would show a profit of over a million dollars, a new record. William had to announce a considerably smaller profit for the same period. The abruptness of Tony Simmons's return to favor left William with only a year in which to persuade the board that they should support him before his opponent's momentum became unstoppable.

Kate listened for hours to William's problems, occasionally offering an understanding comment or a sympathetic reply or chastising him for being overdramatic. Matthew, acting as William's eyes and ears, reported that the voting would fall, as far as was ascertainable, 50-50, split between those who considered William too young to hold such a responsible post as the chairmanship and those who still held Tony Simmons to blame for the extent of the bank's losses

in 1929. It seemed that most of the nonexecutive members
of the board, who had not worked directly with William,
would be more influenced by the age difference between the
two contenders than by any other single factor. Again and
again Matthew heard: "William's time will come." Once,
tentatively, he played the role of Satan the tempter to
William: "With your holdings in the bank, William, you
could remove the entire board, replace them with men of
your own choosing and get yourself elected chairman."

William was only too aware of this route to the top, but
he had already dismissed such tactics without needing seriously to consider them; he wished to become chairman
solely on his merits. That was, after all, the way his father
had achieved the position and it was nothing less than Kate
would expect of him.

On January 2, 1934, Alan Lloyd circulated to every
member the notice of a board meeting that would be held on
his sixty-fifth birthday, its sole purpose being to elect his
successor. As the day for the crucial vote drew nearer,
Matthew found himself carrying the investment department
almost single-handedly, and Kate found herself feeding
them both while they went over the latest state of his campaign again and again. Matthew did not complain once
about the extra workload that was placed on him while
William spent hours planning his bid to capture the chair.
William, conscious that Matthew had nothing to gain by his
success, as he would one day take over his father's bank in
New York—a far bigger proposition than Kane and Cabot—
hoped a time might come when he could offer Matthew the
same unselfish support.

It was to come sooner than he imagined.

When Alan Lloyd's sixty-fifth birthday was celebrated, all
seventeen members of the board were present. The meeting
was opened by the chairman, who made a farewell speech of
only fourteen minutes, which William thought would never
come to an end. Tony Simmons was nervously tapping the

yellow legal pad in front of him with his pen, occasionally looking up at William. Neither was listening to Alan's speech. At last Alan sat down, to loud applause, or as loud as is appropriate for sixteen Boston bankers. When the clapping had died away, Alan Lloyd rose for the last time as chairman of Kane and Cabot.

"And now, gentlemen, we must elect my successor. The board is presented with two outstanding candidates, the director of our overseas division, Mr. Anthony Simmons, and the director of the American investment department, Mr. William Kane. They are both well known to you, gentlemen, and I have no intention of speaking in detail on their respective merits. Instead I have asked each candidate to address the board on how he would see the future of Kane and Cabot were he to be elected chairman."

William rose first, as had been agreed between the two contestants the night before on the toss of a coin, and addressed the board for twenty minutes, explaining in detail that it would be his intention to move into fields where the bank had not previously ventured. In particular he wanted to broaden the bank's base and to get out of a depressed New England, moving close to the center of banking, which he believed was now in New York. He even mentioned the possibility of opening a holding company that might specialize in commercial banking (the heads of some of the older board members shook in disbelief). He wanted the bank to consider more expansion, to challenge the new generation of financiers now leading America and to see Kane and Cabot enter the second half of the twentieth century as one of the largest financial institutions in the United States. When he sat down he was satisfied by the murmurs of approbation; his speech had, on the whole, been well received by the board.

When Tony Simmons rose, he took a far more conservative line: the bank should consolidate its position for the next few years, moving only into carefully selected areas and sticking to the traditional modes of banking that had given Kane and Cabot the reputation it currently enjoyed.

He had learned his lesson during the crash and his main concern, he added—to laughter—was to be certain that Kane
and Cabot did enter the second half of the twentieth century
at all. Tony spoke prudently and with an authority that
William was aware he was too young to match. When Tony
sat down, William had no way of knowing in whose favor
the board might swing, though he still believed that the majority would be more inclined to opt for expansion rather
than standing still.

Alan Lloyd informed the other directors that neither he
nor the two contestants intended to vote. The fourteen voting
members received their little ballots, which they duly filled
in and passed back to Alan, who, acting as teller, began to
count slowly. William found he could not look up from his
doodle-covered pad, which also bore the imprint of his
sweating hand. When Alan had completed the task of counting, a hush came over the room.

He announced six votes for Kane, six votes for Simmons,
with two abstentions. Whispered conversation broke out
among the board members, and Alan called for order.
William took a deep and audible breath in the silence that
followed.

Alan Lloyd paused and then said, "I feel that the appropriate course of action given the circumstances is to have a
second vote. If any member who abstained on the first ballot
finds himself able to support a candidate on this occasion,
that might give one of the contestants an overall majority."

The little slips were passed out again. William could not
bear even to watch the process this time. While members
wrote their choices, he listened to the steel-nibbed pens
scratching across the voting papers. Once again the ballots
were returned to Alan Lloyd. Once again he opened them
slowly one by one, and this time he called out the names as
he read them.

" 'William Kane.' "

" 'Anthony Simmons,' 'Anthony Simmons,' 'Anthony
Simmons.' "

Three votes to one for Tony Simmons.

" 'William Kane,' 'William Kane.'

" 'Anthony Simmons.'

" 'William Kane,' 'William Kane,' 'William Kane.' "

Six votes to four in favor of William.

" 'Anthony Simmons,' 'Anthony Simmons.'

" 'William Kane.'

" 'Seven votes to six in favor of William."

It seemed to William, holding his breath, to take Alan Lloyd a lifetime to open the final voting slip.

" 'Anthony Simmons,' " he declared. "The vote is seven all, gentlemen."

William knew that Alan Lloyd would now be obliged to cast the deciding vote, and although he had never told anyone whom he supported for the chair, William had always assumed that if the vote came to a deadlock, Alan would back him against Tony Simmons.

"As the voting has twice resulted in a dead heat and since I assume that no member of the board is likely to change his mind, I must cast my vote for the candidate whom I feel should succeed me as chairman of Kane and Cabot. I know none of you will envy my position, but I have no alternative except to stand by my own judgment and back the man I feel should be the next chairman of the bank. That man is Tony Simmons."

William could not believe the words he heard, and Tony Simmons looked almost as shocked. He rose from his seat opposite William to a round of applause, changed places with Alan Lloyd at the head of the table and addressed Kane and Cabot for the first time as the bank's new chairman. He thanked the board for its support and praised William for never having used his strong financial and familial position to try to influence the vote. He invited William to be vice chairman of the board and suggested that Matthew Lester should replace Alan Lloyd as a director; both suggestions received unanimous support.

William sat staring at the portrait of his father, acutely conscious of having failed him.

CHAPTER
TWENTY

Abel stubbed out the Corona for a second time and swore that he would not light another cigar until he had cleared the $2 million that he needed for complete control of the Richmond Group. This was no time for big cigars, with the Dow Jones index at its lowest point in history and long soup lines forming in every major city in America. He gazed at the ceiling and considered his priorities. First, he needed to salvage the best of the staff from the Chicago Richmond.

He climbed off the bed, put on his jacket and walked over to the hotel annex, where most of those who had not found employment since the fire were still living. Abel re-employed everyone whom he trusted, giving all those who were willing to leave Chicago work in one of the remaining ten hotels. He made his position very clear that in a period of record unemployment their jobs were secure only as long as the hotels started to show a profit. He realized all the other hotels in the group were being run as dishonestly as the old Chicago Richmond had been; he wanted that changed—and changed quickly. He put his three assistant managers in Chicago in charge of one hotel each, the Dallas Richmond, the Cincinnati Richmond and the St. Louis Richmond. He appointed new assistant managers for the remaining seven hotels—in Houston, Mobile, Charleston, Atlanta, Memphis, New Orleans and Louisville. The original Leroy hotels had all been situated in the South and Midwest. The Chicago

Richmond was the only one Davis Leroy himself had been responsible for building. It took Abel another three weeks to get the old Chicago staff settled into their new hotels.

Abel decided to set up his own headquarters in the Chicago Richmond annex and to open a small restaurant on the ground floor. It made sense to be near his backer and his banker rather than settling in one of the hotels in the South. Moreover, Zaphia was in Chicago, and Abel felt with certainty that given a little time she would drop the pimply youth and fall in love with him. She was the only woman he had ever known with whom he felt self-assured. When Abel was about to leave for New York to recruit more specialized staff, he exacted a promise from her that she would no longer see the pimply boyfriend.

The night before Abel's departure he and Zaphia slept together for the first time. She was soft, plump, giggly and delicious.

Abel's attentive care and gentle expertise took Zaphia by surprise.

"How many girls have there been since the *Black Arrow*?" she teased him.

"None that I really cared about," he replied.

"Enough of them to forget *me*," she added.

"I never forgot you," he said untruthfully, leaning over to kiss her, convinced it was the only way to stop the conversation.

When Abel arrived in New York, the first thing he did was to look up George, whom he found out of work and living in a garret on East Third Street. Abel had forgotten what the houses in this neighborhood could be like when shared by twenty families. The smell of stale food in every room, toilets that didn't flush and beds that were slept in by three different people every twenty-four hours. The bakery, it seemed, had been closed down, and George's uncle had had to find employment at a large mill on the outskirts of New York. The mill could not take on George as well. George leaped at the chance to join Abel and the Richmond Group—in any capacity.

Abel recruited three new employees: a pastry chef, a comptroller and a headwaiter before he and George traveled back to Chicago to set up base in the Richmond annex. Abel was pleased with the outcome of his trip. Most hotels on the East Coast had cut their staff to a bare minimum, which had made it easy to pick up experienced people, one of them from the Plaza itself.

In early March, Abel and George set out for a tour of the remaining hotels in the group. Abel asked Zaphia to join them on the trip, even offering her the chance to work in any of the hotels she chose, but she would not budge from Chicago, the only place in America familiar to her. As a compromise she went to live in Abel's rooms at the Richmond annex while he was away. George, who had acquired middle-class morals along with his American citizenship, and who had had a Catholic upbringing as well, urged the advantages of matrimony on Abel, who, lonely in impersonal hotel rooms, was a ready listener.

It came as no surprise to Abel to find that the other hotels were still being incompetently, and in most cases dishonestly, run, but high national unemployment encouraged most of the staff to welcome his arrival as the savior of the group's fortunes. Abel did not find it necessary to fire staff in the grand manner he adopted when he had first arrived in Chicago. Most of those who knew of his reputation and feared his methods had already departed. Some heads had to fall and they inevitably were attached to the necks of those people who had worked with the Richmond Group for a considerable time and who could not or would not change their unorthodox ways merely because Davis Leroy was dead. In several cases, Abel found that moving personnel from one hotel to another engendered a new attitude. By the end of his first year as president the Richmond Group was operating with only half the staff it had employed in the past and showed a net loss of only a little over $100,000. The voluntary turnover among the staff was very low; Abel's confidence in the future of the group was infectious.

Abel set himself the target of breaking even in 1932. He felt that the only way he could achieve such a rapid profitability was to let every manager in the group take the responsibility for his own hotel with a share in the profits, much in the way that Davis Leroy had treated him when he had first come to the Chicago Richmond.

Abel moved from hotel to hotel, never letting up, and never staying in one particular place for more than three weeks at a time. He did not allow anyone, other than the faithful George, his surrogate eyes and ears in Chicago, to know at which hotel he might arrive next. For months he broke this exhausting routine only to visit Zaphia or Curtis Fenton.

After a full assessment of the group's financial position, Abel had to make some more unpleasant decisions. The most drastic was to close temporarily the two hotels, in Mobile and Charleston, that were losing so much money that he felt they would become a hopeless drain on the rest of the group's finances. The staff at the other hotels watched the ax fall and worked even harder. Every time he arrived back at his little office in the Richmond annex in Chicago there was a clutch of memos demanding immediate attention—burst pipes in washrooms, cockroaches in kitchens, flashes of temperament in dining rooms and the inevitable dissatisfied customer who was threatening a lawsuit.

Henry Osborne reentered Abel's life with a welcome offer of a settlement of $750,000 from Great Western Casualty, which had found no evidence to implicate Abel with Desmond Pacey in the fire at the Chicago Richmond. Lieutenant O'Malley's evidence had proved very telling on this point and Abel realized he owed him more than a milk shake.

Abel had been happy to settle with Great Western at what he considered a fair price. Osborne, however, had suggested to him that he hold out for a larger amount and give him a percentage of the difference. Abel, whose shortcomings had never included peculation, regarded him somewhat warily afterward: if Osborne could so readily be disloyal to his own company, there was little doubt that he would have no qualms about ditching Abel when it suited him.

In the spring of 1932 Abel was somewhat surprised to receive a friendly letter from Melanie Leroy, more cordial in tone than she had ever been in person. He was flattered, even excited, and called her to make a date for dinner at the Stevens, a decision he regretted the moment they entered the dining room, for there, looking unsophisticated, tired and vulnerable, was Zaphia. Melanie, in contrast, looked ravishing in a long mint-green dress that revealed quite clearly what her body would be like if the mint were removed. Her eyes, perhaps, taking courage from the dress, seemed greener and more captivating than ever.

"It's wonderful to see you looking so well, Abel," she remarked as she took her seat in the center of the dining room, "and of course everybody knows how well you're doing with the Richmond Group."

"The Baron Group," said Abel.

She flushed slightly. "I didn't realize you had changed the name."

"Yes, I changed it last year," lied Abel. He had in fact decided at that very moment that every hotel in the group would be known as a Baron hotel. He wondered why he had never thought of it before.

"An appropriate name," said Melanie, smiling.

Abel was aware that Zaphia was staring at them from the other side of the room, but it was too late to do anything about it.

"You're not working?" asked Abel, scribbling the words "Baron Group" on the back of his menu.

"No, not at the moment, but things are looking up a little. A woman with a liberal arts degree in this city has to sit around and wait for every man to be employed before she can hope to find a job."

"If you ever want to work for the Baron Group," said Abel, emphasizing the name slightly, "you only have to let me know."

"No, no," said Melanie. "I'm just fine."

She quickly changed the subject to music and the theater. Talking to her was an unaccustomed and pleasant challenge for Abel; she still teased him, but with intelligence, making him feel more confident in her company than he had ever been in the past. The dinner went on until well after eleven, and when everyone had left the dining room, including Zaphia, ominously red-eyed, he drove Melanie home to her apartment and this time she invited him in for a drink. He sat on the end of the sofa while she poured him a prohibited whiskey and put a record on the phonograph.

"I can't stay long," Abel said. "Busy day tomorrow."

"That's what *I'm* supposed to say, Abel. Don't rush away. This evening has been such fun—just like old times."

She sat down beside him, her dress rising above her knees. Not quite like old times, he thought. Incredible legs. He made no attempt to resist when she edged toward him. In moments he found he was kissing her—or was she kissing him? His hands wandered onto those legs and then to her breasts and this time she seemed to respond willingly. It was she who eventually led him by the hand to her bedroom, folded back the coverlet neatly, turned around and asked him to unzip her. Abel obliged in nervous disbelief and switched out the light before he undressed. After that it was easy for him to put Joyce's careful tutelage into practice. Melanie certainly was not lacking in experience herself; Abel had never enjoyed more the act of making love and fell into a deep, contented sleep.

In the morning Melanie made him breakfast and attended to his every need, right up to the moment Abel had to leave.

"I shall watch the Baron Group with renewed interest," she told him. "Not that anyone doubts that it's going to be a huge success."

"Thank you," said Abel, "for breakfast and a memorable night."

"I hope we'll be seeing each other again sometime soon," Melanie added.

"I'd like that," said Abel.

She kissed him on the cheek as a wife might who is seeing her husband off to work.

"I wonder what kind of woman you'll end up marrying," she asked innocently as she helped Abel on with his overcoat.

He looked at her and smiled sweetly. "When I make that decision, Melanie, you can be certain I shall be influenced by your views."

"What do you mean?" asked Melanie coyly.

"Simply that I shall heed your advice," replied Abel as he reached the front door, "to be sure to find myself a nice Polish girl."

Abel and Zaphia were married a month later. Zaphia's cousin Janek gave her away and George was the best man. The reception was held at the Stevens and the drinking and dancing went on far into the night. By tradition, each man paid a token sum to dance with Zaphia and George perspired as he battled around the room, photographing the guests in every possible permutation and combination. After a midnight supper of *barszcz, pierogi* and *bigos* downed with wine, brandy and Danzig vodka, Abel and Zaphia were allowed to retire to the bridal suite.

Abel was pleasantly surprised to be told by Curtis Fenton the next morning that the bill for his reception at the Stevens had been covered by Mr. Maxton and was to be treated as a wedding gift. Abel used the money he had saved for the reception as a down payment on a little house on Rigg Street.

For the first time in his life he possessed a home of his own.

PART FOUR
1932–1941

CHAPTER
TWENTY-ONE

William decided to take a month's vacation in England before making any firm decision about his future; he even considered resigning from the board of Kane and Cabot, but
Matthew convinced him that that was not the course of action his father would have taken in the same circumstances.
Matthew appeared to take his friend's defeat even harder
than William himself. Twice in the following week he came
into the bank with the obvious signs of a hangover and left
important work unfinished.

William decided to let these incidents pass without comment and invited Matthew to join him and Kate for dinner
that night. Matthew declined, claiming that he had a back-
load of letters to catch up on. William wouldn't have given
the refusal a second thought if Matthew hadn't been dining
at the Ritz-Carlton that night with an attractive woman who
William could have sworn was married to one of Kane and
Cabot's departmental managers. Kate said nothing except
that Matthew didn't look very well.

William, preoccupied with his impending departure for
Europe, took less notice of his friend's strange behavior
than he might otherwise have taken. At the last moment
William couldn't face a month in England alone and asked
Kate to accompany him. To his surprise and delight she
agreed.

William and Kate sailed for England on the *Mauretania*

in separate cabins. Once they had settled into the Ritz, in separate rooms, even on separate floors, William reported to the London branch of Kane and Cabot in Lombard Street and fulfilled the ostensible purpose of his trip to England by reviewing the bank's European activities. Morale was high and Tony Simmons had evidently been a well-liked manager; there was little for William to do but murmur his approval.

He and Kate spent a glorious month together in London, then Hampshire and Lincolnshire, looking at some land William had acquired a few months previously, more than twelve thousand acres in all. The financial return from farming land is never high, but as William explained to Kate, "It will always be there if things ever go sour again in America."

A few days before they were due to travel back to the United States, Kate decided she wanted to see Oxford, and William agreed to drive her down early the next morning. He hired a new Morris, a car he had never driven before. In the university city, they spent the day wandering around the colleges: Magdalen, superb against the river; Christ Church, grandiose but cloisterless; and Merton, where they just sat on the grass and dreamed.

"Can't sit on the grass, sir," said the voice of a college porter.

They laughed and walked hand in hand like undergraduates beside the Cherwell, watching eight Matthews straining to push their boat along as swiftly as possible. William could no longer imagine a life separated in any way from Kate.

They started back for London in midafternoon and when they reached Henley on Thames, they stopped to have tea at the Bell Inn overlooking the river. After scones and a large pot of strong English tea (Kate was adventuresome and drank it with only milk, but William added hot water to dilute it), Kate suggested that they should hurry on before it was too dark to see the countryside; but when William had inserted a crank into the Morris, he could not get the engine to turn over, despite strenuous effort. Finally he gave up and, since it was getting late, decided that they would have to spend the night in Henley. He returned to the front desk of the Bell Inn and requested two rooms.

"Sorry, sir, I have only one double room left," said the receptionist.

William hesitated for a moment and then said, "We'll take it."

Kate looked somewhat surprised but said nothing; the receptionist looked suspiciously at her.

"Mr. and Mrs.—er——?"

"Mr. and Mrs. William Kane," said William firmly. "We'll be back later."

"Shall I put your cases in the room, sir?" the hall porter asked.

"We don't have any," William replied, smiling.

"I see, sir."

A bewildered Kate followed William up Henley's High Street until he came to a halt in front of the parish church.

"May I ask what we're doing, William?" Kate asked.

"Something I should have done a long time ago, my darling."

Kate asked no more questions. When they entered the Norman vestry, William found a church warden piling up some hymnals.

"Where can I find the Vicar?" demanded William.

The church warden straightened himself to his full height and regarded William pityingly.

"In the vicarage, I dare say."

"Where's the vicarage?" asked William, trying again.

"You're an American gentleman, aren't you, sir?"

"Yes," said William, becoming impatient.

"The vicarage will be next door to the church, won't it?" said the church warden.

"I suppose it will," said William. "Can you stay here for the next ten minutes?"

"Why should I want to do that, sir?"

William extracted a large, white £5 note from his inside pocket and unfolded it. "Make it fifteen minutes to be on the safe side, please."

The church warden studied the £5 carefully and said, "Americans. Yes, sir."

William left the man with his £5 note and hurried Kate out of the church. As they passed the main notice board in the porch, he read: " 'The Vicar of this Parish is The Very Reverend Simon Tukesbury, M.A. (Cantab),' " and next to that pronouncement, hanging by one nail, was an appeal concerning a new roof for the church. Every penny toward the necessary £500 will help, declared the notice, not very boldly. William hastened up the path to the vicarage with Kate a few yards behind. A smiling, pink-cheeked, plump woman answered his sharp rap on the door.

"Mrs. Tukesbury?" inquired William.

"Yes." She smiled.

"May I speak to your husband?"

"He's having his tea at the moment. Would it be possible for you to come back a little later?"

"I'm afraid it's rather urgent," William insisted.

Kate had caught up with him but said nothing.

"Well, in that case I suppose you'd better come in."

The vicarage was early sixteenth century and the small stone front room was warmed by a welcoming log fire. The Vicar, a tall, spare man who was eating wafer-thin cucumber sandwiches, rose to greet them.

"Good afternoon, Mr. . . . ?"

"Kane, sir, William Kane."

"What can I do for you, Mr. Kane?"

"Kate and I," said William, "want to get married."

"Oh, how nice," said Mrs. Tukesbury.

"Yes, indeed," said the Vicar. "Are you a member of this parish? I don't seem to remember . . ."

"No, sir, I'm an American. I worship at St. Paul's in Boston."

"Massachusetts, I presume, not Lincolnshire," said the Very Reverend Tukesbury.

"Yes," said William, forgetting for a moment that there was a Boston in England.

"Splendid," said the Vicar, his hands raised as if he were about to give a blessing. "And what date did you have in mind for this union of souls?"

"Now, sir."

"Now, sir?" said the startled Vicar. "I am not aware of the traditions in the United States that surround the solemn, holy and binding institution of marriage, Mr. Kane, though one reads of some very strange incidents involving some of your compatriots from California. I do, however, consider it nothing less than my duty to inform you that those customs have not yet become acceptable in Henley on Thames. In England, sir, you must reside for a full calendar month in any parish before you can be married and the banns must be posted on three separate occasions, unless there are very special and extenuating circumstances. Even did such circumstances exist, I would have to seek the bishop's dispensation, and I couldn't do that in under three days," Mr. Tukesbury added, his hands firmly at his side.

Kate spoke for the first time. "How much do you still need for the church's new roof?"

"Ah, the roof. Now there is a sad story, but I won't embark upon its history at this moment—early eleventh century, you know——"

"How much do you need?" asked William, tightening his grasp on Kate's hand.

"We are hoping to raise five hundred pounds. We've done commendably so far; we've reached twenty-seven pounds four shillings and four pence in only seven weeks."

"No, no dear," said Mrs. Tukesbury. "You haven't counted the one pound eleven shillings and two pence I made from my 'Bring and Buy' sale last week."

"Indeed I haven't, my dear. How inconsiderate of me to overlook your personal contribution. That will make altogether . . . ," began the Reverend Tukesbury as he tried to add the figures in his head, raising his eyes toward Heaven for inspiration.

William took his wallet from his inside pocket, wrote out a check for £500 and silently proffered it to the Very Reverend Tukesbury.

"I—ah, I see there are special circumstances, Mr. Kane," said the surprised Vicar. The tone changed. "Has either of you ever been married before?"

"Yes," said Kate. "My husband was killed in a plane crash some four years ago."

"Oh, how terrible," said Mrs. Tukesbury. "I am so sorry, I didn't——"

"Shush, my dear," said the man of God, now more interested in the church roof than in his wife's sentiments. "And you, sir?"

"I have never been married before," said William.

"I shall have to telephone the bishop." Clutching William's check, the Very Reverend disappeared into the next room.

Mrs. Tukesbury invited Kate and William to sit down and offered them the plate of cucumber sandwiches. She chatted on, but William and Kate did not hear the words as they sat gazing at each other.

The Vicar returned three cucumber sandwiches later.

"It's highly irregular, highly irregular, but the bishop has agreed, on the condition, Mr. Kane, that you will confirm everything at the American embassy tomorrow morning and then with your own bishop at St. Paul's in Boston—Massachusetts, when you return home."

He was still clutching the £500 check.

"All we need now is two witnesses," the Vicar continued. "My wife can act as one and we must hope that the church warden is still on duty, so that he can be the other."

"He is still on duty, I assure you," said William.

"How can you be so certain, Mr. Kane?"

"He cost me one percent."

"One percent?" said the Very Reverend Tukesbury, baffled.

"One percent of your church roof," said William.

The minister ushered William, Kate and his wife down the little path to the church and blinked at the waiting church warden.

"Indeed, I perceive that Mr. Sprogget has remained on duty. . . . He has never done so for me; you obviously have a way with you, Mr. Kane."

Simon Tukesbury put on his vestments and a surplice while the church warden stared at the scene in disbelief.

William turned to Kate and kissed her gently. "I know it's a damn silly question in the circumstances, but will you marry me?"

"Good God!" said the Very Reverend Tukesbury, who had never blasphemed in the fifty-seven years of his mortal existence. "You mean you haven't even asked her?"

Fifteen minutes later, Mr. and Mrs. William Kane left the parish church of Henley on Thames, Oxfordshire. Mrs. Tukesbury had had to supply the ring at the last moment, which she twitched from a curtain in the vestry. It was a perfect fit. The Very Reverend Tukesbury had a new roof, and Mr. Sprogget a yarn to tell them down at the Green Man, where he spent most of his £5.

Outside the church the minister handed William a piece of paper. "Two shillings and sixpence, please."

"What for?" asked William.

"Your marriage certificate, Mr. Kane."

"You should have taken up banking, sir," said William, handing Mr. Tukesbury half a crown. He walked his bride in blissful silence back down the High Street to the Bell Inn. They had a quiet dinner in the fifteenth-century oak-beamed dining room and went to bed at a few minutes past nine. As they disappeared up the old wooden staircase to their room, the chief receptionist turned to the hall porter and winked. "If they're married, I'm the King of England."

William started to hum "God Save the King."

The next morning Mr. and Mrs. Kane had a leisurely breakfast while the car was being fixed. A young waiter poured them both coffee.

"Do you like it black or shall I add some milk?" asked William innocently.

An elderly couple at the next table smiled benignly at them.

"With milk, please," said Kate as she reached across and touched William's hand gently.

He smiled back at her, suddenly aware the whole room was now staring at them.

They returned to London in the cool early spring air, traveling through Henley, over the Thames, and then on through Berkshire and Middlesex into London.

"Did you notice the look the porter gave you this morning, darling?" asked William.

"Yes, I think perhaps we should have shown him our marriage certificate."

"No, no, you'd have spoiled his whole image of the wanton American woman. The last thing he wants to tell his wife when he gets home tonight is that we were really married."

When they arrived back at the Ritz in time for lunch, the desk manager was surprised to find William canceling Kate's room. He was heard to comment later: "Young Mr. Kane appeared to be such a gentleman. His late and distinguished father would never have behaved in such a way."

William and Kate took the *Aquitania* back to New York, having first called at the American embassy in Grosvenor Gardens to inform a consul of their marital status. The consul gave them a long official form to fill out, charged them one pound and kept them waiting for well over an hour. The American embassy, it seemed, was not in need of a new roof. William wanted to go to Cartier's in Bond Street and buy a gold wedding ring, but Kate would not hear of it— nothing was going to make her part with the precious brass curtain ring.

William found it difficult to settle down in Boston under his new chairman. The precepts of the New Deal were passing into law with unprecedented rapidity, and William and Tony

Simmons found it impossible to agree on whether the implications for investment were good or bad. Expansion—on one front at least—became unstoppable when Kate announced soon after their return from England that she was pregnant, news that gave her parents and husband great joy. William tried to modify his working hours to suit his new role as a married man but to begin with he found himself at his desk increasingly often throughout the hot summer evenings. Kate, cool and happy in her flowered maternity smock, methodically supervised the decoration of the nursery of the Red House. William found for the first time in his life that he could leave his work desk and look forward to going home. If he had work left over he just picked up the papers and took them to the Red House, a pattern to which he adhered throughout his married life.

While Kate and the baby, which was due about Christmastime, brought William great happiness at home, Matthew was making him increasingly uneasy at work. He had taken to drinking and coming to the office late without explanation. As the months passed, William found he could no longer rely on his friend's judgment. At first, he said nothing, hoping it was little more than an odd out-of-character reaction—which might quickly pass—to the repeal of Prohibition. But it wasn't and the problem went from bad to worse. The last straw came one November morning when Matthew arrived two hours late, obviously suffering from a hangover, and made a simple, needless mistake, selling off an important investment, which resulted in a small loss for a client who should have made a handsome profit. William knew the time had come for an unpleasant but necessary head-on confrontation. Matthew admitted his error and apologized regretfully. William was thankful to have the row out of the way and was about to suggest they go to lunch together when his secretary uncharacteristically rushed into his office.

"It's your wife, sir, she's been taken to the hospital."

"Why?" asked William, puzzled.

"The baby," said his secretary.

"But it's not due for at least another six weeks," said William incredulously.

"I know, sir, but Dr. MacKenzie sounded rather anxious and wanted you to come to the hospital as quickly as possible."

Matthew, who a moment before had seemed a broken reed, took over and drove William to the hospital. Memories of William's mother's death and her unborn daughter came flooding back to both of them.

"Pray God, not Kate," said Matthew as he drew into the hospital parking lot.

William did not need to be guided to the Richard Kane maternity wing, which Kate had officially opened only six months before. He found a nurse standing outside the delivery room; she informed him that Dr. MacKenzie was with his wife and that Kate had lost a lot of blood. William paced up and down the corridor helplessly, numbly waiting, exactly as he had done years before. The scene was all too familiar. How unimportant being chairman of the bank was compared with losing Kate. When had he last said to her "I love you"? Matthew sat with William, paced with William, stood with William, but said nothing. There was nothing to be said. William checked his watch each time a nurse ran in or out of the delivery room. Seconds turned into minutes and minutes into hours. Finally Dr. MacKenzie appeared, his forehead shining with little beads of sweat, a surgical mask covering his nose and mouth. William could see no expression on the doctor's face until he removed the white mask, revealing a large smile.

"Congratulations, William, you have a boy, and Kate is just fine."

"Thank God," breathed William, clinging onto Matthew.

"Much as I respect the Almighty," said Dr. MacKenzie, "I feel I had a little to do with this birth myself."

William laughed. "Can I see Kate?"

"No, not right now. I've given her a sedative and she's fallen asleep. She lost rather more blood than was good for her, but she'll be fine by morning. A little weak, perhaps, but well ready to see you. But there's nothing to stop your seeing your son. But don't be surprised by his size; remember, he's quite premature."

The doctor guided William and Matthew down the corridor to a room in which they stared through a pane of glass at a row of six little pink heads in cribs.

"That one," said Dr. MacKenzie, pointing to the infant on the end.

William stared dubiously at the ugly little face, his vision of a fine, upstanding son receding rapidly.

"Well, I'll say one thing for the little devil," said Dr. MacKenzie cheerfully, "he's better-looking than you were at that age and you haven't turned out too badly."

William laughed out of relief.

"What are you going to call him?"

"Richard Higginson Kane."

The doctor patted the new father affectionately on the shoulder. "I hope I live long enough to deliver Richard's firstborn."

William immediately wired the rector of St. Paul's, who put the boy down for a place in 1943, and the new father and Matthew got thoroughly drunk and were both late arriving at the hospital the next morning to see Kate. William took Matthew for another look at young Richard.

"Ugly little bastard," said Matthew. "Not at all like his beautiful mother."

"That's what I thought," said William.

"Spitting image of you though."

William returned to Kate's flower-filled room.

"Do you like your son?" Kate asked her husband. "He's so like you."

"I'll hit the next person who says that," William said. "He's the ugliest little thing I've ever seen."

"Oh, no," said Kate in mock indignation, "he's beautiful."

"A face only a mother could love," said William, and he hugged his wife.

She clung to him, happy in his happiness.

"What would Grandmother Kane have said about our firstborn entering the world after less than eight months of marriage? 'I don't want to appear uncharitable, but anyone born in under fifteen months must be considered of dubious parentage, under nine months definitely unacceptable,'" William mimicked. "By the way, Kate, I forgot to tell you something before they rushed you into the hospital."

"What was that?"

"I love you."

Kate and young Richard had to stay in the hospital for nearly three weeks. Not until after Christmas did Kate fully recover her vitality. Richard, on the other hand, grew like an uncontrollable weed, no one having informed him that he was a Kane, and one was not supposed to do that sort of thing. William became the first male Kane to change a diaper and push a perambulator. Kate was very proud of him, and somewhat surprised. William told Matthew that it was high time he found himself a good woman and settled down.

Matthew laughed defensively. "You're getting positively middle-aged. I shall be looking for gray hairs next."

One or two had already appeared during the chairmanship battle. Matthew hadn't noticed.

William was not able to put a finger on exactly when his relationship with Tony Simmons began to deteriorate badly. Tony would continually veto one policy suggestion after another and his negative attitude made William seriously reconsider resignation. Matthew was not helping matters by returning to his old drinking habits. The period of reform had not lasted more than a few months and if anything he was now drinking more heavily than before and arriving at the bank a few minutes later each morning. William wasn't quite sure how to handle the new situation and found himself continually covering Matthew's work. At the end of each day William would double-check Matthew's mail and return his unanswered calls.

By the spring of 1936, as investors gained more confidence and depositors returned, William decided the time had come to go tentatively back into the stock market, but Tony vetoed the suggestion in an offhand interoffice memorandum to the Financial Committee. William stormed into Tony's office to ask if his resignation would be welcome.

"Certainly not, William. I merely want you to recognize that it has always been my policy to run this bank in a conservative manner and that I am not willing to charge headlong back into the market with our investors' money."

"But we're losing business hand over fist to other banks while we sit on the sidelines watching them take advantage of the present situation. Banks we wouldn't even have considered as rivals ten years ago will soon be overtaking us."

"Overtaking us in what, William? Not in reputation. Quick profits perhaps, but not reputation."

"But I'm interested in profits," said William. "I consider it a bank's duty to make good returns for its investors, not to mark time in a gentlemanly fashion."

"I would rather stand still than lose the reputation that this bank built up under your grandfather and father over the better part of half a century."

"Yes, but both of them were always looking for new opportunities to expand the bank's activities."

"In good times," said Tony.

"And in bad," said William.

"Why are you so upset, William? You still have a free hand in the running of your own department."

"Like hell I do. You block anything that even suggests enterprise."

"Let's start being honest with each other, William. One of the reasons I have had to be particularly cautious lately is that Matthew's judgment is no longer reliable."

"Leave Matthew out of this. It's me you're blocking; *I* am head of the department."

"I can't leave Matthew out of it. I wish I could. The final overall responsibility to the board for anyone's actions is mine, and he is the number two man in the bank's most important department."

"Yes, and therefore my responsibility because I am the number one man in that department."

"No, William, it cannot remain your responsibility alone when Matthew comes into the office drunk at eleven o'clock in the morning—no matter how long and close your friendship has been."

"Don't exaggerate."

"I am not exaggerating, William. For over a year now this bank has been carrying Matthew Lester, and the only thing that stopped me from mentioning it to you before is your close personal relationship with him and his family. I wouldn't be sorry to see *him* hand in his resignation. A bigger man would have done so long ago and his friends would have told him so."

"Never," said William. "If he goes, I go."

"So be it, William," said Tony. "My first responsibility is to our investors, not to your old school chums."

"You'll live to regret that statement, Tony," said William. He stormed out of the chairman's office and returned to his own room in a furious temper.

"Where is Mr. Lester?" William demanded as he passed his secretary.

"He's not in yet, sir."

William looked at his watch, exasperated. "Tell him I'd like to see him the moment he arrives."

"Yes, sir."

William paced up and down his office, cursing. Everything Tony Simmons had said about Matthew was true, which only made matters worse. He began to think back to when it had all begun, searching for a simple explanation. His thoughts were interrupted by his secretary.

"Mr. Lester has just arrived, sir."

Matthew entered the room looking rather sheepish, displaying all the signs of another hangover. He had aged badly in the past year and his skin had lost its fine, athletic glow. William hardly recognized him as the man who had been his closest friend for nearly twenty years.

"Matthew, where the hell have you been?"

"I overslept," Matthew replied, uncharacteristically scratching at his face. "Rather a late night, I'm afraid."

"You mean you drank too much."

"No, I didn't have that much. It was a new girlfriend who kept me awake all night. She was insatiable."

"When will you stop, Matthew? You've slept with nearly every single woman in Boston."

"Don't exaggerate, William. There must be one or two left—at least I hope so. And then don't forget all the thousands of married ones."

"It's not funny, Matthew."

"Oh, come on, William. Give me a break."

"Give you a break? I've just had Tony Simmons on my back because of you, and what's more, I know he's right. You'll sleep with anything wearing a skirt, and worse, you're drinking yourself to death. Your judgment has gone to pieces. Why, Matthew? Tell me why. There must be some simple explanation. Up until a year ago you were one of the most reliable men I had ever met in my life. What is it, Matthew? What am I supposed to tell Tony Simmons?"

"Tell Simmons to go to hell and mind his own business."

"Matthew, be fair, it *is* his business. We're running a bank, not a bordello, and you came here as a director on my personal recommendation," said William, unable to hide the anger in his voice.

"And now I'm not measuring up to your standards, is that what you're saying?"

"No, I'm not saying that."

"Then what the hell are you saying?"

"Buckle down and do some work for a few weeks. In no time everyone will have forgotten all about it."

"Is that all you want?"

"Yes," said William.

"I shall do as you command, O Master," said Matthew, and he clicked his heels and walked out of the door.

"Oh, hell," said William.

That afternoon William wanted to go over a client's portfolio with Matthew, but nobody seemed to be able to find him. He had not returned to the office after lunch and was not seen again that day.

Even the pleasure of putting young Richard to bed in the evening could not distract William from his worries about Matthew. Richard could already say "two" and William was trying to make him say "three," but he insisted on saying "tree."

"If you can't say 'three,' Richard, how can you ever hope to be a banker," William demanded of his son as Kate entered the nursery.

"Perhaps he'll end up doing something worthwhile," said Kate.

"What's more worthwhile than banking?" William inquired.

"Well, he might be a musician, or a baseball player, or even President of the United States."

"Of those three I'd prefer him to be a ball player—it's the only one of the three that pays a decent salary," said William as he tucked Richard into bed. Richard's last words before sleeping were "Tree, Daddy." William gave up. It wasn't his day.

"You look exhausted, darling. I hope you haven't forgotten that we're having drinks later at Andrew MacKenzie's."

"Hell, Andrew's party had totally slipped my mind. What time is he expecting us?"

"In about an hour."

"Well, first I'm going to take a long, hot bath."

"I thought that was a woman's privilege," said Kate.

"Tonight I need a little pampering. I've had a nerve-racking day."

"Tony bothering you again?"

"Yes, but I am afraid this time he's in the right. He's been complaining about Matthew's drinking. I was only thankful he didn't mention the womanizing. It's become impossible to take Matthew to any party nowadays unless the eldest daughter—not to mention the occasional wife—has been locked away. Will you run my bath?"

William sat in the tub for more than half an hour and Kate had to drag him out before he fell asleep. Despite her prompting they arrived at the MacKenzies' twenty-five minutes late, only to find that Matthew, already well on the way to being inebriated, was trying to pick up a congressman's wife. William wanted to intervene, but Kate prevented him from doing so.

"Don't say anything," she said.

"I can't stand here and watch him going to pieces in front of my eyes," said William. "He's my closest friend. I have to do something."

But in the end he took Kate's advice and spent an unhappy evening watching Matthew become progressively drunker. Tony Simmons, from the other side of the room, was glancing pointedly at William, who was relieved at Matthew's early departure, even though it was in the company of the only unattached woman left at the party. Once Matthew had gone, William started to relax for the first time that day.

"How is little Richard?" Andrew MacKenzie asked.

"He can't say 'three,'" said William.

"That's good news," said Dr. MacKenzie. "He might end up doing something worthwhile after all."

"Exactly what I said," said Kate. "What a good idea, William: he can be a doctor."

"Pretty safe," said Andrew. "Don't know many doctors who can count past two."

"Except when they send their bills," said William.

Andrew laughed. "Will you have another drink, Kate?"

"No thank you, Andrew. It's time we went home. If we stay any longer, only Tony Simmons and William will be left, and they can both count past two so we would all have to talk banking the rest of the night."

"Agreed," said William. "Thank you for a lovely party, Andrew. By the way, I must apologize for Matthew's behavior."

"Why?" said Dr. MacKenzie.

"Oh, come on, Andrew, not only was he drunk, but there wasn't a woman in the room who felt safe with him."

"I might well do the same if I were in his predicament," said Andrew MacKenzie.

"What makes you say that?" said William. "You can't approve of his conduct just because he's single."

"No, I don't, but I try to understand them and realize I might be a little irresponsible faced with the same problem."

"What do you mean?" asked Kate.

"My God!" said Dr. MacKenzie. "He's your closest friend and he hasn't told you?"

"Told us what?" they said together.

Dr. MacKenzie stared at them both, a look of disbelief on his face.

"Come into my study."

William and Kate followed the doctor into a small room, lined almost wall to wall with medical books, interspersed only with occasional, sometimes unframed, photographs of student days at Cornell.

"Please sit down," he said. "William, I make no apologies for what I am about to say, because I assumed you knew that Matthew was gravely ill—dying, in fact, of Hodgkin's disease. He has known about his condition for over a year."

William fell back in his chair, for a moment unable to speak. "Hodgkin's disease?"

"An almost invariably fatal inflammation and enlargement of the lymph nodes," said the doctor rather formally.

William shook his head incredulously. "Why didn't he tell me?"

"You've known each other since you were at school together. My guess is he's far too proud to burden anyone else with his problems. He'd rather die in his own way than let anyone know what he's going through. I have begged him for the last six months to tell his father and I have certainly broken my professional promise to him by letting you know, but I can't let you go on blaming him for something over which he has absolutely no control."

"Thank you, Andrew," said William. "How can I have been so blind and so stupid?"

"Don't blame yourself," said Dr. MacKenzie. "There's no way you could have known."

"Is there really no hope?" asked William. "Are there no clinics, no specialists? Money would be no problem——"

"Money can't buy everything, William, and I have consulted the three best men in America and one in Switzerland. I'm afraid they're all in agreement with my diagnosis. Medical science hasn't yet discovered a cure for Hodgkin's disease."

"How long has he to live?" asked Kate in a whisper.

"Six months at the outside, more likely three."

"And I thought I had problems," said William. He held tightly onto Kate's hand as if it were a lifeline. "We must be going, Andrew. Thank you for telling us."

"Do what you can for him," said the doctor, "but for God's sake, be understanding. Let him do what he wants to do. It's Matthew's last few months, not yours. And don't ever let him know I told you."

William and Kate drove home in silence. As soon as they reached the Red House, William called the girl Matthew had left the party with.

"Would it be possible to speak to Matthew Lester?"

"He's not here," said a rather irritable voice. "He dragged me off to the Revue Club, but he was already drunk by the time we got there and I refused to go in that place with him." Then she hung up.

The Revue Club. William had a hazy recollection of having seen the sign swinging from an iron bar, but he couldn't remember exactly where the place was. He looked it up in the phone book, drove over to the north side of town and— after questioning a passerby—eventually found the club. William knocked on the door. A hatch slid back.

"Are you a member?"

"No," said William firmly, and passed a ten-dollar bill through the grille.

The hatch slid closed and the door opened. William walked across the middle of the dance floor, looking slightly incongruous in his three-piece banker's suit. The dancers, twined around each other, swayed incuriously away from him. William's eyes searched the smoke-filled room for Matthew, but he wasn't there. Finally he thought he recognized one of Matthew's many recent casual girlfriends, one he felt certain he'd seen coming out of his friend's house early one morning. She was sitting cross-legged in a corner with a sailor. William went over to her.

"Excuse me, miss," he said.

She looked up but obviously didn't recognize William.

"The lady's with me, so beat it," said the sailor.

"Have you seen Matthew Lester?"

"Matthew?" said the girl. "Matthew who?"

"I told you to get lost," said the sailor, rising to his feet.

"One more word out of you and I'll knock your block off," said William.

The sailor had seen anger like that in a man's eyes once before in his life and had nearly lost an eye for his trouble. He sat back down.

"Where is Matthew?"

"I don't know a Matthew, darling." Now she, too, was frightened.

"Six feet two, blond hair, dressed like me and probably drunk."

"Oh, you mean Martin. He calls himself Martin here, darling, not Matthew." She began to relax. "Now let me see, who did he go off with tonight?" She turned her head toward the bar and shouted at the bartender. "Terry, who did Martin leave with?"

The bartender removed a dead cigarette butt from the corner of his mouth. "Jenny," he said, and put the unlit cigarette back in place.

"Jenny, that's right," said the girl. "Now let me see, she's short sessions. Never lets a man stay for more than half an hour, so they should be back fairly soon."

"Thank you," said William.

He waited for almost an hour at the bar, sipping a Scotch with a lot of water, feeling more and more out of place by the minute. Finally the bartender, the unlit cigarette still in his mouth, gestured to a girl who was coming through the door.

"That's Jenny," he said. Matthew was not with her.

The bartender waved for Jenny to join them. A slim, short, dark, not unattractive girl, she winked at William and walked toward him swinging her hips.

"Looking for me, darling? Well, I am available, but I charge ten dollars for half an hour."

"No, I don't want you," said William.

"Charming," said Jenny.

"I'm looking for the man who's been with you, Matthew—I mean Martin."

"Martin, he was too drunk to get it up with the help of a crane, darling, but he paid his ten dollars—he always does. A real gentleman."

"Where is he now?" asked William impatiently.

"I don't know. He gave it up as a bad job and started walking home."

William ran into the street. The cold air hit him, not that he needed to be awakened. He drove his car slowly away from the club, following the route toward Matthew's apartment, looking carefully at each person he passed. Some hurried on when they saw his watchful eyes; others tried to engage him in conversation. When he stopped for a traffic light outside an all-night diner, he caught sight of Matthew through the steamy window, weaving his way through the tables with a cup in his hand. William parked the car, went into the diner and sat down beside him. Matthew had slumped onto the table next to a cup of spilled, untouched coffee. He was so drunk that he didn't even recognize William.

"Matthew, it's me," said William, looking at the crumpled man. Tears started to run down William's cheeks.

Matthew looked up and spilled some more of his coffee. "You're crying, old fellow. Lost your girl, have you?"

"No, my closest friend," said William.

"Ah, they're much harder to come by."

"I know," said William.

"I have a good friend," said Matthew, slurring his words. "He's always stood by me until we quarreled for the first time today. My fault though. You see, I've let him down rather badly."

"No, you haven't," said William.

"How can you know?" said Matthew angrily. "You're not even fit to know him."

"Let's go home, Matthew."

"My name is Martin," said Matthew.

"I'm sorry, Martin, let's go home."

"No, I want to stay here. There's this girl who may come by later. I think I'm ready for her now."

"I have some fine old malt whiskey at my house," said William. "Why don't you join me?"

"Any women at your place?"

"Yes, plenty of them."

"You're on, I'll come."

William hoisted Matthew up and put his arm under his shoulder, guiding him slowly through the diner toward the door. It was the first time he'd ever realized how heavy Matthew was. As they passed two policemen sitting at the corner of the counter, William heard one say to the other, "Goddamn fairies."

He helped Matthew into the car and drove him to Beacon Hill. Kate was waiting up for them.

"You should have gone to bed, darling."

"I couldn't sleep," she said.

"I'm afraid he's nearly incoherent."

"Is this the girl you promised me?" said Matthew.

"Yes, she'll take care of you," said William, and he and

Kate helped him up to the guest room and put him on the bed. Kate started to undress him.

"You must undress as well, darling," he said. "I've already paid my ten dollars."

"When you're in bed," said Kate lightly.

"Why are you looking so sad, beautiful lady?" said Matthew.

"Because I love you," said Kate, tears beginning to form in her eyes.

"Don't cry," said Matthew, "there's nothing to cry about. I'll manage it this time, you'll see."

When they had undressed Matthew, William covered him with a sheet and a blanket. Kate turned the light out.

"You promised you'd come to bed with me," Matthew said drowsily.

She closed the door quietly.

William slept on a chair outside Matthew's room for fear he might wake up in the night and try to leave. Kate woke him in the morning before taking some breakfast in to Matthew.

"What am I doing here, Kate?" were Matthew's first words.

"You came back with us after Andrew MacKenzie's party last night," Kate replied rather feebly.

"No, I didn't. I went to the Revue Club with that awful girl, Patricia something or other, who refused to come in with me. God, I feel lousy. Can I have a tomato juice? I don't want to be unsociable, but the last thing I need is breakfast."

"Of course, Matthew."

William came in. Matthew looked up at him. They stared at each other in silence.

"You know, don't you?" said Matthew finally.

"Yes," said William, "and I've been a fool and I hope you'll forgive me."

"Don't cry, William. I haven't seen you do that since you were twelve and Covington was beating you up and I had to drag him off you. Remember? I wonder what Covington is up to now? Probably running a brothel in Tijuana; it's about all he was fit for. Mind you, if Covington is running it, the place will be damned efficient, so lead me to it. Don't cry, William. Grown men don't cry. Nothing can be done. I've seen all the specialists from New York to Los Angeles to Zurich and there is nothing they can do. Do you mind if I skip the office this morning? I still feel bloody awful. Wake me if I stay too long or if I'm any more trouble and I'll find my own way home."

"This is your home," said William.

Matthew's face changed. "Will you tell my father, William? I can't face him. You're an only son, too—you understand the problem."

"Yes, I will," said William. "I'll go down to New York tomorrow and let him know if you'll promise to stay with Kate and me. I won't stop you from getting drunk if that's what you wish to do, or from having as many women as you want, but you must stay here."

"Best offer I've had in weeks, William. Now I think I'll sleep some more. I get so tired nowadays."

William watched Matthew fall into a deep sleep and removed the half-empty glass from his hand. A tomato stain was forming on the sheets.

"Don't die," he said quietly. "Please don't die, Matthew. Have you forgotten that you and I are going to run the biggest bank in America?"

William went to New York the following morning to see Charles Lester. The great man aged visibly at William's news and seemed to shrink into his seat.

"Thank you for coming, William, and telling me personally. I knew something had to be wrong when Matthew stopped his monthly visits to see us. I'll come up every weekend. He'll want to be with you and Kate and I'll try not to make it too obvious how hard I took the news. God knows what he's done to deserve this. Since Matthew's mother died, I've built everything for him, and now there is no one to leave it to."

"Come to Boston whenever you want to, sir—you'll always be most welcome."

"Thank you, William, for everything you're doing for my son." The old man looked up at him. "I wish your father were alive to see how worthy his son is of the name Kane. If only I could change places with Matthew, and let him live . . ."

"I ought to be getting back to him soon, sir."

"Yes, of course. Tell him I love him, tell him I took the news stoically. Don't tell him anything different."

"Yes, sir."

William traveled back to Boston that night to find that Matthew had stayed at home with Kate and had started reading America's latest best seller, *Gone with the Wind*, as he sat out on the veranda. He looked up as William came through the French doors.

"How did the old man take it?"

"He cried," said William.

"The chairman of Lester's bank cried?" said Matthew. "Never let the shareholders know that."

Matthew stopped drinking and worked as hard as he could right up until the last few days. William was amazed by his determination and continually had to make him slow down. He kept well on top of his work and would tease William by checking *his* mail at the end of each day. In the evenings before the theater or a large dinner, Matthew would play tennis with William or row against him on the Charles. "I'll know I'm dead when I can't beat you," he mocked.

Matthew never entered the hospital, preferring to stay at the Red House. For William, the weeks went so slowly and yet so quickly, waking each morning and wondering if Matthew was still alive.

Matthew died on a Thursday, forty pages still to read of *Gone with the Wind*.

. . .

The funeral was held in New York and William and Kate stayed with Charles Lester. In six months he had become an old man, and as he stood by the graves of his wife and only son, he told William that he no longer saw any purpose in this life. William said nothing; no words of his could help the grieving father. William and Kate returned to Boston the next day. The Red House seemed strangely empty without Matthew. The past few months had been at once the happiest and unhappiest period in William's life. Death had brought him a closeness, both to Matthew and to Kate, that normal life would never have allowed.

When William returned to the bank after Matthew's death, he found it difficult to get back into any sort of normal routine. He would get up and start to head toward Matthew's office for advice or a laugh, or merely to be assured of his existence, but he was no longer there. It was weeks before William could prevent himself from doing this.

Tony Simmons was very understanding, but it didn't help. William lost all interest in banking, even in Kane and Cabot itself, as he went through months of remorse over Matthew's death. He had always taken it for granted that he and Matthew would grow old together and share a common destiny. No one commented that William's work was not up to its usual high standard. Even Kate grew worried by the hours William would spend alone.

Then one morning she awoke to find him sitting on the edge of the bed staring down at her. She blinked up at him. "Is something wrong, darling?"

"No, I'm just looking at my greatest asset and making sure I don't take it for granted."

CHAPTER
TWENTY-TWO

Toward the end of 1932, with America still in the grip of the Depression, Abel was becoming more than a little apprehensive about the future of the Baron Group. Two thousand banks had been closed during the past two years, and more were shutting their doors every week. Nine million people were still unemployed, which seemed to have as its only virtue the assurance that Abel could maintain a highly professional staff in all his hotels. Despite this, the Baron Group lost $72,000 in 1932, the year in which he had predicted they would break even, and he began to wonder whether his backer's purse and patience would hold out long enough to allow him the chance to turn things around.

Earlier, Abel had begun to take an active interest in American politics during Anton Cermak's successful campaign to become mayor of Chicago. Cermak had talked Abel into joining the Democratic party, which had launched a virulent campaign against Prohibition; Abel had thrown himself wholeheartedly behind Cermak because Prohibition had proved very damaging to the hotel trade. The fact that Cermak was himself an immigrant, from Czechoslovakia, had created an immediate bond between the two men, and Abel had been delighted when he was chosen as a delegate to the Democratic National Convention held in Chicago in 1932, where Cermak had brought a packed audience to its feet with the words: "It's true I didn't come over on the *Mayflower*, but I came over as soon as I could."

At the convention Cermak had introduced Abel to Franklin D. Roosevelt, who had made a lasting impression on him. FDR went on to win the Presidential election easily, sweeping Democratic candidates into office all over the country. One of the newly elected aldermen at Chicago City Hall was Henry Osborne. When Anton Cermak was killed in early 1933 in Miami by an assassin's bullet intended for FDR, Abel decided to contribute a considerable amount of time and money to the cause of the Polish Democrats in Chicago.

During 1933 the group lost only $23,000, and one of the hotels, the St. Louis Baron, actually showed a profit. When President Roosevelt had delivered his first fireside chat on March 12, exhorting his countrymen "to once again believe in America," Abel's confidence soared and he decided to reopen the two hotels he had closed.

Zaphia grew querulous about his long sojourns in Charleston and Mobile while he took the two hotels out of mothballs. Zaphia had never wanted Abel to be more than the deputy manager of the Stevens, a level at which she felt she could keep pace. The pace was quickening as every month passed, and she became conscious of falling behind Abel's ambitions and feared he was beginning to lose interest in her.

She was also becoming anxious about her childlessness and started to see doctors, who reassured her that there was nothing to prevent her from becoming pregnant. One offered the suggestion that Abel also be examined, but Zaphia demurred, knowing he would regard the very mention of the subject as a slur on his manhood. Finally, after the subject had become so charged that it was difficult for them to discuss it at all, Zaphia missed her period.

She waited hopefully for another month before saying anything to Abel or even seeing the doctor again. He confirmed that she was at last pregnant. To Abel's delight, Zaphia gave birth to a daughter, on New Year's Day 1934. They named her Florentyna, after Abel's sister. Abel was besotted the moment he set eyes on the child, and Zaphia knew then that she could no longer be the first love of his life. George and Zaphia's cousins were the child's *Kums*, and Abel gave a traditional ten-course Polish dinner on the evening of the christening. Many gifts were presented to the child, including a beautiful antique ring from Abel's unknown backer. He returned the gift in kind when the Baron Group had made a profit of $63,000 at the end of the year. Only the Mobile Baron was still losing money.

Several months after Florentyna's birth Abel, who found he was spending much more of his time in Chicago, decided that the time had come to build a new Baron there. Hotels in the city were booming in the aftermath of the World's Fair. Abel intended to make his new hotel the flagship of the group in memory of Davis Leroy. The company still owned the site of the old Richmond hotel on Michigan Avenue, and although Abel had had several offers for the land, he had always held out, hoping that one day he would be in a strong enough financial position to rebuild the hotel. The project required capital, and Abel decided to use the $750,000 he had eventually received from Great Western Casualty for the old Chicago Richmond to start construction. As soon as his plans were formulated he told Curtis Fenton of his intention, with the sole reservation that if David Maxton did not want a rival to the Stevens, Abel would drop the whole project—a gesture he felt he owed Mr. Maxton. A few days later, Curtis Fenton advised him that Abel's backer was delighted by the idea of the Chicago Baron.

It took Abel twelve months to build the new Baron with a large helping hand from Alderman Henry Osborne, who hurried through the permits required from City Hall in the shortest possible time. The building was opened in 1936 by the mayor of the city, Edward J. Kelly, who, after the death of Anton Cermak, had become the leader of the Democratic machine. In memory of Davis Leroy, the hotel had no seventeenth floor—a tradition Abel continued in every new Baron he built.

Both Illinois senators were also in attendance to address the two thousand assembled guests. The Chicago Baron was superb both in design and construction. Abel had eventually spent well over a million dollars on the hotel and it looked as though every penny had been put to good use. The public rooms were large and sumptuous, with high stucco ceilings and decorations in pastel shades of green, pleasant and relaxing; the carpets were thick. The dark green embossed B was discreet but ubiquitous, adorning everything from the flag that fluttered on the top of the forty-two-story building to the neat lapel of the most junior bellhop.

"This hotel already bears the hallmark of success," said J. Hamilton Lewis, the senior senator from Illinois, "because, my friends, it is the man, not the building, who will always be known as 'The Chicago Baron.'"

Abel beamed with undisguised pleasure as the two thousand guests roared their approval.

His reply of acknowledgment was well turned and confidently delivered and it earned him a standing ovation. He was beginning to feel very much at home among big-business men and senior politicians. Zaphia hovered uncertainly in the background during the lavish celebration: the occasion was a little too much for her. She neither understood nor cared for success on Abel's scale; and even though she could now afford the most expensive clothes, she still looked unfashionable and out of place and she was only too aware that this annoyed Abel. She stood by while Abel chatted with Henry Osborne.

"This must be the high point of your life," Henry was saying, slapping Abel on the back.

"High point—I've just turned thirty," said Abel. A camera flashed as he placed an arm around Henry's shoulder. Abel beamed, realizing for the first time how pleasant it was to be treated as a public figure. "I'm going to put Baron hotels right across the globe," he said, just loud enough for the eavesdropping reporter to hear. "I intend to be to America what César Ritz was to Europe. Stick with me, Henry, and you'll enjoy the ride."

CHAPTER
TWENTY-THREE

At breakfast the next morning, Kate pointed to a small item on page 17 of the *Globe*, reporting the opening of the Chicago Baron.

William smiled as he read the article. Kane and Cabot had been foolish not to listen when he had advised them to support the Richmond Group. It pleased him that his own judgment on Rosnovski had turned out to be right even though the bank had missed out on the deal. His smile broadened as he read the nickname "The Chicago Baron." Then, suddenly, he felt sick. He examined the accompanying photograph more closely, but there was no mistake, and the caption confirmed his first impression: "Abel Rosnovski, the chairman of the Baron Group, talking with Mieczyslaw Szymczak, a governor of the Federal Reserve Board, and Alderman Henry Osborne."

William dropped the paper onto the breakfast table and thought for a moment. As soon as he arrived at his office, he called Thomas Cohen at Cohen, Cohen and Yablons.

"It's been a long time, Mr. Kane" were Thomas Cohen's first words. "I was very sorry to learn of the death of your friend, Matthew Lester. How are your wife and your son—Richard—isn't that his name?"

William always admired Thomas Cohen's instant recall of names and relationships.

"Yes, it is. They're both well, thank you, Mr. Cohen."

"What can I do for you this time, Mr. Kane?" Thomas Cohen also remembered that William could only manage about one sentence of small talk.

"I want to employ, through you, the services of a reliable investigator. I do not wish my name to be associated with this inquiry, but I need an update on Henry Osborne. Everything he's done since he left Boston, and in particular whether there is any connection between him and Abel Rosnovski of the Baron Group."

There was a pause before the lawyer said, "Yes."

"Can you report to me in one week?"

"Two please, Mr. Kane, two," said Mr. Cohen.

"Full report on my desk at the bank in two weeks, Mr. Cohen?"

"Two weeks, Mr. Kane."

Thomas Cohen was as reliable as ever and a full report was on William's desk on the fifteenth morning. William read the dossier with care. There appeared to be no formal business connections between Abel Rosnovski and Henry Osborne. Rosnovski, it seemed, found Osborne useful as a political contact but nothing more. Osborne himself had bounced from job to job since leaving Boston, ending up in the main office of the Great Western Casualty Insurance Company. In all probability, that was how Osborne had come in contact with Abel Rosnovski, as the old Chicago Richmond had always been insured by Great Western. When the hotel burned down, the insurance company had originally refused to pay the claim. A certain Desmond Pacey, the manager, had been sent to prison for ten years, after pleading guilty to arson, and there was some suspicion that Abel Rosnovski might himself have been involved. Nothing was proved and the insurance company settled later for three-quarters of a million dollars. Osborne, the report went on, was now an alderman and full-time politician at City Hall, and it was common knowledge that he hoped to become a congressman for Chicago. He had not long ago married a Miss Marie Axton, the daughter of a wealthy drug manufacturer, and as yet they had no children.

William went over the report again to be sure that he had
not missed anything however inconsequential. Although
there did not seem to be a great deal to connect the two men,
he couldn't help feeling that the association between Abel
Rosnovski and Henry Osborne, both of whom hated him, for
totally disparate reasons, was potentially dangerous to him.
He mailed a check to Thomas Cohen and requested that he
update the file every quarter, but as the months passed, and
the quarterly reports revealed nothing new, he began to stop
worrying, thinking perhaps he had overreacted to the photograph in the Boston *Globe*.

Kate presented her husband with a daughter in the spring of
1937; they christened her Virginia. William started changing
diapers again, and such was his fascination for "the little
lady" that Kate had to rescue the child each night for fear
she would never get any sleep. Richard, now two and a half,
didn't care too much for the new arrival to begin with, but
time and a set of wooden soldiers combined to allay his
jealousy.

By the end of the year William's department at Kane and
Cabot had made a handsome profit for the bank. He had
emerged from the lethargy that had overcome him on
Matthew's death and was fast regaining his reputation as a
shrewd investor in the stock market, not least when Sell'em
Short Smith admitted he had only perfected a technique developed by William Kane of Boston. Even Tony Simmons's
direction had become less irksome. Nevertheless, William
was secretly worried by the prospect that he could not become chairman of Kane and Cabot until Simmons retired in
seventeen years' time, and he began to consider looking
around for employment in another bank.

William and Kate had taken to visiting Charles Lester in
New York about once a month on weekends. The great man
had grown very old over the three years since Matthew's

death, and rumors in financial circles were that he had lost all interest in his work and was rarely seen at the bank. William was beginning to wonder how much longer the old man would live, and then a few weeks later he died. The Kanes traveled down to the funeral in New York. Everyone seemed to be there including the Vice President of the United States, John Nance Garner. After the funeral William and Kate took the train back to Boston, numbly conscious that they had lost their last real link with the Lester family.

It was some six months later that William received a communication from Sullivan and Cromwell, the distinguished New York lawyers, asking him if he would be kind enough to attend the reading of the will of the late Charles Lester at their offices in Wall Street. William went to the reading, more from loyalty to the Lester family than from any curiosity to know what Charles Lester had left him. He hoped for a small memento that would remind him of Matthew and would join the "Harvard Oar" that still hung on the wall of the guest room of the Red House. He also looked forward to the opportunity to renew his acquaintance with many members of the Lester family whom he had come to know during school and college holidays spent with Matthew.

William drove down to New York in his newly acquired Daimler the night before the reading and stayed at the Harvard Club. The will was to be read at ten o'clock the following morning, and William was surprised to find on his arrival in the offices of Sullivan and Cromwell that more than fifty people were already present. Many of them glanced up at William as he entered the room, and he greeted several of Matthew's cousins and aunts, looking rather older than he remembered them; he could only conclude that they must be thinking the same about him. His eyes searched for Matthew's sister, Susan, but he couldn't find her. At ten o'clock precisely Mr. Arthur Cromwell entered the room, accompanied by an assistant carrying a brown leather folder. Everyone fell silent in hopeful expectation. The lawyer began by explaining to the assembled would-be beneficiaries that the contents of the will had not been disclosed until six months after Charles Lester's death at Mr. Lester's specific instruction: having no son to whom to leave his fortune, he had wanted the dust to settle after his death before his final intentions were made clear.

William looked around the room at the faces intent on every syllable issuing from the lawyer's mouth. Arthur Cromwell took nearly an hour to read the will. After reciting the usual bequests to family retainers, charities and Harvard University, Cromwell went on to reveal that Charles Lester had divided his personal fortune among all his relatives, treating them more or less according to their degree of kinship. His daughter, Susan, received the largest share of the estate, while the five nephews and three nieces each received an equal portion of the remainder. All their money and stock were to be held in trust by the bank until they were thirty. Several other cousins, aunts and distant relatives were given immediate cash payments.

William was surprised when Mr. Cromwell announced: "That disposes of all the known assets of the late Charles Lester."

People began to shuffle around in their seats as a murmur of nervous conversation broke out.

"That is not, however, the end of Mr. Charles Lester's Last Will and Testament," said the imperturbable lawyer, and everyone sat still again, fearful of some late and unwelcome thunderbolt.

Mr. Cromwell went on. "I shall now continue in Mr. Charles Lester's own words: 'I have always considered that a bank and its reputation are only as good as the people who serve it. It was well known that I had hoped my son Matthew would succeed me as chairman of Lester's, but his tragic and untimely death has intervened. Until now, I have never divulged my choice of a successor for Lester's Bank. I therefore wish it be known that I desire William Lowell Kane, son of one of my dearest friends, the late Richard Lowell Kane, and at present the vice chairman of Kane and Cabot, be appointed chairman of Lester's Bank and Trust Company following the next full board meeting.' "

There was an immediate uproar. Everyone looked around the room for the mysterious William Lowell Kane, of whom few but the immediate Lester family had ever heard.

"I have not yet finished," said Arthur Cromwell quietly.

Silence fell once more as the members of the audience, anticipating another bombshell, exchanged fearful glances.

The lawyer continued: "All the above grants and divisions of stock in Lester and Company are expressly conditional upon the beneficiaries' voting for Mr. Kane at the next annual general meeting and continuing to do so for at least the following five years, unless Mr. Kane himself indicates that he does not wish to accept the chairmanship."

Uproar broke out again. William wished he were a million miles away, not sure whether to be deliriously happy or to concede that he must be the most detested person in that room.

"That concludes the Last Will and Testament of the late Charles Lester," said Mr. Cromwell, but only the front row heard him. William looked up. The puppy fat had disappeared while the attractive freckles remained. Susan Lester was walking toward him. He smiled, but she walked straight past him, without even acknowledging his presence. William frowned.

Ignoring the babble, a tall, gray-haired man wearing a pin-striped suit and a silver tie moved quickly toward William.

"You are William Kane, are you not, sir?"

"Yes, I am," said William nervously.

"My name is Peter Parfitt," said the stranger.

"One of the bank's vice chairmen," said William.

"Correct, sir," he said. "I do not know you, but I do know something of your reputation and I count myself lucky to have been acquainted with your distinguished father. If Charles Lester thought you were the right man to be chairman of his bank, that's good enough for me."

William had never been so relieved in his life.

"Where are you staying in New York?" continued Peter Parfitt before William could reply.

"At the Harvard Club."

"Splendid. May I ask if you are free for dinner tonight by any chance?"

"I had intended to return to Boston this evening," said William, "but I expect I'll now have to stay in New York for a few days."

"Good. Why don't you come to my house for dinner, say about eight o'clock?"

The banker handed William his card with an address embossed in copperplate script. "I shall enjoy the opportunity of chatting with you in more convivial surroundings."

"Thank you, sir," said William, pocketing the card as others began crowding around him. Some stared at him in hostility; others waited to express their congratulations.

When William eventually managed to make his escape and return to the Harvard Club, the first thing he did was to call Kate and tell her the news.

She said very quietly, "How happy Matthew would be for you, darling."

"I know," said William.

"When are you coming home?"

"God knows. I'm dining tonight with a Mr. Peter Parfitt, a vice chairman of Lester's. He's being most considerate and cordial, which can make life much easier. I'll spend the night here at the club and call you sometime tomorrow to let you know how things are working out."

"All right, darling."

"All quiet on the Eastern Seaboard?"

"Well, Virginia has cut a tooth and seems to think she deserves special attention, Richard was sent to bed early for being rude to Nanny, and we all miss you."

William laughed. "I'll call you tomorrow."

"Yes, please do. By the way, many congratulations. I approve of Charles Lester's judgment even if I'm going to hate living in New York."

It was the first time William had thought about living in New York.

William arrived at Peter Parfitt's home on East Sixty-fourth Street at eight o'clock that night and was taken by surprise to find that his host had dressed for dinner. William felt slightly embarrassed and ill at ease in his dark banker's suit. He quickly explained to his hostess that he had originally intended to return to Boston that evening. Diana Parfitt, who turned out to be Peter's second wife, could not have been more charming to her guest and she seemed delighted that William was to be the next chairman of Lester's. During an excellent dinner, William could not resist asking Peter Parfitt how he thought the rest of the board would react to Charles Lester's wishes.

"They'll all fall in line," said Parfitt. "I've spoken to most of them already. There's a full board meeting on Monday morning to confirm your appointment and I can only see one small cloud on the horizon."

"What's that?" said William, trying not to sound anxious.

"Well, between you and me, the other vice chairman, Ted Leach, was rather expecting to be appointed chairman himself. In fact, I think I would go as far as to say he anticipated it. We had all been informed that no nomination could be made until after the will had been read, but Charles Lester's wishes must have come as rather a shock to Ted."

"Will he put up a fight?" asked William.

"I'm afraid he might, but there's nothing for you to worry about."

"I don't mind admitting," said Diana Parfitt as she studied the rather flat soufflé in front of her, "that he has never been my favorite man."

"Now, dear," said Parfitt reprovingly, "we mustn't say anything behind Ted's back before Mr. Kane has had a chance to judge for himself. There is no doubt in my mind that the board will confirm Mr. Kane's appointment at the meeting on Monday, and there's even the possibility that Ted Leach will resign."

"I don't want anyone to feel he has to resign because of me," said William.

"A very creditable sentiment," said Parfitt. "But don't bother yourself about a puff of wind. I'm confident that the whole matter is well under control. You go quietly back to Boston tomorrow and I'll keep you informed on the lay of the land."

"Perhaps it might be wise if I dropped in at the bank in the morning. Won't your fellow officers find it a little curious if I make no attempt to meet any of them?"

"No, I don't think that would be advisable given the circumstances. In fact, I feel it would be wiser for you to stay out of their way until the Monday board meeting is over. They won't want to seem any less independent than necessary and they may already feel like glorified rubber stamps. Take my advice, Bill—you go back to Boston. I'll call you with the good news before noon on Monday."

William reluctantly agreed to Peter Parfitt's suggestion and went on to spend a pleasant evening discussing with both Parfitts where he and Kate might stay in New York while they were looking for a permanent home. William was somewhat surprised to find that Peter Parfitt seemed to have no desire to discuss his own views on banking, but he assumed the reason was because of Diana Parfitt's presence. An excellent evening ended with a little too much brandy and William did not arrive back at the Harvard Club until after one o'clock.

Once William had returned to Boston he made an immediate report to Tony Simmons of what had transpired in New York; he did not want him to hear about the appointment from anyone else. Tony turned out to be surprisingly sanguine about the news.

"I'm sorry to learn that you'll be leaving us, William. Lester's may well be two or three times the size of Kane and Cabot, but I'll be unable to replace you and I hope you'll consider very carefully before accepting the appointment."

William was surprised and couldn't help showing it. "Frankly, Tony, I would have thought you'd have been only too glad to see the last of me."

"William, when will you ever believe that my first interest has always been the bank, and there has never been any doubt in my mind that you are one of the shrewdest investment advisors in America today? If you leave Kane and Cabot now, many of the bank's most important clients will naturally want to follow you."

"I would never transfer my own trust funds to Lester's," said William, "any more than I would expect any of the bank's clients to move with me."

"Of course you wouldn't solicit them to join you, William, but some of them will want you to continue managing their portfolios. Like your father and Charles Lester, they believe quite rightly that banking is about people and reputations."

William and Kate spent a tense weekend waiting for Monday and the result of the board meeting in New York. William sat nervously in his office the whole of Monday morning, answering every telephone call personally, but he heard nothing as the morning dragged into the afternoon. He didn't even leave the office for lunch. Peter Parfitt finally called a little after five.

"I'm afraid there's been some unexpected trouble, Bill" were his opening words.

William's heart sank.

"Nothing for you to worry about since I still feel I have the situation well under control, but the board wants the right to oppose your nomination with their own candidate. Some of them have produced legal opinions that go as far as saying the relevant clause of the will has no real validity. I've been given the unpleasant task of asking if you would be willing to fight an election against the board's candidate."

"Who would be the board's candidate?" asked William.

"No names have been mentioned by anyone yet, but I imagine their choice will be Ted Leach. No one else has shown the slightest interest in running against you."

"I'd like a little time to think about it," William replied. "When will the next board meeting be?"

"A week from today," said Parfitt. "But don't you go and get yourself all worked up about Ted Leach; I'm still confident you'll win easily and I'll keep you informed of any further developments as the week goes by."

"Do you want me to come down to New York, Peter?"

"No, not for the moment. I don't think that would help matters."

William thanked him and put the phone down. He packed his old leather briefcase and left the office, feeling more than a little depressed. Tony Simmons, carrying a suitcase, caught up with him in the private parking lot.

"I didn't know you were going out of town, Tony."

"It's only the monthly bankers' dinner in New York. I'll be back by tomorrow afternoon. I think I can safely leave Kane and Cabot for twenty-four hours in the capable hands of the next chairman of Lester's."

William laughed. "I may already be the ex-chairman," he said, and explained the latest development. Once again William was surprised by Tony Simmons's reaction.

"It's true that Ted Leach has always expected to be the next chairman of Lester's," he said. "That's common knowledge in financial circles. But he's a loyal servant of the bank and I can't believe he would oppose Charles Lester's express wishes."

"I didn't realize you even knew him," said William.

"I don't know him all that well," said Tony. "He was a class ahead of me at Yale, and now I see him from time to time at these damned bankers' dinners, which you'll have to attend when you're a chairman. He's bound to be there tonight. I'll have a word with him if you like."

"Yes, please do, but be very careful, won't you?" said William.

"My dear William, you've spent ten years of your life telling me I'm far too careful."

"I'm sorry, Tony. Funny how one's judgment is impaired

when one is worrying about personal problems, however sound the same judgment might be considered when dealing with other people's. I'll put myself in your hands and do whatever you advise."

"Good, then. You leave it to me. I'll see what Leach has to say for himself and call you first thing in the morning."

Tony called from New York a few minutes after midnight and woke William from a deep sleep.

"Have I awoken you, William?"

"Yes. Who is it?"

"Tony Simmons."

William switched on the light by his side of the bed and looked at his alarm clock. "Well, you did say you would call first thing in the morning."

Tony laughed. "I'm afraid what I have to tell you won't seem quite so funny. The man opposing you for chairman of Lester's is Peter Parfitt."

"What?" said William, suddenly awake.

"He's been trying to push the board into supporting him behind your back. Ted Leach, as I expected, is in favor of your appointment as chairman, but the board is now split down the middle."

"Hell. First, thank you, Tony, and second, what do I do now?"

"If you want to be the next chairman of Lester's, you'd better get down here fast before the members of the board wonder why you're hiding away in Boston."

"Hiding away?"

"That's what Parfitt has been telling the directors for the past few days."

"The bastard!"

"Now that you mention the subject, I am unable to vouch for his parentage," said Tony.

William laughed.

"Come and stay at the Yale Club. Then we can talk the whole thing out first thing in the morning."

"I'll be there as quickly as I can," said William.

"I may be asleep when you arrive. It'll be your turn to wake me."

William put the phone down and looked over at Kate, blissfully oblivious to his new problems. She had slept right through the entire conversation. How he wished he could manage that. A curtain had only to flutter in the breeze and he was awake. She would probably sleep right through the Second Coming. He scribbled a few lines of explanation to her and put the note on her bedside table; then he dressed, packed—this time including a dinner jacket—and set off for New York.

The roads were clear and the run in the Daimler seemed the quickest he had ever made. He drove into New York with cleaners, mailmen, newsboys and the morning sun and checked in at the Yale Club as the hall clock chimed once. It was six-fifteen. He unpacked and decided to rest for an hour before waking Tony. The next thing he heard was an insistent tapping on his door. Sleepily, he got up to open it, only to find Tony Simmons standing outside.

"Nice dressing gown, William," said Tony, grinning. He was fully dressed.

"I must have fallen asleep. If you wait a minute, I'll be right with you," said William.

"No, no, I have to catch a train back to Boston. You take a shower and get yourself dressed while we talk."

William went into the bathroom and left the door open.

"Now your main problem," started Tony.

William put his head around the bathroom door. "I can't hear you while the water's running."

Tony waited for it to stop. "Peter Parfitt is your main problem. He assumed he was going to be the next chairman and that his would be the name that was read out in Charles Lester's will. He's been maneuvering the directors against you and playing boardroom politics ever since. Ted Leach can fill you in on the finer details and would like you to join him for lunch today at the Metropolitan Club. He may bring two or three other board members with him on whom you can rely. The board, by the way, still seems to be split right down the middle."

William nicked himself with his razor. "Damn. Which club?"

"Metropolitan, just off Fifth Avenue on East Sixtieth Street."

"Why there and not somewhere down in Wall Street?"

"William, when you're dealing with the Peter Parfitts of this world, you don't telegraph your intentions. Keep your wits about you and play the whole thing very coolly. From what Leach tells me, he believes you can still win."

William came back into the bedroom with a towel around his waist. "I'll try," he said. "To be cool, that is."

Tony smiled. "Now I must get back to Boston. My train leaves Grand Central in ten minutes." He looked at his watch. "Damn, six minutes."

Tony paused at the bedroom door. "You know, your father never trusted Peter Parfitt. Too smooth, he always used to say. Never anything more, just a little too smooth." He picked up his suitcase. "Good luck, William."

"How can I begin to thank you, Tony?"

"You can't. Just put it down to my trying to atone for the lousy way I treated Matthew."

William watched the door close as he put in his collar stud. As he straightened his tie he reflected on how curious it was that he had spent years working closely with Tony Simmons without ever really getting to know him but that now, in only a few days of personal crisis, he found himself instantly liking and trusting a man he had never before really been aware of. He went down to the dining room and had a typical club breakfast: a cold boiled egg, one piece of hard toast, butter and English marmalade from someone else's table. The porter handed him a copy of *The Wall Street Journal*, which hinted on an inside page that everything was not running smoothly at Lester's following the nomination of William Kane as its next chairman. At least the *Journal* did not seem to have any inside information.

William returned to his room and asked the operator for a number in Boston. He was kept waiting for a few minutes before he was put through.

"I do apologize, Mr. Kane. I had no idea it was you on the line. May I congratulate you on your appointment as chairman of Lester's. I hope this means our New York office will be seeing a lot more of you in the future."

"That may well depend on you, Mr. Cohen."

"I don't think I quite understand," the lawyer replied.

William explained what had happened over the past few days and read out the relevant section of Charles Lester's will.

Thomas Cohen spent some time taking down each word and then going over his notes carefully.

"Do you think his wishes would stand up in court?" asked William.

"Who knows? I can't think of a precedent for such a situation. A nineteenth-century Member of Parliament once bequeathed his constituency in a will and no one objected, and the beneficiary went on to become Prime Minister. But that was over a hundred years ago—and in England. Now in this case, if the board decided to contest Mr. Lester's will and you took their decision to court, I wouldn't care to predict which way the judge might jump. Lord Melbourne didn't have to contend with a surrogate of New York County. Nevertheless, a nice legal conundrum, Mr. Kane."

"What do you advise?" asked William.

"I am a Jew, Mr. Kane. I came to this country on a ship from Germany at the turn of the century and I have always had to fight hard for anything I've wanted. Do you want to be chairman of Lester's that badly?"

"Yes, Mr. Cohen, I do."

"Then you must listen to an old man who has, over the years, come to view you with great respect and, if I may say so, with some affection. I'll tell you exactly what I'd do if I were faced with your predicament."

. . .

An hour later William put the phone down and, having some time to kill, strolled up Park Avenue. Along the way he passed a site on which a huge building was well into construction. A large, neat billboard announced: "The next Baron Hotel will be in New York. When the Baron has been your host, you'll never want to stay anywhere else." William smiled and walked with a lighter step toward the Metropolitan Club.

Ted Leach, a short, dapper man with dark brown hair and a lighter mustache, was standing in the foyer of the club, waiting for him. He ushered William into the bar. William admired the Renaissance style of the club, built by Otto Kuhn and Stanford White in 1891. J. P. Morgan had founded the club when one of his closest friends was blackballed at the Union League.

"A fairly extravagant gesture even for a very close friend," Ted Leach suggested, trying to make conversation. "What will you have to drink, Mr. Kane?"

"A dry sherry, please," said William.

A boy in a smart blue uniform returned a few moments later with a dry sherry and a scotch and water; he hadn't needed to ask Mr. Leach for his order.

"To the next chairman of Lester's," said Ted Leach, raising his glass.

William hesitated.

"Don't drink, Mr. Kane. As you know, you should never drink to yourself."

William laughed, unsure of what to say.

A few minutes later two older men were walking toward them, both tall and confident in the bankers' uniform of gray three-piece suits, stiff collars and dark, unpatterned ties. Had they been strolling down Wall Street, William would not have given them a second glance. In the Metropolitan Club he studied them carefully.

"Mr. Alfred Rodgers and Mr. Winthrop Davies," said Ted Leach as he introduced them.

William's smile was reserved, unsure as he was whose side anyone was on. The two newcomers studied him with care. No one spoke for a moment.

"Where do we start?" said the one named Rodgers, a monocle falling from his eye as he spoke.

"By going on up to lunch," said Ted Leach.

The three of them turned, obviously knowing exactly where they were going. William followed. The dining room on the second floor was vast, with another magnificent high ceiling. The maitre d' placed them in the window seat, over-looking Central Park, where no one could overhear their conversation.

"Let's order and then talk," said Ted Leach.

Through the window William could see the Plaza Hotel. Memories of his celebration with the grandmothers and Matthew came flooding back to him—and there was some-thing else he was trying to recall about that tea at the Plaza. . . .

"Mr. Kane, let's put our cards on the table," said Ted Leach. "Charles Lester's decision to appoint you as chair-man of the bank came as a surprise, not to put too fine a point on it. But if the board ignores his wishes, the bank could be plunged into chaos and that is an outcome none of us needs. He was a shrewd old man and he had his reasons for wanting you as the bank's next chairman, and that's good enough for me."

William had heard those words before—from Peter Parfitt.

"All three of us," said Winthrop Davies, taking over, "owe everything we have to Charles Lester, and we will carry out his wishes if it's the last thing we do as members of the board."

"It may turn out to be just that," said Ted Leach, "if Peter Parfitt does succeed in becoming chairman."

"I'm sorry, gentlemen," said William, "to have caused so much consternation. If my appointment as chairman came as a surprise to you, I can assure you it was nothing less than a bolt from the blue for me. I imagined I would receive some

minor personal memento of Matthew's from Charles
Lester's will, not the responsibility of running the bank."

"We understand the position you've been placed in, Mr.
Kane," said Ted Leach, "and you must trust us when we say
we're here to help you. We are aware that you'll find that difficult to believe after the treatment that has been meted out
to you by Peter Parfitt and the tactics he's been using behind
your back."

"I have to believe you, Mr. Leach, because I have no
choice but to place myself in your hands. How do you view
the current situation?"

"The situation is clear to me," said Leach. "Peter Parfitt's
campaign is well organized and he now feels he's acting
from a position of strength. We, therefore, Mr. Kane, must
be entirely open with each other if we are to have any chance
of beating him. I am assuming, of course, that you have the
stomach for such a fight."

"I wouldn't be here if I didn't, Mr. Leach. And now that
you've summed up the position so succinctly, perhaps you'll
allow me to suggest how we should go about defeating Mr.
Parfitt."

"Certainly," said Ted Leach.

The three other men all listened intently.

"You are undoubtedly right in saying that Parfitt feels he
is now in a strong position because to date he has always
been the one on the attack, always knowing what is going to
happen next. Might I suggest that the time has come for us
to reverse that trend and take up the attack ourselves where
and when he least expects it—in his own boardroom."

"How do you propose we go about that, Mr. Kane?" inquired Winthrop Davies, looking somewhat surprised.

"I'll tell you if you'll first permit me to ask you two questions. How many full-time executive directors are there with
a vote on the board?"

"Sixteen," said Ted Leach instantly.

"And with whom does their allegiance lie at this moment?" William asked.

"Not the easiest question to answer, Mr. Kane," Winthrop

Davies chipped in. He took a crumbled envelope from his inside pocket and studied the back of it before he continued. "I think we can count on six sure votes, and Peter Parfitt can be certain of five. It came as a shock for me to discover this morning that Rupert Cork-Smith—he was Charles Lester's closest friend—is unwilling to support you, Mr. Kane. Really strange, because I know he doesn't care for Parfitt. I think that may make the voting six apiece."

"That gives us until Thursday," added Ted Leach, "to find out how the other four board members are likely to vote."

"Why Thursday?" asked William.

"Day of the next board meeting," answered Leach, stroking his mustache, which William had noticed he did every time he started to speak. "And more important, Item One on the agenda is the election of a new chairman."

"I was told the next meeting would not take place until Monday," said William in astonishment.

"By whom?" Davies asked.

"Peter Parfitt," said William.

"His tactics," Ted Leach commented, "have not been altogether those of a gentleman."

"I've learned enough about that gentleman," William said, placing an ironic stress on the word, "to make me realize I'll have to take the battle to him."

"Easier said than done, Mr. Kane. He is very much in the driver's seat at this moment," said Winthrop Davies, "and I'm not sure how we go about removing him from it."

"Switch the traffic lights to red," replied William. "Who has the authority to call a board meeting?"

"While the board is without a chairman, either vice chairman," said Ted Leach. "Which in reality means Peter Parfitt or myself."

"How many board members form a quorum?"

"Nine," said Davies.

"And if you are one of the two vice chairmen, Mr. Leach, who is the Company Secretary?"

"I am," said Alfred Rodgers, who until then had hardly

opened his mouth, the exact quality William always looked for in a company secretary.

"How much notice do you have to give to call an emergency board meeting, Mr. Rodgers?"

"Every director must be informed at least twenty-four hours beforehand, although that has never actually happened except during the crash of twenty-nine. Charles Lester always tried to give at least three days' notice."

"But the bank's rules do allow for an emergency meeting to be held on twenty-four hours' notice?" asked William.

"They do, Mr. Kane," Alfred Rodgers affirmed, his monocle now firmly in place and focused on William.

"Excellent, then let's call our own board meeting."

The three bankers stared at William as if they had not quite heard him clearly.

"Think about it, gentlemen," William continued. "Mr. Leach, as vice chairman, calls the board meeting, and Mr. Rodgers, as company secretary, informs all the directors."

"When would you want this board meeting to take place?" asked Ted Leach.

"Tomorrow afternoon." William looked at his watch. "Three o'clock."

"Good God, that's cutting it a bit fine," said Alfred Rodgers. "I'm not sure——"

"Cutting it very fine for Peter Parfitt, wouldn't you say?" said William.

"That's true," said Ted Leach, "if you know precisely what you have planned for the meeting?"

"You leave the meeting to me. Just be sure that it's correctly convened and that every director is properly informed."

"I wonder how Peter Parfitt is going to react," said Ted Leach.

"Don't worry about Parfitt," said William. "That's the mistake we've made all along. Let him start worrying about us for a change. As long as he's given the full twenty-four hours' notice and he's the last director informed, we have nothing to fear. We don't want him to have any more time than necessary to stage a counterattack. And gentlemen, do not be surprised by anything I do or say tomorrow. Trust my judgment and be there to support me."

"You don't feel we ought to know exactly what you have in mind?"

"No, Mr. Leach. You must appear at the meeting as disinterested directors doing no more than carrying out your duty."

It was beginning to dawn on Ted Leach and his two colleagues why Charles Lester had chosen William Kane to be their next chairman. They left the Metropolitan Club a good deal more confident than when they had arrived, despite their being totally in the dark about what would actually happen at the board meeting they were about to instigate. William, on the other hand, having carried out the first part of Thomas Cohen's instructions, was now looking forward to the harder second part.

He spent most of the afternoon and evening in his room at the Yale Club, meticulously considering his tactics for the next day's meeting and taking only a short break to call Kate.

"Where are you, darling?" she said. "Stealing away in the middle of the night to I know not where."

"To my New York mistress," said William.

"Poor girl," said Kate, "she probably doesn't know the half of it. What's her advice on the devious Mr. Parfitt?"

"Haven't had time to ask her, we've been so busy doing other things. While I have you on the phone, what's your advice?"

"Do nothing Charles Lester or your father wouldn't have done in the same circumstances," said Kate, suddenly serious.

"They're probably playing golf together on the eighteenth cloud and taking a side bet while watching us the whole time."

"Whatever you do, William, you won't go far wrong if you do remember they are watching you."

. . .

When dawn broke, William was already awake, having managed to sleep only fitfully. He rose a little after six, had a cold shower, went for a long walk through Central Park to clear his head and returned to the Yale Club for a light breakfast. There was a message waiting for him in the front hall—from his wife. When he read it for a second time, William laughed at the line "If you're not too busy could you remember to buy a baseball glove for Richard." William picked up *The Wall Street Journal*, which was still running the story of trouble in Lester's boardroom over the selection of a new chairman. It now had Peter Parfitt's version of the story, hinting that his appointment as chairman would probably be confirmed at Thursday's meeting. William wondered whose version would be reported in tomorrow's paper. Oh, for a look at tomorrow's *Journal* now. He spent the morning double-checking the articles of incorporation and bylaws of Lester's Bank. He had no lunch but did find time to visit F.A.O. Schwarz and buy a baseball glove for his son.

At two-thirty he took a cab to the bank in Wall Street and arrived a few minutes before three. The young doorman asked him if he had an appointment to see anyone.

"I'm William Kane."

"Yes, sir, you'll want the boardroom."

Good God, thought William, I can't even remember where it is.

The doorman observed his embarrassment. "You take the corridor on the left, sir, and then it's the second door on the right."

"Thank you," said William, and walked confidently as he could down the corridor. Until that moment, he had always thought the expression "a stomach full of butterflies" a stupid one. He felt that his heartbeat must be louder than the clock in the front hall; he would not have been surprised to hear himself chiming three o'clock.

Ted Leach was standing alone at the entrance to the

boardroom. "There's going to be trouble" were his opening words.

"Good," said William. "That's the way Charles Lester would have liked it and he would have faced the trouble head-on."

William strode into the impressive oak-paneled room and did not need to count heads to be sure that every director was present. This was not going to be one of those board meetings a director could occasionally afford to skip. The conversation stopped the moment William entered the room, and there was an awkward silence as they all stood around and stared at him. William quickly took the chairman's seat at the head of the long mahogany table before Peter Parfitt could realize what was happening.

"Gentlemen, please be seated," said William, hoping his voice sounded firm.

Ted Leach and some of the other directors took their seats immediately; others were more reluctant. Murmuring started.

William could see that two directors whom he didn't know were about to rise and interrupt him.

"Before anyone else says anything I would, if you will allow me, like to make an opening statement, and then you can decide how you wish to proceed from there. I feel that is the least we can do to comply with the wishes of the late Charles Lester."

The two men sat down.

"Thank you, gentlemen. To start with I would like to make it clear to all those present that I have absolutely no desire to be the chairman of this bank"—William paused for effect—"unless it is the wish of the majority of its directors."

Every eye in the room was now fixed on William.

"I am, gentlemen, at present vice chairman of Kane and Cabot and I own fifty-one percent of their stock. Kane and Cabot was founded by my grandfather, and I think it compares favorably in reputation, though not in size, with Lester's. Were I required to leave Boston and move to New York to become the next chairman of Lester's, in compliance with Charles Lester's wishes, I cannot pretend the move would be an easy one for myself or for my family. However, as it was Charles Lester's wish that I should do just that—and he was not a man to make such a proposition lightly—I am, gentlemen, bound to take his wishes seriously myself. I would also like to add that his son, Matthew Lester, was my closest friend for over fifteen years, and I consider it a tragedy that it is I, and not he, who is addressing you today as your nominated chairman."

Some of the directors were nodding their approval.

"Gentlemen, if I am fortunate enough to secure your support today, I will sacrifice everything I have in Boston in order to serve you. I hope it is unnecessary for me to give you a detailed account of my banking experience. I shall assume that any director present who has read Charles Lester's will must have taken the trouble to find out why he thought I was the right man to succeed him. My own chairman, Anthony Simmons, whom many of you know, has asked me to stay on at Kane and Cabot.

"I had intended to inform Mr. Parfitt yesterday of my final decision—had he taken the trouble to call me and seek out that information. I had the pleasure of dining with Mr. and Mrs. Parfitt last week at their home, and on that occasion Mr. Parfitt informed me that he had no interest in becoming the next chairman of this bank. My only rival, in his opinion, was Mr. Edward Leach, your other vice chairman. I have since consulted with Mr. Leach himself and he informs me that I have always had his support for the chair. I assumed, therefore, that both vice chairmen were backing me. After reading *The Wall Street Journal* this morning, not that I have ever trusted their forecasting since I was eight"—a little laughter—"I felt I should attend today's meeting to assure myself that I had not lost the support of the two vice chairmen, and that the *Journal*'s account was inaccurate. Mr. Leach called this board meeting and I must ask him at this juncture if he still supports me to succeed Charles Lester as the bank's next chairman."

William looked toward Ted Leach, whose head was

bowed. The wait for his verdict was palpable. A thumbs-down from him would mean the Parfittlians could eat the Christian.

Ted Leach raised his head slowly and said, "I support Mr. Kane unreservedly."

William looked directly at Peter Parfitt for the first time that day. The man was sweating profusely and when he spoke he did not take his eyes off the yellow pad in front of him.

"Well, some members of the board," he began, "felt I should throw my hat into the ring——"

"So you have changed your mind about supporting me and complying with Charles Lester's wishes?" interrupted William, allowing a small note of surprise to enter his voice.

Peter Parfitt raised his head a little. "The problem is not quite that easy, Mr. Kane."

"Yes or no, Mr. Parfitt?"

"Yes, I shall stand against you," said Peter Parfitt suddenly, forcefully.

"Despite telling me last week you had no interest in being chairman yourself?"

"I would like to be able to state my own position," said Parfitt, "before you assume too much. This is not your boardroom yet, Mr. Kane."

"Certainly, Mr. Parfitt."

So far the meeting had gone exactly as William had planned. His own speech had been carefully prepared and delivered, and Peter Parfitt now labored under the disadvantage of having lost the initiative, to say nothing of having been publicly called a liar.

"Gentlemen," he began, as if searching for words. "Well," he said.

The eyes had turned their gaze from William and were now fixed on Parfitt. This gave William the chance to relax a little and study the faces of the other directors.

"Several members of the board approached me privately after I had dinner with Mr. Kane, and I felt that it was no more than my duty to consider their wishes and offer myself for election. I have never at any time wanted to oppose the wishes of Mr. Charles Lester, whom I always admired and respected. Naturally, I would have informed Mr. Kane of my intention before tomorrow's scheduled board meeting, but I confess to have been taken somewhat by surprise by today's events."

He drew a deep breath and started again. "I have served Lester's for twenty-two years, six of them as your vice chairman. I feel, therefore, that I have the right to be considered for the chair. I would be delighted if Mr. Kane were to join the board, but I now find myself unable to back his appointment as chairman. I hope my fellow directors will find it possible to support someone who has worked for this bank for over twenty years rather than elect an unknown outsider on the whim of a man distraught over the death of his only son. Thank you, gentlemen."

He sat down.

In the circumstances, William was rather impressed by the speech, but Parfitt did not have the benefit of Mr. Cohen's advice on the power of the last word in a close contest. William rose again.

"Gentlemen, Mr. Parfitt has pointed out that I am personally unknown to you. I, therefore, want none of you to be in any doubt as to the type of man I am. I am, as I said, the grandson and the son of bankers. I've been a banker all my life and it would be less than honest of me to pretend I would not be delighted to serve as the next chairman of Lester's. If, on the other hand, after all you have heard today, you decide to back Mr. Parfitt as chairman, so be it. I shall return to Boston and serve my own bank quite happily. I will, moreover, announce publicly that I have no wish to be the chairman of Lester's, and that will ensure you against any claims that you have been derelict in fulfilling the provisions of Charles Lester's will.

"There are, however, no conditions on which I would be willing to serve on your board under Mr. Parfitt. I have no intention of being less than frank with you on that point. I come before you, gentlemen, at the grave disadvantage of being, in Mr. Parfitt's words, 'an unknown outsider.' I have, however, the advantage of being supported by a man who cannot be present today. A man whom all of you respected and admired, a man not known for yielding to whims or making hasty decisions. I therefore suggest this board waste no more of its valuable time in deciding whom they wish to serve as the next chairman of Lester's. If any of you have any doubts in your mind about my ability to run this bank, then I can only suggest you vote for Mr. Parfitt. I shall not vote in this election myself, gentlemen, and I assume Mr. Parfitt will not do so either."

"You *cannot* vote," said Peter Parfitt angrily. "You are not a member of this board yet. I am, and I shall vote."

"So be it, Mr. Parfitt. No one will ever be able to say you did not have the opportunity to gain every possible vote."

William waited for the effect of his words to sink in and, as a director who was a stranger to William was about to interrupt, he continued: "I will ask Mr. Rodgers as company secretary to carry out the electoral procedure, and when you have completed your vote, gentlemen, perhaps you could pass the ballot papers back to him."

Alfred Rodgers' monocle had been popping out periodically during the entire meeting. Nervously, he passed voting slips around to each director. When each had written down the name of the candidate whom he supported, the slips were returned to him.

"Perhaps it might be prudent, given the circumstances, Mr. Rodgers, if the votes were counted aloud, thus making sure no inadvertent error is made that might lead the directors to require a second ballot."

"Certainly, Mr. Kane."

"Does that meet with your approval, Mr. Parfitt?"

Peter Parfitt nodded his agreement without looking up.

"Thank you. Perhaps you would be kind enough to read the votes out to the board, Mr. Rodgers."

The company secretary opened the first voting slip.

" 'Parfitt.' "

And then the second.

" 'Parfitt,' " he repeated.

The game was now out of William's hands. All the years of waiting for the prize he had told Charles Lester such a long time ago would be his would be over in the next few seconds.

" 'Kane. Parfitt. Kane.' "

Three votes to two against him; was he going to meet the same fate as he had in his contest with Tony Simmons?

" 'Kane. Kane. Parfitt.' "

Four votes all. He could see that Parfitt was still sweating profusely and he didn't exactly feel relaxed himself.

" 'Parfitt.' "

No expression crossed William's face. Parfitt allowed himself a smile.

Five votes to four.

" 'Kane. Kane. Kane.' "

The smile disappeared.

Just two more, two more, pleaded William, nearly out loud.

" 'Parfitt. Parfitt.' "

The company secretary took a long time opening a voting slip which someone had folded and refolded several times.

" 'Kane.' " Eight votes to seven in William's favor.

The last piece of paper was now being opened. William watched Alfred Rodgers's lips. The company secretary looked up; for that one moment he was the most important man in the room.

" 'Kane.' " Parfitt's head sank into his hands.

"Gentlemen, the tally is nine votes for Mr. William Kane, seven votes for Mr. Peter Parfitt. I therefore declare Mr. William Kane to be the duly elected chairman of Lester's bank."

A respectful silence fell over the room as every head except Peter Parfitt's turned toward William and waited for the new chairman's first move.

William exhaled a great rush of air and stood once again, this time to face his board.

"Thank you, gentlemen, for the confidence you have

placed in me. It was Charles Lester's wish that I be your next chairman and I am delighted you have confirmed that wish with your vote. I now intend to serve this bank to the best of my ability, which I shall be unable to do without the wholehearted support of the board. If Mr. Parfitt would be kind enough . . ."

Peter Parfitt looked up hopefully.

". . . to join me in the chairman's office in a few minutes' time, I would be much obliged. After I have seen Mr. Parfitt, I would like to see Mr. Leach. I hope, gentlemen, that tomorrow I shall have the opportunity of meeting all of you individually. The next board meeting will be the monthly one. This meeting is now adjourned."

The directors began to rise and talk among themselves. William walked quickly into the corridor, avoiding Peter Parfitt's stare. Ted Leach caught up with him and directed him to the chairman's office.

"That was a great risk you took," said Ted Leach, "and you only just pulled it off. What would you have done if you'd lost the vote?"

"Gone back to Boston," said William, sounding unperturbed.

Ted Leach opened the door to the chairman's office for William. The room was almost exactly as he remembered it; perhaps it had seemed a little larger when, as a prep school boy, he had told Charles Lester that he would one day run the bank. He stared at the portrait of the great man behind his desk and winked at the late Chairman. Then he sat down in the big red leather chair and put his elbows on the mahogany desk. As he took a small leather-bound book out of his jacket pocket and placed it on the desk in front of him, there was a knock on the door. An old man entered, leaning heavily on a black stick with a silver handle. Ted Leach left them alone.

"My name is Rupert Cork-Smith," he said, with a hint of an English accent.

William rose to greet him. He was the oldest member of the board. His gray hair, long sideburns and heavy gold watch all came from a past era, but his reputation for probity was legendary in banking circles. No man needed to sign a contract with Rupert Cork-Smith: his word had always been his bond. He looked William firmly in the eye.

"I voted against you, sir, and naturally you can expect my resignation to be on your desk within the hour."

"Will you have a seat, sir?" William said gently.

"Thank you, sir," he replied.

"I think you knew my father and grandfather."

"I had the privilege. Your grandfather and I were at Harvard together and I still remember with regret your father's tragic death."

"And Charles Lester?" said William.

"Was my closest friend. The provisions in his will have preyed upon my conscience. It was no secret that my choice would not have been Peter Parfitt. I would have had Ted Leach for chairman, but as I have never abstained from anything in my life, I felt I had to support the candidate who stood against you, as I found myself unable to vote for a man I had never even met."

"I admire your honesty, Mr. Cork-Smith, but now I have a bank to run. I need you at this moment far more than you need me, so I, as a younger man, beg you not to resign."

The old man raised his head and stared into William's eyes. "I'm not sure it would work, young man. I can't change my attitudes overnight," said Cork-Smith, both hands resting on his stick.

"Give me six months, sir, and if you still feel the same way, I won't put up a fight."

They both sat in silence before Cork-Smith spoke again: "Charles Lester was right: you are the son of Richard Kane."

"Will you continue to serve this bank, sir?"

"I will, young man. There's no fool like an old fool, don't you know."

Rupert Cork-Smith rose slowly with the aid of his stick. William moved to help him but was waved away.

"Good luck, my boy. You can rely on my total support."

"Thank you, sir," said William.

When he opened the door, William saw Peter Parfitt waiting in the corridor. As Rupert Cork-Smith left, the two men did not speak.

Peter Parfitt blustered in. "Well, I tried and I lost. A man can't do more," he said, laughing. "No hard feelings, Bill?" He extended his hand.

"There are no hard feelings, Mr. Parfitt. As you so rightly say, you tried and you lost, and now you will resign from your post at this bank."

"I'll do what?" said Parfitt.

"Resign," said William.

"That's a bit rough, isn't it, Bill? My action wasn't at all personal. I simply felt——"

"I don't want you in my bank, Mr. Parfitt. You'll leave by tonight and never return."

"And if I say I won't go? I own a good many shares in the bank and I still have a lot of support on the board. What's more, I could take you to court."

"Then I would recommend that you read the bank's by-laws, Mr. Parfitt, which I spent some considerable time studying only this morning."

William picked up the small leather-bound book that was still lying on the desk in front of him and turned a few pages over. Having found a paragraph he had marked that morning, he read aloud. " 'The chairman has the right to remove any office holder in whom he has lost confidence.' " He looked up. "I have lost confidence in you, Mr. Parfitt, and you will therefore resign, receiving two years' pay. If, on the other hand, you force me to remove you, I shall see that you leave the bank with nothing other than your stock. The choice is yours."

"Won't you give me a chance?"

"I gave you a chance last week at dinner and you lied and cheated. Not traits I am looking for in my next vice chairman. Will it be resignation or do I throw you out, Mr. Parfitt?"

"Damn you, Kane, I'll resign."

"Good. Sit down and write the letter now."

"No, I'll let you have it in the morning in my own good time." He started walking toward the door.

"Now—or I fire you," said William.

Peter Parfitt hesitated and then came back and sank heavily into a chair by the side of William's desk. William handed him a piece of the bank's stationery and proffered him a pen. Parfitt took out his own pen and started writing. When he had finished, William picked up the letter and read it through carefully.

"Good day, Mr. Parfitt."

Peter Parfitt left without speaking. Ted Leach came in a few moments later.

"You wanted to see me, Mr. Chairman?"

"Yes," said William. "I want to appoint you as the bank's overall vice chairman. Mr. Parfitt felt he had to resign."

"Oh, I'm surprised to hear that, I would have thought . . ."

William passed him the letter. Ted Leach read it and then looked at William.

"I shall be delighted to be overall vice chairman. Thank you for your confidence in me."

"Good. I'll be obliged if you will arrange for me to meet every director during the next two days. I'll start work at eight o'clock tomorrow morning."

"Yes, Mr. Kane."

"Perhaps you will also be kind enough to give Mr. Parfitt's letter of resignation to the company secretary?"

"As you wish, Mr. Chairman."

"My name is William—another mistake Mr. Parfitt made."

Ted Leach smiled tentatively. "I'll see you tomorrow morning,"—he hesitated— "William."

When he had left, William sat in Charles Lester's chair and whirled himself around in an uncharacteristic burst of sheer glee till he was dizzy. Then he looked out of the window onto Wall Street, elated by the bustling crowds, enjoying the view of the other great banks and brokerage houses of America. He was part of all of it now.

"And who, pray, are you?" said a female voice from behind him.

William swiveled around and there standing in front of him was a middle-aged woman, primly dressed, looking very irate.

"Perhaps I may ask you the same question," said William.

"I am the chairman's secretary," the woman said stiffly.

"And I," said William, "am the chairman."

During the next few weeks William moved his family to New York where they found a four-story house on East Sixty-eighth Street. It had everything Kate needed, even a small garden in the back. Settling in took longer than they had anticipated. For the first three months William wished, as he tried to extricate himself from Boston in order to carry out his job in New York, that every day had forty-eight hours in it, and he found the umbilical cord was hard to sever completely. Tony Simmons was most helpful, and William began to appreciate why Alan Lloyd had backed him to be chairman of Kane and Cabot. For the first time he was willing to admit that Alan had been right.

Kate's life in New York was soon fully occupied. Virginia could already crawl across a room and get into William's study before Kate could turn her head, and Richard wanted a new windbreaker like every other boy in New York. As the wife of the chairman of a New York bank Kate was expected to give cocktail parties and dinners regularly, subtly making certain that directors and major clients were always given the chance to catch the private ear of William to seek his advice or voice their opinions. Kate handled all situations with great charm, and William was eternally grateful to the liquidation department of Kane and Cabot for supplying his greatest asset. When she informed William that she was going to have another baby, all he could ask was "When did I find the time?" Virginia was thrilled by the news, not fully understanding why Mummy was getting so fat, and Richard refused to discuss it.

Within six months the clash with Peter Parfitt was a thing of the past, and William had become the undisputed chairman of Lester's bank and a figure to be reckoned with in New York financial circles. Not many more months had passed before he began to wonder in which direction he should start to set himself a new goal. He had achieved his life's ambition by becoming chairman of Lester's at the age of thirty-three although, unlike Alexander, he felt there were more worlds still to conquer, and he had neither the time nor the inclination to sit down and weep.

Kate gave birth to their third child at the end of William's first year as chairman of Lester's, a second girl, whom they named Lucy. William taught Virginia, who was now walking, how to rock Lucy's cradle; while Richard, almost six years old and due to enter the first grade at the Buckley School, used the new arrival as the opportunity to talk his father into a new baseball bat. Lucy, unable to make an articulate demand, nevertheless became the third woman who could twist William around her little finger.

In William's first year as chairman of Lester's the bank's profits were slightly up and he was forecasting a considerable improvement in his second year.

On September 1, 1939, Hitler marched into Poland.

One of William's first reactions was to think of Abel Rosnovski and his new Baron on Park Avenue, already becoming the toast of New York. Quarterly reports from Thomas Cohen showed that Rosnovski went from strength to strength, although his latest ideas for expansion to Europe looked as if they might be in for a slight delay. Cohen continued to find no direct association between Henry Osborne and Abel Rosnovski, but he admitted that it was becoming increasingly difficult to ascertain all the facts William required.

William never thought that America would involve herself in another European war, but he kept the London branch of Lester's open to show clearly which side he was on and never for one moment considered selling his twelve thousand acres in Hampshire and Lincolnshire. Tony Simmons in Boston, on the other hand, informed William that he intended to close Kane and Cabot's London branch. William used the problems created in London by the war as an excuse to visit his beloved Boston and have a meeting with Tony.

The two chairmen now met on extremely easy and friendly terms since they no longer had any reason to see themselves as rivals. In fact, each had come to use the other as a springboard for new ideas. As Tony had predicted, Kane and Cabot had lost some of its more important clients when William became the chairman of Lester's, but William always kept Tony fully informed whenever an old client expressed a desire to move his account and he never solicited a single one. When they sat down at a corner table of Locke-Ober's for lunch, Tony Simmons lost little time in repeating his intent to close the London branch of Kane and Cabot.

"My first reason is simple," he said as he sipped the imported burgundy, apparently not giving a moment's thought to the strong likelihood that German boots were about to trample on the grapes in most of the vineyards in France. "I think the bank will lose more money if we don't cut our losses and get out of England."

"Of course, you will lose a little money,"said William, "but we must support the British."

"Why?" asked Tony. "We're a bank, not a boosters' club."

"Britain's not a baseball team, Tony; it's a nation of people to whom we owe our entire heritage——"

"You should take up politics," said Tony. "I'm beginning to think your talents are wasted in banking. Nevertheless, I feel there's a far more important reason why we should close the branch. If Hitler marches into Britain the way he has into Poland and France—and I'm sure that is exactly what he intends to do—the bank will be taken over and we would lose every penny we have in London."

"Over my dead body," said William. "If Hitler puts so

much as a foot on British soil, America will enter the war the same day."

"Never," said Tony. "FDR has said all aid short of war. And the America Firsters would raise an almighty hue and cry."

"Never listen to a politician," said William. "Especially Roosevelt. When he says 'never,' that only means not today or at least not this morning. You only have to remember what Wilson told us in 1916."

Tony laughed. "When are you going to run for the Senate, William?"

"Now, there is a question to which I can safely answer 'never.'"

"I respect your feelings, William, but I want out."

"You're the chairman," replied William. "If the board backs you, you can close the London branch tomorrow and I would never use my position to act against a majority decision."

"Until you join the two banks together, and it becomes your decision."

"I told you once, Tony, that I would never attempt to do that while you are still chairman."

"But I think we *ought* to merge."

"What?" said William, spilling his burgundy on the tablecloth, unable to believe what he had just heard. "Good heavens, Tony, I'll say one thing for you, you're never predictable."

"I have the best interests of the bank at heart, as always, William. Think about the present situation for a moment. New York is now, more than ever, the center of U.S. finance, and when England goes under to Hitler, it will be the center of world finance, so that's where Kane and Cabot needs to be. Moreover, if we merged we would create a more comprehensive institution because our specialties are complementary. Kane and Cabot has always done a great deal of ship and heavy-industry financing, while Lester's does very little. Conversely, you do a lot of underwriting and we hardly touch it. Not to mention the fact that in many cities we have unnecessary duplicating offices."

"Tony, I agree with everything you've said, but I would still want to stay in Britain."

"Exactly proving my point, William. Kane and Cabot's London branch would be closed, but we would still keep Lester's. Then if London goes through a rough passage, it won't matter as much, because we will be consolidated and therefore stronger."

"But how would you feel if I said that while Roosevelt's restrictions on merchant banks will only allow us to work out of one state, a merger could succeed only if we ran the entire operation from New York, treating Boston as nothing more than a holding office."

"I'd back you," said Tony and added: "You might even consider going into commercial banking and dropping the straight investment work."

"No, Tony. FDR has made it impossible for an honest man to do both, and in any case my father believed that you could either serve a small group of rich people or a large group of poor people, so Lester's will always remain in traditional merchant banking as long as I'm chairman. But if we did decide to merge the two banks, don't you foresee major problems?"

"Very few we couldn't surmount given goodwill on both sides. However, you will have to consider the implications carefully, William, as you would undoubtedly lose overall control of the new bank as a minority shareholder, which would always make you vulnerable to a takeover bid."

"I'd risk that to be chairman of one of the largest financial institutions in America."

William returned to New York that evening, elated by the discussion with Tony, and called a board meeting of Lester's to outline Tony Simmons' proposal. When he found that the board approved of a merger in principle, he instructed each manager in the bank to consider the whole plan in greater detail.

The departmental heads took three months before they reported back to the board, and to a man they came to the same conclusion: a merger was no more than common sense, because the two banks were complementary in so many ways. With different offices all over America and branches in Europe, they had a great deal to offer each other. Moreover, the chairman of Lester's had continued to own 51 percent of Kane and Cabot, making the merger simply a marriage of convenience. Some of the directors on Lester's board could not understand why William hadn't thought of the idea before. Ted Leach was of the opinion that Charles Lester must have had it in his mind when he nominated William as his successor.

The details of the merger took nearly a year to negotiate and lawyers were kept at work into the small hours to complete the necessary paperwork. In the exchange of shares, William ended up as the largest stockholder with 8 percent of the new company and was appointed the new bank's president and chairman. Tony Simmons remained in Boston as one vice chairman and Ted Leach in New York as the other. The new merchant bank was renamed Lester, Kane and Company but continued to be referred to as Lester's.

William decided to hold a press conference in New York to announce the successful merger of the two banks, and he chose Monday, the eighth of December, 1941, to inform the financial world at large. The press conference had to be canceled because the morning before, the Japanese had launched an attack on Pearl Harbor.

The prepared press release had already been mailed to the newspapers some days before, but the Tuesday-morning financial pages understandably allocated the announcement of the merger only a small amount of space. This lack of coverage was, however, far from foremost in William's mind.

He couldn't quite work out how or when he was going to

tell his wife that he intended to enlist. When Kate heard the news she was horrified by its implications and immediately tried to talk him out of the decision.

"What do you imagine you can do that a million others can't?" she demanded.

"I'm not sure," William replied, "but all I can be certain of is that I must do what my father or grandfather would have done given the same circumstances."

"They undoubtedly would have done what was in the best interest of the bank."

"No," William said firmly. "They would have done what was in the best interest of America."

PART FIVE
1941–1952

CHAPTER
TWENTY-FOUR

Abel studied the news item on Lester, Kane and Company in the financial section of the *Chicago Tribune*. With all the space devoted to the probable consequences of the Japanese attack on Pearl Harbor, he would have missed the brief article had it not been accompanied by a small out-of-date photograph of William Kane, so out of date that Kane looked much as he had when Abel had visited him in Boston more than ten years before. Certainly Kane appeared too young in this photograph to fit the journal's description of him as the brilliant chairman of the newly formed Lester, Kane and Company. The article went on to predict: "The new bank, a joining together of Lester and Company of New York and Kane and Cabot of Boston, two old established family banks, could well become one of the most important financial institutions in America. As far as the *Trib* could ascertain, the stock would be in the hands of about twenty people related to, or closely associated with, the two families."

Abel was delighted by this particular piece of information, realizing that Kane must have sacrificed overall control. He read the news item again. Even so, William Kane had obviously risen even higher in the world since they had crossed swords, but then so had Abel, and he still had an old score to settle with the newly designated chairman of Lester, Kane.

So handsomely had the Baron Group's fortunes pros-

pered over the decade that Abel had repaid all the loans to
his backer and honored every original letter of the agreement, thus securing 100 percent ownership of the company
within the stipulated ten-year period.

By the last quarter of 1939, not only had Abel paid off the
loan, but the profits for 1940 had passed the half-million
mark. This milestone coincided with the opening of two new
Barons, one in Washington, the other in San Francisco.

Though Abel had become a less devoted husband during
this period, caused as much by Zaphia's unwillingness to
keep pace with his ambitions as by anything else, he could
not have been a more doting father. Zaphia, longing for a
second child to occupy her more fully, finally goaded him
into seeing his doctor. When Abel learned that, because of a
low sperm count, probably caused by sickness and malnutri-
tion in his days under the Germans and Russians, Florentyna
would almost certainly be his only child, he gave up all hope
for a son and proceeded to lavish everything on her.

Abel's fame was now spreading across America, and the
press had taken to referring to him as "The Chicago Baron."
He no longer cared about jokes behind his back. Wladek
Koskiewicz had arrived and, more important, he was here to
stay. The profits from his thirteen hotels for the last fiscal
year were just short of $1 million and, with his new surplus
of capital, he decided the time had come for even further
expansion.

Then the Japanese attacked Pearl Harbor.

Since the dreadful day of September 1, 1939, on which
the Nazis had marched into Poland, later to meet the Russians at Brest Litovsk and once again divide his homeland
between them, Abel had been sending considerable sums of
money to the British Red Cross for the relief of his homeland. He had waged a fierce battle, both within the Democratic party and in the press, to push an unwilling America
into the war even if now it had to be on the side of the Russians. His efforts so far had been fruitless, but on that December Sunday, with every radio station across the country
blaring out the details of the Japanese attack to an incredu-

lous nation, Abel knew that America must now be committed to the war. On December 11 he listened to President Roosevelt tell the nation that Germany and Italy had declared war on the United States. Abel had every intention of joining up, but first he had a private declaration of war he wished to make, and to that end he placed a call to Curtis Fenton at the Continental Trust Bank. Over the years Abel had grown to trust Fenton's judgment and had kept him on the board of the Baron Group after he gained overall control in order to keep a close link between the Baron group and Continental Trust.

Curtis Fenton came on the line, his usual formal and always polite self.

"How much spare cash am I holding in the group's reserve account?" asked Abel.

Curtis Fenton picked out the file marked "Number 6 Account," remembering the days when he could put all Mr. Rosnovski's affairs into one file. He scanned some figures.

"A little under two million dollars," he said.

"Good," said Abel. "I want you to look into a newly formed bank called Lester, Kane and Company. Find out the name of every shareholder, what percentage they control and if there are any conditions under which they would be willing to sell. All this must be done without the knowledge of the bank's chairman, Mr. William Kane, and without any mention of my name."

Curtis Fenton held his breath and said nothing. He was glad that Abel Rosnovski could not see his surprised face. Why did Abel Rosnovski want to put money into anything to do with William Kane? Fenton had also read in *The Wall Street Journal* about the merging of the two famous family banks. What with Pearl Harbor and his wife's headache, he too had nearly missed the item. Rosnovski's request jogged his memory—he must send a congratulatory wire to William Kane. He penciled a note on the bottom of the Baron Group file while listening to Abel's instructions.

"When you have a full rundown, I want to be briefed in person, nothing on paper."

"Yes, Mr. Rosnovski."

I suppose someone knows what's going on between those two, Curtis Fenton thought to himself, but I'm damned if I do.

Abel continued. "I'd also like you to add to your quarterly reports the details of every official statement issued by Lester's and which companies they are involved with."

"Certainly, Mr. Rosnovski."

"Thank you, Mr. Fenton. By the way, my market research team is advising me to open a new Baron in Montreal."

"The war doesn't worry you, Mr. Rosnovski?"

"Good God, no. If the Germans reach Montreal we can all close down, Continental Trust included. In any case, we beat the bastards last time and we'll beat them again. The only difference is that this time I'll be able to join the action. Good day, Mr. Fenton."

Will I ever understand what goes on in the mind of Abel Rosnovski? Curtis Fenton wondered as he hung up the phone. His thoughts switched back to Abel's other request, for the details on Lester's stock. This worried him even more. Although William Kane no longer had any connection with Rosnovski, Fenton feared where this might all end if his client obtained a substantial holding in Lester's. He decided against expressing those fears to Rosnovski for the time being, supposing the day would come when one of them would explain what they were both up to.

Abel also wondered if he should tell Curtis Fenton why he wanted to buy stock in Lester's but came to the conclusion that the fewer the number of people who were privy to his plan, the better.

He put William Kane temporarily out of his mind and asked his secretary to find George, who had been recently appointed a vice president of the Baron Group. He had grown along with Abel and was now his most trusted lieutenant. Sitting in his office on the forty-second floor of the Chicago Baron, Abel looked down on Lake Michigan, on what was known as the Gold Coast, and his thoughts returned to Poland. He wondered if he would ever live to see his castle again, now well inside the Russian borders under Stalin's control. Abel knew he could never settle in Poland, but he still wanted his castle restored to him. The idea of the Germans or Russians once again occupying his magnificent home made him want to . . . His thoughts were interrupted by George.

"You wanted to see me, Abel?"

George was the only member of the group who called the Chicago Baron by his first name.

"Yes, George. Do you think you could keep the hotels ticking along for a few months if I were to take a leave of absence?"

"Sure I can," said George. "Why, are you finally going to take a vacation?"

"No," replied Abel. "I'm going to war."

"What?" said George. "What?"

"I'm going to New York tomorrow morning to enlist in the Army."

"You're crazy—you could get yourself killed."

"That isn't what I had in mind," replied Abel. "Killing some Germans is what I plan to do. The bastards didn't get me the first time around and I have no intention of letting them get me now."

George continued to protest that America could win the war without Abel. Zaphia protested too; she hated the very thought of war. Florentyna, almost eight years old, did not quite know what war meant, but she did understand that Daddy would have to go away for a very long time and she burst into tears.

Despite their combined protests, Abel took his first plane flight to New York the next day. All America seemed to be going in different directions, and he found the city full of young men in khaki or Navy blues saying their farewells to parents, sweethearts and wives, all assuring one another— but not believing—that the war would be over in a few weeks.

Abel arrived at the New York Baron in time for dinner.
The dining room was packed with young people, girls clinging desperately to soldiers, sailors, and airmen, while Frank
Sinatra crooned to the rhythms of Tommy Dorsey's big
band. As Abel watched the young people on the dance floor,
he wondered how many of them would ever have a chance to
enjoy an evening like this again. He couldn't help remembering Sammy's explanation of how he had become maître
d' at the Plaza. The three men senior to him had returned
from the western front with one leg among them. None of
the young people dancing now could begin to know what
war was really like. He couldn't join in the celebration—if
that's what it was. He went to his room instead.

In the morning he dressed in a plain dark suit and went
down to the recruiting office in Times Square. He had chosen to enlist in New York because he feared someone might
recognize him in Chicago and he would end up with a
swivel chair. The office was even more crowded than the
dance floor had been the night before, but here no one was
clinging to anyone else. He couldn't help noticing that the
other recruits looked fitter than he. The entire morning had
passed before Abel was given and filled out one form—a
task he estimated would have taken ten minutes in his own
office. He then stood in line for two more hours, waiting to
be interviewed by a recruiting sergeant, who asked him what
he did for a living.

"Hotel management," said Abel, and went on to tell the
officer of his experiences during the first war. The sergeant
stared in silent incredulity at the five foot seven, 190-pound
man before him. If Abel had told him he was The Chicago
Baron, the officer would not have doubted his stories of im-
prisonment and escape, but Abel chose to keep this information to himself so that he would not be given any special
treatment.

"You'll have to take a full physical tomorrow morning"
was all the recruiting sergeant said at the end of Abel's
monologue, adding, as though he felt the comment was no
less than his duty, "Thank you for volunteering."

The next day Abel had to wait several more hours for his physical examination. The doctor in charge was fairly blunt about Abel's general condition. He had been protected from such comments for several years by his position and success. It came as a rude awakening when the doctor classified him 4F.

"You're overweight, your eyes are not too good and you limp. Frankly, Rosnovski, you're plain unfit. We can't take soldiers into battle who are likely to have a heart attack even before they find the enemy. That doesn't mean we can't use your talents; there's a lot of paperwork to be done in this war if you are interested."

Abel wanted to hit him, but he knew that wouldn't help him to get him into uniform.

"No, thank you—sir," he said. "I want to fight the Germans, not send them letters."

He returned to his hotel that evening depressed—until he decided he wasn't licked yet. The next day he tried again, going to another recruiting office, but he came back to the Baron with the same result. The second doctor had been a little more polite, but he was every bit as firm as the first one about Abel's condition, and once again Abel ended up with a 4F. It was obvious to Abel that he was not going to be allowed to fight anybody in his present state of health.

The next morning, he found a gymnasium on West Fifty-seventh Street where he engaged a private instructor to do something about his physical condition. For three months he worked every day on his weight and general fitness. He boxed, wrestled, ran, jumped, skipped, pressed weights and starved. When he was down to 155 pounds, the instructor assured him he was never going to be much fitter or thinner. Abel returned to the first recruiting office and filled in the same form under the name of Wladek Koskiewicz. Another recruiting sergeant was a lot more hopeful this time and the medical officer who gave him several tests finally accepted him as a reserve, waiting to be called up.

"But I want to go to war now," said Abel. "I want to fight the bastards."

"We'll be in touch with you, Koskiewicz," said the sergeant. "Please keep yourself fit. You can never be sure when we'll need you."

Abel left, furious as he watched younger, leaner Americans being readily accepted for active service, and as he barged through the door, not sure what his next ploy should be, he walked straight into a tall, gangling man wearing a uniform adorned with stars on the shoulders.

"I'm sorry, sir," said Abel, looking up and backing away.

"Young man," said the general.

Abel walked on, not thinking that the officer could be addressing him, as no one had called him young man for—he didn't want to think for how long, even though he was still only thirty-five.

The general tried again. "Young man," he said a little louder.

This time Abel turned around. "Me, sir?" he asked.

"Yes, you, sir."

Abel walked over to the general.

"Will you come to my office please, Mr. Rosnovski?"

Damn, thought Abel, the man knows who I am and now nobody's going to let me fight. The general's temporary office turned out to be at the back of the building, a small room with a desk, two wooden chairs, peeling green paint and an open door. Abel would not have allowed the most junior member of his staff at a Baron to work in such conditions.

"Mr. Rosnovski," the general began, exuding energy, "my name is Mark Clark and I command the U.S. Fifth Army. I'm over from Governors Island for the day on an inspection tour, so literally bumping into you is a pleasant surprise. I've been an admirer of yours for a long time. Your story is one to gladden the heart of any American. Now, tell me what you are doing in a recruiting office."

"What do you think?" said Abel, not thinking. "I'm sorry, sir," he corrected himself quickly. "I didn't mean to be rude, it's only that no one wants to let me into this damn war."

"What do you want to do in this damn war?" asked the general.

"Sign up and fight the Germans."

"As a foot soldier?" inquired the incredulous general.

"Yes," said Abel. "Don't you need every man you can get?"

"Naturally," said the general, "but I can put your particular talents to a far better use than as a foot soldier."

"I'll do anything," said Abel. "Anything."

"Will you, now?" said the general. "Anything? If I asked you to place your New York hotel at our disposal as Army headquarters here, how would you react to that? Because frankly, Mr. Rosnovski, that would be of far more use to us than if you personally managed to kill a dozen Germans."

"The Baron is yours," said Abel. "Now will you let me go to war?"

"You know you're mad, don't you?" said General Clark.

"I'm Polish," said Abel, and they both laughed. "You must understand," Abel continued, his tone once again serious, "I was born near Slonim, in Poland. I saw my home taken over by the Germans, my sister raped by the Russians. I later escaped from a Russian labor camp and was lucky enough to reach America. I'm not mad. This is the only country in the world where you can arrive with nothing and become a millionaire through damned hard work, regardless of your background. Now those same bastards want another war. I'm not mad, General—I'm human."

"Well, if you're so eager to join up, Mr. Rosnovski, I could use you, but not in the way you imagine. General Demers needs someone to take overall responsibility as quartermaster for the Fifth Army while they're fighting in the front line. If you believe Napoleon was right when he said an army marches on its stomach, you could play a vital role. The job carries the rank of major. That is one way in which you could unquestionably help America to win the war. What do you say?"

"I'll do it, General."

"Thank you, Mr. Rosnovski."

The general pressed a buzzer on his desk, and a very young lieutenant came in and saluted smartly.

"Lieutenant, will you take Major Rosnovski to personnel and then bring him back to me?"

"Yes, sir." The lieutenant turned to Abel. "Will you come this way, please, Major?"

Abel followed him, turning as he reached the door.

"Thank you, General," he said.

Abel spent the weekend in Chicago with Zaphia and Florentyna. Zaphia asked him what he wanted her to do with his fifteen suits.

"Hold on to them," he replied, wondering what she meant. "I'm not going to war to get killed."

"I'm sure you're not, Abel," she said. "That wasn't what was worrying me. It's just that now they're all three sizes too large for you."

Abel laughed and took the suits to the Polish refugee center. He then returned to New York, went to the Baron, canceled the advance guest list and twelve days later handed the building over to the American Fifth Army. The press hailed Abel's decision as a "selfless gesture" of a man who had been a refugee of the First World War.

It was another three months before Abel was called to active duty, during which time he organized the smooth running of the New York Baron for General Clark and then reported to Fort Benning, to complete an officers' training program. When he finally did receive his orders to join General Demers of the Fifth Army, his destination turned out to be somewhere in North Africa. He began to wonder if he would ever get to Germany.

The day before Abel left to go overseas, he drew up a will, instructing his executors to offer the Baron Group to David Maxton on favorable terms if he was killed and divide the rest of his estate between Zaphia and Florentyna. It was the first time in nearly twenty years that he had contemplated death, not that he was sure how he could get himself killed in the regimental canteen.

As his troop ship sailed out of New York harbor, Abel

stared at the Statue of Liberty. He could well remember how he had felt on seeing the statue for the first time nearly twenty years before. Once the ship had passed the Lady, he did not look at her again, but said out loud, "Next time I see you, you French bitch, America will have won this war."

Abel crossed the Atlantic, taking with him two of his top chefs and five others of the kitchen staff who had enlisted. The ship docked at Algiers on February 1, 1943. Abel spent almost a year in the heat and the dust and the sand of the desert, making sure that every member of the division was as well fed as possible.

"We eat badly, but we eat a damn sight better than anyone else" was General Clark's comment.

Abel commandeered the only good hotel in Algiers and turned the building into a headquarters for General Clark. Although Abel could see he was playing a valuable role in the war, he itched to get into a real fight, but a major-quartermaster in charge of catering is rarely sent into the front line other than to feed the troops.

He wrote to Zaphia and George and watched by photograph as his beloved daughter Florentyna grew up. He even received an occasional letter from Curtis Fenton, reporting that the Baron Group was making an ever larger profit, every hotel in America being packed because of the continual movement of troops and civilians. Abel was sad not to have been at the opening of the new hotel in Montreal, where George had represented him. It was the first time he had not been present at the opening of a Baron, but George wrote at reassuring length of the new hotel's great success. Abel began to realize how much he had built in America and how much he wanted to return to the land he now felt was his home.

He soon became bored with Africa and its mess kits, baked beans, blankets and fly swatters. There had been one or two spirited skirmishes out there in the western desert, or so the men returning from the front assured him, but he never saw any real action, although often when he took the food to the front, he would hear the firing, and it made him even angrier. One day to his excitement General Clark's Fifth Army was posted to Southern Europe. Abel hoped this would be his chance to see Poland once again.

The Fifth Army, while American, landed on the Italian coast in amphibious craft. Aircraft gave tactical cover. They met considerable resistance, first at Anzio and then at Monte Cassino, but the action never involved Abel and he began to dread the end of a war in which he had seen no combat. But he could never devise a plan that would get him into the fighting. His chances were not improved when he was promoted to lieutenant colonel and sent to London to await further orders.

With D Day, the great thrust into Europe began. The Allies marched into France and liberated Paris on August 25, 1944. As Abel paraded with the American and Free French soldiers down the Champs Elysées behind General de Gaulle to a hero's welcome, he studied the still magnificent city and decided exactly where he was going to build his first Baron hotel in France.

The Allies moved on up through northern France and across the German border in a final drive toward Berlin. Abel was posted to the First Army under General Omar Bradley. Food was coming mainly from England; local supplies were almost nonexistent, because each succeeding town at which the Allies arrived had already been ravaged by the retreating German army. When Abel arrived in a new city, it would take him only a few hours to commandeer the entire remaining food supply before other American quartermasters had worked out exactly where to look. British and American officers were always happy to dine with the 9th Armored Division and wondered how the 9th had managed to requisition such excellent supplies. On one occasion when General George S. Patton joined General Bradley for dinner, Abel was introduced to the famous Patton, who always led his troops into battle brandishing an ivory-handled revolver.

"The best meal I've had in the whole damn war," said Patton.

By February 1945, Abel had been in uniform for nearly three years and he knew the war would be over in a matter of months. General Bradley kept sending him congratulatory notes and meaningless decorations to adorn his ever-expanding uniform, but they didn't help. Abel begged the general to let him fight in just one battle, but Bradley wouldn't hear of it.

Although it was the duty of a junior officer to lead the food trucks up to the front lines and then supervise mess for the troops, Abel often carried out the responsibility himself. And as in the running of his hotels, he would never let any of his staff know when or where he next intended to pounce.

It was the continual flow of blanket-covered stretchers into camp that March day which made Abel want to go to the front and take a look for himself. When it reached a point where he could no longer bear the one-way traffic of bodies, Abel rounded up his men and personally organized the fourteen food trucks. He took with him one lieutenant, one sergeant, two corporals and twenty-eight privates.

The drive to the front, although only twenty miles, was tiresomely slow that morning. Abel took the wheel of the first truck—it made him feel a little like General Patton—through heavy rain and thick mud; he had to pull off the road several times to allow ambulance details the right of way in their return from the front. Wounded bodies took precedence over empty stomachs. Abel hoped that most were no more than wounded, but only an occasional nod or wave suggested any sign of life. It became obvious to Abel with each mud-tracked mile that something big was going on near Remagen, and he could feel the beat of his heart quicken. Somehow, he knew this time he was going to be involved.

When he finally reached the command post he could hear the enemy fire in the near distance, and he started pounding his leg in anger as he watched stretchers bringing back yet more dead and wounded comrades from he knew not where. Abel was sick of learning nothing about the real war until it was part of history. He suspected that any reader of *The New York Times* was better informed than he was.

Abel brought his convoy to a halt by the side of the field kitchen and jumped out of the truck, shielding himself from the heavy rain, feeling ashamed that others only a few miles away were shielding themselves from bullets. He began to supervise the unloading of 100 gallons of soup, a ton of corned beef, 200 chickens, half a ton of butter, 3 tons of potatoes and 100 ten-pound cans of baked beans—plus the inevitable K rations—in readiness for those going to, or returning from, the front. When Abel arrived in the mess tent he found it full of long tables and empty benches. He left his two chefs to prepare the meal and the orderlies to start peeling 1,000 potatoes while he went off in search of the commanding officer.

Abel headed straight for Brigadier General John Leonard's tent to find out what was going on, continually passing stretchers of dead and nearly dead soldiers. Looking upon the torn, mangled wounded would have made any man sick in ordinary circumstances, but now at Remagen the condition of the injured took the air of being commonplace. As Abel was about to enter the tent, General Leonard, accompanied by his aide, was rushing out. He conducted a conversation with Abel while continuing to walk.

"What can I do for you, Colonel?"

"I have started preparing the food for your battalion as requested in overnight orders, sir. What——?"

"You needn't bother with the food for now, Colonel. At first light this morning Lieutenant Burrows of the Ninth discovered an undamaged railroad bridge north of Remagen— the Ludendorff bridge—and I gave orders that it should be crossed immediately and every effort made to establish a bridgehead on the east bank of the river. Up to now, the Germans have been successful in blowing up every bridge across the Rhine long before we reached it, so we can't hang around waiting for lunch before they demolish this one."

"Did the Ninth get across?" asked Abel.

"Sure did," replied the general, "but they encountered heavy resistance when they reached the forest on the far side. The first platoons were ambushed and God knows how many men we lost. So you better stow that food, Colonel, because my only interest is seeing as many of my men get back alive as possible."

"Is there anything I can do to help?" asked Abel.

The fighting commander stopped walking for a moment and studied the fat colonel. "How many men have you under your direct command?"

"One lieutenant, one sergeant, two corporals, and twenty-eight privates. Thirty-three in all including myself, sir."

"Good. Report to the field hospital with your men and bring back as many dead and wounded as you can find."

"Yes, sir," said Abel, and he ran all the way back to the field kitchen, where he found most of his own men sitting in a corner smoking. None of them noticed Abel when he entered the tent.

"Get up, you bunch of lazy bastards. We've got real work to do for a change."

Thirty-two men snapped to attention.

"Follow me!" shouted Abel. "On the double!"

He turned and started running again, this time toward the field hospital. A young doctor was briefing sixteen medical corpsmen when Abel and his out-of-breath, unfit men appeared at the entrance to the tent.

"Can I help you, sir?" asked the doctor.

"No, I hope I can help you," replied Abel. "I have thirty-two men here who have been detailed by General Leonard to join your group." It was the first time his men had heard it.

The doctor stared in amazement at the Colonel. "Yes, sir."

"Don't call me sir," said Abel. "We're here to find out how we can assist *you*."

"Yes, sir," the doctor said again.

He handed Abel a carton of Red Cross armbands, which the chefs, kitchen orderlies and potato peelers proceeded to put on as they listened to the doctor's briefing. He gave them details on the action in the forest across the Ludendorff bridge.

"The Ninth has sustained heavy casualties," he continued. "Those soldiers with medical expertise will remain in the battle zone, while the rest of you will bring back here as many of the wounded as possible."

Abel was delighted to be taking an active part at last. The doctor, now in command of a team of forty-nine men, passed out eighteen stretchers, and each soldier received a full medical pack. He then led his motley band toward the Ludendorff bridge. Abel was only a yard behind him. They started singing as they marched through the mud and rain; they stopped singing when they reached the bridge and saw stretcher after stretcher that showed clearly the outline of a lifeless body. They marched silently across the bridge in single file by the side of the railroad track, where they could see the results of the German explosion that had failed to destroy the foundations of the bridge. On up toward the forest and the sound of fire, Abel found he was excited by being so near the enemy and horrified by what that enemy was capable of inflicting on his fellow man. From everywhere cries of anguish came from his comrades. Comrades who until that day had wistfully thought the end of the war was near. . . .

He watched the young doctor stop again and again, doing the best he could for each man. Sometimes, when there was not the slightest hope of patching up a wounded man, he would mercifully kill him quickly. Abel ran from soldier to soldier, organizing the stretcher-bearers for those unable to help themselves and guiding the ambulatory wounded back toward the Ludendorff bridge. By the time their group had reached the edge of the forest only the doctor, one of the potato peelers and Abel were left of the original party; all the others were carrying the dead or wounded back to the hospital.

As the three of them dashed into the forest, they could hear enemy guns close by. Abel could see the outline of a big gun, hidden in undergrowth and still pointing toward the bridge, but now damaged beyond repair. Then he heard a volley of bullets that sounded so loud he realized for the first time that the enemy was only a few hundred yards ahead of him. Abel quickly crouched down on one knee, expectant, his senses heightened to screaming pitch. Suddenly there was another burst of fire in front of him. Abel jumped up and ran forward, reluctantly followed by the doctor and the potato peeler. They ran on for another hundred yards, until they came across a lush green hollow covered with white crocuses and littered with the bodies of American soldiers. Abel and the doctor ran from corpse to corpse. "It must have been a massacre," screamed Abel in anger as he heard the retreating fire. The doctor made no comment: he had screamed three years before.

"Don't worry about the dead" was all he said. "Just see if you can find anyone who is still alive."

"Over here," shouted Abel as he knelt beside a sergeant lying in the German mud. Both his eyes were missing. Abel placed little bits of gauze in the sockets and waited impatiently.

"He's dead, Colonel," said the doctor, not giving the sergeant a second glance. Abel ran on to the next body and then the next, but it was always the same, and only the sight of a severed head standing upright in the mud stopped Abel in his tracks. He kept having to look back at its passive stare like that of the bust of some Roman god. Abel recited like a child words he had learned at the feet of the Baron: " 'Blood and destruction shall be so in use and dreadful objects so familiar that mothers shall but smile when they behold their infants quartered by the hands of war.' Does nothing change?" he asked, outraged.

"Only the battlefield," replied the doctor.

When Abel had checked thirty—or was it forty?—men, he once again turned to the doctor, who was trying to save the life of a captain whose head, but for a closed eye and his mouth, was already swathed in blood-soaked bandages.

Abel stood over the doctor watching helplessly, studying the captain's shoulder patch—the 9th Armored—and remembered General Leonard's words: "God knows how many men we lost."

"Fucking Germans," said Abel.

"Yes, sir," said the doctor.

"Is he dead?" asked Abel.

"Might as well be," the doctor replied mechanically. "He's losing so much blood it can only be a matter of time." He looked up. "There's nothing left for you to do here, Colonel. Why don't you try to get this one back to the field hospital. He might have a chance. And let the base commander know that I intend to go forward and I need every man he can spare."

"Right," said Abel, and he helped the doctor carefully lift the captain onto a stretcher. Abel and the potato peeler tramped slowly back toward the camp, the doctor having warned him that any sudden movement to the stretcher could only result in an even greater loss of blood. Abel didn't let the potato peeler rest for one moment during the entire two-mile trek to the hospital. He wanted to give the captain every chance to live. Then he would return to the doctor in the forest.

For over an hour they trudged through the mud and the rain, and Abel felt certain the captain had died. When they finally reached the field hospital both men were exhausted as they handed the stretcher over to a medical team.

As the captain was wheeled slowly away he opened his unbandaged eye, which focused on Abel. He tried to raise his arm. Abel saluted and could have leaped with joy at the sight of the open eye and the moving hand. How he prayed that that man would live.

He ran out of the hospital, eager to return to the forest with his little band of men, when he was stopped by the duty officer.

"Colonel," he said, "I've been looking for you everywhere. There are over three hundred men who need feeding. Christ, man, where have you been?"

"Doing something worthwhile for a change."

Abel thought about the young captain as he slowly headed back to the field kitchen.

For both men the war was over.

CHAPTER
TWENTY-FIVE

The stretcher-bearers took the captain into a tent and laid him gently on an operating table. Captain William Kane of the 9th Armored Division could see a nurse looking sadly down at him, but he was unable to hear anything she was saying. He wasn't sure if it was because his head was swathed in bandages or because he was now deaf. He watched her lips move but learned nothing. He shut his eye and thought. He thought a lot about the past; he thought a little about the future; he thought quickly in case he died. He knew that if he lived, there would be a long time for thinking. His mind turned to Kate in New York. The nurse could see a tear trickling out of the corner of the one eye.

Kate had refused to accept his determination to enlist. He had known that she would never understand, and that he would never be able to justify his reasons to her, so he had stopped trying. The memory of her desperate face now haunted him. He had never really considered death—no man does—and now he wanted only to live and return to his family.

William had left Lester's under the joint control of Ted Leach and Tony Simmons until he returned. Until he returned . . . He had given no instructions for them to follow if he did not come home. Both of them had begged him not to go. Two more men who didn't understand. When he had finally signed up, he couldn't face the children. Richard, aged seven, had held back the tears until his father said that he could not go along with him to fight the Germans.

They sent him first to an Officers' Candidate School in Vermont. Last time he had seen Vermont, he had been skiing with Matthew, slowly up the hills and quickly down. The course lasted for three months and made him fit again for the first time since he had left Harvard.

His first assignment was in a London full of Yanks, where he acted as a liaison officer between the Americans and the British. He was put up at the Dorchester, which the British War Office had taken over and seconded for use by the American Army. William had read somewhere that Abel Rosnovski had done the same thing with the Baron in New York and he had thoroughly approved. The blackouts, the doodlebugs and the air raid warnings all made him believe that he was involved in a war, but he felt strangely detached from what was going on only a few hundred miles south of Hyde Park Corner. Throughout his life he had always taken the initiative; he had never been an onlooker. Moving between Eisenhower's staff headquarters in St. James's and Churchill's War Operations room in Storey's Gate wasn't William's idea of initiative. It didn't look as if he was going to meet a German face-to-face for the entire duration of the war unless Hitler invaded Trafalgar Square.

When part of the First Army was posted to Scotland for training exercises with the Black Watch, William was sent along as an observer and told to report back with his findings. During the long, slow journey to Scotland by train he began to suspect that he was fast becoming a glorified messenger boy, and to wonder why he had ever signed up. But once in Scotland, William found everything different. There, at least the air held the excitement of preparing for war, and when he returned to London, he put in a request for an immediate transfer to the First Army. His commanding officer, who never believed in keeping behind a desk a man who wanted to see action, released him.

Three days later William returned to Scotland to join his new regiment and began his training with the American troops at Inveraray for the invasion they all knew had to come soon. Training was hard and intense. Nights spent in the Scottish hills fighting mock battles with the Black Watch were a marked contrast to evenings at the Dorchester writing reports.

Three months later they were parachuted into northern France to join Omar N. Bradley's army, moving across Europe. The scent of victory was in the air and William wanted to be the first soldier in Berlin.

The First Army advanced toward the Rhine, determined to cross any bridge they could find. Captain Kane received orders that morning that his division was to advance over the Ludendorff bridge ahead of them and engage the enemy a mile northeast of Remagen in a forest on the far side of the river. He stood on the crest of a hill and watched the 9th Armored cross the bridge, expecting it to be blown sky high at any moment.

His colonel led his own division in behind them. William followed with the 120 men under his command, most of them, like William, going into action for the first time. No more exercises with wily Scots pretending to kill him with blank cartridges—followed by a meal together. Germans, with real bullets, death—and perhaps no meal afterward.

When William reached the edge of the forest, he and his men met with no resistance, so they decided to press farther into the woods. The going was slow and without event and William was beginning to think the 9th must have done such a thorough job that his division would only have to follow them through, when from nowhere they were suddenly ambushed by a hail of bullets and mortars. Everything seemed to be coming at them at once. William's men went down, trying to protect themselves among the trees, but he lost over half the platoon in a matter of seconds. The battle, if that's what it could be called, had lasted for less than a minute and he hadn't even seen a German. William crouched in the wet undergrowth for a few more seconds and then saw, to his horror, the next wave of the 9th Division coming through the forest. He ran from his shelter behind a tree to warn them of the ambush. The first bullet hit him in the head and, as he sank to his knees in the German mud and continued to wave and shout a frantic warning to his advancing comrades, the second hit him in the neck and a third in the chest. He lay still in the mud and waited to die not having ever seen the enemy—a dirty, unheroic death.

The next thing William knew, he was being carried on a stretcher, but he couldn't hear or see anything and he wondered if it was night or whether he was blind.

It seemed a long journey, and then his eye opened, focusing on a colonel, limping out of the tent. There was something familiar about him, but he couldn't think what. The stretcher-bearers took him into the operating tent and placed him on the table. He tried to fight off sleep for fear that it might be death.

William woke. He was conscious that two people were trying to move him. They were turning him over as gently as they could and then they stuck a needle into him. William dreamed of seeing Kate, and then his mother, and then Matthew playing with his son Richard. He slept.

He woke. He knew they had moved him to another bed; slight hope replaced the thought of inevitable death. He lay motionless, his one eye fixed on the canvas roof of the tent, unable to move his head. A nurse came over to study a chart and then him. He slept.

He woke. How much time had passed? Another nurse. This time he could see a little more and—joy, oh joy!—he could move his head, if only with great pain. He lay awake as long as he possibly could; he wanted to live. He slept.

He woke. Four doctors were studying him, deciding what? He could not hear them and so learned nothing. They moved him once again. He was able to watch as they put him in an ambulance. The doors closed behind him, the engine revved up and the ambulance began to move over rough ground while a new nurse sat by his side holding him steady. The journey felt like an hour, but he no longer could be sure of time. The ambulance reached smoother ground and then came to a halt. Once again they moved him. This time they were walking on a flat surface and then up some stairs into a dark room. They waited again and then the room began to move, another car perhaps. The room took off. The nurse stuck another needle into him and he remembered nothing until he felt the plane landing and taxiing to a halt. They moved him yet again. Another ambulance, another nurse, another smell, another city. New York, or at least America, he thought; no other smell like that in the world. The new ambulance took him over another smooth surface, continually stopping and starting, until it finally arrived at where it wanted to be. They carried him out once again and up more steps into a small white-walled room. They placed him in a comfortable bed. He felt his head touch the pillow and when he next woke, he thought he was totally alone. But then his eye focused and he thought he saw Kate standing in front of him. He tried to lift his hand and touch her, to speak, but no words came. She smiled, but he knew she could not see his smile, and when he woke again, Kate was still there but wearing a different dress. Or had she come and gone many times? She smiled again. How long had it been? He tried to move his head a little, and saw his son Richard, so tall, so good-looking. He wanted to see his daughters but couldn't turn his head any further. They moved into his line of vision, Virginia—she couldn't be that old—and Lucy—it wasn't possible. Where had the years gone? He slept.

He woke. No one was there, but now he could move his head; some bandages had been removed and he could see more clearly. He tried to say something, but no words came. Kate just watched, her fair hair longer now, falling to her shoulders, her soft brown eyes and unforgettable smile, looking beautiful, so beautiful. He said her name. She smiled. He slept.

He woke. Fewer bandages than before. This time his son spoke.

Richard said, "Hello, Daddy."

He heard him and replied, "Hello, Richard," but didn't recognize the sound of his own voice. The nurse helped him to sit up, ready to greet the rest of his family. He thanked her. A doctor touched his shoulder.

"The worst is over, Mr. Kane. You'll soon be well and then you can return home."

He smiled as Kate came into the room, followed by Virginia and Lucy. So many questions to ask them. Where should he begin? There were gaps in his memory that demanded filling in. Kate told him that he had nearly died. He knew that but had not realized that over a year had passed since his division had been ambushed in the forest at Remagen.

Where had the months of unawareness gone, life lost resembling death? Richard was almost twelve, already preparing for St. Paul's. Virginia was nine and Lucy nearly seven.

Their dresses seemed rather short. He would have to get to know them all over again.

Kate was somehow even more beautiful than William remembered her. She told William how she had never accepted the possibility that he would die, how well Richard was doing at Buckley and how Virginia and Lucy needed a father. She braced herself to tell him of the scars on his face and chest; they would take time to heal. She thanked God that the doctors felt certain there would be nothing wrong with his mind, and his sight would be fully restored. Now all she wanted was to help that recovery. Kate slowly, William quickly.

Each member of the family played a part in the recovery process. Richard helped his father to walk until he no longer needed crutches. Lucy helped him with his food until he could once again feed himself. Virginia read Mark Twain to him—William was not sure if the reading was for her benefit or his, they both enjoyed it so much. Kate stayed by his side at night when William could not get to sleep. And then at last, after Christmas had passed, they allowed him to return to his own home.

Once William was back in East Sixty-eighth Street, his recovery accelerated, and his doctors were predicting that he would be able to return to work at the bank within six months. A little scarred, but very much alive. He was allowed to see visitors.

The first was Ted Leach, somewhat taken aback by William's appearance—something Ted would have to live with for the time being. From Ted, William had news that Lester's had progressed in the past year and his colleagues looked forward to welcoming him back as their chairman. A visit from Tony Simmons brought him news that made him sad. Alan Lloyd and Rupert Cork-Smith had both died. He would miss their prudent wisdom. And then Thomas Cohen called to say how glad he was to learn of William's recovery and to prove, as if it were still necessary, that time had marched on by informing William that he was now semiretired and had turned over many of his clients to his son

Thaddeus, who had opened an office in New York. William remarked on their both being named after apostles. Thomas Cohen laughed and expressed the hope that Mr. Kane would continue to use the firm. William assured him he would.

"By the way, I do have one piece of information you ought to have."

William listened to the old lawyer in silence and became angry, very angry.

CHAPTER
TWENTY-SIX

General Alfred Jodl signed the unconditional surrender at Reims on May 7, 1945, as Abel arrived back into a New York preparing for victory celebrations and an end to the war. Once again, the streets were filled with young people in uniform, but this time their faces showed true elation, not forced gaiety. Abel was saddened by the sight of so many men with one leg, one arm, blind or badly scarred. For them the war would never be over, no matter what piece of paper had been signed four thousand miles away.

When Abel walked into the Baron in his colonel's uniform, no one recognized him. When they had last seen him in civilian clothes three years before, there were no lines on his then youthful face. The face they now saw was older than its thirty-nine years, and the deep, worn ridges on his forehead showed that the war had left its mark on him. He took the elevator to his forty-second-floor office, and a security guard told him firmly he was on the wrong floor.

"Where's George Novak?" asked Abel.

"He's in Chicago, Colonel," the guard replied.

"Well, get him on the phone," said Abel.

"Who shall I say is calling him?"

"Abel Rosnovski."

The guard moved quickly.

George's familiar voice crackled down the line with welcome. At once Abel realized just how good it was to be back—and how much he wanted to be home. He decided not to stay in New York that night but to fly the eight hundred miles on to Chicago. He took with him George's up-to-date reports to study on the plane. He read every detail of the Baron Group's progress during the late stages of the war, and it became obvious that George had done well in keeping the group on an even keel during Abel's absence. His cautious stewardship left Abel with no complaints; the profits were still high because so many of the staff had been called up during the war, while the hotels had remained full because of the continual movement of personnel across America. Abel decided to start employing new staff immediately, before other hotels picked up the best of those returning from the service.

When he arrived at Midway Airport, Terminal 11C, George was standing by the gate waiting to greet him. He had hardly changed—a little more weight, a little less hair perhaps—and within an hour of swapping stories and bringing each other up to date on the past three years, it was almost as though Abel had never been away. Abel would always be thankful to the *Black Arrow* for the introduction to his senior vice president.

George, however, was uncharitable about Abel's limp, which seemed more pronounced than when he had gone away.

"The Hopalong Cassidy of the hotel business," he said mockingly. "Now you don't have a leg to stand on."

"Only a Pole would make such a dumb crack," replied Abel.

George grinned at Abel, who was looking slightly like a puppy that had been scolded by its master.

"Thank God I had a dumb Polack to take care of everything while I was away looking for Germans."

Abel couldn't resist checking once around the Chicago Baron before he drove home. The veneer of luxury had worn rather thin during the wartime shortages. He could see several things that needed renovation, but it could all wait; right now all he wanted to do was see his wife and daughter. It was then that the first shock came. In George there had been little change in three years, but Florentyna was now eleven and had blossomed into a beautiful young girl, while Zaphia, although only thirty-eight, had become plump, dowdy and distinctly middle-aged.

To begin with, Zaphia and Abel were not sure quite how to treat one another, and after only a few weeks Abel began to realize that their relationship would never again be what it had been. Zaphia made little effort to excite Abel or take any pride in his achievements. It saddened him to observe her lack of interest and he tried to get her involved in his life and work, but she did not respond. She seemed contented only at home and with as little to do with the Baron Group as possible. He resigned himself to her attitude and wondered how long he could remain faithful to her. While he was enchanted with Florentyna, Zaphia, her looks and figure gone, left him cold. When they slept together he began to avoid making love, and on the rare occasions when he did, he thought of other women. Soon he began to find any excuse to be away from Chicago and Zaphia's listlessness and silently accusing face.

He began making long trips to his other hotels, taking Florentyna along with him during her school vacations. He spent the first six months after his return to America visiting every hotel in the Baron Group in the same way he had when he had taken over the Richmond Group after Davis Leroy's death. Within the year, they were all back to the high standard he expected of them, but Abel wanted to move forward again. He informed Curtis Fenton at the group's next quarterly meeting that his market research team was now advising him to build a hotel in Mexico and another in Brazil, and they were searching for other new lands on which to erect a Baron.

"The Mexico City Baron and the Rio de Janeiro Baron," said Abel. He liked the ring of those names.

"Well, you have adequate funds to cover the building costs," said Curtis Fenton. "The cash has certainly been accumulating in your absence. You could build a Baron almost anywhere you choose. Heaven knows where you'll stop, Mr. Rosnovski."

"One day, Mr. Fenton, I'll put a Baron in Warsaw and then I'll think about stopping," Abel told him. "I might have helped lick the Germans, but I still have a little score to settle with the Russians."

Curtis Fenton laughed. (Only later that evening when he repeated the story to his wife did he decide that Abel Rosnovski had meant exactly what he had said—a Baron in Warsaw.)

"Now, where do I stand with Kane's bank?"

The sudden change in Abel's tone bothered Curtis Fenton. It worried him that Abel Rosnovski still clearly held William Kane responsible for Davis Leroy's premature death. He opened the special file and started reading.

"Lester, Kane and Company's stock is divided among fourteen members of the Lester family and six past and present employees, while Mr. Kane himself is the largest stockholder with eight percent in his family trust."

"Are any of the Lester family willing to sell their stock?" inquired Abel.

"Perhaps if we can offer the right price. Miss Susan Lester, the late Charles Lester's daughter, has given us reason to believe she might consider parting with her stock, and Mr. Peter Parfitt, a former vice chairman of Lester's, has also showed some interest in our approaches."

"What percentage do they hold?"

"Susan Lester holds six percent. Peter Parfitt has only two percent."

"How much do they want?"

Curtis Fenton looked down at his file again while Abel glanced at Lester's latest annual report. His eyes came to a halt at Article Seven.

"Miss Susan wants two million dollars for her six percent and Mr. Parfitt one million dollars for his two percent."

"Mr. Parfitt is greedy," said Abel. "We will therefore wait

until he is hungry. Buy Miss Susan Lester's stock immediately without revealing whom you represent and keep me briefed on any change of heart by Mr. Parfitt."

Curtis Fenton coughed.

"Is something bothering you, Mr. Fenton?" asked Abel.

Curtis Fenton hesitated. "No, nothing," he said unconvincingly.

"Good, because I'm putting someone in overall charge of the account whom you will know or certainly know of—Henry Osborne."

"Congressman Osborne?" asked Curtis Fenton.

"Yes—do you know him?"

"Only by reputation," said Fenton, with a faint note of disapproval, his head bowed.

Abel ignored the implied comment. He was only too aware of Henry's reputation, but he also had the ability to cut out all the middle men of bureaucracy and ensure quick political decisions, so Abel considered him a worthwhile risk. There was, in addition, the band of common loathing for Kane.

"I'm also inviting Mr. Osborne to be a director of the Baron Group with special responsibility for the Kane account. This information must, as always, be treated in the strictest confidence."

"As you wish," said Fenton unhappily, wondering if he should express his personal misgivings to Abel Rosnovski.

"Brief me as soon as you have closed the deal with Miss Susan Lester."

"Yes, Mr. Rosnovski," said Curtis Fenton without raising his head.

Abel returned to the Baron for lunch, where Henry Osborne was waiting to join him.

"Congressman," said Abel as they met in the foyer.

"Baron," said Henry, and they laughed and went arm in arm into the dining room and sat at a corner table. Abel chastised a waiter because a button was missing from his tunic.

"How's your wife, Abel?"

"Swell. And yours, Henry?"

"Just great." They were both lying.

"Any news to report?"

"Yes. That concession you needed in Atlanta has been taken care of," said Henry in a conspiratorial voice. "The necessary documents will be pushed through sometime in the next few days. You'll be able to start building the new Atlanta Baron around the first of the month."

"We're not doing anything too illegal, are we?"

"Nothing your competitors aren't up to—that I can promise you, Abel." Henry Osborne laughed.

"I'm glad to hear that, Henry. I don't want any trouble with the law."

"No, no," said Henry. "Only you and I know all the facts."

"Good," said Abel. "You've made yourself very useful to me over the years, Henry, and I have a little reward for your past services. How would you like to become a director of the Baron Group?"

"I'd be flattered, Abel."

"Don't give me that. You know you've been invaluable with those state and city building permits. I never have had time to deal with politicians and bureaucrats. In any case, Henry, they prefer to deal with a Harvard man—even if he doesn't so much open doors as simply kick them down."

"You've been very generous in return, Abel."

"It's no more than you've earned. Now, I want you to take on an even bigger job, which should be close to both our hearts. This little exercise will also require complete secrecy, but it shouldn't take too much of your time while giving us some revenge on our mutual friend from Boston, Mr. William Kane."

The maître d'hotel arrived with two large sirloin steaks, medium rare. Henry listened intently as Abel unfolded his plans for William Kane.

A few days later, on May 8, 1946, Abel traveled to New York to celebrate the first anniversary of V-E day. He had laid out a dinner for more than a thousand Polish veterans at the Baron Hotel and had invited General Kazimierz Sosnkowski, commander in chief of the Polish Forces in France after 1943, to be the guest of honor. Abel had looked forward impatiently to the event for weeks and took Florentyna with him to New York. Zaphia stayed behind in Chicago.

On the night of the celebration, the banquet room of the New York Baron looked magnificent, each of the 120 tables decorated with the stars and stripes of America and the white, red and white of the Polish national flag. Huge photographs of Eisenhower, Patton, Bradley, Clark, Paderewski and Sikorsky festooned the walls. Abel sat at the center of the head table with the general on his right and Florentyna on his left.

When General Sosnkowski rose to address the gathering, he announced that Lieutenant Colonel Rosnovski had been made a Life President of the Polish Veterans' Society, in acknowledgment of the personal sacrifices he had made for the Polish-American cause, and in particular for his generous gift of use of the New York Baron throughout the entire duration of the war. Someone who had drunk a little too much shouted from the back of the room:

"Those of us who survived the Germans had to survive Abel's food as well."

The thousand veterans laughed and cheered, toasted Abel in Danzig vodka and then fell silent as the general talked of the plight of postwar Poland, in the grip of Stalinist Russia, urging his fellow expatriates to be tireless in their campaign to secure ultimate sovereignty for their native land. Abel wanted to believe that Poland could one day be free again and that he might even live to see his castle restored to him, but doubted if that would ever be possible after Stalin's success at Yalta.

The general went on to remind the guests that Polish-Americans had, per capita, sacrificed more lives and given more money to the war than any other single ethnic group in the United States. ". . . how many Americans would believe that Poland lost six million of her countrymen while Czechoslovakia lost one hundred thousand? Some observers declare we were stupid not to surrender when we must have known we were beaten. How could a nation that staged a cavalry charge against the might of the Nazi tanks ever believe they were beaten? And, my friends, I tell you we are not beaten now."

Abel felt sad to think that most Americans would still laugh at the thought of the Polish war effort, or, funnier still, a Polish war hero. The general then told his intent audience the story of how Abel had led a band of men to rescue troops who had been killed or wounded at the battle of Remagen. When the general had finished his speech and sat down, the veterans stood and cheered the two men resoundingly. Florentyna was very proud of her father.

Abel was surprised when the story hit the papers the next morning, because Polish achievements were rarely reported in any medium other than *Dziennik Zwiazkiwy*. He doubted that the press would have bothered on this occasion had he not been The Chicago Baron. Abel basked in his newfound glory as an unsung American hero and spent most of the day posing for photographers and giving interviews to newsmen.

By the evening, Abel felt a sense of anticlimax. The general had flown on to Los Angeles and another function, Florentyna had returned to school in Lake Forest, George was in Chicago, and Henry Osborne had gone to Washington. The New York Baron suddenly seemed large and empty to Abel, but he felt no desire to return to Zaphia in Chicago.

He decided to have an early dinner downstairs, then go over the weekly reports from the other hotels in the group before retiring to the penthouse adjoining his office. He seldom ate alone in his private suite, welcoming instead almost any opportunity of being served in one of the dining rooms—a sure way of keeping in constant contact with hotel operations. The more hotels he acquired and built, the more he feared losing touch with his staff on the ground.

Abel took the elevator downstairs and stopped at the reception desk to ask how many people were booked for the night, but he was distracted by a striking woman signing a registration form. He could have sworn he knew her, but it was difficult from where he stood. Midthirties, he thought. When she had finished writing, she turned and looked at him.

"Abel," she said. "How marvelous to see you."

"Good God, Melanie! I hardly recognized you."

"No one could fail to recognize you, Abel."

"I didn't know you were in New York."

"Only overnight. I'm here on business for my magazine."

"You're a journalist?" asked Abel with a hint of disbelief.

"No, I'm the economic advisor to a group of magazines with headquarters in Dallas. I'm here on a market research project."

"Very impressive."

"I can assure you it isn't," said Melanie, "but it keeps me out of mischief."

"Are you free for dinner by any chance?"

"What a nice idea, Abel. But I need a bath and a change of clothes if you don't mind waiting."

"Sure, I can wait. I'll meet you in the main dining room whenever you're ready. Come to my table, say in about an hour."

She smiled in agreement and followed a bellhop to the elevator. Abel noticed her perfume as she walked away.

Abel checked the dining room to be sure his table had fresh flowers, then went to the kitchen to select the dishes he would order for Melanie. Finally, for lack of anything better to do, he sat down. He found himself glancing at his watch and looking at the dining room door every few moments to see when Melanie would walk in. She took a little over an hour, but it turned out to be worth the wait. When at last she appeared at the doorway, in a long, clinging dress that shimmered and sparkled in the dining room lights in an unmistakably expensive way, she looked ravishing. The maître d' ushered her to Abel's table. He rose to greet her as a waiter opened a bottle of vintage Krug and poured them both a glass.

"Welcome, Melanie," said Abel as he raised his goblet. "It's good to see you in the Baron."

"It's good to see the Baron," she said, "especially on his day of celebration."

"What do you mean?" asked Abel.

"I read all about your big dinner in the *New York Post* and how you risked your life to save the wounded at Remagen. Fascinating story. They made you sound like a cross between Audie Murphy and the Unknown Soldier."

"It's all exaggerated," said Abel.

"I've never known you to be modest about anything, Abel, so I can only believe every word must be true."

He poured her a second glass of champagne.

"The truth is, I've always been a little frightened of you, Melanie."

"The Baron is frightened of someone? I don't believe it."

"Well, I'm no southern gentleman, as you once made very clear, my dear."

"And you'll never stop reminding me." She smiled, teasingly. "Did you marry your nice Polish girl?"

"Yes, I did."

"How did that work out?"

"Not so well. She's now fat and forty and no longer has any appeal for me."

"You'll be telling me next that she doesn't understand you," said Melanie, the tone of her voice betraying her pleasure at his reply.

"And did you find yourself a husband?" asked Abel.

"Oh, yes," replied Melanie. "I married a real southern gentleman with all the right credentials."

"Many congratulations," said Abel.

"I divorced him last year—with a large settlement."

"Oh, I'm sorry," said Abel, sounding pleased. "More champagne?"

"Are you by any chance trying to seduce me, Abel?"

"Not before you've finished your soup, Melanie. Even first-generation Polish immigrants have some standards, although I must admit it's my turn to do the seducing."

"Then I must warn you, Abel, I haven't slept with another man since my divorce came through. No lack of offers, but no one's been quite right. Too many groping hands and not enough affection."

After smoked salmon, young lamb, crême brulée and a prewar Mouton Rothschild, they had both thoroughly reviewed their lives since their last meeting.

"Coffee in the penthouse, Melanie?"

"Do I have any choice, after such an excellent meal?" she inquired.

Abel laughed and escorted her out of the dining room and into the elevator. She was teetering very slightly on her high heels as she entered. Abel touched the button marked "42." Melanie looked up at the numbers as they ticked by. "Why no seventeenth floor?" she asked innocently. Abel couldn't find the words to reply.

"The last time I had coffee in your room—" Melanie tried again.

"Don't remind me," said Abel, remembering his own vulnerability. They stepped out of the elevator on the forty-second floor and the bellhop opened the door of the suite.

"Good God!" said Melanie as her eyes swept around the penthouse for the first time. "I must say, Abel, you've learned how to adjust to the style of a multimillionaire. I've never seen anything more extravagant in my life."

A knock at the door stopped Abel as he was about to reach out for her. A young waiter appeared with a pot of coffee and a bottle of Remy Martin.

"Thank you, Mike," said Abel. "That will be all for tonight."

"Will it?" Melanie said, smiling.

The waiter would have turned red if he hadn't been black. He left quickly.

Abel poured coffee and brandy. She sipped slowly, sitting cross-legged on the floor. Abel would have sat cross-legged as well, but he couldn't quite manage the position, so instead he lay down beside her. She stroked his hair and tentatively he began to move his hand up her leg. God, how well he remembered those legs. As they kissed for the first time, Melanie kicked a shoe off and knocked her coffee all over the Persian rug.

"Oh, hell!" she said. "Your beautiful rug."

"Forget it," said Abel as he pulled her back into his arms and started to unzip her dress. Melanie unbuttoned his shirt, and Abel tried to take it off while he was still kissing her, but his cufflinks stopped him, so he helped her out of her dress instead. Her figure had lost none of its beauty and was exactly as he remembered it, except that it was enticingly fuller. Those firm breasts and long, graceful legs. He gave up the one-handed battle with the cufflinks and released her from his grasp to undress himself, aware what an abrupt physical contrast he must have appeared compared with her beautiful body. He hoped all he had read about women being fascinated by powerful men was true. She didn't seem to grimace as she once had at the sight of him. Gently, he caressed her breasts and began to part her legs. The Persian rug was proving better than any bed. It was her turn to try to undress completely while they were kissing. She too gave up and finally freed herself to take off everything except for—at Abel's request—her garter belt and nylon stockings.

When he heard her moan, he was aware how long it had been since he had experienced such ecstasy, and then, how quickly the sensation was passed. Neither of them spoke for several moments, both breathing heavily.

Then Abel chuckled.

"What are you laughing at?" Melanie asked.

"Nothing," said Abel, recalling Dr. Johnson's observation about the position being ridiculous and the pleasure momentary.

Abel rolled over and Melaine rested her head on his shoulder. Abel was surprised to find that he no longer found her desirable, and as he lay there wondering how he could get her to leave without actually being rude, she said, "I'm afraid I can't stay all night, Abel. I have an early appointment tomorrow and I must get *some* sleep. I don't want to look as if I spent the night on your Persian rug."

"Must you go?" said Abel, sounding desperate, but not too desperate.

"I'm sorry, darling, yes." She stood up and walked to the bathroom.

Abel watched her dress and helped her with her zipper. How much easier the garment was to fasten at leisure than it had been to unfasten in haste. He kissed her gallantly on the hand as she left.

"I hope we'll see each other again soon," he said, lying.

"I hope so, too," she said, aware that he did not mean it.

He closed the door behind her and walked over to the phone by his bed.

"Which room was Miss Melanie Leroy booked into?" he asked.

There was a moment's pause; he could hear the flicking of the registration cards.

Abel tapped impatiently on the table.

"There's no one registered under that name, sir," came the eventual reply. "We have a Mrs. Melanie Seaton from Dallas, Texas, who arrived this evening, sir, and checks out tomorrow morning."

"Yes, that will be the lady," said Abel. "See that her bill is charged to me."

"Yes, sir."

Abel replaced the phone and took a long cold shower before preparing for bed. He felt relaxed as he walked over to the fireplace; then, in bed, he turned out the lamp that had illuminated his first adulterous act and noticed that the large coffee stain had now dried on his rug.

"Silly bitch," he said out loud as he switched off the light.

After that night, Abel found that several more coffee stains appeared on the Persian rug during the next several months, some caused by compliant waitresses, some by other non-paying guests, as he and Zaphia grew further apart. What he hadn't anticipated was that she would hire a private detective to check on him and then sue for divorce. Divorce was al-

most unknown in Abel's circle of Polish friends, separation
or desertion being far more common. Abel even tried to talk
Zaphia out of her decided course, only too aware it would do
nothing to enhance his standing in the Polish community,
and worse, it would put back any social or political ambitions he had started to nurture. But Zaphia was determined
to carry the divorce proceedings to their bitter conclusion.
Abel was surprised to find that the woman who had been so
unsophisticated in *his* triumph was, to use George's words, a
little demon in *her* revenge.

When Abel consulted his own lawyer, he found out for
the second time just how many waitresses and nonpaying
guests there had been during the last year. He gave in and the
only thing he fought for was the custody of Florentyna, now
thirteen, and the first true love of his life. Zaphia agreed to
his demands after a long struggle, accepting a settlement of
$500,000, the deed to the house in Chicago, and the right to
see Florentyna on the last weekend in every month.

Abel moved his headquarters and permanent home to
New York, and George dubbed him "The Chicago Baron-in-
Exile" as he roamed America north and south building new
hotels, returning to Chicago only when he had to see Curtis
Fenton.

CHAPTER
TWENTY-SEVEN

The letter lay open on a table by William's chair in the living room. He sat in his dressing gown reading it for the third time, trying to figure out why Abel Rosnovski would want to buy so heavily into Lester's, and why he had appointed Henry Osborne as a director of the Baron Group. William felt he could no longer take the risk of guessing and picked up the phone.

The new Mr. Cohen turned out to be a younger version of his father. When he arrived at East Sixty-eighth Street, he had no need to introduce himself; the hair was beginning to go gray and thin in exactly the same places as his father's, and the round body was encased in a similar suit. Perhaps it was in fact the same suit. William stared at him, but not simply because he looked so like his father.

"You don't remember me, Mr. Kane," said the lawyer.

"Good God!" said William. "The great debate at Harvard. Nineteen twenty——"

"Twenty-eight. You won the debate and sacrificed your membership in the Porcellian."

William burst out laughing. "Maybe we'll do better on the same team if your brand of socialism will allow you to act for an unabashed capitalist."

He rose to shake hands with Thaddeus Cohen. For a moment they both might have been undergraduates again.

William smiled. "You never did get that drink at the Porcellian. What would you like?"

Thaddeus Cohen declined the offer. "I don't drink," he said, blinking in the same disarming way that William recalled so well. "—and I'm afraid I'm now an unabashed capitalist, too."

He turned out to have his father's head on his shoulders. Clearly he was fully briefed on the Rosnovski-Osborne file and well ready to face William. William explained exactly what he now required.

"An immediate report and a further updated one every three months as in the past. Secrecy is still of paramount importance," he said, "but I want every fact you can lay your hands on. Why is Abel Rosnovski buying Lester stock? Does he still feel I am responsible for Davis Leroy's death? Is he continuing his battle with Kane and Cabot even now that they are part of Lester's? What role does Henry Osborne play in all this? Would a meeting between myself and Rosnovski help, especially if I tell him that it was the bank, not I, who refused to support the Richmond Group?"

Thaddeus Cohen's pen was scratching away as furiously as his father's had before him.

"All these questions must be answered as quickly as possible so that I can decide if it's necessary to brief my board."

Thaddeus Cohen gave his father's shy smile as he shut his briefcase. "I'm sorry that you should be troubled in this way while you're still convalescing. I'll be back to you as soon as I can ascertain the facts." He paused at the door. "I greatly admire what you did at Remagen."

William recovered his sense of well-being and vigor rapidly in the following months, and the scars on his face and chest faded into relative insignificance. At night Kate would sit up with him until he fell asleep and whisper, "Thank God you were spared." The terrible headaches and periods of amnesia grew to be things of the past, and the strength returned to his right arm. Kate would not allow him to return to work until they had taken a long and refreshing cruise in the West

Indies. On the sea voyage William relaxed with Kate more than at anytime since their month together in London. Kate reveled in the fact that there were no banks on the ship for William to do business with, although she feared that if they stayed on board another week William would acquire the floating vessel as one of Lester's latest assets, reorganizing the crew, routes, timings and even the way they sailed "the boat," as William insisted on calling the great liner. He was tanned and restless once the ship docked in New York Harbor and Kate could not dissuade him from returning to the bank at the first opportunity.

William soon became deeply involved again in Lester's problems. A new breed of men, toughened by war, enterprising and fast-moving, seemed to be running America's modern banks. President Truman had won a surprise victory for a second term in the White House after headlines in the *Chicago Tribune* had informed the world that Thomas E. Dewey had actually won. William knew very little about the diminutive ex-senator from Missouri, except what he read in the newspapers, and as a staunch Republican, he hoped that his party would find the right man to lead them into the 1952 campaign.

When the first report came in from Thaddeus Cohen, it left no doubt that Abel Rosnovski was still looking for stock to buy in Lester's bank; he had approached all the other benefactors of Charles Lester's will, but only one agreement had been concluded. Susan Lester refused to see William's lawyer when he approached her, so he was unable to discover why she had sold her six percent. All he could ascertain was that she had had no financial reason for doing so.

The Cohen document was admirably comprehensive.

Henry Osborne, it seemed, had been appointed a director of the Baron Group in May of 1946, with special responsibility for the Lester account. More important, Abel Rosnovski had secured Susan Lester's stock in such a way that it was impossible to prove the acquisition went back to either him or to Osborne. Rosnovski now owned six percent of Lester's bank and appeared to be willing to pay at least another $750,000 to obtain Peter Parfitt's 2 percent. William was only too aware of what Abel Rosnovski could do once he was in possession of eight percent. Even more worrisome to William, the growth rate of Lester's compared unfavorably with that of the Baron Group, which was already catching up to its main rivals, Hilton and Sheraton. William began to wonder again if it would now be wise to brief his board of directors on this newly acquired information, and even whether he ought not contact Abel Rosnovski directly. After some sleepless nights, he turned to Kate for advice.

"Do nothing," was Kate's reaction, "until you can be absolutely certain his intentions are as disruptive as you fear. The whole affair may turn out to be a tempest in a teapot."

"With Henry Osborne as his hatchet man, you can be certain that the tempest will pour far beyond the teacup. I don't have to sit around and wait to find out what he is planning for me."

"He might have changed, William. It must be over twenty years since you've had any personal dealings with him."

Kate said nothing more, but William let himself be persuaded and did nothing except keep a close eye on Thaddeus Cohen's quarterly reports—and hope that Kate's intuition would prove to be accurate.

CHAPTER
TWENTY-EIGHT

The Baron Group profited greatly from the postwar explosion in the American economy. Not since the twenties had it been so easy to make so much money so quickly—and by the early fifties, people were beginning to believe that this time it was going to last. But Abel was not content with financial success alone; as he grew older, he began to worry about Poland's place in the postwar world and to feel that his success did not allow him to be a bystander four thousand miles away. What had Pawel Zaleski, the Polish Consul in Turkey, said? "Perhaps in your lifetime you will see Poland rise again."

Abel did everything he could to influence and persuade the United States Congress to take a more militant attitude toward Russian control of its Eastern European satellites. It seemed to Abel, as he watched one puppet Communist government after another come into being, that he had risked his life for nothing. He began to lobby Washington politicians, brief journalists and organize dinners in Chicago and New York and other centers of the Polish-American community, until the Polish cause itself became synonymous with "The Chicago Baron."

Dr. Teodor Szymanowski, formerly professor of history at the University of Cracow, wrote a glowing editorial about Abel's "Fight to Be Recognized" in the journal *Freedom*, which prompted Abel to contact him. The professor was now an old man, and when Abel was ushered into his study he was surprised by his physical frailty, knowing only the vigor of his opinions. He greeted Abel warmly and poured him a Danzig vodka without asking what he would like. "Baron Rosnovski," he said, handing Abel the glass. "I have long admired you and the way you continue to work for our cause. Although we make such little headway, you never seem to lose faith."

"Why should I? I have always believed anything is possible in America."

"But I fear, Baron, that the very men you are now trying to influence are the same ones who have allowed these things to take place. They will never do anything positive to free our people."

"I do not understand what you mean, Professor. Why will they not help us?" asked Abel.

The professor leaned back in his chair. "You are surely aware, Baron, that the American armies were given specific orders to slow down their advance east to allow the Russians to take as much of central Europe as they could lay their hands on. Patton could have been in Berlin long before the Russians, but Eisenhower told him to hold back. It was our leaders in Washington—the same men you are trying to persuade to put American guns and troops back into Europe—who gave those orders to Eisenhower."

"But they couldn't have known then what the U.S.S.R. would eventually become. The Russians had been our Allies. I accept we were too weak and conciliatory with them in 1945, but it was not the Americans who directly betrayed the Polish people."

Before Szymanowski spoke, he leaned back once more and closed his eyes wearily.

"I wish you could have known my brother, Baron Rosnovski. I had word only last week that he died six months ago in a Soviet camp not unlike the one from which you escaped."

Abel moved forward as if to offer sympathy, but Szymanowski raised his hand.

"No, don't say anything. You have known the camps yourself. You would be the first to realize that sympathy is no longer important. We must change the world while others sleep." Szymanowski paused. "My brother was sent to Russia by the Americans."

Abel looked at him in astonishment.

"By the Americans? How is that possible? If your brother was captured in Poland by Russian troops——"

"My brother was never taken prisoner in Poland. He was liberated from a German war camp near Frankfurt. The Americans kept him in a DP camp for a month and then handed him over to the Russians."

"It can't be true. Why would they do that?"

"The Russians wanted all Slavs repatriated. Repatriated so that they could then be exterminated or enslaved. The ones that Hitler didn't get, Stalin did. And I can prove my brother was in the American Sector for over a month."

"But," Abel began, "was he an exception or were there many others like him?"

"Oh yes, there were others," said Syzmanowski without apparent emotion. "Hundreds of thousands. Perhaps as many as a million. I don't think we will ever know the true figures. It's most unlikely the American authorities kept careful records of Operation Kee Chanl."

"Operation Kee Chanl—why don't people ever talk about this? Surely if others realized that we, the Americans, had been sending liberated prisoners back to die in Russia, they would be horrified."

"There is no proof, no known documentation of Operation Kee Chanl. Mark Clark, God bless him, disobeyed his orders and a few of the prisoners were warned in advance by some kindly disposed G.I.'s, and they managed to escape before the Americans could send them to the camps. But they are still lying low and would never admit as much. One of the unlucky ones was with my brother." The Professor paused. "Anyway, it's too late now."

"But the American people must be told. I'll form a committee, print pamphlets, make speeches. Surely Congress will listen to us if we tell them the truth."

"Baron Rosnovski, I think this one is too big even for you."

Abel rose from his seat.

"No, no, I would never underestimate you," said the professor. "But you do not yet understand the mentality of world leaders. America agreed to hand over those poor devils because Stalin demanded it. I am sure they never thought that there would be trials, labor camps and executions to follow. But now, as we approach the fifties, no one's going to admit they were indirectly responsible. No, they will never do that. Not for a hundred years and by then all but a few historians will have forgotten that Poland lost more lives in the war than any other single nation on earth, including Germany. I had hoped the one conclusion you might come to was that you must play a more direct role in politics."

"I've already been considering the idea but cannot decide how. In what way."

"I have my own views on the subject, Baron, so keep in touch." The old man raised himself slowly to his feet and embraced Abel. "In the meantime, do what you can for our cause, but don't be surprised when you meet closed doors."

The moment Abel returned to the Baron he picked up the phone and told the hotel operator to get him Senator Douglas's office. Paul Douglas was Illinois's liberal Democratic senator, elected with the help of the Chicago machine, and he had always been helpful and responsive to any of Abel's past requests, mindful that his constituency contained the largest Polish community in the country. His assistant, Adam Tomaszewicz, dealt with his Polish constituents.

"Hello, Adam, it's Abel Rosnovski. I have something very disturbing to discuss with the senator. Could you arrange an early meeting with him?"

"I'm afraid he's out of town today, Mr. Rosnovski. I know he'll be glad to speak with you as soon as he returns on Thursday. I'll ask him to call you direct. Can I let him know what it's about?"

"Yes. As a Pole you will be interested. I've heard reports from reliable sources that the U.S. authorities in Germany assisted in the return of displaced Polish citizens to territories occupied by the Soviet Union and that many of these Polish citizens were then sent on to Russian labor camps and have never been heard of since."

There was a moment's silence from the other end of the line.

"I'll brief the senator on his return, Mr. Rosnovski. Thank you for calling."

The senator did not get in touch with Abel on Thursday. Nor did he call on Friday or over the weekend. On Monday morning Abel put through another call to his office. Again, Adam Tomaszewicz answered the telephone.

"Oh, yes, Mr. Rosnovski." Abel could almost hear him blushing. "The senator did leave a message for you. He's been very busy, you know, what with so many bills to be acted on before Congress recesses. He asked me to let you know that he'll call back just as soon as he has a spare moment."

"Did you give him my message?"

"Yes, of course. He asked me to assure you he felt certain the rumor you heard was nothing more than a piece of anti-American propaganda. He added that he'd been told personally by one of the Joint Chiefs that American troops had orders not to release any of the DP's under their supervision."

Tomaszewicz sounded as if he was reading a carefully prepared statement and Abel sensed that he had encountered the first of those closed doors. Senator Douglas had never evaded him in the past.

Abel put down the phone and asked his secretary to contact another senator who did make news, who was unafraid to sit in judgment on anybody.

Senator Joseph McCarthy's office came on the line asking who was calling. "I'll try and find the Senator," said a young voice when she heard who was calling and why.

McCarthy was approaching the peak of his power and Abel realized he would be lucky to have more than a few moments on the phone with him.

"Mr. Rosenevski" were McCarthy's first words.

Abel wondered if he had mangled his name on purpose or if it was a bad connection. "What is this matter of grave urgency you wanted to discuss with me?" the Senator asked. Abel hesitated; the realization that he was actually speaking to McCarthy directly had slightly taken him aback.

"Your secrets are safe with me," he heard the Senator say, sensing his hesitation.

"Of course," said Abel, pausing again to collect his thoughts. "You, Senator, have been a forthright spokesman for those of us who would like to see the Eastern European nations freed from the yoke of communism."

"So I have. So I have. And I'm glad to see you appreciate the tack, Mr. Rosenevski."

This time Abel was sure he had mispronounced his name on purpose, but resolved not to comment on it.

"As for Eastern Europe," the Senator continued, "you realize that only after the traitors have been driven from within our own government can any real action be taken to free your captive country."

"That is exactly what I want to speak to you about, Senator. You've had brilliant success in exposing treachery within our own government. But to date, one of the communists' greatest crimes has gone unpublicized."

"Just what great crime did you have in mind, Mr. Rosenevski? I have found so many since I came to Washington."

"I am referring"—Abel drew himself up a little straighter in his chair—"to the forced repatriation of thousands of displaced Polish citizens by the American authorities after the war ended. Innocent enemies of communism who were sent back to Poland and then on to the U.S.S.R., to be enslaved and sometimes murdered." Abel waited for a response, but none was forthcoming. He heard a click and wondered if someone else had been listening to the conversation.

"How can you be so stupid, Rosenevski?" said the Senator, his tone completely changed. "You dare to phone me to say that Americans—loyal United States soldiers—sent thousands of Poles back to Russia and nobody heard a word about it? Are you asking me to believe that? Even a Polack couldn't be that much of a fool. And I wonder what kind of person accepts a lie like that without any proof? Do you want me also to believe that American soldiers are disloyal? Is that what you want? Tell me, Rosenevski, tell me what it is with you people? Are you too stupid to recognize Communist propaganda even when it hits you right in the face? Do you have to waste the time of an overworked United States senator because of a rumor cooked up by the *Pravda* Red slime to create unrest in America's immigrant communities?"

Abel sat motionless, stunned by the outburst. Before half of the tirade was over, Abel realized that any counterargument was going to be pointless. As he waited for the histrionic speech to end, he was glad the senator couldn't see his startled face.

"Senator, I'm sure you're right and I'm sorry to have wasted your time," Abel said quietly. "I hadn't thought of it in quite that light before."

"Well, it just goes to show you how tricky these Commie bastards can be," said McCarthy, his tone softening. "You have to keep an eye on them all the time. Anyway, I hope you're more alert now to the continual danger the American people face."

"I am indeed, senator. Thank you once again for taking the trouble to speak to me personally. Good-bye, senator."

"Good-bye, Rosenevski."

Abel heard the phone click and realized it was the same sound as a closing door.

CHAPTER
TWENTY-NINE

William became aware of feeling older when Kate teased him about his graying hair, hairs which he used to be able to count and no longer could—and when Richard started to bring girls home. William almost always approved of Richard's choice of young ladies, as he called them, perhaps because they were all rather like Kate, who, he considered, was more beautiful in middle age than she had ever been. His daughters, Virginia and Lucy, now becoming young ladies, brought him great happiness as they grew in the image of their mother. Virginia was developing into quite an artist, and the walls of the kitchen and children's bedrooms were covered in her latest works of genius—as Richard mockingly described them. Virginia's revenge came the day Richard started cello lessons, when even the servants murmured unkind comments whenever the bow came in contact with the strings. Lucy adored them both and considered Virginia, with uncritical prejudice, the new Picasso, and Richard the new Casals. William began to wonder what the future would hold for all three of them when he was no longer around to control their lives.

In Kate's eyes all three children advanced satisfactorily. Richard, now at St. Paul's, had improved enough at the cello to be chosen to play in a school concert, while Virginia was painting well enough for one of her pictures to be hung in the front room. But it became obvious to all the family that

Lucy was going to be the beauty when, aged only eleven, she started receiving love notes from boys who until then had only shown an interest in baseball.

In 1951, Richard was accepted at Harvard and although he did not win the top mathematics scholarship, Kate was quick to point out to William that he had played baseball and the cello for St. Paul's, two accomplishments William had never so much as attempted. William was secretly proud of Richard's achievements but mumbled to Kate something about not knowing many bankers who played baseball or the cello.

Banking was moving into an expansionist period as Americans began to believe in a lasting peace. William soon found himself overworked, and for a short time, the threat of Abel Rosnovski and the problems associated with him had to be pushed into the background.

The flow of quarterly reports from Thaddeus Cohen indicated that Rosnovski had embarked on a course he had no intention of abandoning; through a third party he had let every stockholder other than William know of his interest in Lester stock. William wondered if this course was heading toward a direct confrontation between himself and the Pole. He began to feel that the time was fast approaching when he would have to inform the Lester board of Rosnovski's actions and perhaps even offer his resignation if the bank looked to be under siege, a move that would result in a complete victory for Abel Rosnovski, which was the one reason William did not seriously contemplate it. He decided that if he had to fight for his life, fight he would, and if one of the two had to go under, he would do everything in his power to ensure that it wasn't William Kane.

The problem of what to do about Abel Rosnovski's investment program was finally taken out of William's hands.

Early in 1951 the bank had been invited to represent one of America's new airline companies, Interstate Airways, when the Federal Aviation Administration granted it a franchise for flights between the East and West coasts. The airline approached Lester's bank when it needed to raise $30 million, the financial backing required by governmental regulations.

William considered the airline and the whole project to be well worth supporting and he spent virtually his entire time setting up a public offering to raise the necessary $30 million. The bank, acting as the sponsor for the project, put its full financial resources behind the new venture. The project became William's biggest since he had returned to Lester's, and he realized that his personal reputation was at stake when he went to the market for the $30 million. In July, when the details of the offering were announced, the stock was snapped up in a matter of days. William received lavish praise from all quarters for the way he had handled the project and carried it through to such a successful conclusion. He could not have been happier about the outcome himself, until he read in Thaddeus Cohen's next report that 10 percent of the airline's stock had been obtained by one of Abel Rosnovski's dummy corporations.

William realized then that the time had come to acquaint Ted Leach and Tony Simmons with his worst fears. He asked Tony to come to New York, where he related to both of the vice chairmen the saga of Abel Rosnovski and Henry Osborne.

"Why didn't you let us know about all this before?" was Tony Simmons's first reaction.

"I dealt with a hundred companies the size of the Richmond Group when I was at Kane and Cabot, Tony, and I couldn't know at the time that he was that serious about revenge. I was only finally convinced of his obsession when Rosnovski purchased ten percent of Interstate Airways."

"I suppose it's possible you may be overreacting," said Ted Leach, "because there is one thing of which I am certain: it would be unwise to inform the rest of the board of all this information. The last thing we want a few days after launching a new company is a panic of selling."

"That's for sure," said Tony Simmons. "Why don't you see this fellow Rosnovski and have it out with him?"

"I expect that's exactly what he'd like me to do," replied

William. "It would leave him in no doubt that the bank feels it is under siege."

"Don't you think his attitude might change if you told him how hard you tried to talk the bank into backing the Richmond Group but they wouldn't support you and——?"

"I am convinced it wouldn't make any difference."

"Well, what do you feel the bank should do?" asked Ted Leach. "We certainly can't stop Rosnovski from buying Lester stock if he can find a willing seller. If we went in for purchasing our own stock, far from stopping him, we would play right into his hands by pushing up the price and raising the value of his holding, thus jeopardizing our own financial position. I think you can be certain he would enjoy watching us sweat that one out. We are about the perfect size to be taken on by Harry Truman and there's nothing the Democrats would enjoy more than a banking scandal with an election in the offing."

"I realize there's little I can do about it," said William, "but I had to let you know what Rosnovski was up to in case he springs another surprise on us."

"I suppose there's still an outside chance," said Tony Simmons, "that the whole thing is innocent and he simply respects your talent as an investor."

"How can you say that, Tony, when you know my stepfather is involved? Do you think Rosnovski employed Henry Osborne to further my career? Then you obviously don't understand Rosnovski. I've watched him operating now for over twenty years. He's not used to losing; he simply goes on throwing the dice until he wins. I couldn't know him much better if he were one of my own family. He will . . ."

"Now don't become paranoid, William. I expect——"

"Don't become paranoid, Tony? Remember the power our Articles of Incorporation give to anyone who gets his hands on eight percent of the bank's stock—an article I originally inserted to protect myself from being removed. The man already owns six percent, and if that's not a bad enough prospect for the future, remember that Rosnovski could wipe out Interstate Airways overnight just by placing his entire block of stock on the market at once."

"But he would gain nothing from that," said Ted Leach. "On the contrary, he'd stand to lose a great deal of money."

"Believe me, you don't understand how Abel Rosnovski's mind works," said William. "He has the courage of a lion and the loss would mean nothing to him. I'm fast becoming convinced his only interest is in getting even with me. Yes, of course he'd lose money if he dumped his Interstate stock, but he always has his hotels to fall back on. There are twenty-one of them now, you know, and he must realize that if Interstate stock collapses overnight, we'll also be knocked backward. As bankers, our credibility depends on the fickle confidence of the public, confidence Abel Rosnovski can now shatter as and when it suits him."

"Calm down, William," said Tony Simmons. "It hasn't come to that yet. Now that we know what Rosnovski is up to, we can keep a closer watch on him. We can counter his moves as and when we need to. The first thing we must be sure of is that no one else sells their stock in Lester's before first offering them to you. The bank is always going to support any action you take. My own feeling is still that you should speak to Rosnovski personally and have it out in the open with him. At least that way we'd know how serious his intentions are and we could prepare ourselves accordingly."

"Is that also your opinion, Ted?"

"Yes, it is. I agree with Tony. I think you should contact the man directly. It can only be in the bank's best interests to discover how innocent or otherwise his intentions really are."

William sat in silence for a few moments. "If you both feel that way, I'll give it a try," he eventually said. "I must add that I don't agree with you, but I may be too personally involved to make a dispassionate judgment. Give me a few days to think about how I should best approach him and I'll let you know the outcome."

After the two vice chairmen had left his office, William sat alone, thinking about the action he had agreed to take, certain there could be little hope of success with Abel Rosnovski as long as Henry Osborne was involved.

Four days later William again sat alone in his office, having given instructions that he was not to be interrupted under any circumstances. He knew that Abel Rosnovski was also sitting in his office in the New York Baron: he had had a man posted at the hotel all morning whose only task had been to report the moment Rosnovski showed up. The waiting man had phoned; Abel Rosnovski had arrived that morning at eight twenty-seven, had gone straight up to his office on the forty-second floor and had not been seen since. William picked up his telephone and asked the operator to get him the Baron hotel.

"New York Baron."

"Mr. Rosnovski, please," said William nervously. He was put through to a secretary.

"Mr. Rosnovski, please," he repeated. This time his voice was a little steadier.

"May I ask who is calling?" the secretary said.

"My name is William Kane."

There was a long silence—or did it simply seem long to William?

"I'm not sure if he's in, Mr. Kane. I'll find out for you."

Another long silence.

"Mr. Kane?"

"Mr. Rosnovski?"

"What can I do for you, Mr. Kane?" asked a very calm, lightly accented voice.

Although William had prepared his opening remarks carefully, he was aware that he sounded anxious.

"I'm a little worried about your holdings in Lester's bank, Mr. Rosnovski," he said, "and indeed in the strong position you've been building in one of the companies we represent. I thought perhaps the time had come for us to meet and discuss your full intentions. There is also a private matter I should like to make known to you."

Another long silence. Had he been cut off?

"There are no conditions which would ever make a meeting with you possible, Kane. I know enough about you already without wanting to hear your excuses for the past. You keep your eyes open all the time and you'll find out only too clearly what my intentions are, and they differ greatly from those you will find in the Book of Genesis, Mr. Kane. One day you're going to want to jump out of the seventeenth-floor window of one of my hotels, because you'll be in deep trouble with Lester's bank over your own holdings. I only need two more percent to invoke Article Seven, and we both know what that means, don't we? Then perhaps you'll appreciate for the first time what it felt like for Davis Leroy, wondering for months what the bank might do with his life. Now you can sit and wonder for years what I am going to do with yours once I own eight percent."

Abel Rosnovski's words chilled William, but somehow he forced himself to carry on calmly while at the same time banging his fist angrily on his desk. "I can understand how you feel, Mr. Rosnovski, but I still think it would be wise for us to get together and talk this thing out. There are one or two aspects of the whole affair I know you can't be aware of."

"Like the way you swindled Henry Osborne out of five hundred thousand dollars, Mr. Kane?"

William was momentarily speechless and wanted to explode but once again managed to control his temper.

"No, Mr. Rosnovski, what I wanted to talk to you about has nothing to do with Mr. Osborne. It's a personal matter and involves only you. However, I most emphatically assure you that I have never swindled Henry Osborne out of one red cent."

"That's not Henry's version. He says you were responsible for the death of your own mother, to make sure that you didn't have to honor a debt to him. After your treatment of Davis Leroy, I find that only too easy to believe."

William had never had to fight harder to control his emotions—who the hell did this man think he was—and it took him several seconds to muster a reply. "May I suggest we clear this whole misunderstanding up by meeting at a neutral place of your choice where no one would recognize us?"

"There's only one place left where no one would recognize you, Mr. Kane."

"Where's that?" asked William.

"Heaven," said Abel, and placed the phone back on the hook.

CHAPTER
THIRTY

"Get me Henry Osborne at once," he said to his secretary.

He drummed his fingers on his desk while the girl took nearly fifteen minutes to find Congressman Osborne, who, it turned out, had been showing some of his constituents around the Capitol building.

"Abel, is that you?"

"Yes, Henry, I thought you'd want to be the first to hear that Kane knows everything, so now the battle is out in the open."

"What do you mean, he knows everything? Do you think he knows I'm involved?" Henry asked anxiously.

"He sure does, and he also seems to be aware of the special company accounts, my holdings in Lester's bank and Interstate Airways."

"How could he possibly know everything? Only you and I know about the special accounts."

"And Curtis Fenton," said Abel, interrupting him.

"Right. But he would never inform Kane."

"He must have. There's no one else. Don't forget that Kane dealt directly with Curtis Fenton when I bought the Richmond Group from his bank. I suppose they must have maintained some sort of contact all along."

"Jesus."

"You sound worried, Henry."

"If William Kane knows everything, it's a different ball game. I'm warning you, Abel, he's not in the habit of losing."

"Nor am I," said Abel, "and William Kane doesn't frighten me, not while I have all the aces in my hand. What is our latest holding in Kane's stock?"

"Off the top of my head, you own six percent of Lester's and ten percent of Interstate Airways, plus odd bits of other companies they're involved with. You only need another two percent of Lester's to invoke Article Seven, and Peter Parfitt is still nibbling."

"Excellent," said Abel. "I don't see how the situation could be better. Continue talking to Parfitt, remembering that I'm in no hurry, while Kane can't even approach him. For the time being, we'll let Kane wonder what we're up to. And be sure you do nothing until I return from Europe. After my phone conversation with Mr. Kane this morning, I can assure you that—to use a gentleman's expression—he's perspiring. But I'll let you in on a secret, Henry: I'm not sweating. He can go on that way because I have no intention of making a move until I'm good and ready."

"Fine," said Henry. "I'll keep you informed if anything comes up that we should worry about."

"You must get it through your head, Henry, that there's nothing for *us* to worry about. We have your friend, Mr. Kane by the balls and I now intend to squeeze them very slowly."

"I'll enjoy watching that," said Henry, sounding a little happier.

"Sometimes I think you hate Kane more than I do."

Henry laughed nervously. "Have a good time in Europe."

Abel put the phone back on the hook and sat staring into space as he considered his next move, his fingers still tapping noisily on the desk. His secretary came in.

"Get Mr. Curtis Fenton at the Continental Trust Bank," he said without looking at her. His fingers continued to tap. His eyes continued to stare. A few moments later the phone rang.

"Fenton?"

"Good morning, Mr. Rosnovski, how are you?"

"I want you to close all my accounts with your bank."

There was no reply from the other end.

"Did you hear me, Fenton?"

"Yes," said the stupefied banker. "May I ask why, Mr. Rosnovski?"

"Because Judas never was my favorite apostle, Fenton, that's why. As of this moment, you are no longer on the board of the Baron Group. You will shortly receive written instructions confirming this conversation and telling you to which bank the accounts should be transferred."

"But I don't understand why, Mr. Rosnovski. What have I done . . . ?"

Abel hung up as his daughter walked into the office.

"That didn't sound very pleasant, Daddy."

"It wasn't meant to be pleasant, but it's nothing to concern yourself with, darling," said Abel, his tone changing immediately. "Did you manage to find all the clothes you'll need?"

"Yes, thank you, Daddy, but I'm not absolutely sure what they're wearing in London and Paris. I can only hope I've got it right. I don't want to be a sore thumb."

"You'll stick out, all right, my darling—anyone would with your taste. You'll be the most beautiful thing Europe's seen in years. They'll know your clothes didn't come out of a ration book. Those young Europeans will be falling all over themselves to get at you, but I'll be there to stop them. Now, let's go and have some lunch and discuss what we're going to do while we're in London."

Ten days later, after Florentyna had spent a long weekend with her mother—Abel never inquired after her—father and daughter flew from New York's Idlewild Airport to London's Heathrow. The flight in a Boeing 377 took nearly fourteen hours, and although they had private berths, when they arrived at Claridge's in Brook Street, the only thing they both wanted was another long sleep.

Abel was making the trip for three reasons: first, to confirm building contracts for new Baron hotels in London, Paris and possibly Rome; second, to give Florentyna her first view of Europe before she went to Radcliffe to study modern languages; and third, and most important, to revisit his castle in Poland to see if there was even an outside chance of proving his ownership.

London turned out to be a success for both of them. Abel's advisors had found a site on Hyde Park corner, and he instructed his solicitors to begin negotiations immediately for the land and the permits that would be needed before England's capital could boast a Baron. Florentyna found the austerity of postwar London forbidding after the excess of her own home, but the Londoners seemed to be undaunted by their war-damaged city, still believing themselves to be a world power. She was invited to lunches, dinners and balls, and her father was proved right about her taste in clothes and the effect she had on young male Europeans. She returned each night with sparkling eyes and stories of new conquests—most forgotten by the following morning, but not all: she couldn't make up her mind whether she wanted to marry an Etonian from the Grenadier Guards who liked to salute her, or a member of the House of Lords who was in waiting to the King. She wasn't quite sure what "in waiting" meant, but he certainly knew exactly how to treat a lady.

In Paris the pace never slackened and because they both spoke good French, they got along as well with the Parisians as they had with the English. Abel was normally bored by the end of the second week of any vacation and would start counting the days until he could return home to work. But not while he had Florentyna as his companion. She had, since his separation from Zaphia, become the center of his life and the sole heir to his fortune.

When the time came to leave Paris, neither of them wanted to go, so they stayed on a few more days, claiming as an excuse that Abel was still negotiating to buy a famous but now run-down hotel on the Boulevard Raspail. He did not inform the owner, a M. Neuffe, who looked, if it were possible, even more run-down than the hotel, that he planned to demolish the building and start again from scratch. When M. Neuffe signed the papers a few days later, Abel ordered the building razed while he and Florentyna, with no more excuses left for remaining in Paris, reluctantly departed for Rome.

After the friendliness of the British and the gaiety of the French capital, the sullen and dilapidated Eternal City immediately dampened their spirits, for the Romans felt they had nothing to celebrate. For the two travelers, the pleasures of London and Paris seemed infinitely far behind them. In London they had strolled through the magnificent Royal parks together and admired historic buildings, and Florentyna had danced until the wee hours. In Paris they had been to the Opera, lunched on the banks of the Seine and taken a boat down the river past Notre Dame and on to supper in the Latin Quarter. In Rome, Abel found only an overpowering sense of financial instability and decided that he would have to shelve his plans to build a Baron in the Italian capital. Florentyna sensed her father's growing impatience to see his castle in Poland once again, so she suggested they leave Italy a day early.

Abel had found bureaucracy more reluctant to grant a visa for Florentyna and himself to enter an Iron Curtain country than it had been to issue a permit to build a new 500-room hotel in London. A less persistent visitor would probably have given up, but with the appropriate visas firmly stamped in their passports, Abel and Florentyna set off in a hired car for Slonim. They were kept waiting for hours at the Polish border, helped along only by the fact that Abel was fluent in the language. Had the border guards known why his Polish was so good, they would doubtless have taken an entirely different attitude toward allowing his entry. Abel changed $500 into zlotys—that at least seemed to please the Poles—and motored on. The nearer they came to Slonim, the more Florentyna was aware of how much the journey meant to her father.

"Daddy, I can never remember you so excited about anything."

"This is where I was born," Abel explained. "After such a long time in America, where things change every day, it's almost unreal to be back where it looks as if nothing has changed since I left."

As they drove on toward Slonim, Abel's senses heightened in anticipation of seeing his birthplace once again. Across a time span of nearly forty years he heard his childish voice ask the Baron whether the hour of the submerged peoples of Europe had arrived and would he be able to play his part, and tears came to his eyes to think how short that hour had been, and what a little part he had played.

At last they rounded the final corner before approaching the Baron's estate and saw the great iron gates that led to the castle. Abel laughed aloud in excitement as he brought the car to a halt.

"It's all just as I remember it. Nothing's changed. Come on, let's go see the cottage where I spent the first five years of my life—I don't expect anyone is living there now. Then we'll go and see my castle."

Florentyna followed her father as he marched confidently down a small track into the forest of moss-covered birches and oaks that was not going to change in a hundred years. After they had walked for about twenty minutes, they came into a small clearing, and there in front of them was the trapper's cottage. Abel stood and stared. He had forgotten how tiny his first home was: could nine people really have lived there? The thatched roof was now in disrepair, its stone eroded, its windows broken. The once tidy vegetable garden was indistinguishable in the matted overgrowth.

Had the cottage been deserted? Florentyna took her father by the arm and led him slowly to the front door. Abel stood there motionless, so Florentyna knocked. They waited in silence. Florentyna knocked again, this time a little more loudly, and they heard someone moving within.

"All right, all right," said a querulous voice in Polish, and a few moments later the door inched open. They were being studied by an old woman, bent and thin, dressed entirely in black. Wisps of untidy snow-white hair escaped from her kerchief, and her gray eyes looked vacantly at the visitors.

"It's not possible," Abel said softly in English.

"What do you want?" asked the old woman suspiciously. She had no teeth, and the line of her nose, mouth and chin formed a perfect concave arc.

Abel answered in Polish, "May we come in and talk to you?"

Her eyes looked from one to the other fearfully. "Old Helena hasn't done anything wrong," she said in a whine.

"I know," said Abel gently. "I have brought good news for you."

With some reluctance the woman allowed them to enter the bare, cold room, but she didn't offer them a seat. The room hadn't changed—two chairs, one table and the memory that until he had left the cottage he hadn't known what a carpet was. Florentyna shuddered.

"I can't get the fire going," wheezed the old woman, prodding the grate with her stick. The faintly glowing log refused to rekindle and she scrabbled ineffectually in her pocket. "I need paper." She looked at Abel, showing a spark of interest for the first time. "Do you have any paper?"

Abel looked at her steadily. "Don't you remember me?" he said.

"No, I don't know you."

"You do, Helena. My name is—Wladek."

"You knew my little Wladek?"

"I am Wladek."

"Oh, no," she said with sad and distant finality. "He was too good for me—the mark of God was upon him. The Baron took him away to be an angel. Yes, he took away Matka's littlest one—"

Her old voice cracked and died away. She sat down, but the ancient, lined hands were busy in her lap.

"I have returned," said Abel, more insistently, but the old woman paid him no attention and her old voice quavered on as though she were quite alone in the room.

"They killed my husband, my Jasio, and all my lovely children were taken to the camps except little Sophia. I hid her and they went away." Her voice was even and resigned.

"What happened to little Sophia?" asked Abel.

"The Russians took her away in the other war," she said dully.

Abel shuddered.

The old woman roused herself from her memories. "What do you want? Why are you asking me these questions?" she demanded.

"I wanted you to meet my daughter, Florentyna."

"I had a daughter called Florentyna once, but now there's only me."

"But I—" began Abel, starting to unbutton his shirt.

Florentyna stopped him. "We know," she said, smiling at the old lady.

"How can you possibly know? It was all so long before you were even born."

"They told us in the village," said Florentyna.

"Have you any paper with you?" the old lady asked. "I need paper for the fire."

Abel looked at Florentyna helplessly. "No," he replied, "I am sorry we didn't bring any with us."

"Then, what do you want?" reiterated the old woman, once again hostile.

"Nothing," said Abel, now resigned to the impossibility that she might remember him. "We just wanted to say hello." He took out his wallet, removed all the new zloty notes he had acquired at the border and handed them over to her.

"Thank you, thank you," she said as she took each note, her old eyes watering with pleasure.

Abel bent over to kiss his foster mother, but she backed away.

Florentyna took her father's arm and led him out of the cottage and back down the forest track in the direction of their car.

The old woman watched from her window until she was sure they were out of sight. Then she took the new bank

notes, crumpled each one into a little ball and placed them
all carefully in the grate. They kindled immediately. She
placed twigs and small logs on top of the blazing zlotys and
sat slowly down by her fire, the best in weeks, rubbing her
hands together at the comfort of the warmth.

Abel did not speak on the walk back to the car until the iron
gates were once again in sight. Then he promised Florentyna, trying his best to forget the little cottage, "You are
about to see the most beautiful castle in the world."

"You must stop exaggerating, Daddy."

"In the world," Abel repeated quietly.

Florentyna laughed. "I'll let you know how it compares
with Versailles."

They climbed back into the car and Abel drove through
the gates, remembering the vehicle he had been in when he
last passed through them, and up the mile-long drive to the
castle. Memories came flooding back to him. Happy days as
a child with the Baron and Leon, unhappy days in the dungeon under the Germans' command, and the worst days of
his life when he was taken away from his beloved castle by
the Russians, imagining he would never see the building
again. But now he, Wladek Koskiewicz, was returning, returning in triumph to reclaim what was his.

The car bumped up the winding road and both remained
silent in anticipation as they rounded the final bend to the
first sight of Baron Rosnovski's home. Abel brought the car
to a halt and gazed at his castle. Neither of them spoke—
what was there to say?—but simply stared in disbelief at the
devastation, at the bombed-out remains of his dream.

Abel and Florentyna climbed slowly out of the car. Still
neither spoke. Florentyna held her father's hand very, very
tightly as the tears rolled down his cheeks. Only one wall remained, precariously standing in a semblance of its former
glory; the rest was nothing more than a pile of rubble and
red stone. He could not bear to tell her of the great halls, the
wings, the kitchens, the bedrooms. Abel walked over to the

three mounds, now smooth with thick green grass, that were the graves of the Baron and his son Leon and the other beloved Florentyna. He paused at each one and couldn't help but think that Leon and Florentyna should still be alive today. He knelt at their heads, the dreadful visions of their final moments returning to him vividly. His daughter stood by his side, her hand now resting on his shoulder, saying nothing. A long time passed before Abel rose slowly and then they tramped over the ruins together, broken slabs of stone masking the places where once magnificent rooms had been filled with laughter. Abel still said nothing. Holding hands, they reached the dungeons. There Abel sat down on the floor of the damp little room near the grille, or the half of the grille that was still left. He twisted the silver band around and around on his arm.

"This is where your father spent four years of his life."

"It can't be possible," said Florentyna, who did not sit down.

"It's better now than it was then," said Abel. "At least now there is fresh air, birds, the sun and a feeling of freedom. Then there was nothing, only darkness, death, the stench of death and worst of all the hope of death."

"Come on, Daddy, let's get out of here. Staying can only make you feel worse."

Florentyna led her reluctant father to the car and she drove him slowly down the long drive. Abel didn't look back toward the ruined castle as they passed for the last time through its iron gates.

On the return journey to Warsaw, Abel hardly spoke and Florentyna abandoned attempts at vivacity. When her father said, "There is now only one thing left that I must achieve in this life," Florentyna wondered what he could possibly mean. But she did not press him to explain. She did, however, manage to coax him into spending another weekend in London on the return journey, which she convinced herself would cheer her father up a little and perhaps even help him to forget his demented old foster mother and the bombed-out remains of his castle in Poland.

. . .

They flew to London the next day. Abel was glad to be back in a country where he could communicate quickly with America. Once they had booked into Claridge's, Florentyna went off to see old friends and make new ones. Abel spent his time reading the back-number newspapers that had been accumulating at the hotel. He did not like knowing that things could happen while he was away; it reminded him only too clearly that the world would keep turning without him. An item on an inside page of that day's *Times* caught his eye. Something *had* happened while he was away. An Interstate Airways Vickers Viscount had crashed immediately after takeoff at the Mexico City airport the previous morning. The seventeen passengers and crew had all been killed. The Mexican authorities had been quick to place the blame on Interstate's bad servicing of its aircraft. Abel picked up the phone and asked the girl for the overseas operator.

Saturday, he's probably back in Chicago, thought Abel. He thumbed through his little address book to find the home number.

"There'll be a delay of about thirty minutes," said a precise English voice.

"Thank you," said Abel, and he lay down on the bed with the phone by his side, thinking. It rang twenty minutes later.

"Your overseas call is on the line, sir," said the same precise voice.

"Abel, is that you? Where are you?"

"Sure is, Henry. I'm in London."

"Are you through?" said the girl, who was back on the line.

"I haven't even started," said Abel.

"I'm sorry, sir, I mean are you speaking to America?"

"Oh yes, sure. Thank you. Jesus, Henry, they speak a different language over here."

Henry Osborne laughed.

"Now listen. Did you hear about that Interstate Vickers Viscount that crashed at Mexico City?"

"Yes, I did," said Henry, "but there's nothing for you to worry about. The plane was properly insured and the company is completely covered, so they incurred no loss and the stock has remained steady."

"The insurance is the last thing I'm interested in," said Abel. "This could be our best chance yet for a little trial run to discover just how strong Mr. Kane's constitution is."

"I don't think I understand, Abel. What do you mean?"

"Listen carefully and I'll explain exactly what I want you to do when the Stock Exchange opens on Monday morning. I'll be back in New York by Tuesday to orchestrate the final crescendo myself."

Henry Osborne listened attentively to Abel Rosnovski's instructions. Twenty minutes later, Abel replaced the phone on its hook.

He was through.

CHAPTER
THIRTY-ONE

William realized he could expect more trouble from Abel Rosnovski the morning that Curtis Fenton phoned to let him know that the Chicago Baron was closing all the group's bank accounts with Continental Trust and was accusing Fenton himself of disloyalty and unethical conduct.

"I thought I did the correct thing in writing to you about Mr. Rosnovski's acquisitions in Lester's," said the banker unhappily, "and it has ended with my losing one of my biggest customers. I don't know what my board of directors will say."

William calmed Fenton down a little by promising him he would speak to his superiors. He was, however, more preoccupied with wondering what Abel Rosnovski's next move would be.

Nearly a month later, he found out. He was going through the bank's Monday morning mail when a call came through from his broker, telling him that someone had placed a million dollars' worth of Interstate Airway's stock on the market. William had to make the instant decision that his personal trust should pick up the shares and he issued an immediate buy order for them. At two o'clock that afternoon, another million dollars' worth was put on the market. Before William had a chance to pick them up, the price had started falling. By the time the New York Stock Exchange closed at three o'clock, the price of Interstate Airways had fallen by a third.

At ten minutes past ten the next morning, William received a call from his now agitated broker. Another million dollars' worth of Interstate stock had been placed on the market at the opening bell. The broker reported that the latest dumping had had an avalanche effect: Interstate sell orders were coming onto the floor from every quarter, the bottom had fallen out, and the stock was now trading at a few cents a share. Only twenty-four hours previously, Interstate had been quoted at four and a half.

William instructed Alfred Rodgers, the company secretary, to call a board meeting for the following Monday. He needed the time to confirm who was responsible for the dumping, not that he was in much doubt. By Wednesday he had to abandon any attempt at shoring up Interstate by buying all the shares that came on the market himself. At the close of business that day, the Securities and Exchange Commission announced that it would be conducting an inquiry into all Interstate transactions. William knew that Lester's board would now have to decide whether to support the airline for the three to six months it would take the S.E.C. to complete its investigation or whether to let the company go under. The alternatives looked extremely damaging, both to William's pocket and to the bank's reputation.

It came as no surprise to William to discover from Thaddeus Cohen the next day that the company that had dumped the three million dollars' worth of Interstate shares was one of those fronting for Abel Rosnovski, Guaranty Investment Corporation by name. A corporation spokesman had issued a plausible little press release explaining their reasons for selling: they had been very concerned for the company's future after the Mexican government's "responsible" statement about inadequate servicing facilities and procedures on the part of Interstate Airways.

" 'Responsible statement,' " said William, outraged. "The Mexican government hasn't made a responsible statement since they claimed Speedy Gonzales would win the one hundred meters at the Helsinki Olympics."

The media made the most of Guaranty Investment's press release and on Friday the Federal Aviation Administration grounded the airline until the agency could conduct an in-depth investigation of its servicing facilities and procedures.

William was confident Interstate had nothing to fear from such an inspection, but grounding the airline proved disastrous to short-term passenger bookings. No aviation company can afford to leave aircraft on the ground; it can make money only when its planes are in the air.

To compound William's problems, other major companies represented by Lester's were reconsidering future commitments. The press had been quick to point out that Lester's was Interstate Airways' underwriters. Surprisingly, Interstate's shares began to pick up again late Friday afternoon, and it did not take William long to guess why—a guess that was later confirmed by Thaddeus Cohen: the buyer was Abel Rosnovski. He had sold his Interstate shares at the top and was now buying them back in small amounts while they were still at the bottom. William shook his head in grudging admiration. Rosnovski was making a small fortune for himself while bankrupting William both in reputation and in financial terms.

William worked out that although the Baron Group must have risked over $3 million, it might well end up making a huge profit. Moreover, it was evident that Rosnovski was unconcerned about a temporary loss, which he could in any case use as a tax write-off; his only interest was in the total destruction of Lester's reputation.

When the Lester board met on Monday, William explained the entire history behind his clash with Rosnovski and offered his resignation. It was not accepted, nor was a vote taken, but there were murmurings, and William knew that if Rosnovski attacked again, his colleagues might not take the same tolerant attitude a second time.

The board went on to consider whether the bank should

continue to support Interstate Airways. Tony Simmons convinced them that the F.A.A.'s findings would be in Interstate's favor and that the bank and William would in time recover all their money. Tony had to admit to William after the meeting that their decision could only help Rosnovski in the long run, but the bank had no choice if it wished to protect its reputation.

He proved right on both counts. When the S.E.C. finally published its findings, it declared Lester's "reproach-proof" although it had some stern words for Guaranty Investment Corporation. When the market started trading in Interstate shares that morning, William was surprised to find the stock rising steadily. It was soon back up to its original four and a half.

Thaddeus Cohen informed William that the principal purchaser was once again Abel Rosnovski.

"That's all I need at the moment," said William. "Not only does he make a large profit on the whole transaction, but now he can repeat the same exercise whenever it suits him."

"In fact," said Thaddeus Cohen, "that is exactly what you do need."

"Whatever do you mean, Thaddeus?" said William. "I've never known you speak in riddles."

"Mr. Abel Rosnovski has made his first error in judgment, because he's breaking the law, and now it's your turn to go after him. He probably doesn't even realize that what he's involved in is illegal, because he's doing it for all the wrong reasons."

"What are you talking about?" asked William.

"Simple," said Thaddeus Cohen. "Because of your obsession with Rosnovski—and his with you—it seems that both of you have overlooked the obvious: if you sell shares with the sole intention of causing the market to drop in order to pick up those same shares at the bottom and therefore be certain of a profit, you're breaking Rule 10b-5 of the Securities and Exchange Commission and you are committing the crime of fraud. There's no doubt in my mind that making a quick profit was not Mr. Rosnovski's original intention; in fact, we know very well he only wanted to embarrass you personally. But who's going to believe him if his explanation is that he dumped the stock because he thought the company was unreliable, when he has bought it back when they reached rock bottom. Answer: Nobody—and certainly not the S.E.C. I'll have a full written report sent around to you by tomorrow, William, explaining the legal implications."

"Thank you," said William, jubilant over the news.

Thaddeus Cohen's report was on William's desk at nine the next morning and after William had read over the contents very carefully, he called another meeting. The directors agreed with the course of action William wanted to take. Thaddeus Cohen was instructed to draft a carefully written press release to be issued that evening. *The Wall Street Journal* ran a front-page article the following morning.

William Kane, the Chairman of Lester's Bank, has reason to believe that the sell orders placed by Guaranty Investment Corporation in November 1952 on Interstate Airways shares, a company underwritten by Lester's, were issued for the sole purpose of making an illegal profit.

It has been established that Guaranty Investment Corporation was responsible for placing a million dollars' worth of Interstate stock on the market when the exchange opened on Monday, May 12, 1952. A further million dollars' worth was on the market five hours later. A third million dollars' worth was placed on a sell order by Guaranty Investment Corporation when the exchange reopened on Tuesday, May 13, 1952. This caused the stock to fall to a record low. After an S.E.C. inquiry showed there had been no illegal dealing within either Lester's Bank or Interstate Airways, the market picked up again with the stock trading at the depressed price. Guaranty Investment was quickly back in the market to purchase the shares at as low a price as possible. They continued to buy until they had

replaced the three million dollars' worth of stock they
had originally released onto the market.

The Chairman and Directors of Lester's Bank have
sent a copy of all the relevant documents to the Fraud
Division of the Securities and Exchange Commission,
and have asked them to proceed with a full inquiry.

The story below the statement gave S.E.C. Rule 10b-5 in
full and commented that this was exactly the sort of test case
that President Truman had been looking for. A cartoon below the article showed Harry S. Truman catching a businessman with his hand in the cookie jar.

William smiled as he read through the item, confident
that he had heard the last from Abel Rosnovski.

Abel Rosnovski frowned and said nothing as Henry Osborne
read the statement again for him. Abel looked up, his fingers
tapping in irritation on his desk.

"The boys in Washington," said Osborne, "are determined to get to the bottom of this one."

"But Henry, you know very well I didn't sell Interstate to
make a quick killing on the market," said Abel. "The profit I
made was of no interest to me at all."

"I know that," said Henry, "but you try and convince the
Senate Finance Committee that the Chicago Baron had no
interest in financial gain, that all he really wanted to do was
settle a personal grudge against one William Kane, and
they'll laugh you right out of court—or out of the Senate, to
be more exact."

"Damn," said Abel. "Now what the hell do I do?"

"Well, first you'll have to lie very low until this has had
time to blow over. Start praying that some bigger scandal
comes along for Truman to get himself worked up about, or
that the politicians become so involved in the election that
they haven't time to press for an inquiry. With luck, a new
administration may even drop the whole thing. Whatever
you do, Abel, don't buy any more stocks in any way con-

nected with Lester's bank, or the least you're going to end up with is a very large fine. Let me swing what I can with the Democrats in Washington."

"Remind Harry Truman's office that I gave fifty thousand dollars to his campaign fund during the last election and I intend to do the same for Adlai."

"I've already done that," said Henry. "In fact I would advise you to give fifty thousand to the Republicans as well."

"They're making a mountain out of a molehill," said Abel. "A molehill that Kane will turn into a mountain if we give him the chance." His fingers continued to tap on his desk.

CHAPTER
THIRTY-TWO

Thaddeus Cohen's next quarterly report revealed that Abel Rosnovski had stopped buying or selling stock of any of Lester's companies. It seemed he was now concentrating all his energies on building more hotels in Europe. Cohen's opinion was that Rosnovski was lying low until a decision had been made by the S.E.C. on the Interstate affair.

Representatives of the S.E.C. had visited William at the bank on several occasions. He had spoken to them with complete frankness, but they had never revealed how their inquiries were progressing as to who had caused the share collapse.

The S.E.C. finally finished its investigation and thanked William for his cooperation. He heard nothing more from the Commission.

As the Presidential election grew nearer and Truman seemed to be concentrating his own efforts on the dissolution of the Du Pont industrial combine, William began to fear that Abel Rosnovski might have been let off the hook. He couldn't help feeling that Henry Osborne must have been able to pull a few strings in Congress. He remembered that Cohen had once underlined a note about a $50,000 donation from the Baron Group to Harry Truman's campaign fund and was surprised to read in Cohen's latest report that Rosnovski had repeated the donation for Adlai Stevenson, the Democrats' choice for President, along with another $50,000 for the Eisenhower campaign fund. Again Cohen had underlined the item.

William, who had never considered supporting anyone for public office who wasn't a Republican, wanted General Eisenhower, the surprise candidate who had emerged on the first ballot at the convention in Chicago, to defeat Adlai Stevenson, although he was aware that a Republican administration was less likely than a Democratic one to press for a share-manipulation inquiry.

When General Dwight D. Eisenhower (it appeared that the nation did "like Ike") was elected the thirty-fourth President of the United States on November 4, 1952, William assumed that Abel Rosnovski had escaped any charge and could only hope that the experience would persuade him to leave Lester's affairs alone in the future. The one small compensation to come out of the election for William was that Congressman Henry Osborne lost his congressional seat to a Republican candidate. The Eisenhower jacket had turned out to have coattails, and Osborne's rival had clung to them. Thaddeus Cohen was inclined to think that Henry Osborne no longer exerted quite the same influence over Abel Rosnovski that he had in the past. The rumor in Chicago was that, since divorcing his wealthy wife, Osborne owed large sums of money to Rosnovski and was gambling heavily again.

William was happier and more relaxed than he had been for some time and looked forward to joining the prosperous and peaceful era that Eisenhower had promised in his Inauguration speech.

As the first years of the new President's Administration went by, William began to put Rosnovski's threats at the back of his mind and to think of them as a thing of the past. He informed Thaddeus Cohen that he believed they had heard the last of Abel Rosnovski. The lawyer made no comment. He wasn't asked to.

William put all his efforts into building Lester's, both in

size and reputation, increasingly aware that he was now doing it as much for his son as for himself. Some of his staff at
the bank had already started referring to him as the "old
man."

"It had to happen," said Kate.

"Then why hasn't it happened to you?" William asked
tenderly.

Kate looked up at William and smiled. "Now I know the
secret of how you have closed so many deals with vain
men."

William laughed. "And one beautiful woman," he added.

With Richard's twenty-first birthday only a year away,
William revised the provisions of his will. He set aside $5
million for Kate and $2 million for each of the girls and left
the rest of the family fortune to Richard, noting ruefully the
bite that would come out for inheritance taxes. He also left
$1 million to Harvard.

Richard had been making good use of his four years at
Harvard. By the start of his senior year, he not only appeared
set for a summa cum laude, but he was also playing the cello
in the university orchestra and was a pitcher with the varsity
baseball team, which even William had to admire. As Kate
liked to ask rhetorically, How many students spent Saturday
afternoon playing baseball for Harvard against Yale and
Sunday evening playing the cello in the Lowell concert hall
for the university string quartet?

The final year passed quickly, and when Richard left Harvard, armed with a Bachelor of Arts degree in mathematics,
a cello and a baseball bat, all he required before reporting to
the Business School on the other side of the Charles River
was a good holiday. He flew to Barbados with a girl named
Mary Bigelow, of whose existence Richard's parents were
blissfully unaware. Miss Bigelow had studied music, among
other things, at Vassar, and when they returned two months
later almost the same color as the natives, Richard took her
home to meet his parents. William approved of Miss
Bigelow; after all, she was Alan Lloyd's great-niece.

Richard reported to the Harvard Business School on October 1, 1955, to start his graduate work, taking residence in the Red House. He threw out all William's cane furniture and removed the paisley wallpaper that Matthew Lester had once found so modern and installed wall-to-wall carpet in the living room, an oak table in the dining room, a dishwasher in the kitchen and, more than occasionally, Miss Bigelow in the bedroom.

PART SIX
1952–1963

CHAPTER
THIRTY-THREE

Abel returned from a trip to Istanbul in October 1952 immediately upon hearing the news of David Maxton's fatal heart attack. He attended the funeral in Chicago with George and Florentyna and later told Mrs. Maxton that she could be a guest at any Baron in the world whenever she so pleased for the rest of her life. She did not understand why Abel had made such a generous gesture.

When Abel returned to New York the next day, he was delighted to find on the desk of his forty-second-floor office a report from Henry Osborne indicating that the heat was now off. In Henry's opinion, the new Eisenhower Administration was unlikely to pursue an inquiry into the Interstate Airways fiasco, especially since the stock had held steady for nearly a year. There therefore had been no further incidents to renew interest in the scandal. Eisenhower's Vice President, Richard M. Nixon, seemed more involved in chasing the spectral communists whom Joe McCarthy had missed.

Abel spent the next two years concentrating on building his hotels in Europe. Florentyna opened the Paris Baron in 1953 and the London Baron at the end of 1954. Barons were also in various stages of development in Brussels, Rome, Amsterdam, Geneva, Edinburgh, Cannes and Stockholm in a ten-year expansion program.

Abel had become so overworked that he had little time to consider William Kane's continued prosperity. He had not made any further attempt to buy stock in Lester's bank or its subsidiary companies, although he had held on to those he already owned in the hope that opportunity would be forthcoming to deal a blow against William Kane from which he would not recover so easily. The next time, Abel promised himself, he'd make sure he didn't unwittingly break the law.

During Abel's increasingly frequent absences abroad, George ran the Baron Group. Abel hoped that Florentyna would join them on the board as soon as she left Radcliffe in June of 1955. He had already decided that she should take over responsibility for all the shops in the hotels and consolidate their buying, as they were fast becoming an empire in themselves.

Florentyna was very excited by the prospect but was insistent that she wanted some outside expertise before joining her father's group. She did not think that her natural gifts for design, color coordination, and organization were any substitute for experience. Abel suggested that she train in Switzerland under M. Maurice at the famed Ecole Hotelière in Lausanne. Florentyna balked at the idea, explaining that she wanted to work for two years in a New York store before she would decide on whether or not to take over the shops. She was determined to be worth employing, ". . . and not just as my father's daughter," she informed him. Abel thoroughly approved.

"A New York store, that's easily enough done," he said, "I'll ring up Walter Hoving at Tiffany's and you can start at the top."

"No," said Florentyna, revealing that she'd inherited her father's streak of stubbornness. "What's the equivalent of a junior waiter at the Plaza Hotel?"

"A salesgirl at a department store," said Abel, laughing.

"Then that's exactly what I'm going to be," she said.

Abel stopped laughing. "Are you serious? With a degree from Radcliffe and all the traveling you've done, you want to be an anonymous salesgirl?"

"Being an anonymous waiter at the Plaza didn't do you

any harm when you were building up one of the most successful hotel groups in the world," replied Florentyna.

Abel knew when he was beaten. He had only to look into the steel gray eyes of his beautiful daughter to realize she had made up her mind and that no amount of persuasion, gentle or otherwise, was going to change it.

After Florentyna had graduated from Radcliffe, she spent a month in Europe with her father, checking progress on the latest Baron hotels. She officially opened the Brussels Baron, where she made a conquest of the handsome young French-speaking managing director whom Abel accused of smelling of garlic. She had to give him up three days later when it reached the kissing stage, but she never admitted to her father that garlic had been the reason.

When Florentyna returned to New York with her father, she immediately applied for the vacant position (the words used in the classified advertisement) of "junior sales assistant" at Bloomingdale's. When she filled in the application form, she gave her name as Jessie Kovats, well aware that no one would leave her in peace if they thought she was the daughter of the Chicago Baron.

Despite protests from her father, she also left her suite in the New York Baron and started looking for her own place to live. Once again Abel gave in and presented Florentyna with a small but elegant cooperative apartment on Fifty-seventh Street near the East River as a twenty-second birthday present.

Florentyna already knew her way around New York and enjoyed a full social life, but she had long before resolved not to let her friends know that she was going to work at Bloomingdale's. She feared they would all want to visit her and her cover would be blown in days, making it impossible to be treated like any other trainee.

When her friends did inquire, she merely told them that she was helping to run some shops in her father's hotels. None of them gave her reply a second thought.

Jessie Kovats—it took her some time to get used to the

name—started in cosmetics. After six months, she was ready to run her own cosmetics shop. The girls in Blooming-dale's worked in pairs, which Florentyna immediately turned to her advantage by choosing to work with the laziest girl in the department. This arrangement suited both girls as Florentyna's choice was a gorgeous, unenlightened blonde named Maisie who had only two interests in life: the clock when it pointed to six and men. The former happened once a day, the latter all the time.

The two girls soon became comrades without exactly being friends. Florentyna learned a lot from her partner about how to avoid work without being spotted by the floor manager, and also how to get picked up by a man.

The cosmetic counter's profits were well up after the girls' first six months together even though Maisie had spent most of her time trying out the products rather than selling them. She could take two hours just to repaint her finger-nails. Florentyna, in contrast, had found that she had a natural gift for selling—and that she thoroughly enjoyed it. This combination worked well for her, and after only a few weeks her manager considered her as knowing as some employees who had been around for years.

The partnership with Maisie suited Florentyna ideally, and when they moved her to Better Dresses, Maisie went along by mutual agreement and passed much of her time trying on dresses while Florentyna sold them. Maisie would have been able to attract men—in tow with their wives or sweethearts—no matter what the quality of the merchandise simply by looking at them. Once they were ensnared, Florentyna could move in and sell them something. It seemed hardly possible that the combination could work in Better Dresses, but Florentyna nearly always coaxed Maisie's victims into a purchase. Few escaped with untapped wallets.

The profits for the first six months in the department were up by 30 percent and the floor supervisor decided that the two girls obviously worked well together. Florentyna said nothing to contradict that impression. While other assistants in the shop were always complaining about how little work their partners did, Florentyna continually praised Maisie as the ideal workmate, who had taught her so much about how a big store operated. She didn't mention the useful advice that Maisie also imparted on how to deal with overamorous men.

The greatest compliment an assistant can receive at Bloomingdale's is to be put on one of the counters facing a Lexington Avenue entrance, one of the first persons to be seen by customers coming in through the main doors. To be moved to one of these counters was considered as a small promotion and it was rare for a girl to be invited to sell there until she had been with the store at least five years. Maisie had been with Bloomingdale's since she was seventeen, a full five years, while Florentyna had only just completed her first. But because their sales record together had been so impressive, the manager decided to try the two girls out on the ground floor in the stationery department. Maisie was unable to derive any personal advantage from the stationery department, for although she didn't care much for reading she cared even less for writing. Florentyna wasn't sure after a year with her that she could read or write. Nevertheless, the new post pleased Maisie greatly because she adored attention. So the two girls continued their perfect partnership.

Abel admitted to George that he had once gone to Bloomingdale's and covertly watched Florentyna at work and he had to confess that she was damned good. He assured his vice president that he was looking forward to her finishing the two years' training so that he could employ her himself. They had both agreed that when Florentyna left Bloomingdale's, she would be made a vice president of the group with special responsibility for the hotel stores. Florentyna was a chip off a formidable old block, and Abel had no doubt that she would have few problems taking on the responsibilities he was planning for her.

Florentyna spent her last six months at Bloomingdale's on the ground floor in charge of six counters with the new title of Junior Supervisor. Her duties now included stock check-ing, the cash desks and overall supervision of eighteen sales clerks. Bloomingdale's had already decided that Jessie Kovats was an ideal candidate to be a buyer.

Florentyna had not yet informed her employees that she would be leaving shortly to join her father as a vice president of the Baron Group. As the six months were drawing to their conclusion, she began to wonder what would happen to poor Maisie after she had left. Maisie assumed that Jessie was at Bloomingdale's for life—wasn't everybody?—and never gave the question a second thought. Florentyna even considered offering her a job at one of the shops in the New York Baron. As long as it was behind a counter at which men spent money, Maisie was an asset.

One afternoon when Maisie was waiting on a customer—she was now in gloves, scarves and woolly hats—she pulled Florentyna aside and pointed to a young man who was loitering over the mittens.

"What do you think of him?" she asked, giggling.

Florentyna glanced up at Maisie's latest desire with her customary uninterest, but on this occasion she had to admit that the man was rather attractive. For once she was almost envious of Maisie.

"They only want one thing, Maisie," said Florentyna.

"I know," she said, "and he can have it."

"I'm sure he'll be pleased to hear that," said Florentyna, laughing as she turned to wait on a customer who was becoming impatient at Maisie's indifference to her presence. Maisie took advantage of Florentyna's move and rushed off to serve the gloveless young man. Florentyna watched them both out of the corner of her eye. She was amused that he kept glancing nervously toward her, checking that Maisie wasn't being spied on by her supervisor. Maisie giggled away and the young man departed with a pair of dark blue leather gloves.

"Well, how did he measure up to your hopes?" asked Florentyna, conscious she felt a little jealous of Maisie's new conquest.

"He didn't," replied Maisie. "But I'm sure he'll be back," she added, grinning.

Maisie's prediction turned out to be accurate, for the next day the young man was there again, thumbing among the gloves, looking even more uncomfortable than before.

"I suppose you had better go and wait on him," said Florentyna.

Maisie hurried obediently away. Florentyna nearly laughed out loud when, a few minutes later, the young man departed with another pair of dark blue gloves.

"Two pairs," declared Florentyna. "On behalf of Bloomingdale's I think I can say he deserves you."

"But he still didn't ask me out," said Maisie.

"What?" said Florentyna in mock disbelief. "He must have a glove fetish."

"It's very disappointing," said Maisie, "because I think he's neat."

"Yes, he's not bad," said Florentyna.

The next day when the young man arrived, Maisie leaped forward, leaving an old lady in midsentence. Florentyna quickly replaced her and once again watched Maisie out of the corner of her eye. This time customer and salesgirl appeared to be in deep conversation and the young man finally departed with yet another pair of dark blue leather gloves.

"It must be the real thing," ventured Florentyna.

"Yes, I think it is," replied Maisie, "but he still hasn't suggested a date."

Florentyna was flabbergasted.

"Listen," said Maisie desperately, "if he comes in tomorrow could you serve him? I think he's scared to ask me directly. He might find it easier to make a date through you."

Florentyna laughed. "A Viola to your Orsino."

"What?" said Maisie.

"It doesn't matter," said Florentyna. "I wonder if I'll be able to sell him a pair of gloves."

As the young man pushed his way through the doors at exactly the same time the next day, and immediately headed

toward the glove counter, she thought that if he was anything, he was consistent.

Maisie dug Florentyna in the ribs, and Florentyna decided the time had come to enjoy herself.

"Good afternoon, sir."

"Oh, good afternoon," said the young man, looking surprised—or was it disappointment.

"Can I help you?" offered Florentyna.

"No. I mean, yes. I would like a pair of gloves," he added
unconvincingly.

"Yes, sir. Have you considered dark blue? In leather? I'm
sure we have your size—unless we're all sold out."

The young man looked at her suspiciously as she handed
him the gloves. He tried them on. They were a little too big.
Florentyna offered him another pair; they were a little too
tight. He looked toward Maisie. She was almost surrounded
by a sea of male customers, but she wasn't sinking because
she glanced toward the young man and grinned. He grinned
back nervously. Florentyna handed him another pair of
gloves. They fitted perfectly.

"I think that's what you're looking for," said Florentyna.

"No, it's not really," replied the customer, now visibly
embarrassed.

Florentyna decided the time had come to help the poor
man off the hook. Lowering her voice, she said, "I'll go and
rescue Maisie. Why don't you ask her out? I'm sure she'll
say yes."

"Oh no," said the young man. "You don't understand. It's
not her I want to take out—it's you."

Florentyna was speechless. The young man seemed to
muster courage.

"Will you have dinner with me tonight?"

She heard herself saying yes.

"Shall I pick you up at your home?"

"No," said Florentyna, perhaps a little too firmly, but the
last thing she wanted was to be met at her apartment where it
would be obvious to anyone that she was something more

than a salesgirl. "Let's meet at a restaurant," she added quickly.

"Where would you like to go?"

Florentyna tried to think quickly of a place that would not be too ostentatious.

"Allen's at Seventy-third and Third?" he ventured.

"Yes, fine," said Florentyna, thinking how much better Maisie would have been at handling the whole situation.

"Around eight o'clock suit you?"

"Around eight," replied Florentyna.

The young man left with a smile on his face. As Florentyna watched him disappear onto the street, she suddenly realized he had left without buying a pair of gloves.

Florentyna took a long time choosing which dress she should wear that evening. She wanted to be certain that the outfit didn't scream Bergdorf Goodman. She had acquired a small wardrobe especially for Bloomingdale's, but it was strictly for business use and she had never worn anything from that selection in the evening. If her date—heavens she didn't even know his name—thought she was a salesgirl she mustn't disillusion him. She couldn't help feeling that she was actually looking forward to the evening more than she ought to.

She left her apartment on East Fifty-seventh Street a little before eight and had to wait several minutes before she managed to hail a taxi.

"Allen's, please," she said to the taxi driver.

"On Third Avenue?"

"Yes."

"Sure thing, miss."

When Florentyna arrived at the restaurant, she was a few minutes late. Her eyes began to search for the young man. He was standing at the bar, waving. He had changed into a pair of gray flannel slacks and a blue blazer. Very Ivy League, thought Florentyna, and very good-looking.

"I'm sorry to be late," began Florentyna.

"It's not important. What's important is that you came."

"You thought I wouldn't?" said Florentyna.

"I wasn't sure." He smiled. "I'm sorry I don't know your name."

"Jessie Kovats," said Florentyna, determined to retain her alias. "And yours?"

"Richard Kane," said the young man, thrusting out his hand.

She took it and he held on to it a little longer than she had expected.

"And what do you do when you're not buying gloves at Bloomingdale's?" she teased.

"I'm at Harvard Business School."

"I'm surprised they didn't teach you that most people only have two hands."

He laughed and smiled in such a relaxed and friendly way that she wished she could start again and tell him they might have met in Cambridge when she was at Radcliffe.

"Shall we sit down?" he said, taking her arm and leading her to a table.

Florentyna looked up at the menu on the blackboard.

"Salisbury steak?" she queried.

"A hamburger by any other name," said Richard.

They both laughed in the way two people do when they don't know each other but want to. She could see he was surprised that she might have known his out-of-context quote.

Florentyna had rarely enjoyed anyone's company more. Richard chatted about New York, the theater and music—so obviously his first love—with such grace and charm that she was soon fully at ease. He might have thought she was a salesgirl, but he was treating her as if she'd come from one of the oldest Brahmin families. He hoped he didn't seem too surprised that she shared his interests. When he inquired, she told him nothing more than that she was Polish and lived in New York with her parents. As the evening progressed she found the deception becoming increasingly intolerable. Still, she thought, we may never see each other again after tonight and then it will all be irrelevant.

When the evening did come to an end and neither of them could drink any more coffee, they left Allen's and Richard looked for a taxi, but they were all taken or off duty.

"Where do you live?" he asked.

"Fifty-seventh Street," she said, not thinking about her reply.

"Then let's walk," said Richard, taking Florentyna's hand.

She smiled her agreement. They started walking, stopping and looking in shop windows, laughing and talking. Neither of them noticed the empty taxis that now rushed past. It took them almost an hour to cover the sixteen blocks and Florentyna nearly told him the truth. When they reached Fifty-seventh Street she stopped outside a small old apartment house, some hundred yards from her own building.

"This is where my parents live," she said.

He seemed to hesitate; then he let go of her hand.

"I hope you will see me again," said Richard.

"I'd like that," replied Florentyna in a polite, dismissive way.

"Tomorrow?" Richard asked diffidently.

"Tomorrow?" asked Florentyna.

"Yes. Why don't we go to the Blue Angel and see Bobby Short?" He took her hand again. "It's a little more romantic than Allen's."

Florentyna was momentarily taken aback. Her plans for Richard had not included any provisions for tomorrows.

"Not if you don't want to," he added before she could recover.

"I'd love to," she said quietly.

"I'm having dinner with my father, so why don't I pick you up at ten o'clock?"

"No, no," said Florentyna, "I'll meet you there. It's only two blocks away."

"Ten o'clock then." He bent forward and kissed her gently on the cheek. "Good night, Jessie," he said, and disappeared into the night.

Florentyna walked slowly to her apartment, wishing she hadn't told so many lies about herself. Still it might be over in a few days. She couldn't help feeling that she hoped it wouldn't.

Maisie, who had not yet forgiven her, spent a considerable part of the next day asking all about Richard. Florentyna kept trying unsuccessfully to change the subject.

Florentyna left Bloomingdale's the moment the store closed, the first time in nearly two years that she had left before Maisie. She had a long bath, put on the prettiest dress she thought she could get away with and walked to the Blue Angel. When she arrived, Richard was waiting for her outside the checkroom. He held her hand as they walked into the lounge, where the voice of Bobby Short came floating through the air: " '*Are you telling me the truth, or am I just another lie?*' "

As Florentyna walked in, Short raised his arm in acknowledgment. Florentyna pretended not to notice. Mr. Short had been a guest performer at the Baron on two or three occasions and it never occurred to Florentyna that he would remember her. Richard had seen the gesture and looked puzzled, then assumed that Short had been greeting someone else. When they took a table in the dimly lit room, Florentyna sat with her back to the piano to be certain it couldn't happen again.

Richard ordered a bottle of wine without letting go of her hand and then asked about her day. She didn't want to tell him about her day; she wanted to tell him the truth. "Richard, there is something I must——"

"Hi, Richard." A tall, handsome man stood at Richard's side.

"Hi, Steve. May I introduce Jessie Kovats—Steve Mellon. Steve and I were at Harvard together."

Florentyna listened to them chat about the New York Yankees, Eisenhower's golf handicap and why Yale was going from bad to worse. Steve eventually left with a gracious "Nice to have met you, Jessie."

Florentyna's moment had passed.

Richard began to tell her of his plans once he had left business school. He hoped to come to New York and join his father's bank, Lester's. She had heard the name before but couldn't remember in what connection. For some reason, this worried her.

They spent a long evening together, laughing, eating, talking, and just sitting holding hands listening to Bobby Short. When they walked home, Richard stopped on the corner of Fifty-seventh and kissed her for the first time. She couldn't recall any other occasion when she was so aware of a first kiss. When he left her in the shadows of Fifty-seventh Street, she was aware that this time he had not mentioned tomorrow. She felt slightly wistful about the whole nonaffair.

She was taken aback by how pleased she felt when Richard phoned her at Bloomingdale's on Monday, asking if she would go out with him on Friday.

They spent most of that weekend together: a concert, a film—even the New York Knicks did not escape them. When the weekend was over Florentyna realized that she had told so many white lies about her background that she had become inconsistent and had puzzled Richard more than once by contradicting herself. It seemed to make it all the more impossible to tell him now another entirely different albeit true story. When Richard returned to Harvard on Sunday night she persuaded herself that the deception would seem unimportant with the relationship ended. But Richard phoned every day during the week and spent the next two weekends in her company, and she began to realize it wasn't going to end easily because she was falling in love with him. Once she had admitted this to herself, she realized she had to tell him the truth the following weekend.

CHAPTER
THIRTY-FOUR

Richard daydreamed through his morning lecture. He was so much in love with that girl that he could not even concentrate on the "twenty-nine crash." How could he tell his father he intended to marry a Polish girl who worked behind the scarf, glove and woolly hats counter at Bloomingdale's? Richard was unable to fathom why she was so unambitious for herself when she was obviously very bright; he was certain that if she had had the chances he had been given, she would not have ended up in Bloomingdale's. Richard decided that his parents would have to learn to live with his choice, because that weekend he was going to ask Jessie to be his wife.

Whenever Richard returned to his parents' home in New York on a Friday evening, he would always leave the house on East Sixty-eighth Street to go to pick up something from Bloomingdale's, normally a little-wanted item, simply so that Jessie would see that he was back in town (over the past ten weeks he had already given a pair of gloves to every relative he possessed). That Friday he told his mother that he was going out to buy razor blades.

"Don't bother, darling, you can use your father's," she said.

"No, no, it's all right," Richard said. "I'll go and get some of my own. We don't use the same brand in any case," he added feebly. "I'll only be a few minutes."

He almost ran the eight blocks to Bloomingdale's and managed to rush in just as they were closing the doors. He knew he would be seeing Jessie at seven-thirty, but he could never resist a chance just to look at her. Steve Mellon had told him once that love was for suckers and Richard had written on his steamed-up shaving mirror that morning, "I am a sucker."

But when Richard reached Bloomingdale's this Friday, Jessie was nowhere to be seen. Maisie was standing in a corner filing her fingernails, and he asked her if Jessie was still around. Maisie looked up as if she had been interrupted from the one important task of her day.

"No, she's already gone home, Richard. Left a few seconds early. She can't have gone far. I thought you were meeting her later."

Richard ran out onto Lexington Avenue. He searched for Jessie's among the faces hurrying home, then spotted her on the other side of the street, walking toward Fifth Avenue. She obviously wasn't headed home and he somewhat guiltily decided to follow her. When she reached Scribner's at Forty-eighth Street, he stopped and watched her go into the bookshop. If she wanted something to read, surely she could have got it at Bloomingdale's. He was puzzled. He peered through the window as Jessie talked to a salesclerk, who left her for a few moments and then returned with two books. He could just make out their titles: *The Affluent Society* by John Kenneth Galbraith and *Inside Russia Today* by John Gunther. Jessie signed for them—which surprised Richard—and left as he ducked around the corner.

"Who *is* she?" said Richard out loud as he watched her enter Bendel's. The doorman saluted respectfully, leaving a distinct impression of recognition. Once again Richard peered through the window to see salesladies fluttering around Florentyna with more than casual respect. An older lady appeared with a package, which Jessie had obviously been expecting. She opened it, to reveal a simple yet stunning evening dress. Florentyna smiled and nodded as the saleslady placed the dress in a brown-and-white box. Florentyna mouthed the words "Thank you" and turned toward the door without even signing for her purchase. Richard was mesmerized by the scene and barely managed to avoid colliding with her as she ran out of the shop and jumped into a cab.

He grabbed one himself, telling the driver to follow her. When the cab passed the small apartment house outside of which they normally parted, he began to feel queasy. No wonder she had never asked him in. The cab in front of him continued for another hundred yards and stopped in front of a spanking-new apartment house complete with a uniformed doorman, who opened the door for her. With astonishment and anger, Richard jumped out of his cab and started to march up to the door through which she had disappeared.

"That'll be ninety-five cents, fella," said a voice behind him.

"Oh, sorry," said Richard, and thrust five dollars at the cab-driver, forgetting his change.

"Thanks, buddy," said the driver. "Someone sure is happy today."

Richard hurried through the door of the building and managed to catch Florentyna at the elevator. Florentyna stared at him speechlessly.

"Who are you?" demanded Richard as the elevator door closed.

"Richard," she stammered. "I was going to tell you everything this evening. I never seemed to find the right opportunity."

"Like hell you were going to tell me," he said, following Florentyna out of the elevator to her apartment. "Stringing me along with a pack of lies for nearly three months. Well, now the time has come for the truth."

Florentyna had never seen Richard angry before and suspected that it was very rare. He pushed his way past her brusquely and she opened the door. He looked over the apartment. At the end of the entrance hall, there was a large living room with a fine Oriental rug. A superb grandfather clock stood opposite a side table on which there was a bowl of fresh flowers. The room was beautiful, even by the standards of Richard's own home.

"Nice place you've got yourself for a salesgirl," said Richard. "I wonder which of your lovers pays for this."

Florentyna slapped him so hard that her own palm stung. "How dare you?" she said. "Get out of my home."

As she heard herself saying the words, she started to cry. She didn't want him to leave—ever. Richard took her in his arms.

"Oh, God, I'm sorry," he said. "That was a terrible thing to say. Please forgive me. It's just that I love you so much and thought I knew you so well, and now I find I don't know anything about you."

"Richard, I love you too and I'm sorry I hit you. I didn't want to deceive you, but there's no one else—I promise you that." Her voice cracked.

"I deserved it," he said as he kissed her.

Clasped tightly in one another's arms, they sank onto the couch and remained almost motionless for some moments. Gently, he stroked her hair until her tears subsided. Help me take my clothes off, she wanted to say, but remained silent, slipping her fingers through the gap between his two top shirt buttons. Richard seemed unwilling to make the next move.

"Do you want to sleep with me?" she asked quietly.

"No," he replied. "I want to stay awake with you all night."

Without speaking further, they undressed and made love, gently and shyly afraid to hurt each other, desperately trying to please. Finally, with her head on his shoulder, they talked.

"I love you," said Richard. "I have since the first moment I saw you. Will you marry me? Because I don't give a damn who you are, Jessie, or what you do, but I know I must spend the rest of my life with you."

"I want to marry you too, Richard, but first I have to tell you the truth."

Florentyna pulled Richard's jacket over their naked bodies and told him all about herself, ending by explaining her job at Bloomingdale's. When she had completed her story, Richard did not speak.

"Have you stopped loving me already?" she said. "Now that you know who I really am?"

"Darling," said Richard very quietly, "my father hates your father."

"What do you mean?"

"Just that the only time I ever heard your father's name mentioned in his presence, he flew completely off the handle, saying your father's sole purpose in life seemed to be a desire to ruin the Kane family."

"What? Why?" said Florentyna, shocked. "I've never heard of your father. How do they even know each other?"

It was Richard's turn to tell Florentyna everything his mother had told him about the quarrel with her father.

"Oh, my God. That must have been the 'Judas' my father referred to when he changed banks after twenty-five years," she said. "What shall we do?"

"Tell them the truth," said Richard. "That we met innocently, fell in love and now we're going to be married, and nothing they can do will stop us."

"Let's wait for a few weeks," said Florentyna.

"Why?" asked Richard. "Do you think your father can talk you out of marrying me?"

"No, Richard," she said, touching him gently as she placed her head back on his shoulder. "Never, my darling, but let's find out if we can do anything to break it gently before we present them both with a *fait accompli*. Anyway, maybe they won't feel as strongly as you imagine. After all, you said the affair with the airline company was nearly five years ago."

"They still feel every bit as strongly, I promise you that. My father would be outraged if he saw us together, let alone thought we were considering marriage."

"All the more reason to leave it for a little before we break the news to them. That will give us time to consider the best way to go about it."

He kissed her again. "I love you, Jessie."

"Florentyna."

"That's something else I'm going to have to get used to," he said. "I love you, Florentyna."

During the next four weeks, Florentyna and Richard found out as much as they possibly could about their fathers' feud: Florentyna, by traveling to Chicago to ask her mother, who was surprisingly informative on the subject, and then quizzing George Novak with a set of carefully worded questions that revealed George's personal despair with what he described as "your father's obsession"; Richard from his father's filing cabinet and another talk with his mother, which only emphasized more graphically that the hatred was mutual. It became more obvious with each discovery that there was no gentle way to break the news of their love.

Richard was always attentive and kind and nothing was too much trouble. He went to extremes to take Florentyna's mind off the problem that they knew they would eventually have to face. They went to the theater, spent an afternoon skating and on Sundays took long walks through Central Park, always ending up in bed long before it was dark. Florentyna even accompanied Richard to a New York Yankees game, which she "couldn't understand," and they attended the New York Philharmonic, which she "adored." She refused to believe that Richard could play the cello until he gave her a private recital in her apartment. She applauded enthusiastically when he had finished his favorite Brahms sonata, without noticing that he was staring into her gray eyes.

"We have got to tell them soon," he said, placing his bow on a table and taking her into his arms.

"I know we must. I just don't want to hurt my father."

It was his turn to say "I know."

She avoided his eyes. "Next Friday Daddy will be back from Washington."

"Then it's next Friday," said Richard, holding her so close she could hardly breathe.

Richard returned to Harvard on Monday morning and they spoke to each other on the phone every night, never weakening, determined that nothing would stop them now.

On Friday, Richard arrived in New York earlier than usual and spent an hour alone with Florentyna, who had asked for a half-day off. As they walked to the corner of Fifty-seventh and Park, they stopped at the red "Don't Walk" sign and Richard turned to Florentyna and asked her once again to marry him. He took a small red leather box out of his pocket, opened it and placed a ring on the third finger of her left hand, a sapphire set with diamonds, so beautiful that tears came to Florentyna's eyes. It was a perfect fit. Passersby looked at them strangely as they stood on the corner, clinging to each other, ignoring the green "Walk" sign. When eventually they did notice its command, they kissed before parting and walked in opposite directions to confront their parents. They had agreed to meet again at Florentyna's apartment as soon as the ordeal was over. She tried to smile through her tears.

Florentyna walked toward the Baron Hotel, occasionally looking at her ring. It felt new and strange on her finger and she imagined that the eyes of all who passed by would be drawn to the magnificent sapphire, and to her, it looked so beautiful next to the antique ring that was her favorite from the past. She had been astonished when Richard placed the sapphire on her finger. She touched the ring and found that it gave her courage, although she was aware that she was walking more and more slowly as she came nearer and nearer the hotel.

When she reached the reception desk, the clerk told her that her father was in the penthouse with George Novak and called to say that Florentyna was on her way up. The elevator reached the forty-second floor far too quickly, and Florentyna hesitated before leaving its safety. She stepped out onto the green carpet and heard the elevator door slide closed behind her. She stood alone in the corridor for a moment before knocking quietly at her father's door. Abel opened it immediately.

"Florentyna, what a pleasant surprise. Come on in, my darling. I wasn't expecting to see you today."

George Novak was standing by the window in the living room, looking down at Park Avenue. He turned to greet his goddaughter. Florentyna's eyes pleaded with him to leave. If he stayed, she knew she would lose her nerve. Go, go, go, she said inside her brain. George had sensed her anxiety immediately.

"I must get back to work, Abel. There's a goddamn maharajah checking in tonight."

"Tell him to park his elephants at the Plaza," said Abel genially. "Now that Florentyna's here, stay and have another drink."

George looked at Florentyna. "No, Abel, I have to go. The man's taken the whole of the thirty-third floor. The least he'll expect is the vice president to greet him. Good night, Florentyna," he said, kissing her on the cheek and briefly clasping her arm, almost as though he knew that she needed strength. He left them alone and suddenly Florentyna wished he had not gone.

"How's Bloomingdale's?" said Abel, ruffling his daughter's hair affectionately. "Have you told them yet they're going to lose the best junior supervisor they've had in years? They're sure going to be surprised when they hear that Jessie Kovats's next job will be to open the Edinburgh Baron." He laughed out loud.

"I'm going to be married," said Florentyna, shyly extending her left hand. She could think of nothing to add, so she simply waited for his reaction.

"This is a bit sudden, isn't it?" said Abel, more than a little shocked.

"Not really, Daddy. I've known him for some time."

"Do I know the boy? Have I ever met him?"

"No, Daddy, you haven't."

"Where does he come from? What's his background? Is he Polish? Why have you been so secretive about him, Florentyna?"

"He's not Polish, Daddy. He's the son of a banker."

Abel went white and picked up his drink, swallowing the liquor in one gulp. Florentyna knew exactly what must be going through his mind as he poured himself another drink, so she got the truth out quickly.

"His name is Richard Kane, Daddy."

Abel swung around to face her. "Is he William Kane's son?" he demanded.

"Yes, he is," said Florentyna.

"You could consider marrying William Kane's son? Do you know what that man did to me?"

"I think so," said Florentyna.

"You couldn't even begin to know," shouted Abel as he let forth a tirade that seemed to go on forever and only served to convince Florentyna that both men had gone mad. In the end she interrupted her father to tell him that she was well aware of all the facts.

"Are you, young lady, and did you know the *fact* that William Kane was the man who was responsible for the death of my closest friend? Yes, he's the man who made Davis Leroy commit suicide and, not satisfied with that, he tried to bankrupt me. If David Maxton hadn't rescued me in time, Kane would have taken away my hotels and sold them without a second thought. And where would I be now if William Kane had had his way? You'd have been lucky to end up as a shop-girl at Bloomingdale's. Have you thought about that, Florentyna?"

"Yes, Daddy, I've thought of little else these past few weeks. Richard and I are horrified about the hatred that exists between you and his father. He's facing him now."

"Well, I can tell you how he'll react," said Abel. "He'll go berserk. That man would never allow his precious WASP son to marry you, so you might as well forget the whole crazy idea, young lady."

His voice had risen again to a shout.

"I can't forget it, Father," she said evenly. "We love each other and we both need your blessing, not your anger."

"Now you listen to me, Florentyna," said Abel, his face

now red with fury. "I forbid you to see the Kane boy ever again. Do you hear me?"

"Yes, I hear you. But I will see him. I'll not be parted from Richard because you hate his father."

She found herself clutching her ring finger and trembling slightly.

"It will not happen," said Abel, the color in his face deepening. "I will never allow the marriage. My own daughter deserting me for the son of that bastard Kane. I say you will not marry him."

"I am not deserting you. I would have run away with him if that were true, but I couldn't marry anyone behind your back." She was aware of the tremble in her voice. "But I'm over twenty-one and I will marry Richard. I intend to spend the rest of my life with him. Please help us, Daddy. Won't you meet him, and then you'll begin to understand why I feel the way I do about him?"

"He will never be allowed to enter my home. I do not want to meet any child of William Kane. Never, do you hear me?"

"Then I must leave you."

"Florentyna, if you leave me to marry the Kane boy, I'll cut you off without a penny. Without a penny, do you hear me?" Abel's voice softened. "Now, use your common sense, girl—you'll get over him. You're still young and there are lots of other men who'd give their right arm to marry you."

"I don't want lots of other men," said Florentyna. "I've met the man I'm going to marry and it's not his fault that he's his father's son. Neither of us chose our fathers."

"If my family isn't good enough for you, then go," roared Abel. "And I swear I won't have your name mentioned in my presence again." He turned away and stared out of the window. "For the last time, I warn you, Florentyna—do not marry that boy."

"Daddy, we are going to be married. Although we're both past the stage of needing your consent, we do ask for your approval."

Abel looked away from the window and walked toward her. "Are you pregnant? Is that the reason? Do you have to get married?"

"No, Father."

"Have you ever slept with him?" Abel demanded.

The question shook Florentyna, but she didn't hesitate. "Yes," she replied. "Many times."

Abel raised his arm and hit her full across the face. Blood started to trickle down her chin and she nearly fell. She turned, ran out of the room crying and leaned on the elevator button, holding a hand over her bleeding lip. The door slid open and George stepped out. She had a fleeting glimpse of his shocked expression as she stepped quickly into the car and jabbed repeatedly at the Close Door button. As George stood and watched her crying, the elevator doors closed slowly.

Once Florentyna had reached the street, she took a cab straight to her own apartment. On the way, she dabbed at her cut lip with a Kleenex. Richard was already there, standing under the marquee, head bowed and looking miserable.

She jumped out of the cab and ran to him. Once they were upstairs, she opened the door and quickly closed it behind them, feeling blessedly safe.

"I love you, Richard."

"I love you, too," said Richard, as he threw his arms around her.

"I don't have to ask how your father reacted," said Florentyna, clinging to him desperately.

"I've never seen him so angry," said Richard. "Called your father a liar and a crook, nothing more than a jumped-up Polish immigrant. He asked me why I didn't marry somebody from my own background."

"What did you say to that?"

"I told him someone as wonderful as you couldn't be replaced by a suitably Brahmin family friend, and he completely lost his temper."

Florentyna didn't let go of Richard as he spoke.

"Then he threatened to cut me off without a penny if I

married you," he continued. "When will they understand we don't care a damn about their damn money?

"I tried appealing to my mother for support, but even she could not control his temper. He insisted that she leave the room. I have never seen him treat my mother that way before. She was weeping, which only made my resolve stronger. I left him in midsentence. God knows I hope he doesn't take it out on Virginia and Lucy. What happened when you told your father?"

"He hit me," said Florentyna very quietly. "For the first time in my life. I think he'll kill you if he finds us together. Richard darling, we must get out of here before he finds out where we are, and he's bound to try the apartment first. I'm so frightened."

"No need for you to be frightened, Florentyna. We'll leave tonight and go as far away as possible and to hell with them both."

"How quickly can you pack?" asked Florentyna.

"I can't," said Richard. "I can never return home now. You pack your things and then we'll go. I've got about a hundred dollars with me. How do you feel about marrying a hundred-dollar man?"

"As much as a salesgirl can hope for, I suppose—and to think I dreamed of being a kept woman. Next you'll be wanting a dowry," Florentyna added while rummaging in her bag. "Well, I've got two hundred and twelve dollars and an American Express card. You owe me fifty-six dollars, Richard Kane, but I'll consider repayment at a dollar a year."

In thirty minutes Florentyna was packed. Then she sat down at her desk, scrawled a note and left the envelope on the table by the side of her bed.

Richard hailed a cab. Florentyna was delighted to find how capable Richard was in a crisis and it made her feel more relaxed. "Idlewild," he said after placing Florentyna's three suitcases in the trunk.

At the airport he booked a flight to San Francisco; they chose the Golden Gate city simply because it seemed the best very distant point on the map of the United States.

At seven-thirty the American Airlines Super Constellation 1049 taxied out onto the runway to start its seven-hour flight.

Richard helped Florentyna with her seatbelt. She smiled at him.

"Do you know how much I love you, Mr. Kane?"

"Yes, I think so—Mrs. Kane," he replied.

CHAPTER
THIRTY-FIVE

Abel and George arrived at Florentyna's apartment on East Fifty-seventh Street a few minutes after she and Richard had left for the airport. Abel was already regretting the blow he had struck his daughter. He did not care to conjecture about what his life would be like without his only child. He thought if he could only reach her before it was too late, he might, with gentle persuasion, still talk her out of marrying the Kane boy. He was willing to offer her anything to stop the marriage.

George rang the bell as he and Abel stood outside her door. No one answered. George pressed the button again and they waited for some time before Abel used the key Florentyna had left with him for emergencies. They looked in all the rooms, neither really expecting to find her.

"She must have left already," said George as he joined Abel in the bedroom.

"Yes, but where?" said Abel, and then he saw an envelope addressed to him on the night table. He remembered the last letter left for him by the side of a bed that had not been slept in. He ripped it open:

Dear Daddy,

Please forgive me for running away but I do love Richard and will not give him up because of your ha-

*tred for his father. We will be married right away and
nothing you can do will prevent it. If you ever try to
harm him in any way, you will be harming me. Neither
of us intend to return to New York until you have ended
the senseless feud between our family and the Kanes.
I love you more than you will ever realize and I shall
always be thankful for everything you have done for
me. I pray that this is not the end of our relationship
but until you can change your mind, "Never seek the
wind in the field—it is useless to try and find what is
gone."*

*Your loving daughter,
Florentyna*

Abel passed the letter to George and collapsed onto the
bed. George read the handwritten note and asked helplessly,
"Is there anything I can do?"

"Yes, George. I want my daughter back even if it means
dealing directly with that bastard Kane. There's only one
thing I feel certain of: He will want this marriage stopped
whatever sacrifice he has to make. Get him on the phone."

It took George some time to locate William Kane's un-
listed number. The night security officer at Lester's bank finally gave it to him when George insisted that it was a
family emergency. Abel sat on the bed in silence, Florentyna's letter in his hand, remembering how when she was a
little girl he had taught her the old Polish proverb that she
had now quoted to him. When George was put through to the
Kane residence, a male voice answered the phone.

"May I speak to Mr. William Kane?" asked George.

"Who shall I say is calling?" asked the imperturbable
voice.

"Mr. Abel Rosnovski," said George.

"I'll see if he is in, sir."

"I think that was Kane's butler. He's gone to look for
him," said George as he passed the receiver over to Abel.
Abel waited, his fingers tapping on the bedside table.

"William Kane speaking."

"This is Abel Rosnovski."

"Indeed?" William's tone was icy. "And when exactly did you think of setting up your daughter with my son? At the time no doubt when you failed so conspicuously to cause the collapse of my bank perhaps?"

"Don't be such a damn—" Abel checked himself. "I want this marriage stopped every bit as much as you do. I never tried to take away your son. I only learned of his existence today. I love my daughter even more than I hate you and I don't want to lose her. Can't we get together and work something out between us?"

"No," said William. "I asked you that same question once in the past, Mr. Rosnovski, and you made it very clear when and where you would meet me. I can wait until then, because I am confident you will find it is you who are there not me."

"What's the good of raking over the past now, Kane? If you know where they are, perhaps we can stop them. That's what you want too. Or are you so goddamn proud that you'll stand by and watch your son marry my girl rather than help . . . ?"

The telephone clicked as he spoke the word *help*. Abel buried his face in his hands and wept. George took him back to the Baron.

Through that night and the following day, Abel tried every way he could think of to find Florentyna. He even rang her mother, who admitted that her daughter had told her all about Richard Kane.

"He sounded rather nice," she added spitefully.

"Do you know where they are right now?" Abel asked impatiently.

"Yes."

"Where?"

"Find out for yourself." Another telephone click.

Abel placed advertisements in newspapers and even bought radio time. He tried to get the police involved, but they could only put out a general call since she was over twenty-one. No word came from her. Finally he had to admit to himself that she would undoubtedly be married to the Kane boy by the time her father found her.

He reread her letter many times and resolved that he would never attempt to harm the boy in any way. But the father—that was a different matter. He, Abel Rosnovski, had gone down on his knees and pleaded and the bastard hadn't even listened. Abel vowed that when the chance presented itself, he would finish William Kane off once and for all. George became fearful at the intensity of his old friend's passion.

"Shall I cancel your European trip?" he asked.

Abel had completely forgotten that he had intended to accompany Florentyna to Europe when she had finished her two years with Bloomingdale's at the end of the month. She had been going to open the Edinburgh Baron and the Cannes Baron.

"I can't cancel," replied Abel, although he now barely cared who opened what or whether the hotels were opened at all. "I'll have to go and open the hotels myself. But while I'm away, George, keep trying to find out exactly where Florentyna is. And don't let her know. She mustn't think I'm spying on her; she would never forgive me if she found out. Your best bet may well be Zaphia, but be careful because you can be sure she'll take every advantage of what has happened. It is obvious she has already briefed Florentyna on everything she knew about Kane."

"Do you want Osborne to do anything about the Kane stock?"

"No, nothing for the moment. Now is not the appropriate time for finishing Kane off. When I do, I want to be certain that it's once and for all. Leave Kane alone for the time being—I can always come back to him. For now, concentrate on finding Florentyna."

George promised that he would have found her by the time Abel returned.

Abel opened the Edinburgh Baron three weeks later. The hotel looked quite magnificent as it stood on the hill dominating the Athens of the North. It was always little things that annoyed Abel most when he opened a new hotel and he would always check them on arrival. A small electric shock caused by nylon carpets when you touched a light switch. Room service that took forty minutes to materialize or a bed that was too small for anyone who was either fat or tall.

The press was quick to point out that it had been expected that Florentyna Rosnovski, daughter of the Chicago Baron, would perform the opening ceremony. One of the gossip columnists, on the *Sunday Express*, hinted at a family rift and reported that Abel had not been his usual exuberant, bouncy self. Abel denied the suggestion unconvincingly, retorting that he was over fifty—not an age for bouncing, his public relations man had told him to say. The press remained unconvinced and the following day the *Daily Mail* printed a photograph of a discarded engraved bronze plaque, discovered on a rubbish heap, that read:

The Edinburgh Baron
opened by
Florentyna Rosnovski
October 17, 1958

Abel flew on to Cannes. Another splendid hotel, this time overlooking the Mediterranean, but it didn't help him get Florentyna out of his mind. Another discarded plaque, this one in French. The openings were ashes without her.

Abel was beginning to dread that he might spend the rest of his life without seeing his daughter again. To kill the loneliness, he slept with some very expensive and some rather cheap women. None of them helped. William Kane's son now possessed the one person Abel Rosnovski truly loved.

France no longer held an excitement for him, and once he had finished his business there, Abel flew on to Bonn, where he completed negotiations for the site on which he would build the first Baron in Germany. He kept in constant touch with George by phone, but Florentyna had not been found and there was some very disturbing news concerning Henry Osborne.

"He's got himself in heavy debt with the bookmakers again," said George.

"I warned him last time that I was through bailing him out," said Abel. "He's been no damn use to anyone since he lost his seat in Congress. I suppose I'll have to deal with the problem when I get back."

"He's making threats," said George.

"There's nothing new about that. I've never let them worry me in the past," said Abel. "Tell him whatever it is he wants, it will have to wait until my return."

"When do you expect to be back?" asked George.

"Three weeks, four at the most. I want to look at some sites in Turkey and Egypt. Hilton's already started building there and I'm going to find out why. Which reminds me, George, the experts tell me you'll never be able to reach me once the plane has landed in the Middle East. The Arabs still haven't worked out how to find each other, let alone visitors from foreign countries, so I'll leave you to run everything as usual until you hear from me."

Abel spent more than three weeks looking for sites for new hotels in the Arab states. His advisors were legion, most of them claiming the title of Prince, each assuring Abel that he had real influence as a very close personal friend of the key minister, a distant cousin, in fact. However, it always turned out to be the wrong minister or too distant a cousin. The only solid conclusion Abel reached, after twenty-three days in the dust, sand and heat with soda but no whiskey, was that if his advisors' forecasts on the Middle East oil reserves were accurate, the Gulf States were going to want a lot of hotels in the long term and the Baron Group needed to start planning carefully if they were not going to be left behind.

Abel managed to find several sites on which to build hotels, through his several princes, but he did not have the time to discover which of them had the real power to fix the officials. He objected to bribery only when the money reached the wrong hands. At least in America, Henry Osborne had always known which officials needed to be taken care of. Abel set up a small office in Bahrain, leaving his local representatives in no doubt that the Baron Group was looking for hotel sites throughout the Arab world but not for princes or the cousins of ministers.

He flew on to Istanbul, where he almost immediately found the perfect place to build a hotel, overlooking the Bosphorus, only a hundred yards from the old British embassy. He mused as he stood on the barren ground that was his latest acquisition, recalling when he had last been here. He clenched his fist and held the wrist of his right hand. He could hear again the cries of the mob—it still made him feel frightened and sick although more than thirty years had passed.

Exhausted from his travels, Abel flew home to New York. During the interminable journey he thought of little but Florentyna. As always, George was waiting outside the customs gate to meet him. His expression indicated nothing.

"What news?" asked Abel as he climbed into the back of the Cadillac while the chauffeur put his bags in the trunk.

"Some good, some bad," said George as he pressed a button by the side window. A sheet of glass glided up between the driver and passenger sections of the car. "Florentyna has been in touch with her mother. She's living in a small apartment in San Francisco."

"Married?" said Abel.

"Yes," said George.

Neither spoke for some moments.

"And the Kane boy?" asked Abel.

"He's found a job in a bank. It seems a lot of people turned him down because word got around that he didn't finish at the Harvard Business School and his father wouldn't supply a reference. Not many people will employ him if as a consequence they antagonize his father. He finally was hired as a teller with the Bank of America. Way below what he might have expected with his qualifications."

"And Florentyna?"

"She's working as the assistant manager in a fashion shop

called 'Wayout Columbus' near Golden Gate Park. She's also been trying to borrow money from several banks."

"Why? Is she in any sort of trouble?" asked Abel anxiously.

"No, she's looking for capital to open her own shop."

"How much is she looking for?"

"She needs thirty-four thousand dollars for the lease on a small building on Nob Hill."

Abel sat thinking about what George had said, his short fingers tapping at the car window. "See that she gets the money, George. Make it look as if the transaction is an ordinary bank loan and be sure that it's not traceable back to me." He continued tapping. "This must always remain simply between the two of us, George."

"Anything you say, Abel."

"And keep me informed of every move she makes, however trivial."

"What about him?"

"I'm not interested in him," said Abel. "Now, what's the bad news?"

"Trouble with Henry Osborne again. It seems he owes money everywhere. I'm also fairly certain his only source of income is now you. He's still making threats—about revealing that you condoned bribes in the early days when you had taken over the group. Says he's kept all the papers from the first day he met you, when he claims he fixed an extra payment after the fire at the old Richmond in Chicago. Says he now has a file three inches thick."

"I'll deal with Henry in the morning," said Abel.

George spent the remainder of the drive into Manhattan bringing Abel up to date on the rest of the group's affairs. Everything was satisfactory, except that there had been a takeover of the Baron in Lagos after yet another coup. That never worried Abel.

The next morning Abel saw Henry Osborne. He looked old and tired, and the once smooth and handsome face was now heavily lined. He made no mention of the three-inch-thick file.

"I need a little money to get me through a tricky period," said Henry. "I've been a bit unlucky."

"Again, Henry? You should know better at your age. You're a born loser with horses and women. How much do you need this time?"

"Ten thousand would see me through," said Henry.

"Ten thousand!" said Abel, spitting out the words. "What do you think I am, a gold mine? It was only five thousand last time."

"Inflation," said Henry, trying to laugh.

"This is the last time, do you understand me?" said Abel as he took out his checkbook. "Come begging once more, Henry, and I'll remove you from the board as a director and turn you out without a penny."

"You're a real friend, Abel. I swear I'll never come back again—I promise you that. Never again." Henry plucked a Romeo y Julieta from the humidor on the table in front of Abel and lit it. "Thanks, Abel. You'll never regret this."

Henry left, puffing away at the cigar, as George came in. George waited for the door to be closed.

"What happened with Henry?"

"I gave in for the last time," said Abel. "I don't know why—it cost me ten thousand."

"Jesus, I feel like the brother of the prodigal son," said George. "He'll be back again. I'd be willing to put money on that."

"He'd better not," said Abel, "because I'm through with him. Whatever he's done for me in the past, it's now quits. Anything new about my girl?"

"Florentyna's fine, but it looks as though you were right about Zaphia. She's been making regular monthly trips to the Coast to see them both."

"Bloody woman," said Abel.

"Mrs. Kane had been out a couple of times as well," added George.

"And Kane?"

"No sign that he's relenting."

"That's one thing we have in common," said Abel.

"I've set up a facility for Florentyna with the Crocker National Bank of San Francisco," continued George. "She made an approach to the loan officer there less than a week ago. The agreement will appear to her as one of the bank's ordinary loan transactions, with no special favors. In fact, they're charging her half a percent more than usual so there can be no reason for her to be suspicious. What she doesn't know is that the loan is covered by your guarantee."

"Thanks, George, that's perfect. I'll bet you ten dollars she pays off the loan within two years and never needs to go back for another."

"I'd want odds of five to one on that," said George. "Why don't you try Henry; he's more of a sucker."

Abel laughed. "Keep me briefed, George, on everything she's up to. Everything."

CHAPTER
THIRTY-SIX

William felt he had been briefed on everything as he studied Thaddeus Cohen's quarterly report, and only one thing now worried him. Why was Abel Rosnovski still doing nothing with his vast holdings in Lester's? William couldn't help remembering that Rosnovski still owned six percent of the bank and with two more percent he could invoke Article Seven of Lester's bylaws. It was hard to believe that Rosnovski still feared S.E.C. regulations, especially as the Eisenhower Administration was settled into its second term and had never shown any interest in pursuing the original inquiry.

William was fascinated to read that Henry Osborne was once again in financial trouble and that Rosnovski still kept bailing him out. William wondered for how much longer that would go on, and what Henry had on Rosnovski. Was it possible that Rosnovski had enough problems of his own, leaving him no time to worry further about the downfall of William Kane? Cohen's report reviewed progress on the eight new hotels Rosnovski was building across the world. The London Baron was losing money and the Lagos Baron was out of commission; otherwise, he continued to grow in strength. William reread the attached clipping from the *Sunday Express*, reporting that Florentyna Rosnovski had not opened the Edinburgh Baron, and he thought about his son. Then he closed the report and locked the file in his safe, convinced there was nothing in it of importance to concern himself with.

William regretted his earlier loss of temper with Richard. Although he did not want the Rosnovski girl in his life, he wished he had not turned his back so irrevocably on his only son. Kate had pleaded on Richard's behalf and she and William had had a long and bitter argument—so rare in their married life—which they had been unable to resolve. Kate tried every tactic from gentle persuasion to tears, but nothing seemed to move William. Virginia and Lucy also missed their brother. "There's no one who will be critical of my paintings," said Virginia. "Don't you mean rude?" asked Kate.

Virginia tried to smile.

Lucy began locking herself in the bathroom, turning on the water and writing secret letters to Richard, who could never figure out why they always gave the appearance of being damp. No one dared to mention Richard's name in the house in front of William, and the strain was creating a sad rift within the family.

William had tried spending more time at the bank, even working late into the night, in the hope that it might help. It didn't. The bank was once again making heavy demands on his energies at the very time when he most felt like a rest. He had appointed six new vice presidents during the previous two years, hoping they would take some of the load off his shoulders. The reverse had turned out to be the case. They had created more work and more decisions for him to make, and the brightest of them, Jake Thomas, already looked like the most likely candidate to take William's place as chairman if Richard did not give up the Rosnovski girl. Although the profits of the bank continued to rise each year, William found he was no longer interested in making money for money's sake. Perhaps he now faced the same problem that Charles Lester had encountered: he had no son to leave his fortune and the chairmanship to. William had cut Richard out of his life, rewritten his will and dismantled Richard's trust.

. . .

In the year of their silver wedding anniversary, William decided to take Kate and the girls for a long vacation to Europe in the hope that it might help to put Richard out of their minds. They flew to London for the first time in a jet, a Boeing 707, and stayed at the Ritz. The hotel brought back many happy memories of William's first trip to Europe with Kate. They made a sentimental journey to Oxford and showed Virginia and Lucy the university city and then went to Stratford-on-Avon to see a Shakespeare play: *Richard III* with Laurence Olivier. They could have wished for a king with another name.

On the return journey from Stratford they stopped at the church in Henley on Thames where William and Kate had been married. They would have stayed at the Bell Inn again, but it still had only one vacant room. An argument started between William and Kate in the car on the way back to London as to whether it had been the Reverend Tukesbury or the Reverend Dukesbury who had married them. They came to no satisfactory conclusion before reaching the Ritz. On one thing they had been able to agree; the new roof on the parish church had worn well. William kissed Kate gently when he climbed into bed that night.

"Best five hundred pounds I ever invested," he said.

They flew on to Italy a week later, having seen every English sight any self-respecting American tourist is meant to visit and many they usually miss. In Rome the girls drank too much bad Italian wine and made themselves ill on the night of Virginia's birthday, while William ate too much good pasta and put on seven pounds. All of them would have been so much happier if they could have talked of Richard. Virginia cried that night and Kate tried to comfort her. "Why doesn't someone tell Daddy that some things are more important than pride?" Virginia kept asking. Kate had no reply.

When they returned to New York, William was refreshed and eager once again to plunge back into his work at the bank. He lost the seven pounds in seven days.

As the months passed by, he felt things were becoming quite routine again. Routine disappeared from his mind when Virginia, just out of Sweet Briar, announced she was going to marry a student from the University of Virginia Law School. The news shook William.

"She's not old enough," he said.

"Virginia's twenty-two," said Kate. "She's not a child any longer, William. How do you feel about becoming a grand-father?" she added, regretting the sequence of her words as soon as she had spoken them.

"What do you mean?" said William, horrified. "Virginia isn't pregnant, is she?"

"Good gracious, no," said Kate, and then she spoke more softly, as if she had been found out. "Richard and Florentyna have had a baby."

"How do you know?"

"Richard wrote to tell me the good news," replied Kate. "Hasn't the time come for you to forgive him, William?"

"Never," said William, and he marched out of the room in anger.

Kate sighed wearily. He had not even asked if his grand-child was a boy or a girl.

Virginia's wedding took place in Trinity Church, Boston, on a beautiful spring afternoon in late March of the following year. William thoroughly approved of David Telford, the young lawyer with whom Virginia had chosen to spend the rest of her life.

Virginia had wanted Richard to be an usher and Kate had begged William to invite him to the wedding, but he had steadfastly refused. Although it was meant to be the happiest day in Virginia's life, she would have given back all her presents to have her father and Richard standing together in the photograph that was taken outside the church. William had wanted to say yes, but he knew that Richard would never agree to coming without the Rosnovski girl, though William had been proud when he learned that Richard had been promoted to assistant manager at the bank. On the day of the wedding, Richard sent a present and a telegram to his sister. William put the present in the trunk of Virginia's car and would not allow the telegram to be read at the reception afterward.

CHAPTER
THIRTY-SEVEN

Abel was sitting alone in his office in the New York Baron, waiting to see a fund-raiser for the Kennedy campaign. The man was already twenty minutes late. Abel was tapping his fingers impatiently on his desk when his secretary came in.

"Mr. Vincent Hogan to see you, sir."

Abel sprang out of his chair. "Come in, Mr. Hogan," he said, slapping the good-looking young man on the back. "How are you?"

"I'm fine, Mr. Rosnovski. I'm sorry I'm a little late," said the unmistakably Bostonian voice.

"I didn't notice," said Abel. "Would you care for a drink, Mr. Hogan?"

"No, thank you, Mr. Rosnovski. I try not to drink when I have to see many people in one day."

"Absolutely right. I hope you won't mind if I have one," said Abel. "I'm not planning on seeing many people today."

Hogan laughed like a man who knew he was in for a day of other people's jokes. Abel poured a whiskey.

"Now, what can I do for you, Mr. Hogan?"

"Well, Mr. Rosnovski, we were hoping the Party could once again count on your support."

"I've always been a Democrat, as you know, Mr. Hogan. I supported Franklin D. Roosevelt, Harry Truman and Adlai Stevenson, although I couldn't understand what Adlai was talking about half the time."

Both men laughed falsely.

"I also helped my old friend, Dick Daley, in Chicago and I've been backing young Ed Muskie—the son of a Polish immigrant, you know—since his campaign for governor of Maine back in fifty-four."

"You've been a loyal supporter of the Party in the past, there's no denying that, Mr. Rosnovski," said Vincent Hogan in a tone that indicated that the statutory time for small talk had run out. "We also know the Democrats, not least of all former Congressman Osborne, have done the odd favor for you in return. I don't think it's necessary for me to go into any details of the unpleasant little incident with Interstate Airways."

"That's long since past," said Abel, "and well behind me."

"I agree," said Mr. Hogan, "and although most self-made multimillionaires couldn't face having their affairs looked into too closely, you will be the first to appreciate that we have to be especially careful. The candidate, as you will understand, cannot afford to take any personal risks so near the election. Nixon would love a scandal at this stage of the race."

"We understand each other clearly, Mr. Hogan. Now that's out of the way, how much were you expecting from me for the campaign?"

"I need every penny I can lay my hands on." Hogan's words came across clipped and slow. "Nixon is gathering a lot of support across the country and it's going to be a very close thing getting our man into the White House."

"Well, I'll support Kennedy," said Abel, "if he supports me. It's as simple as that."

"He's delighted to support you, Mr. Rosnovski. We all realize you're a pillar of the Polish community, and Senator Kennedy is personally aware of the brave stand you took on behalf of your countrymen who are still in slave labor camps behind the Iron Curtain, not to mention the service you gave in the war. I've been authorized to let you know that the candidate has already agreed to open your new hotel in Los Angeles during his campaign trip."

"That's good news," said Abel.

"The candidate is also fully aware of your desire to grant Poland most favored nation status in foreign trade with the United States."

"No more than we deserve after our service in the war," said Abel, and he paused briefly. "What about the other little matter?" he asked.

"Senator Kennedy is canvasing Polish-American opinion at the moment and we haven't met with any objections. He naturally cannot come to a final decision until after he is elected."

"Naturally. Would two hundred and fifty thousand dollars help him make that decision?" asked Abel.

Vincent Hogan didn't speak.

"Two hundred and fifty thousand dollars it is then," said Abel. "The money will be in your campaign fund headquarters by the end of the week, Mr. Hogan. You have my word on it."

The business was over, the bargain struck. Abel rose. "Please give Senator Kennedy my best wishes and add that of course I hope he'll be the next President of the United States. I always loathed Richard Nixon after his despicable treatment of Helen Gahagan Douglas, and in any case, there are personal reasons why I don't want Henry Cabot Lodge as vice president."

"I shall be delighted to pass on your message," said Mr. Hogan, "and thank you for your continued support of the Democratic party and, in particular, of the candidate." The Bostonian thrust out his hand. Abel grasped it.

"Keep in touch, Mr. Hogan. I don't part with that sort of money without expecting a return on my investment."

"I fully understand," said Vincent Hogan.

Abel showed his guest to the elevator and returned smiling to his office. His fingers started to tap the desk again. His secretary reappeared.

"Ask Mr. Novak to come in," said Abel.

George came through from his office a few moments later.

"I think I've pulled it off, George."

"Congratulations, Abel. I'm delighted. If Kennedy becomes the next President, then one of your biggest dreams will be fulfilled. How proud Florentyna will be of you."

Abel smiled when he heard her name. "Do you know what the little minx has been up to?" he said, laughing. "Did you see the Los Angeles *Times* last week, George?"

George shook his head and Abel passed him a copy of the paper. A picture was circled in red ink. George read the caption aloud: " 'Florentyna Kane opens her third shop, this one in Los Angeles. She already owns two in San Francisco and is hoping to open another in San Diego before the end of the year. "Florentyna's," as they are known, are fast becoming to California what Balenciaga is to Paris.' "

George laughed as he put the paper down.

"She must have written the piece herself," said Abel. "I can't wait for her to open a Florentyna's in New York. I'll bet she achieves that within five years, ten at the most. Do you want to take another bet on that, George?"

"I didn't take the first one, if you remember, Abel. Otherwise I would already have been out ten dollars."

Abel looked up, his voice quieter. "Do you think she'd come and see Senator Kennedy open the new Baron in Los Angeles, George? Do you think she might?"

"Not unless the Kane boy is invited as well."

"Never," said Abel. "That Kane boy is nothing. I read all the facts in your last report. He's left the Bank of America to work with Florentyna; couldn't even hold down a good job, had to fall back on her success."

"You're becoming a selective reader, Abel. You know very well that's not the way it was. I made the circumstances crystal clear: Kane is in charge of finances while Florentyna runs the shops. It's proving to be an ideal partnership. Don't ever forget that a major bank offered Kane the chance to head up its European department, but Florentyna begged him to join her when she no longer found she could control the finances herself. Abel, you'll have to face the fact that their marriage is a success. I know it's hard for you to stomach, but why don't you climb down off your high horse and meet the boy?"

"You're my closest friend, George. No one else in the world would dare to speak to me like that. So no one knows better than you why I can't climb down, not until that bastard Kane shows he is willing to meet me halfway. Until then I won't crawl again while he's still alive to watch me."

"What if you were to die first, Abel? You're exactly the same age."

"Then I'd lose and Florentyna inherits everything."

"You told me she wouldn't get a thing. You were going to change your will in favor of your grandson."

"I couldn't do it, George. When the time came to sign the documents, I just couldn't do it. What the hell—that damned grandson is going to end up with both our fortunes in the end."

Abel removed a billfold from his inside pocket, shuffled through several old pictures of Florentyna and took out a new one of his grandson, which he proffered to George.

"Good-looking little boy," said George.

"Sure is," said Abel. "The image of his mother."

George laughed. "You never give up, do you, Abel?"

"What do you think they call him?"

"What do you mean?" said George. "You know very well what his name is."

"I mean what do you think they actually call him?"

"How should I know?" said George.

"Find out," said Abel. "I care."

"How am I supposed to do that?" said George. "Have someone follow them while they're pushing the stroller around Golden Gate Park? You left clear instructions that Florentyna must never find out that you're still taking an interest in her or the Kane boy."

"That reminds me, I still have a little matter to settle with his father," said Abel.

"What are you going to do about the Lester stock?" asked George. "Peter Parfitt has been showing new interest in selling his two percent and I wouldn't trust Henry with the negotiations. With those two working on the sale, everybody will be in on the deal except you."

"I'm doing nothing. Much as I hate Kane, I don't want any trouble with him until we know if Kennedy wins the election. I'm leaving the whole situation dormant for the moment. If Kennedy fails, I'll buy Parfitt's two percent and go ahead with the plan we've already discussed. And don't worry yourself about Henry—I've already taken him off the Kane file. From now on I'm handling it myself."

"I do worry, Abel. I know he's in debt again to half the bookmakers in Chicago and I wouldn't be surprised if he arrived in New York on the scrounge any minute now."

"Henry won't be coming here. I made the situation very clear last time I saw him that he wouldn't get another dime out of me. If he does come begging, he'll only lose his seat on the board and his only source of income."

"That worries me even more," said George. "Let's say he took it on himself to go to Kane direct for money."

"Not possible, George. Henry is the one man alive who hates Kane even more than I do, and not without reason."

"How can you be so sure of that?"

"William Kane's mother was Henry's second wife," said Abel, "and young William, aged only sixteen, threw him out of his own home."

"Good God, how did you come across that piece of information?"

"There's nothing I don't know about William Kane," said Abel. "Or Henry, for that matter. Absolutely nothing—from the fact that Kane and I started life on the same day—and I'd be willing to bet my good leg there's nothing he doesn't know about me. So we have to be very careful for the time being, but you need have no fear that Henry will turn stool pigeon. He'd lie before he had to admit his real name is Vittorio Togna and he once served a jail sentence."

"Good God, does Henry realize you know all this?"

"No, he doesn't. I've kept it to myself for years, always believing, George, that if you think a man might threaten you at some time, then you should keep a little more up your sleeve than your arm. I've never trusted Henry since the days he suggested swindling Great Western Casualty while he was still actually working for them, although I'd be the first to admit he's been very useful to me in the past. And I'm confident he isn't going to cause me any trouble in the future, because without his director's salary he becomes penniless overnight. So forget Henry and let's be a little more positive. What's the latest date for the completion of the Los Angeles Baron?"

"Middle of September," replied George.

"Perfect. That will be six weeks before the election. When Kennedy opens that hotel, the news will hit every front page in America."

CHAPTER
THIRTY-EIGHT

When William returned to New York, after a bankers' conference in Washington, he found a message awaiting him, requesting that he contact Thaddeus Cohen immediately. He hadn't spoken to Cohen for a considerable time, because Abel Rosnovski had caused no direct trouble since the abortive telephone conversation on the eve of Richard and Florentyna's marriage, nearly three years ago. The successive quarterly reports had merely confirmed that Rosnovski was trying neither to buy nor to sell any of the bank's stock. Nevertheless, William called Thaddeus Cohen immediately and somewhat apprehensively. The lawyer told William that he had stumbled across some information that he did not wish to divulge over the phone. William asked him to come over to the bank as soon as it was convenient.

Thaddeus Cohen arrived forty minutes later. William heard him out in attentive silence.

When Cohen had finished his revelation, William said, "Your father would never have approved of such underhanded methods."

"Neither would yours," said Thaddeus Cohen, "but they didn't have to deal with the likes of Abel Rosnovski."

"What makes you think your plan will work?"

"Look at the Bernard Goldfine and Sherman Adams case. Only one thousand six hundred and forty-two dollars involved in hotel bills and a vicuna coat, but it sure embar-

rassed the hell out of the President when Adams was accused of preferred treatment because he was a Presidential
assistant. We know Mr. Rosnovski is aiming a lot higher
than that. It should, therefore, be easier to bring him down."

"How much is it going to cost me?"

"Twenty-five thousand at the outside, but I may be able to
pull the whole deal off for less."

"How can you be sure that Rosnovski doesn't realize that
I'm personally involved?"

"I'd use a third person who won't even know your name
to act as an intermediary."

"And if you pull it off, what would you recommend we
do then?"

"You send all the details to Senator John Kennedy's office, and I guarantee it will finish off Abel Rosnovski's ambitions once and for all. The moment his credibility has been
shattered he will be a spent force and find it quite impossible
to invoke Article Seven of the bank's bylaws—even if he did
control eight percent of Lester's."

"Maybe—if Kennedy becomes President," said William.
"But what happens if Nixon wins? He's way ahead in the
opinion polls and I'd certainly back his chances against
Kennedy. Can you really imagine America would ever send
a Roman Catholic to the White House? I can't, but I admit
that an investment of twenty-five thousand is small enough
if there's better than an outside chance the move will finish
Abel Rosnovski off once and for all and leave me secure at
the bank."

If Kennedy becomes President . . .

"I'm quite confident," said Thaddeus Cohen.

William opened the drawer of his desk, took out a large
checkbook marked "Private Account" and wrote out the figures two, five, zero, zero, zero.

CHAPTER
THIRTY-NINE

Abel's prediction that Kennedy's opening of the Baron would hit every front page in America did not turn out to be wholly accurate. Although the candidate did indeed open the hotel, he had to appear at dozens of other events in Los Angeles that day and face Nixon for a televised debate the following evening. Nevertheless, the opening of the newest Baron gained fairly wide coverage in the national press, and Vincent Hogan assured Abel privately that Kennedy had not forgotten the other little matter. Florentyna's shop was only a few hundred yards from the new Baron, but father and daughter did not meet.

After the Illinois returns came in, when John F. Kennedy looked certain to be the thirty-fifth President of the United States, Abel drank to Mayor Daley's health and celebrated at the Democratic National Headquarters on Times Square. He didn't get home until nearly five the next morning.

"Hell, I have a lot to celebrate," he told George. "I'm going to be the next—" He fell asleep before he finished the sentence. George smiled and put him to bed.

William watched the results of the election in the peace of his study on East Sixty-eighth Street. After the Illinois returns, which were not confirmed until ten o'clock the next morning (William never had trusted Mayor Daley), Walter

Cronkite declared it was all over but the shouting and William picked up his phone and dialed Thaddeus Cohen's home number.

All he said was, "The twenty-five thousand dollars has turned out to be a wise investment, Thaddeus. Now let us be sure that there is no honeymoon period for Mr. Rosnovski. Don't do anything until he makes his trip to Turkey."

William placed the phone back on the hook and went to bed. He was disappointed that Richard Nixon had failed to beat Kennedy and that his distant cousin, Henry Cabot Lodge, would not be the vice president, but it is an ill wind. . . .

When Abel received his invitation to be a guest at one of President Kennedy's inaugural balls in Washington, D.C., there was only one person he wanted to share the honor with. He talked the idea over with George and had to agree that Florentyna would never be willing to accompany him unless she was convinced that the feud with Richard's father could finally be resolved. So he knew he would have to go alone.

In order to be in Washington to attend the celebrations, Abel had to postpone a trip to Europe and the Middle East. He could not afford to miss the inauguration, whereas he could always put back the opening of the Istanbul Baron.

Abel had a new, rather conservative dark blue suit made especially for the occasion and took over the Presidential Suite at the Washington Baron for the day of the Inauguration. He enjoyed watching the vital young President deliver his inaugural speech, full of hope and promise for the future.

"A new generation of Americans, born in this century"— Abel only just qualified—"tempered by war"—Abel certainly qualified—"disciplined by a hard and bitter peace"—Abel qualified again. "Ask not what your country can do for you. Ask what you can do for your country."

The crowd rose to a man, everyone ignoring the snow

that had failed to dampen the impact of John F. Kennedy's brilliant oration.

Abel returned to the Washington Baron exhilarated. He showered before changing for dinner into white tie and tails, also made especially for the occasion. When he studied his ample frame in the mirror, Abel had to admit to himself that he was not the last word in sartorial elegance. His tailor had done the best he could (he had had to make three new and ever larger evening suits for Abel in the past three years). Florentyna would have chastised her father for the unnecessary inches, as she used to call them, and for her he would have done something about it. Why did his thoughts always return to Florentyna? He checked his medals. First the Polish Veterans' Medal, next the decorations for his service in the desert and in Europe, and then his cutlery medals, as Abel called them, for distinguished service with knives and forks.

In all, seven inaugural balls were held in Washington that evening, and Abel's invitation directed him to the D.C. Armory. He sat in a corner reserved for Polish Democrats from New York and Chicago. They had a lot to celebrate. Edmund Muskie was in the Senate and ten more Polish Democrats had been elected to Congress. No one mentioned the two newly elected Polish Republicans. Abel spent a happy evening with two old friends who, along with him, were founding members with him of the Polish-American Congress. They both asked for Florentyna.

The ball was interrupted by the entrance of John F. Kennedy and his beautiful wife, Jacqueline. They stayed about fifteen minutes, chatted with a few carefully selected people and then moved on. Although Abel didn't actually speak with the President, even though he had left his table and placed himself strategically in Kennedy's path, he did manage to have a word with Vincent Hogan as he was leaving with the Kennedy entourage.

"Mr. Rosnovski, what a fortuitous meeting."

Abel would have liked to explain to the boy that with him

nothing was fortuitous, but now was neither the time nor the place. Hogan took Abel's arm and guided him quickly behind a large marble pillar.

"I can't say too much at the moment, Mr. Rosnovski, as I must stick with the President, but I think you can expect a call from us in the near future. Naturally, the President has rather a lot of appointments to deal with at the moment."

"Naturally," said Abel.

"But I am hoping," continued Vincent Hogan, "that in your case everything will be confirmed by late March or early April. May I be the first to offer my congratulations, Mr. Rosnovski? I am confident you will serve the President well."

Abel watched Vincent Hogan literally run off to be sure he caught up with the Kennedy party, which was already climbing into a fleet of open-doored limousines.

"You look pleased with yourself," said one of Abel's Polish friends as he returned to his table and sat down to attack a tough steak, which would not have been allowed inside a Baron. "Did Kennedy invite you to be his new Secretary of State?"

They all laughed.

"Not yet," said Abel. "But he did tell me the accommodation in the White House was not in the same class as the Barons."

Abel flew back to New York the next morning after first visiting the Polish Chapel of Our Lady of Czestochowa in the National Shrine. It made him think of both Florentynas. Washington National airport was chaos and Abel eventually arrived at the New York Baron three hours later than planned. George joined him for dinner and knew that all had gone well when Abel ordered a magnum of Dom Pérignon.

"Tonight we celebrate," said Abel. "I saw Hogan at the ball and my appointment will be confirmed in the next few weeks. The official announcement will probably be made soon after I get back from the Middle East."

"Congratulations, Abel. I know of no one who deserves the honor more."

"Thank you, George. I can assure you your reward will not be in heaven, because when it's all official, I'm going to appoint you acting president of the Baron Group in my absence."

George drank another glass of champagne. They were already halfway through the bottle.

"How long do you think you'll be away this time, Abel?"

"Only three weeks. I want to check that those Arabs aren't robbing me blind and then go on to Turkey to open the Istanbul Baron. I think I'll take in London and Paris on the way."

George poured more champagne.

Abel spent three more days in England than he had originally planned, trying to sort out the London Baron's problems with a manager who seemed to blame everything on the British unions. The London Baron had turned out to be one of Abel's few failures, although he never could put his finger on why the hotel continually lost money. He would have considered closing it, but the Baron Group had to have a presence in England's capital city, so once again he fired the manager and made a new appointment.

Paris presented a striking contrast. The hotel was one of his most successful in Europe and he'd once admitted to Florentyna, as reluctantly as a parent admits to having a favorite child, that the Paris Baron was his favorite hotel. Abel found everything on the Boulevard Raspail well organized and spent only two days in Paris before flying on to the Middle East.

Abel now had sites in five of the Persian Gulf States, but only the Riyadh Baron had actually started construction. If he'd been a younger man, Abel would have stayed in the Middle East for a couple of years himself and straightened the Arabs out. But he couldn't abide the sand or the heat or the uncertainty of the availability of a whiskey. He couldn't stand the natives either. He left them to one of his young assistant vice presidents, who had been told that he would be

allowed to return and manage the infidels in America only
when Abel was sure he had proved a success with the holy
and blessed ones in the Middle East.

He left the poor assistant vice president in the richest private hell in the world and flew on to Turkey.

Abel had visited Turkey several times during the past few
years to watch the progress of the Istanbul Baron. For Abel,
there would always be something special about Constantinople, as he remembered the city. He was looking forward
to opening a new Baron in the country he had finally left to
start a new life in America.

While he was unpacking his suitcase in yet another Presidential Suite, Abel found fifteen invitations awaiting his reply. There always were several invitations about the time of
a hotel opening; a galaxy of freeloaders who wanted to be
invited to any opening night party appeared on the scene as
if by magic. On this occasion, however, two of the dinner invitations came as an agreeable surprise to Abel from men
who certainly could not be classified as freeloaders: namely,
the ambassadors of America and Britain. The invitation to
the old British embassy was particularly irresistible as he
had not been inside the building for nearly forty years.

That evening, Abel dined as the guest of Sir Bernard Burrows, Her Majesty's Ambassador to Turkey. To his surprise
he found that he had been placed at the right of the Ambassador's wife, a privilege Abel had never been afforded in any
other embassy in the past. When the dinner was over he observed the quaint English tradition by which the ladies left
the room while the gentlemen sat together to smoke cigars
and drink port or brandy. Abel was invited to join the American ambassador, Fletcher Warren, for port in Sir Bernard's
study. Sir Bernard was taking the American Ambassador to
task for allowing him to have The Chicago Baron to dinner
before he had.

"The British have always been a presumptuous race,"
said the American Ambassador, lighting a large Cuban cigar.

"I'll say one thing for the Americans," said Sir Bernard, "they don't know when they're fairly beaten."

Abel listened to the two diplomats' banter, wondering why he had been included in such a private gathering. Sir Bernard offered Abel some vintage port, and the American Ambassador raised his glass.

"To Abel Rosnovski," he said.

Sir Bernard also raised his glass. "I understand that congratulations are in order," he said.

Abel reddened and looked hastily toward Fletcher Warren, hoping he would help him out.

"Oh, have I let the cat out of the bag, Fletcher?" said Sir Bernard, turning to the American Ambassador. "You told me the appointment was common knowledge, old chap."

"Fairly common," said Fletcher Warren. "Not that the British could ever keep a secret for very long."

"Is that why your lot took such a devil of a time to discover we were at war with Germany?" said Sir Bernard.

"And then moved in to make sure of the victory?"

"And the glory," said Sir Bernard.

The American Ambassador laughed. "I'm told the official announcement will be made in the next few days."

Both men looked at Abel, who remained silent.

"Well then, may I be the first to congratulate you, Your Excellency," said Sir Bernard. "I wish you every happiness in your new appointment."

Abel flushed to hear aloud the appellation he had whispered so often to his shaving mirror during the past few months. "You'll have to get used to being called Your Excellency, you know," continued the British Ambassador, "and a whole lot of worse things than that. Particularly all the damned functions you'll be made to attend one after another. If you have a weight problem now, it will be nothing compared to the one you'll have when you finish your term of office. You may yet live to be grateful for the Cold War. It's the one thing that might keep your social life within bounds."

The American Ambassador smiled. "Well done, Abel,

and may I add my best wishes for your continued success. When were you last in Poland?" he inquired.

"I've only been back home once, for a short visit a few years ago," said Abel. "I've wanted to return ever since."

"Well, you will be returning in triumph," said Fletcher Warren. "Are you familiar with our embassy in Warsaw?"

"No, I'm not," admitted Abel.

"Not a bad building," said Sir Bernard. "Remembering you colonials couldn't get a foothold in Europe until after the Second World War. But the food is appalling. I shall expect you to do something about that, Mr. Rosnovski. I'm afraid the only thing for it is that you'll have to build a Baron hotel in Warsaw. As ambassador, that's the least they'll expect from an old Pole."

Abel sat in a state of euphoria, laughing and enjoying Sir Bernard's feeble jokes. He found he was drinking a little more wine than usual and felt at ease with himself and the world. He couldn't wait to return to America and tell Florentyna his news, now that the appointment seemed to be official. She would be so proud of him. He decided then and there that the moment he arrived back in New York he would reserve a seat for San Francisco, where he would make everything up with her. It was what he had wanted to do all along and now he had an excuse. Somehow he'd force himself to like the Kane boy. He must stop referring to him as the Kane boy. What was his name—Richard? Yes, Richard. Abel felt a sudden rush of relief at having made the decision.

After the three men had returned to the ladies in the main reception room, Abel reached up and touched the British Ambassador on the shoulder. "I should be getting back, Your Excellency."

"Back to the Baron," said Sir Bernard. "Allow me to accompany you to your car, my dear fellow."

The Ambassador's wife bade Abel good night at the door.

"Good night, Lady Burrows, and thank you for a memorable evening."

She smiled. "I know I'm not meant to know, Mr. Rosnovski, but many congratulations on your appointment. You must be so proud to be returning to the land of your birth as your country's senior representative."

"I am," Abel said simply.

Sir Bernard accompanied him down the marble steps of the British embassy to the waiting car. The chauffeur opened the door.

"Good night, Rosnovski," said Sir Bernard, "and good luck in Warsaw. By the way, I hope you enjoyed your first meal in the British embassy."

"My second actually, Sir Bernard."

"You've been here before, old boy? When we checked through the guest book we couldn't find your name."

"No," said Abel. "Last time I had dinner in the British embassy, I ate in the kitchen. I don't think they keep a guest book down there, but the meal was the best I'd had in years."

Abel smiled as he climbed into the back of the car. He could see that Sir Bernard wasn't sure whether to believe him or not.

As Abel was driven back to the Baron, his fingers tapped on the side windows and he hummed to himself. He would have liked to return to America the next morning, but he couldn't cancel the invitation to dine with Fletcher Warren at the American embassy the following evening. Hardly the sort of thing a future ambassador does, old fellow, he could hear Sir Bernard saying.

Dinner with the American Ambassador turned out to be another pleasant occasion. Abel was made to explain to the assembled guests how he had come to eat in the kitchen of the British Embassy. When he told them the truth, they looked on in surprised admiration. He wasn't sure if many of them believed the story of how he had nearly lost his hand, but they all admired the silver band, and that night, everyone called him "Your Excellency."

The next day, Abel was up early, ready for his flight to America. The DC-8 flew into Belgrade, where he was grounded for sixteen hours, waiting for the plane to be ser-

viced. Something wrong with the landing gear, they told
him. He sat in the airport lounge, sipping undrinkable Yugo-
slavian coffee. The contrast between the British embassy
and the snack bar in a Communist-controlled country was
not entirely lost on Abel. At last the plane took off, only to
be delayed again in Amsterdam. This time the passengers
were made to change planes.

When he finally arrived at Idlewild, Abel had been traveling for nearly thirty-six hours. He was so tired he could
hardly walk. As he left the Customs area, he suddenly found
himself surrounded by newsmen, and the cameras started
flashing and clicking. Immediately he smiled. The announcement must have been made, he thought; now it's official. He stood as straight as he could and walked slowly and
with dignity, disguising his limp. There was no sign of
George as the cameramen jostled each other unceremoniously to be sure of a picture.

Then he saw George standing at the edge of the crowd,
looking like death. Abel's heart lurched as he passed the barrier, and a journalist, far from asking him what it felt like to
be the first Polish-American to be appointed ambassador to
Warsaw, shouted: "Do you have any answers to the
charges?"

The cameras went on flashing and so did the questions.

"Are the accusations true, Mr. Rosnovski?"

"How much did you actually pay Congressman Osborne?"

"Do you deny the charges?"

"Have you returned to America to face trial?"

They wrote down Abel's replies although he had not
spoken.

Then he shouted above the crowd: "Get me out of here!"

George squeezed forward and managed to reach Abel and
then pushed his way back through the crowd and bundled
him into the waiting Cadillac. Abel bent over and hid his
head in his hands as the cameras' flashbulbs kept popping.
George shouted at the chauffeur to get moving.

"To the Baron, sir?" he asked.

"No, to Miss Rosnovski's apartment on East Fifty-seventh Street."

"Why?" said Abel.

"Because the press is crawling all over the Baron."

"I don't understand," said Abel. "In Istanbul they treat me as if I were the ambassador-elect and I return home to find I'm a criminal. What the hell is going on, George?"

"Do you want to hear it all from me or wait until you've seen your lawyer?" asked George.

"My lawyer? You got someone to represent me?" asked Abel.

"H. Trafford Jilks, the best."

"And the most expensive."

"I didn't think you would be worrying about money at a time like this, Abel."

"You're right, George. I'm sorry. Where is he now?"

"I left him at the courthouse, but he said he'd come to the apartment as soon as he was through."

"I can't wait that long, George. For God's sake, put me in the picture. Tell me the worst."

George drew a deep breath. "There's a warrant out for your arrest," he said.

"What the hell's the charge?"

"Bribery of government officials."

"I've never been directly involved with a government official in my whole life," protested Abel.

"I know, but Henry Osborne has, and what he did seems to have been in your name or on your behalf."

"Oh my God!" said Abel. "I should never have employed the man. I let the fact that we both hated Kane cloud my judgment. But I still find it hard to believe Henry has told everything, because he would only end up implicating himself."

"But Henry has disappeared," said George, "and the big surprise is that suddenly, mysteriously, all his debts have been cleared up."

"William Kane," said Abel, spitting the words out.

"We've found nothing that points in that direction," said George. "There's no proof he's involved in this at all."

"Who needs proof? You tell me how the authorities got hold of the details."

"We do know that much," said George. "It seems an anonymous package containing a file was sent direct to the Justice Department in Washington."

"Postmarked New York, no doubt," said Abel.

"No, Chicago."

Abel was silent for a few moments. "It couldn't have been Henry who sent the file to them," he said finally. "That doesn't make any sense."

"How can you be so sure?" asked George.

"Because you said all his debts have been cleared up and the Justice Department wouldn't pay out that sort of money unless they thought they were going to catch Al Capone. Henry must have sold his file to someone else. But who? The one thing we can be certain of is that he would never have released any information directly to Kane."

"Directly?" said George.

"Directly," repeated Abel. "Perhaps he didn't sell it directly. Kane could have arranged for an intermediary to deal with the whole thing if he already knew that Henry was heavily in debt and the bookmakers were threatening him."

"That might be right, Abel. And it certainly wouldn't take an ace detective to discover the extent of Henry's financial problems. They were common knowledge to anyone sitting on a bar stool in Chicago, but don't jump to hasty conclusions just yet. Let's find out what your lawyer has to say."

The Cadillac came to a halt outside Florentyna's former home, which Abel had retained and maintained in the hope that his daughter would one day return. George saw H. Trafford Jilks waiting in the foyer and opened the apartment door to let them all in. Once they had settled down, George poured Abel a large whiskey. He drank it in one gulp and gave the empty glass back to George, who refilled it.

"Tell me the worst, Mr. Jilks. Let's get it over with."

"I am sorry, Mr. Rosnovski," he began. "Mr. Novak told me about Warsaw."

"That's all over now, so we may as well forget 'Your Excellency.' You can be sure if Vincent Hogan were asked, he wouldn't even remember my name. Come on, Mr. Jilks, what am I facing?"

"You've been indicted on seventeen charges of bribery and corruption of officials in fourteen different states. I've made provisional arrangements with the Justice Department for you to be arrested here at the apartment tomorrow morning, and they will make no objection to the granting of bail."

"Very cozy," said Abel, "but what if they can prove the charges?"

"Oh, they should be able to prove some of the charges," said H. Trafford Jilks matter-of-factly. "But as long as Henry Osborne stays tucked away, they're going to find it very difficult to nail you on most of them. But you're going to have to live with the fact, Mr. Rosnovski, that most of the real damage has already been done whether you're convicted or not."

"I can see that only too well," said Abel, glancing at a picture of himself on the front page of the *Daily News*, which H. Trafford Jilks obviously had brought with him. "So you find out, Mr. Jilks, who the hell bought that file from Henry Osborne. Put as many people to work on it as you need. I don't care about the cost. But you find out and find out quickly, because if it turns out to be William Kane, I'm going to finish him once and for all."

"Don't get yourself into any more trouble than you are already in," said H. Trafford Jilks. "You're knee deep in it as it is."

"Don't worry," said Abel. "When I finish Kane, it'll be legal and way aboveboard."

"Now listen carefully, Mr. Rosnovski. You forget about William Kane for the time being and start worrying about your impending trial. It will be the most important event in your life unless you don't mind spending the next ten years in jail. Now, there's not much more you can do tonight. I'll get my men looking for Henry Osborne, and I'll issue a short press statement denying the charges and saying we have a full explanation that will exonerate you completely."

"Do we?" George asked hopefully.

"No," said Jilks, "but it will give me some much needed time to think. When Mr. Rosnovski has had a chance to check through that file of names, it wouldn't surprise me to discover he's never had direct contact with anyone in it. It's possible that Henry Osborne always acted as an intermediary without ever putting Mr. Rosnovski fully in the picture. Then my job will be to prove that Osborne exceeded his authority as a director of the group. Mind you, Mr. Rosnovski, if you did meet any of the people mentioned in the file, for God's sake let me know, because you can be sure the Justice Department will put them on the stand as witnesses against us. I'll leave a copy of the file for you and we'll start worrying about that tomorrow. You go to bed and get some sleep. You must be exhausted after your trip. I will see you first thing in the morning."

Abel was arrested quietly in his daughter's apartment at 8:30 A.M. and driven away by a U.S. marshal to the Federal District Court for the Southern District of New York. The brightly colored St. Valentine's Day decorations in store windows heightened Abel's sense of loneliness. Jilks had hoped that his arrangements had been so discreet that the press would not have discovered them, but when Abel reached the courthouse, he was once again surrounded by photographers and reporters. He ran the gauntlet into the courtroom with George in front of him and Jilks behind. They sat silently in an anteroom waiting for their case to be called.

When they were called, the indictment hearing lasted only a few minutes and was a strange anticlimax. The clerk read the charges, H. Trafford Jilks answered "Not Guilty" to each one on behalf of his client and requested bail. The Government, as agreed, made no objection. Jilks asked Judge

Prescott for at least three months to prepare his defense. The judge set a trial date of May 17.

Abel was free again, free to face the press and more of their flashing bulbs. The chauffeur had the car waiting for him at the bottom of the steps with the back door open. The engine was already running and the driver had to do some very skillful maneuvering to escape the reporters who were still pursuing their story. When the car pulled to a stop on East Fifty-seventh Street, Abel turned to George and put his arm on his shoulder.

"Now listen, George, you're going to have to run the group for at least three months while I get my defense worked out with Mr. Jilks. Let's hope you don't have to run it alone after that," said Abel, trying to laugh.

"Of course I won't have to, Abel. Mr. Jilks will get you off, you'll see." George picked up his briefcase and touched Abel on the arm. "Keep smiling," he said, and left the other two men as they entered the apartment building.

"I don't know what I'd do without George," Abel told his lawyer as they settled down in the living room. "We came over on the boat together nearly forty years ago and we've been through a hell of a lot since then. Now it looks as if there's a whole lot more ahead of us, so let's get on with it, Mr. Jilks. Nothing new on Henry Osborne?"

"No, but I have six men working on it, and I understand the Justice Department has at least another six, so we can be pretty sure he'll turn up, not that we want them to find him first."

"What about the man Osborne sold the file to?" asked Abel.

"I have some people I trust in Chicago detailed to run that down."

"Good," said Abel. "Now the time has come to go over that file of names you left with me last night."

Trafford Jilks began by reading the indictment and then he went over each of the charges in detail with Abel.

After nearly three weeks of constant meetings, when Jilks was finally convinced there was nothing else Abel could tell him, he left his client to rest. The three weeks had failed to turn up any leads to the whereabouts of Henry Osborne, for either Trafford Jilks's men or the Justice Department. Jilks's men had also had no breakthrough on finding the person to whom Henry had sold his information, and the lawyer was beginning to wonder if Abel had guessed right.

As the trial date drew nearer, Abel started to face the possibility of actually going to jail. He was now fifty-five and afraid of the prospect of spending the last few years of his life the same way he had spent three of the first few. As H. Trafford Jilks had pointed out, if the Government could prove it had a case, there was enough in Osborne's file to send Abel to prison for a very long time. The injustice—as it seemed to him—of his predicament angered Abel. The malfeasances that Henry Osborne had committed in his name had been substantial but not exceptional; Abel doubted that any new business could have grown or any new money made without the kinds of handout and bribe to different people documented with sickening accuracy to Trafford Jilks's file. He thought bitterly of the smooth, impassive face of the young William Kane, sitting in his Boston office all those years ago on a pile of inherited money whose probably disreputable origins were safely buried under generations of respectability. Then Florentyna wrote, a touching letter enclosing some photographs of her son, saying that she still loved and respected Abel and believed in his innocence.

Three days before the trial was due to open, the Justice Department found Henry Osborne in New Orleans. They undoubtedly would have missed him completely if he hadn't landed in a local hospital with two broken legs. A zealous policeman discovered that Henry had received his injuries for welching on gambling debts. They don't like that in New Orleans. The policeman put two and two together and later that night, after the hospital had put plaster casts on Osborne's legs, the Justice Department wheeled him onto an Eastern Airlines flight to New York.

Henry Osborne was charged the next day with conspiracy

to defraud and he was denied bail. H. Trafford Jilks asked the court's permission to be allowed to question him. The court granted his request, but Jilks gained very little satisfaction from the interview. It became obvious that Osborne had already made his deal with the Government, promising to turn state's evidence against Abel in return for lesser charges against him.

"No doubt, Mr. Osborne will find the charges against him surprisingly minor," the lawyer commented drily.

"So that's his game," said Abel. "I take the rap while he escapes. Now we'll never find out who he sold that goddamn file to."

"No, there you are wrong, Mr. Rosnovski. That was the one thing he was willing to talk about," said Jilks. "He said it wasn't William Kane. He would never have sold the file to Kane under any circumstances. A man from Chicago called Harry Smith paid Mr. Osborne cash for the evidence and, would you believe it, Harry Smith turns out to be an alias: there are dozens of Harry Smiths in the Chicago area and not a single one of them fits the description."

"Find him," said Abel. "And find him before the trial starts."

"We're already working on that," said Jilks. "If the man is still in Chicago we'll pin him down within the week. Osborne also added that this so-called Smith assured him he only wanted the file for private purposes. He had no intention of revealing the contents to anyone in authority."

"Then why did 'Smith' want the details in the first place?" asked Abel.

"The inference was blackmail. That's why Henry Osborne disappeared, to avoid you. If you think about that, Mr. Rosnovski, he could be telling the truth. After all, the disclosures are extremely damaging to him and he must have been as distressed as you when he heard the file was in the hands of the Justice Department. It's no wonder he decided to stay out of sight and turned state's evidence when he was eventually caught."

"Do you know," said Abel, "the only reason I ever employed that man was because he hated William Kane as much as I did, and now Kane has done us both."

"There's no proof that Mr. Kane was in any way involved," said Jilks.

"I don't need proof."

The trial was delayed at the request of the Government, which claimed it needed more time to question Henry Osborne before presenting its case. He was now the principal witness for the prosecution. Trafford Jilks objected strongly and informed the court that the health of his client, who was no longer a young man, was failing under the strain of false accusations. The plea did not move Judge Prescott, who agreed to the Government's request and postponed the trial for a further four weeks.

The month dragged on for Abel and two days before the trial again was due to open, he resigned himself to being found guilty and facing a long jail sentence. Then H. Trafford Jilks's investigator in Chicago found the man called Harry Smith, who turned out to be a local private detective who had used an alias under strict instructions from his client, a firm of lawyers in New York. It cost Jilks one thousand dollars and another twenty-four hours before Harry Smith revealed that the firm concerned had been Cohen, Cohen and Yablons.

"Kane's lawyer," said Abel immediately on being told.

"Are you sure?" asked Jilks. "I would have thought from all we know about William Kane that he would be the last person to use a Jewish firm."

"Way back, when I bought the hotels from Kane's bank, some of the paper work was covered by a man named Thomas Cohen. For some reason, the bank used two lawyers for the transaction."

"What do you want me to do about it?" George asked Abel.

"Nothing," said Trafford Jilks. "We must have no more trouble before the trial. Do you understand, Mr. Rosnovski?"

"Yes," said Abel. "I'll deal with Kane when the trial's

over. Now, Mr. Jilks, listen and listen carefully. You must go back to Osborne immediately and tell him the file was sold by Harry Smith to William Kane and that Kane used the contents to gain revenge on both of us, and stress the 'both of us.' I promise you when Osborne hears that, he's not going to open his mouth in the witness chair, no matter what promises he's made to the Justice Department. Henry Osborne's the one man alive who may hate Kane more than I do."

"Anything you say," said Jilks, who clearly wasn't convinced. "But I feel I must warn you, Mr. Rosnovski, that he's still putting the blame firmly on your shoulders and to date he's been no help to our side at all."

"You can take my word for this, Mr. Jilks. His attitude will change the moment he knows about Kane's involvement."

H. Trafford Jilks obtained permission to spend ten minutes that night with Henry Osborne in his cell. Osborne listened but said nothing. Jilks was sure that his news had made no impression on the Government's star witness and he decided he would wait until the next morning before telling Abel Rosnovski. He preferred that his client try to get a good night's sleep before the trial opened the next day.

Four hours before the trial was due to start, Henry Osborne was found hanging in his cell by the guard bringing in his breakfast.

He had used a Harvard tie.

The trial opened for the Government without its star witness and it appealed for a further extension. After hearing another impassioned plea by H. Trafford Jilks on the state of his client's health, Judge Prescott refused the request. The public followed every word of The Chicago Baron Trial on television and in the newspapers—and, to Abel's horror, Zaphia sat in the public gallery seeming to enjoy every moment of his discomfort. After nine days in court, the prosecution knew that their case was not standing up well and offered to make a deal with H. Trafford Jilks. During an adjournment, Jilks briefed Abel on the offer.

"They will drop all the main indictments of bribery if you will plead guilty to the misdemeanors on two of the minor counts of attempting to improperly influence a public official."

"What do you estimate are my chances of getting off completely if I turn them down?"

"Fifty-fifty, I would say," said Jilks.

"And if I don't get off?"

"Judge Prescott is tough. The sentence wouldn't be a day under six years."

"And if I agree to the deal and plead guilty to the two minor charges, what then?"

"A heavy fine. I would be surprised if it came to anything more than that," said Jilks.

Abel sat and considered the alternatives for a few moments.

"I'll plead guilty. Let's get the damn thing over with."

The Government lawyers informed the judge that they were dropping fifteen of the charges against Abel Rosnovski. H. Trafford Jilks rose from his place and told the court that his client wished to change his plea to guilty on the two remaining misdemeanor charges. The jury was dismissed and Judge Prescott was very hard on Abel in his summing up, reminding him that the right to do business did not include the right to suborn public officials. Bribery was a crime and a worse crime when condoned by an intelligent and competent man, who should not need to stoop to such levels. In other countries, the judge added pointedly, making Abel feel like a raw immigrant once again, bribery might be an accepted way of going about one's daily life, but such was not the case in the United States of America. Judge Prescott gave Abel a six months' suspended sentence and a $25,000 fine plus costs.

George took Abel back to the Baron and they sat in the

penthouse drinking whiskey for more than an hour before Abel spoke.

"George, I want you to contact Peter Parfitt and pay him the one million dollars he asked for his two percent of Lester's, because once I have my hands on eight percent of that bank I am going to invoke Article Seven and kill William Kane in his own boardroom."

George nodded sadly, fearing the battle wasn't over yet.

A few days later the State Department announced that Poland had been granted most favored nation status in foreign trade with the United States and that the next American Ambassador to Warsaw would be John Moors Cabot.

CHAPTER
FORTY

On a bitter February evening, William Kane sat back and reread Thaddeus Cohen's report. Henry Osborne had released all the information he had needed to finish Abel Rosnovski and had taken his $25,000 and disappeared. Very much in character, thought William as he replaced the well-worn copy of the Rosnovski file back in his safe. The original had been sent to the Justice Department in Washington, D.C., some days before by Thaddeus Cohen.

When Abel Rosnovski had returned from Turkey and was subsequently arrested, William had waited for him to retaliate, expecting him to dump all his Interstate stock on the market immediately. This time, William was prepared. He had already warned his broker that Interstate might come onto the open market in large amounts with little warning. His instructions were clear. They were to be bought immediately so that the price would not drop. Again he was prepared to put up the money from his trust as a short-term measure, to avoid any unpleasantness at the bank. William had also circulated a memo among all the stockholders of Lester's asking them not to sell any Interstate stock without consulting him.

As the weeks passed and Abel Rosnovski made no move, William began to believe that Thaddeus Cohen had been correct in assuming that nothing had been traceable back to him. Rosnovski must surely be placing the blame firmly on Henry Osborne's shoulders.

Thaddeus Cohen was certain that with Osborne's evidence, Abel Rosnovski would end up behind bars for a very long time, preventing him from ever finding it possible to invoke Article 7 and again be a threat to the bank or William Kane. William hoped that the verdict might also make Richard come to his senses and return home. Surely these latest revelations about that family could only make him embarrassed by the Rosnovski girl and realize that his father had been right all along.

William would have welcomed Richard back. There was now a gap on the board of Lester's created by the retirement of Tony Simmons and the untimely death of Ted Leach. Richard would have to return to New York before William's sixty-fifth birthday in ten years or it would be the first time in over a century that a Kane had not sat in a bank's boardroom. Cohen had reported that Richard had made a series of brilliant takeover bids for shops that Florentyna needed, but surely the opportunity to become the next chairman of Lester's would mean more to Richard than working with that Rosnovski girl.

Another factor that was bothering William was that he did not care much for the new breed of directors now working at the bank. Jake Thomas, the new vice chairman, was still the firm favorite to succeed William as chairman. He might have been educated at Princeton and graduated Phi Beta Kappa, but he was flashy—too flashy—thought William, and far too ambitious, not at all the right sort to be the next chairman of Lester's. William would have to hang on until his sixty-fifth birthday, trying in the meantime to convince Richard that he should join Lester's long before then. William was only too aware that Kate would have had Richard back on any terms, but as the years passed, he had found it harder to give way to his better judgment. Thank heaven Virginia's marriage was going well, and now she was pregnant. If Richard refused to return home and give up that

Rosnovski girl, he could still leave everything to Virginia—
if she produced a grandson.

William was at his desk in the bank when he had his first
heart attack. Not a very serious one. The doctors told him he
should rest a short time but that he would still live another
twenty years. He told his doctor, another bright young
man—how William missed Andrew MacKenzie!—that he
wanted to survive only for ten years to see out his term of office as chairman of the bank.

For the few weeks in which he convalesced at home,
William reluctantly allowed Jake Thomas the overall responsibility for the bank's decisions, but as soon as William
returned he quickly reestablished his position as chairman
for fear that Thomas might have taken on too much authority in his absence. From time to time, Kate plucked up the
courage to beg him to let her make some direct approach to
Richard, but William remained obstinate, saying, "The boy
knows he can come home whenever he wants to. All he has
to do is end his relationship with that scheming girl."

The day Henry Osborne killed himself, William had a
second heart attack but never commented on the pain. Kate
sat by his bedside all through the night, fearing he would
die, but his interest in Abel Rosnovski's forthcoming trial
kept him alive. William followed the various developments
devoutly and he knew Osborne's suicide could only put Rosnovski in a far stronger position. When Rosnovski was finally released with nothing more than a six months'
suspended sentence and a $25,000 fine, the lightness of the
penalty did not come as a surprise to William. It wasn't hard
to figure out that the Government must have agreed to a deal
with Rosnovski's brilliant lawyer.

William was, however, surprised to find himself feeling
slightly guilty and somewhat relieved that Abel Rosnovski
had not been sent to prison.

Once the trial was over, William didn't care if Rosnovski
dumped his Interstate Airways stock or not. He was still

ready for him. But nothing happened, and as the weeks passed, William began to lose interest in the Chicago Baron and think only of Richard, whom he now desperately wanted to see again. "Old age and fear of death allows for sudden changes of the heart," he had once read. One morning in September he informed Kate of his wish. She didn't ask why he had changed his mind; it was enough for her that William wanted to see his only son.

"I'll call Richard immediately and invite them both," she told him, and was pleasantly surprised that the word *both* didn't seem to faze her husband.

"That will be fine," said William quietly. "Please tell Richard that I want to see him again before I die."

"Don't be silly, darling. The doctor said that if you slow down you'll still live another twenty years."

"I only want to complete my term as chairman and see Richard take my place. That will be enough. Why don't you fly to the Coast again and tell Richard of my request, Kate?"

"What do you mean, again?" Kate asked nervously.

William smiled. "I know you've been to San Francisco several times already, my darling. Whenever I've gone away on a business trip the last few years, you've always used the excuse that you were visiting your mother. When she died last year, your excuses became increasingly improbable. We've been married for twenty-seven years and by now I think I'm aware of all your habits. You're still as lovely as the day I met you, my darling, but I do believe that at fifty-four you're unlikely to have a lover. So it wasn't all that hard for me to conclude that you had been visiting Richard."

"Yes, I have been," said Kate. "Why didn't you mention that you knew before?"

"In my heart I was glad," said William. "I hated the thought of his losing contact with us both. How is he?"

"Both of them are well and you have a granddaughter now as well as a grandson."

" 'A granddaughter as well as a grandson.' " William repeated.

"Yes, she's called Annabel," said Kate.

"And my grandson?" said William, inquiring for the first time.

When Kate told him his name, he had to smile.

It was only half a lie.

"Good," said William. "Well, you fly to San Francisco and see what can be done. Tell him I love him." He had once heard another old man say that, one who was going to lose his son.

Kate was more content that night than she had been in years. She called Richard to say she would be flying out to stay with them the following week, bringing good news with her.

When Kate returned to New York three weeks later, William was pleased to learn that Richard and Florentyna could visit them early the next year, which was the first opportunity for them to get away from San Francisco together. Kate was full of stories of how successful they both were, how William's grandson was the image of his grandfather and how Richard and Florentyna were so much looking forward to coming back to New York for a visit.

William listened intently and found he was happy, too, and at peace with himself. He liked everything he heard about Florentyna and had begun to fear that if Richard did not return home soon, he never would, and then the chairmanship of the bank would fall into Jake Thomas's lap. William did not care to think about that.

William returned to work the following Monday in high spirits after his lengthy absence, having made a good recovery from his second heart attack and now feeling he had something worth living for.

"You must pace yourself a little more carefully," the clever young doctor had told him, but William was determined to reestablish himself as chairman and president of the bank so that he could pave the way for his only son. On his arrival at the bank he was greeted by the doorman, who told him that Jake Thomas was looking for him and had tried to reach him at home earlier. William thanked the senior employee of the bank, the only person who had served Lester's more years than the Chairman himself.

"Nothing's so important that it can't wait," he said.

"No, sir."

William walked slowly to the chairman's office. When he opened his door, he found three of his directors already in conference and Jake Thomas sitting firmly in William's chair.

"Have I been away that long?" said William, laughing. "Am I no longer chairman of the board?"

"Yes, of course you are," said Jake Thomas, moving quickly out of the chairman's seat. "Welcome back, William."

William had found it impossible to get used to Jake Thomas's use of his first name. The new generation were all too familiar. They had known each other only a few years, and the man couldn't have been a day over forty.

"What's the problem?" he asked.

"Abel Rosnovski," said Jake Thomas without expression.

William felt a sick feeling in the pit of his stomach and sat down in the nearest leather seat.

"What does he want this time?" he said wearily. "Won't he let me finish my days in peace?"

Jake Thomas walked toward William.

"He intends to invoke Article Seven and hold a proxy meeting with the sole purpose of removing you from the chair."

"He can't. He doesn't have the necessary eight percent and the bank's bylaws state clearly that the chairman must be informed immediately if any outside person comes into possession of eight percent of the stock."

"He says he'll have the eight percent by tomorrow morning."

"No, no," said William. "I've kept a careful check on all the stock. No one would sell to Rosnovski. No one."

"Peter Parfitt," said Jake Thomas.

"No," said William, smiling triumphantly. "I bought his stock a year ago through a third party."

Jake Thomas looked shocked and no one spoke for several moments.

William realized for the first time just how much Thomas wanted to be the next chairman of Lester's.

"Well," said Jake Thomas, "the fact is that he claims he'll have eight percent by tomorrow, which would entitle him to elect three directors to the board and hold up any major policy decision for three months. The very provisions you put into the articles of incorporation to project your long-term position. He also intends to announce his decision in advertisements all across the country. For good measure, he's threatening to make a reverse takeover bid for Lester's using the Baron Group as the vehicle if he receives any opposition to his plans. He has made it clear that there is only one way he'll drop the whole scheme."

"What's that?" said William.

"That you submit your resignation as chairman of the bank," replied Jake Thomas.

"It's blackmail," said William, nearly shouting.

"Maybe, but if you do not resign by noon next Monday, he intends to make his announcement to all shareholders. He has already reserved space in forty newspapers and magazines."

"The man's gone mad," said William. He took his handkerchief from his breast pocket and mopped his brow.

"That's not all he said," Jake Thomas added. "He has also demanded that no Kane replace you on the board during the next ten years and that your resignation should not give ill health or, indeed, any reason for your sudden departure."

He held out a lengthy document bearing "The Baron Group" letterhead.

"Mad," repeated William, when he had skimmed the letter.

"Nevertheless, I've called a board meeting for tomorrow," said Jake Thomas. "At ten o'clock. I think we should discuss his demands in detail then, William."

The three directors left William alone in his office and no one visited him during the day. He sat at his desk trying to contact some of the other directors, but he only managed to have a word with one or two of them and couldn't feel certain of their support. He realized the meeting was going to be a close-run thing, but as long as no one else had eight percent he was safe, and he began to prepare his strategy to retain control of his own boardroom. He checked the list of stockholders: As far as he could see, not one of them intended to release his stock. He laughed to himself. Abel Rosnovski had failed with his coup. William went home early that night, and retired to his study to consider his tactics for defeating Abel Rosnovski for the last time. He didn't go to bed until 3 A.M., but he had decided what had to be done. Jake Thomas must be removed from the board so that Richard could take his place.

William arrived early for the board meeting the next morning and sat waiting in his office looking over his notes, confident of victory. He felt that his plan had taken everything into account. At five to ten his secretary buzzed. "A Mr. Rosnovski is on the phone for you," she said.

"What?" said William.

"Mr. Rosnovski."

" 'Mr. Rosnovski.' " William repeated the name in disbelief. "Put him through," he said, his voice quavering.

"Yes, sir."

"Mr. Kane?" The slight accent that William could never forget.

"Yes, what are you trying to achieve this time?" he asked wearily.

"Under the bylaws of the bank I have to inform you that I now own eight percent of Lester's shares and intend to invoke Article Seven unless my earlier demands are met by noon Monday."

"From whom did you get the final two percent?" stammered William.

The phone clicked. He quickly studied the list of share-holders, trying to work out who had betrayed him. William was still trembling when it rang again.

"The board meeting is just about to begin, sir."

As ten o'clock struck William entered the boardroom. Looking around the table, he suddenly realized how few of the younger directors he knew well. Last time he'd had a fight in this same room, he hadn't known any of the directors and he'd still won. He smiled to himself, reasonably confi-dent he could still beat Abel Rosnovski, and rose to address the board.

"Gentlemen, this meeting has been called because the bank has received a demand from Mr. Abel Rosnovski of the Baron Group, a convicted criminal who has had the effron-tery to issue a direct threat to me, namely, that he will use his eight percent holding in my bank to embarrass us and if this tactic fails he will attempt a reverse takeover bid, unless I re-sign from the presidency and chairmanship of this board without explanation. You all know that I have only nine years left to serve this bank until my retirement and, if I were to leave before then, my resignation would be totally misinterpreted in the financial world."

William looked down at his notes, deciding to lead with his ace.

"I am willing, gentlemen, to pledge my entire sharehold-ing and a further ten million dollars from my private trust to be placed at the disposal of the bank in order that you can counter any move Mr. Rosnovski makes while still insuring Lester's against any financial loss. I hope, gentlemen, in these circumstances, I can expect your full support in my battle against Abel Rosnovski. I am sure you are not men to give in to vulgar blackmail."

The room went silent. William felt certain he had won, but then Jake Thomas asked if the board might question him about his relationship with Abel Rosnovski. The request took William by surprise, but he agreed without hesitation. Jake Thomas didn't frighten him.

"This vendetta between you and Abel Rosnovski," said

Jake Thomas, "has been going on for over thirty years. Do you believe if we followed your plan that would be the end of the matter?"

"What else can the man do? What else can he do?" stuttered William, looking around the room for support.

"We can't be sure until he does it, but with an eight percent holding in the bank he has powers every bit as great as yours," said the new company Secretary—not William's choice, he talked too much. "And all we know is that neither of you seems able to give up this personal feud. Although you have offered ten million to protect our financial position, if Rosnovski were continually to hold up policy decisions, call proxy meetings, arrange takeover bids with no interest in the goodwill of the bank, it would undoubtedly cause panic. The bank and its subsidiary companies, to whom we have a duty as directors, would, at best, be highly embarrassed and, at worst, might eventually collapse."

"No, no," said William. "With my personal backing we could meet him head-on."

"The decision we have to make today," continued the company secretary, "is whether there are any circumstances in which this board wants to meet Mr. Rosnovski head-on. Perhaps we are bound to be the losers in the long run."

"Not if I cover the cost from my private trust," said William.

"That you could do," said Jake Thomas, "but it's not just money we're discussing—much bigger problems arise for the bank. Now that Rosnovski can invoke Article Seven, he can play with us as he pleases. The bank could be spending its entire time doing nothing but trying to anticipate Abel Rosnovski's every move."

Jake Thomas waited for the effect of what he had said to sink in. William remained silent. Then Thomas looked at William and continued: "Now I must ask you a very serious personal question, Mr. Chairman, which worries every one of us around this table, and I hope you'll be nothing less than frank with us when answering it, however unpleasant that may be for you."

William looked up, wondering what the question could be. What had they been discussing behind his back? Who the hell did Jake Thomas think he was? William felt he was losing the initiative.

"I will answer anything that the board requires," said William. "I have nothing and no one to fear," he said looking pointedly at Jake Thomas.

"Thank you," said Jake Thomas. "Mr. Chairman, were you in any way involved with sending a file to the Justice Department in Washington that caused Abel Rosnovski to be arrested and charged with fraud when at the same time you knew he was a major shareholder of the bank's?"

"Did he tell you that?" demanded William.

"Yes, he claims you were the sole reason for his arrest."

William stayed silent for a few moments, considering his reply, while he looked down at his notes. They didn't help. He had not thought that question would arise, but he had never lied to the board in over twenty-three years. He wouldn't start now.

"Yes, I did," he said, breaking the silence. "The information came into my hands and I considered that it was nothing less than my duty to pass it on to the Justice Department."

"How did the information come into your hands?"

William did not reply.

"I think we all know the answer to that question, Mr. Chairman," said Jake Thomas. "Moreover, you let the authorities know without briefing the board of your action and by so doing you put all of us in jeopardy. Our reputations, our careers, everything this bank stands for, over a personal vendetta."

"But Rosnovski was trying to ruin me," said William, aware he was now shouting.

"So in order to ruin him you risked the bank's stability and reputation."

"It's my bank," said William.

"It is not," said Jake Thomas. "You own eight percent of the stock, as does Mr. Rosnovski, and at the moment you are president and chairman of Lester's, but the bank is not yours to use for your own personal whim without consulting the other directors."

"Then I will have to ask the board for a vote of confidence," said William. "I'll ask you to support me against Abel Rosnovski."

"That is not what a vote of confidence would be about," said the company secretary. "The vote would be about whether you are the right man to run this bank in the present circumstances. Can't you see that, Mr. Chairman?"

"So be it," said William, turning his eyes away. "This board must decide whether it wishes to end my career in disgrace now, after nearly a quarter of a century's service, or to yield to the threats of a convicted criminal."

Jake Thomas nodded to the company secretary, and voting slips were passed around to every board member. It looked to William as if everything had been decided before the meeting. He glanced around the crowded table at the twenty-nine men. Many of them he had chosen himself. He had once heard that a small group of the younger directors openly supported the Democratic party and John Kennedy. Some of them wouldn't let Rosnovski beat him. Not now. Please let me finish my term as chairman, he said to himself. Then I'll go quietly and without any fuss—but not this way.

He watched the members of the board as they passed their voting slips back to the secretary. He was opening them slowly. The room was silent and all eyes were turned toward the secretary as he began opening the last few slips, noting down each aye and nay meticulously on a piece of paper placed in front of him that revealed two columns. William could see that one list of names was considerably longer than the other, but his eyesight did not permit him to decipher which was which. He could not accept that the day could have come when there would be a vote in his own boardroom between himself and Abel Rosnovski.

The secretary was saying something. William couldn't believe what he heard. By seventeen votes to twelve he had lost the confidence of the board. He managed to stand up. Abel Rosnovski had beaten him in the final battle. No one spoke as

William left the boardroom. He returned to the chairman's office and picked up his coat, stopping only to look at the portrait of Charles Lester for the last time, and then walked slowly down the long corridor and out the front entrance.

The doorman said, "Nice to have you back again, Mr. Chairman. See you tomorrow, sir."

William realized he would never see him again. He turned around and shook hands with the man who had directed him to the boardroom twenty-three years before.

The rather surprised doorman said, "Good night, sir," as he watched William climb into the back of his car for the last time.

His chauffeur took him home and when he reached East Sixty-eighth Street, William collapsed on his front door step. The chauffeur and Kate helped him into the house. Kate could see he was crying and she put her arms around him.

"What is it, William? What's happened?"

"I've been thrown out of my own bank," he wept. "My own board no longer have confidence in me. When it mattered, they supported Abel Rosnovski."

Kate managed to get him up to bed and sat with him through the night. He never spoke. Nor did he sleep.

The announcement in *The Wall Street Journal* the following Monday morning said simply: "William Lowell Kane, the President and Chairman of Lester's Bank, resigned after yesterday's board meeting."

No mention of illness or any explanation was given for his sudden departure, and there was no suggestion that his son would take his place on the board. William knew that rumors would sweep through Wall Street and that the worst would be assumed. He sat in bed alone, caring no longer for this world.

Abel read the announcement of William Kane's resignation in *The Wall Street Journal* the same day. He picked up the phone, dialed Lester's bank and asked to speak to the new chairman. A few seconds later Jake Thomas came on the line. "Good morning, Mr. Rosnovski."

"Good morning, Mr. Thomas. I'm just phoning to confirm that I shall release all my Interstate Airways shares to the bank at the market price this morning and my eight percent holding in Lester's to you personally for two million dollars."

"Thank you, Mr. Rosnovski, that's most generous of you."

"No need to thank me, Mr. Chairman, it's no more than we agreed on when you sold me your two percent of Lester's," said Abel Rosnovski.

PART SEVEN
1963–1967

CHAPTER
FORTY-ONE

Abel was surprised to find how little satisfaction his final triumph had given him.

George tried to persuade him to go to Warsaw to look over sites for the new Baron, but Abel didn't want to. As he grew older, he became fearful of dying abroad and never seeing Florentyna again, and for months Abel showed no interest in the group's activities. When John F. Kennedy was assassinated on November 22, 1963, Abel became even more depressed and feared for America. Eventually George did convince him that a trip abroad could do no harm, and that things would perhaps seem a little easier for him when he returned.

Abel traveled to Warsaw, where he obtained a highly confidential agreement to build the first Baron in the Communist world. His command of the language impressed the Warszawians and he was pleased to beat Holiday Inn and Intercontinental behind the Iron Curtain. He couldn't help thinking . . . and it didn't help when Lyndon Johnson appointed John Gronowski to be the first Polish-American ambassador to Warsaw. But now nothing seemed to give him any satisfaction. He had defeated Kane and lost his own daughter and he wondered if the man felt the same way about his son. After Warsaw, he roamed the world, staying in his old hotels, watching the construction of new ones. He opened the first Baron in Cape Town, South Africa, and flew back to Germany to open one in Düsseldorf.

Abel then spent six months in his favorite Baron, in Paris, roaming the streets by day, and attending the opera and the theater at night, hoping to revive happy memories of Florentyna.

He eventually left Paris and returned to America, after his long exile. As he descended the metal steps of an Air France 707 at Kennedy International Airport, his back hunched and his bald head covered with a black hat, nobody recognized him. George was there to greet him, loyal, honest George, looking quite a bit older. On the ride to the New York Baron, George, as always, brought him up to date on group news. The profits, it seemed, were even higher as his keen young executives thrust forward in every major country in the world. Seventy-two hotels run by a staff of 22,000. Abel didn't seem to be listening. He only wanted news of Florentyna.

"She's well," said George, "and coming to New York early next year."

"Why?" said Abel, suddenly excited.

"She's opening one of her shops on Fifth Avenue."

"Fifth Avenue?"

"The eleventh Florentyna," said George.

"Have you seen her, George?"

"Yes," he admitted.

"Is she well, is she happy?"

"Both of them are very well and happy, and so successful. Abel, you should be very proud of them. Your grandson is quite a boy, and your granddaughter's beautiful. The image of Florentyna when she was that age."

"Will she see me?"

"Will you see her husband?"

"No, George. I can never meet that boy, not while his father is still alive."

"What if you die first?"

"You mustn't believe everything you read in the Bible."

Abel and George drove in silence back to the hotel and Abel dined alone in his suite that night.

For the next six months, he never left the penthouse.

CHAPTER
FORTY-TWO

When Florentyna Kane opened her new boutique on Fifth Avenue in March 1967, everyone in New York seemed to be there, except William Kane and Abel Rosnovski.

Kate and Lucy had left William in bed muttering to himself while they went off to the opening of Florentyna's.

George left Abel in his suite so that he could attend the celebrations. He had tried to talk Abel into going along with him. Abel grunted that his daughter had opened ten shops without him and one more wouldn't make any difference. George told him he was a stubborn old fool and left for Fifth Avenue on his own. When he arrived at the shop, a magnificent modern boutique with thick carpets and the latest Swedish furniture— he was reminded of the way Abel used to do things. He found Florentyna wearing a long blue gown with the now famous F on the high collar. She gave George a glass of champagne and introduced him to Kate and Lucy Kane, who were chatting with Zaphia. Kate and Lucy were clearly happy and they surprised George by inquiring after Abel Rosnovski.

"I told him he was a stubborn old fool to miss such a good party. Is Mr. Kane here?" he asked.

George was surprised by Kate Kane's reply.

William was still muttering angrily at *The New York Times*, something about Johnson's pulling his punches in Vietnam, when he folded the newspaper and got himself out of bed. He started to dress slowly, staring at himself in the mirror when he had finished. He looked like a banker. He scowled. How else should he look? He put on a heavy black overcoat and his old Homburg hat, picked up his black walking stick with the silver handle, the one Rupert Cork-Smith had left him, and somehow got himself out onto the street. The first time he had been out on his own, he thought, for the best part of three years, since that last serious heart attack. The maid was surprised to see him leaving the house unaccompanied.

It was an unusually warm spring evening, but William felt the cold after being in the house so long. It took him a considerable time to reach Fifth Avenue and Fifty-sixth Street, and when he eventually did arrive, the crowd was so large outside Florentyna's that he felt he didn't have the strength to fight his way through it. He stood at the curb, watching the people enjoying themselves. Young people, happy and excited, thrusting their way into Florentyna's beautiful shop. Some of the girls were wearing the new mini skirts from London. What next, thought William, and then he saw his son talking to Kate. He had grown into such a fine-looking man—tall, confident and relaxed; he had an air of authority about him that reminded William of his own father. But in the bustle and continual movement, he couldn't quite work out which one was Florentyna. He stood there for nearly an hour enjoying the comings and goings, regretting the stubborn years he had thrown away.

The wind was beginning to race down Fifth Avenue. He'd forgotten how cold that March wind could be. He turned his collar up. He must get home, because they were all coming to dinner that night, and he was going to meet Florentyna and the grandchildren for the first time. His grandson and little Annabel and their father, his beloved son. He had told Kate what a fool he'd been and begged her forgiveness. All he remembered her saying was "I'll always love you." Florentyna had written to him. Such a generous letter. She had been so understanding and kind about the past. She had ended with "I can't wait to meet you."

He must get home. Kate would be cross with him if she ever discovered he'd been out on his own in that cold wind. But he had to see the opening of the shop and in any case tonight he would be with them all. He must leave now and let them enjoy their celebrations. They could tell him all about the opening tonight. He wouldn't tell them he'd been there—that would always be his secret.

He turned to go home and saw an old man standing a few yards away in a black coat, with a hat pulled way down on his head, and a scarf around his neck. He, too, was cold. Not a night for old men, thought William, as he walked toward him. And then he saw the silver band on his wrist, just below his sleeve. In a flash it all came back to him, fitting into place for the first time. First the Plaza, then Boston, then Germany, and now Fifth Avenue. The man turned and started to walk toward him. He must have been standing there for a long time because his face was red from the wind. He stared at William out of those unmistakable blue eyes. They were now only a few yards apart. As they passed, William raised his hat to the old man. He returned the compliment, and they continued on their separate ways without a word.

I must get home, thought William, before they do. The joy of seeing Richard and his two grandchildren would make everything worthwhile again. He must come to know Florentyna, ask for her forgiveness, and trust that she would understand what he could scarcely understand himself now. Such a fine girl, they all told him.

When he reached East Sixty-eighth Street, he fumbled for his key and opened the front door. Must turn on all lights, he told the maid, and build the fire up to make them feel welcome. He was very contented and very, very tired.

"Draw the curtains," he said, "and light the candles on the dining room table. There's so much to celebrate."

William couldn't wait for them all to return. He sat in the old crimson leather chair by a blazing fire and thought happily of the evening that lay ahead of him. Grandchildren around him, the years he had missed. When had his little grandson first said "three"? A chance to bury the past and earn forgiveness in the future. The room was so nice and warm after that cold wind, but the journey had been well worthwhile.

A few minutes later there was an excited bustle downstairs and the maid came in to tell William that his son had arrived. He was in the hall with his mother and his wife and two of the loveliest children the maid had ever seen. And then she ran off to be sure that dinner would be ready on time. He would want everything to be perfect for them that night.

When Richard came into the room, Florentyna was by his side. She looked quite radiant.

"Father," he said. "I would like you to meet my wife."

William Lowell Kane would have turned to greet them, but he could not. He was dead.

CHAPTER
FORTY-THREE

Abel placed the envelope on the table by the side of his bed. He hadn't dressed yet. Nowadays he rarely rose before noon. He tried to remove his breakfast tray from his knees onto the floor—a bending movement that demanded too much dexterity for his stiff body to accomplish. He inevitably ended by dropping the tray with a bang. It was no different today. He no longer cared. He picked up the envelope once more and read the covering note for a second time.

"We were instructed by the late Mr. Curtis Fenton, sometime manager of the Continental Trust Bank, LaSalle Street, Chicago, to send you the enclosed letter when certain circumstances had come about. Please acknowledge receipt of this letter by signing the enclosed copy, returning it to us in the stamped addressed envelope supplied herewith."

"Goddamn lawyers," said Abel, and tore open the letter.

Dear Mr. Rosnovski:

This letter has been in the keeping of my lawyers until today for reasons that will become more apparent to you as you read on.

When in 1951 you closed your accounts at the Continental Trust after a period of over twenty years with the bank, I was naturally very unhappy and very concerned. My concern was engendered not by losing one of the bank's most valued customers, sad though that was, but because I know you felt that I had acted in a dishonorable fashion. What you were not aware of at the time was that I had specific instructions from your backer not to reveal certain facts to you.

When you first visited me at the bank in 1929, you requested financial help to clear the debt incurred by Mr. Davis Leroy, in order that you might take posses- sion of the hotels which then formed the Richmond Group. I was unable to find a backer, despite ap- proaching several leading financiers myself. I took a personal interest, as I believed that you had an excep- tional flair for your chosen career. It has given me a great deal of satisfaction to observe in old age that my confidence was not misplaced. I might add at this point that I also felt some responsibility, having ad- vised you to buy twenty-five percent of the Richmond Group from my client, Miss Amy Leroy, when I did not know the financial predicament that was facing Mr. Leroy at that time. I digress.

I did not succeed in finding a backer for you and had given up all hope when you came to visit me on that Monday morning. I wonder if you remember that day. Only thirty minutes before your appointment I had a call from a financier who was willing to put up the necessary money, who, like me, had great confi- dence in you personally. His only stipulation was, as I advised you at the time, that he insisted on remaining anonymous because of a potential conflict between his professional and private interests. The terms he of- fered, allowing you to gain eventual control of the Richmond Group, I considered at the time to be ex- tremely generous, and you rightly took full advantage of them. Indeed, your backer was delighted when you found it possible, through your own diligence, to repay his original investment.

I lost contact with you both after 1951, but soon af- ter I retired from the bank, I read a distressing story in the newspapers concerning your backer, which prompted me to write this letter, in case I died before either of you.

I write not to prove my good intentions in this whole affair, but so that you should not continue to live under the illusion that your backer and benefactor was Mr. David Maxton of the Stevens Hotel. Mr. Maxton was a great admirer of yours, but he never approached the bank in that capacity. The gentleman who made the Baron Group possible, by his foresight and personal generosity, was William Lowell Kane, the Chairman of Lester's Bank, New York.

I begged Mr. Kane to inform you of his personal involvement, but he refused to break the clause in his trust deed that stipulated that no benefactor should be privy to the investments of the family trust. After you had paid off the loan and he later learned of Henry Osborne's personal involvement with the Baron Group he became even more adamant that you should never be informed.

I had left instructions that this letter is to be destroyed if you die before Mr. Kane. In those circumstances, he will receive a letter, explaining your total lack of knowledge of his personal generosity.

Whichever one of you receives a letter from me, it was a privilege to have served you both.

As ever,
Your faithful servant,
Curtis Fenton

Abel picked up the phone by the side of his bed. "Find George for me," he said. "I need to get dressed."

CHAPTER
FORTY-FOUR

William Lowell Kane's funeral was well attended. Richard and Florentyna stood on one side of Kate; Virginia and Lucy were on the other. Grandmother Kane would have approved of the turnout. Three senators, five congressmen, two bishops, most of the leading banks' chairmen, and the publisher of *The Wall Street Journal* were all there. Jake Thomas and every director of the Lester board was also present, their heads bowed in prayer to the God whom William had never really needed.

No one noticed two old men, standing at the back of the gathering, their heads also bowed, looking as if they were not attached to the main party. They had arrived a few minutes late and left quickly at the end of the service. Florentyna recognized the limp as the shorter old man hurried away. She told Richard. They didn't mention the respectful mourner to Kate Kane.

A few days later, the taller of the two old men went to see Florentyna in her shop on Fifth Avenue. He had heard she was returning to San Francisco and needed to seek her help before she left. She listened carefully to what he had to say and agreed to his request with joy.

Richard and Florentyna Kane arrived at the Baron Hotel the next afternoon. George Novak was there to meet and escort them to the forty-second floor. After ten years, Florentyna hardly recognized her father, now propped up in bed, half-moon glasses on the end of his nose, still no pillows, but smiling defiantly. They talked of happier days and both laughed a little and cried a lot.

"You must forgive us, Richard," said Abel, "the Polish are a sentimental race."

"I know. My children are half Polish," said Richard.

Later that evening they dined together—magnificent roast veal, appropriate for the return of the prodigal daughter, said Abel.

He talked of the future and how he saw the progress of his group.

"We ought to have a Florentyna's in every hotel," he said. She laughed and agreed.

He told Richard of his sadness concerning his father, revealing in detail the mistakes he had made for so many years and how it had never crossed his mind even for a moment that William Kane could have been his benefactor, and how he would have liked one chance to thank him personally.

"He would have understood," said Richard.

"We met, you know, the day he died," said Abel.

Florentyna and Richard stared at him in surprise.

"Oh yes," said Abel. "We passed each other on Fifth Avenue—he had come to watch the opening of your shop. He raised his hat to me. It was enough, quite enough."

Abel had only one request of Florentyna. That she and Richard would accompany him on his journey to Warsaw in nine months' time for the opening of the latest Baron.

"Can you imagine," he said, again excited, his fingers tapping the side table. "The Warsaw Baron. Now there is a hotel that could only be opened by the president of the Baron Group."

During the following months the Kanes visited Abel regularly and Florentyna grew very close to her father again. Abel came to admire Richard and the common sense that tempered all his daughter's ambitions. He adored his grandson. And little Annabel was—what was that awful modern expression?—she was something else. Abel had rarely been happier in his life and began elaborate plans for his triumphant return to Poland to open the Warsaw Baron.

The president of the Baron Group opened the Warsaw Baron six months later than had been originally scheduled. Building contracts run late in Warsaw just as they do in every other part of the world.

In her first speech, as president of the Group, she told her guests that her pride in the magnificent hotel was mingled with a feeling of sadness that her late father could not have been present to open the Warsaw Baron himself.

In his will, Abel had left everything to Florentyna, with the single exception of a small bequest. The inventory described the gift as a heavy engraved silver bracelet, rare, but of unknown value, bearing the legend "Baron Abel Rosnovski."

The beneficiary was his grandson, William Abel Kane.

SONS OF FORTUNE

To Ed and Priscilla

CONTENTS

BOOK ONE

GENESIS

1

SUSAN PLONKED THE ice cream firmly on Michael Cartwright's head. It was the first occasion the two of them had met, or that was what Michael's best man claimed when Susan and Michael were married twenty-one years later.

Both of them were three years old at the time, and when Michael burst into tears, Susan's mother rushed over to find out what the problem was. All Susan was willing to say on the subject, and she repeated it several times, was, "Well, he asked for it, didn't he?" Susan ended up with a spanking. Not the ideal start for any romance.

The next recorded meeting, according to the best man, was when they both arrived at their elementary school. Susan declared with a knowing air that Michael was a cry-baby, and what's more, a sneak. Michael told the other boys that he would share his graham crackers with anyone who was willing to pull Susan Illingworth's pigtails. Few boys tried a second time.

At the end of their first year, Susan and Michael were jointly awarded the class prize. Their teacher considered it the best course of action if she hoped to prevent another ice-cream incident. Susan told her friends that Michael's mother did his homework for him, to which Michael responded that at least it was in his own handwriting.

The rivalry continued unabated through junior and senior high until they departed for different universities, Michael to Connecticut State and Susan to Georgetown. For the next four years, they both worked hard at avoiding each other. In fact the next occasion their paths crossed was, ironically, at Susan's home, when her parents threw a surprise graduation party for their daughter. The biggest surprise was not that Michael accepted the invitation, but that he turned up.

Susan didn't recognize her old rival immediately, partly because he had grown four inches and was, for the first time, taller than her. It wasn't until she offered him a glass of wine and Michael remarked, "At least this time you didn't pour it all over me," that she realized who the tall handsome man was.

"God, I behaved dreadfully, didn't I," said Susan, wanting him to deny it.

"Yes, you did," he said, "but then I expect I deserved it."

"You did," she said, biting her tongue.

They chatted like old friends, and Susan was surprised at how disappointed she felt when a classmate from Georgetown joined them and started flirting with Michael. They didn't speak to each other again that evening.

Michael phoned the following day and invited her to see Spencer Tracy and Katharine Hepburn in *Adam's Rib*. Susan had already seen the movie, but still heard herself accepting, and couldn't believe how long she spent trying on different dresses before he arrived for that first date.

Susan enjoyed the film, even though it was her second time, and wondered if Michael would put an arm around her shoulder when Spencer Tracey kissed Katharine Hepburn. He didn't. But when they left the movie house, he took her hand as they crossed the road, and didn't let it go until they reached the coffee shop. That was when they had their first row, well, disagreement. Michael admitted that he was going to vote for Thomas Dewey in November, while Susan made it clear that she wanted the incumbent Democrat, Harry Truman, to remain in the White House. The waiter placed the ice cream in front of Susan. She stared down at it.

"Don't even think about it," Michael said.

Susan wasn't surprised when he called the following day, although she had been sitting by the phone for over an hour pretending to be reading.

Michael admitted to his mother over breakfast that morning it had been love at first sight.

"But you've known Susan for years," remarked his mother.

"No, I haven't, Mom," he replied, "I met her for the first time yesterday."

Both sets of parents were delighted, but not surprised, when they became engaged a year later, after all, they'd hardly spent a day apart since Susan's graduation party. Both had landed jobs within days of leaving college, Michael as a trainee with the Hartford Life Insurance Co. and Susan as a history teacher at Jefferson High, so they decided to get married during the summer vacation.

What they hadn't planned was that Susan would become pregnant while they were on their honeymoon. Michael couldn't hide his delight at the thought of being a father, and when Dr. Greenwood told them in the sixth month that it was going to be twins he was doubly delighted.

"Well, at least that will solve one problem," was his first reaction.

"Namely?" asked Susan.

"One can be a Republican, and the other a Democrat."

"Not if I have anything to do with it," said Susan, rubbing her stomach.

Susan continued teaching until her eighth month, which happily coincided with the Easter vacation. She arrived at the hospital on the twenty-eighth day of the ninth month carrying a small suitcase. Michael left work early and joined her a few minutes later, with the news that he had been promoted to account executive.

"What does that mean?" asked Susan.

"It's a fancy title for an insurance salesman," Michael told her. "But it does include a small pay raise, which can only help now we're going to have two more mouths to feed."

Once Susan was settled in her room, Dr. Greenwood suggested to Michael that he wait outside during the delivery, as with twins there just might be complications.

Michael paced up and down the long corridor. Whenever he reached the portrait of Josiah Preston hanging on the far wall, he turned and retraced his steps. On the first few of these route marches, Michael didn't stop to read the long biography printed below the portrait of the hospital's founder. By the time the doctor emerged through the double doors, Michael knew the man's entire life history by heart.

The green-clad figure walked slowly toward him before removing his mask. Michael tried to fathom the expression on his face. In his profession it was an advantage to be able to decipher expressions and second-guess thoughts, because when it came to selling life insurance you needed to anticipate any anxieties a potential client might have. However, when it came to this life insurance policy, the doctor gave nothing away. When they came face-to-face, he smiled and said, "Congratulations, Mr. Cartwright, you have two healthy sons."

Susan had delivered two boys, Nat at 4:37 and Peter at 4:43 that afternoon. For the next hour, the parents took turns cuddling them, until Dr. Greenwood suggested that perhaps mother and babies should be allowed to rest. "Having to feed two children will prove exhausting enough. I shall put them both in the special care nursery overnight," he added. "Nothing to worry about, because it's something we always do with twins."

Michael accompanied his two sons to the nursery, where once again he was asked to wait in the corridor. The proud father pressed his nose up against the pane of glass that divided the corridor from the row of cribs, gazing at the boys as they lay sleeping, wanting to tell everyone who passed, "they're both mine." He smiled at the nurse who was standing by their side keeping a watchful eye over the latest arrivals. She was placing name tags around their tiny wrists.

Michael couldn't remember how long he remained there before eventually returning to his wife's bedside. When he opened the door, he was pleased to find that Susan was fast asleep. He kissed her gently on the forehead. "I'll see you in the morning, honey, just before I go to work," ignoring the fact that she couldn't hear a word. Michael left her, walked down the corridor and stepped into the elevator to find Dr. Greenwood had exchanged his green scrubs for a sports jacket and gray flannels.

"I wish they were all that easy," he told the proud father as the elevator stopped on the ground floor. "Still, I'll drop by this evening, Mr. Cartwright, to check on your wife and see how the twins are doing. Not that I anticipate any problems."

"Thank you, doctor," said Michael. "Thank you."

Dr. Greenwood smiled, and would have left the hospital and driven home had he not spotted an elegant lady coming through the swing doors. He walked quickly across to join Ruth Davenport.

Michael Cartwright glanced back to see the doctor holding open the elevator doors for two women, one heavily pregnant. An anxious look had replaced Dr. Greenwood's warm smile. Michael only hoped that the doctor's latest charge would have as uncomplicated a birth as Susan had managed. He strolled across to his car, trying to think about what needed to be done next, still unable to remove the broad grin from his face.

The first thing he must do was phone his parents . . . grandparents.

2

RUTH DAVENPORT HAD already accepted that this would be her last chance. Dr. Greenwood, for professional reasons, would not have put it quite so bluntly, although after two miscarriages in as many years, he could not advise his patient to risk becoming pregnant again.

Robert Davenport, on the other hand, was not bound by the same professional etiquette and when he learned that his wife was expecting for a third time, he had been characteristically blunt. He simply issued an ultimatum: "this time you will take it easy," a euphemism for don't do anything that might harm the birth of our son. Robert Davenport assumed his firstborn would be a boy. He also knew that it would be difficult, if not impossible, for his wife to "take it easy." She was, after all, the daughter of Josiah Preston, and it was often said that if Ruth had been a boy, she, and not her husband, would have ended up as president of Preston Pharmaceuticals. But Ruth had to settle for the consolation prize when she succeeded her father as chairman of St. Patrick's Hospital Trust, a cause with which the Preston family had been associated for four generations.

Although some of the older fraternity at St. Patrick's needed to be convinced that Ruth Davenport was of the same mettle as her father, it was only weeks before they acknowledged that not only had she inherited the old man's energy and drive, but he had also passed on to her his considerable knowledge and wisdom, so often lavished on an only child.

Ruth hadn't married until the age of thirty-three. It certainly wasn't for lack of suitors, many of whom went out of their way to claim undying devotion to the heir of the Preston millions. Josiah Preston hadn't needed to explain the meaning of fortune hunters to his daughter, because the truth was that she simply hadn't fallen in love with any of them. In fact, Ruth was beginning to doubt if she would ever fall in love. Until she met Robert.

Robert Davenport had joined Preston Pharmaceuticals from Roche via Johns Hopkins and Harvard Business School, on what Ruth's father described as the "fast track." In Ruth's recollection, it was the nearest the old man had come to using a modern expression. Robert had been made a vice-president by the age of twenty-seven, and at thirty-three was appointed the youngest deputy chairman in the company's history, breaking a record that had been set by Josiah himself. This time Ruth did fall in love, with a man who was neither overwhelmed nor overawed by the Preston name or the Preston millions. In fact when Ruth suggested that perhaps she should become Mrs. Preston-Davenport, Robert had simply inquired, "When do I get to meet this Preston-Davenport fellow who hopes to prevent me from becoming your husband?"

Ruth announced she was pregnant only weeks after their wedding, and the miscarriage was almost the only blemish in an otherwise charmed existence. However, even this quickly began to look like a passing cloud in an otherwise clear blue sky, when she became pregnant again eleven months later.

Ruth had been chairing a board meeting of the Hospital Trust when the contractions began, so she only needed to take the elevator up two floors to allow Dr. Greenwood to carry out the necessary check-up. However, not even his expertise, his staff's dedication or the latest medical equipment could save the premature child. Kenneth Greenwood couldn't help recalling how, as a young doctor, he had faced a similar problem when he had delivered Ruth, and for a week the hospital staff didn't believe the baby girl would survive. And now the family was going through the same trauma thirty-five years later.

Dr. Greenwood decided to have a private word with Mr. Davenport, suggesting that perhaps the time had come for them to consider adoption. Robert reluctantly agreed, and said he would raise the subject with his wife just as soon as he felt she was strong enough.

Another year passed before Ruth agreed to visit an adoption society and with one of those coincidences that fate decides, and novelists are not allowed to consider, she became pregnant on the day she was due to visit a local children's home. This time Robert was determined to ensure that human error would not be the reason for their child failing to enter this world.

Ruth took her husband's advice, and resigned as chairman of the Hospital Trust. She even agreed that a full-time nurse should be employed—in Robert's words—to keep a watchful eye on her. Mr. Davenport interviewed several applicants for the post and short-listed those whom he considered held the necessary qualifications. But his final choice would be based solely on whether he was convinced the applicant was strong-willed enough to make sure that Ruth kept to her agreement to "take it easy," and to insist she didn't lapse into any old habits of wanting to organize everything she came across.

After a third round of interviews, Robert settled on a Miss Heather Nichol, who was a senior nurse on the maternity wing of St. Patrick's. He liked her no-nonsense approach and the fact that she was neither married nor graced with the kind of looks that would ensure that situation was likely to change in the foreseeable future. However, what finally tipped the balance was that Miss Nichol had already delivered over a thousand children into the world.

Robert was delighted by how quickly Miss Nichol settled into the household, and as each month slipped by, even he started to feel confident that they wouldn't be facing the same problem a third time. When Ruth passed first five, six, and then seven months without incident, Robert even raised the subject of possible Christian names: Fletcher Andrew if it was a boy, Victoria Grace if it was a girl. Ruth expressed only one preference; that were it a boy he should be known as Andrew, but all she hoped for was to be delivered of a healthy child.

Robert was in New York attending a medical conference, when Miss Nichol called him out of a seminar to report that his wife's contractions had begun. He assured her he would return by train immediately and then take a cab straight to St. Patrick's.

Dr. Greenwood was leaving the building, having successfully delivered the Cartwright twins, when he spotted Ruth Davenport coming through the swing doors accompanied by Miss Nichol. He turned around and caught up with the two ladies before the elevator doors closed.

Once he had settled his patient into a private room, Dr. Greenwood quickly assembled the finest obstetrics team the hospital could muster. Had Mrs. Davenport been a normal patient, he and Miss Nichol could have delivered the child without having to call on any extra assistance. However, following an examination, he realized that Ruth would require a Caesarean section if the child was to be delivered safely. He looked toward the ceiling and sent up a silent prayer, acutely aware that this was going to be her last chance.

The delivery took just over forty minutes. At the first glimpse of the baby's head, Miss Nichol let out a sigh of relief, but it wasn't until the doctor cut the umbilical cord that she added "Alleluia." Ruth, who was still under a general anesthetic, was unable to see the relieved smile on Dr. Greenwood's face. He quickly left the theater to tell the expectant father, "It's a boy."

While Ruth slept peacefully it was left to Miss Nichol to take Fletcher Andrew off to the special care unit where he would share his first few hours with several other progeny. Once she had tucked up the child in his little crib, she left the nurse to watch over him before returning to Ruth's room. Miss Nichol settled herself into a comfortable chair in the corner and tried to stay awake.

Just as night was contemplating day, Miss Nichol woke with a start. She heard the words, "Can I see my son?"

"Of course you can, Mrs. Davenport," replied Miss Nichol, rising quickly from her chair. "I'll just go and fetch little Andrew." As she closed the door behind her, she added, "I'll be back in a few moments."

Ruth pulled herself up, plumped up her pillow, switched on the bedside lamp and waited in eager anticipation.

As Miss Nichol walked along the corridor, she checked her watch. It was 4:31 A.M. She took the stairs down to the fifth floor and made her way to the nursery. Miss Nichol opened the door quietly so as not to wake any of the sleeping offspring, As she entered the room, illuminated by a small fluorescent light glowing overhead, her eyes settled on the night nurse dozing in the corner. She didn't disturb the young woman as it was probably the only few moments of slumber that she would manage during her eight-hour shift.

Miss Nichol tiptoed between the two rows of cots, stopping only for a moment to glance at the twins in the double crib that had been placed next to Fletcher Andrew Davenport.

She stared down at a child who would want for nothing for the rest of his life. As she bent over to lift the little boy from his crib, she froze. After a thousand births, you are well qualified to recognize death. The pallor of the skin and the stillness of the eyes made it unnecessary for her to check the pulse.

It is often spur-of-the-moment decisions, sometimes made by others, that can change our whole lives.

3

WHEN DR. GREENWOOD was woken in the middle of the night to be told that one of his new charges had died, he knew exactly which child it was. He also realized that he would have to return to the hospital immediately.

Kenneth Greenwood had always wanted to be a doctor. After only a few weeks at medical school, he had known in which field he would specialize. He thanked God every day for allowing him to carry out his vocation. But then from time to time, as if somehow the Almighty felt it was necessary to balance the scales, he had to tell a mother that she had lost her child. It was never easy, but having to tell Ruth Davenport for a third time . . .

There were so few cars on the road at five o'clock in the morning that Dr. Greenwood was parked in his reserved spot at the hospital twenty minutes later. He pushed through the swing doors, strode past the reception desk and had stepped into the elevator before any of the staff had the chance to say good morning.

"Who's going to tell her?" asked the nurse who was waiting for him as the elevator doors opened on the fifth floor.

"I will," said Dr. Greenwood. "I've been a friend of the family for years," he added.

The nurse looked surprised. "I suppose we must be thankful that the other baby survived," she said, interrupting his thoughts.

Dr. Greenwood stopped in his tracks. "The other baby?" he repeated.

"Yes, Nathaniel's just fine, it was Peter who died."

Dr. Greenwood remained silent for a moment as he tried to take in this piece of information. "And the Davenport boy?" he ventured.

"Doing well, as far as I know," replied the nurse. "Why do you ask?"

"I delivered him just before I went home," he said, hoping the nurse hadn't spotted the hesitation in his voice.

Dr. Greenwood walked slowly between the rows of cribs, passing offspring who were sleeping soundly and others who were yelling, as if to prove they had lungs. He stopped when he came to the double crib where he had left the twins only a few hours before. Nathaniel lay peacefully asleep while his brother was motionless. He glanced across to check the name on the headboard of the next crib, Davenport, Fletcher Andrew. That little boy was also sleeping soundly, his breathing quite regular.

"Of course I couldn't move the child until the doctor who had delivered . . ."

"You don't have to remind me of hospital procedure," snapped Dr. Greenwood uncharacteristically. "What time did you come on duty?" he asked.

"Just after midnight," she replied.

"And have you been in attendance since then?"

"Yes, sir."

"Did anyone else enter the nursery during that time?"

"No, doctor," the nurse replied. She decided not to mention that about an hour ago she thought she'd heard a door close, or at least not while he was in such a foul mood. Dr. Greenwood stared down at the two cribs marked Cartwright, Nathaniel and Peter. He knew exactly where his duty lay.

"Take the child to the morgue," he said quietly. "I'll write up a report immediately, but I won't inform the mother until the morning. No purpose will be served waking her at this hour."

"Yes, sir," said the nurse meekly.

Dr. Greenwood left the nursery, walked slowly down the corridor and stopped outside Mrs. Cartwright's door. He opened it noiselessly, relieved to discover that his patient was fast asleep. After climbing the staircase up to the sixth floor, he carried out the same exercise when he reached Mrs. Davenport's private room. Ruth was also sleeping. He glanced across the room to see Miss Nichol seated awkwardly in her chair. He could have sworn that she opened her eyes, but he decided not to disturb her. He pulled the door closed, walked to the far end of the corridor and slipped out onto the fire escape stairs that led to the parking lot. He didn't want to be seen leaving by those on duty at the front desk. He needed some time to think.

Dr. Greenwood was back in his bed twenty minutes later, but he didn't sleep.

When his alarm went off at seven he was still awake. He knew exactly what his first course of action must be, although he feared the repercussions could reverberate for many years.

Dr. Greenwood took considerably longer to drive back to St. Patrick's for a second time that morning, and it wasn't just because of the increased traffic. He dreaded having to tell Ruth Davenport that her child had died during the night, and only hoped it could be done without any accompanying scandal. He knew he would have to go straight to Ruth's room and explain what had happened, otherwise he would never be able to go through with it.

"Good morning, Dr. Greenwood," said the nurse on reception, but he didn't respond.

When he stepped out on the sixth floor and began walking toward Mrs. Davenport's room, he found his pace became slower and slower. He came to a halt in front of her door, hoping she would still be asleep. He eased it open, to be greeted with the sight of Robert Davenport sitting beside his wife. Ruth was holding a baby in her arms. Miss Nichol was nowhere to be seen.

Robert jumped up from his side of the bed.

"Kenneth," he said shaking him by the hand, "we will be eternally in your debt."

"You owe me nothing," the doctor replied quietly.

"Of course we do," said Robert, turning back to face his wife. "Shall we let him know what we've decided, Ruth?"

"Why not, then we'll both have something to celebrate," she said, kissing the boy's forehead.

"But first I have to tell you . . ." began the doctor.

"No buts," said Robert, "because I want you to be the first to know that I've decided to ask the board of Preston's to finance the new maternity wing that you have always hoped would be completed before you retire."

"But . . ." repeated Dr. Greenwood.

"I thought we agreed on no buts. After on, the plans have been drawn up for years," he said, looking down at his son, "so I can't think of any reason why we shouldn't start on the building program right away." He turned to face the hospital's senior obstetrician. "Unless of course you . . . ?"

Dr. Greenwood remained silent.

When Miss Nichol saw Dr. Greenwood coming out of Mrs. Davenport's private room, her heart sank. He was carrying the little boy in his arms and walking back toward the elevator that would take him to the special care nursery. As they passed each other in the corridor their eyes met, and although he didn't speak, she was in no doubt that he was aware of what she must have done.

Miss Nichol accepted that if she was going to make a run for it, it had to be now. Once she had taken the child back to the nursery, she'd lain awake in the corner of Mrs. Davenport's room for the rest of the night, wondering if she would be found out. She had tried not to stir when Dr. Greenwood had looked in. She had no idea what time it was because she didn't dare glance down at her watch. She had quite expected him to call her out of the room and tell her he knew the truth, but he had left just as silently as he had come, so she was none the wiser.

Heather Nichol went on walking toward the private room, while her eyes remained firmly fixed on the fire escape exit at the far end of the corridor. Once she had passed Mrs. Davenport's door she tried not to quicken her pace. She had only a couple of paces to go when she heard a voice she immediately recognized say, "Miss Nichol?" She froze on the spot, still staring toward the fire escape, as she considered her options. She swung around to face Mr. Davenport. "I think we need to have a private word," he said.

Mr. Davenport stepped into an alcove on the other side of the corridor, assuming she would follow. Miss Nichol thought her legs would give way long before she collapsed into the chair opposite him. She couldn't tell from the expression on his face if he also realized she was the guilty party. But then with Mr. Davenport you never could. It wasn't in his nature to give anything away, and that was something he found difficult to change, even when it came to his private life. Miss Nichol couldn't look him in the eye, so she stared over his left shoulder and watched Dr. Greenwood as the elevator doors closed.

"I suspect you know what I'm about to ask you," he said.

"Yes, I do," Miss Nichol admitted, wondering if anyone would ever employ her again, and even if she might end up in prison.

When Dr. Greenwood reappeared ten minutes later, Miss Nichol knew exactly what was going to happen to her and where she would end up.

"When you've thought about it, Miss Nichol, perhaps you could give me a call at my office, and if your answer is yes, then I'll need to have a word with my lawyers."

"I've already thought about it," said Miss Nichol. This time she did look Mr. Davenport directly in the eye. "The answer is yes," she told him, "I'd be delighted to continue working for the family as nanny."

4

MISS NICHOL STUDIED the photograph when it was published in *The Hartford Courant.* She was relieved to find that although both boys had inherited their father's square jaw, Andrew had curly fair hair, while Nat's was straight and already turning dark. But it was Josiah Preston who saved the day, by frequently remarking that his grandson had inherited his nose and pronounced forehead in the great tradition of the Prestons. Miss Nichol constantly repeated these observations to fawning relatives and sycophantic employees, prefaced with the words, "Mr. Preston often remarks . . ."

Within two weeks of returning home, Ruth had been reappointed as Chairman of the Hospital Trust, and immediately set about honoring her husband's pledge to build a new maternity wing for St. Patrick's.

Miss Nichol meanwhile took on any job, however menial, that allowed Ruth to resume her outside activities while she took charge of Andrew. She became the boy's nanny, mentor, guardian and governess. But not a day went by without her dreading that the truth might eventually come out.

Miss Nichol's first real anxiety arose when Mrs. Cartwright phoned to say that she was holding a birthday party for her son, and as Andrew had been born on the same day, would she like him to be included.

"How kind of you to ask," Miss Nichol replied, without missing a beat, "but Andrew is having his own birthday party, and I'm only sorry that Nat won't be able to join us."

"Well, please pass on my best wishes to Mrs. Davenport, and tell her how much we appreciate being invited to the opening of the new maternity wing next month." An invitation Miss Nichol could not cancel. When Susan put the phone down, her only thought was how did Miss Nichol know her son's name.

Within moments of Mrs. Davenport arriving home that evening, Miss Nichol suggested that she should organize a party for Andrew's first birthday. Ruth thought it was a splendid idea, and was only too happy to leave all the arrangements, including the guest list, in nanny's hands. Organizing a birthday party where you can control who should or should not be invited is one thing, but trying to make sure that her employer and Mrs. Cartwright did not meet up at the opening of the Preston Maternity Wing was quite another.

In fact, it was Dr. Greenwood who introduced the two women while giving his guided tour of the new facility. He couldn't believe that no one would notice that the two little boys looked so alike. Miss Nichol turned away when he glanced in her direction. She quickly placed a bonnet over Andrew's head, which made him look more like a girl, and before Ruth could comment, said, "It's turning quite cold and I wouldn't want Andrew to catch a chill."

"Will you be staying in Hartford once you've retired, Dr. Greenwood?" Mrs. Cartwright asked.

"No, my wife and I plan to retire to our family home in Ohio," the doctor replied, "but I'm sure we'll return to Hartford from time to time."

Miss Nichol would have let out a sigh of relief had the doctor not stared pointedly at her. However, with Dr. Greenwood out of the way, Miss Nichol felt a little more confident that her secret would not be discovered.

Whenever Andrew was invited to join in any activity, become a member of any group, participate in any sport or just sign up for the summer pageant, Miss Nichol's first priority was to ensure that her charge didn't come into contact with any member of the Cartwright family. This she managed to achieve with considerable success throughout the child's formative years, without arousing the suspicions of either Mr. or Mrs. Davenport.

It was two letters that arrived in the morning mail that persuaded Miss Nichol that she need no longer be apprehensive. The first was addressed to Andrew's father and confirmed that the boy had been admitted to Hotchkiss, Connecticut's oldest private school. The second, postmarked Ohio, was opened by Ruth.

"How sad," she remarked as she turned the hand-written page. "He was such a fine man."

"Who?" asked Robert, looking up from his copy of *The New England Journal of Medicine.*

"Dr. Greenwood. His wife has written to say that he passed away last Friday, aged seventy-four."

"He was a fine man," Robert repeated, "perhaps you should attend the funeral."

"Yes, of course I will," said Ruth, "and Heather might like to accompany me," she added. "After all, she used to work for him."

"Of course," said Miss Nichol, hoping that she looked suitably distressed.

Susan read the letter a second time, saddened by the news. She would always recall how personally Dr. Greenwood had taken Peter's death, almost as if he felt somehow responsible. She remembered how tired she had grown, hearing friends and relations telling her to thank God that one of them had survived. Didn't they understand that Peter was dead, and she had lost a son? Dr. Greenwood had understood. Michael had hoped that his wife would begin to recover from the loss once she'd left the hospital and returned home. But it wasn't to be. Susan still talked endlessly of her other son, and kept a photograph of the two boys by her bedside.

Perhaps she should go to the doctor's funeral. She was about to share the news of his death with Michael, when her husband suddenly leaped in the air and shouted, "Well done, Nat."

"What is it?" asked Susan, surprised by such uncharacteristic exuberance.

"Nat's won a scholarship to Taft," said her husband, waving his letter in the air.

Susan didn't share the same enthusiasm as her husband for Nat being sent away at such an early age to board with children whose parents came from a different world. How could a child of fourteen begin to understand that they couldn't afford so many of the things that his school friends would take for granted. She had long felt that Nathaniel should follow in Michael's footsteps and go to Jefferson High. If it was good enough for her to teach at, why wasn't it good enough for their child to be taught at?

Nat had been sitting on his bed rereading his favorite book when he heard his father's outburst. He'd reached the chapter where the whale was about to escape yet again. He reluctantly jumped off the bed and put his head around the door to find out what was causing the commotion. His parents were furiously debating—they never argued, despite the much-reported incident with the ice cream—which school he should attend. He caught his father in mid-sentence . . . "chance of a lifetime," he was saying. "Nat will be able to mix with children who will end up as leaders in every field, and therefore influence the rest of his life."

"Rather than go to Jefferson High and mix with children who he might end up leading and influence for the rest of *their* lives?"

"But he's won a scholarship, so we wouldn't have to pay a penny."

"And we wouldn't have to pay a penny if he went to Jefferson."

"But we must think of Nat's future. If he goes to Taft, he might well end up at Harvard or Yale . . ."

"But Jefferson has produced several pupils who have attended both Harvard and Yale."

"If I had to take out an insurance policy on which of the two schools would be more likely . . ."

"It's a risk I'm willing to take."

"Well, I'm not," said Michael, "and I spend every day of my life trying to eliminate risks like that." Nat listened intently as his mother and father continued their debate, never once raising their voices or losing their tempers.

"I'd rather my son graduate as an egalitarian than a patrician," Susan retorted with passion.

"Why should they be incompatible?" asked Michael.

Nat disappeared back into his room without waiting to hear his mother's reply. She had taught him to immediately look up any word that he'd never heard before; after all, it was a Connecticut man who had compiled the greatest lexicography in the world. Having checked all three words in his Webster's dictionary, Nat decided that his mother was more egalitarian than his father, but that neither of them was a patrician. He wasn't sure if he wanted to be a patrician.

When Nat had finished the chapter, he emerged from his room for a second time. The atmosphere seemed to be more settled, so he decided to go downstairs and join his parents.

"Perhaps we should let Nat decide," said his mother.

"I already have," said Nat, as he took a seat between them. "After all, you've always taught me to listen to both sides of any argument before coming to a conclusion."

Both parents were speechless as Nat nonchalantly unfolded the evening paper, suddenly aware that he must have overheard their conversation.

"And what decision have you come to?" his mother asked quietly.

"I would like to go to Taft rather than Jefferson High," Nat replied without hesitation.

"And may we know what helped you come to that conclusion?" asked his father.

Nat, aware that he had a spellbound audience, didn't hurry his reply. "*Moby-Dick,*" he finally announced, before turning to the sports page.

He waited to see which of his parents would be the first to repeat his words.

"*Moby-Dick?*" they pronounced together.

"Yes," he replied, "after all, the good folks of Connecticut considered the great whale to be the *patrician* of the sea."

5

"Every inch a Hotchkiss man," Miss Nichol said as she checked Andrew's appearance in the hall mirror. White shirt, blue blazer with tan corduroy trousers. Miss Nichol straightened the boy's blue and white striped tie, removing a speck of dust from his shirt. "Every inch," she repeated. I'm only five foot three, Andrew wanted to say as his father joined them in the hall. Andrew checked his watch, a present from his maternal grandfather—a man who still sacked people for being late.

"I've put your suitcases in the car," his father said, touching his son on the shoulder. Andrew turned cold when he heard his father's words. The casual remark only reminded him that he really was leaving home. "It's less than three months until Thanksgiving," his father added. Three months is a quarter of a year—a not insignificant percentage of your life when you're only fourteen years old, Andrew wanted to remind him.

Andrew strode out of the front door and onto the gravel courtyard, determined not to look back at the house he loved, and would not see again for a quarter of a year. When he reached the car, he held the back door open for his mother. He then shook hands with Miss Nichol as if she were an old friend, and said that he looked forward to seeing her at Thanksgiving. He couldn't be sure, but he thought she had been crying. He looked away and waved to the housekeeper and cook, before he jumped into the car.

As they drove through the streets of Farmington, Andrew

stared at the familiar buildings he had considered until that moment to be the center of the whole world.

"Now make sure you write home every week," his mother was saying. He ignored the redundant comment, not least because Miss Nichol had issued the same instruction at least twice a day for the past month.

"And if you need any extra cash, don't hesitate to give me a call," his father added.

Someone else who hadn't read the rule-book. Andrew didn't remind his father that boys in their first year at Hotchkiss were only allowed ten dollars a term. It was spelled out on page seven, and had been underlined in red by Miss Nichol.

No one spoke again during the short journey to the station, each anxious in his own particular fashion. His father brought the car to a halt next to the station and jumped out. Andrew remained seated, reluctant to leave the safety of the car, until his mother opened the door on his side. Andrew quickly joined her, determined not to let anyone know how nervous he was. She tried to take his hand, but he quickly ran to the back of the car to help his father with the cases.

A blue cap arrived by their side pushing a trolley. Once the cases were loaded, he led them onto the station platform and came to a halt at car eight. As the porter lifted the cases onto the train, Andrew turned to say goodbye to his father. He had insisted that only one parent accompany him on the train journey to Lakeville, and as his father was a Taft man, his mother seemed the obvious choice. He was already regretting his decision.

"Have a good journey," his father said, shaking his son's outstretched hand. What silly things parents say at stations, Andrew thought; surely it was more important that he worked hard when he got there. "And don't forget to write."

Andrew boarded the train with his mother and as the engine pulled out of the station he didn't once look back at his father, hoping it would make him appear more grown up.

"Would you like some breakfast?" his mother asked as the porter placed his cases on the overhead rack.

"Yes, please," replied Andrew, cheering up for the first time that morning.

Another uniformed man showed them to a table in the dining car. Andrew studied the menu and wondered if his mother would allow him to have the full breakfast.

"Have anything you like," she said, as if reading his thoughts.

Andrew smiled when the waiter reappeared. "Double hash browns, two eggs, sunny side up, bacon and tomatoes." He only left out the mushrooms because he didn't want the waiter to think that his mother never fed him.

"And you, ma'am?" inquired the waiter, turning his attention to the other side of the table.

"Just coffee and toast, thank you."

"The boy's first day?" asked the waiter.

Mrs. Davenport smiled and nodded.

How does he know? wondered Andrew.

Andrew munched nervously through his breakfast, not sure if he would be fed again that day. There had been no mention of meals in the handbook, and Grandpa had told him that when he was at Hotchkiss, they were only fed once a day. His mother kept telling him to put his knife and fork down while he was eating. "Knives and forks are not airplanes and shouldn't remain in mid-air longer than is necessary," she reminded him. He had no way of knowing that she was almost as nervous as he was.

Whenever another boy, dressed in the same smart uniform, passed by their table, Andrew looked out of the window, hoping they wouldn't notice him, because none of their uniforms were as new as his. His mother was on her third cup of coffee when the train pulled into the station.

"We've arrived," she announced, unnecessarily.

Andrew sat staring at the sign for Lakeville as several boys leaped off the train, greeting each other with "Hi there, how was your vacation? And good to see you again," followed by much shaking of hands. He finally glanced across at his mother, and wished she would disappear in a cloud of smoke. Mothers were just another announcement that it was his first day.

Two tall boys dressed in double-breasted blue blazers and gray slacks began shepherding the new boys onto a waiting bus. Andrew prayed that parents were banned from the bus, otherwise everyone would realize he was a new boy.

"Name?" said one of the young men in a blue blazer as Andrew stepped off the train.

"Davenport, sir," said Andrew, staring up at him. Would he ever be that tall?

The young man smiled, almost a grin. "You don't call me sir, I'm not a master, just a senior proctor." Andrew's head dropped. The first words he'd uttered, and he'd made a fool of himself. "Has your luggage been placed on the bus, Fletcher?"

Fletcher? thought Andrew. Of course, Fletcher Andrew Davenport; he didn't correct the tall young man for fear of making another mistake.

"Yes," Andrew replied.

The god turned his attention to Andrew's mother. "Thank you, Mrs. Davenport," he said, checking his list, "I hope you have a pleasant journey back to Farmington. Fletcher will be just fine," he added kindly.

Andrew thrust out his hand, determined to stop his mother cuddling him. If only mothers could read thoughts. He shuddered as she threw her arms around him. But then he couldn't begin to understand what she was going through. When his mother finally released him, Andrew quickly joined the flow of boys who were jumping onto the waiting bus. He spotted a boy, even smaller than himself, who was sitting on his own looking out the window. He quickly sat down beside him.

"I'm Fletcher," he said, reverting to the name bestowed on him by the god. "What's yours?"

"James," he replied, "but my friends call me Jimmy."

"Are you a new boy?" asked Fletcher.

"Yes," said Jimmy quietly, still not looking around.

"Me too," replied Fletcher.

Jimmy took out a handkerchief and pretended to blow his nose, before he finally turned to face his new companion.

"Where are you from?" he asked.

"Farmington."

"Where's that?"

"Not far from West Hartford."

"My dad works in Hartford," said Jimmy, "he's in the government. What does your dad do?"

"He sells drugs," said Fletcher.

"Do you like football?" asked Jimmy.

"Yes," said Fletcher, but only because he knew Hotchkiss had an unbeaten record for the past four years, something else Miss Nichol had underlined in the handbook.

The rest of the conversation consisted of a series of unrelated questions to which the other rarely knew the answer. It was a strange beginning for what was to become a lifelong friendship.

6

"Spotless," said his father as he checked the boy's uniform in the hall mirror. Michael Cartwright straightened his son's blue tie, and removed a hair from his jacket. "Spotless," he repeated.

Five dollars for a pair of corduroys was all Nathaniel could think about, even if his father had said they were worth every cent.

"Hurry up, Susan, or we'll be late," his father called, glancing up toward the landing. But Michael still found time to pack the case in the trunk and move the car out of the driveway before Susan finally appeared to wish her son luck on his first day. She gave Nathaniel a big hug, and he was only grateful that there wasn't another Taft man in sight to witness the event. He hoped that his mother had got over her disappointment that he hadn't chosen Jefferson High, because he was already having second thoughts. After all, if he'd gone to Jefferson High he could have gone home every night.

He took the seat next to his father in the front of the car, and checked the clock on the dashboard. It was nearly seven o'clock. "Let's get going, Dad," he said, desperate not to be late on his first day and to be remembered for all the wrong reasons.

Once they reached the highway, his father moved across to the outside lane and put the speedometer up to sixty-five, five miles an hour over the limit, calculating that the odds of being pulled over at that time in the morning were in his favor. Although Nathaniel had visited Taft to be interviewed, it was still a terrifying moment when his father drove their old Studebaker through the vast iron gates and slowly up the mile-long drive. He was relieved to see two or three other cars filing in behind them, though he doubted if they were new boys. His father followed a line of Cadillacs and Buicks into a parking lot, not altogether sure where he should park; after all, he was a new father. Nathaniel jumped out of the car, even before his father had pulled on the hand brake. But then he hesitated. Did he follow the stream of boys heading toward Taft Hall, or were new boys expected to go somewhere else?

His father didn't hesitate in joining the throng, and only came to a halt when a tall, self-assured young man carrying a clipboard looked down at Nathaniel and asked, "Are you a new boy?"

Nathaniel didn't speak, so his father said, "Yes."

The young man's gaze was not averted. "Name?" he said.

"Cartwright, sir," Nathaniel replied.

"Ah yes, a lower mid; you've been assigned to Mr. Haskins, so you must be clever. All the bright ones start off with Mr. Haskins." Nathaniel lowered his head while his father smiled. "When you go into Taft Hall," continued the young man, "you can sit anywhere in the front three rows on the left-hand side. The moment you hear nine chimes on the clock, you will stop talking and not speak again until the principal and the rest of the staff have left the hall."

"What do I do then?" asked Nathaniel, trying to hide the fact that he was shaking.

"You will be briefed by your form master," said the young man who turned his attention to the new father. "Nat will be just fine, Mr. Cartwright. I hope you have a good journey home, sir."

That was the moment Nathaniel decided in the future he would always be known as Nat, even though he realized it wouldn't please his mother.

As he entered Taft Hall Nat lowered his head and walked quickly down the long aisle, hoping no one would notice him. He spotted a place on the end of the second row, and slipped into it. He glanced at the boy seated on his left, whose head was cupped in his hands. Was he praying, or could he possibly be even more terrified than Nat? "My name's Nat," he ventured.

"Mine's Tom," said the boy, not raising his head.

"What happens next?"

"I don't know, but I wish it would," said Tom as the clock struck nine, and everyone fell silent.

A crocodile of masters proceeded down the aisle—no mistresses, Nat observed. His mother wouldn't approve. They walked up onto the stage, and took their places, leaving only two seats unoccupied. The faculty began to talk quietly among themselves, while those in the body of the hall remained silent.

"What are we waiting for?" whispered Nat, and a moment later his question was answered as everyone rose, including those seated on the stage. Nat didn't dare look around when he heard the footsteps of two men proceeding down the aisle. Moments later, the school chaplain followed by the principal passed him on their way up to the two vacant seats. Everyone remained standing as the chaplain stepped forward to conduct a short service, which included the Lord's Prayer, and ended with the assembly singing the "Battle Hymn of the Republic."

The chaplain then returned to his seat, allowing the principal to take his place. Alexander Inglefield paused for a moment, before gazing down at the assembled gathering. He then raised his hands, palms down, and everyone resumed their seat. Three hundred and eighty pairs of eyes stared up at a man of six foot two with thick bushy eyebrows and a square jaw, who presented such a frightening figure that Nat hoped they would never meet.

The principal gripped the edge of his long black gown before addressing the gathering for fifteen minutes. He began by taking his charges through the long history of the school, extolling Taft's past academic and sporting achievements. He stared down at the new boys and reminded them of the school's motto, *Non ut sibi ministretur sed ut ministret.*

"What does that mean?" whispered Tom.

"Not to be served, but to serve," muttered Nat.

The principal concluded by announcing that there were two things a Bearcat could never afford to miss—an exam, or a match against Hotchkiss—and, as if making clear his priorities, he promised a half-day's holiday if Taft beat Hotchkiss in the annual football game. This was immediately greeted by a rousing cheer from the whole assembly, although every boy beyond the third row knew that this had not been achieved for the past four years.

When the cheering had died down, the principal left the stage, followed by the chaplain and the rest of the staff. Once they had departed, the chattering began again as the upper classmen started to file out of the hall, while only those boys in the front three rows remained seated, because they didn't know where to go.

Ninety-five boys sat waiting to see what would happen next. They did not have long to wait, because an elderly master—well actually he was only fifty-one, but Nat thought he looked much older than his dad—came to a halt in front of them. He was a short, thick-set man, with a semicircle of gray hair around an otherwise bald pate. As he spoke, he clung onto the lapels of his tweed jacket, imitating the principal's pose.

"My name is Haskins," he told them. "I am master of the lower middlers," he added with a wry smile. "We'll begin the day with orientation, which you will have completed by first break at ten thirty. At eleven you will attend your assigned classes. Your first lesson will be American history." Nat frowned, as history had never been his favorite subject. "Which will be followed by lunch. Don't look forward to that," Mr. Haskins said with the same wry smile. A few of the boys laughed. "But then that's just another Taft tradition," Mr. Haskins assured them, "which any of you who are following in your father's footsteps will have already been warned about." One or two of the boys, including Tom, smiled.

Once they had begun what Mr. Haskins described as the nickel and dime tour, Nat never left Tom's side. He seemed to have prior knowledge of everything Haskins was about to say. Nat quickly discovered that not only was Tom's father a former alumni, but so was his grandfather.

By the time the tour had ended and they had seen everything from the lake to the sanatorium, he and Tom were best friends. When they filed into the classroom twenty minutes later, they automatically sat next to each other.

As the clock chimed eleven, Mr. Haskins marched into the room. A boy followed in his wake. He had a self-assurance about him, almost a swagger, that made every other boy look up. The master's eyes also followed the new pupil as he slipped into the one remaining desk.

"Name?"

"Ralph Elliot."

"That will be the last time you will be late for my class while you're at Taft," said Haskins. He paused. "Do I make myself clear, Elliot?"

"You most certainly do." The boy paused, before adding, "Sir."

Mr. Haskins turned his gaze to the rest of the class. "Our first lesson, as I warned you, will be on American history, which is appropriate remembering that this school was founded by the brother of a former president." With a portrait of William H. Taft in the main hall and a statue of his brother in the quadrangle, it would have been hard for even the least inquisitive pupil not to have worked that out.

"Who was the first president of the United States?" Mr. Haskins asked. Every hand shot up. Mr. Haskins nodded to a boy in the front row.

"George Washington, sir."

"And the second?" asked Haskins. Fewer hands rose, and this time Tom was selected.

"John Adams, sir."

"Correct, and the third?"

Only two hands remained up, Nat's and the boy who had arrived late. Haskins pointed to Nat.

"Thomas Jefferson, 1800 to 1808."

Mr. Haskins nodded, acknowledging that the boy also knew the correct dates, "And the fourth?"

"James Madison, 1809 to 1817," said Elliot.

"And the fifth, Cartwright?"

"James Monroe, 1817 to 1825."

"And the sixth, Elliot?"

"John Quincy Adams, 1825 to 1829."

"And the seventh, Cartwright?"

Nat racked his brains. "I don't remember, sir."

"You don't remember, Cartwright, or do you simply not know?"

Haskins paused. "There is a considerable difference," he added. He turned his attention back to Elliot.

"William Henry Harrison, I think, sir."

"No, he was the ninth president, Elliot, 1841, but as he died of pneumonia only a month after his inauguration, we won't be spending a lot of time on him," added Haskins. "Make sure everyone can tell me the name of the ninth president by tomorrow morning. Now let's go back to the founding fathers. You may all take notes as I require you to produce a three-page essay on the subject by the time we next meet."

Nat had filled three long sheets even before the lesson had ended, while Tom barely managed a page. As they left the classroom at the end of the lesson, Elliot brushed quickly past them.

"He already looks like a real rival," remarked Tom.

Nat didn't comment.

What he couldn't know was that he and Ralph Elliot would be rivals for the rest of their lives.

7

THE ANNUAL FOOTBALL game between Hotchkiss and Taft was the sporting highlight of the semester. As both teams were undefeated that season, little else was discussed once the midterms were over, and for the jocks, long before midterms began.

Fletcher found himself caught up in the excitement, and in his weekly letter to his mother named every member of the team, although he realized that she wouldn't have a clue who any of them were.

The game was due to be played on the last Saturday in October and once the final whistle had been blown, all boarders would have the rest of the weekend off, plus an extra day should they win.

On the Monday before the match, Fletcher's class sat their first midterms, but not before the principal had declared at morning assembly that, "Life consists of a series of tests and examinations, which is why we take them every term at Hotchkiss."

On Tuesday evening Fletcher phoned his mother to tell her he thought he'd done well.

On Wednesday he told Jimmy he wasn't so sure.

By Thursday, he'd looked up everything he hadn't included, and wondered if he had even achieved a pass grade.

On Friday morning, class rankings were posted on the school notice board and the preps were headed by the name of Fletcher Davenport. He immediately ran to the nearest phone and rang his mother. Ruth couldn't hide her delight when she learned her son's news, but didn't tell him that she wasn't surprised. "You must celebrate," she said. Fletcher would have done so, but felt he couldn't when he saw who had come bottom of the class.

At the full school assembly on Saturday morning, prayers were offered by the chaplain "for our undefeated football team, who played only for the glory of our Lord." Our Lord was then vouch-safed the name of every player and asked if his Holy Spirit might be bestowed on each and every one of them. The principal was obviously in no doubt which team God would be supporting on Saturday afternoon.

At Hotchkiss, everything was decided on seniority, even a boy's place in the bleachers. During their first term, preps were relegated to the far end of the field so both boys sat in the right-hand corner of the stand every other Saturday, and watched their heroes extend the season's unbeaten run, a record they realized Taft also enjoyed.

As the Taft game fell on a homecoming weekend, Jimmy's parents invited Fletcher to join them for a tailgate picnic before the kickoff. Fletcher didn't tell any of the other boys in preps, because he felt it would only make them jealous. It was bad enough being top of the class, without being invited to watch the Taft game with an old boy who had seats on the center line.

"What's your dad like?" asked Jimmy, after lights-out the night before the game.

"He's great," said Fletcher, "but I should warn you that he's a Taft man, and a Republican. And how about your dad? I've never met a senator before."

"He's a politician to his fingertips, or at least that's how the press describe him," said Jimmy. "Not that I'm sure what it means."

On the morning of the game no one was able to concentrate during chemistry, despite Mr. Bailey's enthusiasm for testing the effects of acid on zinc, not least because Jimmy had turned the gas off at the main, so Mr. Bailey couldn't even get the Bunsen burners lit.

At twelve o'clock a bell rang, releasing 380 screaming boys to charge out into the courtyard. They resembled nothing less than a warring tribe, with their cries of, "Hotchkiss, Hotchkiss, Hotchkiss will win, death to all Bearcats."

Fletcher ran all the way to the assembly point to meet his parents, as cars and taxis came streaming in past the lake. Fletcher scanned every vehicle, searching for his father and mother.

"How are you, Andrew my darling?" were his mother's first words as she stepped out of the car.

"Fletcher, I'm Fletcher at Hotchkiss," he whispered, hoping that none of the other boys had heard the word "darling." He shook hands with his father, before adding, "We must leave for the field immediately, because we've been invited to join Senator and Mrs. Gates for a tailgate lunch."

Fletcher's father raised an eyebrow. "If I remember correctly, Senator Gates is a Democrat," he said with mock disdain.

"And a former Hotchkiss football captain," said Fletcher. "His son Jimmy and I are in the same class, and he's my best friend, so Mom had better sit next to the senator, and if you don't feel up to it, Dad, you can sit on the other side of the field with the Taft supporters."

"No, I think I'll put up with the senator. It will be so rewarding to be seated next to him when Taft scores the winning touchdown."

It was a clear autumnal day and the three of them strolled through a golden carpet of leaves all the way to the field. Ruth tried to take her son's hand, but Fletcher stood just far enough away to make it impossible. Long before they reached the field, they could hear the cheers erupting from the pre-game rally.

Fletcher spotted Jimmy standing behind an Oldsmobile wagon, its open tailgate covered in far more sumptuous food than anything he'd seen for the past two months. A tall elegant man stepped forward. "Hello, I'm Harry Gates." The senator thrust out his politician's hand to welcome Fletcher's parents.

Fletcher's father grasped the outstretched hand. "Good afternoon, Senator, I'm Robert Davenport and this is my wife, Ruth."

"Call me Harry. This is Martha, my first wife." Mrs. Gates stepped forward to welcome them both. "I call her my first wife—well, it keeps her on her toes."

"Would you like a drink?" asked Martha, not laughing at a joke she had heard so many times before.

"It had better be quick," said the senator, checking his watch, "that is if we still hope to eat before the kick-off. Let me serve you, Ruth, and we'll let your husband fend for himself. I can smell a Republican at a hundred paces."

"I'm afraid it's worse than that," said Ruth.

"Don't tell me he's an old Bearcat, because I'm thinking of making that a capital offense in this state." Ruth nodded. "Then Fletcher, you'd better come and talk to me because I intend to ignore your father."

Fletcher was flattered by the invitation, and soon began grilling the senator on the workings of the Connecticut legislature.

"Andrew," said Ruth.

"Fletcher, mother."

"Fletcher, don't you think the senator might like to talk about something other than politics?"

"No, that's fine by me, Ruth," Harry assured her. "The voters rarely ask such insightful questions, and I'm rather hoping it might rub off on Jimmy."

After lunch had been cleared away they walked quickly across to the bleachers, sitting down only moments before the game was due to begin. The seats were better than any prep could have dreamed of, but then Senator Gates hadn't missed the Taft match since his own graduation. Fletcher couldn't contain his excitement as the clock on the score board edged toward two. He stared across at the far stand, to be greeted with the enemy's cries of, "Give me a T, give me an A, give me a . . ." and fell in love.

—◇—

Nat's eyes remained on the face above the letter A.

"Nat's the brightest boy in our class," Tom told Nat's father. Michael smiled.

"Only just," said Nat a little defensively; "don't forget I only beat Ralph Elliot by one grade."

"I wonder if he's Max Elliot's son?" said Nat's father, almost to himself.

"Who's Max Elliot?"

"In my business he's what's known as an unacceptable risk."

"Why?" asked Nat, but his father didn't expand on the bland statement, and was relieved when his son was distracted by the cheerleaders, who had blue and white pom-poms attached to their wrists and were performing their ritual war dance. Nat's eyes settled on the second girl on the left, who seemed to be smiling up at him, although he realized to her he could only be a speck at the back of the stand.

"You've grown, if I'm not mistaken," said Nat's father, noting that his son's trousers were already an inch short of his shoes. He only wondered how often he would have to buy him new clothes.

"Well, it can't be the school food that's responsible," suggested Tom, who was still the smallest boy in the class. Nat didn't reply. His eyes remained fixed on the group of cheerleaders.

"Which one of them have you fallen for?" inquired Tom, punching his friend on the arm.

"What?"

"You heard me the first time."

Nat turned away so that his father couldn't overhear his reply. "Second one from the left, with the letter A on her sweater."

"Diane Coulter," said Tom, pleased to discover that he knew something his friend didn't.

"How do you know her name?"

"Because she's Dan Coulter's sister."

"But he's the ugliest player on the team," said Nat. "He's got cauliflower ears and a broken nose."

"And so would Diane if she'd played on the team every week for the past five years," said Tom with a laugh.

"What else do you know about her?" Nat asked his friend conspiratorially.

"Oh, it's that serious is it?" said Tom. It was Nat's turn to punch his friend. "Having to revert to physical violence, are we? Hardly part of the Taft code," added Tom. "Beat a man with the strength of your argument, not the strength of your arm; Oliver Wendell Holmes, if I remember correctly."

"Oh, stop droning on," said Nat, "and just answer the question."

"Don't know a lot more about her, to be honest. All I remember is that she goes to Westover and plays right wing on their hockey team."

"What are you two whispering about?" asked Nat's father.

"Dan Coulter," said Tom without missing a beat, "one of our running backs—I was just telling Nat that he eats eight eggs for breakfast every morning."

"How do you know that?" asked Nat's mother.

"Because one of them is always mine," said Tom ruefully.

As his parents burst out laughing, Nat continued to gaze down at the A in TAFT. The first time he'd really noticed a girl. His concentration was distracted by a sudden roar, as everyone on his side of the stadium rose to greet the Taft team as they ran out onto the field. Moments later the Hotchkiss players appeared from the other side of the field and just as enthusiastically their supporters leaped to their feet.

—◦—

Fletcher was also standing, but his eyes remained fixed on the cheerleader with an A on her sweater. He felt guilty that the first girl he'd ever fallen for was a Taft supporter.

"You don't seem to be concentrating on our team," said the senator, leaning over and whispering in Fletcher's ear.

"Oh, yes I am, sir," said Fletcher, immediately turning his attention back to the Hotchkiss players as they began to warm up.

The two team captains jogged across to join the umpire, who was waiting for them on the center line. The Zebra flicked a silver coin into the air that flashed in the afternoon sun before landing in the mud. The Bearcats clapped each other on the back when they saw the profile of Washington.

"He should have called heads," said Fletcher.

At half time, Fletcher asked Jimmy's father, "Can I borrow your binoculars, sir?"

"Of course, my boy," said the senator, passing them across. "Let me have them back when the game re-starts." Fletcher missed the irony in his host's voice as he focused on the girl with an A on her sweater and wished she would turn around and face the opposition more often.

"Which one are you interested in?" whispered the senator.

"I was just checking on the Tafties, sir."

"I don't think they've come back onto the field yet," said the senator. Fletcher turned scarlet. "T, A, F or T?" inquired Jimmy's father.

"A, sir," admitted Fletcher.

The senator retrieved his binoculars, focused on the second girl from the left, and waited for her to turn around. "I approve of your choice, young man, but what do you intend to do about it?"

"I don't know, sir," said Fletcher helplessly. "To be honest, I don't even know her name."

"Diane Coulter," said the senator.

"How do you know that?" asked Fletcher, wondering if senators knew everything.

"Research, my boy. Haven't they taught you that at Hotchkiss yet?" Fletcher looked bewildered. "All you need to know is on page eleven of the program," added the senator as he passed the open booklet across. Page eleven had been devoted to the cheer-leaders supporting each school. "Diane Coulter," repeated Fletcher, staring at the photo. She was a year younger than Fletcher—women are still willing to admit their age at thirteen—and she also played the violin in her school orchestra. How he wished he'd taken his mother's advice and learned to play the piano.

The whistle blew for the third quarter, and after a series of brilliant passes, it was Hotchkiss's turn to make it over the end zone, putting them back into the lead, which they clung onto until the end of the third quarter.

"Hello Taft, Hello Taft, you're back where you belong," sang the senator out of tune, while the teams took a timeout.

"There's still the final quarter to come," Fletcher reminded the senator as his host passed the glasses across to him.

"Have you decided which side you're supporting, young man, or have you been ensnared by the Tafties' Mata Hari?" Fletcher looked puzzled. He would have to check on who Mata Hari was just as soon as he got back to his room. "She probably lives locally," continued the senator, "in which case it will take a member of my staff about two minutes to find out everything you need to know about her."

"Even her address and telephone number?" asked Fletcher.

"Even whether she has a boyfriend," replied the senator.

"Wouldn't that be abusing your position?" asked Fletcher.

"Damn right I would," replied Senator Gates, "but then any politician would do as much if he felt it might ensure two extra votes at some future election."

"But that doesn't solve the problem of meeting her while I'm stuck in Farmington."

"That can also be solved if you'd come and spend a few days with us after Christmas, and then I'll make sure that she and her parents are invited to some function at the Capitol."

"You'll do that for me?"

"Sure will, but at some time you'll have to learn about trade-offs if you're going to deal with a politician."

"What's the trade-off?" asked Fletcher. "I'll do anything."

"Never admit to that, my boy, because it immediately puts you in the weaker bargaining position. However, all I want in return on this occasion is for you to make sure Jimmy somehow scrapes off the bottom of the class. That will be your part of the bargain."

"It's a deal, Senator," said Fletcher, shaking hands.

"That's good to hear," said the senator, "because Jimmy seems only too willing to follow your lead."

It was the first time anyone had suggested that Fletcher might be a leader. Until that moment it hadn't even crossed his mind. He thought about the senator's words, and failed to notice Taft's winning touchdown until Diane rushed up out of the bleachers and began a ritual that unfortunately resembled a victory ceremony. There would be no extra day off this year.

‹◦›

As the game began, Nat had continued to stare as Diane climbed back into the bleachers. He wondered how he could possibly meet her. It wouldn't be easy. Dan Coulter was a god. How could a new boy possibly hope to scale Olympus?

"Good run," hollered Tom.

"Who?" said Nat.

"Coulter, of course. He's just picked up the first down."

"Coulter?"

"Don't tell me you were still staring at his sister when the Kissies fumbled?"

"No, I wasn't."

"Then you'll be able to tell me how many yards we gained," Tom said, looking at his friend. He paused. "I thought so, you weren't even watching." He let out an exaggerated sigh, "I do believe that the time has come to put you out of your misery."

"What do you mean?"

"I shall have to arrange a meeting."

"You can do that?"

"Sure, her father's a local auto dealer, and we always buy our cars from him, so you'll just have to come and stay with me during the holidays."

Tom didn't hear if his friend accepted the invitation, because his reply was drowned by another roar from the Taft supporters as the Bearcats intercepted.

When the whistle blew at the end of the first quarter, Nat let out the biggest cheer, having forgotten that his team was trailing. He remained standing in the hope that the girl with the head of curly fair hair and the most captivating smile might just notice him. But how could she, as she leaped energetically up and down, encouraging the Taft supporters to cheer even louder.

The whistle for the start of the second quarter came all too quickly, and when A disappeared back in the bleachers to be replaced by thirty muscle-bound heavies, Nat reluctantly resumed his place and pretended to concentrate on the game.

After gaining painful yard upon painful yard, Taft finally crossed the line and took the lead. Dutifully Diane reappeared on the sidelines to perform her energetic routine.

"You've got it bad," said Tom, "I guess I'm going to have to introduce you."

"You really know her?" said Nat in disbelief.

"Sure do," said Tom. "We've been going to the same parties since the age of two."

"I wonder if she has a boyfriend," said Nat.

"How should I know? Why don't you come and spend a week with us during vacation, and then you can leave the rest to me."

"You'd do that?"

"It'll cost you."

"What do you have in mind?"

"Make sure you finish the holiday assignments before you turn up—then I won't have to bother double-checking all the facts."

"It's a deal," said Nat.

—◇—

After the game, on the other side of the stadium, Nat and Tom stood outside the locker rooms, along with a multitude of Taft supporters who, with one exception, were waiting to greet their heroes. Nat nudged his friend in the ribs as she came out. Tom stepped quickly forward. "Hi, Diane," he said and, not waiting for a reply, added, "I want you to meet my friend Nat. Actually, the truth is he wanted to meet you." Nat blushed, and not just because he thought Diane was even prettier than her photo. "Nat lives in Cromwell," added Tom helpfully, "but he's coming to spend a few days with us after Christmas, so you can get to know him better then."

Nat only felt confident of one thing; Tom's chosen career wasn't destined to be in the diplomatic corps.

8

NAT SAT AT his desk, trying to concentrate on the Great Depression. He managed about half a page, but he found his mind kept wandering. He went over the short meeting he'd had with Diane, again and again. This didn't take long because she'd hardly said a word before his father had joined them and suggested they ought to be leaving.

Nat had cut out her picture from the football program, and carried it around with him wherever he went. He was beginning to wish he'd picked up at least three programs, because the little photo was becoming so worn. He'd rung Tom the following morning on the pretense of discussing the Wall Street crash, and then casually threw in, "Did Diane say anything about me after I'd left?"

"She thought you were very nice."

"Nothing else?"

"What else could she say? You only had about two minutes together before your father dragged you off."

"Did she like me?"

"She thought you were very nice, and if I remember correctly, she said something about James Dean."

"No, she didn't—did she?"

"No, you're right—she didn't."

"You're a rat."

"True, but a rat with a telephone number."

"You have her telephone number?" said Nat in disbelief.

"You catch on quickly."

"What is it?"

"Have you completed that essay on the Great Depression?"

"Not quite, but I'll have it finished by the weekend, so hold on while I get a pencil." Nat wrote the number down on the back of Diane's photograph. "Do you think she'll be surprised if I give her a call?"

"I think she'll be surprised if you don't."

—◇—

"Hi, I'm Nat Cartwright. I don't suppose you remember me."

"No, I don't. Who are you?"

"I'm the one you met after the Hotchkiss game and thought looked like James Dean."

Nat glanced in the mirror. He'd never thought about his looks before. Did he really look like James Dean?

It took another couple of days, and several more rehearsals, before Nat had the courage to dial her number. Once he'd completed his essay on the Great Depression he prepared a list of questions, which varied according to who picked up the phone. If it was her father, he would say, "Good morning, sir, my name is Nat Cartwright. May I please speak to your daughter," if it was her mother he would say, "Good morning, Mrs. Coulter, my name is Nat Cartwright. May I please speak to your daughter." If Diane answered the phone, he had prepared ten questions, in a logical order. He placed three sheets of paper on the table in front of him, took a deep breath, and carefully dialed the digits. He was greeted by a busy signal. Perhaps she was talking to another boy. Had she already held his hand, even kissed him? Was he her regular date? Fifteen minutes later he phoned again. Still busy. Had another suitor called in between? This time he only waited ten minutes before he tried again. The moment he heard the ringing tone he felt his heart thumping in his chest, and wanted to put the phone right back down. He stared at his list of questions. The ringing stopped. Someone picked up the phone.

"Hello," said a deep voice. He didn't need to be told it was Dan Coulter.

Nat dropped the phone on the floor. Surely gods don't answer phones, and in any case, he hadn't prepared any questions for

45

Diane's brother. Hastily he picked the receiver up off the floor and placed it back on the phone.

Nat read through his essay before he dialed a fourth time. At last a girl's voice answered.

"Diane?"

"No, it's her sister Tricia," said a voice that sounded older, "Diane's out at the moment, but I'm expecting her back in about an hour. Who shall I say called?"

"Nat," he replied, "would you tell her I'll phone again in about an hour?"

"Sure," said the older voice.

"Thank you," said Nat and put the receiver down. He hadn't any questions or answers prepared for an older sister.

Nat must have looked at his watch sixty times during the next hour, but he still added another fifteen minutes before he re-dialed the number. He'd read in *Teen* magazine that if you like a girl, don't appear too keen, it puts them off. The phone was eventually picked up.

"Hello," said a younger voice. Nat glanced down at his script. "Hello, can I speak to Diane?"

"Hi, Nat, it's Diane. Tricia told me you'd called, how are you?"

How are you wasn't in the script. "I'm fine," he eventually managed, "how are you?"

"I'm fine too," she replied, which was followed by another long silence while Nat searched for an appropriate question.

"I'm coming over to Simsbury next week to spend a few days with Tom," he read out in a monotone.

"That's great," replied Diane, "then let's hope we bump into each other." There certainly wasn't anything in the script about bumping into each other. He tried to read all ten questions at once. "Are you still there, Nat?" asked Diane.

"Yes. Any hope of seeing you while I'm in Simsbury?" Question number nine.

"Yes, of course," said Diane, "I'd like that very much."

"Goodbye," said Nat looking at answer number ten.

During the rest of the evening, Nat tried to recall the conversation in detail, and even wrote it down line by line. He underlined three times her words—yes, of course, I'd like that very much. As there were still four days before he was due to visit Tom, he wondered if he should call Diane again—just to confirm. He returned to *Teen* magazine to seek their advice, as they seemed to have anticipated all his previous problems. *Teen* gave no help on calling a second time, but did suggest for a first date he should dress casually, be relaxed, and whenever he got the chance, talk about other girls he'd been out with. He'd never been out with another girl, and worse, he didn't have any casual clothes, other than a plaid shirt that he had hidden in a bottom drawer half an hour after he'd bought it. Nat checked to see how much money he'd saved from his paper route—seven dollars and twenty cents—and wondered if that was enough to purchase a new shirt and a casual pair of slacks. If only he had an older brother.

He put the finishing touches to his essay only hours before his father drove him across to Simsbury.

As they traveled north, Nat kept asking himself why he hadn't called Diane back and fixed a time and place to meet her. She might have gone away, decided to stay with a friend—a boyfriend. Would Tom's parents mind if he asked to use their phone the moment he arrived?

"Oh, my God," said Nat as his father swung his car into a long drive and drove past a paddock full of horses. Nat's father would have chastised him for blaspheming, but was somewhat taken aback himself. The driveway must have stretched for over a mile before they turned into a gravel courtyard to be greeted by the most magnificent white pillared colonial home surrounded by evergreens.

"Oh, my God," said Nat a second time. This time his father did remonstrate with him.

"Sorry, Dad, but Tom never mentioned he lived in a palace."

"Why should he?" replied his father, "when it's all he's ever known. By the way, he's not your closest friend because of the size of his house, and if he had felt it was necessary to impress you, he would have mentioned it some time ago. Do you know what his father does, because one thing's for sure, he doesn't sell life insurance."

"I think he's a banker."

"Tom Russell, of course. Russell's Bank," said his father as they pulled up in front of the house.

Tom was waiting on the top step to greet them. "Good afternoon, sir, how are you?" asked Tom as he opened the door on the driver's side.

"I'm well, thank you, Tom," replied Michael Cartwright as his son climbed out of the car, clinging to a small battered suitcase with the initials M. C. printed next to the lock.

"Would you care to join us for a drink, sir?"

"That's kind of you," said Nat's father, "but my wife will be expecting me back in time for supper, so I ought to be on my way."

Nat waved as his father circled the courtyard and began his return journey to Cromwell.

Nat looked up at the house to see a butler standing on the top step. He offered to take the suitcase, but Nat hung on to it as he was escorted up a magnificent wide circular staircase to the second floor, where he was shown into a guest bedroom. In Nat's home they only had one spare bedroom, which would have passed as a broom closet in this house. Once the butler had left him, Tom said, "When you've unpacked, come down and meet my mother. We'll be in the kitchen."

Nat sat at the end of one of the twin beds, painfully aware that he would never be able to invite Tom to stay with him.

It took Nat about three minutes to unpack as all he had were two shirts, one spare pair of trousers and a tie. He spent some considerable time checking out the bathroom before finally bouncing up and down on the bed. It was so springy. He waited for a couple more minutes before he left the room to stroll back down the wide staircase, wondering if he would ever be able to find the kitchen. The butler was waiting on the bottom step and escorted him along the corridor. Nat stole a quick glance into each room he passed.

"Hi," said Tom, "your room OK?"

"Yes, it's great," said Nat, aware that his friend was not being sarcastic.

"Mom, this is Nat. He's the cleverest boy in the class, damn him."

"Please don't swear, Tom," said Mrs. Russell. "Hello, Nat, how nice to meet you."

"Good evening, Mrs. Russell, it's nice to meet you too. What a lovely home you have."

"Thank you, Nat, and we were delighted that you were able to join us for a few days. Can I get you a Coke?"

"Yes, please."

A uniformed maid went straight to the fridge, took out a Coke and added some ice.

"Thank you," he repeated, as he watched the maid return to the sink and continue chopping potatoes. He thought of his mother back in Cromwell. She would also be chopping up potatoes, but only after a full day's teaching.

"Want me to show you around?" asked Tom.

"Sounds great," said Nat, "but can I make a phone call?"

"You don't need to, Diane's already called."

"She's already called?"

"Yea, she phoned this morning, to ask what time you'd be arriving. She begged me not to tell you, so I think we can assume she's interested."

"Then I'd better call her back immediately."

"No, that's the last thing you should do," said Tom.

"But I said I would."

"Yes, I know you did, but I think we'll walk around the grounds first."

—◦—

The next day at the Coulters', Tricia answered the door. She was dressed for a game of tennis.

"Is Diane home?" Nat asked.

"No, she's gone to some party at the Capitol with my parents. She should be back in about an hour. I'm Tricia, by the way. I spoke to you on the phone. I was just going to have a Coke. Want to join me?"

"Is your brother at home?"

"No, he's training down at the gym."

"Yes, please."

Tricia led Nat through to the kitchen and pointed toward a stool on the other side of the table. Nat sat down and didn't speak as Tricia pulled open the fridge door. As she bent over to remove two Cokes, her short skirt rose. Nat couldn't stop staring at her white tennis panties.

"What time are you expecting them back?" he asked as she added some ice cubes to his drink.

"No idea, so for the time being, you're stuck with me."

Nat sipped his drink, not sure what to say, because he thought he and Diana had agreed to see *To Kill a Mockingbird*.

Nat was sipping his Coke when he felt a hand on his thigh. He blushed, but made no attempt to remove it. Tricia smiled across the table at him. "You can put your hand on my leg if you want to." Nat thought she might consider him rude if he didn't comply, so he reached under the table and placed a hand on her thigh. "Good," she said as she sipped her Coke, "that's a little more friendly." Nat didn't comment as her hand moved farther up his newly pressed slacks. "Just follow my lead," she said. He moved his hand farther up her thigh, but came to a halt when he reached the hem of her skirt. Tricia didn't stop until she had reached his crotch.

"You've still got some way to go to catch up with me," Tricia said, as she began to undo the top button of his slacks. "Under the skirt, not over," she added, without any trace of mockery. He slipped his hand under her skirt as she continued to unbutton his slacks. He hesitated again when his fingers reached her panties. He couldn't remember anything in *Teen* magazine about what he was expected to do next.

9

WHEN FLETCHER'S MOTHER dropped him off at Senator and Mrs. Gates's home in East Hartford, it was Jimmy who answered the door.

"Now don't forget to always address Mr. Gates as Senator or sir."

"Yes, Mom."

"And don't bother him with too many questions."

"No, Mom."

"Remember that a conversation conducted by two people should be fifty percent talking and fifty percent listening."

"Yes, Mom."

"Hello, Mrs. Davenport, how are you?" asked Jimmy as he opened the door to greet them.

"I'm well, thank you, Jimmy, and you?"

"Just great. I'm afraid Mom and Dad are out at some function, but I could make you a cup of tea?"

"No thank you, I have to be back in time to chair a meeting of the Hospital Trust, but please remember to pass on my best wishes to your parents."

Jimmy carried one of Fletcher's suitcases up to the spare room. "I've put you next to me," he said, "which means we have to share the same bathroom."

Fletcher put his other suitcase on the bed, before studying the pictures on the walls—prints of the Civil War, just in case a southerner should come to stay and might have forgotten who won. They reminded Jimmy to ask Fletcher if he'd finished his essay on Lincoln.

"Yes, but have you found out Diane's phone number?"

"I've gone one better. I've discovered which coffee shop she goes to most afternoons. So I thought we might just drop in casually, say around five, and should that fail, my father has invited her parents to a reception at the Capitol tomorrow evening."

"But they might not come."

"I've checked the guest list, and they've accepted."

Fletcher suddenly remembered the trade-off he'd agreed on with the senator. "How far have you got with your homework?"

"Haven't even started," admitted Jimmy.

"Jimmy, if you don't get a pass grade next term, Mr. Haskins will put you on probation and then I won't be able to help."

"I know, but I'm also aware of the deal you struck with my father."

"Then if I'm to keep it, we'll have to start work first thing tomorrow. We'll begin by doing two hours every morning."

"Yes sir," said Jimmy, snapping to attention. "But before we worry about tomorrow, perhaps you should get changed," said Jimmy.

Fletcher had packed half a dozen shirts and a couple pairs of slacks, but still hadn't a clue what to wear on his first date. He was about to seek his friend's advice, when Jimmy said, "Once you've unpacked why don't you come down and join us in the living room? The bathroom's at the end of the hall."

Fletcher changed quickly into the shirt and slacks he'd bought the previous day at a local tailor his father had recommended. He checked himself in the long mirror. He had no idea how he looked, because he'd never taken any interest in clothes before. Act casual, look sharp, he'd heard a disc jockey telling his radio audience, but what did that mean? He'd worry about it later. As Fletcher walked downstairs, he could hear voices coming from the front room, one of which he didn't recognize.

"Mom, you remember Fletcher," Jimmy said as his friend strolled into the room.

"Yes, of course I do. My husband never stops telling everyone about the fascinating conversation the two of you had at the Taft game."

"That's kind of him to remember," said Fletcher, not looking at her.

"And I know he's looking forward to seeing you again."

"That's kind of him," said Fletcher a second time.

"And this is my kid sister, Annie," said Jimmy.

Annie blushed, and not only because she hated being described by Jimmy as his kid sister: his friend hadn't taken his eyes off her from the moment he'd walked into the room.

—◇—

"Good evening, Mrs. Coulter, how nice to meet you and your husband, and this must be your daughter Diane, if I remember correctly." Mr. and Mrs. Coulter were impressed because they had never met the senator before, and not only had their son scored the winning touchdown against Hotchkiss, but they were registered Republicans. "Now, Diane," continued the senator, "I have someone I want you to meet." Harry Gates's eyes swept the room searching for Fletcher, who had been standing by his side only a moment before. "Strange," he said, "but you mustn't leave without meeting him. Otherwise I won't have kept my end of the bargain," he added without explanation.

"Where's Fletcher disappeared off to?" Harry Gates asked his son once the Coulters had joined the other guests.

"If you can spot Annie, you won't find Fletcher behind; he hasn't left her side since he arrived in Hartford. In fact I'm thinking of buying him a dog leash and calling him Fletch."

"Is that right?" said the senator. "I hope he doesn't think that releases him from our deal."

"No, he doesn't," said Jimmy. "In fact we studied *Romeo and Juliet* for two hours this morning, and guess who he sees himself as."

The senator smiled. "And which part do you imagine fits your character?" he asked.

"I think I'm Mercutio."

"No," said Harry Gates, "you can only be Mercutio if he starts to chase Diane."

"I don't understand."

"Ask Fletcher. He'll explain it to you." Jimmy left his father to walk across and join his friend.

"I don't know what you see in her," said Jimmy.

"She's got everything you haven't," said Fletcher smiling. "She's bright, pretty, fun to be with and . . ."

"Are you sure we're talking about my sister?"

"Yes, which is why you're the one who has to wear glasses."

"By the way, Diane Coulter has just turned up with her parents. Dad wants to know if you're still hoping to meet her."

"Not particularly, she's gone from A to Z, so she's now a natural for you."

"No thanks," said Jimmy, "I don't need your cast-offs. By the way, I told Dad about *Romeo and Juliet,* and said I saw myself as Mercutio."

"Only if I start to date Dan Coulter's sister, but I'm no longer interested in the daughter of that house."

"I still don't understand."

"I'll explain tomorrow morning," said Fletcher, as Jimmy's sister reappeared carrying two Dr. Peppers. Annie scowled at her brother, and he quickly disappeared.

For some time, neither of them spoke, until Annie said, "Would you like me to show you the Senate Chamber?"

"Sure, that would be great," said Fletcher. She turned and began walking toward the door, with Fletcher following a pace behind.

"Do you see what I see?" said Harry Gates, turning to his wife as Fletcher and his daughter disappeared out of the room.

"I certainly do," replied Martha Gates, "but I shouldn't get too worried about it, as I doubt if either of them is capable of seducing the other."

"It didn't stop me trying at that age, as I feel sure you remember."

"Typical politician. That's another story you've embellished over the years. Because if I remember correctly, it was me who seduced you."

—◇—

"This is the Senate Chamber," said Annie as they looked down from the gallery onto a semicircle of blue leather chairs.

"It's very impressive," said Fletcher.

"Daddy says you'll end up here one day, or perhaps go even further." Fletcher didn't reply, because he had no idea what exams you had to pass to become a politician. "I heard him tell my mother he'd never met a more brilliant boy."

"Well, you know what they say about politicians," said Fletcher.

"Yes, I do, but I can always tell when Daddy doesn't mean it because he smiles at the same time, and this time he didn't smile."

"Where does your father sit?" asked Fletcher trying to change the subject.

"As the majority leader, he sits third along from the left in the front row," she said pointing down, "but I'd better not tell you too much because I know he's looking forward to showing you around the Capitol himself." He felt her hand touch his.

"Sorry," he said, quickly removing his hand, thinking it had been a mistake.

"Don't be silly," she said. She took his hand again, this time holding on to it.

"Don't you think we ought to go back and join the party?" asked Fletcher. "Otherwise they might start to wonder where we are."

"I suppose so," said Annie, but she didn't move. "Fletcher, have you ever kissed a girl?" she asked quietly.

"No, I haven't," he admitted, turning scarlet.

"Would you like to?"

"Yes, I would," he said.

"Would you like to kiss me?"

He nodded and then turned and watched as Annie closed her eyes and pursed her lips. He checked to make sure that all the doors were closed, before he leaned forward and kissed her gently on the mouth. Once he'd stopped, she opened her eyes.

"Do you know what a French kiss is?" she asked.

"No, I don't," said Fletcher.

"No, neither do I," admitted Annie. "If you find out, will you tell me?"

"Yes, I will," said Fletcher.

BOOK TWO

EXODUS

10

"ARE YOU GOING to run for president?" asked Jimmy.

"Haven't decided yet," Fletcher replied.

"Everyone assumes you will."

"That's one of the problems."

"My father wants you to."

"But my mother doesn't," said Fletcher.

"Why not?" asked Jimmy.

"She thinks I should spend my final year concentrating on getting a place at Yale."

"But if you become student president, it will only assist your application. It's me who's going to find it a struggle."

"I'm sure your father has several markers to call in," said Fletcher with a grin.

"What does Annie think?" asked Jimmy, ignoring the comment.

"She's happy to go along with whatever I decide."

"Then perhaps I should be the deciding factor."

"What do you have in mind?"

"If you hope to win, you'll have to appoint me as your campaign manager."

"That should certainly lengthen the odds," said Fletcher. Jimmy picked up a cushion from the sofa and threw it at his friend. "In fact, if you really want to guarantee my victory," added Fletcher as he caught it, "you should volunteer your services as campaign manager for my closest rival."

Their sparring was interrupted when Jimmy's father walked into the room. "Fletcher, could you spare me a moment?"

"Of course, sir."

"Perhaps we could have a chat in my study." Fletcher quickly rose and followed the senator out of the room. He looked back at Jimmy, but his friend just shrugged his shoulders. He wondered if he had done something wrong.

"Have a seat," said Harry Gates as he took his place behind the desk. He paused before he added, "Fletcher, I need a favor."

"Anything, sir. I'll never be able to repay you for all you've done for me."

"You've more than honored our agreement," said the senator. "For the past three years, Jimmy has somehow kept his place in the top stream, and he wouldn't have had a prayer without your continued vigilance."

"That's kind of you to say so, but . . ."

"It's no more than the truth, but all I want for the boy now is to see that he has a fair shot at getting into Yale."

"But how can I help when I'm not even certain of a place myself?"

The senator ignored the comment. "Pork barrel politics, my boy."

"I'm not sure I understand, sir."

"If you become student government president, as I'm confident you will, the first thing you'll have to do is appoint a vice-president." Fletcher nodded. "And that could just tip the balance for Jimmy when the admissions office at Yale decides who gets those last few places."

"And it's just tipped the balance for me, sir."

"Thank you, Fletcher, I appreciate that, but please don't let Jimmy know that we've had this conversation."

As soon as he woke the following morning, Fletcher went next door and sat on the end of Jimmy's bed. "This had better be good," said Jimmy, "because I was dreaming about Daisy Hollingsworth."

"Dream on," said Fletcher, "half the football team are in love with her."

"So why did you wake me?"

"I've decided to run for president, and I don't need a campaign manager who lies in bed all morning."

"Was it something my father said?"

"Indirectly." He paused. "So who do you think will be my main rival?"

"Steve Rodgers," said Jimmy without hesitation.

"Why Steve?"

"He's a three-letter man, so they'll try to run him as the popular jock up against the austere academic. You know, Kennedy against Stevenson."

"I had no idea you knew what the word austere meant."

"No more jokes, Fletcher," said Jimmy as he rolled off the bed. "If you're going to beat Rodgers, you'll have to be prepared for anything and everything they throw at you. I think we ought to begin by having a breakfast meeting with Dad; he always has breakfast meetings before he starts a campaign."

◆

"I lost my first campaign," said Senator Gates, when he heard Fletcher's news, "so let's be sure that you don't make the same mistakes. For a start, who's your campaign manager?"

"Jimmy, of course."

"Never 'of course'; only select someone who you are convinced can do the job, even if you're not close friends."

"I'm convinced he can do the job," said Fletcher.

"Good. Now, Jimmy, you will be of no value to the candidate"— it was the first time Fletcher thought of himself as the candidate— "unless you're always open and frank with Fletcher, however unpleasant it might be." Jimmy nodded. "Who's your main rival?"

"Steve Rodgers."

"What do we know about him?"

"A nice enough guy, but not a lot between his ears," said Jimmy.

"Except a good-looking face," said Fletcher.

"And several touchdowns last season, if I remember correctly," added the senator. "So now we know who the enemy is, let's start working on our friends. First, you must pick an inner circle—six, eight at most. They only need two qualities, energy and loyalty— if they've got brains as well, that's a bonus. How long is the campaign?"

"Just over a week. School reassembles at nine o'clock on Monday, and the vote takes place on the Tuesday morning of the following week."

"Don't think week," said the senator, "think hours, 192 of them, because every hour will count."

Jimmy began making notes.

"So who's allowed to vote?" was the senator's next question.

"Every student."

"Then make sure you spend as much time with the boys in the lower grades as with your contemporaries. They'll be flattered that you're taking so much interest in them. And, Jimmy, get your hands on an up-to-date list of the voters, so that you can be certain to make contact with every one of them before election day. And don't forget, new boys will vote for the last person who speaks to them."

"There are 380 students," said Jimmy, unfolding a large sheet of paper on the floor, "I've marked the ones we already know in red, everyone I feel confident will support Fletcher in blue, new boys in yellow and left the rest blank."

"And if you're in any doubt," said the senator, "leave them blank, and don't forget younger brothers."

"Younger brothers?" said Fletcher.

"I've marked them in green," said Jimmy. "Every one of our supporters who has a brother in a lower grade will be appointed a rep. Their only job will be signing up support in their class and reporting back to their brothers."

Fletcher looked on with admiration. "I'm not sure it shouldn't be you who's running for president," he said. "You're a natural."

"No, I'm a natural campaign manager," said Jimmy, "it's you who should be president."

Although the senator agreed with his son's assessment, he didn't offer an opinion.

—◦—

"How do you think it's going?" asked Fletcher as they walked around the lake.

"Can't be sure," Jimmy replied. "A lot of the upper-mids are telling both camps that they'll be supporting their candidate, simply because they want to be seen backing the winner. Just be thankful that the vote isn't on Saturday evening," Jimmy added.

"Why?" asked Fletcher.

"Because we play Kent on Saturday afternoon, and if Steve Rodgers scores the winning touchdown, we could kiss goodbye to any chance of you becoming president. It's just a pity it's a home game. If you'd been born a year earlier or a year later, it would have been an away match, and the impact would have been negligible. But as it is, every voter will be in the stadium watching the encounter, so pray we lose, or at least that Rodgers has a bad game."

By two o'clock on Saturday, Fletcher was seated in the stand, prepared for four quarters that would make up the longest hour of his life. But even he couldn't have predicted the outcome.

―◦―

"I'm not sure how it will affect the vote," said Jimmy, as the two of them ran toward the exit to join up with the rest of the team. "At least Steve Rodgers can't shake hands with everyone as they leave the stadium."

"I wonder how long he'll be in the hospital." Fletcher said.

"Three days is all we need," said Jimmy. Fletcher laughed.

Fletcher was delighted to find that his team were already well spread out by the time he joined them, and several boys came up to say they would be supporting him, although it still felt close. He never moved beyond the main exit as he continued to shake hands with any boy over the age of fourteen and under the age of eighteen, including, he suspected, a few supporters from the visiting team. Fletcher and Jimmy didn't leave until they were sure the stadium was empty of everyone except the groundsmen.

As they walked back to their rooms, Jimmy admitted that no one could have predicted a tie, or that Rodgers would have been on his way to the local hospital before the end of the first quarter. "If the vote was tonight he'd win on sympathy. If no one sees him again before Tuesday at nine o'clock, you'll be the president."

"Doesn't ability to do the job come into the equation?"

"Of course not, you fool," said Jimmy. "This is politics."

Fletcher was invited to read the lesson in chapel that Sunday morning, making it abundantly clear who the principal would have voted for. During lunch, he and Jimmy visited every dorm, to ask the boys how they felt about the food. "A sure vote winner," the senator had assured them, "even if you can't do anything about it." That evening, they climbed into bed exhausted. Jimmy set the alarm for five thirty. Fletcher groaned.

"A master stroke," said Jimmy as they stood outside assembly the following morning waiting for the boys to go off to their classrooms.

"Brilliant," admitted Fletcher.

"I'm afraid so," said Jimmy. "Not that I can complain, because I would have recommended that you do exactly the same thing, given the circumstances."

The two of them stared across at Steve Rodgers, who was standing on crutches by the exit to the hall allowing the boys to sign their autographs on his plastered leg.

"A master stroke," repeated Jimmy. "It brings a new meaning to the sympathy vote. Perhaps we should ask the question, do you want a cripple for president?"

"One of the greatest Presidents in the history of this country was a cripple," Fletcher reminded his campaign manager.

"Then there's only one thing for it," said Jimmy, "you'll have to spend the next twenty-four hours in a wheelchair."

Although everyone knew the result wouldn't be announced until nine o'clock, the assembly hall was packed long before the principal made his entrance.

Fletcher sat in the back row, with his head bowed, while Jimmy stared directly in front of him. "I should have got up earlier every morning," said Fletcher.

"I should have broken your leg," Jimmy responded.

The principal, accompanied by the chaplain, marched down the aisle as if to show God was somehow involved in who became president of student government at Hotchkiss. The principal walked to the front of the stage and cleared his throat.

"The result of the election for student government president," said Mr. Fleming, "is Fletcher Davenport 207 votes, Steve Rodgers 173 votes. I therefore declare Fletcher Davenport to be the new president."

Fletcher immediately walked across and shook hands with Steve, who smiled warmly, looking almost relieved. Fletcher turned around to see Harry Gates standing by the door. The senator bowed respectfully to the new president.

"You never forget your first election victory," was all he said.

They both ignored Jimmy, who was leaping up and down, unable to contain himself.

"I believe you know my vice-president, sir," Fletcher replied.

◄○►

"Will anyone bother to stand against you?" asked Diane Coulter.

"No one I can't beat."

"What about Nat Cartwright?"

"Not while it's known that he's the principal's favorite, and if elected will simply carry out his wishes; at least that's what my supporters are telling everyone."

"And don't let's forget the way he treated my sister."

"I thought it was you who dumped him? I didn't even realize he knew your sister."

"He didn't, but that didn't stop him trying to make a move on her when he came around to the house to see me."

"Does anyone else know about this?"

"Yes, my brother Dan. He caught him in the kitchen with his hand up her skirt. My sister complained bitterly she just couldn't stop him."

"Did she?" He paused. "Do you think your brother would be willing to back me for president?"

"Yes, but there's not much he can do while he's at Princeton."

"Oh yes there is," said Elliot. "To start with . . ."

◄○►

"Who's my main rival?" asked Nat.

"Ralph Elliot, who else?" said Tom. "He's been working on his campaign since the beginning of last term."

"But that's against the rules."

"I don't think Elliot has ever cared much about rules, and as he knows you're far more popular than he is, we can look forward to a dirty campaign."

"But I'm not going down that road . . ."

"So we'll have to take the Kennedy route."

"What do you have in mind?"

"You should open your campaign by challenging Elliot to a debate."

"He'll never accept."

"Then you win either way. If he does accept, you'll wipe the floor with him. If he doesn't, we can play the 'he flunked it' card."

"So how would you set up such a challenge?"

"Send him a letter, a copy of which I'll post on the bulletin board."

"But you're not allowed to post notices without the principal's permission."

"By the time they take it down, most people will have read it, and those that haven't will want to know what it said."

"And by then I'll have been disqualified."

"Not while the principal thinks Elliot might win."

It was six thirty on the first day of term when Nat and Tom stood alone in the parking lot. The first vehicle to come through the gates was the principal's.

"Good morning, Cartwright," he barked, as he climbed out of his car, "from your excess of enthusiasm at this early hour, am I to assume that you're running for president?"

"Yes, sir."

"Excellent, and who is your main rival?"

"Ralph Elliot."

The principal frowned. "Then it will be a fiercely fought competition, because Elliot won't roll over easily."

"True," admitted Tom as the principal disappeared toward his study, leaving the two of them to greet the second car. The occupant turned out to be a terrified new boy, who ran away when Nat approached him, and worse, the third car was full of Elliot supporters, who quickly fanned across the parking lot, obviously having already been through a dress rehearsal.

"Damn," said Tom, "our first team meeting isn't scheduled until the ten o'clock break. Elliot obviously briefed his team during the vacation."

"Don't worry," said Nat, "just grab our people as they get out of their cars, and put them to work immediately."

By the time the last car had disgorged its occupants, Nat had answered nearly a hundred questions and shaken hands with over three hundred boys, but only one fact became clear. Elliot was happy to promise them anything in exchange for their vote.

"Shouldn't we be letting everyone know what a sleaze-bag Elliot really is?"

"What do you have in mind?" Nat asked.

"How he cajoles new boys into parting with their allowances?"

"There's never been any proof."

"Just endless complaints."

"If there's that many, they'll know where to put their cross, won't they," said Nat. "In any case, that's not the sort of campaign I want to run," he added. "I'd prefer to assume the voters can make up their own minds which one of us can be trusted."

"That's an original idea," said Tom.

"Well, at least the principal is making it clear that he doesn't want Elliot to be president," said Nat.

"I don't think we should tell anyone that," said Tom. "It may well swing a few more votes to Elliot."

◄○►

"Damn, how did he manage to pull that off?" growled Nat.

"Bribery and corruption would be my bet," said Jimmy. "Elliot has always been a useful player, but never good enough to make the school team."

"Do you think they'll risk putting him in the game?"

"Why not? St. George's often fields a weak side, so they could leave him out there for a few minutes once they're confident it won't affect the result. Then Elliot will spend the rest of the game running up and down the sidelines, waving at the voters, while all we can do is stare down at him from the bleachers."

"Then let's make sure all our workers are in position outside the stadium a few minutes before the game ends, and don't let anyone see our new hand-held placards until Saturday afternoon. That way Elliot won't have time to come up with his own."

"You're learning fast," said Tom.

"When Elliot's your opponent, you're not left with a lot of choice."

When Nat arrived at the game, his placards were to be seen everywhere, and all that the Elliot supporters could do was cry foul play. Nat and Tom couldn't hide their smiles as they took their places in the bleachers. The smiles broadened when St. George's scored early in the first quarter. Nat didn't want Taft to lose, but no coach was going to risk putting Elliot on the field while St. George's remained in the lead. And that didn't change until the final quarter.

Nat shook hands with everyone as they left the stadium, but he knew that Taft's last-minute victory over St. George's hadn't helped his cause, even if Elliot had only been able to run up and down the sideline until the last person had left the bleachers.

"Just be thankful he never got into the game," said Tom.

Over the final weekend, Nat's workers tried to project an air of confidence, even though they realized it was too close to call. Neither candidate stopped smiling, until Monday evening when the school bell struck six.

"Let's go back to my room," said Tom, "and tell stories of the death of kings."

"Sad stories," said Nat.

The team all crowded into Tom's little room and swapped anecdotes of the roles they had played in the campaign, and laughed at jokes that weren't funny, as they waited impatiently to learn the result.

A loud rap on the door interrupted their noisy exuberance. "Come in," called Tom.

They all stood up the moment they saw who it was standing in the doorway.

"Good evening, Mr. Anderson," said Nat.

"Good evening, Cartwright," replied the dean of students formally. "As the returning officer in the election for president of student government, I have to inform you that due to the closeness of the result, I will be calling for a recount. Assembly has therefore been postponed until eight o'clock."

"Thank you, sir," was all Nat could think of saying.

When eight o'clock had struck every boy was seated in his place. They rose dutifully when the dean of students entered the hall. Nat tried to read any sign of the result from the expression on his face, but even the Japanese would have been proud of Mr. Anderson's inscrutability.

The dean walked to the center of the stage and invited the assembly to be seated. There was a hush, rarely experienced at a normal gathering.

"I must tell you," began the dean, "that this was the closest result in the school's seventy-five-year history." Nat could feel the palms of his hands sweating, as he tried to remain calm. "The voting for president of student council was Nat Cartwright, 178, Ralph Elliot, 181."

Half the gathering leaped to their feet and cheered, while the other half remained seated and silent. Nat rose from his place, walked across to Elliot and offered his outstretched hand.

The new president ignored it.

11

Nat's mother seemed to be one of the few people who wasn't disappointed that her son hadn't been elected president. She felt it would give him more time to concentrate on his work. And if Susan Cartwright could have seen the hours Nathaniel was putting in, she would have stopped worrying. Even Tom found it difficult to pry Nat away from his books for more than a few minutes, unless it was to go on his daily five-mile run. And even when he broke the school cross-country record, Nat only allowed himself a couple of hours off to celebrate.

Christmas Eve, Christmas Day, New Year's Eve—it made no difference. Nat remained in his room, head buried in his books. His mother only hoped that when he left to spend a long weekend in Simsbury with Tom, he would take a real break. He did. Nat cut his workload down to two hours in the morning and another two in the afternoon. Tom was grateful that his friend kept him to the same routine, even if he declined the invitation to join him for his daily run. It amused Nat that he could complete the five miles without ever leaving Tom's estate.

"One of your many sweethearts?" asked Nat over breakfast the following morning as his friend tore open a letter.

"I only wish," said Tom. "No, it's from Mr. Thompson asking if I want to be considered for a part in *Twelfth Night*."

"And do you?" asked Nat.

"No. It's more your world than mine. I'm a producer by nature, not a performer."

"I would have put my name down for a part if I was confident about my Yale application, but I haven't even completed my independent study."

"I haven't even started mine," admitted Tom.

"Which of the five subjects did you select?" asked Nat.

"Control of the lower Mississippi during the Civil War," replied Tom. "And you?"

"Clarence Darrow and his influence on the trade union movement."

"Yeah, I considered Mr. Darrow, but wasn't sure I could manage five thousand words on the subject. No doubt you've already written ten."

"No, but I've almost finished a first draft, and should have a final copy ready by the time we return in January."

"Yale's deadline isn't until February; you really ought to consider taking a part in the school play. At least read for the audition. After all, it doesn't have to be the lead."

Nat thought about his friend's suggestion as he buttered himself a piece of toast. Tom was right, of course, but Nat felt it would be just another distraction if he was hoping to win a scholarship to Yale. He glanced out of the window across acres of land and wondered what it must be like to have parents who didn't have to worry about tuition payments, pocket money, and whether he could get a holiday job during the summer vacation.

—◦—

"Do you wish to read for any particular role, Nat?" asked Mr. Thompson as he stared up at the six-foot-two boy with a mop of black hair, whose trousers always seemed to be a couple of inches too short.

"Antonio, possibly Orsino," replied Nat.

"You're a natural Orsino," said Mr. Thompson, "but I have your friend, Tom Russell, in mind for that part."

"I'm hardly Malvolio," said Nat with a laugh.

"No, Elliot would be my first choice for Malvolio," said Thompson with a wry smile. Mr. Thompson, like so many others at Taft, wished Nat had become the student government president. "But sadly he's not available, whereas in truth, you are best suited for the role of Sebastian."

Nat wanted to protest, although when he first read the script he had to admit he thought the part would be a challenge. However, its sheer length would demand hours of learning, not to mention time spent in rehearsals. Mr. Thompson sensed Nat's reservations. "I think the time has come for a little bribery, Nat."

"Bribery, sir?"

"Yes, my boy. You see the admissions director at Yale is one of my oldest friends. We studied classics together at Princeton, and he always spends a weekend with me every year. I think I'll make it the weekend of the school play," he paused, "that is, if you feel able to play Sebastian." Nat didn't respond. "Ah, I see bribery is not enough for someone of your high moral standards, so I shall have to stoop to corruption."

"Corruption, sir?" said Nat.

"Yes, Nat, corruption. You will have observed that there are three parts in the play for females—the fair Olivia, your twin Viola, and the feisty Maria, not to mention understudies and maid-servants, and don't let's forget that they all fall in love with Sebastian." Nat still didn't respond. "And," continued Mr. Thompson, revealing his trump card, "my opposite number at Miss Porter's has suggested that I should take a boy over on Saturday to read the male parts while we decide who should audition for the females." He paused again. "Ah, I see I have finally caught your attention."

—◇—

"Do you believe it's possible to spend your whole life loving only one person?" Annie asked.

"If you're lucky enough to find the right person, why not?" responded Fletcher.

"I suspect that when you go to Yale in the fall you'll be surrounded by so many bright and beautiful women, I'll pale by comparison."

"Not a chance," said Fletcher. He sat down next to her on the sofa and put an arm around her shoulder. "And in any case, they'll quickly discover that I'm in love with somebody else, and once you're at Vassar, they'll discover why."

"But that won't be for another year," said Annie, "and by then . . ."

"Shh . . . haven't you noticed that every man who meets you is immediately jealous of me?"

"No, I haven't," she replied honestly.

Fletcher turned to look at the girl he'd fallen in love with when she'd had a flat chest and braces on her teeth. But even then he couldn't resist that smile, her black hair, inherited from an Irish grandmother, and steel-blue eyes from the Swedish side of the family. But now, four years later, time had added a slim, graceful figure and legs that made Fletcher grateful for the new fashion of mini skirts.

Annie put a hand on Fletcher's thigh, "Do you realize that half the girls in my class are no longer virgins?" she said.

"So Jimmy tells me," said Fletcher.

"And he should know." Annie paused, "I'm seventeen next month, and you've never once suggested . . ."

"I've thought about it many times, of course I have," said Fletcher as she moved her body so that his hand touched her breast, "but when it happens, I want it to be right for both of us and for there never to be any regrets."

Annie nestled her head in his shoulder. "For me there wouldn't be any regrets," she said, placing a hand on his leg.

He took her in his arms. "When are you expecting your parents back?"

"Around midnight. They're attending another of those never-ending functions politicians seem to thrive on."

Fletcher didn't move as Annie began to unbutton her blouse. When she reached the last button, she slipped it off and let it fall to the floor. "Your turn I think," she said. Fletcher quickly unbuttoned his shirt and cast it aside. Annie stood up and faced him, amused by the sudden power she seemed to have over him. She unzipped her skirt slowly in the way she had seen Julie Christie do in *Darling*. Like Miss Christie, she hadn't bothered with a petticoat. "Your turn I think," she said again.

Oh my God, thought Fletcher, I daren't take off my trousers. He slipped off his shoes and socks.

"That's cheating," said Annie, who had removed her shoes even before Fletcher knew what she had in mind. He reluctantly pulled down his trousers, and she burst out laughing. Fletcher blushed as he looked down at his pants.

"It's good to know I can do that to you," said Annie.

"Would it be possible for you to concentrate on the words, Nat?" asked Mr. Thompson, not attempting to disguise his sarcasm. "Take it from *'But here the lady comes.'*"

Even dressed in her school uniform, Rebecca stood out from the rest of the girls Mr. Thompson was auditioning. The tall, slim girl with fair hair cascading down her shoulders had an air of self-confidence that captivated Nat, and a smile that made him respond immediately. When she returned his smile, he turned away, embarrassed to have embarrassed her. All he knew about her was her name. *"What's in a name,"* he said.

"Wrong play Nat, try again."

Rebecca Armitage waited as Nat stumbled through his words, *"But here the lady comes . . ."* Rebecca was surprised because when she'd stood at the back of the hall and heard him earlier, he had sounded so totally self-assured. She looked down at her script and read, *"Blame not this haste of mine. If you mean well, now go with me and with this holy man into the chantry by: there, before him, and underneath that consecrated roof, plight me the full assurance of your faith; that my most jealous and too doubtful soul may live at peace. He shall conceal it while you are willing it shall come to note, what time we will our celebration keep according to my birth. What do you say?"*

Nat said nothing.

"Nat, had you thought of joining in?" suggested Mr. Thompson. "So that Rebecca can at least deliver a few more lines? I admit that the adoring look is most effective, and for some might pass as acting, but this is not a mime we're performing. One or two of the audience might even have come to hear the familiar words of Mr. Shakespeare."

"Yes, sir, sorry sir," said Nat, returning to the script. *"I'll follow this good man, and go with you; and having sworn truth, ever will be true."*

"Then lead the way, good father; and heavens so shine, that they may fairly note this act of mine."

"Thank you, Miss Armitage, I don't think I need to hear any more."

"But she was wonderful," said Nat.

"Ah, you can deliver an entire line without pausing," said Mr.

Thompson. "That's a relief to discover at this late stage, but then I had no idea you wanted to be the director as well as play the lead. However, Nat, I think I have already made up my mind who will play the fair Olivia."

Nat watched Rebecca as she quickly left the stage. "Then what about Viola?" he persisted.

"No, if I've understood the plot correctly, Nat, Viola is your twin sister, and unfortunately or fortunately Rebecca bears absolutely no resemblance to you."

"Then Maria, she'd make a wonderful Maria."

"I'm sure she would, but Rebecca is far too tall to play Maria."

"Have you thought of playing Feste as a woman?" asked Nat.

"No, to be honest, Nat, I hadn't, partly because I don't have the time to rewrite the entire script."

Nat didn't notice Rebecca slip behind a pillar, trying to hide her embarrassment as he blundered on. "What about the maid-servant in Olivia's household?"

"What about her?"

"Rebecca would make a wonderful maidservant."

"I'm sure she would, but she can't play Olivia and be her maid-servant at the same time. Someone in the audience might notice." Nat opened his mouth but didn't speak. "Ah, silence at last, but I feel confident that you will be rewriting the play overnight, in order to ensure that Olivia has several new scenes with Sebastian that Mr. Shakespeare hadn't even considered." Nat heard a giggle from behind the pillar. "Anyone else you fancy for the maidser-vant, Nat, or can I carry on with casting the play?"

"Sorry, sir," said Nat. "Sorry."

Mr. Thompson leaped onto the stage, smiled at Nat and whis-pered, "If you were considering playing hard to get, Nat, I'm bound to say I think you've blown it. You've made yourself more available than a whore in a Las Vegas casino. And I feel sure you'll be interested to learn that next year's play will be *The Taming of the Shrew,* which I feel might have been more appropriate. If only you'd been born a year later, how different your life would have been. However, good luck with Miss Armitage."

"The boy must be expelled," said Mr. Fleming. "No other punishment would be appropriate."

"But, sir," said Fletcher, "Pearson is only fifteen, and he apologized to Mrs. Appleyard immediately."

"I would have expected nothing less," said the chaplain, who until that moment had not offered an opinion.

"And in any case," said the principal, rising from behind his desk, "can you imagine the effect on school discipline if it became known that you could get away with swearing at a master's wife?"

"And because of the words, 'bitchy woman,' the boy's entire future is to be determined?"

"That's the consequence of such ill manners," said the principal, "and at least, this way, one can be certain he'll learn from it."

"But what will he learn?" asked Fletcher. "That you can never afford to make a mistake in life, or that you must never swear?"

"Why are you defending the boy so vehemently?"

"In the first lecture I ever heard you deliver, sir, you told us that not to stand up and be counted when an injustice had been done was the act of a coward."

Mr. Fleming glanced at the chaplain, who made no comment. He remembered the lecture well. After all he delivered the same text to every new entering class.

"May I be allowed to ask you an impertinent question?" asked Fletcher, turning to face the chaplain.

"Yes," said Dr. Wade a little defensively.

"Have you ever wanted to swear at Mrs. Appleyard, because I have, several times."

"But that's the point, Fletcher, you showed some self-restraint. Pearson didn't, and therefore he must be punished."

"If that punishment is to be expulsion, sir, then I must resign as president of the student government, Principal, because the Bible tells us that the thought is as evil as the deed."

Both men stared at him in disbelief. "But why, Fletcher? Surely you realize that if you were to resign it could even affect your chances of being offered a place at Yale?"

"The type of person who would allow that to influence him isn't worthy of a place at Yale."

Both men were so stunned by this remark that neither spoke for some time. "Isn't that a bit extreme, Fletcher?" the chaplain eventually managed.

"Not for the boy in question it isn't, Dr. Wade, and I am not willing to stand and watch this student sacrificed on the altar of a woman who gets her kicks from goading pubescent boys."

"And you would resign as president to prove your point?" asked the principal.

"Not to do it, sir, would be only one step away from what your generation condoned at the time of McCarthy."

Another long silence followed, before the chaplain said quietly, "Did the boy apologize in person to Mrs. Appleyard?"

"Yes, sir," said Fletcher, "and he followed it up with a letter."

"Then perhaps probation for the remainder of the term would be more appropriate," suggested the principal, glancing at the chaplain.

"Along with the loss of all privileges, including weekend leaves, until further notice," added Dr. Wade.

"Does that seem to you a fair compromise, Fletcher?" asked the principal, raising an eyebrow.

It was Fletcher's turn to remain silent. "Compromise, Fletcher," interjected the chaplain, "is something you will have to learn to live with if you hope to become a successful politician."

Fletcher didn't respond immediately. "I accept your judgment, Dr. Wade," he eventually said, and, turning to the principal, added, "and thank you for your indulgence, sir."

"Thank you, Fletcher," said Mr. Fleming as the student president rose from his place and left the principal's study.

"Wisdom, courage and conviction are rare enough in a grown man," said the principal quietly as the door closed, "but in a child . . ."

—◦—

"Then what *is* your explanation, Mr. Cartwright?" asked the dean of Yale's examination board.

"I don't have one, sir," Nat admitted. "It must be a coincidence."

"It's quite a coincidence," said the dean of academic affairs, "that large sections of your paper on Clarence Darrow are word for word identical to those of another student in your class."

"And what's his explanation?"

"As he submitted his independent study a week before yours, and it was hand-written, while yours was typed, we haven't felt it necessary to ask him for an explanation."

"Would his name be Ralph Elliot, by any chance?" asked Nat.

No one on the board commented.

"How did he manage it?" asked Tom, when Nat returned to Taft later that evening.

"He must have copied it out word for word while I was over at Miss Porter's rehearsing for *Twelfth Night.*"

"But he still had to remove the thesis from your room."

"That wouldn't have been difficult," said Nat. "If it wasn't on my desk, he would have found it filed under Yale."

"But he still took a hell of a risk going into your room when you weren't there."

"Not when you're the student president; he has the run of the place—no one questions his coming or going. He would easily have had enough time to copy out the text and return the original to my room the same evening without anyone being any the wiser."

"So what have the board decided?"

"Thanks to the principal going overboard on my behalf, Yale has agreed to defer my application for a year."

"So Elliot gets away with it once again."

"No, he does not," said Nat finally. "The principal worked out what must have happened, because Yale has also withdrawn Elliot's place."

"But that only delays the problem for a year," said Tom.

"Happily not," said Nat, smiling for the first time. "Mr. Thompson also decided to step in, and rang the admissions tutor, with the result that Yale has not offered Elliot the chance to reapply."

"Good old Thomo," said Tom. "So what are you planning to do in your year? Join the Peace Corps?"

"No, I'm going to spend the year at the University of Connecticut."

"Why UConn?" asked Tom, "when you could . . ."

"Because it was Rebecca's first choice."

12

THE PRESIDENT OF Yale stared down at a thousand expectant freshmen. In a year's time, some of them would have found the going too tough and moved on to other universities, while others would have simply given up. Fletcher Davenport and Jimmy Gates sat in the body of the hall and listened intently to every word President Waterman had to say.

"Do not waste a moment of your time while you are at Yale, or you will regret for the rest of your life not having taken advantage of all this university has to offer. A fool leaves Yale with only a degree, a wise man with enough knowledge to face whatever life throws at him. Seize every opportunity that is offered to you. Do not be frightened of any new challenge, and should you fail, there is no reason to be ashamed. You will learn far more from your mistakes than from your triumphs. Do not be afraid of your destiny. Be afraid of nothing. Challenge every writ, and let it not be said of you, I walked a path but never left an imprint."

The president of Yale resumed his place after nearly an hour on his feet, and received a prolonged standing ovation. Trent Waterman, who did not approve of such displays, rose and left the stage.

"I thought you weren't going to join in the standing ovation?" said Fletcher to his friend as they filed out of the hall. "'Just because everyone else has for the past ten years, doesn't mean I shall join in the ritual,' if I remember your sentiments correctly."

"I admit it, I was wrong," said Jimmy. "It was even more impressive than my father had assured me it would be."

"I feel confident your endorsement will come as a relief to Mr.

Waterman," said Fletcher, as Jimmy spotted a young woman laden with books walking a few paces ahead of them.

"Seize every opportunity," he whispered in Fletcher's ear. Fletcher wondered whether to stop Jimmy making a complete fool of himself, or just let him find out the hard way.

"Hi, I'm Jimmy Gates. Would you like me to help you with your books?"

"What did you have in mind, Mr. Gates? Carrying them, or reading them to me?" replied the woman, who didn't break her stride.

"I was thinking of carrying them to begin with, and then why don't we see how it goes from there?"

"Mr. Gates, I have two rules I never break: dating a freshman and dating someone with red hair."

"Don't you think the time has come," said Jimmy, "to break them both at once? After all, the president did tell us to never be frightened of a new challenge."

"Jimmy," said Fletcher, "I think . . ."

"Ah yes, this is my friend Fletcher Davenport, he's very clever, so he could help you with the reading part."

"I don't think so, Jimmy."

"And he's also very modest, as you can see."

"Not a problem you suffer from, Mr. Gates."

"Certainly not," said Jimmy. "By the way, what's your name?"

"Joanna Palmer."

"So you're obviously not a freshman, Joanna," said Jimmy.

"No, I'm not."

"Then you're the ideal person to help and succor me."

"What do you have in mind?" asked Miss Palmer, as they climbed the steps to Sudler Hall.

"Why don't you invite me to supper this evening, and then you can tell me everything I should know about Yale," ventured Jimmy just as they came to a halt outside the lecture hall. "Hey," he said, turning to Fletcher, "isn't this where we're meant to be?"

"Yes, it is, and I did try to warn you."

"Warn me? About what?" asked Jimmy, as he opened the door for Miss Palmer and followed her into the room, hoping he could sit next to her. The undergraduates immediately stopped talking, which took Jimmy by surprise.

"I apologize for my friend, Miss Palmer," whispered Fletcher, "but I can assure you he has a heart of gold."

"And the balls to go with it, it would seem," Joanna replied. "By the way, never let him know, but I was extremely flattered that he thought I might be a freshman."

Joanna Palmer placed her books on the long desk and turned to face the packed lecture theater. "The French Revolution is the turning point of modern European history," she began to a rapt audience. "Although America had already removed a monarch," she paused, "without having to remove his head . . ." Her eyes swept the tiered benches as her pupils laughed, before coming to rest on Jimmy Gates. He winked.

—◦—

They held hands as they walked across the campus to their first lecture. They had become friends during the rehearsals of the play, inseparable in the week of the performance, and had both lost their virginity together during spring vacation. When Nat told his lover that he would not be going to Yale, but joining her at the University of Connecticut, Rebecca felt guilty about how happy the news made her.

Susan and Michael Cartwright liked Rebecca the moment they met her, and their disappointment over Nat not being offered an immediate place at Yale was softened by seeing their son so relaxed for the first time in his life.

The opening lecture in Buckley Hall was on the subject of American literature, and delivered by Professor Hayman. During the summer vacation, Nat and Rebecca had read all the authors on the assigned list—James, Steinbeck, Hemingway, Fitzgerald and Bellow—and then discussed in detail *Washington Square, The Grapes of Wrath, For Whom the Bell Tolls, The Great Gatsby,* and *Herzog.* So by the time they took their places in the lecture theater that Tuesday morning, they both felt confident they were well prepared. Within moments of Professor Hayman delivering his opening salvo, they both realized that they had done little more than read the texts. They had not considered the different influences on the authors that birth, upbringing, education, religion and mere circumstance had brought to their work, nor given any thought to the fact that the gift of storytelling was not bestowed on any particular class, color or creed.

"Take, for example, Scott Fitzgerald," continued the professor, in his short story, 'Bernice Bobs Her Hair.'"

Nat looked up from his notes and saw the back of his head. He felt sick. He stopped listening to Professor Hayman's views on Fitzgerald and continued to stare for some time before the student turned and began talking to his neighbor. Nat's worst fears were confirmed. Ralph Elliot was not only at the same university, but taking the same course. Almost as if conscious of being stared at, Elliot suddenly turned around. He didn't acknowledge Nat, as his attention settled on Rebecca. Nat glanced across at her, but she was too busy taking notes on Fitzgerald's drinking problems during his time in Hollywood to register Elliot's unsubtle interest.

Nat waited until Elliot had left the lecture theater before he collected his books and rose from his place.

"Who was that who kept turning around and staring at you?" asked Rebecca, as they strolled over to the dining hall.

"His name's Ralph Elliot," said Nat. "We were both at Taft, and I think he was staring at you, not me."

"He's very good looking," said Rebecca with a grin. "He reminds me a little of Jay Gatsby. Is he the one Mr. Thompson thought would make a good Malvolio?"

"A natural, I think were Thomo's exact words."

Over lunch, Rebecca pressed Nat to tell her more about Elliot, but he said that there wasn't that much to tell, and continually tried to change the subject. If enjoying Rebecca's company also meant having to be at the same university as Ralph Elliot, it was something he'd learn to live with.

Elliot didn't attend the afternoon lecture on the Spanish influence over the colonies, and by the time Nat accompanied Rebecca back to her room that evening, he had almost forgotten the unwelcome presence of his old rival.

The women's dorms were on south campus, and Nat's freshman

advisor had warned him that it was against the regulations for men to be found in residence after dark.

"Whoever fixed the regulations," said Nat, as he lay next to Rebecca on her single bed, "must have thought that students could only make love in the dark." Rebecca laughed as she pulled her sweater back on.

"Which means that during the spring semester you won't have to go back to your room until after nine o'clock," she said.

"Perhaps the regulations will allow me to stay with you after the spring semester," said Nat without explanation.

During his first term, Nat was relieved to discover that he rarely came into contact with Ralph Elliot. His rival showed no interest in cross-country running, acting or music, so it came as a surprise when Nat found him chatting to Rebecca outside the chapel on the last Sunday of the term. Elliot quickly walked away the moment he saw Nat approaching them.

"What did he want?" asked Nat defensively.

"Just going over his ideas to improve the student council. He's running as the freshman representative, and wanted to know if you were thinking of putting your name forward."

"No, I'm not," said Nat firmly. "I've had enough of elections."

"I think that's a pity," said Rebecca, squeezing Nat's hand, "because I know a lot of our class hope you will run."

"Not while he's in the field," said Nat.

"Why do you hate him so much?" asked Rebecca. "Is it just because he beat you in that silly school election?" Nat stared across at Elliot and watched him chatting to a group of students— the same insincere smile, and no doubt the same glib promises. "Don't you think it's possible that he might have changed?" said Rebecca.

Nat didn't bother to reply.

—◇—

"Right," said Jimmy, "the first election you can run for is as freshman representative on the Yale college council."

"I thought I'd skip elections during my first year," said Fletcher, "and just concentrate on work."

"You can't risk it," declared Jimmy.

"And why not?" asked Fletcher.

"Because it's a statistical fact that whoever gets elected to the college council in his first year, is almost certain to end up as president three years later."

"Perhaps I don't want to be president of the college council," said Fletcher with a grin.

"Perhaps Marilyn Monroe didn't want to win an Oscar," said Jimmy, as he produced a booklet from his briefcase.

"What's that?"

"The freshman yearbook—there's 1,021 of them."

"I see you've once again begun the campaign without consulting the candidate."

"I had to, because I can't afford to hang around waiting for you to make up your mind. I've done some research and discovered that you have little or no chance of even being considered for the college council unless you speak in the freshman's debate in the sixth week."

"Why's that?" asked Fletcher.

"Because it's the only occasion when all the frosh come together in one room and are given the chance to listen to any prospective candidate."

"So how do you get selected as a speaker?"

"Depends which side of the motion you want to support."

"So what's the motion?"

"I'm glad to see you're finally warming to the challenge, because that's our next problem." Jimmy removed a leaflet from an inside pocket. "Resolved: America should withdraw from the Vietnam War."

"I don't see any problem with that," said Fletcher, "I'd be quite happy to oppose such a motion."

"That's the problem," said Jimmy, "because anyone who opposes is history, even if they look like Kennedy and speak like Churchill."

"But if I present a good case, they might feel I was the right person to represent them on the council."

"However persuasive you are, Fletcher, it would still be suicide, because almost everyone on campus is against the war. So why not leave that to some madman who never wanted to be elected in the first place?"

"That sounds like me," said Fletcher, "and in any case, perhaps I believe . . ."

"I don't care what you believe," interrupted Jimmy. "My only interest is getting you elected."

"Jimmy, do you have any morals at all?"

"How could I?" Jimmy replied. "My father's a politician and my mother sells real estate."

"Despite your pragmatism, I still couldn't get myself to speak in favor of such a motion."

"Then you're doomed to a life of endless study and holding hands with my sister."

"Sounds pretty good to me," said Fletcher, "especially as you seem quite incapable of having a serious relationship with any woman for more than twenty-four hours."

"That isn't Joanna Palmer's opinion," said Jimmy.

Fletcher laughed, "And what about your other friend, Audrey Hepburn? I haven't seen her on campus lately."

"Neither have I," said Jimmy, "but it will only be a matter of time before I capture Miss Palmer's heart."

"In your dreams, Jimmy."

"You will in time, apologize, O ye of little faith, and I predict that it will be before your disastrous contribution to the freshman debate."

"You won't change my mind, Jimmy, because if I take part in the debate, it will be to oppose the motion."

"You do like to make life difficult for me, don't you, Fletcher. Well, one thing's for certain, the organizers will welcome your participation."

"Why's that?" asked Fletcher.

"Because they haven't been able to find anyone half electable who is willing to put the case against withdrawal."

—◦—

"Are you sure," asked Nat quietly.

"Yes, I am," replied Rebecca.

"Then we must get married as soon as possible," said Nat.

"Why?" asked Rebecca. "We live in the sixties, the age of the Beatles, pot, and free love, so why shouldn't I have an abortion?"

"Is that what you want?" asked Nat in disbelief.

"I don't know what I want," said Rebecca. "I only found out this morning. I need some more time to think about it."

Nat took her hand. "I'd marry you today if you'd have me."

"I know you would," said Rebecca, squeezing his hand, "but we have to face the fact that this decision will affect the rest of our lives. We shouldn't rush into it."

"But I have a moral responsibility to you and our child."

"And I have my future to consider," said Rebecca.

"Perhaps we should tell our parents, and see how they react?"

"That's the last thing I want to do," said Rebecca. "Your mother will expect us to get married this afternoon, and my father will turn up on campus with a shotgun under his arm. No, I want you to promise you won't mention that I'm pregnant to anyone, especially our parents."

"But why?" pressed Nat.

"Because here's another problem . . ."

"How's the speech coming on?"

"Just finished the third draft," said Fletcher cheerfully, "and you'll be happy to learn that it's likely to make me the most unpopular student on campus."

"You do like making my task more difficult . . ."

"Impossible is my ultimate aim," admitted Fletcher. "By the way, who are we up against?"

"Some guy called Tom Russell."

"What have you found out about him?"

"Went to Taft."

"Which means that we have a head start," said Fletcher with a grin.

"No, I'm afraid not," said Jimmy. "I met him at Mory's last night, and I can tell you he's bright and popular. I can't find anyone who doesn't like him."

"Have we got anything going for us?"

"Yes, he admitted that he's not looking forward to the debate. He'd rather support another candidate, if the right one came forward. Sees himself as more of a campaign organizer than a leader."

"Then perhaps we could ask Tom to join our team," said Fletcher. "I'm still looking for a campaign organizer."

"Funnily enough, he offered *me* that job," said Jimmy.

Fletcher stared at his friend. "Did he really?"

"Yes," replied Jimmy.

"Then I'll have to take him seriously, won't I?" Fletcher paused, "Perhaps we should start by going over my speech tonight, then you can tell me if . . ."

"Not possible tonight," said Jimmy. "Joanna's invited me over to her place for supper."

"Ah yes, that reminds me, I can't make it either. Jackie Kennedy has asked me to accompany her to the Met."

"Now you mention it, Joanna did wonder if you and Annie would like to join us for a drink next Thursday. I told her that my sister was coming over to New Haven for the debate."

"Are you serious?" said Fletcher.

"And if you do decide to join us, please tell Annie not to hang around for too long, because Joanna and I like to be tucked up in bed by ten."

❦

When Nat found Rebecca's hand-written note slipped under his door, he ran all the way across campus, wondering what could possibly be that urgent.

When he walked into her room she turned away as he tried to kiss her, and without explanation locked the door. Nat sat by the window, while Rebecca perched herself on the edge of the bed. "Nat, I have to tell you something that I've been avoiding for the past few days." Nat just nodded, as he could see that Rebecca was finding it difficult to get the words out. There followed what seemed to him to be an interminable silence.

"Nat, I know you'll hate me for this . . ."

"I'm incapable of hating you," said Nat, now looking directly at her.

She met his gaze but then lowered her head. "I'm not sure you're the father."

Nat gripped the sides of his chair. "How's that possible?" he eventually asked.

"That weekend you went over to Penn for the cross-country meet, I ended up at a party and I'm afraid I drank a little too much." She paused again. "Ralph Elliot joined us and I don't remember a great deal after that, except waking up in the morning, and finding him sleeping next to me."

It was Nat's turn not to speak for some time. "Have you told him that you're pregnant?"

"No," said Rebecca. "What's the point? He's hardly spoken to me since."

"I'll kill the bastard," said Nat, rising from his chair.

"I don't think that will help," said Rebecca quietly.

"It doesn't change anything," said Nat, walking across to take her in his arms, "because I still want to marry you. In any case, the odds are far more likely that it's my child."

"But you could never be sure," said Rebecca.

"That's not a problem for me," said Nat.

"But it's a problem for me," said Rebecca, "because there's something else I haven't told you . . ."

＊

The moment Fletcher entered the packed Woolsey Hall he regretted not heeding Jimmy's advice. He took his place on the bench opposite Tom Russell, who greeted him with a warm smile, as a thousand students began to chant, "Hey, hey LBJ, how many kids have you killed today?"

Fletcher looked up at his opponent as he rose from his place to open the debate. Tom was welcomed by the assembled throng with acclamation even before he'd opened his mouth. To Fletcher's surprise he appeared to be just as nervous as he was, beads of sweat appearing on his forehead.

The crowd fell silent the moment Tom began to speak, but he had only delivered two words when it turned to boos. "Lyndon Johnson," he waited. "Lyndon Johnson has told us that it is America's duty to defeat the North Vietnamese and save the world from creeping communism. I say it's the president's duty not to sacrifice one American life on the altar of a doctrine that, given time, will defeat itself."

Once again the throng erupted, this time into cheers, and it was nearly a minute before Tom could continue. In fact the remainder of his words were punctuated with so many interruptions of approval, that he'd barely delivered half his speech before he came to the end of his allotted time.

The cheers turned to boos the moment Fletcher rose from his place. He had already decided that this was the last public speech he would ever make. He waited for a silence that never came, and when someone shouted, "Get on with it," he delivered his first faltering words.

"The Greeks, the Romans and the British have all, in their time, taken on the mantle of world leadership," Fletcher began.

"That's no reason why we should!" hollered someone from the back of the hall.

"And after the breakup of the British Empire following the Second World War," continued Fletcher, "that responsibility has been passed on to the United States. The greatest nation on the earth." A smattering of applause broke out in the hall. "We can of course sit back and admit that we are unworthy of that responsibility, or we can offer leadership to millions around the world, who admire our concept of freedom and wish to emulate our way of life. We could also walk away, allowing those same millions to suffer the yoke of communism as it engulfs the free world, or we could support them as they too try to embrace democracy. Only history will be left to record the decision we make, and history must not find us wanting."

Jimmy was amazed that they had thus far listened with only the occasional interruption, and surprised by the respectful applause Fletcher received when he resumed his place some twenty minutes later. At the end of the debate everyone in the hall recognized that Fletcher had won the argument, even if it was Tom who won the motion by over two hundred votes.

Jimmy somehow managed to look cheerful after the result had been read out to the cheering mob. "It's nothing less than a miracle," said Jimmy.

"Some miracle," said Fletcher. "Didn't you notice that we lost by two hundred and twenty-eight votes?"

"But I was expecting to be beaten by a landslide, so I consider two hundred and twenty-eight to be nothing less than a miracle. We've got five days to change the minds of a hundred and four-teen voters, because most frosh accept that you're the obvious choice to represent them on the student council," said Jimmy as they walked out of Woolsey Hall, with several people whispering to Fletcher, "Well done" and "Good luck."

"I thought Tom Russell spoke well," said Fletcher, "and more important, he represents their views."

"No, he won't do anymore than keep the seat warm for you."

"Don't be too sure of that," said Fletcher. "Tom might quite like the idea of becoming president."

"Not a chance with what I have planned for him."

"Dare I ask what you have in mind?" said Fletcher.

"I had a member of our team present whenever he gave a speech. During the campaign he made forty-three pledges, most of which he will not be able to keep. After he's been reminded of that fact twenty times a day, I don't think his name will be appear-ing on the ballot paper for president."

"Jimmy, have you ever read Machiavelli's *The Prince*?" asked Fletcher.

"No, should I?"

"No, don't bother, he has nothing to teach you. What are you doing for dinner tonight?" he added, as Annie came across to join them. She gave Fletcher a big hug. "Well done," she said, "your speech was brilliant."

"Too bad a couple of hundred others didn't agree with you," said Fletcher.

"They did, but most of them had decided how they were going to vote long before they entered the hall."

"That's exactly what I've been trying to tell him." Jimmy turned to Fletcher. "My kid sister's right, and what's more . . ."

"Jimmy, I'll be eighteen in a few weeks' time," said Annie, scowling at her brother, "just in case you haven't noticed."

"I've noticed, and some of my friends even tell me that you're passably pretty, but I can't see it myself."

Fletcher laughed. "So are you going to join us at Dino's?"

"No, you've obviously forgotten that Joanna and I invited you both to dinner at her place."

"I hadn't forgotten," said Annie, "and I can't wait to meet the woman who's tied my brother down for more than a week."

"I haven't looked at another woman since the day I met her," said Jimmy quietly.

—◇—

"But I still want to marry you," said Nat, holding on to her.

"Even if you can't be sure who the father is?"

"That's all the more reason for us to get married, then you'll never doubt my commitment."

"I've never doubted it for a moment," said Rebecca, "or that you're a good and decent man, but haven't you considered the possibility that I might not love you enough to want to spend the rest of my life with you?" Nat let go of her and looked into her eyes. "I asked Ralph what he would do if it turned out to be his child, and he agreed with me that I should have an abortion." Rebecca placed the palm of her hand on Nat's cheek. "Not many of us are good enough to live with Sebastian, and I'm certainly no Olivia." She took her hand away and quickly left the room without another word.

Nat lay on her bed unaware of the darkness setting in. He couldn't stop thinking about his love for Rebecca, and of his loathing for Elliot. He eventually fell asleep, and woke only when the telephone rang.

Nat listened to the familiar voice and congratulated his old friend when he heard the news.

13

WHEN NAT WENT to pick up his mail from the student union, he was pleased to find he had three letters: a bumper crop. One of them bore the unmistakable hand of his mother. The second was postmarked New Haven, so he assumed it had to be from Tom. The third was a plain brown envelope containing his monthly scholarship check, which he would bank immediately as his funds were running low.

He walked across to McConaughy and grabbed a bowl of corn-flakes and a couple of slices of toast, avoiding the powdered scrambled eggs. He took a vacant seat in the far corner of the room, and tore open his mother's letter. He felt guilty that he hadn't written to her for at least two weeks. There were only a few days to go before the Christmas vacation, so he hoped she would understand if he didn't reply immediately. He'd had a long conversation with her on the phone the day after he had broken up with Rebecca. He hadn't mentioned her being pregnant or given a particular reason for them breaking up.

My dear Nathaniel—she never called him Nat. If anyone ever read a letter from his mother, Nat reckoned that they would quickly learn everything they needed to know about her. Neat, accurate, informative, caring but somehow leaving an impression of being late for her next appointment. She always ended with the words, *Must dash, love Mother.* The only piece of real news she had to impart was Dad's promotion to regional manager, which meant he would no longer have to spend endless hours on the road, but in future would be working in Hartford.

Dad is delighted about the promotion and the pay rise, which means we can just about afford a second car. However, he's already missing the personal contact with the customers.

Nat took another spoonful of cereal before he opened the letter from New Haven. Tom's missive was typed and contained the occasional spelling mistake, probably caused by the excitement of describing his election victory. In his usual disarming way, Tom reported that he had won only because his opponent had made a passionate speech defending America's involvement in the Vietnam War, which hadn't helped his cause when it came to the ballot. Nat liked the sound of Fletcher Davenport, and realized that he might well have run up against him had he gone to Yale. He bit into his toast as he continued to read Tom's letter: *I was sorry to hear about your breakup with Rebecca. Is it irreconcilable?* Nat looked up from the letter not sure of the answer to that question, although he realized his old friend wouldn't be at all surprised once he discovered Ralph Elliot was involved.

Nat buttered a second piece of toast and for a moment considered whether a reconciliation was still possible, but quickly returned to the real world. After all, he still planned to go on to Yale just as soon as he'd completed his first year.

Finally Nat turned his attention to the brown envelope and decided he would drop his monthly check off at the bank before his first lecture—unlike some of his fellow students, he couldn't afford banking his meager funds until the last moment. He slit open the envelope, and was surprised to find that there was no check enclosed, just a letter. He unfolded the single sheet of paper, and stared at the contents in disbelief.

—◇—

Nat placed the letter on the table in front of him, and considered its consequences. He accepted that the draft was a lottery, and his number had come up. Was it morally right to apply for an exemption simply because he was a student, or should he, as his old man had done in 1942, sign up and serve his country? His father had spent two years in Europe with the Eightieth Division before

93

SELECTIVE SERVICE SYSTEM

ORDER TO REPORT FOR

ARMED FORCES PHYSICAL EXAMINATION

To:

Nathaniel Cartwright
University of Connecticut
North Eagleville Road
Storrs, Connecticut

Local Board No 21
Selective Service System
205 Walter Street
Rockville, CT

December 14th, 1967

SELECTIVE SERVICE NO.

6   21   48   270

You are hereby directed to present yourself for
Armed Forces Physical Examination
to the Local Board named above by reporting at:

Routes 195 & 44 (Mansfield Corners), Storrs, Connecticut

(Place of reporting)

at   7.58 a.   m.,   on the   5th   of   January   19   68

(Hour of reporting)   (Day)   (Month)   (Year)

Greg Rodgers

(Member or clerk at Local Board)

returning home with the Purple Heart. Over twenty-five years later he felt just as strongly that America should be playing a role in Vietnam. Did such sentiments apply only to those uneducated Americans who were given little choice?

Nat immediately phoned home, and was not surprised when his parents had one of their rare disagreements on the subject. His mother was in no doubt that he should complete his degree, and then reconsider his position; the war could be over by then. Hadn't President Johnson promised as much during the election campaign? His father, on the other hand, felt that though it might have been an unlucky break, it was nothing less than Nat's duty to answer the call. If everyone decided to burn their draft card, a state of anarchy would prevail, was his father's final word on the subject.

He next phoned Tom at Yale to find out if he'd received a draft notice.

"Yes I have," said Tom.

"Did you burn it?" Nat asked.

"No, I didn't go that far, though I know several students who have."

"Does that mean you're going to sign up?"

"No, I don't have your moral fiber, Nat. I'm going to take the legal route. My father's found a lawyer in Washington who specializes in exemption, and he's pretty confident he can get me deferred, at least until I've graduated."

"What about that guy who ran against you for freshman rep and felt so strongly about America's responsibility to those 'who wished to participate in democracy'—what decision has he come to?" asked Nat.

"I've no idea," said Tom, "but if his name comes up in the ballot, you'll probably meet up with him in the front line."

As each month passed, and no plain brown envelope appeared in his mail slot, Fletcher began to believe that he had been among the fortunate ones that hadn't made the ballot. However, he had already decided what his reply would be should the slim brown envelope appear.

When Jimmy was called up, he immediately consulted his father, who advised him to apply for an exemption while he was still an undergraduate, but to make it clear that he would be willing to reconsider his position in three years' time. He also reminded Jimmy that by then there might well be a new president, new legislation and a strong possibility that Americans would no longer be in Vietnam. Jimmy took his father's advice, and was outspoken when he discussed the moral issue with Fletcher.

"I have no intention of risking my life against a bunch of Vietcong, who will, in the end, succumb to capitalism, even if they fail in the short term to respond to military superiority."

Annie agreed with her brother's views, and was relieved that Fletcher hadn't received a draft notice. She wasn't in any doubt how he would respond.

On January 5, 1968, Nat reported to his local draft board.

After a rigorous medical examination, he was interviewed by a Major Willis. The major was impressed; Cartwright scored ninety-two percent in his preinduction physical, having spent a morning with young men who came up with a hundred different reasons why he should find them medically unfit to serve. In the afternoon, Nat sat the General Classification Test, and scored ninety-seven percent.

The following night, along with fifty other inductees, Nat boarded a bus destined for New Jersey. During the slow, interminable journey across the state lines, Nat toyed with little plastic trays of food that made up his boxed lunch, before falling into a fitful sleep.

The bus finally came to a halt at Fort Dix in the early hours of the morning. The would, and would not be, soldiers off-loaded to be greeted by the yells of drill sergeants. They were quickly billeted in prefabricated huts, and then allowed to sleep for a couple of hours.

The following morning, Nat rose—he had no choice—at five, and after being given a "buzz cut," was issued fatigues. All fifty new recruits were then ordered to write a letter to their parents, while at the same time returning every item of civilian origin to their home of record.

During the day, Nat was interviewed by Specialist Fourth Class Jackson, who, having checked through his papers, had only one question, "You do realize, Cartwright, that you could have applied for exemption?"

"Yes, I do, sir."

Specialist Jackson raised an eyebrow. "And having taken advice, you made the decision not to?"

"I didn't need to take advice, sir."

"Good, then just as soon as you've completed your basic training, Private Cartwright, I'm sure you'll want to apply for officer cadet school." He paused. "About two in fifty make it, so don't get your hopes up. By the way," he added, "you don't call me sir. Specialist Fourth Class will be just fine."

After years of cross-country running Nat considered himself in good shape, but he quickly discovered that the army had a totally different meaning for the word, not fully explained in Webster's. And as for the other word—basic—everything was basic: the food, the clothing, the heating, and especially the bed he was expected to sleep on. Nat could only assume that the army were importing their mattresses direct from North Vietnam, so that they could experience the same hardship as the enemy.

For the next eight weeks Nat rose every morning at five, took a cold shower—heat simply didn't exist in army parlance—was dressed, fed and had his clothes neatly folded on the end of the bed before standing at attention on the parade ground by six A.M. along with all the other members of Second Platoon, Alpha Company.

The first person to address him each morning was Drill Sergeant Al Quamo, who always looked so smart that Nat assumed he must have risen at four to press his uniform. And if Nat attempted to speak to anyone else during the next fourteen hours, Quamo wanted to know who and why. The drill sergeant was the same height as Nat, and there the resemblance ended. Nat never stood still long enough to count the sergeant's medals. "I'm your mother, your father, and your closest friend," he bellowed at the top of his voice. "Do you hear me?"

"Yes, sir," shouted back thirty-six raw recruits from the Second Platoon. "You're my mother, my father and my closest friend."

Most of the platoon had applied for exemption and been turned down. Many of them considered Nat was crazy to volunteer, and it took several weeks before they changed their minds about the boy from Cromwell. Long before the course had ended, Nat had become the platoon counselor, letter writer, advisor and confidant. He even taught a couple of the recruits to read. He didn't choose to tell his mother what they had taught him in return. Halfway through the course, Quamo made him squad leader.

At the end of the two-month stint, Nat came first in everything which involved spelling. He also surprised his fellow rookies by beating them all around the cross-country course and, although he had never fired a weapon before basic training, he even out-shot the boys from Queens when it came to mastering the M60 machine gun and the M70 grenade launcher. They were more practiced in smaller weapons.

It didn't take eight weeks for Quamo to change his mind about Nat's chances of making Officer Cadet School. Unlike most of the other "sadsacks" who were destined for 'Nam, he found that Nat was a born leader.

"Mind you," Quamo warned Nat, "a butter bar second lieutenant is just as likely to have his ass blown off as a private soldier, because one thing's for certain, the VC can't tell the difference." Sergeant Quamo turned out to be right, because only two soldiers were selected to go to Fort Benning. The other was a college boy from Third Platoon named Dick Tyler.

—◦—

For the first three weeks at Fort Benning, the main outdoor activity was alongside the black hats. The parachute instructors took their new recruits through their landing falls, first from a thirty-five-foot wall, and later from the dreaded three-hundred-foot tower. Of the two hundred soldiers who began the course, less than a hundred made it through to the next stage. Nat was among the final ten chosen to wear a white helmet during jump week. Fifteen jumps later, and it was his turn to have silver jump wings pinned to his chest.

When Nat returned home for a week's furlough, his mother hardly recognized the child who had left her three months earlier. He had been replaced by a man, an inch taller and seven pounds lighter, with a crew cut that made his father reminisce about his days in Italy.

After the short break, Nat returned to Fort Benning, pulled back on his glistening Corcoran jump boots, threw his barrack bag over his shoulder, and took the short walk from airborne to the other side of the road.

Here he began his training as an infantry officer. Although he rose just as early each morning, he now spent far more of his time in the classroom, studying military history, map reading, tactics and command strategy, along with seventy other would-be officers who were also preparing to be sent to Vietnam. The one statistic no one would talk about was that more than fifty percent of them could expect to return in a body bag.

"Joanna's going to have to face a disciplinary inquiry," said Jimmy as he sat on the end of Fletcher's bed. "Whereas it's me who should be suffering the wrath of the ethics committee," he added.

Fletcher tried to calm his friend, but he had never seen him so incensed. "Why can't they understand that it's not a crime to fall in love?"

"I think you'll find that they are more worried about the consequences of it happening the other way around," said Fletcher.

"What do you mean?" asked Jimmy, looking up.

"Simply that the administration is genuinely concerned about male teachers taking advantage of young, impressionable female undergraduates."

"But can't they tell when it's genuine?" asked Jimmy. "Anyone can see that I adore Joanna, and she feels the same way about me."

"And they might even have turned a blind eye in your case if you both hadn't made it so public."

"I would have thought you of all people would have respected Joanna for her refusal to be disingenuous on the subject," said Jimmy.

"I do," said Fletcher, "but she's left the authorities with no option but to respond to that honesty, given the university regulations."

"Then it's the regulations that need changing," said Jimmy. "Joanna believes as a teacher, you shouldn't have to hide your true feelings. She wants to make sure that the next generation never have to face the same predicament."

"Jimmy, I'm not disagreeing with you, and knowing Joanna, she will have thought about those regulations carefully and also have a strong view on the relevance of rule 17b."

"Of course she does, but Joanna isn't going to become engaged just to let the board off the hook."

"That's some woman you asked if you could carry her books," said Fletcher.

"Don't remind me," Jimmy replied. "You know that they're now cheering her at the beginning and end of every lecture she gives."

"So when does the ethics committee convene to make its decision?"

"Next Wednesday at ten o'clock. It's going to be a media field day. I just wish my father wasn't coming up for reelection in the fall."

"I wouldn't worry about your father," said Fletcher. "My bet is that he'll have already found a way of turning the problem to his advantage."

❖

Nat had never expected to come into contact with his commanding officer, and wouldn't have done so if his mother hadn't parked her car in the colonel's reserved space. When Nat's father spotted the sign COMMANDANT, he suggested she should quickly reverse. Susan reversed a little too quickly, and collided with Colonel Tremlett's jeep just as he swung in.

"Oh, God," said Nat as he leaped out of the car.

"I wouldn't go that far," said Tremlett. "Colonel will do just fine."

Nat leaped to attention and saluted as his father surreptitiously checked the commandant's medals. "We must have served together," he said, staring at a red and green ribbon among the cluster on his chest. The colonel looked up from studying the dent in his fender. "I was with the Eightieth in Italy," Nat's father explained.

"I hope you maneuvered those Shermans a damn sight better than you drive a car," said the colonel as the two men shook hands. Michael didn't mention that it was his wife who was driving. Tremlett looked at Nat. "Cartwright, isn't it?"

"Yes, sir," said Nat, surprised that the commanding officer knew his name.

"Your son looks as though he's going to be top of his class when he graduates next week," Tremlett said, turning his attention back to Nat's father. He paused, "I may have an assignment in mind for him," he added without explanation. "Report to my office at eight tomorrow morning, Cartwright." The colonel smiled at Nat's mother, and shook hands once again with his father, before turning back to Nat. "And if I can see a dent in that fender when I leave tonight, Cartwright, you can forget your next furlough." The colonel winked at Nat's mother as the boy sprang to attention and saluted again.

Nat spent the afternoon on his knees with a hammer and a pot of khaki paint.

The following morning, Nat arrived at the colonel's office at seven forty-five, and was surprised to be ushered straight through to see the commandant. Tremlett pointed to a chair on the other side of his desk.

"So you've stood up and been counted, Nat," were the colonel's first words as he glanced down at his file. "What do you want to do next?"

Nat looked across at Colonel Tremlett, a man with five rows of ribbons on his chest. He'd seen action in Italy and Korea and had recently returned from a tour of duty in Vietnam. His nickname was "the terrier," because he enjoyed getting so close to the enemy that he could bite their ankles. Nat responded to his question immediately. "I expect to be among those posted to Vietnam, sir."

"It's not necessary for you to serve in the Asian sector," said his

CO. "You've proved your point, and there are several other postings I can recommend, ranging from Berlin to Washington, D.C., so that once you've completed your two years, you can return to university."

"That rather defeats the object, doesn't it, sir?"

"But it's almost unknown to send an enlisted officer to 'Nam," said the CO, "especially one of your caliber."

"Then perhaps the time has come for someone to break the mold. After all, that's what you keep reminding us leadership is all about."

"What if I asked you to complete your service as my staff officer, then you could assist me here at the academy with the next intake of recruits?"

"So that they can all go off to Vietnam and get themselves killed?" Nat stared across the table at his CO. He immediately regretted overstepping the mark.

"Do you know who the last person was who sat there and told me he was determined to go to 'Nam, and nothing I could say would change his mind?"

"No, sir."

"My son, Daniel," replied Tremlett, "and on that occasion I had no choice but to accept his decision." The colonel paused, glancing at a photo on his desk that Nat couldn't see. "He survived for eleven days."

⌐◦⌐

WOMAN LECTURER SEDUCES SENATOR'S SON, screamed the banner headline in the *New Haven Register.*

"That's a bloody insult," said Jimmy.

"What do you mean?" asked Fletcher.

"I seduced her."

When Fletcher stopped laughing, he continued to read the front page article:

> Joanna Palmer, a lecturer in European history at Yale, has had her contract terminated by the University Ethics Committee, after admitting that she was having an affair with James Gates, a freshman she has been teaching for the past six months. Mr. Gates is the son of

Senator Harry Gates. Last night, from their home in East Hartford . . .

Fletcher looked up. "How has your father taken it?"

"Tells me he'll win by a landslide," said Jimmy. "All the women's rights groups are backing Joanna, and all the men think I'm the coolest thing since Dustin Hoffman's *Graduate*. Dad also believes that the committee will be left with no choice but to reverse their decision long before the term ends."

"And if they don't?" asked Fletcher. "What chance is there of Joanna being offered another job?"

"That's the least of her problems," Jimmy replied, "because the phone hasn't stopped ringing since the committee announced their decision. Both Radcliffe, where she did her undergraduate degree, and Columbia, where she completed her Ph.D., have offered her jobs, and that was before the opinion poll on the *Today Show* reported that eighty-two percent of their viewers thought she should be reinstated."

"So what does she plan to do next?"

"Appeal, and my bet is that the committee won't be able to ignore public opinion."

"But where does that leave you?"

"I still want to marry Joanna, but she won't hear of it until she know the result of her arbitration. She refuses to become engaged in case it influences the committee in her favor. She's determined to win the case on its merits, not on public sentiment."

"That's a remarkable woman you've got yourself involved with," said Fletcher.

"I agree," said Jimmy. "And you only know the half of it."

14

LT. NAT CARTWRIGHT had been stenciled on the door of his little office at MACV headquarters even before he'd arrived in Saigon. It quickly became clear to Nat that he was to be desk-bound for his entire watch, not even allowed to discover where the front line was. On arrival, he did not join his regiment in the field, but was assigned to Combat Service Support. Colonel Tremlett's dispatches had obviously landed in Saigon long before he had.

Nat was described on the daily manifest as a quartermaster, which allowed those above him to pile up the paperwork, and those below him to take their time carrying out his orders. They all seemed to be involved in the plot, a plot that resulted in Nat spending every working hour filling in regulation forms for items as varied as baked beans and Chinook helicopters. Seven hundred and twenty-two tons of supplies were flown into the capital every week, and it was Nat's duty to see they reached the front line. In any one month, he handled over nine thousand items. Everything managed to get there except him. He even resorted to sleeping with the commanding officer's secretary, but quickly discovered that Mollie had no real influence over her boss, although he did find out about her considerable expertise in unarmed combat.

Nat began leaving the office later and later each evening, and even began to wonder if he was in a foreign country. When you have a Big Mac and Coke for lunch, Kentucky Fried Chicken with a Budweiser for dinner, and return to the officers' quarters every evening to watch the *ABC News* and reruns of *77 Sunset Strip*, what proof is there that you ever left home?

Nat made several surreptitious attempts to join his regiment in the front line, but as the weeks passed he came to realize that Colonel Tremlett's influence permeated everywhere; his applications would land back on his desk, rubber-stamped: *Refused, reapply in one month.*

Whenever Nat requested an interview to discuss the issue with a field officer, he never managed to see anyone above the rank of staff major. On each occasion, a different officer would spend half an hour trying to convince Nat that he was doing a valuable and worthwhile job in requisition. His combat file was the thinnest in Saigon.

Nat was beginning to realize that his stand on "a matter of principle" had served no purpose. In a month's time Tom would be starting his second year at Yale, and what did he have to show for his efforts other than a crew cut and an inside knowledge of how many paper clips the army required in Vietnam in any one month?

Nat was sitting in his office, preparing for the new intake of recruits due to report the following Monday, when all that changed.

Accommodation, clothing and travel documents had kept him occupied all day and well into the evening. *Urgent* was stamped on several of them, as the CO always wanted to be fully briefed on the background of any new intake before they landed in Saigon. Nat hadn't noticed how long the task had taken, and when he had completed the final form, he decided to drop them off in the adjutant's office before grabbing something to eat in the officers' mess.

As he strolled past the ops room, he experienced a surge of anger; all the training he had been put through at Fort Dix and Fort Benning had been a complete waste of time. Although it was nearly eight o'clock, there were still a dozen or so operatives, some of whom he recognized, manning the phones and updating a large operational map of North Vietnam.

On his way back from the adjutant's office, Nat dropped into the ops room to see if anyone was free to join him for dinner. He found himself listening to the troop movements of the Second Battalion, 503rd Parachute Infantry Regiment. He would have slipped back out and gone to the mess alone if it hadn't been his own regiment. The Second Battalion was facing a barrage of mortar fire from the Vietcong and was holed up on the wrong side of the Dyng River, defending itself from a further onslaught. The red phone on the desk in front of Nat began to ring insistently. Nat didn't move a muscle.

"Don't just stand there, Lieutenant, pick it up and find out what they want," demanded the operations officer. Nat quickly obeyed the order.

"Mayday, Mayday, this is Captain Tyler, do you read me?"

"I do, Captain, this is Lieutenant Cartwright. How can I help, sir?"

"My platoon has been ambushed by Victor Charlie just above the Dyng River, grid reference SE42 NNE71. I need a flight of Hueys with full medical backup. I have ninety-six men, eleven of them are already down, three dead, eight injured."

A staff sergeant came off another phone. "How do I reach emergency rescue?" asked Nat.

"Contact Blackbird base at the Eisenhower field. Pick up the white phone and give the officer of the watch the grid reference."

Nat grabbed the white phone, and a sleepy voice answered.

"This is Lieutenant Cartwright. We have a Mayday call. Two platoons trapped on the north side of the Dyng River, grid reference SE42 NNE71; they've been ambushed and require immediate assistance."

"Tell them we'll be off the ground and on our way in five minutes," said a voice now fully alert.

"Can I join you?" asked Nat, cupping his hand over the mouthpiece, expecting the inevitable rejection.

"Are you authorized to fly in Hueys?"

"Yes, I am," lied Nat.

"Any parachute experience?"

"Trained at Fort Benning," said Nat, "sixteen jumps at six hundred feet from S-123s, and in any case, it's my regiment out there."

"Then if you can get here in time, Lieutenant, be my guest."

Nat replaced the white phone and returned to the red one. They're on their way, Captain," was all he said.

Nat ran out of the ops room and into the parking lot. A duty corporal was dozing behind the wheel of a jeep. Nat leaped in beside him, banged the palm of his hand on the horn and said, "Blackbird base in five minutes."

"But that's about four miles away, sir," said the driver.

"Then you'll have to get moving, won't you, Corporal," shouted Nat.

The corporal switched on the engine, threw the jeep into gear, and accelerated out of the parking lot, lights on, leaving the palm of one hand on the horn and the other on the steering wheel. "Faster, faster," repeated Nat, as those who were still on the streets of Saigon after curfew leaped out of their way along with several startled chickens. Three minutes later, Nat spotted a dozen Huey helicopters perched on the airfield up ahead. The blades on one of them were already rotating.

"Put your foot down," Nat repeated.

"It's already touching the floor, sir," replied the corporal as the gates of the airfield came into sight. Nat counted again: seven of the helicopters now had their blades whirring.

"Shit," he said as the first one took off.

The jeep screeched to a halt at the gates to the compound, where an MP asked to see their identity cards.

"I have to be on one of those choppers in under a minute," shouted Nat passing over his papers. "Can't you speed it up?"

"Just doing my job, sir," said the MP as he checked both men's papers.

Once both identity cards had been handed back, Nat pointed to the one helicopter whose blades were not yet rotating, and the corporal shot off toward it, skidding to a halt by an open door, just as its blades began to turn.

The pilot looked down and grinned, "You only just made it, Lieutenant," he said. "Climb aboard." The helicopter had lifted off even before Nat had been given a chance to click on his safety harness. "You want to hear the bad news, or the bad news?" asked the pilot.

"Try me," said Nat.

"The rule in any emergency is always the same. Last off the ground is the first to land in enemy territory."

"And the bad news?"

"Will you marry me?" asked Jimmy.

Joanna turned and looked at the man who had brought her more happiness in the past year than she could ever have imagined possible. "If you still want to ask me the same question on the day you graduate, freshman, my reply will be yes, but today the answer is still no."

"But why? What could have possibly changed in a year or two's time?"

"You'll be a little older, and hopefully a little wiser," replied Joanna with a smile. "I'm twenty-five and you're not yet twenty."

"What difference can that make if we want to spend the rest of our lives together?"

"Just that you might not feel that way when I'm fifty and you're forty-five."

"You've got it all wrong," said Jimmy. "At fifty you'll be in your prime, and I'll be a debauched husk, so you'd better grab me while I've still got some energy left."

Joanna laughed. "Try not to forget, freshman, that what we've been through during the past few weeks may also be affecting your judgment."

"I don't agree. I believe the experience can only have strengthened our relationship."

"That's possible," said Joanna, "but in the long run, you should never make an irreversible decision on the back of good or bad news, because it's just possible that one of us will feel differently when this all blows over."

"Do you feel differently?" asked Jimmy quietly.

"No, I don't," said Joanna firmly, as she touched his cheek. "But my parents have been married for nearly thirty years, and my grandparents lived to celebrate their golden wedding anniversary, so when I get married I want it to be for life."

"All the more reason for us to get married as quickly as possible," said Jimmy. "After all, I'm going to have to live to the age of seventy if we hope to celebrate our golden wedding."

Joanna laughed. "I'll bet your friend Fletcher would agree with me."

"You could be right, but you're not marrying Fletcher. In any case, my bet is that he and my sister will be together for at least fifty years."

"Freshman, I couldn't love you anymore if I wanted to, but remember that I'll be at Columbia next fall, and you'll still be at Yale."

"But you can still change your mind about taking that job at Columbia."

"No, it was only public opinion that forced the board to reverse their decision. If you'd seen the look on their faces when they delivered their verdict, you'd have realized they couldn't wait to see the back of me. We've made our point, freshman, so I think it would be better for everyone if I moved on."

"Not everyone," said Jimmy quietly.

"Because once I'm no longer around to haunt them, they're going to find it far easier to amend the rules," said Joanna, ignoring his comment. "In twenty years' time, students will never believe such a ridiculous regulation even existed."

"Then I'll have to get myself a commuter ticket to New York, because I'm not going to let you out of my sight."

"I'll be at the station to meet you, freshman, but while I'm away, I hope you'll take out other women. Then, if you still feel the same way about me on the day you graduate, I'll be happy to say yes," she added as the alarm went off.

"Hell," said Jimmy, as he leaped out of bed, "can I use the bathroom first, because I've a nine o'clock lecture, and I don't even know what the subject is."

"Napoleon and his influence on the development of American law," said Joanna.

"I thought you told us that American law was more influenced by the Romans and the English than any other nation?"

"Half a mark, freshman, but you'll still need to attend my nine o'clock lecture if you hope to find out why. By the way, do you think you could do two things for me?"

"Only two?" said Jimmy as he turned on the shower.

"Could you stop staring at me like a lost puppy whenever I give a lecture?"

Jimmy stuck his head back around the door, "No," he said, as he watched Joanna slip out of her nightie. "What's the second?"

"Well, could you at least look interested in what I'm saying, and perhaps even take the occasional note?"

"Why should I bother to take notes when it's you who grades my papers?"

"Because you won't be pleased with the grade I've given your latest effort," said Joanna, as she joined him in the shower.

"Oh, and I was hoping for an A for that particular masterpiece," said Jimmy as he began soaping her breasts.

"Do you by any chance recall who you suggested was the biggest influence on Napoleon?"

"Josephine," said Jimmy without hesitation.

"That might even have been the correct answer, but it isn't what you wrote in your essay."

Jimmy stepped out of the shower and grabbed a towel. "What did I write?" he asked, turning to face her.

"Joanna."

⟶

Within minutes, all twelve helicopters were flying in a V formation. Nat looked behind him at the two rear gunners, who were staring intently out into the black cloudless night. He slipped on a pair of earphones and listened to the flight lieutenant.

"Blackbird One to group, we'll be out of allied air space in four minutes, then I anticipate an ETA of twenty-one hundred hours."

Nat found himself sitting bolt upright as he listened to the young pilot. He glanced out of a side window at stars that would never be seen on the American continent. He could feel the adrenalin pumping through his body as they flew nearer to the enemy lines. At last he felt he was part of this damn man's war. His only surprise was that he sensed no fear. Perhaps that would come later.

"We're moving into enemy territory," said the flight lieutenant as if he were crossing a busy road. "Are you receiving me, ground leader?"

There was a crackling on the line before a voice said, "I hear you, Blackbird One, what's your position?" Nat recognized the southern drawl of Captain Dick Tyler.

"We're approximately fifty miles south of you."

"Copy that, expect you to rendezvous in fifteen minutes."

"Roger. You won't see us until the last moment, because we're keeping all our external lights off."

"Copy that," came back the same drawl.

"Have you identified a possible landing spot?"

"There's a small piece of sheltered land on a ridge just below me," replied Tyler, "but it will only take one helicopter at a time, and because of the rain, not to mention the mud, landing could be a hell of a problem."

"What's your current position?"

"I'm still at my same grid reference just north of the Dyng River," Tyler paused, "and I'm fairly sure that the VC have begun crossing the river."

"How many men do you have with you?"

"Seventy-eight." Nat knew that the full complement of two platoons was ninety-six. "And how many bodies?" asked the flight lieutenant, as if he were asking how many eggs the captain wanted for breakfast.

"Eighteen."

"OK, be ready to put six men and two bodies into each chopper, and make sure you're able to climb on board the moment you see me."

"We'll be ready," said the captain. "What time do you have?"

"Twenty thirty-three," said the flight lieutenant.

"Then at twenty forty-eight, I'll put up one red flare."

"Twenty forty-eight, one red flare," repeated the flight lieutenant, "Roger and out."

Nat was impressed by how calm the flight lieutenant appeared to be when he, his co-pilot and both rear gunners could be dead in twenty minutes. But as he had been reminded so often by Colonel Tremlett, more lives are saved by calm men than brave ones. No one spoke for the next fifteen minutes. It gave Nat time to think about the decision he'd made; would he also be dead in twenty minutes?

Nat then endured the longest fifteen minutes of his life, staring out across acres of dense jungle lit only by a half moon while radio silence was maintained. He looked back at the rear gunners as the chopper skimmed above the tree line. They were already clasping their guns, thumbs on the buttons, alert for any trouble. Nat was looking out of a side window when suddenly a red flare shot high into the sky. He couldn't help thinking that he would have been having coffee in the mess around now.

"This is Blackbird One to flight," said the pilot, breaking radio silence. "Don't switch on your underbelly lights until you're thirty seconds from rendezvous, and remember, I'm going in first."

A green tracer of bullets shot in front of the cockpit, and the rear gunners immediately returned fire.

"The VC have identified us," said the flight leader crisply. He dipped his helicopter to the right and Nat saw the enemy for the first time. The VC were advancing up the hill, only a few hundred yards away from where the chopper would try to land.

—◦—

Fletcher read the article in the *Washington Post*. It was an heroic episode that had caught the imagination of the American public in a war no one wanted to know about. A group of seventy-eight infantrymen, cornered in the North Vietnamese jungle, easily outnumbered by the Vietcong, had been rescued by a fleet of helicopters that had flown over dangerous terrain, unable to land while encountering enemy fire. Fletcher studied the detailed diagram on the opposite page. Flight Lieutenant Chuck Philips had been the first to swoop down and rescue half a dozen trapped men. He had hovered only a few feet above the ground while the rescue took place. He hadn't noticed that another officer, Lieutenant Cartwright, had leaped off the aircraft just as he dipped his nose and rose back up into the sky to allow the second helicopter to take his place.

Among the bodies on the third helicopter was that of the officer in command, Captain Dick Tyler. Lieutenant Cartwright had immediately assumed command, and taken over the counterattack while at the same time coordinating the rescue of the remaining men. He was the last person to leave the field of battle and climb on board the remaining rescue helicopter. All twelve helicopters headed back to Saigon, but only eleven landed at Eisenhower airfield.

Brigadier General Hayward immediately dispatched a rescue party, and the same eleven pilots and their crews volunteered to go in search of the missing Huey, but despite making repeated sorties into enemy territory, they could find no sign of Blackbird Twelve. Hayward later described Nat Cartwright—an enlisted man, who had left the University of Connecticut in his freshman year to sign up—as an example to all Americans of someone who, in Lincoln's words, had given "the last full measure of devotion." "Alive or dead, we'll find him," vowed Hayward.

Fletcher scoured every paper for articles that mentioned Nat Cartwright after reading a profile that revealed he had been born on the same day, in the same town and in the same hospital.

—◦—

Nat leaped off the first helicopter as it continued to hover a few feet above the ground. He assisted Captain Tyler as he sent back the first group to board the Huey while a wave of bullets and mortars shrieked across the nose cone.

"You take over here," said Tyler, "while I go back and organize my men. I'll send up half a dozen at a time."

"Go," shouted Nat as the first helicopter dipped to the left before ascending into the sky. As the second helicopter flew in, despite being under constant fire, Nat calmly organized the next group to take their place on board. He glanced down the hill to see Dick Tyler still leading his men in a rearguard action while at the same time giving orders for the next group to join Nat. When Nat turned back, the third chopper was dropping into place to hover above the small square of muddy ground. A staff sergeant and five soldiers ran up to the side of the helicopter and began to clamber on board.

"Shit," said the staff sergeant looking back, "the captain's hit."

Nat turned to see Tyler lying facedown in the mud, two soldiers lifting him up. They quickly carried his body toward the waiting helicopter.

113

"Take over here, sergeant," said Nat, and then ran down toward the ridge. He grabbed the captain's M60, took cover and began firing at the advancing enemy. Somehow he selected six more men to run up the hill and join the fourth helicopter. He was only on that ridge for about twenty minutes, as he continued to try and repel the waves of advancing VC, while his own support group became fewer and fewer because he kept sending them up the hill to the safety of the next helicopter.

The last six men on that ridge didn't retreat until they saw Blackbird Twelve swoop in. As Nat finally turned and began to run up the hill, the bullet ripped into his leg. He knew he should have felt pain, but it didn't stop him running as he had never run before. When he reached the open door of the aircraft, firing as he ran, he heard the staff sergeant say, "For fuck's sake, sir, get your ass on board."

As the staff sergeant yanked him up, the helicopter dipped its nose and lurched starboard, throwing Nat across the floor before swinging quickly away.

"Are you OK?" asked the skipper.

"I think so," gasped Nat, finding himself lying across the body of a private.

"Typical of the army, can't even be sure if they're still alive. With luck and a tail wind," he added, "we should be back in time for breakfast."

Nat stared down at the body of the soldier, who had stood by his side only moments before. His family would now be able to attend his burial, rather than having to be informed that he had been left to an unceremonious death in an unceremonious land.

"Christ Almighty," he heard the flight lieutenant say.

"Problem?" Nat managed.

"You could say that. We're losing fuel fast; the bastards must have hit my fuel tank."

"I thought these things had two fuel tanks," said Nat.

"What do you imagine I used on the way out, soldier?"

The pilot tapped the fuel gauge and then checked his milometer. A flashing red light showed he had less than thirty miles left before he would be forced to put down. He turned around to see

Nat still lying on top of the dead soldier as he clung to the floor. "I'm going to have to look for somewhere to land."

Nat stared out of an open door, but all he could see was acres of dense forest.

The pilot switched on all his lights, searching for a break in the trees, and then Nat felt the helicopter shudder. "I'm going down," said the pilot, sounding just as calm as he had throughout the whole operation. "I guess we'll have to postpone breakfast."

"Over to your right," shouted Nat as he spotted a clearing in the forest.

"I see it," said the pilot as he tried to swing the helicopter toward the open space, but the three-ton juggernaut just wouldn't respond. "We're going down, whether we like it or not."

The whirring of the blades became slower and slower, until it began to feel to Nat as if they were gliding. He thought of his mother and felt guilty that he hadn't replied to her latest letter, and then of his father, who he knew would be so proud of him, of Tom and his triumph of being elected to the Yale student council—would he in time become president? And of Rebecca, whom he still loved and feared he always would. As he clung to the floor, Nat suddenly felt very young; he was, after all, still only nineteen. He discovered some time later that the flight lieutenant, known as Blackbird Twelve, was only a year older.

As the helicopter blades stopped whirring and the aircraft glided silently toward the trees, the staff sergeant spoke, "Just in case we don't meet again, sir, my name's Speck Foreman, it's been an honor to know you."

They shook hands, as one does at the end of any game.

◆

Fletcher stared at the picture of Nat on the front page of the *New York Times* below the headline AN AMERICAN HERO. A man who had signed up the moment he'd received the draft notice, although he could have cited three different reasons for claiming exemption. He'd been promoted to lieutenant and later, as a warrant officer, he'd taken command of an operation to rescue a stranded platoon on the wrong side of the Dyng River. No one seemed to be able to explain what a warrant officer was doing on a helicopter during a front-line operation.

Fletcher knew he would spend the rest of his life wondering what decision he would have made if that plain brown envelope had ended up in his mailbox, a question that could only be properly answered by those who had been put to the test. But even Jimmy conceded that Lieutenant Cartwright must have been a remarkable man. "If this had happened a week before the vote," he told Fletcher, "you might even have beaten Tom Russell—it's all in the timing."

"No, I wouldn't," said Fletcher.

"Why not?" asked Jimmy.

"That's the weird thing," Fletcher replied. "He turns out to be Tom's closest friend."

—◦—

A fleet of eleven helicopters had returned to search for the missing men, but all they could come up with a week later were the remains of an aircraft that must have exploded the moment it hit the trees. Three bodies had been identified, one of them Flight Lieutenant Carl Mould's, but despite an extensive search of the area, no trace could be found of Lieutenant Cartwright or Staff Sergeant Speck Foreman.

Henry Kissinger, the national security advisor, asked the nation to both mourn and honor men who exemplified the courage of every fighting soldier at the front.

"He shouldn't have said mourn," remarked Fletcher.

"Why not?" asked Jimmy.

"Because Cartwright's still alive."

"What makes you so sure of that?"

"I don't know how I know," Fletcher replied, "but I promise you, he's still alive."

—◦—

Nat couldn't recall hitting the trees, or being thrown from the helicopter. When he eventually woke, the blazing sun was burning down on his parched face. He lay there, wondering where he was, and then the memory of that dramatic hour came flooding back.

For a moment a man who wasn't even sure there was a God prayed. Then he raised his right arm. It moved like an arm should move, so he wiggled the fingers, all five of them. He lowered the arm and raised the left one. It too obeyed the telegraphed message from his brain, so he wiggled his fingers, and, once again, all five of them responded. He lowered the arm and waited. He slowly raised his right leg and carried out the same exercise with the toes. He lowered the leg before raising the other one, and that's when he felt the pain.

He turned his head from side to side, and then placed the palms of his hands on the ground. He prayed again and pressed down on his hands to push himself giddily up. He waited for a few moments in the hope that the trees would stop spinning, and then tried to stand. Once he was on his feet he tentatively placed one foot in front of the other, as a child would do, and as he didn't fall over, he tried to move the other one in the same direction. Yes, yes, yes, thank you, yes, and then he felt the pain again, almost as if until that moment he had been anesthetized.

He fell to his knees, and examined the calf of his left leg where the bullet had torn straight through. Ants were crawling in and out of the wound, oblivious to the fact that this human thought he was still alive. It took Nat some time to remove them one by one, before binding his leg with a sleeve of his shirt. He looked up to see the sun retreating toward the hills. He only had a short time to discover if any of his colleagues had survived.

He stood and turned a complete circle, only stopping when he spotted smoke coming from the forest. He began to limp toward it, vomiting when he stumbled across the charred body of the young pilot, whose name he didn't know, the jacket of his uniform hanging from a branch. Only the lieutenant's bars on his epaulet indicated who it had been. Nat would bury him later, but for now he had a race with the sun. It was then that he heard the groan.

"Where are you?" shouted Nat. The groan went up a decibel. Nat swung around to see the massive frame of Staff Sergeant Foreman lodged in the trees, only a few feet above the wreckage. As he reached the man, the groan rose yet another decibel. "Can you hear me?" asked Nat. The man opened and closed his eyes as Nat lowered him onto the ground. He heard himself saying, "Don't worry, I'll get you home," like some schoolboy hero from the pages of a comic book. Nat removed the compass from the staff sergeant's belt, looked up at the sun, and then he spotted an object in the trees. He would have cheered if only he could have thought of some way of retrieving it. Nat dragged himself over to the base of the tree. He somehow jumped up and down on one foot as he grabbed at a branch and shook it, hoping to dislodge its load. He was about to give up when it shifted an inch. He tugged at the branch even more vigorously, and then it moved again and suddenly, without warning, came crashing down. It would have landed on Nat's head if he hadn't quickly fallen to one side. He couldn't jump.

Nat rested for a moment, before slowly lifting the staff sergeant up and gently placing him on the stretcher. He then sat on the ground and watched the sun disappear behind the highest tree, having completed its duty for the day in that particular land.

He had read somewhere about a mother who had kept her child alive after a car crash by talking to him all through the night. Nat talked to the staff sergeant all night.

Fletcher read in sheer disbelief how, with the help of local peasants, Lieutenant Nat Cartwright had dragged that stretcher from village to village for two hundred and eleven miles, and seen the sun rise and fall seventeen times before he reached the outskirts of the city of Saigon, where both men were rushed to the nearest field hospital.

Staff Sergeant Speck Foreman died three days later, never discovering the name of the lieutenant who had rescued him and who was now fighting for his own life.

Fletcher followed every snippet of news he could find about Lieutenant Cartwright, never doubting he would live.

A week later they flew Nat to Camp Zama in Japan, where they operated on him to save his leg. The following month, he was allowed to return home to the Walter Reed Army Medical Center in Washington, D.C., to complete his recuperation.

The next time Fletcher saw Nat Cartwright was on the front page of the *New York Times*, shaking hands with President Johnson in the Rose Garden at the White House.

He was receiving the Medal of Honor.

15

MICHAEL AND SUSAN Cartwright were "bowled over" by their visit to the White House to witness their only son being decorated with the Medal of Honor in the Rose Garden. After the ceremony, President Johnson listened attentively to Nat's father as he explained the problems Americans would be facing if they all lived to the age of ninety and were not properly covered by life insurance. "In the next century, Americans will spend as long in retirement as they do in work," were the words LBJ repeated to his cabinet the following morning.

On their journey back to Cromwell, Nat's mother asked him what plans he had for the future.

"I can't be sure, because it's not in my hands," he replied. "I've received orders to report to Fort Benning on Monday, when I'll find out what Colonel Tremlett has in mind for me."

"Another wasted year," said his mother.

"Character building," said his father, who was still glowing from his long chat with the president.

"I hardly think Nat's in need of much more of that," was his mother's response.

Nat smiled as he glanced out of the window and took in the Connecticut landscape. While pulling a stretcher for seventeen days and seventeen nights with snatches of sleep and little food, he had wondered if he would ever see his homeland again. He thought about his mother's words, and had to agree with her. The idea of a wasted year of form-filling, making and returning salutes before training someone else to take his place angered him. The top brass had made it clear that they weren't going to let him return to Vietnam and thereby risk the life of one of America's few recognized heroes.

Over dinner that night, after his father had repeated the conversation he'd had with the president several times, he asked Nat to tell them more about 'Nam.

For over an hour, Nat described the city of Saigon, the countryside and its people, rarely referring to his job as a warrant officer. "The Vietnamese are hard-working and friendly," he told his parents, "and they seem genuinely pleased that we're there, but no one, on either side, believes that we can stay forever. I fear history will regard the whole episode as pointless, and once it's over it will be quickly erased from the national psyche." He turned to his father. "At least your war had a purpose." His mother nodded her agreement, and Nat was surprised to see that his father didn't immediately offer a contrary view.

"Did you come away with any particular abiding memory?" asked his mother, hoping that her son might talk about his experience at the front.

"Yes, I did. The inequality of man."

"But we're doing everything we can to assist the people of South Vietnam," said his father.

"I'm not referring to the Vietnamese, father," Nat replied, "I'm talking about what Kennedy described as 'my fellow Americans.'"

"Fellow Americans?" his mother repeated.

"Yes, because my abiding memory will be our treatment of the poor minorities, in particular the blacks. They were on the battlefield in great numbers for no other reason than that they couldn't afford a smart lawyer who could show them how to avoid the draft."

"But your closest friend . . ."

"I know," said Nat, "and I'm glad Tom didn't sign up, because he might well have suffered the same fate as Dick Tyler."

"So do you regret your decision?" asked his mother quietly.

Nat took some time before he responded. "No, but I often think of Speck Foreman, his wife and three children in Alabama, and wonder what purpose his death served."

Nat rose early the next morning to catch the first train bound for Fort Benning. When the locomotive pulled into Columbus station, he checked his watch. There was still another hour before his meeting with the colonel, so he decided to walk the two miles up to the academy. On the way, he was continually reminded that he was on a military base, by how regularly he had to return salutes from everyone below the rank of captain. Some even smiled in recognition when they spotted the Medal of Honor, as they might with a college football hero.

He was standing outside Colonel Tremlett's office a full fifteen minutes before his appointment.

"Good morning, Captain Cartwright. The colonel told me to take you straight through to his office the moment you arrived," said an even younger aide.

Nat marched into the colonel's office, stood to attention, and saluted. Tremlett came around from behind his desk, and threw his arms around Nat. The aide was unable to hide his surprise, as he thought only the French greeted their fellow officers in that way. The colonel motioned Nat to a seat on the other side of his desk. After returning to his chair, Tremlett opened a thick file and began studying its contents. "Do you have any idea what you want to do for the next year, Nat?"

"No, I don't, sir, but as I'm not being allowed to return to Vietnam, I'd be happy to take up your earlier offer, and remain at the academy to assist you with any new recruits."

"That job has already been taken," said Tremlett, "and I'm no longer sure if that's what's best for you in the long term."

"Do you have something else in mind?" asked Nat.

"Now you mention it, I do," admitted the colonel. "Once I knew you were coming home, I called in the academy's top lawyers to advise me. Normally, I despise lawyers—a breed who only fight their battles in a courtroom—but I have to admit on this occasion one of them has come up with a most ingenious scheme." Nat didn't comment, as he was keen to learn what the colonel had in mind. "Rules and regulations can be interpreted in so many ways. How else would lawyers keep their jobs?" asked the colonel. "A year ago, you signed up for the draft without question, and having been commissioned, you were sent to Vietnam, where you proved me wrong, thank God."

Nat wanted to say, get on with it, Colonel, but restrained himself.

"By the way, Nat, I forgot to ask if you'd like a coffee."

"No thank you, sir," said Nat, trying not to sound impatient.

The colonel smiled, "I think I'll have one." He picked up his phone. "Fix me up with a coffee, will you, Dan," he said, "and perhaps even some doughnuts." He looked across at Nat. "Are you sure you won't change your mind?"

"You're enjoying yourself, aren't you, sir?" said Nat with a smile.

"To be honest, I am," said the colonel. "You see, it's taken me several weeks to get Washington to fall in line with my proposal, so I hope you'll forgive me if I indulge myself for a few more minutes."

Nat smiled wryly, and settled back in his chair.

"It appears that there are several avenues left open to you, and most of them in my view are a complete waste of time. You could, for example, apply for a discharge on the grounds of an injury sustained in action. If we went down that path you would end up with a small pension, and be out of here in about six months—after your spell as a warrant officer you don't need to be told how long the paperwork would take. You could, of course, as you suggested, complete your service here at the academy, but do I really want a cripple on my staff?" the colonel asked with a grin, as his aide entered the room with a tray of piping hot coffee and two cups. "You could on the other hand take up some other posting, in a more friendly environment, like Honolulu, but I don't expect you need to go that far to find yourself a dancing girl. But whatever I have to offer," he once again glanced down at Nat's file, "you would still only end up clicking your heels for another year. So now I need to ask you a question, Nat. What had you planned to do, once you'd completed your two years?"

"Return to college, sir, and continue with my studies."

"Exactly what I thought you'd say," said the colonel, "so that's exactly what you're going to do."

"But the new term starts next week," said Nat, "and as you pointed out, the paperwork alone . . ."

"Unless you were to sign up for another six years, then you might find that the paperwork moves surprisingly quickly."

"Sign up for another six years?" repeated Nat in disbelief. "I was hoping to get out of the army, not stay in it."

"And you will," said the colonel, "but only if you sign up for six years. You see, with your qualifications, Nat," he added as he stood up and began to pace around the room, "you can immediately apply for any course of higher education and what's more, the army will pay for it."

"But I already have a scholarship," Nat reminded his commanding officer.

"I'm well aware of that, it's all in here," said the colonel, looking down at the open file in front of him. "But the university doesn't offer you a captain's pay to go with it."

"I would be paid to go to college?" said Nat.

"Yes, you would receive a full captain's pay, plus an added allowance for an overseas posting."

"An overseas posting? But I'm not applying for a place at the University of Vietnam—I want to return to Connecticut, and then go on to Yale."

"And so you will, because the regulations state that if, and only if, you have served abroad, in a war sector, and, I quote," the colonel turned another page in his file, "then an application for advanced education will be given the same status as your last posting. I've decided I now love lawyers," said the colonel, looking up, "because, can you believe it, they've come up with something even better." Tremlett sipped his coffee while Nat remained silent. "Not only will you receive your full captain's salary as well as an overseas allowance," the colonel continued, "but because of your injury, at the end of six years, you will automatically be discharged, when you will qualify for a captain's pension."

"How did they ever get that through Congress?" asked Nat.

"I don't suppose they worked out that anyone would qualify in all four categories at the same time," replied the colonel.

"There has to be a downside," said Nat.

"Yes, there is," said the colonel gravely, "because even Congress has to cover its backside." Once again, Nat didn't bother to hold him up. "First, you will have to return to Fort Benning every year for two weeks' intensive training to bring you up to scratch."

"But I'd enjoy that," said Nat.

"And at the end of the six years," said the colonel, ignoring the interruption, "you will remain on the active list until your forty-fifth birthday, so in the event of another war, you could be called up."

"That's it?" said Nat in disbelief.

"That's it," repeated the colonel.

"So what do I have to do next?"

"Sign all six documents that the lawyers have prepared, and we'll have you back at the University of Connecticut by this time next week. By the way, I've already spoken to the provost, and he tells me that they're looking forward to seeing you next Monday. He asked me to inform you that the first lecture begins at nine o'clock. Sounds a bit late to me," he added.

"You even knew how I would respond, didn't you?" said Nat.

"Well, I admit," said Tremlett, "that I did think you would consider it a better alternative to brewing my coffee for the next twelve months. By the way, are you sure you won't join me?" the colonel asked, as he poured himself a second cup.

⊸◦⊷

"Will you take this woman to be your lawful wedded wife?" intoned the bishop of Connecticut.

"I will," said Jimmy.

"Will you take this man to be your lawful wedded husband?"

"I will," said Joanna.

"Will you take this woman to be your lawful wedded wife?" repeated the bishop.

"I will," said Fletcher.

"Will you take this man to be your lawful wedded husband?"

"I will," said Annie.

Double weddings were a rare event in Hartford, and the bishop admitted that it was the first he'd ever conducted.

Senator Gates stood at the head of a long receiving line, smiling at each new guest. He knew almost all of them. After all, both of his children were being married on the same day.

"Who would have thought Jimmy would end up marrying the smartest girl in the class?" said Harry proudly.

"Why shouldn't he?" asked Martha. "You did. And don't forget, thanks to Joanna, he also managed *cum laude*."

"We'll cut the cake, just as soon as everyone is seated at their tables," announced the maître d', "and I'll need the brides and grooms in front, and the parents behind the cake when the photographs are taken."

"You won't have to round up my husband," said Martha Gates. "If a flashbulb goes off, he'll be on the other side of the camera within moments—it's an occupational hazard."

"How right she is," admitted the senator. He turned his attention to Ruth Davenport, who was looking wistfully at her daughter-in-law.

"I sometimes wonder if they aren't both a little too young."

"She's twenty," said the senator, "Martha and I were married when she was twenty."

"But Annie still hasn't graduated."

"Does it matter? They've been together for the past six years." The senator turned to greet another guest.

"I sometimes wish ... ." began Ruth.

"What do you sometimes wish?" inquired Robert, who was standing on the other side of his wife.

Ruth turned so that the senator couldn't overhear her. "No one could love Annie more than I do, but I sometimes wish they, well," she hesitated, "they had both dated more."

"Fletcher met lots of other girls, he just didn't want to date them, and by the way," said Robert, allowing his champagne glass to be refilled yet again, "how often have I gone shopping with you, only to find you end up buying the dress you first looked at?"

"That didn't stop me considering several other men before I settled for you," said Ruth.

"Yes, but that was different, because none of the others wanted you."

"Robert Davenport, I would have you know . . ."

"Ruth, have you forgotten how many times I asked you to

marry me before you finally accepted? I even tried to make you pregnant."

"You never told me that," said Ruth, turning to face her husband.

"You've obviously forgotten how long it was before you eventually had Fletcher."

Ruth looked back at her daughter-in-law. "Let's hope she doesn't have to face the same problem."

"No reason why they should," said Robert. "It's not Fletcher who is going to have to give birth. And my bet is," he continued, "that Fletcher, like me, will never look at another woman for the rest of his life."

"You've never looked at another woman since we've been married?" said Ruth after shaking hands with two more guests.

"No," said Robert, before he took another gulp of champagne, "I slept with several of them, but I never looked at them."

"Robert, how much have you had to drink?"

"I haven't counted," Robert admitted, as Jimmy broke away from the line.

"What are you two laughing about, Mr. Davenport?"

"I was telling Ruth about my many conquests, but she refuses to believe me. So tell me, Jimmy, what are you hoping to do when you graduate?"

"I'll be joining Fletcher at law school. It's likely to be a tough ride, but with your son to get me through the day, and Joanna the night, I might just about manage it. You must be very proud of him," said Jimmy.

"*Magna cum laude* and president of the college council," said Robert. "We sure are," he added as he held out his empty glass to a passing waiter.

"You're drunk," said Ruth, trying not to smile.

"You're right as always, my darling, but that won't stop me being inordinately proud of my only son."

"But he would never have become president without Jimmy's contribution," said Ruth firmly.

"It's very kind of you to say so, Mrs. Davenport, but don't forget, Fletcher won by a landslide."

"But only after you had convinced Tom . . . whatever his name was, that he should concede and back Fletcher."

"It may have helped, but it was Fletcher who instigated the changes that will affect a generation of Yalies," said Jimmy as Annie came over to join them. "Hi, kid sister."

"When I'm chairman of General Motors, will you still address me in that tiresome manner?"

"Sure will," said Jimmy, "and what's more, I'll stop driving Caddies."

Annie was just about to hit him, when the maître d' suggested that the time had come to cut the cake.

Ruth put an arm around her daughter-in-law. "Take no notice of your brother," she said, "because once you've graduated, he'll have been put firmly in his place."

"It's not my brother I need to prove anything to," said Annie. "It's always been your son who sets the pace."

"Then you'll just have to beat him as well," said Ruth.

"I'm not sure I want to," said Annie. "You know he's talking about going into politics once he's obtained his law degree."

"That shouldn't stop you having your own career."

"It won't, but I'm not too proud to make sacrifices if it will help him to achieve his ambitions."

"But you've the right to a career of your own," said Ruth.

"Why?" said Annie. "Because it's suddenly become fashionable? Perhaps I'm not like Joanna," she said, glancing across at her sister-in-law. "I know what I want, Ruth, and I'll do whatever is necessary to achieve it."

"And what's that?" asked Ruth quietly.

"Support the man I love for the rest of my life, bring up his children, delight in his success, and with all the pressures of the seventies, that may prove a lot harder than gaining a *magna cum laude* from Vassar," said Annie as she picked up the silver knife with an ivory handle. "You know, I suspect there are going to be far fewer golden wedding anniversaries in the twenty-first century than there have been in the twentieth."

"You're a lucky man, Fletcher," said his mother as Annie placed the knife on the bottom layer of the cake.

"I knew that even before the braces had been removed from her teeth," said Fletcher.

Annie passed the knife across to Joanna. "Make a wish," whispered Jimmy.

"I already have, freshman," she replied, "and what's more, it's been granted."

"Ah, you mean the privilege of being married to me?"

"Good heavens no, it's far more significant than that."

"What could possibly be more significant than that?"

"The fact that we're going to have a baby."

Jimmy threw his arms around his wife. "When did that happen?"

"I don't know the exact moment, but I stopped taking the pill a while ago once I was convinced you'd graduate."

"That's wonderful. Come on, let's share the news with our guests."

"You say a word, and I'll plant this knife in you instead of the cake. Mind you, I always knew it was a mistake to marry a freshman with red hair."

"I bet the baby has red hair."

"Don't be too sure, freshman, because if you mention it to anyone, I'll tell them I'm not certain who the father is."

"Ladies and gentlemen," said Jimmy, as his wife raised the knife, "I have an announcement to make." The room fell silent. "Joanna and I are going to have a baby." The silence continued for a moment, before the five hundred guests broke into spontaneous applause.

"You're dead, freshman," said Joanna, as she plunged the knife into the cake.

"I knew that the moment I met you, Mrs. Gates, but I think we should have at least three children before you finally kill me."

"Well, Senator, you're about to become a grandfather," said Ruth. "My congratulations. I can't wait to be a grandmother, although I suspect it will be some time before Annie has her first child."

"She won't even consider it until she's graduated, would be my bet," said Harry Gates, "especially when they find out what I have planned for Fletcher."

"Is it possible that Fletcher might not fall in with your plans?" suggested Ruth.

"Not as long as Jimmy and I continue to make him feel that it was always his idea in the first place."

"Don't you think by now he might just have worked out what you're up to?"

"He's been able to do that since the day I met him at the Hotchkiss versus Taft game nearly a decade ago. I knew then he was capable of raising the bar far higher than I ever could."

The senator placed an arm around Ruth. "However, there's one problem I may need your help with."

"And what's that?" asked Ruth.

"I don't think Fletcher has made up his mind yet if he's a Republican or a Democrat, and I know how strongly your husband . . ."

"Isn't it wonderful news about Joanna?" said Fletcher to his mother-in-law.

"Sure is," said Martha, "Harry's already counting the extra votes he'll pick up once he becomes a grandfather."

"What makes him so confident of that?" asked Fletcher.

"Senior citizens are the fastest growing section of the electorate, so it must be worth at least a percentage point for the voters to see Harry wheeling a stroller everywhere."

"And if Annie and I have a child, will that be worth another percentage point?"

"No, no," said Martha, "it's all in the timing. Just try to remember that Harry will be up for reelection again in two years' time."

"Do you think we should plan the birth of our first child simply to coincide with the date of Harry's next election?"

"You'd be surprised how many politicians do," replied Martha.

"Congratulations, Joanna," said the senator, giving his daughter-in-law a hug.

"Will your son ever be able to keep a secret?" Joanna hissed as she extracted the knife from the cake.

"No, not if it will make his friends happy," admitted the senator, "but if he thought it would harm someone he loved, he would carry the secret to his grave."

16

PROFESSOR KARL ABRAHAMS entered the lecture theater as the clock struck nine. The professor gave eight lectures a term, and it was rumored that he had never missed one in thirty-seven years. Many of the other rumors about Karl Abrahams could not be substantiated, and so he would have dismissed them as hearsay and therefore inadmissible.

However, such rumors persisted, and thus became part of folklore. There was no doubting his sardonic wit should any student be foolish enough to take him on; that could be testified to on a weekly basis. Whether it was the case that three presidents had invited him to join the Supreme Court, only the three presidents knew. However it was recorded that, when questioned about this, Abrahams said he felt the best service he could give the nation was to instruct the next generation of lawyers and create as many decent, honest counselors as possible, rather than clear up the mess made by so many bad ones.

The *Washington Post,* in an unauthorized profile, observed that Abrahams had taught two members of the present Supreme Court, twenty-two federal judges and several of the deans of leading law schools.

When Fletcher and Jimmy attended the first of Abrahams's eight lectures, they weren't under any illusion about how much work lay ahead of them. Fletcher was, however, under the illusion that during his final year as an undergraduate, he had put in sufficiently long hours, often ending up in bed after midnight. It took

Professor Abrahams about a week to familiarize him with hours when he normally slept.

Professor Abrahams continually reminded his first-year students that not all of them would attend his final address to the law graduates at the end of the course. Jimmy bowed his head. Fletcher began to spend so many hours researching that Annie rarely saw him before the library doors had been locked and bolted. Jimmy would sometimes leave a little earlier so that he could be with Joanna, but he rarely departed without several books under his arm. Fletcher told Annie that he'd never known her brother to work so hard.

"And it won't be any easier for him once the baby arrives," Annie reminded her husband one evening after she had come to pick him up from the library.

"Joanna will have planned for the child to be born during the vacation so she can be back at work on the first day of the term."

"I don't want our first child to grow up like that," said Annie. "I intend to raise my children in our home as a full-time mother and with a father who will be back early enough in the evening to read to them."

"Suits me," said Fletcher. "But if you change your mind and decide to become the chairman of General Motors, I'll be happy to change the diapers."

⋘⊙⋙

The first thing that surprised Nat when he returned to the university was how immature his former classmates seemed to be. He had sufficient credits to allow him to move on to his sophomore year, but the students he had mixed with before signing up were still discussing the latest pop group or movie star, and he'd never even heard of The Doors. It wasn't until he attended his first lecture that he became aware just how much the experience of Vietnam had changed his life.

Nat was also aware that his fellow students didn't treat him as if he was one of them, not least because a few of the professors also appeared somewhat in awe. Nat enjoyed the respect he was afforded, but quickly discovered there was another side to that coin. Over the Christmas vacation, he discussed the problem with

132

Tom, who told him that he understood why some of them were a bit wary of him; after all, they believed he had killed at least a hundred Vietcong. "At least a hundred?" repeated Nat.

"While others have read what our soldiers did to the Vietnamese women," said Tom.

"I should have been so lucky; if it hadn't been for Mollie, I'd have remained celibate."

"Well, don't disillusion them would be my advice," said Tom, "because my bet is that the men are envious and the women intrigued. The last thing you want them to discover is that you're a normal law-abiding citizen."

"I sometimes wish they'd remember that I'm also only nineteen," Nat replied.

"The trouble is," said Tom, "that Captain Cartwright, holder of the Medal of Honor, doesn't sound as if he's only nineteen, and I'm afraid the limp only reminds them."

Nat took his friend's advice, and decided to dissipate his energy in the classroom, in the gym and on the cross-country course. The doctors had warned him that it could take at least a year before he would be able to run again—if ever. After their pessimistic prediction, Nat never spent less than an hour a day in the gym, climbing ropes, lifting weights and even playing the occasional game of paddle tennis. By the end of the first term back he was able to jog slowly around the course—even if it did take him an hour and twenty minutes to cover six miles. He looked up his old training schedule, and found that his record as a freshman remained on the books at thirty-four minutes, eighteen seconds. He promised himself that he would break that by the end of his sophomore year.

The next problem Nat faced was the response he got whenever he asked a woman out on a date. They either wanted to jump straight into bed with him or simply turned him down out of hand. Tom had warned him that his scalp in bed was probably a prize several undergraduates wanted to claim, and Nat quickly discovered that some he hadn't even met were already doing so.

"Reputation has its disadvantages," complained Nat.

"I'll swap places with you if you like," said Tom.

The one exception turned out to be Rebecca, who made it clear from the day Nat arrived back on campus that she wanted to be given a second chance. Nat was circumspect about rekindling that particular old flame, and concluded that if they were to rebuild any relationship, it would have to be done slowly. Rebecca, however, had other plans.

After their second date, she invited him back to her room for coffee, and started trying to undress him only moments after she'd closed the door. Nat broke away, and could only come up with the lame excuse that he was running a time trial the following day. She wasn't put off that easily, and when she reappeared a few minutes later carrying two cups of coffee, Rebecca had already changed into a silk robe that revealed she was wearing little if anything underneath. Nat suddenly realized that he no longer felt anything for her, and quickly drank his coffee, repeating that he needed an early night.

"Time trials never worried you in the past," teased Rebecca.

"That was when I had two good legs," replied Nat.

"Perhaps I'm no longer good enough for you," said Rebecca, "now that everybody thinks you're some kind of hero."

"It's got nothing to do with that. It's just . . ."

"It's just that Ralph was right about you from the start."

"What do you mean by that?" asked Nat sharply.

"You're simply not in his class. In or out of bed." She paused.

Nat was about to respond but decided it wasn't worth it. He left without saying another word. Later that night he lay awake, realizing that Rebecca, like so many other things, was part of his past life.

One of Nat's more surprising discoveries on returning to the university was how many students pressed him to run against Elliot for the president of the student senate. But Nat made it clear that he had no interest in fighting an election while he still needed to make up for the time he'd lost.

When he returned home at the end of his sophomore year, Nat told his father that he was just as pleased that his cross-country time was now down to under an hour as to discover he was placed in the top six on the class list.

During the summer, Nat and Tom traveled to Europe. Nat found that one of the many advantages of a captain's salary was that it allowed him to accompany his closest friend without ever feeling he couldn't afford to pay his way.

Their first stop was London, where they watched the guards march down Whitehall. Nat was left in no doubt that they would have been a formidable force in Vietnam. In Paris, they strolled along the Champs Elysées and regretted having to turn to a phrase book every time they saw a beautiful woman. They then traveled on to Rome, where in tiny back-street cafés they discovered for the first time how pasta really should taste, and swore they would never eat at McDonald's again.

But it wasn't until they reached Venice that Nat fell in love, and overnight became promiscuous, his taste ranging from nudes to virgins. It began with a one-day stand—Da Vinci, followed by Bellini, and then Luini. Such was the intensity of these affairs that Tom agreed they should spend a few more days in Italy and even add Florence to their itinerary. New lovers were quickly picked up on every street corner—Michelangelo, Caravaggio, Canaletto, Tintoretto. Almost anyone with an o at the end of their name qualified to join Nat's harem.

—◇—

Professor Karl Abrahams stood in front of his desk for the fifth lecture of the term and stared up at the semicircle of tiered seats that rose above him.

He began his lecture, not a book, not a file, not even a note in front of him, as he took them through the landmark case of *Carter v. Amalgamated Steel*.

"Mr. Carter," began the professor, "lost an arm in an industrial accident in 1923, and was sacked without receiving a cent in compensation. He was unable to seek further employment, as no other steel company would consider offering work to a one-armed man, and when he was turned down for a job as doorman at a local hotel, he realized that he would never work again. There wasn't an Industry Compensation Act until 1927, so Mr. Carter decided to take the rare and almost unheard-of step at that time of suing his employers. He wasn't able to afford a lawyer—that hasn't changed over the years—however, a young law student who felt that Mr. Carter had not received fair recompense volunteered to represent him in court. He won the case and Carter was awarded one hundred dollars in compensation—not a large amount for such a grievance, you might well feel. However, together these two men were responsible for bringing about a change in the law. Let us hope that one of you might at some time in the future cause the law to be changed when faced with such an injustice. Subtext, the young lawyer's name was Theo Rampleiri. He only narrowly avoided being thrown out of law school for spending too much time on the Carter case. Later, much later, he was appointed to the Supreme Court."

The professor frowned. "Last year General Motors paid a Mr. Cameron five million dollars for the loss of a leg. This was despite the fact that GM was able to prove that it was Mr. Cameron's negligence that was the cause of the injury." Abrahams took them through the case slowly, before adding, "The law so often is, as Mr. Charles Dickens would have us believe, an ass, and perhaps more importantly, indiscriminately imperfect. I have no brief for counsel who look only for a way around the law, especially when they know exactly what the Senate and Congress intended in the first place. There will be those among you who forget these words within days of joining some illustrious firm, whose only interest is to win at all cost. But there will be others, perhaps not so many, who will remember Lincoln's dictum, 'let justice be done.'" Fletcher looked up from his notes and stared down at his mentor. "By the time we next meet, I expect you to have researched the five cases that followed *Carter* versus *Amalgamated Steel,* through to *Demetri* versus *Demetri,* all of which resulted in changes in the law. You may work in pairs, but not consult any other pair. I hope I make myself clear." The clock struck eleven. "Good morning, ladies and gentlemen."

Fletcher and Jimmy shared the workload as they trawled through case after case, and by the end of the week, they had found three that were relevant. Joanna pulled from the recesses of her memory a fourth that had been heard in Ohio when she was a child. She refused to give them any more clues.

"What does love, honor and obey mean?" demanded Jimmy.

"I never agreed to obey you, freshman," was all she said, "and by the way, if Elizabeth wakes up during the night, it's your turn to change her diaper."

"*Sumner* versus *Sumner*," Jimmy told her triumphantly as he slipped into bed just after midnight.

"Not bad, freshman, but you still have to find the fifth by ten o'clock on Monday if you're hoping to get a smile out of Professor Abrahams."

"I think we'd have to do a whole lot more than that to move the lips on that block of granite," said Jimmy.

⟐

As Nat climbed the hill, he spotted her running ahead of him. Nat assumed he would pass her on the downward slope. He checked his watch as he reached the halfway mark. Seventeen minutes and nine seconds. Nat felt confident that he would break his personal best, and be back on the team for the first meet of the season.

He felt full of energy as he surged over the brow of the hill and then he swore out loud. The stupid woman had taken the wrong path. She had to be a freshman. He began to shout at her back, but she didn't respond. He cursed again, changed direction and chased after her. As he came bounding down the slope, she suddenly turned and looked startled.

"You're going the wrong way," shouted Nat, ready to turn and quickly retrace his steps, but even at twenty yards he wanted to take a closer look. He jogged quickly up to her, and kept running on the spot.

"Thank you," she said, "it's only my second time on the course, and I couldn't remember which path to take at the top of the hill."

Nat smiled. "You have to take the smaller path; the wider one leads you into the woods."

"Thank you," she repeated, and began running back up the hill without another word.

He chased after her, and once he had caught up jogged by her side until they reached the top. He waved goodbye once he was certain she had returned to the straight and narrow. "See you later," he said, but if she replied, Nat didn't hear her.

Nat checked his watch as he crossed the finishing line. Forty-three minutes, fifty-one seconds. He cursed again, wondering how much time he'd lost redirecting the wrong-path woman. He didn't mind. He began to cool down, and took longer over his stretching exercises than he normally would have done, as he waited for the young woman to return.

Suddenly she appeared at the top of the hill, running down toward the finishing line. "You made it," Nat said with a smile as he jogged over to join her. She didn't return his smile. "I'm Nat Cartwright," he said.

"I know who you are," she replied curtly.

"Have we met before?"

"No," she said, "I know you only by reputation." She jogged off in the direction of the women's locker room without offering any further explanation.

—◦—

"Stand up, those who managed to find all five cases."

Fletcher and Jimmy rose triumphantly, an emotion that deflated when they discovered at least seventy percent of the class were also on their feet. "Four?" said the professor, trying not to sound too disdainful. Most of those remaining rose, leaving around ten percent still seated. Fletcher could only wonder how many of them would complete the course. "Sit down," he said. "Let us begin with *Maxwell River Gas* versus *Pennstone*; what change in the law came about because of that particular case?" He pointed to a student in the third row.

"In 1932 it became the company's responsibility to ensure that all equipment complied with safety regulations, and all employees understood any emergency procedure." The professor moved his finger on.

"Any written instructions had to be posted where every employee could read them."

"When did that become redundant?"

The finger moved again, another voice, "*Reynolds* versus *McDermond Timber*."

"Correct." The finger moved again. "And why?"

"Reynolds lost three fingers when cutting a log, but his defense counsel was able to show he couldn't read, and had not been given any verbal instruction on how to operate the machine."

"What was the basis of the new law?" The finger moved again.

"The Industry Act, 1934, when it became an employer's responsibility to instruct all staff, verbally and in writing, how to use any equipment."

"When did that need further amendments?" Someone else was selected.

"*Rush* versus the *government*."

"Correct, but why did the government still win the case despite being in the wrong?"

Yet another selection. "I don't know, sir." The finger moved scornfully on, in search of someone who did.

"The government was able to defend its position when it was shown that Rush had signed an agreement stating . . ." The finger moved.

". . . that he'd received full instructions as demanded by law." The finger moved again.

"That he had also been in their employ beyond the statutory three-year period." The finger continued moving . . .

". . . but the government went on to prove they were not a company in the strict meaning of the word, as the bill had been badly drafted by the politicians."

"Don't blame the politicians," said Abrahams. "Lawyers draft legislation, so they must take the responsibility. The politicians were not culpable on this occasion, so once the courts accepted that the government was not subject to its own legislation, who caused the law to be changed yet again?" He pointed the finger at another terrified face. "*Demetri* versus *Demetri*," came the reply.

"How did this differ from past laws?" The finger came to rest on Fletcher.

"It was the first time that one member of a family sued another for negligence while they were still married, as well as being fifty-fifty shareholders in the company concerned."

"Why did that action fail?" he continued to stare at Fletcher.

"Because Mrs. Demetri refused to give evidence against her husband."

The finger moved on to Jimmy. "Why did she refuse?" demanded Abrahams.

"Because she was stupid."

"Why was she stupid?" demanded the professor again.

"Because her husband probably made love to her, or hit her, the night before or possibly even both, so she caved in." A little laughter broke out.

"Were you present to witness the lovemaking, Mr. Gates, or the attack on her?" asked Abrahams, to even more laughter.

"No, sir," said Jimmy, "but I'll bet it's what happened."

"You may well be right, Mr. Gates, but you would not have been able to prove what took place in the bedroom that night unless you could provide a reliable witness. Had you made such a rash statement in court, opposing counsel would have objected, the judge would have sustained his objection, and the jury would have dismissed you as a fool, Mr. Gates. And more importantly, you would have let down your client. Don't ever rely on what might have happened, however likely it appears, unless you can prove it. If you can't, remain silent."

"But . . ." began Fletcher. Several students quickly bowed their heads, others held their breath, while the rest just stared at Fletcher in disbelief.

"Name?"

"Davenport, sir."

"No doubt you feel able to explain what you mean by the word 'but,' Mr. Davenport?"

"Mrs. Demetri was advised by her counsel that if she won the case, as neither of them owned a majority holding, the company would have to cease trading. The Kendall Act, 1941. She then placed her shares on the open market and they were picked up by her husband's greatest rival, a Mr. Canelli, for $100,000. I cannot prove that Mr. Canelli was, or wasn't, sleeping with Mrs. Demetri, but I do know that the company went into liquidation a year later, when she repurchased her shares for ten cents each, at a cost of $7,300, and then immediately signed a new partnership deal with her husband."

"Was Mr. Canelli able to prove the Demetris were acting in collusion?" Fletcher thought carefully. Was Abrahams setting him a trap? "Why do you hesitate?" demanded Abrahams.

"It wouldn't constitute proof, professor."

"Nevertheless, what is it you wish to tell us?"

"Mrs. Demetri produced a second child a year later, and the birth certificate indicated that Mr. Demetri was the father."

"You're right, that is not proof, so what charge was brought against her?"

"None; in fact, the new company went on to be very successful."

"Then how did they cause the law to be changed?"

"The judge brought this case to the attention of the attorney general of that state."

"Which state?"

"Ohio, and as a consequence, they passed the Marriage Partnership Act."

"Year?"

"1949."

"Changes of relevance?"

"Husbands and wives could no longer repurchase shares sold in a former company in which they had been partners, if that directly benefited them as individuals."

"Thank you, Mr. Davenport," said the professor, as the clock struck eleven. "Your 'but' was well qualified." A ripple of applause broke out. "But not that well qualified," added Abrahams, as he left the lecture theater.

—◦—

Nat sat on the wall opposite the dining hall and waited patiently. After he had seen about five hundred young women leave the building, he decided the reason she was so slim was because she simply didn't eat. Then she suddenly came rushing through the swing doors. Nat had been given more than enough time to rehearse his lines, but still felt nervous when he caught up with her. "Hi, I'm Nat." She looked up, but didn't smile. "We met the other day." She still didn't respond.

"On the top of the hill."

"Yes, I do remember," she said.

"But you didn't tell me your name."

"No, I didn't."

"Have I done something to annoy you?"

"No."

"Then can I ask what you meant by 'your reputation'?"

"Mr. Cartwright, you may be surprised to learn that there are some women on this campus who don't think you have the automatic right to claim their virginity simply because you've won the Medal of Honor."

"I never thought I did."

"But you must be aware that half the women on campus claim they've slept with you."

"They may well claim it," said Nat, "but the truth is that only two of them can prove it."

"But everyone knows how many girls chase after you."

"And most of them can't keep up, as I'm sure you remember." He laughed, but she didn't respond. "So why can't I fall for someone just like anyone else?"

"But you're not just like anyone else," she said quietly. "You're a war hero on a captain's salary, and as such you expect everyone else to fall in line."

"Who told you that?"

"Someone who's known you since your school days."

"Ralph Elliot, no doubt?"

"Yes, the man you tried to cheat out of the Taft student government presidency . . ."

"I did *what*?" said Nat.

". . . and then passed off his essay as yours when you applied for Yale," she said ignoring his interruption.

"Is that what he told you?"

"Yes," the young woman replied calmly.

"Then perhaps you should ask him why he isn't at Yale."

"He explained that you transferred the blame on to him so he lost his place as well." Nat was about to explode again, when she added, "And now you want to be president of the student senate, and your only strategy seems to be to sleep your way to victory."

Nat tried to control his temper. "First, I don't want to run for president, second, I've only slept with three women in my life: a student I also knew when I was at school, a secretary in Vietnam, and a one-night stand I now regret. If you can find anyone else, please introduce me because I'd like to meet them." She stopped and looked at Nat for the first time. "Anyone else," he repeated. "Now can I at least know your name?"

"Su Ling," she said quietly.

"Su Ling, if I promise never to try and seduce you until after I've asked for your hand in marriage, sought your father's permission, produced a ring, booked the church, and had the banns read, will you at least let me take you out to dinner?"

Su Ling laughed. "I'll think about it," she said. "I'm sorry to rush, but I'm already late for my afternoon lecture."

"But how do I find you?" asked Nat desperately.

"You managed to find the Vietcong, Captain Cartwright, surely it shouldn't be too difficult to find me?"

17

"ALL RISE. The *State* versus *Mrs. Anita Kirsten*. His Honor Mr. Justice Abernathy presiding."

The judge took his place and looked toward the defense counsel's table. "How do you plead, Mrs. Kirsten?"

Fletcher rose from behind the defense table. "My client pleads Not Guilty, your honor."

The judge looked up, "Are you representing the defendant?"

"Yes, I am, your honor."

Judge Abernathy glanced down at the charge sheet. "I don't think I've come across you before, Mr. Davenport?"

"No, your honor, it's my first appearance in your court."

"Will you please approach the bench, Mr. Davenport?"

"Yes, sir." Fletcher stepped out from behind the little table and walked toward the judge, where the prosecution counsel joined them.

"Good morning, gentlemen," said Mr. Justice Abernathy. "May I inquire what legal qualifications you have that are recognized in my court, Mr. Davenport?"

"None, sir."

"I see. Is your client aware of this?"

"Yes, sir, she is."

"But she still wants you to represent her, despite this being a capital charge?"

"Yes, sir."

The judge turned to face the attorney general for Connecticut.

144

"Do you have any objection to Mr. Davenport representing Mrs. Kirsten?"

"None whatsoever, your honor; in fact the state welcomes it."

"I feel sure they do," said the judge, "but I must ask you, Mr. Davenport, if you have any experience of the law at all."

"Not a great deal, your honor," Fletcher admitted. "I'm a second-year law student at Yale, and this will be my first case." The judge and the attorney general smiled.

"May I ask who your director of studies is?" asked the judge.

"Professor Karl Abrahams."

"Then I am proud to preside over your first case, Mr. Davenport, because that is something you and I have in common. How about you, Mr. Stamp?"

"No, sir, I qualified in South Carolina."

"Although it is most irregular, in the end it must be the defendant's decision, so let us proceed with the case in hand." The attorney general and Fletcher returned to their places.

The judge looked down at Fletcher. "Will you be applying for bail, Mr. Davenport?"

Fletcher rose from his place. "Yes, sir."

"On what grounds?"

"That Mrs. Kirsten has no previous record, and constitutes no danger to the public. She is the mother of two children, Alan aged seven, and Della aged five, who are currently living with their grandmother in Hartford."

The judge turned his attention to the attorney general. "Does the state have any objection to grant bail to Mr. Stamp?"

"We most certainly do, your honor. We oppose bail not only on the grounds that this is a capital charge, but because the murder itself was premeditated. We therefore contend that Mrs. Kirsten constitutes a danger to society, and may also try to leave the state's jurisdiction."

Fletcher shot up. "I must object, your honor."

"On what grounds, Mr. Davenport?"

"This is indeed a capital charge, so leaving the state is hardly relevant, your honor, and in any case, Mrs. Kirsten's home is in

JEFFREY ARCHER

Hartford, where she earns her living working as a hospital custodian at St. Mary's, and her children are both at a local school."

"Any further submission, Mr. Davenport?"

"No, sir."

"Bail refused," said the judge, and brought his hammer down. "This court is adjourned until Monday the seventeenth."

"All rise."

Mr. Justice Abernathy winked at Fletcher as he left the courtroom.

—◦—

Thirty-four minutes and ten seconds. Nat couldn't hide his delight that he had not only broken his personal best, but had managed sixth place in the university trials, and was therefore certain to be picked for the opening meet against Boston University.

As Nat cooled down, and went through his usual stretching routine, Tom walked over to join him. "Congratulations," he said, "and my bet is that by the end of the season, you'll have knocked another minute off your time."

Nat stared at the sour red scar on the back of his leg as he pulled on his sweat-pants. "Why don't we have dinner tonight," continued Tom, "and celebrate, because there's something I need to discuss with you before I go back to Yale."

"Can't manage tonight," said Nat as they began to stroll across to the locker rooms. "I've got a date."

"Anyone I know?"

"No," said Nat, "but as it's my first for months, I have to admit I'm quite nervous."

"Captain Cartwright nervous? Whatever next?" mocked Tom.

"That's the problem," admitted Nat. "She thinks I'm a cross between Don Juan and Al Capone."

"She sounds like a good judge of character," said Tom. "So tell me all about her."

"There's not that much to tell. We ran into each other on the top of a hill. She's bright, ferocious, quite beautiful, and thinks I'm a bastard." Nat then recounted their conversation outside the dining hall.

"Ralph Elliot obviously got his version in first," said Tom.

"To hell with Elliot. Do you think I should wear a jacket and tie?"

"You haven't asked for that sort of advice since we were at Taft."

"And in those days I needed to borrow your jacket and your tie, so what do you think?"

"Full dress uniform with medals."

"Be serious."

"Well, it would certainly confirm her opinion of you."

"That's exactly what I'm trying to disabuse her of."

"Well then, try looking at it from her point of view."

"I'm listening."

"What do you think she'll wear?"

"I have no idea, I've only seen her twice in my life, and on one of those occasions she was in her running shorts covered in mud."

"God, that must have been sexy, but I don't suppose she'll turn up in a tracksuit, so what about the other occasion?"

"Smart and understated."

"Then follow her lead, which won't be easy, because there's nothing smart about you, and from what you say, she doesn't believe that you're capable of being understated."

"Answer the question," Nat said.

"I'd go for casual," said Tom. "Shirt, not T-shirt, slacks and a sweater. I could, of course, as your advisor on sartorial elegance, join you both for dinner."

"I don't want you anywhere near the place, because you'll only fall in love with her."

"You really care about this girl, don't you?" said Tom quietly.

"I think she's divine, but that doesn't stop her being very uncertain about me."

"But she's agreed to have dinner with you, so she can't believe you're all bad."

"Yes, but the terms of that agreement were somewhat unusual," said Nat as he told Tom what he had proposed before she would agree to a date.

"As I said, you've got it bad, but that doesn't alter the fact that I need to see you. How about breakfast? Or will you also be having eggs and bacon with this mysterious Oriental lady?"

"I'd be very surprised if she agreed to that," said Nat wistfully. "And disappointed."

—◦—

"How long do you expect the trial to last?" asked Annie.

"If we plead not guilty to murder, but guilty to manslaughter, it could be over in a morning, with perhaps a further court appearance for sentencing."

"Is that possible?" asked Jimmy.

"Yes, the state is offering me a deal."

"What sort of deal?" asked Annie.

"If I agree to a charge of manslaughter, Stamp will only call for three years, no more, which means with good behavior and parole, Anita Kirsten could be out in eighteen months. Otherwise he intends to press for first degree and demand the death penalty."

"They would never send a woman to the electric chair in this state for killing her husband."

"I agree," said Fletcher, "but a tough jury might settle for ninety-nine years, and as the defendant is only twenty-five, I have to accept the fact that she might be better off agreeing to eighteen months; at least that way she could look forward to spending the rest of her life with her family."

"True," said Jimmy. "But I ask myself, why is the attorney general willing to agree to three years if he feels he's got such a strong case? Don't forget this is a black woman, accused of murdering a white man, and at least two members of the jury will be black. If you play your cards right, it could be three, and then you can almost guarantee a hung jury."

"Plus the fact that my client has a good reputation, holds down a responsible job, and has no previous convictions. That's bound to influence any jury, whatever color."

"I wouldn't be so sure of that," said Annie. "Your client poisoned her husband with an overdose of curare, which caused paralysis and then she sat on the staircase waiting for him to die."

"But he'd been beating her up for years—and he also abused their children," said Fletcher.

"Do you have any proof of that, counselor?" asked Jimmy.

"Not a lot, but on the day she agreed to appoint me, I took several photographs of the bruises on her body, and the burn on the palm of her hand will remain with her for the rest of her life."

"How did she get that?" asked Annie.

"That bastard of a husband pressed her hand down on a burning stove, and only stopped when she fainted."

"Sounds like a lovely guy," said Annie. "So what's stopping you pleading manslaughter and pressing for extenuating circumstances?"

"Only the fear of losing, and Mrs. Kirsten having to spend the rest of her life in jail."

"Why did she ask you to be her defense counsel in the first place?" asked Jimmy.

"No one else stepped up to the plate," replied Fletcher. "And in any case, she found my fee irresistible."

"But you're up against the state's attorney."

"Which is a bit of a mystery, because I can't work out why he's bothering to represent the state in a case like this."

"That's simply answered," said Jimmy. "Black woman kills white man in a state where only twenty percent of the population is black, and over half of them don't bother to vote, and surprise, surprise, there's an election coming up in May."

"How long has Stamp given you before you have to tell him your decision?" asked Annie.

"We're back in court next Monday."

"Can you spare the time to be involved in a long trial?" she asked.

"No, but I mustn't make that an excuse for agreeing to any compromise."

"So we'll be spending our holiday in court number three, will we?" asked Annie with a grin.

"It could even be court number four," said Fletcher, putting an arm around his wife.

"Have you thought of asking Professor Abrahams's advice on how she should plead?"

Jimmy and Fletcher stared at her in disbelief. "He advises presidents and heads of state," said Fletcher.

"And possibly the occasional governor," added Jimmy.

"Then perhaps the time has come for him to start advising a second-year law student. After all, that's what he's paid for."

"I wouldn't know where to start," said Fletcher.

"How about picking up the phone and asking if he'll see you," said Annie. "My bet is that he'd be flattered."

—◦—

Nat arrived at Mario's fifteen minutes early. He'd chosen the restaurant because it was unpretentious—tables with red-and-white checked cloths, a small arrangement of flowers, with black-and-white photos of Florence decorating the walls. Tom had also told him the pasta was homemade, cooked by the patron's wife, and this had brought back memories of their trip to Rome. He'd taken Tom's advice and selected a casual blue shirt, gray slacks and a navy sweater, no tie and no jacket—Tom had approved.

Nat introduced himself to Mario, who suggested a quiet table in the corner. After Nat had read the menu several times, he looked at his watch again, becoming ever more nervous. He must have checked a dozen times to be sure he had enough cash on him in case they didn't accept credit cards. Perhaps it would have been more sensible if he had walked around the block a couple of times.

The moment he saw her, he realized he'd blown it. Su Ling was wearing a smart, well-cut blue suit, cream blouse and navy shoes. Nat rose from his place and waved. She smiled—a smile he hadn't experienced until then, which made her look even more captivating. She walked over to join him.

"I apologize," he said, rising from his place as he waited for her to be seated.

"What for?" she asked, looking puzzled.

"My clothes. I confess I spent a lot of time thinking about what I should wear, and still got it wrong."

"Me too," said Su Ling. "I expected you to turn up in a uniform covered in medals," she added as she slipped off her jacket and placed it over the back of her chair.

Nat burst out laughing, and they didn't seem to stop laughing for the next two hours, until Nat asked if she'd like some coffee. "Yes, black please," said Su Ling.

"I've told you about my family, now tell me about yours," Nat said. "Are you, like me, an only child?"

"Yes, my father was a master sergeant in Korea when he met my

150

mother. They were only married for a few months before he was killed at the battle of Yudam-ni."

Nat wanted to lean across and take her hand. "I'm sorry," he said.

"Thank you," she said simply. "Mom decided to emigrate to America so that we could meet up with my grandparents. But we were never able to trace them." This time he did take her hand. "I was too young to know what was going on, but my mother doesn't give up that easily. She took a job in Storrs Laundry, near the bookstore, and the owner allowed us to live above the shop."

"I know that laundry," said Nat. "My father has his shirts done there—it's very efficient and . . ."

". . . And has been ever since my mother took it over, but she's had to sacrifice everything to ensure that I had a good education."

"Your mother sounds just like mine," said Nat as Mario appeared by their side.

"Everything to your satisfaction, Mr. Cartwright?"

"An excellent meal, thank you, Mario," said Nat. "All I need now is the check."

"Certainly, Mr. Cartwright, and may I say what an honor it has been to have you in the restaurant."

"Thank you," said Nat, trying to hide his embarrassment.

"How much did you tip him to say that?" asked Su Ling once Mario had slipped away.

"Ten dollars, and he's word-perfect every time."

"But does it always pay off?" asked Su Ling.

"Oh yes, most of my dates start taking off their clothes even before we get back to the car."

"So do you always bring them here?"

"No. If I think it's likely to be a one-night stand, I take them to McDonald's, followed by a motel—if it's serious, we go to the Altnaveigh Inn."

"So which group are chosen for Mario's?" asked Su Ling.

"I can't answer that," said Nat, "because I've never taken anyone to Mario's before."

"I'm flattered," said Su Ling as he helped her on with her jacket. As they walked out of the restaurant, Su Ling took his hand. "You're really quite shy, aren't you?"

"Yes, I suppose I am," said Nat, as they continued walking toward the campus.

"Not at all like your arch rival, Ralph Elliot." Nat didn't comment. "He asked me for a date within minutes of meeting me."

"To be fair," said Nat, "I would have too, but you walked away."

"I thought I was running at the time," she said. He turned and smiled. "And even more interesting is how much action you actually saw in Vietnam to turn you into such a hero." Nat was about to protest when she added, "Answer, about half an hour."

"How do you know that?" asked Nat.

"Because I did some research on you, Captain Cartwright, and to quote Steinbeck, 'you're sailing under false colors.' I learned that quote today," she said, "just in case you might think I'm well read. When you jumped on the helicopter, you weren't even carrying a gun. You were a warrant officer who shouldn't have been on that aircraft in the first place. In fact, it was bad enough that you jumped on the helicopter without permission, but you also jumped off it without permission. Mind you, if you hadn't, you might well have been court-martialed."

"True," said Nat, "but don't tell anyone else, because it will stop me having my usual three girls a night."

Su Ling placed a hand in front of her mouth and laughed. "But I did read on, and your action after the helicopter crashed in the jungle was that of an extremely brave man. To have dragged that poor soldier on a stretcher with half your leg blown away must have taken immense courage, and then to discover he had later died can only have left an irremediable scar." Nat didn't reply. "I'm sorry," she said as they reached south campus, "that last remark was inconsiderate of me."

"It was kind of you to search for the truth," he said, looking down into her dark brown eyes. "Not many have bothered to do that."

18

"MEMBERS OF THE jury, in most murder trials it is the responsibility of the state, and rightly so, to prove that the defendant is guilty of homicide. That has not proved necessary in this case. Why? Because Mrs. Kirsten signed a confession within an hour of her husband's brutal killing. And even now, eight months later, you will have noted that her legal representative has not at any time during this trial suggested that his client didn't commit the crime, or even challenged how she went about it.

"So let us turn to the facts in this case, because this was not what could be described as a crime of passion where a woman seeks to defend herself with the nearest weapon at hand. No, Mrs. Kirsten was not interested in the nearest weapon at hand, because she spent several weeks planning this cold-blooded murder, well aware that her victim would have no chance of defending himself.

"How did Mrs. Kirsten set about her task? Over a period of nearly three months, she collected several vials of curare from different drug dealers who reside in the shadows of Hartford. The defense tried to suggest that none of the dealers' evidence could be relied upon, which might have influenced you had Mrs. Kirsten herself not confirmed from the witness stand that they were all telling the truth.

"Having collected the vials over several weeks, what does Mrs. Kirsten do next? She waits until a Saturday night, when she knows her husband goes out drinking with his friends, and covertly pours the drug into six bottles of beer, and even replaces the tops. She then puts these bottles on the kitchen table, leaves the light on and goes to bed. She even places a bottle opener and a glass next to them. She does everything except pour out the drink herself.

"Ladies and gentlemen of the jury, this was a well-planned and cleverly executed murder. However, if you can believe it possible, there was even worse to follow.

"When her husband arrives home that night, he does indeed fall into her trap. First he goes to the kitchen, probably to turn off the light, and, seeing the bottles on the table, Alex Kirsten is tempted into having a beer before going to bed. Even before he has put the second bottle to his lips, the drug has begun to take effect. When he calls for help his wife leaves the bedroom and walks slowly down to the hall, where she hears her husband crying out in pain. Does she phone for an ambulance? No, she does not. Does she even go to his assistance? No, she does not. She sits on the staircase and waits patiently until his agonized cries have stopped and she can be certain he's dead. And then, and only then, does she raise the alarm.

"How can we be so sure this is what actually took place? Not just because the neighbors were woken by her husband's haunting screams for help, but because when one of those neighbors came to the door to see if they could assist, in her panic Mrs. Kirsten forgot to dispose of the contents of the other four bottles." He paused for several seconds. "When analyzed, they contained enough curare to kill a football team.

"Members of the jury, the only defense Mr. Davenport has suggested for this crime is that Mrs. Kirsten's husband regularly beat her. If this was the case, why didn't she inform the police? If this was true, why didn't she go and live with her mother, who resides on the other side of the city? If we are to believe her story, why didn't she leave him? I'll tell you why. Because once her husband was out of the way, she would own the house they lived in and collect his pension from the company he worked for, making it possible for her to live in relative comfort for the rest of her life.

"In normal circumstances, the state would not hesitate to call for the death penalty for such a horrendous crime, but we do not feel it is appropriate on this occasion. It is, nevertheless, your duty to send a clear message to any person who believes they can get

away with murder. Such a crime may be lightly regarded in some
other states, but we don't need one of those to be Connecticut.
Do we want to be known as the state that condones murder?"

The attorney general lowered his voice almost to a whisper,
and looked straight at the jury. "When you indulge yourself in a
moment of sympathy for Mrs. Kirsten, and indeed you should, if
only because you are caring human beings, place that on one side
of the scales called justice. On the other side, place the facts—
the cold-blooded murder of a forty-two-year-old man who would
still be alive today if it were not for the premeditated crime cun-
ningly executed by that evil woman." He turned and pointed
directly at the defendant. "The state has no hesitation in asking
you to find Mrs. Kirsten guilty, and sentence her according to the
law." Mr. Stamp returned to his place, the suggestion of a smile
on his his face.

"Mr. Davenport," said the judge, "I intend to break for lunch.
When we return, you may begin your summing up."

—◇—

"You look very pleased with yourself," said Tom as they settled
down for breakfast in the kitchen.

"It was an unforgettable evening."

"From that I assume consummation took place?"

"No, you cannot assume anything of the sort," said Nat. "But I
can tell you that I held her hand."

"You did what?"

"I held her hand," Nat repeated.

"That won't do your reputation any good."

"I'm rather hoping it will ruin my reputation," said Nat as he
poured some milk over his Wheaties. "And how about you?" he
asked.

"If you are referring to my sex life, it is currently nonexistent,
though not through lack of offers, one even persistent. But I'm
just not interested." Nat stared across at his friend and raised an
eyebrow. "Rebecca Thornton has made it all too obvious that she's
available."

"But I thought . . ."

"That she was back with Elliot?"

"Yes."

"Possibly, but whenever I see her, she prefers to talk about you—in very flattering terms, I might add, though I'm told she tells a different story whenever she's with Elliot."

"If that's the case," said Nat, "why do you think she's bothering to chase you?"

Tom pushed aside his empty bowl and began to concentrate on the two boiled eggs in front of him. He cracked the shell and looked at the yolk before he continued. "If it's known that you're an only child and your father is worth millions, most women view you in a completely different light. So I never can be sure if it's me, or my money they're interested in. Just be thankful that you don't suffer from the same problem."

"You'll know when it's the right person," said Nat.

"Will I? I wonder. You're one of the few people who's never shown the slightest interest in my wealth, and you're almost the only person I know who always insists on paying his own way. You'd be surprised by how many people assume I'll pick up the tab just because I can afford it. I despise such people, which means that my circle of friends ends up being very small."

"My latest friend is very small," said Nat, hoping to snap Tom out of his morose mood, "and I know you'll like her."

"The 'I held her hand' girl?"

"Yes, Su Ling—she's about five foot four, and now that thin is fashionable, she'll be the most sought-after woman on the campus."

"Su Ling?" said Tom.

"You know her?" asked Nat.

"No, but my father tells me that she's taken over the new computer lab that his company funded, and the tutors have virtually stopped bothering to try and teach her."

"She never mentioned anything about computers to me last night," said Nat.

"Well, you'd better move quickly, because Dad also mentioned that MIT and Harvard are both trying to tempt her away from UConn, so be warned, there's a big brain on top of that little body."

"And I've made a complete fool of myself again," said Nat, "because I even teased her about her English, when she's obviously mastered a new language that everyone wants to know about. By the way, is that why you wanted to see me?" asked Nat.

"No, I had no idea you were dating a genius."

"I'm not," said Nat, "she's a gentle, thoughtful, beautiful woman, who considers holding hands is one step away from promiscuity." He paused. "So if it wasn't to discuss my sex life, why did you call this high-powered breakfast meeting in the first place?"

Tom gave up on the eggs and pushed them to one side. "Before I return to Yale, I wanted to know if you're going to run for president." He waited for the usual barrage of count me out, not interested, you've got the wrong person, but Nat didn't respond for some time.

"I discussed it with Su Ling last night," he eventually said, "and in her usual disarming way, she told me that it was not so much that they wanted me, as they didn't want Elliot. The lesser of two evils were her exact words, if I remember correctly."

"I'm sure she's right," said Tom, "but that could change if you gave them a chance to get to know you. You've been pretty much of a recluse since you returned to college."

"I've had a lot of catching up to do," said Nat defensively.

"Well that's no longer the case, as your grade point average clearly shows," said Tom, "and now you've been selected to run for the university . . ."

"If you were at UConn, Tom, I wouldn't hesitate to run for president, but while you're at Yale . . ."

—◦—

Fletcher rose from his place to face the jury—ninety-nine years was written on every one of their faces. If he could have turned the clock back and accepted the offer of three years, he would have done so without hesitation. Now he had been left with only one throw of the dice to try and give Mrs. Kirsten the rest of her life back. He touched his client's shoulder, and turned to seek a reassuring smile from Annie, who had felt so strongly that he should defend this woman. The smile disappeared the moment he saw who was seated two rows behind her. Professor Karl Abrahams graced him with a nod. At least Jimmy would discover what it took to get a nod out of Homer.

"Members of the jury," Fletcher began, a slight tremor in his voice. "You have listened to the persuasive advocacy of the attorney general as he poured venom on my client, so perhaps the time has come to show where that venom should have been directed. But first may I spend a moment talking about you. The press have made great play of the fact that I did not object to every white juror who was selected; indeed there are ten of you on this jury. They went further, and suggested that had I achieved an all-black jury with a majority of women, then Mrs. Kirsten would have been certain to walk free. But I didn't want that. I chose each one of you for a different reason." The jury members looked puzzled.

"Even the attorney general couldn't work out why I didn't object to some of you," added Fletcher, turning to face Mr. Stamp. "I crossed my fingers, because neither did any of his vast team fathom why I selected you. So what is it that you all have in common?" The attorney general was now looking just as puzzled as the jurors. Fletcher swung around and pointed to Mrs. Kirsten. "Like the defendant, every one of you has been married for more than nine years." Fletcher turned his attention back to the jury. "No bachelors or spinsters who have never experienced married life, or what goes on between two people behind closed doors." Fletcher spotted a woman in the second row who shuddered. He remembered Abrahams saying that in a jury of twelve, there is a strong possibility that one of them will have suffered the same experience as the defendant. He had just identified that juror.

"Which of you dreads the thought of your spouse returning home after midnight, drunk, with only violence in mind? For Mrs. Kirsten, this was something she had come to expect six nights out of seven, for the past nine years. Look at this frail and fragile woman and ask yourself what chance she would have up against a man of six foot two who weighed two hundred and thirty pounds?"

He focused his attention on the woman juror who had shuddered. "Which of you arrives home at night and expects their husband to grab the bread board, a cheese grater or even a steak knife for use not in the kitchen for preparing a meal, but in the bedroom to disfigure his wife? And what did Mrs. Kirsten have to call on for her defense, this five-foot-four, one-hundred-and-five-pound woman? A pillow? A towel? A flyswatter perhaps?" Fletcher paused. "It's never crossed your mind, has it?" he added, facing the rest of the jurors. "Why? Because your husbands and wives are not evil. Ladies and gentlemen, how can you begin to understand what this woman was being subjected to, day in and day out?

"But not satisfied with such degradation, one night this thug returns home drunk, goes upstairs, drags his wife out of bed by her hair, back down the stairs and into the kitchen; he is bored with simply beating her black and blue." Fletcher began to walk in the direction of his client. "He needs some other thrill to reach new heights of excitement, and what does Anita Kirsten see immediately when she's dragged into the kitchen? The ring on the stove is already red hot, and waiting for its victim." He swung back to face the jury. "Can you imagine what must have been going through her mind when she first saw that ring of fire? He grabs her hand like a piece of raw steak, and slams it down on the stove for fifteen seconds."

Fletcher picked up Mrs. Kirsten's scarred hand and held it up so that the palm was clearly visible to the jury, looked at his watch and counted to fifteen, before he added, "And then she fainted.

"Which of you can even imagine such horror, let alone be asked to endure it? So why did the attorney general demand ninety-nine years? Because, he told us, the killing was premeditated. It was, he assured us, most certainly not a crime of passion carried out by someone defending their life in a moment of rage." Fletcher swung around to face the attorney general and said, "Of course it was premeditated and of course she knew exactly what she was doing. If you were five foot four, being attacked by a man of six foot two, would you rely on a knife, a gun, or some blunt instrument that this thug could so easily turn against you?" Fletcher turned and walked slowly toward the jury. "Which one of you would be that stupid? Which one of you, after what she had been through, *wouldn't* plan it? Think of that poor woman when you next have a row with your spouse. After a few angry words have been exchanged, will you resort to putting the stove on to 350 degrees to prove you've won the argument?" He looked at the seven men on the jury one by one. "Does such a man deserve your sympathy?

"If this woman is guilty of murder, which one of you would not have done the same thing if you had been unfortunate enough to marry Alex Kirsten?" This time he turned his attention to the five women before he continued. " 'But I didn't,' I hear you cry. 'I married a good and decent man.' So now we can all agree on Mrs. Kirsten's crime. She married an evil man."

Fletcher leaned on the rail of the jury box. "I must beg the jury's indulgence for my youthful passion, for passion it is. I chose to take this case as I feared justice would not be done for Mrs. Kirsten, and in my youth I hoped that twelve fair-minded citizens would see what I had seen and would be unable to condemn this woman to spend the rest of her life in jail.

"I must close my summation, by repeating to you the words Mrs. Kirsten said to me when we sat alone in her cell this morning. 'Mr. Davenport, although I am only twenty-five, I would rather spend the rest of my life in jail than have to spend another night under the same roof as that evil man.'

"Thank God she does not have to return home to him tonight. It is in your power, as members of the jury, to send this woman home tonight to her loving children, with the hope that together they might rebuild their lives, because twelve decent people understood the difference between good and evil." Fletcher lowered his voice to almost a whisper. "When you go home to your husbands and wives this evening, tell them what you did today in the name of justice, for I am confident if you bring in a verdict of Not Guilty, your spouses will not turn up the stove to 350 degrees because they don't agree with you. Mrs. Kirsten has already suffered a nine-year sentence. Do you think she deserves another ninety?"

Fletcher returned to his seat, but did not turn around to look at Annie, for fear that Karl Abrahams would notice he was fighting back the tears.

19

"HI, MY NAME'S Nat Cartwright."

"Not *the* Captain Cartwright?"

"Yes, the hero who killed all those Vietcong with his bare hands because he forgot to take any paper clips with him."

"No," said Su Ling in mock admiration. "Not the one who flew a helicopter alone across enemy-infested jungle when he didn't have a pilot's license?"

"And then killed so many of the enemy that they stopped counting them, while at the same time he rescued a whole platoon of stranded men."

"And the people back home believed it, so he was decorated, given vast financial rewards and offered a hundred vestal virgins."

"I only get four hundred dollars a month, and I've never met a vestal virgin."

"Well, you have now," said Su Ling with a smile.

"Well, can you tell her that I have been chosen to run against Boston University."

"No doubt you'd expect her to stand around in the rain and wait until you trail in near the back, like all your other adoring fans?"

"No, the truth is that I need my tracksuit cleaned, and I'm told her mother takes in washing." Su Ling burst out laughing. "Of course I'd like you to come to Boston," said Nat, taking her in his arms.

"I've already booked a place on the supporters' bus."

"But Tom and I are driving up the night before, so why don't you come with us?"

161

"But where would I stay?"

"One of Tom's numerous aunts has a house in Boston, and has offered to put us all up for the night." Su Ling hesitated. "I'm told she has nine bedrooms, and even a separate wing, but if that's not enough, I could always spend the night in the back of the car." Su Ling didn't reply as Mario appeared carrying two cappuccinos.

"This is my friend Mario," said Su Ling. "Very good of you to keep my usual table," she added.

"Do you bring all your men here?"

"No, I tend to select a different restaurant each time, so that way no one finds out about my vestal reputation."

"Like your reputation as a computer whiz?"

Su Ling blushed. "How did you find out about that?"

"What do you mean, how did I find out? It seems everyone on campus knew except me. In fact my closest friend told me, and he's at Yale."

"I was going to tell you, but you never asked the right question."

"Su Ling, you can tell me things without having to be asked the right question."

"Then I must ask if you've also heard that both Harvard and MIT have invited me to join their computer science departments."

"Yes, but I don't know how you responded."

"Tell me, Captain," she said, "can I ask you something first?"

"You're trying to change the subject again, Su Ling."

"Yes, I am, Nat, because I need my question answered before I can reply to yours."

"OK, so what's your question?"

Su Ling lowered her head as she always did when she was slightly embarrassed. "How can two such different people," she hesitated, "end up liking each other so much."

"End up falling in love, I think is what you are trying to say. If I knew the answer to that question, little flower, I'd be a professor of philosophy, and not worrying about my end-of-term exam grades."

"In my country," said Su Ling, "love is something you do not talk about until you have known each other for many years."

"Then I promise not to discuss the matter again for many years—on one condition."

"And what is that?"

"That you will agree to come to Boston with us on Friday."

"Yes, if I can have Tom's aunt's telephone number."

"Of course you can, but why?"

"My mother will need to speak to her." Su Ling lifted her right foot, slipped it under the table and placed it on top of Nat's left foot.

"Now I feel sure that has a significant meaning in your country."

"Yes, it does. It means I wish to walk with you, but not in a crowd."

Nat placed his right foot on her left. "And what does that mean?"

"That you agree to my request," she hesitated. "But I should not have done it first, otherwise I would be considered a loose woman." Nat immediately removed his foot and then replaced it. "Honor restored," she said.

"Then after we have been on our uncrowded walk, what happens next?"

"You must wait for an invitation to take tea with my family."

"How long will that take?"

"Normally a year would be considered appropriate."

"Couldn't we speed up the process a little?" suggested Nat. "How about next week?"

"All right, then you will be invited to tea on Sunday afternoon, because Sunday is the traditional day for a man to have a first meal with a woman under the watchful eye of family."

"But we've already had several meals together."

"I know, so you must come to tea before my mother finds out, otherwise I will be abandoned and disinherited."

"Then I shall not accept your invitation to tea," said Nat.

"Why not?"

"I'll just stand outside your house and grab you when your mother throws you out, and then I won't have to wait for another two years." Nat placed both his feet on hers, and she withdrew them immediately. "What did I do wrong?"

"Two feet means something completely different."

"What?" asked Nat.

"I can't tell you, but as you were clever enough to find out the correct translation of Su Ling, I feel sure you will discover the meaning of two feet, and never do it again, unless . . ."

On Friday afternoon, Tom drove Nat and Su Ling up to his aunt's home in the leafy suburbs of Boston. Miss Russell had obviously spoken to Su Ling's mother, because she'd put her in the bedroom on the main landing, next to hers, while Nat and Tom were relegated to the east wing.

After breakfast the following morning, Su Ling left to keep her appointment with the professor of statistics at Harvard, while Nat and Tom spent some time walking slowly around the cross-country course, something Nat always did whenever he would be running over unfamiliar territory. He checked out all the well-worn paths, and whenever he came to a stream, a gate or a sudden undulation, he practiced crossing it several times.

On the way back across the meadow, Tom asked him what he would do if Su Ling agreed to a transfer to Harvard.

"I'll move at the same time and enroll at the business school."

"You feel that strongly about her?"

"Yes, and I can't risk letting anyone else place both feet on hers."

"What are you talking about?"

"I'll explain another time," said Nat as he came to a halt by a stream. "Where do you imagine they cross it?"

"No idea," said Tom, "but it looks too wide to jump."

"Agreed, so I expect they aim for the large flat pebbles in the middle."

"What do you do if you're not sure?" asked Tom.

"Follow closely behind one of their team, because they'll do the right thing automatically."

"Where are you hoping to end up this early in the season?"

"I'd be satisfied with being a counter."

"I don't understand, doesn't everybody count?"

"No, although there are eight runners on each team, only six count when the final score is calculated. If I come in twelfth or higher, I would be a counter."

"So how is the counting done?"

"First across the line counts as one, second two, and so on. When the race is over, the first six in each team are added together, and the team with the lowest overall score is the winner. That way, seven and eight can only contribute if they stay ahead of any of the first six runners on the other team. Is that clear?"

"Yes, I think so," said Tom, looking at his watch. "I'd better get back, because I promised Aunt Abigail I'd have lunch with her. Are you coming?"

"No, I'm joining the rest of the team for a banana, a lettuce leaf and a glass of water. Could you pick up Su Ling and make sure that she's back in time to watch the race."

"She won't need to be reminded," said Tom.

When Tom strolled to the house, he found his aunt and Su Ling deep in conversation over bowls of clam chowder. Tom sensed that his aunt had changed the subject the moment he'd entered the room. "You'd better grab something to eat," she said, "if you're hoping to be back in time to see the start."

After a second bowl of clam chowder, Tom accompanied Su Ling across to the course. He explained to her that Nat had selected a spot about halfway around, where they could see all the runners for at least a mile and then if they took a shortcut, they would be back in time to watch the winner crossing the finishing line.

"Do you understand what a counter is?" Tom asked.

"Yes, Nat explained it to me—an ingenious system, which makes the abacus look positively modern. Would you like me to explain it to you?" she asked.

"Yes, I think I would," said Tom.

By the time they reached the vantage point that Nat had selected, they didn't have long to wait before the first runner came into view over the brow of the hill. They watched Boston's captain shoot past them, and ten other runners had come and gone before Nat appeared. He gave a wave as he sped off down the hill.

"He's the last counter," said Su Ling as they set off to take the short cut back to the finishing line.

"My bet is that he'll move up two or three places now he knows you're here to watch him," said Tom.

"How flattering," said Su Ling.

"Will you be taking up the Harvard offer?" asked Tom quietly.

"Did Nat ask you to find out?" she inquired.

"No," said Tom, "though he talks of little else."

"I have said yes, but only on one condition." Tom remained silent. Su Ling didn't tell Tom what the condition was, so he didn't ask.

They almost had to jog the last couple of hundred yards to make sure they were back in time to see the Boston captain raise his arms in triumph as he crossed the finishing line. Tom turned out to be right, because Nat ended up in ninth position, and fourth counter for his team. Both of them rushed over to congratulate him as if he were the winner. Nat lay on the ground exhausted, disappointed that he hadn't done better when he learned that Boston had won by 31 to 24.

After supper with Aunt Abigail, they started out on the long drive back to Storrs. Nat rested his head in Su Ling's lap and quickly fell asleep.

"I can't imagine what my mother would say about our first night together," she whispered to Tom as he drove on through the night.

"Why don't you go the whole hog and tell her that it was a *ménage à trois*?"

◆

"Mother thought you were wonderful," said Su Ling as they walked slowly back toward south campus after tea the following afternoon.

"What a woman," said Nat. "She can cook, run a home and is also a successful businesswoman."

"And don't forget," said Su Ling, "that she was shunned in her own land for bearing a foreigner's child and wasn't even welcomed in this country when she first arrived, which is the reason I've been brought up so strictly. Like so many children of immigrants, I'm no cleverer than my mother, but by sacrificing everything to give me a first-class education, she has allowed me a better chance than she ever had. Perhaps you can now understand why I always try to respect her wishes."

"Yes, I can," said Nat, "and now that I've met your mother, I'd like you to meet mine, because I am equally proud of her." Su Ling laughed.

"Why do you laugh, little flower?" asked Nat.

"In my country, for a man to meet a woman's mother is to admit to a relationship. If the man then asks you to meet his mother, it means betrothal. If he then does not marry the girl, she will be a spinster for the rest of her life. However, I will take that risk, because Tom asked me to marry him yesterday when you were running away.

Nat bent down, kissed her on the lips and then placed both his feet gently on top of hers. She smiled. "I love you too," she said.

20

"WHAT DO YOU make of it?" asked Jimmy.

"I've no idea," said Fletcher, who glanced over at the attorney general's table, but none of the state's team gave any sign of looking either anxious or confident.

"You could always ask Professor Abrahams for his opinion," said Annie.

"Why, is he still around?"

"I saw him roaming up and down the corridor only a few moments ago."

Fletcher left the table, pushed open the little wooden gate dividing the court from the public and strode quickly out of the courtroom into the corridor. He glanced up and down the wide marble expanse, but didn't spot the professor until the crowds near the rotunda staircase parted to reveal a distinguished-looking man seated in the corner, head down, writing notes on a legal pad. Court officials and members of the public rushed past him, unaware of his presence. Fletcher walked apprehensively across to join him and watched as the old man continued making notes. He didn't feel he could interrupt, so he waited until the professor eventually looked up.

"Ah, Davenport," he said, tapping the bench beside him. "Take a seat. You have an inquiring look on your face, so how may I assist you?"

Fletcher sat beside him. "I only wanted to ask your opinion on why the jury has been out for so long. Should I read anything into it?"

The professor checked his watch. "Just over five hours," he said. "No, I wouldn't consider that long for a capital charge. Juries like to let you know that they've taken their responsibility seriously, unless of course it's cut and dried, and this case certainly wasn't."

"Do you have any feel for what the outcome might be?" asked Fletcher anxiously.

"You can never second-guess a jury, Mr. Davenport; twelve people chosen at random, with little in common, though I must say, with a couple of exceptions, they looked a fair-minded lot. So what's your next question?"

"I don't know, sir, what is my next question?"

"What should I do if the verdict goes against me?" He paused. "An eventuality you must always prepare for." Fletcher nodded. "Answer? You immediately ask the judge for leave to appeal." The professor tore off one of the sheets of yellow paper and handed it across to his pupil. "I hope you will not consider it presumptuous of me, but I have jotted down a simple form of words for every eventuality."

"Including guilty?" said Fletcher.

"No need to be that pessimistic yet. First we must consider the possibility of a hung jury. I observed in the center of the back row a juror who never once looked at our client while she was on the witness stand. But I noticed that you also spotted the lady on the far end of the front row who lowered her eyes when you held up the scorched palm of Mrs. Kirsten's right hand."

"What do I do if it is a hung jury?"

"Nothing. The judge, although not the brightest legal mind currently sitting on the appellate bench, is meticulous and fair when it comes to points of law, so he will ask the jury if they are able to return a majority verdict."

"Which in this state is ten to two."

"As it is in forty-three other states," the professor reminded him.

"But if they are unable to agree on a majority verdict?"

"The judge is left with no choice but to dismiss the jury and ask the attorney general if he wishes to call for a retrial, and before you ask, I can't second-guess how Mr. Stamp will react to that eventuality."

"You seem to have made a lot of notes," Fletcher said, looking down at line after line of neatly written script.

"Yes, I intend to refer to this case next term when I give my lecture on the legal difference between manslaughter and homicide. It will be for my third-year students, so you should not be too embarrassed."

"Should I have accepted the attorney general's deal of manslaughter, and settled for three years?"

"I suspect we will find out the answer to that question in the not-too-distant future."

"Did I make a lot of mistakes?" asked Fletcher.

"A few," said the professor turning the pages of his pad.

"What was the biggest one?"

"Your only glaring error, in my opinion, was not calling a doctor to describe in graphic detail—something doctors always enjoy doing—how the bruises on Mrs. Kirsten's arms and legs might have been inflicted. Juries admire doctors. They assume that they are honest people, and in the main they are. But like every other group, if you ask them the right question—and it is after all the lawyers who select the questions—they are as prone to exaggeration as the rest of us." Fletcher felt guilty that he had missed such an obvious gambit, and only wished he had taken Annie's advice and sought the professor's counsel earlier.

"Don't worry, the state still has one or two hurdles to cross, because the judge is certain to grant us a stay of execution."

"Us?" said Fletcher.

"Yes," said the professor quietly, "although I have not appeared in court for many years, and may well be a little rusty, I was hoping that you might allow me to assist you on this occasion."

"You would serve as my co-counsel?" said Fletcher in disbelief.

"Yes, Davenport, I would," said the professor, "because you did convince me of one thing. Your client should not be spending the rest of her life in jail."

"Jury's coming back," shouted a voice that echoed down the corridor.

"Good luck, Davenport," added the professor. "And may I say

before I hear the result, that for a second-year student, your defense was a remarkable tour de force."

◄◇►

Nat could sense how nervous Su Ling was the closer they got to Cromwell. "Are you sure your mother will approve of the way I'm dressed?" she asked, pulling her skirt down even farther.

Nat looked across to admire the simple yellow suit that Su Ling had selected, that just hinted how graceful her figure was. "My mother will approve, and my father won't be able to take his eyes off you."

Su Ling squeezed his leg. "How will your father react when he finds not that I'm Korean?"

"I shall remind him of your Irish father," said Nat. "In any case, he's spent his whole life dealing with figures, so it will take him only a few minutes to realize how bright you are."

"It's not too late to turn back," said Su Ling. "We could always visit them next Sunday."

"It is too late," said Nat. "In any case, haven't you considered how nervous my parents might be? After all, I have already told them that I'm desperately in love with you."

"Yes, but my mother adored you."

"And mine will adore you." Su Ling remained silent until Nat told her that they were approaching the outskirts of Cromwell.

"But I don't know what to say."

"Su Ling, it's not an examination that you have to pass."

"Yes, it is, that's exactly what it is."

"This is the town where I was born," said Nat, trying to relax her as they drove down the main street. "When I was a child, I thought it was a great metropolis. But to be fair, I also used to think Hartford was the capital of the world."

"How long before we get there?" she asked.

Nat glanced out of the window. "I'd say about ten minutes. But please don't expect anything too grand, we only live in a small house."

"My mother and I live above the shop," said Su Ling.

Nat laughed, "And so did Harry Truman."

"And look where that got him," she replied.

Nat turned the car into Cedar Avenue. "We're the third house on the right."

"Could we drive around the block a few times?" said Su Ling, "I need to think about what I'm going to say."

"No," said Nat firmly, "try to remember how the professor of statistics at Harvard reacted when he first met you."

"Yes, but I didn't want to marry his son."

"I feel sure he would have agreed to that if he'd thought it might have convinced you to join his team." Su Ling laughed for the first time in over an hour, just as Nat brought the car to a halt outside the house. He went quickly around to Su Ling's side and opened the door for her. She stepped out and lost one of her shoes in the gutter.

"I'm sorry, I'm sorry," she said as she slipped it back on. "I'm sorry."

Nat laughed and took her in his arms.

"No, no," said Su Ling, "your mother might see us."

"I hope she does," said Nat. He smiled and took her by the hand as they walked up the short driveway.

The door was opened long before they'd reached it, and Susan ran out to greet them. She immediately took Su Ling in her arms and said, "Nat didn't exaggerate. You are quite beautiful."

◄◦►

Fletcher walked slowly back down the corridor toward the court room, surprised to find that the professor remained by his side. When they reached the swing doors, the young counselor assumed his mentor would return to his place a couple of rows behind Annie and Jimmy, but he continued walking toward the front of the court room and took the vacant seat next to Fletcher's. Annie and Jimmy could barely conceal their surprise. The court usher announced, "All rise. His Honor Judge Abernathy presiding."

Once he was seated, the judge looked toward the attorney general and acknowledged him, then turned his attention to the defense team, and for the second time during the trial, surprise registered on his face.

"I see you have acquired an assistant, Mr. Davenport. Is his name to be entered on the register before I recall the jury?"

Fletcher turned to the professor, who rose from his place and said, "That would be my wish, your honor."

"Name?" asked the judge, as if he had never seen him before.

"Karl Abrahams, your honor."

"Are you qualified to appear in my court?" asked the judge solemnly.

"I believe I am, sir," said Abrahams, "I first became a member of the Connecticut bar in 1937, though I have never had the privilege of appearing before your honor."

"Thank you, Mr. Abrahams. If the attorney general has no objection, I will enter your name on my register as Mr. Davenport's co-counsel."

The attorney general rose, gave the professor a slight bow, and said, "It is a privilege to be in the same court as Mr. Davenport's assistant."

"Then I think we should waste no more time in recalling the jury," said the judge.

Fletcher examined the faces of the seven men and five women as they filed back to their places. The professor had suggested that Fletcher check to see if any jury members looked directly at their client, which would possibly indicate a verdict of not guilty. He thought two or three of them did, but he couldn't be sure.

The foreman rose. "Have you reached a verdict in this case?" the judge asked.

"No, your honor, we have been unable to do so," the foreman replied.

Fletcher could feel the sweat on the palms of his hands even more intensely than when he had first stood to address the jury. The judge tried a second time. "Are you able to return a majority verdict?"

"No, we are not, your honor," replied the foreman.

"Do you feel, given more time, you might eventually reach a majority verdict?"

"I don't think so, your honor. We have been equally divided for the past three hours."

"Then I have no choice but to declare a mistrial, and dismiss the jury. On behalf of the state, I thank you for your service." He turned his attention to the attorney general, and as he did so Mr. Abrahams rose to his feet.

"I wonder, your honor, if I might seek your guidance on a small matter of protocol."

The judge looked puzzled, as did the attorney general. "I can't wait to hear your small matter of protocol, Mr. Abrahams."

"Allow me first to inquire of your honor, if I am correct in thinking that should there be a retrial, the defense team must be announced within fourteen days?"

"That would be the normal practice, Mr. Abrahams."

"Then may I assist the court by making it clear that should that situation arise, Mr. Davenport and I will continue to represent the defendant."

"I am obliged for your small point of protocol," said the judge, no longer puzzled.

"So I must now ask you, Mr. Stamp," said the judge, turning his attention back to the attorney general, "if it is your intention to apply for a retrial of this case."

The court's attention swung to the state's lawyers, all five of whom were in a huddle, holding an animated conversation. Judge Abernathy made no attempt to hurry them, and it was some time before Mr. Stamp rose from his place. "We do not believe, your honor, that it is in the state's best interest to reopen this case."

Cheering broke out in the well of the court as the professor tore a sheet from his yellow pad and pushed it across to his pupil. Fletcher glanced down at it, rose from his place and read it, word for word. "You honor, in the circumstances, I would ask for the immediate release of my client." He looked down at the professor's next sentence and continued to read, "And may I say how grateful I am for the gracious and professional manner in which Mr. Stamp and his team have conducted the case for the prosecution."

The judge nodded, and Mr. Stamp rose again. "May I in turn congratulate the defense counsel and his assistant on their first case before your honor, and wish Mr. Davenport every success in what I feel certain will be a promising career."

Fletcher beamed at Annie, as Professor Abrahams rose from his place. "Objection, your honor."

Everyone turned to face the professor. "I wouldn't have thought it was that certain," he said. "It is my belief that a lot of work still needs to be done before that promise will be realized."

"Sustained," said Judge Abernathy.

—◇—

"My mother taught me two languages up until the age of nine and by then I was just about ready to be mainstreamed into the Storrs school system."

"That's where I started my academic life," said Susan.

"But I discovered from an early age that I was more at ease with numbers than words." Michael Cartwright nodded his understanding. "And I was most fortunate to have a math teacher whose hobby was statistics, and who was also fascinated by the role the computer might play in the future."

"We're beginning to rely a lot on them in the insurance business," said Michael as he refilled his pipe.

"How big is your firm's computer, Mr. Cartwright?" asked Su Ling.

"About the size of this room."

"The next generation of students will work with computers no larger than the lids of their desks, and the generation after that will be able to hold them in the palm of their hand."

"Do you really believe that's possible?" asked Susan, transfixed.

"The technology is moving at such a pace, and the demand will be so high, that the price must fall quickly. Once that happens, computers will become like the phone and the television were in the forties and fifties, as more people purchase them, the cheaper and smaller they will be."

"But surely some computers will still need to be large?" suggested Michael. "After all, my company has over forty thousand customers."

"Not necessarily," said Su Ling. "The computer that sent the first man to the moon was larger than this house, but we will live to see a space capsule land on Mars controlled by a computer no larger than this kitchen table."

"No larger than the kitchen table?" repeated Susan, trying to grasp the concept.

"In California, Silicon Valley has become the new hotbed of technology. Already IBM and Hewlett Packard are finding that their latest models can be out of date in a matter of months, and once the Japanese are fully up to speed, it might even be weeks."

"Then how can firms like mine be expected to keep up?" asked Michael.

"You'll simply have to replace your computer just as often as you change your car, and in the not-too-distant future, you'll be able to carry in your inside pocket detailed information on every customer you represent."

"But I repeat," said Michael, "our company currently has forty-two thousand clients."

"It won't matter if you have four hundred thousand, Mr. Cartwright, a handheld computer will still be able to do the same job."

"But think of the consequences," said Susan.

"They are very exciting, Mrs. Cartwright," said Su Ling. She paused and blushed, "I apologize, I've been talking far too much."

"No, no," said Susan, "it's fascinating, but I was hoping to ask you about Korea, a country I've always wanted to visit. If it's not a silly question, are you more like the Chinese or the Japanese?"

"Neither," replied Su Ling. "We are as different as a Russian is from an Italian. The Korean nation was originally a tribal one and probably first existed as early as the second century . . ."

"And to think I told them that you were shy," Nat remarked as he slipped in beside her later that night.

"I'm very sorry," said Su Ling. "I broke your mother's golden rule."

"Which one?" said Nat.

"That when two people meet, the conversation should be equally shared, three people, thirty-three percent, four people, twenty-five percent. I talked," she paused, "for about ninety percent of the time. I feel ashamed, because I behaved so disgracefully, I don't know what came over me. I was just so nervous. I feel sure they already regret any suggestion of me as a daughter-in-law."

Nat laughed. "They adored you," he said, "my father was mesmerized by your knowledge of computers, and my mother fascinated by the customs of Korea, though you didn't mention what has to take place if a Korean girl takes tea with her suitor's parents."

"That doesn't apply to a first-generation American, like myself."

"Who wears pink lipstick and mini skirts," said Nat, holding up a tube of pink lipstick.

"I didn't know you used lipstick, Nat. Another habit you picked up in Vietnam?"

"Only on night ops, now turn over."

"Turn over?"

"Yes," said Nat firmly, "I thought Korean women were meant to be subservient, so do as you're told and turn over."

Su Ling turned over, and placed her face down on the pillow. "What is your next order, Captain Cartwright?"

"To take off your nightdress, little flower."

"Does this happen to all American girls on the second night?"

"Take off your nightdress."

"Yes, Captain." She slowly pulled her white silk nightdress over the top of her head, and dropped it on the floor. "What next," she asked. "Is it now that you beat me?"

"No, that doesn't happen until the third date, but I am going to ask you a question." Nat took the pink lipstick and wrote four words on her olive skin, followed by a question mark.

"What have you written, Captain Cartwright?"

"Why don't you find out for yourself?"

Su Ling climbed off the bed and stared over her shoulder into the long mirror. It was some time before a smile spread across her face. She turned to find Nat lying spread-eagled on the bed, holding the lipstick high above his head. Su Ling walked slowly across, grabbed the lipstick, stared down at his broad shoulders for some time, before she wrote the words, YES I WILL.

21

"ANNIE'S PREGNANT."

"That's wonderful news," said Jimmy as they left the dining hall and strolled across the campus for their first lecture of the morning. "How many months is she?"

"Only a couple, so now it will be your turn to give the advice."

"What do you mean?"

"Don't forget, you're the one with all the experience. You're a father of a six-month-old baby daughter. To start with, how can I help Annie during the next seven months?"

"Just try to be supportive. Never forget to tell her that she looks wonderful even when she resembles a beached whale, and if she gets any crazy ideas, just play along with them."

"Such as?" asked Fletcher.

"Joanna liked to eat half-pint tubs of double chocolate chip ice cream just before she went to bed each night, so I had a tub as well, and then if she woke up in the middle of the night she often asked for another one."

"That must have been a real sacrifice," said Fletcher.

"Yes it was, because it always had to be followed by a spoonful of cod liver oil."

Fletcher laughed. "Keep going," he said as they approached the Andersen building.

"Annie will start going to pre-natal classes fairly soon, and the instructors usually recommend that husbands also attend so they can appreciate what their wives are going through."

"I'd enjoy that," said Fletcher, "especially if I'm going to have to eat all that ice cream." They climbed the steps and walked through the swing doors.

"With Annie, it may turn out to be onions or pickle," said Jimmy.

"Then I may not be quite as enthusiastic."

"And then there's the preparation for the birth. Who'll help Annie with this?"

"Mom asked if she wanted Miss Nichol, my old nanny, to come out of retirement, but Annie wouldn't hear of it. She's determined to bring up this child without any outside assistance."

"Joanna would have taken advantage of Miss Nichol without a second thought, because from what I remember of that lady, she would have happily agreed to paint the nursery as well as change the diapers."

"We don't have a nursery," said Fletcher, "just a spare room."

"Then as of today, that becomes the nursery, and Annie will expect you to repaint it, while she goes out and buys a whole new wardrobe."

"She's got more than enough clothes already," said Fletcher.

"No woman has more than enough clothes," said Jimmy, "and in a couple of months' time she won't be able to fit into any of them, and that's before she starts thinking about the baby's needs."

"I'd better start looking for a job as a waiter or bartender right away," said Fletcher, as they walked down the corridor.

"But surely your father will . . ."

"I don't intend to spend my whole life sponging off my old man."

"If my father had that sort of money," said Jimmy, "I wouldn't do a day's work."

"Yes, you would," said Fletcher, "otherwise Joanna would never have agreed to marry you."

"I don't think you'll end up being a bartender, Fletcher, because after your triumph in the Kirsten case you'll get the pick of the summer association jobs. And if there's one thing I know about my kid sister, she won't allow anything to get in the way of you coming out top of our year." Jimmy paused. "Why don't I have a word with my mother? She certainly helped Joanna with a lot of the chores without ever making it at all obvious." He paused. "But I'd expect something in return."

"What do you have in mind?" asked Fletcher.

"Well, for a start, how about your father's money?" he said with a grin.

Fletcher laughed. "You want my father's money in exchange for asking your mother to help her daughter with the birth of her grandchild? You know, Jimmy, I have a feeling you'd make a very successful divorce lawyer."

—◇—

"I've decided to run for president," he said without even announcing who it was on the other end of the line.

"That's good news," said Tom, "but how does Su Ling feel about it?"

"I wouldn't have taken the first step if she hadn't suggested it. And she also wants to play a role in the campaign. She's asked to be responsible for polling and anything to do with figures or statistics."

"Then that's one of your problems solved," said Tom. "Have you appointed a campaign manager?"

"Yes, just after you returned to Yale, I settled on a guy called Joe Stein. He's fought two campaigns in the past, and will also bring in the Jewish vote," said Nat.

"There's a Jewish vote in Connecticut?" said Tom.

"In America, there's always a Jewish vote, and on this campus, there are four hundred and eighteen Jews, and I need the support of every one of them."

"So what's your considered opinion on the future of the Golan Heights?" asked Tom.

"I don't even know where the Golan Heights are," Nat replied.

"Well you'd better find out by this time tomorrow."

"I wonder what Elliot's view is on the Golan Heights?"

"That they should always be part of Israel, and not one inch should ever be sacrificed to the Palestinians, would be my bet," said Tom.

"So what will be his line with the Palestinians?"

"There are probably so few on campus, he won't have an opinion."

"That would certainly make the decision easy for him."

"The next thing you'll have to consider is your opening address, and where you're going to deliver it," said Tom.

"I was thinking of Russell Hall."

"But that only holds four hundred. Isn't there anything bigger?"

"Yes," said Nat, "the Assembly Rooms hold over a thousand, but Elliot made that mistake, because when he gave his opening speech, the place looked half empty. No, I'd rather book the hall and have people sitting on the ledges, hanging from the rafters, even standing on the steps outside unable to get in, which will leave a much better impression with the voters."

"Then you'd better select a date and reserve the hall immediately, and at the same time get on with putting the rest of your team in place."

"What else should I be worrying about?" asked Nat.

"The candidate's bread-and-butter speech, and don't forget to talk to every student you come across—you remember the routine, 'Hi, my name is Nat Cartwright, and I'm running for president, and I hope I can rely on your support.' Then listen to what they have to say, because if they believe you're interested in their views, you have a far better chance of their support."

"Anything else?"

"Be ruthless in using Su Ling, and ask her to carry out the same routine with every female student, because she's bound to be one of the most admired women on campus after her decision to remain at the university. There aren't many people who turn down Harvard."

"Don't remind me," said Nat. "Is that it, because you seem to have thought of just about everything?"

"Yes, I'll come back and help you for the last ten days of the term, but I won't be officially part of your team."

"Why not?"

"Because Elliot will tell everyone your campaign is being run by an outsider and worse, a millionaire banker's son from Yale. Try not to forget you would have won your last election if it hadn't been for Elliot's deceit, so be prepared for him to come up with something that might derail you."

"Like what?"

"If I could work that out, I'd be Nixon's chief of staff."

—◇—

"How do I look?" asked Annie, propped up on the front seat of the car, clutching her seatbelt.

"You look fantastic, honey," said Fletcher, not even glancing across at her.

"No I don't, I look awful, and it's going to be such an important occasion."

"It's probably only one of his get-togethers for a dozen or so students."

"I doubt it," said Annie. "It was a hand-written invitation, and even I couldn't miss the words, 'do try to make it, there's someone I want you to meet.'"

"Well we're about to find out who that is," said Fletcher as he parked his old Ford behind a limousine surrounded by a dozen Secret Service agents.

"Who can that possibly be?" whispered Annie as he helped her from the car.

"I've no idea, but . . ."

"How nice to see you, Fletcher," said the professor, who was standing at the front door. "Good of you to come," he added. It would have been damn stupid of me not to, Fletcher wanted to reply. "And you too, Mrs. Davenport, of course I remember you well, because for a couple of weeks I sat just two rows behind you in court."

Annie smiled. "I was a little slimmer then."

"But no more beautiful," said Abrahams. "May I ask when the baby is due?"

"In ten weeks, sir."

"Please call me Karl," said the professor. "It makes me feel so much younger when an undergraduate from Vassar calls me by my first name. A privilege I might add, that I shall not be extending to your husband for at least another year." He winked as he put an arm around Annie's shoulder. "Come on in, because there's someone I want you both to meet."

Fletcher and Annie followed the professor into the living room, where they found a dozen guests already deep in conversation. It looked as if they were the last to arrive.

"Mr. Vice-President, I should like to introduce Annie Cartwright."

"Good evening, Mr. Vice-President."

"Hi, Annie," said Spiro Agnew thrusting out his hand, "I'm told you've married a very bright guy."

Karl whispered loudly, "Try not to forget, Annie, that politicians have a tendency to exaggerate, because they are always hoping for your vote."

"I know, Karl, my father is a politician."

"Is that right?" said Agnew.

"No, left, sir," she replied with a smile, "he's the majority leader in the Connecticut state senate."

"Are there no Republicans among us this evening?"

"And this, Mr. Vice-President, is Annie's husband, Fletcher Davenport."

"Hi, Fletcher, is your father also a Democrat?"

"No, sir, he's a card-carrying Republican."

"Great, so at least we've got two votes wrapped up in your household."

"No sir, my mother wouldn't allow you across the threshold."

The vice-president burst out laughing. "I don't know what that does for your reputation, Karl."

"I shall continue to remain neutral, Spiro, as I have no politics. However, may I leave Annie with you, sir, as there's someone else I want Fletcher to meet."

Fletcher was puzzled as he had assumed it was the vice-president to whom the professor must have been referring in his letter, but he dutifully followed his host to join a group of men standing by a blazing fire on the far side of the room.

"Bill, this is Fletcher Davenport, Fletcher, this is Bill Alexander of Alexander . . ."

". . . Dupont and Bell," completed Fletcher as he shook hands with the senior partner of one of New York's most prestigious law firms.

"I've been keen to make your acquaintance for some time,

Fletcher," said Bill Alexander. "You have managed something I failed to achieve in thirty years."

"And what was that, sir?"

"Getting Karl to appear as second chair in one of my cases—how did you manage it?"

Both men waited to hear his reply. "I didn't have a lot of choice, sir. He forced himself on me in a most unprofessional manner, but then you must realize he was desperate. No one has offered him any real work since 1938." Both men laughed.

"But I'm bound to ask if he was worth his fee, which must have been handsome, remembering you kept that woman out of jail?"

"It certainly was," said Abrahams, before his young guest could reply. He placed a hand on the bookshelf behind Bill Alexander and removed a hardback copy of *The Trials of Clarence Darrow*. Mr. Alexander studied the book. "I have one myself, of course," said Alexander.

"And so did I," said Abrahams. Fletcher looked disappointed. "But not a signed first edition with a dust jacket in perfect condition. They are indeed a collector's item."

Fletcher thought about his mother, and her invaluable advice: "Try to choose something he'll treasure, it doesn't have to cost a lot of money."

—◇—

Nat went around the circle of eight men and six women who made up his team, asking each of them to give a brief biography for the rest of the group. He then allocated their particular responsibilities in the run-up to the election. Nat could only admire Su Ling's commitment, because following Tom's offstage advice, she had selected a remarkable cross-section of students, most of whom had obviously wanted Nat to stand for some time.

"OK, let's start with updates," said Nat.

Joe Stein rose from his place. "Because the candidate has made it clear that no single contribution can exceed one dollar, I have increased the number in the fund-raising team so we can approach as many of the students as possible. That group currently meets once a week, usually on a Monday. It would be helpful if the candidate was able to address them some time."

"Would next Monday suit you?" asked Nat.

"Fine by me," said Joe. "To date, we've raised $307, most of which was collected after your speech at Russell Hall. Because the room was so packed many of them were convinced that they were backing the winner."

"Thanks, Joe," said Nat. "Next: what's the opposition up to? Tim?"

"My name's Tim Ulrich, and my job is to cover the opposition's campaign, and make sure we know what they're up to the whole time. We have at least two people taking notes whenever Elliot opens his mouth. He's made so many promises during the past few days, that if he tried to keep them all, the university would be bankrupt by this time next year."

"Now how about groups. Ray?"

"Groups fall into three categories, ethnic, religious and club, so I have three deputy leaders to cover each one. There is of course a considerable amount of overlapping, for example, Italians and Catholics."

"Sex?" suggested someone.

"No," said Ray, "we found sex to be universal, and therefore couldn't group it, but opera, food, fashion are examples of where the overlapping came for Italians—but we're on top of it. Mario's even offering free coffee to those customers who promise to vote Cartwright."

"Be careful. Elliot will pick that up as an election expense," said Joe. "Don't let's lose on a technicality."

"Agreed," said Nat. "Sports?"

Jack Roberts, the basketball captain, didn't need to introduce himself. "Track and field is well covered by Nat's personal involvement, especially after his victory in the final cross-country meet against Cornell. I'm covering the baseball team as well as basketball. Elliot already has football sewn up, but the surprise is women's lacrosse—that club has over three hundred members."

"I've got a girlfriend on the second team," said Tim.

"I thought you were homosexual?" said Chris. Some of them laughed.

"Who *is* covering the gay vote?" asked Nat.

No one spoke. "If anyone admits to being openly gay, find a place for them on the team, and no more snide remarks."

Chris nodded his agreement. "Sorry, Nat."

"Finally, polls and statistics, Su Ling."

"My name is Su Ling. There are 9,628 students registered—5,517 men, 4,111 women. A very amateur poll conducted on campus last Saturday morning showed Elliot had 611 votes and Nat 541, but don't forget Elliot's had a head start on us, because he's been campaigning for over a year, and his posters are already displayed everywhere. Ours will be up by Friday."

"And torn down by Saturday."

"Then we replace them immediately," said Joe, "without resorting to the same tactics. Sorry, Su Ling."

"No, that's fine. Every member of the team must be sure to speak to at least twenty voters a day," Su Ling said. "With sixty days still to go, we must try to canvas every student several times before election day. Now this exercise should not be done casually," she continued. "On the wall behind you, you will find a board with the name of every student in alphabetical order. On the table below you will see seventeen crayons. I have allocated a color for each member of the team. Every evening, you will place a tick by the voters that you have spoken to. This is just another way of finding out who are the talkers and who are the workers."

"But you said there were seventeen crayons on the table," said Joe, "when there are only fourteen members of the team?"

"Correct, but there's also one black, one yellow and one red crayon. If the person has said they will be voting for Elliot, you cross him or her out in black, if you're unsure, give them a yellow tick, but if you're confident they will be voting for Nat, then use red. Each evening I'll enter any new data on my computer, and hand you all printouts first thing the following morning. Any questions?" asked Su Ling.

"Will you marry me?" asked Chris.

Everyone burst out laughing. "Yes, I will," said Su Ling. She paused. "And remember not to believe everything you're told, because Elliot has already asked me, and I said yes to him as well."

"What about me?" said Nat.

Su Ling smiled. "Don't forget, I gave you your answer in writing."

—<o>—

"Goodnight, sir, and thank you for a memorable evening."

"Goodnight, Fletcher. I'm glad you enjoyed yourself."

"We certainly did," said Annie. "It was fascinating to meet the vice-president. I'll be able to tease my father for weeks," she added, as Fletcher helped her into the car.

Before he had pulled the door closed on his side, Fletcher said, "Annie, you were fantastic."

"I was only trying to survive," said Annie. "I hadn't expected Karl to place me between the vice-president and Mr. Alexander during dinner. I even wondered if it was a mistake."

"The professor doesn't make that sort of mistake," said Fletcher. "I suspect that Bill Alexander requested it."

"But why would he do that?" asked Annie.

"Because he's the senior partner of an old-fashioned, traditional firm, so he'll figure that he can learn a great deal about me if he gets to know my wife; if you're invited to join Alexander Dupont and Bell, it's nothing short of marriage."

"Then let's hope I didn't hold up a proposal."

"Far from it. What you did was to make sure I reach the courting stage. Don't imagine that it was coincidental that Mrs. Alexander came and sat next to you when coffee was being served in the drawing room."

Annie gave out a slight moan, and Fletcher looked anxiously across. "Oh, my God," she said, "the contractions have begun."

"But you've still got another ten weeks," said Fletcher. "Just relax and I'll have you back home and tucked up in no time."

Annie groaned again, a little louder. "Don't bother with going home," she said, "get me to a hospital."

Speeding across Westville, Fletcher checked the names on the street corners and tried to work out which would be the best route to Yale–New Haven Hospital, when he spotted a taxi stand on the far side of the road. He swung the car sharply across and pulled up alongside the front cab. He wound down the window, and shouted, "My wife's gone into labor, which is the quickest route to Yale–New Haven?"

"Follow me," shouted the cab driver and shot off in front of them.

Fletcher tried to keep up with the taxi as he nipped in and out of the traffic, with a palm pressed down on the horn, while flashing his lights, as he took a route Fletcher didn't even know existed. Annie clutched her stomach, as the groans became louder and louder.

"Don't worry, my darling, we're nearly there," he said, as he jumped another red light to make sure he didn't lose contact with the cab.

When the two cars finally reached the hospital, Fletcher was surprised to see a doctor and nurse standing next to a gurney by an open door, obviously expecting them. As the cab driver jumped out, he gave the nurse a thumbs-up sign, and Fletcher guessed that he must have asked his dispatcher to call ahead; he hoped he had enough money on him to pay the fare, not to mention a large tip for the man's initiative.

Fletcher jumped out of the car, and ran around to help Annie, but the cab driver beat him to it. They took an elbow each and helped to lift her out of the cab and gently onto the gurney. The nurse began to unbutton Annie's dress even before she was wheeled through the open door. Fletcher removed his wallet, turned to the taxi driver and said, "Thank you, you couldn't have been more helpful. How much do I owe you?"

"Not a cent, it's on me," the taxi driver replied.

"But . . ." began Fletcher

"If I told my wife I'd charged you, she'd kill me. Good luck," he shouted and without another word walked back to his cab.

"Thank you," Fletcher repeated before he dashed into the hospital. He quickly caught up with his wife and took her hand. "It's going to be just fine, honey," he assured her.

The orderly asked Annie a series of questions, all of which received a monosyllabic yes in reply. His inquiries complete, he rang through to the operating room to alert Dr. Redpath and the waiting team that they were less than a minute away. The slow, vast elevator lurched to a halt on the fifth floor. Annie was wheeled quickly down the corridor, Fletcher trotting by her side, clinging to her outstretched hand. He could see two nurses in the distance holding open double doors so that the gurney would never lose its momentum.

Annie continued to hold on to Fletcher's hand as she was lifted onto the operating table. Three more people came bursting into the room, their faces hidden behind masks. The first checked the instruments laid out on the table, the second prepared an oxygen mask, while the third tried to ask Annie more questions; although she was now screaming with pain. Fletcher never let go of his wife's hand, until an older man came through the door. He pulled on a pair of surgical gloves and said, "Are we all ready?" even before he'd had a chance to check the patient.

"Yes, Dr. Redpath," replied the nurse.

"Good," he said and turning to Fletcher added, "I'm afraid I'll have to ask you to leave, Mr. Davenport. We'll call for you just as soon as the baby has been delivered."

Fletcher kissed his wife on the forehead. "I'm so proud of you," he whispered.

22

NAT WOKE AT five on the day of the election, only to discover that Su Ling was already in the shower. He checked the schedule on the bedside table. Full team meeting at seven, followed by an hour and a half outside the dining hall to meet and greet voters as they went in and out of breakfast.

"Come and join me," shouted Su Ling, "we haven't any time to waste." She was right, because they arrived at the team meeting only moments before the clock on the bell tower struck seven times. Every other member of the team was already present, and Tom, who had come over from Yale for the day, was passing on the experience of his own recent election. Su Ling and Nat took the two empty seats on each side of their unofficial chief of staff, who continued the briefing as if they weren't there.

"No one stops, even to draw breath, until one minute past six when the last vote will have been cast. Now I suggest that the candidate and Su Ling are outside the dining hall between seven thirty and eight thirty while the rest of you go into breakfast."

"We're expected to go on eating that garbage for an hour?" said Joe.

"No, I don't want you to eat anything, Joe, I need you moving from table to table, never two of you at the same table, and remember that Elliot's team will probably be carrying out exactly the same exercise, so don't waste any time asking for their vote. OK, let's go."

Fourteen people ran out of the room and across the lawn, disappearing through the swing doors and into the dining hall, leaving Nat and Su Ling to hang around near the entrance.

"Hi, I'm Nat Cartwright, and I'm running for student president, and I hope you'll be able to support me in today's election."

Two sleepy-eyed students said, "Fine, man, you've already wrapped up the gay vote."

"Hi, I'm Nat Cartwright, and I'm running for student president, and I hope you'll be able to support me . . ."

"Yes, I know who you are, but how can you possibly understand what it's like to survive on a student loan, when you earn an extra four hundred dollars a month?" came back the sharp reply.

"Hi, I'm Nat Cartwright, I'm running for student president and . . ."

"I won't be voting for either of you," said another student, as he pushed through the swing doors.

"Hi, I'm Nat Cartwright, and I'm running for . . ."

"Sorry, just visiting from another campus, so I don't have a vote."

"Hi, I'm Nat Cartwright and I'm . . ."

"Good luck, but I'm only voting for you because of your girlfriend, I think she's terrific."

"Hi, I'm Nat Cartwright . . ."

"And I'm a member of Ralph Elliot's team, and we're going to kick your butt."

"Hi, I'm Nat . . ."

Nine hours later, Nat could only wonder how many times he had delivered that line, and how many hands he'd shaken. All he knew for certain was that he had lost his voice and was sure his fingers would fall off. At one minute past six, he turned to Tom and said, "Hi, I'm Nat Cartwright and . . ."

"Forget it," said Tom with a laugh, "I'm the president of Yale, and all I know is if it wasn't for Ralph Elliot you'd have my job."

"What have you planned for me now," asked Nat, "because my schedule ends at six, so I don't have a clue what to do next."

"Typical of every candidate," said Tom, "but I thought the three of us could have a relaxed dinner at Mario's."

"What about the rest of the team?" asked Su Ling.

"Joe, Chris, Sue and Tim are acting as observers at the count over in the Commons, while the others are getting a well-earned rest. As the count begins at seven and should take at least a couple of hours, I've suggested that everybody be there by eight thirty."

"Sounds good to me," said Nat. "I could eat a horse."

Mario guided the three of them to their table in the corner, and kept addressing Nat as Mr. President. As the three of them sipped their drinks and tried to relax, Mario reappeared with a large bowl of spaghetti which he covered in a bolognese sauce, before sprinkling parmesan cheese all over it. However many times Nat stuck his fork in the heap of pasta, it never seemed to diminish. Tom noticed that his friend was becoming more and more nervous and eating less and less.

"I wonder what Elliot is up to right now?" asked Su Ling.

"He'll be at McDonald's along with the rest of his wretched gang, eating burgers and fries and pretending to enjoy them," said Tom as he sipped a glass of house wine.

"Well, at least there are no more dirty tricks he can play now," said Nat.

"I wouldn't be so sure of that," said Su Ling, just as Joe Stein came rushing through the door.

"What can Joe want?" asked Tom as he stood and waved at him. Nat smiled as his chief of staff rushed over to their table, but Joe didn't return his smile.

"We've got a problem," said Joe. "You'd better come over to the Commons immediately."

———

Fletcher began pacing up and down the corridor, much in the same way as his father had done over twenty years before, an evening that had been described to him by Miss Nichol on many occasions. It was like the replaying of an old black-and-white movie, always with the same happy ending. Fletcher found he was never more than a few paces from the door of the operating room as he waited for someone—anyone—to come out.

At last the rubber doors swung open and a nurse rushed out, but she hurried quickly past Fletcher without saying a word. It was several more minutes before Dr. Redpath finally emerged. He removed his face mask, but his lips weren't smiling. "They're just settling your wife into her room," he said. "She's fine, exhausted, but fine. You should be able to see her in a few moments."

"What about the baby?"

"Your son has been transferred to the special care nursery. Let me show you," he said, touching Fletcher's elbow and guiding him along the corridor, stopping at a large plate glass window. On the other side were three incubators. Two of them were already occupied. He watched as his son was placed gently in the third. A scrawny, helpless little thing, red and wrinkled. The nurse was inserting a rubber tube down his nose. She then attached a sensor to his chest and plugged the lead into a monitor. Her final task was to place a tiny band around the baby's left wrist, displaying the name Davenport. The screen began to flicker immediately, but even with his slight knowledge of medicine, Fletcher could see that his son's heartbeat was weak. He looked anxiously across at Dr. Redpath.

"What are his chances?"

"He's ten weeks premature, but if we can get him through the night, he'll have a good chance of survival."

"What are his chances?" Fletcher pressed.

"There are no rules, no percentages, no laid-down laws. Every child is unique, your son included," the doctor added as a nurse joined them.

"You can see your wife now, Mr. Davenport," she said, "if you'd like to come with me."

Fletcher thanked Dr. Redpath and followed the nurse down one flight of stairs to the floor below, where he was taken to his wife's bedside. Annie was propped up with several pillows behind her.

"How's our son?" were her opening words.

"He looks terrific, Mrs. Davenport, and he's lucky to begin his life with such an amazing mother."

"They won't let me see him," said Annie quietly, "and I so much want to hold him in my arms."

"They've put him in an incubator for the time being," Fletcher said gently, "but he has a nurse with him the whole time."

"It seems years ago that we were having dinner with Professor Abrahams."

"Yes, it's been quite a night," said Fletcher, "and a double triumph for you. You wowed the senior partner of a firm I want to join, and then produced a son, all on the same evening. What next?"

"That all seems so unimportant now we have a child to take care of." She paused. "Harry Robert Davenport."

"It has a nice ring about it," said Fletcher, "and both our fathers will be delighted."

"What shall we call him," asked Annie, "Harry or Robert?"

"I know what I'm going to call him," said Fletcher as the nurse returned to the room.

"I think you should try and get some sleep, Mrs. Davenport, it's been an exhausting time for you."

"I agree," said Fletcher. He removed several pillows from behind his wife's head, as she lowered herself slowly down the bed. Annie smiled and rested her head on the remaining pillow as her husband kissed her. As Fletcher left, the nurse switched off the light.

Fletcher raced back up the stairs and along the corridor to check if his son's heartbeat was any stronger. He stared through the plate glass window at the monitor, willing it to flicker a little higher, and managed to convince himself that it had. Fletcher kept his nose pressed up against the window. "Keep fighting, Harry," he said, and then began counting the heartbeats per minute. Suddenly he felt exhausted. "Hang in there, you're going to make it."

He took a couple of paces backward and collapsed into a chair on the other side of the corridor. Within minutes, he had fallen into a deep sleep.

Fletcher woke with a start when he felt a hand gently touch his shoulder. His tired eyes blinked open; he had no idea how long he'd been asleep. The first thing he saw was a nurse, her face solemn. Dr. Redpath stood a pace behind her. He didn't need to be told that Harry Robert Davenport was no longer alive.

"So what's the problem?" asked Nat as they ran toward the Commons where the vote was being counted.

"We were leading comfortably until a few minutes ago," said Joe, already out of breath from his trip there and back and unable to keep up with what Nat would have described as a jog. He slowed to a fast walk. "And then suddenly two new ballot boxes appeared, stuffed with votes—and nearly ninety percent of them in favor of Elliot," he added as they reached the bottom step.

Nat and Tom didn't wait for Joe as they bounded up the steps and through the swing doors. The first person they saw was Ralph Elliot—a smug look on his face. Nat turned his attention to Tom, who was already being briefed by Sue and Chris. He quickly joined them.

"We were leading by just over four hundred votes," said Chris, "and we assumed it was all over, when two new boxes appeared out of nowhere."

"What do you mean, out of nowhere?" asked Tom.

"Well, they were discovered under a table, but hadn't been included among those that were registered in the original count. In those two boxes," Chris checked his clipboard, "Elliot polled 319, to Nat's 48, and 322 to Nat's 41, which reversed the original outcome and put him in the lead by a handful of votes."

"Give me a few examples of figures from some of the other boxes," said Su Ling.

"They were all fairly consistent," said Chris, returning to his list. "The most extreme was 209 for Nat, against 176 for Elliot. In fact, Elliot only polled higher in one box, 201 to 196."

"The votes in the last two boxes," said Su Ling, "are not statistically possible, when you compare them with the other ten that have already been counted. Someone must have literally stuffed those boxes with enough ballot papers to reverse the original decision."

"But how could they have managed that?" asked Tom.

"It would be easy enough if you could get your hands on any unused ballots," said Su Ling.

"And that wouldn't have been too difficult," said Joe.

"How can you be so sure?" asked Nat.

"Because when I voted in my dorm during the lunch hour, there was only one teller on duty, and she was writing an essay. I could have removed a handful of ballots without her even noticing."

"But that doesn't explain the sudden appearance of two missing boxes," said Tom.

"You don't need a Ph.D. to work out that one," chipped in Chris, "because once the poll has closed, all they had to do was hold back two of the boxes, and then stuff them with ballots."

"But we have no way of proving that," said Nat.

"The statistics prove it," said Su Ling. "They never lie, though I admit we don't have any first-hand proof."

"So what are we going to do about it?" asked Joe, as he stared across at Elliot, the same self-satisfied look still in place.

"There's not much we can do except pass on our observations to Chester Davies. After all, he is the chief elections officer."

"OK, Joe, why don't you do that, and we'll wait to see what he has to say."

Joe left them to make his submission to the dean of students. They watched as the expression on the elderly academic's face became grimmer and grimmer. Once Joe had made his point, the dean immediately called for Elliot's chief of staff, who did nothing more than shrug his shoulders and point out that every ballot was valid.

Nat watched apprehensively as Mr. Davies questioned both men, and saw Joe nod his agreement, before they broke away to join their respective teams.

"The dean is calling an immediate meeting of the elections committee in his office, and he will report back after they've discussed the matter, which should be in about thirty minutes."

Su Ling took Nat's hand. "Mr. Davies is a good and just man," she said, "he'll come to the right conclusion."

"He may well come to the right conclusion," said Nat, "but in the end he can only follow the election rules whatever his personal reservations."

"I agree," said a voice from behind them. Nat swung around to see Elliot grinning at him. "They won't have to look in the rule book to discover that the person with the most votes is the winner," Elliot added with disdain.

"Unless they come across something about one person, one vote," said Nat.

"Are you accusing me of cheating?" Elliot snapped back, as a group of his supporters drifted over and stood behind him.

"Well, let's put it this way. If you win this election, you can apply for a job in Chicago as a teller in Cook County, because Mayor Daly has nothing to teach you."

Elliot took a step forward and raised his fist just as the dean reentered the room, a single sheet of paper in his hand. He made his way back up onto the stage.

"You just escaped a beating," whispered Elliot.

"And I suspect you're just about to get one," replied Nat, as they both turned to face the stage.

The chattering in the hall died down as Mr. Davies adjusted the height of the microphone and faced those who had hung around to hear the result. He read slowly from a prepared script.

"In the election for president of the student senate, it has been brought to my attention that two ballot boxes were discovered some time after the count had been concluded. When they were opened, the outcome of those votes varied considerably from all the other boxes. Therefore as delegated officials, we were left with no choice but to refer to the rule book on elections. Search as we might, we were unable to find any mention of missing boxes, or what action to take should there be a disproportionate ratio of votes found in any one box."

"Because no one has ever cheated in the past," shouted Joe from the back of the hall.

"And no one did this time," came back the immediate reply, "you're just bad losers."

"How many more boxes have you got hidden away just in case . . . ?"

"We don't need any more."

"Quiet," said the dean. "These outbursts do not reflect well on either side." He waited for silence before he continued to read from his script. "We are, however, mindful of our responsibility as officers, and have come to the conclusion that the result of the election must stand." Elliot's supporters leaped in the air and cheered.

Elliot turned to Nat and said, "I think you'll find it's you who just got the beating."

"It's not over yet," said Nat, his eyes still fixed on Mr. Davies.

It was some time before the dean could continue, as few present realized that he had not yet completed his statement.

"As there have been several irregularities in this election, one of which in our opinion remains unresolved, I have therefore decided that under rule 7B of the Student Senate Charter, the defeated candidate should be given the opportunity to appeal. Should he do so, the committee will be faced with three choices." He opened the rule book and read: "a) to confirm the original result, b) to reverse the original result, or c) to call for a new election, which would be held during the first week of the following term. We therefore propose to give Mr. Cartwright twenty-four hours to appeal."

"We won't need twenty-four hours," called out Joe. "We appeal."

"I shall need that in writing from the candidate," said the dean.

Tom glanced across at Nat, who was looking down at Su Ling.

"Do you remember what we agreed if I didn't win?"

BOOK THREE

CHRONICLES

23

NAT TURNED AND watched Su Ling walk slowly toward him and recalled the day they had first met. He had chased her down a hill, and when she turned on that occasion, she'd taken his breath away.

"Do you have any idea how lucky you are?" whispered Tom.

"Could you please concentrate on your job. Now, where's the ring?"

"The ring, what ring?" Nat turned and stared at his best man. "Hell, I knew there was something I was meant to bring with me," Tom whispered frantically. "Can you hold things up for a moment while I go back to the house and look for it?"

"Do you want me to strangle you?" said Nat, grinning.

"Yes please," said Tom, gazing at Su Ling as she advanced toward them. "Let her be my last memory of this world."

Nat turned his attention to his bride, and she gave him that smile that he remembered when she'd stood at the entrance to the café on their first date. She stepped up and took her place beside him, head slightly bowed as they waited for the priest to begin the service. Nat thought about the decision they had made the day after the election, and knew he would never regret it. Why should he hold up Su Ling's career on the off chance of winning the presidency? The idea of rerunning the ballot during the first week of the following term, and having to ask Su Ling to hang around for another year if he failed, left him in no doubt what he should do. The priest turned to the congregation. "Dearly beloved . . ."

When Su Ling had explained to Professor Mullden that she was getting married, and her future husband was at the University of

Connecticut, they immediately offered him the chance to complete his undergraduate degree at Harvard. They already knew of Nat's record in Vietnam and his success on the cross-country team, but it was his grades that tipped the balance. They remained puzzled as to why he hadn't taken up his place at Yale because it was clear to the admissions office that they would not be carrying Su Ling's husband.

"Do you take this woman to be your lawful wedded wife?"

Nat wanted to shout "I do." "I do," he said quietly.

"Do you take this man to be your lawful wedded husband?"

"I do," said Su Ling, head bowed.

"You may kiss the bride," said the priest.

"I think that means me," said Tom, taking a pace forward. Nat took Su Ling in his arms and kissed her as he lifted his left leg sharply and kicked Tom in the shins.

"So that's what I get for all the sacrifices I've made over the years? Well, at least it's my turn now." Nat swung around and took Tom in his arms and hugged him, while the congregation burst out laughing.

Tom was right, thought Nat. He hadn't even remonstrated with him when he refused to appeal to the elections committee, although Nat knew Tom believed he would have been victorious in a rerun contest. And the following morning Mr. Russell had phoned and offered Nat the use of their home for the reception. How could he even begin to repay them?

"Be warned," said Tom, "Dad will expect you to join him at the bank as a trainee once you've graduated from Harvard Business School."

"That may turn out to be the best offer I get," said Nat.

The bride and groom turned to face their family and friends. Susan made no attempt to hide her tears, while Michael beamed with pride. Su Ling's mother stepped forward and took a photo of the two of them in their first moment as man and wife.

Nat didn't recall much about the reception, other than feeling that Mr. and Mrs. Russell couldn't have done anymore had he been their own son. He moved from table to table, especially thanking those who had traveled a long distance. It was only when he heard the sound of silver against crystal that he checked to make sure his speech was still in his inside pocket.

Nat quickly slipped into his place at the top table just as Tom rose to speak. The best man opened by explaining why the reception was being held in his home. "Don't forget that I proposed to Su Ling long before the bridegroom did, although inexplicably on this occasion she was willing to settle for second best." Nat smiled across at Tom's aunt Abigail from Boston, as the guests applauded.

Nat sometimes wondered if Tom's jokes about his love for Su Ling didn't betray an underlying truth about his real feelings. He looked up at his best man, recalling, because he was late—thank you, mother—how he had come to sit next to the tearful little boy at the end of the row on their first day at Taft. He thought how lucky he was to be blessed with such a friend, and hoped it would not be long before he was carrying out the same duty for him.

Tom received a warm reception when he sat down to make way for the bridegroom.

Nat began his speech by thanking Mr. and Mrs. Russell for their generosity in allowing them the use of their beautiful home for the reception. He thanked his mother for her wisdom and his father for his looks, which brought applause and laughter. "But most of all I thank Su Ling, for going down the wrong path, and my parents for an upbringing that made me follow her, to warn her that she was making a mistake."

"She made a far bigger mistake chasing you back up the hill," said Tom.

Nat waited for the laughter to die down, before he said, "I fell in love with Su Ling the moment I saw her, a feeling that was clearly not reciprocated, but then, as I've already explained, I'm blessed with my father's looks. And so let me end by inviting you all to our golden wedding anniversary on July 11, 2024." He paused. "Only wimps and those who dare to die in between will be excused attendance." He raised his glass. "To my wife, Su Ling."

When Su Ling disappeared upstairs to change, Tom finally asked Nat where they were going on their honeymoon.

"Korea," whispered Nat. "We're planning to find the village where Su Ling was born, and see if we can trace any other members of her family. But don't tell Su Ling's mother—we want to surprise her when we return."

Three hundred guests surged out to join them in the driveway, and applauded as the car carrying the bride and groom disappeared on its journey to the airport.

"I wonder where they're spending their honeymoon," said Su Ling's mother.

"I have no idea," Tom replied.

—◦—

Fletcher held Annie in his arms. A month had passed since the funeral of Harry Robert, and she was still blaming herself.

"But that's just not fair," said Fletcher. "If anyone's to blame, it must be me. Look at the pressure Joanna was under when she gave birth, and it made absolutely no difference to her." But Annie couldn't be consoled. The doctor told him the quickest way to solve the problem, and Fletcher happily acquiesced.

As each day passed, Annie grew a little stronger, but her first interest remained supporting her husband in his determination to be top of his year. "You owe it to Karl Abrahams," she reminded him. "He's invested a lot in you, and there is only one way you can repay him."

Annie inspired her husband to work night and day during his summer vacation before he returned for his final year. She became his assistant and researcher while remaining his lover and friend. And she only ignored his advice when he pressed her to consider going on to graduate school herself.

"No," said Annie, "I want to be your wife and God willing in time . . ."

—◦—

Once he'd returned to Yale, Fletcher accepted it would not be too long before he would have to start the meat run. Although several firms had already invited him for an interview, and one or two had even offered him jobs, Fletcher didn't want to work out of Dallas or Denver, Phoenix or Pittsburgh. But as the weeks passed, and he heard nothing from Alexander Dupont & Bell, his hopes began to fade and he concluded that if he still hoped to be invited to join one of the big firms it would require a full round of interviews.

Jimmy had already sent out over fifty letters and to date had only received three replies; not one of them had offered him a job. He would have settled for Dallas or Denver, Phoenix or Pittsburgh if it hadn't been for Joanna. Annie and Fletcher agreed on the cities they would be happy to live in, and then she carried out some research on the leading firms in those states. Together they composed a letter that was duplicated fifty-four times, and then dispatched on the first day of the term.

When Fletcher returned to college later that morning, he found a letter in his mailbox.

"That was quick," said Annie, "we only posted them an hour ago."

Fletcher laughed until he saw the postmark on the letter. He tore it open. The simple black-embossed heading announced Alexander Dupont & Bell. Of course, the distinguished New York firm always began interviewing candidates during March, so why should it be any different for Fletcher Davenport?

Fletcher didn't stop working during those long winter months leading up to the interview, but he still had every reason to feel apprehensive when he finally set out on the journey to New York. As soon as he stepped off the train at Grand Central Station, Fletcher was intoxicated by the babble of a hundred tongues, and feet that moved more swiftly than he'd experienced in any other city. He spent the cab ride to 54th Street peering out of an open window, taking in a smell that no other city produces.

The cab drew up outside a seventy-two-floor glass skyscraper, and Fletcher knew right away that he didn't want to work anywhere else. He hung around on the ground floor for a few minutes, not wishing to be stuck in a waiting room with several other candidates. When he finally stepped out of the elevator on the thirty-sixth floor, the receptionist ticked off his name. She then handed him a sheet of paper, which listed a schedule of interviews that would take the rest of the day.

His first meeting was with the senior partner, Bill Alexander, which Fletcher felt went well, although Alexander didn't exude the same warmth as he had at Karl Abrahams's party. However, he did ask after Annie, expressing the hope that she had fully recovered from the sad loss of Harry. It also became clear during the meeting that Fletcher was not the only person who was being interviewed—six upside-down names appeared on a list facing Mr. Alexander.

Fletcher then spent an hour with three other partners who specialized in his chosen field, criminal law. When the last interview ended, he was invited to join the rest of the board for lunch. It was the first time he came into contact with the other five applicants, and the lunch conversation left him in no doubt what he was up against. He could only wonder how many days the firm had put aside for interviews with other would-be applicants.

What he couldn't know was that Alexander Dupont & Bell had carried out a rigorous sifting process months before any of the candidates had been invited for interview, and he had made the final six, on recommendation and reputation. He also didn't realize that only one, perhaps two, would be offered a position with the firm. As with a good wine, there were even years when no one was selected, simply because it just wasn't a vintage crop.

More interviews followed in the afternoon, by which time Fletcher was convinced he wouldn't make it, and would soon have to begin the long trek around to those firms who had replied to his letter and offered him an interview.

"They'll let me know by the end of the month if I've made it to the next round," he told Annie, who was waiting for him at the station, "but don't stop sending the letters, although I confess I no longer want to work anywhere but New York."

Annie continued to question Fletcher on the way home, wanting to know every detail of what had taken place. She was touched that Bill Alexander had remembered her; more so that he had even taken the trouble to find out the name of their son.

"Perhaps you should have told him," said Annie as she brought the car to a halt outside their home.

"Told him what?" asked Fletcher.

"That I'm pregnant again."

—◦—

Nat loved the hustle and bustle of Seoul, a city determined to put all memories of war behind it. Skyscrapers loomed on every corner, as the old and new tried to live in harmony. Nat was impressed by the potential of such a well-educated, intelligent workforce who survived on wages a quarter of what would be acceptable back home. Su Ling couldn't help noticing the subservient role women still played in Korean society and silently thanked her mother for having the courage and foresight to set out for America.

Nat rented a car so that they could move from village to village as and when it suited them. Once they'd driven a few miles out of the capital, the first thing that struck them both was how quickly the way of life changed. By the time they had traveled a hundred miles, they had also traveled back a hundred years. The modern skyscrapers were quickly replaced by little wooden shacks, and the hustle and bustle by a slower, more considered pace.

Although Su Ling's mother had rarely talked about her upbringing in Korea, Su Ling knew the village where she had been born, and her family name. She also knew that two of her uncles had been killed in the war, so that when they arrived in Kaping with its population of 7,303—according to the guide book—she wasn't all that hopeful of being able to find anyone who would remember her mother.

Su Ling Cartwright began her quest at the town hall, where a register was kept of all the local citizens. It didn't help that, of the 7,000 inhabitants, over a thousand shared Su Ling's mother's maiden name of Peng. However, the lady at reception also exhibited that name on the plaque on her desk. She told Su Ling that her great-aunt, who was now over ninety, claimed to know every branch of the family, and if she would like to meet her, that could be arranged. Su Ling nodded her agreement, and was asked to return later that day.

She called back in the afternoon, to be told that Ku Sei Peng would be happy to take tea with her the following day. The receptionist apologized before politely explaining that Su Ling's American husband would not be welcome.

Su Ling returned to their little hotel the following night, bearing a piece of paper and a happy smile. "We've traveled all this way out here, only to be told to go back to Seoul," she said.

"How come?" asked Nat.

"It's simple. Ku Sei Peng remembers my mother leaving the village to seek work in the capital, but she never returned. But her younger sister, Kai Pai Peng, still lives in Seoul and Ku Sei has given me her last known address."

"So it's back to the capital," said Nat, who phoned down to reception to warn them they would be checking out immediately. They arrived back in Seoul just before midnight.

"I think it might be wise if I were to visit her on my own," said Su Ling over breakfast the following morning, "as she may not be willing to say a great deal once she discovers I'm married to an American."

"Suits me," said Nat. "I was hoping to visit the market on the other side of the city as I'm searching for something in particular."

"What?" asked Su Ling,

"Wait and see," teased Nat.

Nat took a taxi to the Kiray district, and spent the day roaming around one of the biggest open markets in the world—row upon row of laden stalls crammed with everything from Rolex watches to cultured pearls, from Gucci bags to Chanel perfume, from Cartier bracelets to Tiffany hearts. He avoided the cries of "Over here, American, please to look at my goods, much cheaper," as he could never be sure what, if anything, was the real thing.

By the time he arrived back at the hotel that evening, Nat was exhausted and laden down with six shopping bags, mostly full of presents for his wife. He took the elevator to the third floor, and as he pushed open the door to their room, he hoped to find that Su Ling had returned from visiting her great aunt. As he closed the door, he thought he heard sobbing. He stood still. The unmistakable sound was coming from the bedroom.

Nat dropped the bags on the floor, walked across the room and pushed open the bedroom door. Su Ling was curled up on the bed, like an unsprung coil, weeping. He slipped off his shoes and jacket and climbed onto the bed beside her and took her in his arms.

"What is it, little flower?" he said, caressing her gently.

She didn't reply. Nat held her close, aware that she would tell him in her own time.

When it grew dark and the neon streetlights began to flicker on, Nat drew the curtains. He then sat beside her and took her hand.

"I will always love you," said Su Ling, not looking directly at him.

"And I'll always love you," said Nat, taking her back into his arms.

"Do you remember the night of our marriage, we agreed on no secrets, so I must now tell you what I discovered this afternoon."

Nat had never seen a face so sad. "Nothing you found out could make me love you less," he said, trying to reassure her.

Su Ling pulled her husband toward her while lowering her head on to his chest, as if she didn't want their eyes to meet. "I kept my appointment with my great aunt this morning," she began. "She remembered my mother well, and explained to me why she had left the village to join her in Seoul." As she clung on to Nat, Su Ling repeated everything Kai Pai had told her. When she had finished her story, she eased away and looked up at her husband for the first time.

"Can you still love me now you know the truth?" she asked.

"I didn't believe it was possible to love you any more, and I can only imagine what courage it must have taken to share this news with me." He paused. "It will only strengthen a bond that now no one will ever be able to break."

⬧

"I don't think it would be wise for me to go with you," said Annie.

"But you're my lucky mascot, and . . ."

". . . and Dr. Redpath says it wouldn't be wise." Fletcher reluctantly accepted that he would have to make the journey to New York alone. Annie was in her seventh month of pregnancy, and although there had been no complications, he never argued with the doctor.

Fletcher had been delighted to be invited back for a second interview with Alexander Dupont & Bell, and wondered how many of the other candidates had been short-listed. He had a feeling Karl Abrahams knew, though the professor wasn't sharing any confidences.

When the train pulled into Central Station, Fletcher took a taxi to 54th Street, arriving outside the vast entrance lobby twenty minutes early. He had been told that on one occasion a candidate had arrived three minutes late, so they didn't bother to interview him.

He took the elevator to the thirty-sixth floor and was directed by the receptionist to a spacious room that was almost as smart as the senior partner's office. Fletcher sat alone and wondered if that was a good sign, until a second candidate joined him a few minutes before nine. He smiled at Fletcher.

"Logan Fitzgerald," he said, his hand outstretched. "I heard you address the freshman debate at Yale. Your speech on Vietnam was brilliant, although I didn't agree with a word you said."

"You were at Yale?"

"No, I was visiting my brother. I went to Princeton, and I guess we both know why we're here."

"How many others are there, do you imagine?" asked Fletcher.

"Looking at the clock, I would suggest we're the last two. So all I can say is good luck."

"I am sure you mean that sincerely," said Fletcher with a grin.

The door opened and a woman who Fletcher remembered as Mr. Alexander's secretary addressed them. "Gentlemen, if you'll come this way," she said.

"Thank you, Mrs. Townsend," said Fletcher, whose father had once told him never to forget a secretary's name—after all, they spend more time with the boss than his wife ever does. The two candidates followed her out of the room, and Fletcher wondered if Logan could possibly be as nervous as he was. On either side of the long carpeted corridor the names of the partners were lettered in gold beside each oak-paneled door they passed. William Alexander's was the last before the conference room.

Mrs. Townsend knocked gently on the door, opened it and stood to one side as twenty-five men and three women rose from their places and began to applaud.

"Please be seated," said Bill Alexander, once the applause had died down. "May I be the first to congratulate you both on being offered the opportunity to join Alexander Dupont and Bell, but be warned, the next time you'll hear such approbation from your colleagues will be when you're invited to become a partner, and that won't be for at least seven years. During the morning you will have meetings with different members of the executive committee who between them should be able to answer any of your questions. Fletcher, you have been assigned to Matthew Cunliffe, who heads up our criminal office, while you, Logan, will report directly to Graham Simpson in mergers and acquisitions. At twelve thirty, you will both return and join the partners for lunch."

The midday meal turned out to be a friendly affair after the grueling process of interviews; the partners stopped behaving like Mr. Hyde and reverted to being Dr. Jekyll. Roles they played every day with clients and adversaries.

"They tell me that you are both going to be top of your respective classes," said Bill Alexander, after the main course was served—there had been no first course or drink supplied, other than bottled water. "And I can only hope so, because I haven't yet decided which offices to assign you to."

"And should one of us flunk?" asked Fletcher nervously.

"Then you will spend your first year in the mail room, delivering briefs to other law firms," Mr. Alexander paused. "On foot." No one laughed, and Fletcher couldn't be sure if he meant it. The senior partner was about to continue when there was a knock on the door and his secretary reappeared.

"There's a call for you on line three, Mr. Alexander."

"I said no interruptions, Mrs. Townsend."

"It's an emergency, sir."

Bill Alexander picked up the boardroom phone; the scowl on his face turned to a smile as he listened intently. "I'll let him know," he said and put the phone down.

"Let me be the first to congratulate you, Fletcher," said the senior partner. Fletcher was puzzled because he knew final grades wouldn't be published for at least another week. "You're the proud father of a little girl. Mother and daughter are doing just fine. I knew the moment I met that girl she was just the kind of woman we appreciate at Alexander Dupont and Bell."

24

"Lucy."

"But what about Ruth or Martha?"

"We can give her all three names," said Fletcher, "which will make both our mothers happy, but we'll call her Lucy." He smiled as he gently placed his daughter back in her crib.

"And have you thought about where we're going to live?" asked Annie. "I don't want Lucy brought up in New York."

"I agree," said Fletcher, as he tickled his daughter under the chin, "I've been talking to Matt Cunliffe and he told me he faced the same problem when he joined the firm."

"So what does Matt recommend?"

"He suggested three or four small towns in New Jersey that are less than an hour away by train from Penn Station. So I thought we might drive up there next Friday and spend a long weekend seeing if there's any particular area we like."

"I suppose we'll have to rent a place to begin with," said Annie, "until we've saved enough to buy something of our own."

"It seems not, because the firm would prefer us to purchase our own property."

"It's all very well for the firm to prefer something, but what if we simply can't afford it?"

"That doesn't seem to pose a problem either," said Fletcher, "because Alexander Dupont and Bell will cover the cost with an interest-free loan."

"That's very generous of them," said Annie, "but if I know Bill Alexander, there has to be an ulterior motive."

"There sure is," said Fletcher. "It ties you into the firm, and Alexander Dupont and Bell are very proud of having the smallest turnover of employees of any legal practice in New York. It's becoming obvious to me that once they've gone to all the trouble of selecting you and training you in their ways, they then make damn sure they don't lose you to a rival firm."

"Sounds to me like a shotgun marriage," said Annie. She paused. "Have you ever mentioned your political ambitions to Mr. Alexander?"

"No, I wouldn't have passed first base if I had, and in any case, who knows how I'll feel in two or three years' time?"

"I know exactly how you'll feel," said Annie, "in two years, ten years, twenty years. You're happiest when you're running for something, and I'll never forget when Dad was reelected to the Senate, you were the only person who was more excited about the result than he was."

"Don't ever let Matt Cunliffe hear you say that," said Fletcher with a smile, "because you can be sure Bill Alexander would know about it ten minutes later, and the firm is just not interested in anyone who isn't fully committed. Remember their motto, *there are twenty-five billing hours in every day.*"

–◇–

When Su Ling woke, she could hear Nat on the phone in the next room. She wondered who he could possibly be talking to so early in the morning. She heard the phone click, and a moment later her husband returned to the bedroom.

"I want you up and packed, little flower, because we have to be out of here in under an hour."

"What . . . ?"

"In under an hour."

Su Ling jumped out of bed and ran into the bathroom. "Captain Cartwright, am I allowed to know where you are taking me?" she called above the sound of running water.

"All will be revealed once we're on the plane, Mrs. Cartwright."

"Which direction?" she asked the moment the taps had been turned off.

"I'll tell you when the plane has taken off, not before."

213

"Are we going home?"

"No," said Nat, without offering to elaborate.

Once she was dry, Su Ling concentrated on what to wear while Nat picked up the phone again.

"An hour doesn't give a girl a lot of time," said Su Ling.

"That was the idea," said Nat, who was asking the front desk if they could order him a cab.

"Damn," said Su Ling as she looked at all the presents. "There just isn't going to be enough room to cram them all in."

Nat replaced the receiver, walked over to the cupboard and produced a suitcase she'd never seen before. "Gucci?" she asked, surprised by Nat's unusual extravagance.

"I don't think so," said Nat, "not for ten dollars."

Su Ling laughed as her husband picked up the phone once more. "I need a porter and could the bill be ready by the time we come down, as we'll be checking out." He paused, listened, and said, "Ten minutes."

He turned to see Su Ling buttoning up her blouse. He thought about her finally falling asleep the night before, and his decision to leave Korea as quickly as possible. Every moment spent in that city would only remind her . . .

At the airport Nat waited in line to collect the tickets, and thanked the woman behind the counter for dealing with his early morning request so promptly. Su Ling had gone off to order breakfast while he checked their bags in. Nat then took the escalator to the first-floor restaurant, to find his wife seated in a corner, chatting to a waitress.

"I haven't ordered for you," she said as Nat joined her, "because I told the waitress that after a week of marriage I wasn't sure if you'd turn up."

Nat looked up at the waitress. "Yes, sir?" she said.

"Two eggs, sunny side up, bacon, hash browns and black coffee."

The waitress studied her pad. "Your wife has already ordered that for you."

Nat turned and looked at Su Ling. "Where are we going?" she asked.

"You'll find out once we're at the gate, and if you go on being a nuisance, not until we land."

"But . . ." she began.

"I'll blindfold you if necessary," said Nat as the waitress returned with a pot of steaming coffee. "Now I need to ask you some serious questions," Nat said, and saw that Su Ling immediately tensed. He pretended not to notice. He would have to remember not to tease her too much for the next few days as she so obviously still had one thing uppermost in her mind. "I recall your telling my mother that when Japan came online with the computer revolution, the entire technological process would speed up."

"We're going to Japan?"

"No, we're not," said Nat, as his order was placed in front of him. "Now concentrate, because I may have to rely on your expertise."

"The whole industry is on the gallop right now," said Su Ling, "Canon, Sony, Fujitsu have already overtaken the Americans. Why? Are you thinking of looking into new IT companies? In which case, you should consider . . ."

"Yes and no," said Nat as he turned his head and listened carefully to an announcement on the PA system. He checked the bill and covered it with his last few Korean notes, and then stood up.

"Going somewhere, are we, Captain Cartwright?" asked Su Ling.

"Well, I am," said Nat, "because that was my last call, and by the way, if you have other plans, I've got the tickets and the travelers' checks."

"Then I'm stuck with you, aren't I?" said Su Ling as she quickly drained her coffee and checked the departure board to see which gate was showing final calls. There were at least a dozen. "Honolulu?" she said as she caught up with him.

"Why would I want to take you to Honolulu?" asked Nat.

"To lie on the beach and make love all day."

"No, we're going somewhere where we can meet my former lovers by day, while we still make love all night."

"Saigon?" said Su Ling, as another city flicked up on the departure board. "Are we going to visit the scene of Captain Cartwright's past triumphs?"

"Wrong direction," said Nat, as he continued walking toward the international departure gate. Once their passports and tickets had been checked, Nat didn't bother to stop at duty-free, as he continued heading for the check-in desks.

"Bombay?" hazarded Su Ling as they passed gate number one.

"I don't think there are many of my old lovers to be found in India," Nat assured her as they passed gates two, three and four.

Su Ling continued to study the posted names as they walked toward each gate. "Singapore, Manila, Hong Kong?"

"No, no, and no," he repeated as they passed gates eleven, twelve and thirteen.

Su Ling remained silent as they continued on—Bangkok, Zurich, Paris, London, before Nat came to a halt at gate twenty-one.

"Are you traveling to Rome and Venice with us, sir?" asked the lady behind the Pan Am desk.

"Yes," said Nat. "The tickets are booked in the name of Mr. and Mrs. Cartwright," he said as he turned to face his wife.

"You know something, Mr. Cartwright," Su Ling said, "you are a very special man."

Over the next four weekends Annie lost count of the number of potential homes the two of them viewed. A few were too large, some too small, while others were in a district they didn't want to live in, and when they were in a neighborhood they liked, they simply couldn't afford the asking price, even with Alexander Dupont & Bell's assistance. Then one Sunday afternoon, they found exactly what they were looking for in Ridgewood, and within ten minutes of walking in the front door they had nodded to each other behind the agent's back. Annie immediately phoned her mother. "It's absolutely ideal," she enthused. "It's in a quiet neighborhood with more churches than bars, more schools than movie houses and it's even got a river meandering right through the center of town."

"And the price?" said Martha.

"A little more than we wanted to pay, but the realtor is expecting a call from my agent Martha Gates; if you can't get the price down, Mom, I don't know anyone who can."

"Did you follow my instructions?" asked Martha.

"To the letter. I told the agent we were both schoolteachers, because you said they always hike the price for lawyers, bankers and doctors. He looked suitably disappointed."

Fletcher and Annie spent the afternoon strolling around the town, praying that Martha could get them a sensible deal, because even the station was only a short drive from their front door.

After four long weeks finalizing the deal, Fletcher, Annie and Lucy Davenport spent their first night at their new home in Ridgewood, New Jersey on October 1, 1974. No sooner had they closed the front door than Fletcher announced, "Do you think you can leave Lucy with your mother for a couple of weeks?"

"It doesn't worry me having her around while we're getting the house in shape," said Annie.

"That wasn't what I had in mind," said Fletcher. "I just thought it was time we had a holiday, a sort of second honeymoon."

"But . . ."

"No buts . . . we're going to do something you've always talked about—go to Scotland and trace our ancestors, the Davenports and the Gateses."

"When were you thinking of leaving?" asked Annie.

"Our plane takes off at eleven tomorrow morning."

"Mr. Davenport, you do like to give a girl a lot of notice, don't you?"

—◇—

"What are you up to?" asked Su Ling as she leaned across to watch her husband checking over a column of figures on the financial pages of the *Asian Business News.*

"Studying currency movements over the past year," Nat replied.

"Is that how Japan fits into the equation?" inquired Su Ling.

"Sure is," said Nat, "because the yen is the only major currency in the past ten years that has consistently risen in value against the dollar, and several economists are predicting that the trend will continue for the foreseeable future. They claim the yen is still massively undervalued. If the experts are correct, and you're right about Japan's expanding role in new technology, then I think I've identified a good investment in an uncertain world."

"Is this to be the subject of your business school thesis?"

"No, however that's not a bad idea," said Nat. "I was thinking of making a small currency investment and if I prove to be right, I'll notch it up a few dollars each month."

"A bit of a risk, isn't it?"

"If you hope to make a profit, there's bound to be a certain amount of risk involved. The secret is to eliminate the elements that add to that risk." Su Ling didn't look convinced. "I'll tell you what I have in mind," said Nat. "I'm currently earning $400 a month as a captain in the army. If I sell those dollars a year in advance for yen at today's rate, then convert them back in twelve months' time, and if the dollar-yen exchange rate continues as it has done for the past seven years, I should make an annual profit of around $400 to $500."

"And if it goes the other way?" said Su Ling.

"But it hasn't for the past seven years."

"But if it did?"

"I'd lose around $400, or a month's salary."

"I'd rather have a guaranteed paycheck each month."

"You can never create capital on earned income," said Nat. "Most people live well beyond their means, and their only form of savings ends up as life insurance or bonds, both of which can be decimated by inflation. Ask my father."

"But what do we need all this money for?" asked Su Ling.

"For my lovers," said Nat.

"And where are all these lovers?"

"Most of them are in Italy, but there are a few others hanging around in the world's major capitals."

"So that's why we're going to Venice?"

"And Florence, Milan and Rome. When I left them, many were in the nude, and one of the things I most liked about them is they don't age, other than to crack a little if they're exposed to too much sunlight."

"Lucky women," said Su Ling. "And do you have a favorite?"

"No, I'm fairly promiscuous, though if I were forced to choose, I confess there is a lady in Florence who resides in a small palace, whom I adore, and am longing to meet up with again."

"Is she a virgin, by any chance?" inquired Su Ling.

"You're bright," said Nat.

"Goes by the name of Maria?"

"You've found me out, although there are a lot of Marias in Italy."

"*The Adoration of the Magi,* Tintoretto."

"No."

"Bellini, *Mother and Child*?"

"No, they still reside at the Vatican."

Su Ling went silent for a moment as the stewardess asked them to fasten their seatbelts. "Caravaggio?"

"Very good. I left her in the Pitti Palace on the right-hand wall of the third-floor gallery. She promised she would be faithful until I returned."

"And there she will remain, because such a lover would cost you more than $400 a month, and if you're still hoping to go into politics, you won't even be able to afford the frame."

"I won't be going into politics until I can afford the whole gallery," Nat assured his wife.

◆

Annie began to appreciate why the British could be so dismissive about American tourists who somehow managed to cover London, Oxford, Blenheim and Stratford in three days. It didn't help when she observed busloads of tourists descending on the Royal Shakespeare Theatre in Stratford, take their seats, and then leave during the intermission, to be replaced by another busload of her countrymen. Annie wouldn't have thought it possible, if she hadn't returned after the intermission to find the two rows in front of her full of people with familiar accents whom she had never seen before. She wondered if those who attended the second act told those who watched the first act what had happened to Rosencrantz and Guildenstern or was that busload already on its way back to London?

Annie felt less guilty after they'd spent a leisurely ten days in Scotland. They enjoyed being in Edinburgh for the Festival, where they could choose between Marlowe and Mozart, or Pinter and Orton. However, for both of them, the highlight of the trip was the long drive up and down the two coastlines. The scenery was so breathtaking they thought there could be no more beautiful landscape on earth.

In Edinburgh, they tried to trace the Gates and the Davenport lineage, but all they ended up with was a large colored chart of the clans, and a skirt made in the garish Davenport tartan, which Annie doubted she would ever wear again once they were back in the States.

Fletcher fell asleep within minutes of their plane taking off from Edinburgh for New York. When he woke, the sun that he'd seen dip on one side of the cabin still hadn't risen on the other. As they began their descent into JFK—Annie couldn't get used to it not being called Idlewilde—all Annie could think about was being reunited with Lucy, while Fletcher anxiously looked forward to his first day with Alexander Dupont & Bell.

When Nat and Su Ling returned from Rome, they were also exhausted, but the change of plans could not have been more worthwhile. Su Ling had relaxed more and more as each day passed; in fact during the second week, neither of them even mentioned Korea. They agreed on their flight home to tell Su Ling's mother that they had honeymooned in Italy. Only Tom would be puzzled.

While Su Ling slept, Nat once again studied the currency market in the *International Herald Tribune* and London's *Financial Times*. The trend continued unabated, a dip, a slight recovery, followed by another dip, but the long-term graph was only going one way for the yen, and in the opposite direction from the dollar. This was also true for the yen against the mark, the pound and the lira, and Nat decided to continue researching which of the exchange rates had the greatest disparity. Just as soon as they were back in Boston he would talk to Tom's father, and use the currency department at Russell's Bank rather than reveal his ideas to someone he didn't know.

Nat glanced across at his sleeping wife, grateful for her suggestion that he make exchange rates the subject of his final-year thesis at business school. His time at Harvard would pass all too quickly, and he realized that he could not put off a decision that would affect both their futures. They had already discussed the three possible options: he could look for a job in Boston so that Su Ling could remain at Harvard, but as she had pointed out, that would limit his horizons. He could take up Mr. Russell's offer and join Tom at a large bank in a small town, but that would seriously curtail his future prospects. Or he could apply for a job on Wall Street and find out if he could survive in the big league.

Su Ling wasn't in any doubt which of the three options he should pursue, and although they had some time to consider their future, she was already talking to her contacts at Columbia.

25

LOOKING BACK ON his final year at Harvard, Nat had had few regrets.

Only hours after touching down at Logan International, he'd phoned Tom's father to share his currency ideas. Mr. Russell pointed out that the sums he wished to deal in were too small for any foreign exchange counter to handle. Nat was disappointed until Mr. Russell suggested that the bank put up a thousand-dollar loan, and asked that he and Tom might be allowed to invest a thousand dollars each. This became Nat's first currency fund.

When Joe Stein heard about the project, another thousand appeared on the same day. Within a month, the fund had grown to $10,000. Nat told Su Ling that he was more worried about losing the investors' money than his own. By the end of the term, the Cartwright Fund had grown to $14,000, and Nat had made a clear profit of $726.

"But you could still lose it all," Su Ling reminded him.

"True, but now the fund is more substantial there's less chance of a severe loss. Even if the trend suddenly reverses, I could hedge my position by selling ahead, and so keep the losses to a minimum."

"But doesn't this take a great deal of your time, when you should be writing your thesis?" Su Ling asked.

"It only takes about fifteen minutes a day," said Nat. "I check the Japanese market at six each morning and the closing prices in New York at six every night, and as long as there isn't a run against me for several days in a row, I have nothing to do except reinvest the capital each month."

"It's obscene," said Su Ling.

"But what's wrong with using my skill, knowledge and an ounce of enterprise?" Nat inquired.

"Because you earn more working fifteen minutes a day than I can hope to pick up in a year as a senior researcher at Columbia University—in fact, it may be more than my supervisor earns."

"Your supervisor will still be in place this time next year, whatever happens to the market. That's free enterprise. The downside is that I can lose everything."

Nat didn't tell his wife that he thought the British economist Maynard Keynes had once remarked, *A shrewd man ought to be able to make a fortune before breakfast, so that he can do a proper job during the rest of the day.* He knew how strongly his wife felt about what she called easy money, so he only talked about his investments whenever *she* raised the subject. He certainly didn't let her know that Mr. Russell felt the time had come to consider leverage.

Nat felt no guilt when it came to spending fifteen minutes a day managing his mini-fund, as he doubted if there was any student in his class studying more diligently. In fact the only real break he took from work was to run for an hour every afternoon, and the highlight of his year came when, wearing a Harvard vest, he crossed the finishing line in first place in the meet against UConn.

After several interviews in New York Nat received a plethora of offers from financial institutions, but there were only two he took seriously. In reputation and size there was nothing to choose between them, but once he'd met Arnie Freeman, who headed the currency desk at Morgan's, he was quite happy to sign up there and then. Arnie had a gift for making fourteen hours a day on Wall Street sound like fun.

Nat wondered what else could happen that year, until Su Ling asked how much profit the Cartwright Fund had accumulated.

"Around forty thousand dollars," said Nat.

"And your share?"

"Twenty percent. So what are you planning to spend it on?"

"Our first child," she replied.

Looking back on his first year with Alexander Dupont & Bell, Fletcher also had few regrets. He'd no idea what his responsibilities would be, but first-year associates were not known as "pack horses" for nothing. He quickly found out that his principal responsibility was to make sure that whatever case Matt Cunliffe was working on, he never needed to look beyond his desk for any relevant documents or case histories. It had only taken Fletcher a matter of days to discover that any idea of nonstop appearances in glamorous court cases defending innocent women accused of murder was the stuff of television dramas. Most of his work was painstaking and meticulous and more often than not rewarded by plea bargaining before a trial date had even been set.

Fletcher also discovered that it wasn't until you became a partner that you started earning "the big bucks" and got to go home in the daylight. Despite this, Matt did lighten his workload by not insisting on a thirty-minute lunch break, which allowed him to play squash twice a week with Jimmy.

Although Fletcher took work home on the train, he tried whenever possible to spend an hour in the evening with his daughter. His father frequently reminded him that once those early years had passed, he wouldn't be able to rewind the reel marked "important moments in Lucy's childhood."

Lucy's first birthday party was the noisiest event outside a football stadium that Fletcher had ever attended. Annie had made so many friends in the neighborhood that he found his home full of young children who seemed to all want to laugh or cry at the same time. Fletcher marveled at how calmly Annie handled spilled ice cream, chocolate cake trodden into the carpet, a bottle of milk poured over her dress, without the familiar smile ever leaving her face. When the last brat had finally departed, Fletcher was exhausted, but all Annie said was, "I think that went just fine."

Fletcher continued to see a lot of Jimmy, who, thanks to his father—his own words—had landed a job with a small but well-respected law practice on Lexington Avenue. His hours were almost as bad as Fletcher's, but the responsibility of fatherhood seemed to have given him a new incentive, which only increased when Joanna gave birth to a second child. Fletcher marveled how successful their marriage was, remembering the age gap and academic disparity. But it seemed to make no difference, because the couple simply adored each other and were the envy of many of their contemporaries who had already filed for divorce. When Fletcher heard the news of Jimmy's second child, he hoped it wouldn't be long before Annie followed suit; he so envied Jimmy having a son. He often thought about Harry Robert.

Because of his workload, Fletcher made few new friends, with the exception of Logan Fitzgerald, who had joined the firm on the same day. They would often compare notes over lunch, and have a drink together before Fletcher caught his train home in the evening. Soon the tall, fair-haired Irishman was being invited back to Ridgewood to meet Annie's unmarried girlfriends. Although Fletcher accepted that Logan and he were rivals, it didn't appear to harm their friendship; in fact, if anything, it seemed to make the bond between them even stronger. Both had their minor triumphs and setbacks during the first year, and no one in the firm seemed willing to offer an opinion on which of them would become a partner first.

Over a drink one evening, Fletcher and Logan agreed they were now full-fledged members of the firm. In a few weeks' time a new brace of trainees would appear and they would progress from pack horses to yearlings. They had both studied with interest the CVs of all those who made the short list.

"What do you think of the applicants?" asked Fletcher, trying not to sound superior.

"Not bad," said Logan, as he ordered Fletcher his usual light beer, "with one exception—that guy from Stanford, I couldn't work out how he even got on the shortlist."

"I'm told he's Bill Alexander's nephew."

"Well, that's a good enough reason to put him on the shortlist, but not to offer him a job, so I don't expect we'll ever see him again. Come to think of it," said Logan, "I can't even remember his name."

—◇—

Nat was the youngest in a team of three at Morgan's. His immediate boss was Steven Ginsberg, who was twenty-eight, and his number two, Adrian Kenwright, had just celebrated his twenty-sixth birthday. Between them, they controlled a fund of over a million dollars.

As the currency markets open in Tokyo just as most civilized Americans are going to bed, and close in Los Angeles when the sun no longer shines on the American continent, one of the team had to be on call to cover every hour of the night or day. In fact the only occasion Steven allowed Nat to take an afternoon off was to watch Su Ling receiving her doctorate at Harvard, and even then he had to leave the celebration party so he could take an urgent phone call and explain why the Italian lira was going south.

"They could have a Communist government by this time next week," said Nat, "so start switching into Swiss francs," he added. "And get rid of any pesetas or sterling we have on our books, because they both have left-wing governments, and will be the next to feel the strain."

"And the deutschmark?"

"Hold on to the mark, because the currency will remain under-valued as long as the Berlin Wall is in place."

Although the two senior members of the team had a great deal more financial experience than Nat, and were willing to work just as hard, they both acknowledged that because of his political antennae Nat could read a market more quickly than anyone else they had ever worked with—or against.

The day everyone sold the dollar and went into pounds, Nat immediately sold the pound on the forward market. For eight days it looked as if he might have lost the bank a fortune and his colleagues rushed past him quickly in the corridor without looking him in the eye. A month later, seven other banks were offering him a job and a considerable rise in salary. Nat received a bonus check for eight thousand dollars at the end of the year, and decided the time had come to go in search of a mistress.

He didn't tell Su Ling about the bonus, or the mistress, as she had recently received a pay raise of ninety dollars a month. As for the mistress, he'd had his eye on one particular lady he passed on the street corner every morning as he went to work. And she was still reposing there in the window when he returned to their flat in SoHo every evening. As each day passed, he gave the lady soaking in a bath more than a casual glance, and finally decided to ask her price.

"Six thousand five hundred dollars," the gallery owner informed him, "and if I may say so, sir, you have an excellent eye because not only is it a magnificent picture, but you will also have made a shrewd investment." Nat was quickly coming to the conclusion that art dealers were nothing more than used-car salesmen dressed in Brooks Brothers suits.

"Bonnard is greatly undervalued compared to his contemporaries Renoir, Monet and Matisse," continued the dealer, "and I predict his prices will soar in the near future." Nat didn't care about Bonnard's prices, because he was a lover not a pimp.

◄○►

His other lover called that afternoon to warn him that she was on her way to the hospital. He asked Hong Kong to hold.

"Why?" Nat asked anxiously.

"Because I'm having your baby," his wife replied.

"But it's not due for another month."

"Nobody told the baby that," said Su Ling.

"I'm on my way, little flower," said Nat dropping the other phone.

◄○►

When Nat returned from the hospital that night, he called his mother to tell her she had a grandson.

"Wonderful news," she said, "but what are you going to call him?" she asked.

"Luke," he replied.

"And what do you plan to give Su Ling to commemorate the occasion?"

He hesitated for a moment, and then said, "A lady in a bath."

It was another couple of days before he and the dealer finally agreed on five thousand seven hundred and fifty dollars, and the little Bonnard was transferred from the gallery in SoHo to the bedroom wall in their apartment.

"Do you fancy her?" asked Su Ling the day she and Luke returned from the hospital.

"No, although there would be more of her to cuddle than you. But then I prefer thin women."

◄○►

Su Ling stood and looked at her present for some time before she gave a pronouncement.

"It's quite magnificent. Thank you."

Nat was delighted that his wife seemed to appreciate the painting as much as he did. He was only relieved that she didn't ask how much the lady had cost.

What had begun as a whim on a journey from Rome to Venice to Florence with Tom had quickly turned into an addiction that Nat couldn't kick. Every time he received a bonus he went in search of another picture. Nat might well have been dismissive of the used-car salesman, but his judgment turned out to be correct, because Nat continued to select Impressionists who were still within reach of his pocket—Vuillard, Luce, Pissarro, Camoin and Sisley—only to find that they increased in value as fast as any of the financial investments he selected for his clients on Wall Street.

Su Ling enjoyed watching their collection grow. She took no interest in what Nat paid for his mistresses, and even less in their investment value. Perhaps this was because when, at the age of twenty-five, she was appointed as the youngest associate professor in Columbia's history, she was earning less in a year than Nat was making in a week.

He no longer needed to be reminded that it was obscene.

⚊◇⚊

Fletcher remembered the incident well.

Matt Cunliffe had asked him to take a document over to Higgs & Dunlop for signing. "Normally I'd ask a paralegal to do this," Matt explained, "but it's taken Mr. Alexander weeks to get the terms agreed, and he doesn't want any last-minute hitches that might just give them another excuse for not signing."

Fletcher had expected to be back at the office in less than thirty minutes, because all he needed was to get four agreements signed and witnessed. However, when Fletcher reappeared two hours later and told his boss that the documents had neither been signed nor witnessed, Matt put down his pen and waited for an explanation.

When Fletcher had arrived at Higgs & Dunlop, he was left waiting in reception, and told that the partner whose signature he needed had not yet returned from lunch. This surprised Fletcher, as it was the partner in question, Mr. Higgs, who had scheduled the meeting for one o'clock, and Fletcher had skipped his own lunch to be sure he wouldn't be late.

While Fletcher sat in the reception area, he read through the agreement and familiarized himself with its terms. After a takeover bid had been agreed, a partner's compensation package was challenged, and it had taken some considerable time before both partners had been able to agree on a final figure.

At 1:15 P.M. Fletcher glanced up at the receptionist, who looked apologetic and offered him a second coffee. Fletcher thanked her; after all it wasn't her fault that he was being kept waiting. But once he'd read through the document a second time, and had drunk three coffees, he decided Mr. Higgs was either downright rude or plain inefficient.

Fletcher checked his watch again. It was 1:35 P.M. He sighed and asked the receptionist if he could use the washroom. She hesitated for a moment, before producing a key from inside her desk. "The executive washroom is one floor up," she told him. "It's only meant for partners and their most important clients, so if anyone asks, please tell them you're a client."

The washroom was empty, and, not wishing to embarrass the receptionist, Fletcher locked himself into the end cubicle. He was just zipping up his trousers, when two people walked in, one of them sounding as if he had just arrived back from a long lunch, where water had not been the only drink imbibed.

First voice: "Well I'm glad that's settled. There's nothing I enjoy more than getting the better of Alexander Dupont and Bell."

Second voice: "They've sent over some messenger boy with the agreement. I told Millie to leave him in reception and let him sweat a little."

Fletcher removed a pen from an inside pocket and tugged gently on the toilet roll.

First voice, laughing: "What did you finally settle for?"

Second voice: "That's the good news, $1,325,000, which is a lot more than we anticipated."

First voice: "The client must be delighted."

Second voice: "That's who I was having lunch with. He ordered a bottle of Château Lafitte '52—after all we'd told him to expect half a million, which he would have been quite happy to settle for—for obvious reasons."

First voice, more laughter: "Are we working on a contingency fee?"

Second voice: "We sure are. We pick up fifty percent of anything over half a million."

First voice: "So the firm has netted a cool $417,500. But what did you mean by 'for obvious reasons?'"

A tap was turned on. "Our biggest problem was the client's bank—the company's currently $720,000 overdrawn, and if we don't cover the full sum by close of business on Friday, they're threatening nonpayment, which would have meant we might not even have got . . ."—the tap was turned off—". . . the original $500,000, and that after months of bargaining."

Second voice: "Pity about one thing."

First voice: "What's that?"

Second voice: "That you can't tell those snobs over at Alexander Dupont and Bell that they don't know how to play poker."

First voice: "True, but I think I'll have a little sport with . . ."—a door opened—". . . their messenger boy." The door closed.

Fletcher rolled up the toilet paper and stuffed it in his pocket. He left the cubicle and quickly washed his hands before slipping out and taking the fire escape stairs to the floor below. Once back in reception, he handed over the executive washroom key.

"Thank you," said the receptionist just as the phone rang. She smiled at Fletcher. "That was good timing. If you'll take the elevator to the eleventh floor, Mr. Higgs is available to see you now."

"Thank you," Fletcher said as he walked back out of the room, stepped into the elevator and pressed the button marked "G."

Matt Cunliffe was unraveling the toilet roll when the phone rang.

"Mr. Higgs is on line one," said his secretary.

"Tell him I'm not available." Matt sat back in his chair and winked at Fletcher.

"He's asking when you will be available."

"Not before close of business on Friday."

26

FLETCHER COULDN'T REMEMBER an occasion when he'd disliked someone so much on first meeting him, and even the circumstances didn't help.

The senior partner had asked Fletcher and Logan to join him for coffee in his office—an unusual event in itself. When they arrived, they were introduced to one of the new trainees.

"I want you both to meet Ralph Elliot," were Bill Alexander's opening words.

Fletcher's first reaction was to wonder why he'd singled out Elliot from the two successful applicants. He quickly found out.

"I have decided this year to take on a trainee myself. I'm keen to keep in touch with what the new generation are thinking, and as Ralph's grades at Stanford were exceptional, he seemed to be the obvious choice."

Fletcher recalled Logan's disbelief that Alexander's nephew had even made the shortlist, and they both came to the conclusion that Mr. Alexander must have overruled any objections from the other partners.

"I hope both of you will make Ralph feel welcome."

"Of course," said Logan. "Why don't you join us for lunch?"

"Yes, I feel sure I could fit that in," replied Elliot, as if granting them a favor.

Over lunch, Elliot never missed an opportunity to remind them that he was the nephew of the senior partner, with the unspoken implication that if either Fletcher or Logan should cross him, he could slow their progress to a partnership. The threat only served to strengthen the bond between the two men.

"He's now telling anyone who will listen that he's going to be the first person to make partner in under seven years," Fletcher told Logan over a drink a few days later.

"You know he's such a cunning bastard, it wouldn't surprise me if he pulled it off," was Logan's only response.

"How do you think he became student president of UConn if he treated everyone the same way as he does us?"

"Perhaps no one dared to oppose him."

"Is that how you managed it?" asked Logan.

"How did you know that?" asked Fletcher, as the bartender collected their glasses.

"I checked your CV the day I joined the firm. Don't tell me you didn't read mine?"

"Of course I did," admitted Fletcher, raising his glass, "I even know that you were the Princeton chess champion." Both men laughed. "I must run, or I'll miss my train," said Fletcher, "and Annie might begin to wonder if there's another woman in my life."

"I envy you that," said Logan quietly.

"What do you mean?"

"The strength of your marriage. It wouldn't cross Annie's mind for a second that you could even look at another woman."

"I'm very fortunate," said Fletcher. "Maybe you'll be just as lucky one day. Meg on the reception desk can't take her eyes off you."

"Which one is Meg?" asked Logan as Fletcher left him to pick up his coat.

Fletcher had only walked a few yards down Fifth Avenue, when he spotted Ralph Elliot approaching. Fletcher slipped into a doorway, and waited for him to pass. Stepping back out into a raw cold wind that required ear muffs even if you were only walking a single block, he reached into his pocket to retrieve his scarf, but it wasn't there. He cursed. He must have left it in the bar. He would have to collect it tomorrow, but then he cursed again when he remembered Annie had given it to him for Christmas. He turned around and began to retrace his steps.

Back in the bar, he asked the girl at the coat check if she'd seen a red woolen scarf.

"Yes," she replied, "it must have fallen out of your sleeve when you put your coat on. I found it on the floor."

"Thank you," said Fletcher as he turned to leave, not expecting to see Logan still standing at the bar. He froze when he saw the man he was talking to.

—◦—

Nat was fast asleep.

La dévaluation française—three simple words sent the tapes from a gentle murmur into a chattering panic. The phone by Nat's bed was ringing thirty seconds later, and he immediately gave Adrian the order, "Get out of francs as fast as you can." He listened and then replied, "Dollars."

Nat couldn't remember a day in the last ten years when he hadn't shaved. He didn't shave.

Su Ling was awake by the time he came out of the bathroom a few minutes later. "Is there a problem?" she asked, rubbing her eyes.

"The French have devalued by seven percent."

"Is that good or bad?" she asked.

"Depends how many francs we're holding. I'll be able to make an assessment just as soon as I can get to a screen."

"You'll have one by the side of your bed in a few years' time, so you wouldn't even need to go into your office," said Su Ling, letting her head fall back on the pillow when she saw 5:09 flick up on the bedside clock.

Nat picked up the phone; Adrian was still on the other end of the line. "It's proving difficult to get out of francs; there are very few buyers other than the French government and they won't be able to go on propping up the currency for much longer."

"Keep selling. Pick up yen, deutschmarks or Swiss francs, but nothing else. I'll be with you in fifteen minutes. Is Steven there?"

"No, he's on his way. It took me some time to find out whose bed he was in."

Nat didn't laugh as he replaced the receiver. He leaned over and kissed his wife before running to the door.

"You're not wearing a tie," said Su Ling.

"By tonight I might not be wearing a shirt," Nat replied.

When they had moved from Boston to Manhattan, Su Ling had found an apartment only a cab ride away from Wall Street. As each bonus came in, she'd been able to furnish and decorate the four rooms, so that Nat soon felt able to bring his colleagues and even some clients back for dinner. Seven paintings—few that laymen would have recognized—now adorned the walls.

Su Ling fell back into a half sleep as her husband left. Nat broke with his usual routine as he leaped down the stairs in twos and threes, not bothering to wait for the elevator. On a normal day, he would have risen at six, and phoned the office from his study to ask for an update. He rarely had to make any major decisions over the phone, as most of their positions were locked in for several months. He would then shower, shave and be dressed by six thirty. He would read the *Wall Street Journal* while Su Ling prepared breakfast, and leave the apartment around seven, having looked in on Luke. Rain or shine, he would walk the five blocks to work, picking up a copy of the *New York Times* from a box on the corner of William and John. He immediately turned to the financial section and if the headline grabbed his attention, he would read it on the move, and still be at his desk by seven twenty. The *New York Times* wouldn't be informing its readers of the French devaluation until tomorrow morning, by which time, for most bankers, it would be history.

When Nat reached the street, he hailed the first available cab, and removed a ten-dollar bill for a five-block journey, and said, "I need to be there yesterday." The driver immediately changed lanes, and they pulled up outside his office four minutes later. Nat ran into the building and headed for the first open elevator. It was packed with traders, all talking at the tops of their voices. Nat learned nothing new, except that the simple announcement had been made by the French Ministry of Finance at ten o'clock, central European time. He cursed as the elevator stopped eight times on its slow progress to the eleventh floor.

Steven and Adrian were already at their desks in the trading room.

"Tell me the latest," he shouted as he threw off his coat.

"Everyone's taking a bath," said Steven. "The French have officially devalued by seven percent, but the markets are discounting it as too little too late."

Nat checked his screen. "And the other currencies?"

"The pound, lira and peseta are also going south. The dollar is climbing, the yen and the Swiss franc are holding steady, while the deutschmark is bobbing."

Nat continued to stare at his screen, watching the figures flick up and down every few seconds. "Try and buy some yen," he said as he watched the pound drop another point.

Steven picked up a phone linked directly to the trading desk. Nat stared in his direction. They were losing valuable seconds as they waited for a trader.

"How much is the trade?" barked Steven.

"Ten million at 2068."

Adrian looked away as Steven gave the order.

"And sell any pounds or lire we're still holding because they'll be the next to devalue," said Nat.

"What about the rate?"

"To hell with the rate, just sell," said Nat, "and get into dollars. If it's a real storm, everyone will try to shelter in New York." Nat was surprised how calm he felt amidst the barrage of shouting and cursing around him.

"We're out of lire," said Adrian, "and are being offered yen at 2027."

"Grab them," intoned Nat, his eyes not moving from the screen.

"We're out of the pound," said Steven, "at 2:37."

"Good, transfer half our dollars back into yen."

"I'm out of guilders," shouted Adrian.

"Switch them all into Swiss francs."

"Do you want to sell our deutschmark position?" asked Steven.

"No," said Nat.

"Do you want to buy any?"

"No," repeated Nat. "They're sitting on the equator and don't seem to be moving in either direction."

He'd finished making decisions in less than twenty minutes, and then all he could do was stare at the screens and wait to see how much damage had been done. As most currencies continued their downward trend Nat realized others would be suffering far more than he was. It didn't help.

If only the French had waited until midday, the usual time to announce a devaluation, he would have been at his desk. "Damn the French," said Adrian.

"Clever French," countered Nat, "to devalue when we're asleep."

—◦—

The French devaluation meant little to Fletcher as he read the details in the *New York Times* on the train into work the following morning. Several banks had taken a bath, and one or two were even having to report solvency problems to the Securities and Exchange Commission. He turned the page to read a profile about the man who looked certain to be running against Ford for president. Fletcher knew very little about Jimmy Carter, other than that he'd been governor of Georgia and owned a large peanut farm. He paused for a moment, and thought about his own political ambitions, which he'd put on hold while he tried to establish himself at the firm.

Fletcher decided he would sign up to help the "Back Carter" campaign in New York in whatever spare time he had. Spare time? Harry and Martha complained about never seeing him. Annie had joined yet another nonprofit board, and Lucy had chicken pox. When he'd phoned his mother to ask if he'd ever had chicken pox, the first thing she said was, "Hello, stranger." However, these problems were quickly forgotten only moments after he'd arrived at the office.

The first hint of any trouble came when he said good morning to Meg in reception.

"There's a meeting of all attorneys in the conference room at eight thirty," she said flatly.

"Any idea what it's about?" asked Fletcher, realizing that it was a silly question the moment he'd asked it. Confidentiality was the firm's hallmark.

Several partners were already in their places, talking in hushed tones, when Fletcher entered the boardroom at eight twenty, and he quickly took a seat directly behind Matt's chair. Could the devaluation of the French franc in Paris affect a law firm in New York? He doubted it. Did the senior partner want to talk about the Higgs & Dunlop deal? No, not Alexander's style. He looked around the boardroom table. If any of them knew what was on the agenda, they weren't giving anything away. But it had to be bad news, because good news was always announced at the six o'clock evening meeting.

At eight twenty-four the senior partner walked in.

"I must apologize for keeping you away from your desks," he began, "but this was not something that I felt could be covered by an internal memo, or slipped into my monthly report." He paused and cleared his throat. "The strength of this firm has always been that it has never become involved in scandals of a personal or financial nature; therefore I considered even the hint of such a problem had to be dealt with expeditiously." Fletcher was now even more puzzled. "It has been brought to my notice that a member of this firm was seen in a bar frequented by lawyers from rival institutions." *I do that every day,* thought Fletcher, *it's hardly a crime.* "And although this in itself is not reprehensible, it can lead to other developments that are unacceptable at Alexander Dupont and Bell. Fortunately, one of our number, with the best interest of the firm at heart, felt it his duty to keep me briefed on what might have become an embarrassing situation. The employee I am referring to was seen in a bar talking to a member of a rival firm. He then left with that person at approximately ten o'clock, took a cab to his home on the West Side, and did not reappear again until six thirty the following morning, when he returned to his own apartment. I immediately confronted the employee concerned, who made no attempt to deny his relationship with the member of a rival firm, and I'm pleased to say that he agreed the wisest course of action was to resign immediately." He paused. "I am grateful to the member of staff who reluctantly decided that it was his duty to report this matter to me."

Fletcher glanced across at Ralph Elliot, who was trying to feign surprise as each new sentence was delivered, but no one had ever told him about overacting. It was then that Fletcher recalled seeing Elliot on Fifth Avenue after his evening drink. He felt sick the moment he realized it was Logan the senior partner was referring to.

"May I remind everyone," emphasized Bill Alexander, "that this matter should not be discussed again in public or in private." The senior partner rose from his place and left the room without another word.

Fletcher thought it would be diplomatic to be among the last to leave, and when there were no partners left in the room he rose and walked slowly toward the door. On his way back to his office he could hear footsteps behind him, but he didn't look around, until Elliot caught up with him. "You were in the bar with Logan that night, weren't you?" he paused. "I didn't tell my uncle." Fletcher said nothing as Elliot slipped away, but once he was back at his desk he wrote down the exact words Elliot had threatened him with.

The only mistake he made was not to inform Bill Alexander immediately.

<hr />

One of the many things Nat admired about Su Ling was that she never once said, "I told you so," although after all her warnings, she had every right to do so.

"So what happens next?" she asked, having already put the incident behind her.

"I have to decide whether to resign or wait to be pushed."

"But Steven is the head of your department, and even Adrian is senior to you."

"I know, but they were all my positions, and I signed the buy and sell orders, so no one really believes they made any of the plays."

"How much did the bank lose?"

"A few dollars short of half a million."

"But you've made them much more than that in the past couple of years."

"True, but the other heads of departments will now consider me unreliable, and will always be fearful that it just might happen again. Steven and Adrian are already distancing themselves as quickly as they can; they won't want to lose their jobs as well."

"But you're still capable of making the bank huge profits, so why should they let you go?"

"Because they'll be able to replace me; business schools throw up bright new graduates every year."

"Not of your caliber, they don't," said Su Ling.

"But I thought you didn't approve?"

"I didn't say I approve," replied Su Ling, "but that doesn't mean I don't recognize and admire your ability." She hesitated. "Will anyone else offer you a job?"

"I don't suppose they will be calling me as frequently as they were a month ago, so I'll just have to start calling them."

Su Ling wrapped her arms around her husband. "You've faced far worse than this in Vietnam and so did I in Korea, and you didn't flinch." Nat had almost forgotten what had happened in Korea, although it was obviously still troubling Su Ling.

"What about the Cartwright Fund?" she asked as Nat helped her set the table.

"Lost around fifty thousand, but it's still showing a small profit over the year. Which reminds me, I must ring Mr. Russell and apologize."

"But you've also made them handsome returns in the past."

"Which is why they put so much trust in me in the first place," said Nat, thumping the table. "Damn it, I should have seen it coming." He looked across the table at his wife. "What do you think I should do?"

Su Ling considered his question for some time. "Resign, and get yourself a proper job."

—◇—

Fletcher dialed the number without going through his secretary. "Are you free for lunch?" He paused. "No, we need to meet somewhere where no one will recognize us"—pause—"is that the one on West 57th?"—pause—"see you there at twelve thirty."

Fletcher arrived at Zemarki's a few minutes early. His guest was waiting for him. They both ordered salad, and Fletcher called for a light beer.

"I thought you never drank at lunch?"

"Today is one of those rare exceptions," said Fletcher. After he'd taken a long draft, he told his friend what had taken place that morning.

"This is 1976 not 1776," was all Jimmy said.

"I know, but it seems that there are still one or two dinosaurs roaming around, and God knows what other bile Elliot fed to his uncle."

"Sounds like a nice guy, your Mr. Elliot. You'd better keep your eye on him as you're probably the next one he has in his sights."

"I can take care of myself," said Fletcher. "It's Logan I'm worried about."

"But surely if he's as good as you say he'll be quickly snapped up?"

"Not after a call to Bill Alexander asking why he left so suddenly."

"No lawyer would dare to suggest that being gay was a reason for dismissal."

"He doesn't have to," said Fletcher. "Given the circumstances he need only say, 'I would prefer not to discuss the matter, it's somewhat delicate,' which is far more deadly." He took another swig. "I have to tell you, Jimmy, that if your firm were lucky enough to employ Logan, they would never regret it."

"I'll have a word with the senior partner this afternoon, and let you know how he reacts. Anyway, how's my kid sister?"

"Slowly taking over everything in Ridgewood, including the book club, the neighborhood swim team and the blood donors' drive. Our next problem is going to be which school to send Lucy to."

"Hotchkiss is taking girls now," said Jimmy, "and we intend . . ."

"I wonder how the senator feels about that," said Fletcher as he drained his beer. "How is he, by the way?"

"Exhausted, he never stops preparing for the next election."

"But no one could oust Harry. I don't know a more popular politician in the state."

"You tell him that," said Jimmy. "When I last saw him he'd put on fifteen pounds, and was looking badly out of shape."

Fletcher glanced at his watch. "Send the old warhorse my best, and tell him Annie and I will try and get up to Hartford for a weekend soon." He paused. "This meeting never took place."

"You're becoming paranoid," said Jimmy as he picked up the check, "which is exactly what this Elliot guy will be hoping for."

—◁◦▷—

Nat handed in his resignation the following morning, relieved at how calmly Su Ling had taken the whole debacle. But it was all very well her telling him to get a proper job when there was only one job he felt qualified to do.

When he returned to his office to remove his personal possessions it was as if there were a quarantine notice attached to his desk. Former colleagues walked quickly past, and those occupying desks nearby remained on their phones, their faces turned away.

He took a laden cab back to the apartment, and filled the tiny elevator three times before he had finally deposited everything in his study.

Nat sat alone at his desk. The phone hadn't rung once since he'd arrived home. The apartment felt strangely empty without Su Ling and Luke; he'd got used to them both being there to greet him whenever he came home. Thank God the boy was too young to know what they were going through.

At midday, he went to the kitchen, opened a can of corned beef hash and tipped it into a frying pan, added some butter, cracked two eggs on top and waited until they looked done.

After lunch, he typed out a list of financial institutions that had been in contact with him during the past year, and then settled down to call them one by one. He started with a bank that had phoned him only a few days before.

"Oh hi, Nat, yes sorry, we managed to fill the position last Friday."

"Good afternoon, Nat, that sounds like an interesting proposition, give me a couple of days to think about it, and I'll come back to you."

"It was good of you to call, Mr. Cartwright, but . . ."

When Nat had reached the end of the list, he put the phone down. He'd just been devalued, and there was obviously a sell order out on him. He checked his current account. It was still showing a healthy balance, but for how much longer? He glanced up at the oil painting above his desk, *Reclining Nude* by Camoin. He wondered just how long it would be before he had to return one of his mistresses to the gallery pimp.

The phone rang. Had one of them thought about it and called him back? He picked it up and heard a familiar voice.

"I must apologize, Mr. Russell," Nat said. "I should have called you earlier."

—◦—

Once Logan had left the firm, Fletcher felt isolated and hardly a day went by when Elliot didn't try to undermine him, so when Bill Alexander asked to see him on Monday morning, Fletcher sensed it wasn't going to be a friendly encounter.

Over supper with Annie on Sunday evening, he told his wife everything that had taken place during the past few days, trying hard not to exaggerate. Annie listened in silence.

"If you don't tell Mr. Alexander the truth about his nephew, both of you will live to regret it."

"It's not that easy," said Fletcher.

"The truth is always that easy," said Annie. "Logan has been treated disgracefully, and if it hadn't been for you, he might never have been offered another job. Your only mistake was not telling Alexander the moment the meeting was over; that's given Elliot the confidence to go on undermining you."

"And if he sacks me as well?"

"Then it isn't a firm you should have joined in the first place, Fletcher Davenport, and you would certainly not be the man I chose to marry."

—◦—

When Fletcher arrived outside Mr. Alexander's door a few minutes before nine, Mrs. Townsend ushered him straight through to the senior partner's office.

"Have a seat," said Bill Alexander, pointing to the chair on the other side of the desk. No "nice to see you, Fletcher," just have a seat. No "how's Annie and Lucy," just have a seat. Those three words resolved Fletcher in the belief that Annie was right, and he must not be fearful of standing up for what he believed in.

242

"Fletcher, when you first joined Alexander Dupont and Bell nearly two years ago, I had high hopes for you, and indeed during your first year you more than lived up to my expectations. We all recall with some considerable pleasure the Higgs and Dunlop incident. But of late, you have not shown the same resolution." Fletcher looked puzzled. He had seen Matt Cunliffe's most recent report on him, and the word exemplary had stuck in his mind. "I think we have the right to assume a standard of loyalty second to none in the legal profession," continued Alexander. Fletcher remained silent, not yet sure of the crime he was about to be charged with. "It has been brought to my attention that you were also in the bar with Fitzgerald on the night he was having a drink with his *friend*."

"Information supplied by your nephew, no doubt," said Fletcher, "whose role in this whole affair has been far from impartial."

"What do you mean by that?"

"Quite simply that Mr. Elliot's version of events is based totally on self-interest, as I feel sure a man of your perspicacity has already worked out."

"Perspicacity?" said Alexander. "Was it perspicacious of you to be seen in the company of Fitzgerald's *friend*?" He emphasized the word again.

"I did not meet Logan's friend, as I feel sure Mr. Elliot told you, unless he only wanted you to know half the story. I left for Ridgewood . . ."

"But Ralph told me that you later returned."

"Yes I did, and like any good spy, your nephew must also have reported that I only went back to pick up my scarf, which had fallen out of the sleeve of my overcoat."

"No, he did not report that," said Alexander.

"Which is what I mean by only telling you half the story," said Fletcher.

"So you didn't speak to Logan or his friend?"

"No, I didn't," said Fletcher, "but that was only because I was in a hurry, and didn't have time."

"So you would have spoken to him?"

243

"Yes, I would."

"Even if you'd known that Logan was a homosexual?"

"I neither knew nor cared."

"You didn't care?"

"No, I did not consider Logan's private life was any of my business."

"But it might have been the firm's business, which brings me to more important matters. Are you aware that Logan Fitzgerald has since joined the firm that employs your brother-in-law?"

"Yes, I am," said Fletcher, "I told Mr. Gates that Logan would be looking for a job and they'd be lucky to get a man of his caliber."

"I wonder if that was wise," said Bill Alexander.

"When it comes to dealing with a friend, I have a tendency to put decency and fairness ahead of my own self-interest."

"And ahead of the firm's?"

"Yes, if it's morally right. That's what Professor Abrahams taught me."

"Don't bandy words with me, Mr. Davenport."

"Why not? You've been bandying them with me, Mr. Alexander."

The senior partner turned scarlet. "You must realize that I could have you thrown out of this firm."

"Two of us leaving in the same week may take some explaining, Mr. Alexander."

"Are you threatening me?"

"No, I think it's you who is threatening me."

"It may not be that easy to get rid of you, Mr. Davenport, but I can make damn sure you never become a partner while I'm a member of this firm. Now get out."

As he rose to leave, Fletcher recalled Annie's words. *Then it's not the firm you should have joined in the first place.*

He returned to his office to find the phone ringing. Was Alexander calling him back? He picked it up ready to offer his resignation. It was Jimmy.

"Sorry to bother you at work, Fletcher, but Dad's had a heart attack. He's been taken to St. Patrick's. Can you and Annie get over to Hartford as quickly as possible?"

27

"I'VE GOT MYSELF a proper job," said Nat as Su Ling walked through the door.

"You're going to be a New York cab driver?"

"No," replied Nat. "I don't have the qualifications for that job."

"That's never seemed to hinder anyone in the past."

"But not living in New York might."

"We're leaving New York? Please tell me that we're going somewhere civilized where skyscrapers will be replaced with trees and exhaust fumes by fresh air."

"We're going home."

"Hartford? Then it can only be Russell's."

"You're right, Mr. Russell has offered me a job as vice-president of the bank, working alongside Tom."

"Serious banking? Not just speculating in the currency market?"

"I'll oversee his currency department, but I can promise you that it concentrates mainly on foreign exchange, not speculation. What Mr. Russell most needs is for Tom and me to work on a complete reorganization of the bank. During the past few years Russell's has been falling behind its competitors and . . ." Su Ling placed her bag on the hall table and walked over to the phone. "Who are you calling?" asked Nat.

"My mother, of course, we must start looking for a house, and then we'll have to consider a school for Luke, and once she's got to work on that, I'll need to be in touch with some former colleagues about a job, and then . . ."

"Hold on, little flower," said Nat, taking his wife in his arms. "Am I to assume from this that you approve of the idea?"

"Approve? I can't wait to get out of New York. The idea of Luke starting his education in a school where the kids use machetes to sharpen their pencils horrifies me. I also can't wait . . ." The phone rang and Su Ling picked it up. She cupped her hand over the mouthpiece. "It's someone named Jason, from Chase Manhattan. Shall I tell him you're no longer available?"

Nat smiled and took the phone.

"Hi, Jason, what can I do for you?"

"I've been thinking about your call, Nat, and we may just have an opening for you at Chase."

"That's kind of you, Jason, but I've already accepted another offer."

"Not one of our rivals, I hope?"

"Not yet, but give me a little time," said Nat, smiling.

—◇—

When Fletcher reported to Matt Cunliffe that his father-in-law had been taken to the hospital, he was surprised to find that he was not all that sympathetic.

"Domestic crises arise fairly often," remarked Cunliffe curtly. "We all have families to worry about. Are you sure this can't wait until the weekend?"

"Yes, I'm sure," said Fletcher, "I owe more to this man than anyone other than my parents."

Fletcher had only left Bill Alexander's room for a few moments, and already there was a less than subtle change in the atmosphere. He assumed that, by the time he returned, that change would have spread like a contagious disease to the rest of the staff.

He phoned Annie from Penn Station. She sounded calm, but relieved to know he was on his way home. When Fletcher stepped onto the train, he suddenly realized that he hadn't brought any work with him for the first time since he joined the firm. He used the journey to consider his next move following his meeting with Bill Alexander, but he'd come to no definite conclusions by the time the train pulled into Ridgewood.

Fletcher took a cab from the station, and was not surprised to find the family car parked outside the front door, two suitcases already in the trunk, and Annie walking down the drive with Lucy in her arms. How different from his mother, he thought, yet how similar. He laughed for the first time that day.

On the journey up to Hartford, Annie reported all the details she'd picked up from her mother. Harry had suffered a heart attack a few minutes after arriving at the Capitol that morning, and was immediately rushed to the hospital. Martha was by his side, and Jimmy, Joanna and the children were already on their way down from Vassar.

"What are the doctors saying?"

"That it's too early for anything conclusive, but Dad has been warned that if he doesn't slow down, it could well happen again and next time it might prove fatal."

"Slow down? Harry doesn't know what the words mean. He's one of life's speeding tickets."

"He may have been," said Annie, "but Mom and I are going to tell him this afternoon that he has to withdraw his name as a senate candidate at the next election."

◄○►

Bill Russell stared across his desk at Nat and Tom. "It's what I've always wanted," he said. "I'll be sixty in a couple of years' time, and I feel I've earned the right not to be opening up the bank at ten every morning, and locking the front door before I go home at night. The thought of you two working together—to quote the Good Book—fills my heart with joy."

"I don't know about the Good Book," said Tom, "but we feel the same way, Dad. So where do you want us to start?"

"Of course I'm aware that the bank has fallen behind its rivals during the past few years, perhaps because as a family firm we've put greater emphasis on customer relations than on the bottom line. Something your father would approve of, Nat, which is perhaps why he's had an account with us for over thirty years." Nat nodded his agreement. "You'll also be aware that there have been one or two approaches from other banks with a view to taking us over, but that isn't how I wanted to end my career with Russell's— just ending up as an anonymous branch of some vast corporation.

So I'll tell you what I have in mind. I want both of you to spend your first six months taking the bank apart from top to bottom. I'll give you *carte blanche* to ask any questions, open any doors, read any files, study any accounts. At the end of those six months, you will report back what needs to be done. And don't give a moment's thought to trying to placate my feelings, because I know that if Russell's is to survive into the next century, it will need a complete overhaul. So what's your first question?"

"Can I have the front-door keys?" asked Nat.

"Why?" asked Mr. Russell.

"Because ten o'clock is a little too late for the staff of a progressive bank to be opening."

As Tom drove them back to New York, he and Nat set about dividing their responsibilities.

"Dad was touched that you turned down Chase to join us," said Tom.

"You made exactly the same sacrifice when you left the Bank of America."

"Yes, but the old man has always assumed that I'd take over from him once he reached his sixty-fifth birthday, and I was just about to warn him that I wasn't willing to do so."

"Why not?" inquired Nat.

"I don't have the vision or ideas that are required to rescue the bank, but you do."

"Rescue?" said Nat.

"Yes, don't let's kid ourselves. You've studied the balance sheet, so you know only too well that we're just about clearing enough to allow my parents to maintain their standard of living. But the profits haven't risen for some years; the truth is that the bank needs your particular skills more than it requires an efficient packhorse like me. So it's important to settle one thing before it ever becomes an issue—in banking terms I intend to report to you as chief executive."

"But it will still be necessary for you to become chairman once your father retires."

"Why?" asked Tom. "When you'll obviously be making all the strategic decisions?"

"Because the bank bears your name, and that still matters in a town like Hartford. It's equally important that the customers never find out what the chief executive is up to behind the scenes."

"I'll go along with that on one condition," said Tom, "that all salaries, bonuses and any other financial considerations are allocated on an equal basis."

"That's very generous of you," said Nat.

"No, it's not," said Tom. "Shrewd perhaps, but not generous, because fifty percent of you will bring in a far higher return than one hundred percent of me."

"Don't forget that I've just lost Morgan's a fortune," said Nat.

"And no doubt learned from the experience."

"Just as we did when we were up against Ralph Elliot."

"Now there's a name from the past. Any idea what he's up to?" asked Tom as he turned onto Route 95.

"The last thing I heard was that after Stanford he'd become a hot-shot lawyer in New York."

"I wouldn't want to be one of his clients," said Tom.

"Or go up against him for that matter," said Nat.

"Well, at least that's something we don't have to worry about."

Nat looked out of the grimy window as they traveled through Queens. "Don't be too sure, Tom, because if anything were to go wrong, he'll want to represent the other side."

—◇—

They sat in a circle around his bed, chatting about anything and everything except what was on their minds. The one exception was Lucy, who remained firmly in the middle of the bed and treated Grandpa as if he was a rocking horse. Joanna's children were more restrained. Fletcher couldn't believe how quickly Harry Junior was growing.

"Now before I get too tired," said Harry, "I need to have a private word with Fletcher."

Martha shepherded the family out of the room, clearly aware of what her husband wanted to discuss with his son-in-law.

"I'll see you back at the house later," said Annie, as she dragged a reluctant Lucy away.

"And then we should be starting back for Ridgewood," Fletcher reminded her. "I can't afford to be late for work tomorrow." Annie nodded as she closed the door.

Fletcher drew up a chair and sat by the senator's side. He didn't bother with any small talk, as his father-in-law was looking tired.

"I've given a great deal of thought to what I'm about to say," said the senator, "and the only other person I've discussed it with is Martha, and she is in complete agreement with me. And like so many things over the past thirty years, I can't be sure if it wasn't her idea in the first place." Fletcher smiled. How like Annie, he thought, as he waited for the senator to continue. "I've promised Martha that I won't run for reelection." The senator paused. "I see you're not putting up any protest, so I must assume that you agree with my wife and daughter on this subject."

"Annie would prefer you to live to an old age, rather than die making a speech in the Senate Chamber, however important," said Fletcher, "and I agree with her."

"I know they're right, Fletcher, but by God I'll miss it."

"And they will miss you, sir, as you can see from the flowers and cards already in this room. By this time tomorrow, they'll have filled every other room on this floor and be spilling out onto the pavement." The senator ignored the compliment, clearly not wishing to be diverted from his course.

"When Jimmy was born, I had the crazy notion that one day he would take my place, perhaps even go on to Washington and represent the state. But it wasn't long before I realized that was never going to be a possibility. I couldn't be more proud of him, but he just isn't cut out for public office."

"He made a damn fine job of getting me elected as president," said Fletcher, "Twice."

"He did indeed," said Harry, "but Jimmy should always be in the engine room, because he isn't destined to be the driver." He paused again. "But then some twelve years ago I met a young man at the Hotchkiss-Taft football game, who I knew couldn't wait to be the driver. A meeting, incidentally, that I shall never forget."

"Nor me, sir," said Fletcher.

"As the years passed, I watched that boy grow into a fine young man, and I'm proud he's now my son-in-law and father of my granddaughter. And before I grow too maudlin, Fletcher, I think I ought to come to the point in case one of us falls asleep." Fletcher laughed.

"Pretty soon I shall have to let it be known that I will not be running for reelection to the Senate." He raised his head and looked directly at Fletcher. "I would, at the same time, like to say how proud I am to announce that my son-in-law, Fletcher Davenport, has agreed to run in my place."

28

IT DIDN'T TAKE six months for Nat to discover why Russell's Bank had failed to increase its profits in over a decade. Almost every modern banking tenet had been ignored. Russell's still lived in an age of written ledgers, personalized accounts and a sincerely held belief that the computer was more likely to make mistakes than a human being, and was therefore a waste of the bank's time and money. Nat was in and out of Mr. Russell's office three or four times a day, only to find that something they had agreed on in the morning had been reversed by the afternoon. This usually occurred whenever a longstanding member of the staff was seen leaving the same office an hour later with a smile on his or her face. It was often left for Tom to pick up the pieces; in fact, if he hadn't been there to explain to his father why the changes were necessary, there might never have been a six-month report to present.

Nat would come home most nights exhausted and sometimes infuriated. He warned Su Ling there was likely to be a showdown when his report was finally presented. And he wasn't altogether sure that he would still be the bank's vice-president if the chairman was unable to stomach almost all of the changes he was recommending. Su Ling didn't complain, although she had just about managed to get the three of them settled in their new house, sell the apartment in New York, find a nursery school for Luke, and prepare to take up her new appointment as professor of statistics at UConn in the fall. The idea of moving back to New York didn't appeal to her.

In between, she had advised Nat on which computers would be most cost-effective for the bank, supervised their installation and also given night classes to those members of the staff who appreciated there was more to learn than how to press the ON button. But Nat's biggest problem was the bank's chronic overstaffing. He had already pointed out to the chairman that Russell's currently employed seventy-one staff and that Bennett's, the only other independent bank in town, offered the same services with only thirty-nine employees. Nat wrote a separate report on the financial implications of overstaffing, suggesting an early retirement program that, although it would cut into their profits for the next three years, would be highly beneficial in the long term. This was the sticking point on which Nat was unwilling to budge. Because, as he explained to Tom over dinner with Su Ling, if they waited for another couple of years until Mr. Russell retired, they would all be joining the ranks of the unemployed.

Once Mr. Russell had read Nat's report, he scheduled a Friday evening at six o'clock for the showdown. When Nat and Tom walked into the chairman's office they found him at his desk writing a letter. He looked up as they entered the room.

"I'm sorry to say that I'm unable to go along with your recommendations," said Mr. Russell even before his two vice-presidents had sat down, "because I do not wish to fire employees, some of whom I have known and worked with for the past thirty years." Nat tried to smile as he thought about being sacked twice in six months, and wondered if Jason at Chase might still have an opening for him. "So I have come to the conclusion," continued the chairman, "that if this is going to work," he placed his hands on the report, as if blessing it, "the one person who will have to go is me." He scribbled his signature on the bottom of the letter he had been writing, and handed his resignation over to his son.

Bill Russell left the office at 6:12 that evening, and never entered the building again.

⟶o⟵

"What are your qualifications to run for public office?"

Fletcher looked down from his place on the stage at the small group of journalists seated in front of him. Harry smiled. It was one of the seventeen questions and answers they had prepared the previous evening.

"I don't have a great deal of experience," admitted Fletcher, he hoped disarmingly, "but I was born, brought up and educated in Connecticut before going to New York to join one of the most prestigious law firms in the country. I've come home to put those skills to work for the people of Hartford."

"Don't you feel that twenty-six is a bit young to be telling us how we should be running our lives?" asked a young lady seated in the second row.

"Same age as I was," said Harry, "and your father never complained." One or two of the older hacks smiled, but the young woman wasn't quite so easily put off.

"But you had just returned from a world war, Senator, with three years' experience as an officer at the front, so may I ask, Mr. Davenport, did you burn your draft card during the height of the Vietnam War?"

"No, I did not," said Fletcher, "I was not drafted, but had I been, I would have served willingly."

"Can you prove that?" the journalist snapped back.

"No," said Fletcher, "but if you were to read my speech at the Yale freshman debate, you would be left in no doubt of my feelings on this subject."

"If you are elected," asked another member of the press, "will your father-in-law be pulling the strings?"

Harry glanced across and saw that the question had annoyed Fletcher. "Calm down," he whispered. "He's only doing his job. Stick to the answer we agreed on."

"If I am fortunate enough to be elected," said Fletcher, "it would be foolish of me not to take advantage of Senator Gates's wealth of experience, and I will stop listening to him only when I consider he has nothing left to teach me."

"What do you feel about the Kendrick Amendment to the finance bill currently being debated in the house?" The ball came swinging in from left field, and it certainly wasn't one of the seventeen questions they had prepared for.

'That's a bit rough isn't it, Robin?" said the senator. "After all, Fletcher is . . ."

"In so far as the clause affects senior citizens, I believe it discriminates against those who have already retired and are on fixed incomes. Most of us will have to retire at some time, and the only thing I remember Confucius saying was that a civilized society was one that educated its young and took care of its old. If I am elected, when Senator Kendrick's amendment to the bill comes before the Senate, I will vote against it. Bad laws can be drafted in a legislative session, but then take years to repeal, and I will only ever vote for a bill that I believe can be realistically administered."

Harry sat back in his chair. "Next question," he said.

"In your CV, Mr. Davenport, which I must say was most impressive, you claim you resigned from Alexander Dupont and Bell in order to run in this election."

"That is correct," said Fletcher.

"Did a colleague of yours, a Mr. Logan Fitzgerald, also resign around that time?"

"Yes, he did."

"Is there any connection between his resignation and yours?"

"None whatsoever," said Fletcher firmly.

"What are you getting at?" asked Harry.

"Just a call from our New York office which they asked me to follow up," replied the journalist.

"Anonymous, no doubt," said Harry.

"I'm not at liberty to reveal my sources," the journalist replied, trying hard not to smirk.

"Just in case your New York office didn't tell you who that informant was, I'll let you know his name just as soon as this press conference is over," snapped Fletcher.

"Well, I think that just about wraps it up," said Harry, before anyone could ask a supplementary question. "Thank you all for joining us. You'll get a regular shot at the candidate in his weekly campaign press conferences—which is more than I ever gave you."

"That was awful," said Fletcher as they walked off the stage. "I must learn to control my temper."

"You did just fine, my boy," said Harry, "and by the time I've finished with the bastards, the only thing they will remember about this morning was your answer on the Kendrick Amendment to the finance bill. And frankly, the press are the least of our problems." Harry paused ominously. "The real battle will begin when we discover who the Republican candidate is."

29

"WHAT DO YOU know about her?" asked Fletcher as they walked down the street together.

There wasn't a lot Harry didn't know about Barbara Hunter, as she had been his opponent for the past two elections, and a perpetual thorn in his flesh during the intervening years.

"She's forty-eight, born in Hartford, daughter of a farmer, educated in the local school system, and then at the University of Connecticut, married to a successful advertising executive, with three children, all living in the state, and she's currently a member of the State Congress."

"Any bad news?" asked Fletcher.

"Yes, she doesn't drink and is a vegetarian, so you'll be visiting every bar and butcher in the constituency. And like anyone who has spent a lifetime in local politics, she's made her fair share of enemies on the way, and as she barely won the Republican nomination this time around, you can be sure that several party activists didn't want her in the first place. But more important, she lost the last two elections, so we paint her as a loser."

Harry and Fletcher entered the Democratic headquarters on Park Street to find the front window covered in posters and photos of the candidate, something Fletcher still hadn't become used to. *The Right Man for the Job.* He hadn't thought a lot of the slogan until the media experts explained that it was good to have the words "right" and "man" in the message when your opponent was a Republican woman. Subliminal, they had explained.

Harry walked up the stairs to the conference room on the first floor, and took his seat at the head of the table. Fletcher yawned as he sat down, although they had only been campaigning for seven days; and there were still twenty-six to go. The mistakes you make today are history tomorrow morning, your triumphs forgotten by the early evening news. Pace yourself, was one of Harry's most repeated maxims.

Fletcher looked around at the assembled group, a combination of pros and seasoned amateurs, with Harry no longer their candidate, but instead pressed into being campaign chairman. It was the only concession Martha had allowed, but she had told Fletcher to send him home the moment he showed the slightest sign of fatigue. As each day passed, it became harder to keep to Martha's instructions, as it was Harry who always set the pace.

"Anything new or devastating?" Harry asked as he looked around the team, one or two of whom had played a role in all seven of his election victories. In the last encounter, he'd beaten Barbara Hunter by over five thousand votes, but with the polls now running neck and neck, they were about to find out just how much of that vote had been personal.

"Yes," said a voice from the other end of the table. Harry smiled down at Dan Mason, who had been with him for six of his seven campaigns. Dan had started by working the copier, and was now in charge of press and public relations.

"The floor's all yours, Dan."

"Barbara Hunter has just issued a press release challenging Fletcher to a debate. Presumably I tell her to get lost, and add that it's a sign of someone who is desperate and knows they are going to lose. That's what you always did."

Harry was silent for a moment. "You're right, Dan, I did," he eventually said, "but only because I was the incumbent and treated her as an upstart. In any case, I had nothing to gain from a debate, but that situation has changed now that we're fielding an unknown candidate, so I think we need to discuss the idea more fully before we come to any conclusion. What are the advantages and disadvantages? Opinions?" he said. Voices all started speaking at once.

"Gives our man more exposure."

"Gives her the center stage."

"Proves we have the outstanding debater, which because of his youth will come as a surprise."

"She knows the local problems—we could look inexperienced and ill-informed."

"We look young, dynamic, and energetic."

"She looks experienced, canny and seasoned."

"We represent the youth of tomorrow."

"She represents the women of today."

"Fletcher could wipe the floor with her."

"She wins the debate, and we lose the election."

"Well, now we've heard the committee's views, perhaps it's time to consider the candidate's," said Harry.

"I'm quite happy to debate with Mrs. Hunter," said Fletcher. "People will assume she's more impressive simply because of her past record and my lack of experience, so I must try and turn that to our advantage."

"But if she outshines you on local issues, and makes it look as if you're just not ready to do the job," said Dan, "then the election will be over in one evening. Don't think of it as a thousand people in a hall. Try to remember that the whole event would be covered by local radio and television, and is certain to be plastered over the front page of the *Hartford Courant* the following morning."

"But that could work to our advantage as well," said Harry.

"I agree," said Dan, "but it's one hell of a risk to take."

"How long have I got to think about it?" asked Fletcher.

"Five minutes," said Harry, "perhaps ten, because if she's issued a press statement, they'll want to know our immediate response."

"Can't we say we need a little time to think about it?"

"Certainly not," said Harry, "that would look as if we're debating the debate, and in the end you'd have to give in, so she then wins both ways. We either turn it down firmly, or accept it with enthusiasm. Perhaps we should take a vote on it," he added, looking around the table. "Those in favor?" Eleven hands shot up. "Against?" Fourteen hands were raised. "Well, that's the end of that."

"No, it isn't," said Fletcher. Everyone seated around the table stopped talking and looked at the candidate. "I am grateful for your opinions, but I do not intend to spend my political career being run by a committee, especially when the vote is that close. Dan, you will issue a statement saying I'm delighted to accept Mrs. Hunter's challenge, and look forward to debating the real issues with her, rather than the political posturing that the Republicans seem to have specialized in from the start of this campaign." There was a moment's silence, before the room broke into spontaneous applause.

Harry smiled. "Those in favor of a debate?" Every hand shot up. "Those against?" None. "I declare the motion carried unanimously."

"Why did we have a second vote?" Fletcher asked Harry as they left the room.

"So that we can tell the press that the decision was unanimous."

Fletcher smiled as they headed toward the station. Another lesson learned.

◆

A team of twelve canvassed the station every morning, most of them handing out leaflets, while the candidate shook hands with the early commuters leaving the city. Harry had told him to concentrate on those going into the station, because they almost certainly lived in Hartford, whereas those coming off the trains probably didn't have a vote in the constituency.

"Hi, I'm Fletcher Davenport . . ."

At eight thirty they crossed the road to Ma's and grabbed an egg and bacon sandwich. Once Ma had given her opinion on how the election was going, they headed off for the city's insurance district to shake hands with "the suits" as they arrived at their offices. In the car, Fletcher put on a Yale tie, which he knew many of the executives would identify with.

"Hi, I'm Fletcher Davenport . . ."

At nine thirty, they returned to campaign HQ for the early morning press conference. Barbara Hunter had already held hers an hour earlier, so Fletcher knew that there would only be one subject on the agenda that morning. On the way back, he replaced the Yale tie with something more neutral as he listened to the headlines on the morning news update, to make sure he couldn't be surprised by a piece of breaking news. War had broken out in the Middle East. He would leave that to President Ford, because it wasn't going to end up on the front page of the *Hartford Courant*.

"Hi, I'm Fletcher Davenport . . ."

When Harry opened the morning press conference, he told the assembled journalists even before they could ask the question that it had been a unanimous decision to take on Mrs. Hunter head to head. Harry never referred to her as Barbara. When questioned about the debate—venue, time, format—Harry said this was yet to be decided, as they had only received the challenge earlier that morning, but he added, "I don't foresee any problems." Harry knew only too well that the debate would throw up nothing *but* problems.

Fletcher was surprised by Harry's reply when asked what he thought of the candidate's chances. He had expected the senator to talk about his debating skills, his legal experience and his political acumen, but instead Harry said, "Well of course, Mrs. Hunter starts off with a built-in advantage. We all know that she's a seasoned debater, with a great deal of experience on local issues, but I consider it typical of Fletcher's honest, open approach to this election that he's agreed to take her on."

"Doesn't that make it a tremendous risk, Senator?" asked another journalist.

"Sure does," admitted Harry, "but as the candidate has pointed out, if he wasn't man enough to face Mrs. Hunter, how could the public expect him to take on the bigger challenge of representing them?" Fletcher couldn't remember saying anything like that, although he didn't disagree with the sentiment.

Once the press conference was over, and the last journalist had departed, Fletcher said, "I thought you told me Barbara Hunter was a poor debater, and took forever answering questions?"

"Yep, that's exactly what I said," admitted Harry.

"Then why did you tell the journalists that . . ."

"It's all about expectations, my boy. Now they think you're not up to it," Harry replied, "and that she'll wipe the floor with you, so even if you only manage a draw they'll declare you the winner."

"Hi, I'm Fletcher Davenport . . ." kept repeating itself over and over like some hit song he just couldn't get out of his mind.

30

NAT WAS DELIGHTED when Tom popped his head around the door and asked, "Can I bring a guest to dinner tonight?"

"Sure, business or pleasure?" Nat asked, looking up from his desk.

Tom hesitated, "I'm rather hoping that it might be both."

"Female?" said Nat, now more interested.

"Decidedly female."

"Name?"

"Julia Kirkbridge."

"And what . . ."

"That's enough of the third degree, you can ask her all the questions you want to tonight because she's more than capable of taking care of herself."

"Thanks for the warning," said Su Ling when Nat sprung an extra guest on her only moments after he'd arrived home.

"I should have called, shouldn't I?" he said.

"It would have made life a little easier, but I expect you were making millions at the time."

"Something like that," said Nat.

"What do we know about her?" asked Su Ling.

"Nothing," said Nat. "You know Tom; when it comes to his private life, he's even more secretive than a Swiss banker, but as he's willing to let us meet her one can only live in hope."

"What happened to that gorgeous redhead called Maggie? I'd thought that . . ."

"Disappeared like all the others. Can you ever remember him inviting anyone to join us for dinner a second time?"

Su Ling thought about the question for a moment, and then admitted, "Now you mention it, I can't. I suppose it could just be my cooking."

"No, it's not your cooking, but I'm afraid that you are to blame."

"Me?" said Su Ling.

"Yes, you. The poor man has been besotted with you for years, so everyone he goes out with is dragged along to dinner so that Tom can compare . . ."

"Oh no, not that old chestnut again," said Su Ling.

"It's not an old chestnut, little flower, it's the problem."

"But he's never done more than kiss me on the cheek."

"And he never will. I wonder how many people are in love with someone they have never even kissed on the cheek."

Nat disappeared upstairs to read to Luke as Su Ling set a fourth place at the table. She was polishing an extra glass, when the doorbell rang.

"Can you get it, Nat? I'm a bit tied up. There was no response, so she took off her apron and went to the front door.

"Hi," said Tom as he bent down and kissed Su Ling on the cheek, which only brought Nat's words to mind.

"This is Julia," he said. Su Ling looked up at an elegant woman, who was nearly as tall as Tom, and almost as slim as she was, although her fair hair and blue eyes suggested a heritage nearer Scandinavia than the Far East.

"How nice to meet you," said Julia. "I know it's hackneyed, but I really have heard so much about you."

Su Ling smiled as she took Julia's fur coat. "My husband," she said, "is caught up with . . ."

"Black cats," said Nat as he appeared by Su Ling's side. "I've been reading *The Cat in the Hat* to Luke. Hi, I'm Nat, and you must be Julia."

"Yes, I am," she said, giving Nat a smile that reminded Su Ling that other women found her husband attractive. "Let's go into the living room and have a drink," said Nat, "I've put some champagne on ice."

"Do we have something to celebrate?" asked Tom.

"Other than you being able to find someone who is willing to accompany you to dinner, no, I can't think of anything in particular, unless . . ." Julia laughed. "Unless we include a call from my lawyers to say that the Bennett's takeover has been clinched."

"When did you hear about that?" asked Tom.

"Late this afternoon; Jimmy called to say that they've signed all the documents. All that we have to do now is hand over the check."

"You didn't mention this when you came in," said Su Ling.

"The thought of Julia coming to dinner drove it out of my mind," said Nat, "but I did discuss the deal with Luke."

"And what was his considered opinion?" asked Tom.

"He thought that a dollar was far too much to pay for a bank."

"A dollar?" echoed Julia.

"Yes, Bennett's have been declaring a loss for the past five years and, if you exclude the banking premises, their long-term debt is no longer covered by their assets, so Luke may prove to be right if I can't turn it around in time."

"How old is Luke?" asked Julia.

"Two, but he already has a proper grasp of financial matters."

Julia laughed. "So tell me more about the bank, Nat."

"It's only the beginning," he explained as he poured the champagne, "I still have my eye on Morgan's."

"And how much is that going to cost you?" asked Su Ling.

"Around three hundred million at today's prices, but by the time I'm ready to make a bid, it could be over a billion."

"I can't think in those sort of sums," said Julia, "it's way out of my league."

"Now that's not true, Julia," said Tom. "Don't forget I've studied your company's accounts, and unlike Bennett's, you've made a profit for the past five years."

"Yes, but only just over a million," said Julia, giving him that smile again.

"Excuse me," said Su Ling, "while I check on dinner."

Nat smiled at his wife and then glanced at Tom's guest. He already had the feeling that Julia just might make it to a second date. "What do you do, Julia?" asked Nat.

"What do you think I do?" was thrown back with the same flirtatious smile.

"I'd say you were a model, possibly an actress."

"Not bad. I used to be a model when I was younger, but for the past six years I've been involved in real estate."

Su Ling reappeared. "If you'd like to come through, dinner is just about ready."

"Real estate," said Nat as he accompanied his guest into the dining room, "I would never have guessed."

"But it's true," said Tom. "And Julia wants us to handle her account. There's a site she's looking at in Hartford, and she will be depositing five hundred thousand dollars with the bank, in case she needs to move quickly."

"Why did you select us?" asked Nat, as his wife placed a bowl of lobster bisque in front of her.

"Because my late husband dealt with Mr. Russell over the Robinson Mall site. Although we were the underbidders on that occasion and failed to secure the deal, Mr. Russell didn't charge us," said Julia. "Not even a fee."

"That sounds like my father," said Tom.

"So my late husband said that if we were ever to look at anything else in this area, we should only bank with Russell's."

"Things have changed since then," said Nat, "Mr. Russell has retired and . . ."

"But his son is still there, as chairman."

"And he has me breathing down his neck to make sure people like you are charged when we give them a professional service. Though you'll be interested to know that the mall has been a great success, showing an excellent return for its investors. So what brings you to Hartford?"

"I read that there are plans to build a second mall on the other side of the city."

"That's right. The council is putting the land up for sale with a development permit."

"What sort of figure are they looking for?" asked Julia as she sipped her soup.

"Around three million is the word on the street, but I think it's likely to end up nearer three point three to three point five after the success of the Robinson's site."

"Three point five is our upper limit," said Julia. "My company is by nature cautious, and in any case, there's always another deal around the corner."

"Perhaps we could interest you in some of the other properties we represent," said Nat.

"No, thank you," said Julia. "My firm specializes in malls, and one of the many things my husband taught me was never to stray away from your field of expertise."

"Wise man, your late husband."

"He was," said Julia. "But I think that's enough business for one night, so once my money has been deposited, perhaps the bank would be willing to represent me at the auction? However, I require complete discretion, I don't want anyone else to know who you're bidding for. Something else my husband taught me." She turned her attention to the hostess. "Can I help you with the next course?"

"No, thank you," said Su Ling, "Nat's hopeless, but is just about capable of carrying four plates into the kitchen, and when he remembers, pouring the occasional glass of wine."

"So how did you two meet?" asked Nat while, prompted by Su Ling's comment, he began to refill the glasses.

"You wouldn't believe it," said Tom, "but we met on a building site."

"I'm sure there has to be a more romantic explanation."

"When I was checking over the council land last Sunday, I came across Julia out jogging."

"I thought you were insistent about discretion," said Nat smiling.

"Not many people seeing a woman jogging over a building site on a Sunday morning think she wants to buy it."

"In fact," said Tom, "it wasn't until I'd taken her out for dinner at the Cascade that I discovered what Julia was really up to."

"Corporate real estate must be a tough world for a woman?" said Nat.

"Yes, it is," said Julia, "but I didn't choose it, it chose me. You see, when I left college in Minnesota, I did some modeling for a short time, before I met my husband. It was his idea that I should look at sites whenever I went out jogging, and then report back to him. Within a year I knew exactly what he was looking for and within two, I had a place on the board."

"So you now run the company."

"No," said Julia, "I leave that to my chairman and chief executive officer, but I remain the majority shareholder."

"So you decided to stay involved after your husband's death?"

"Yes, that was his idea, he knew he only had a couple of years to live, and as we didn't have any children he decided to teach me everything about the business. I think even he was surprised by how willing a pupil I turned out to be."

Nat began to clear away the plates.

"Anyone for *crème brûlée*?" asked Su Ling.

"I couldn't eat another mouthful; that lamb was so tender," said Julia. "But don't let that stop you," she added, patting Tom's stomach.

Nat glanced across at Tom, and thought he'd never seen him looking so content. He suspected that Julia might even come to dinner a third time.

"Is that really the time?" asked Julia, looking down at her watch. "It's been a wonderful evening, Su Ling, but please forgive me, I have a board meeting at ten tomorrow morning, so I ought to be leaving."

"Yes, of course," said Su Ling, rising from her place.

Tom leaped up from his chair and accompanied Julia out into the hall, before helping her on with her coat. He kissed Su Ling on the cheek, thanking her for a wonderful evening.

"I'm only sorry that Julia has to rush back to New York. Let's make it my place next time."

Nat glanced across at Su Ling and smiled, but she didn't respond.

Nat found himself chuckling as he closed the front door. "Some woman that," he said when he joined his wife in the kitchen and grabbed a drying-up cloth.

"She's a phony," said Su Ling.

"What do you mean?" asked Nat.

"Exactly what I said, she's a phony—phony accent, phony clothes, and her phony story was altogether too neat and tidy. Don't do any business with her."

"What can go wrong if she deposits five hundred thousand with the bank?"

"I'd be willing to bet a month's salary that the five hundred thousand never turns up."

Although Su Ling didn't raise the subject again that night, when Nat arrived at his office the following morning, he asked his secretary to dig up all the financial details she could find on Kirkbridge & Company of New York. She was back an hour later with a copy of their annual report, and latest financial statement. Nat checked carefully through the report and his eye finally settled on the bottom line. They had made a profit of just over a million the previous year, and all the figures tallied with those Julia had talked about over dinner. He then checked the board of directors. Mrs. Julia Kirkbridge was listed as a director, below the chairman and chief executive. But because of Su Ling's apprehension, he decided to take the inquiry one step further. He dialed the telephone number of their office in New York, without going through his secretary.

"Kirkbridge and Company, how can I help you?" said a voice.

"Good morning, would it be possible to speak to Mrs. Kirkbridge?"

"No, I'm afraid not, sir, she's in a board meeting," Nat glanced at his watch and smiled, it was ten twenty-five, "but if you leave your number, I'll ask her to call you back just as soon as she's free."

"No, that won't be necessary," said Nat. As he put the phone down it rang again immediately. "It's Jeb in new accounts, Mr. Cartwright, I thought you would want to know that we have just received a wire transfer from Chase for the sum of five hundred thousand, to be credited to the account of a Mrs. Julia Kirkbridge."

Nat couldn't resist calling Su Ling to tell her the news.

"She's still a phony," his wife repeated.

31

"HEADS OR TAILS?" asked the moderator.

"Tails," said Barbara Hunter.

"Tails it is," said the moderator. He looked across at Mrs. Hunter and nodded. Fletcher couldn't complain, because he would have called heads—he always did—so he only wondered what decision she would make. Would she speak first, because that would determine at the end of the evening that Fletcher spoke last? If, on the other hand . . .

"I'll speak first," she said.

Fletcher suppressed a smile. The tossing of the coin had proved irrelevant; if he'd won, he would have elected to speak second.

The moderator took his seat behind the desk on the center of the stage. Mrs. Hunter sat on his right, and Fletcher on his left, reflecting the ideology of their two parties. But selecting where they should sit had been the least of their problems. For the past ten days there had been arguments about where the debate should be held, what time it should begin, who the moderator should be, and even the height of the lecterns from which they would speak, because Barbara Hunter was five foot seven, and Fletcher six foot one. In the end, it was agreed there should be two lecterns of different heights, one on either side of the stage.

The moderator acceptable to both was chairman of the journalism department at UConn's Hartford campus. He rose from his place.

"Good evening, ladies and gentlemen. My name is Frank McKenzie, and I will be moderator for this evening's debate. The format calls on Mrs. Hunter to begin with a six-minute opening statement, followed by Mr. Davenport. I feel I should warn both candidates that I will ring this bell," he picked up a small bell by his side and rang it firmly, which caused some laughter in the audience and helped break the tension, "at five minutes to warn' you both that you have sixty seconds left to speak. I will then ring it again after six minutes when you must deliver your final sentence. Following their opening statements, both candidates will then answer questions from a selected panel for forty minutes. Finally, Mrs. Hunter, followed by Mr. Davenport, will each make their closing remarks for three minutes. I now call upon Mrs. Hunter to open proceedings."

Barbara Hunter rose from her place and walked slowly over to her lectern on the right-hand side of the stage. She had calculated that since ninety percent of the audience would be watching the debate on television, she would address the largest number of potential voters if she spoke first, especially as a World Series game was due to be aired at eight thirty, when the majority of viewers would automatically switch channels. Since both of them would have made their opening remarks by that time, Fletcher felt it wasn't that significant. But he also wanted to speak second so that he could pick up on some of the points Mrs. Hunter made during her statement, and if at the end of the evening, he had the last word, perhaps it might be the only thing the audience would remember.

Fletcher listened attentively to a predictable and well-rehearsed opening from Mrs. Hunter. She held the lectern firmly as she spoke. "I was born in Hartford. I married a Hartford man, my children were born at St. Patrick's Hospital and all of them still live in the state capital, so I feel I am well qualified to represent the people of this great city." The first burst of applause flooded up from the floor. Fletcher checked the packed audience carefully, and noted that about half of them were joining in, while the other half remained silent.

Among Jimmy's responsibilities for the evening was the allocation of seats. It had been agreed that both parties would be given three hundred tickets each, with four hundred left over for the general public. Jimmy and a small band of helpers had spent hours urging their supporters to apply for the remaining four hundred, but Jimmy realized that the Republicans would be just as assiduous carrying out the same exercise, so it was always going to end up around fifty–fifty. Fletcher wondered how many genuinely neutral people there were sitting in the auditorium.

"Don't worry about the hall," Harry had told him, "the real audience will be watching you on television and they're the ones you need to influence. Stare into the middle of the camera lens, and look sincere," he added with a grin.

Fletcher made notes as Mrs. Hunter outlined her program, and although the contents were sensible and worthy, she had the sort of delivery that allowed the mind to wander. When the moderator rang the bell at five minutes. Mrs. Hunter was only about halfway through her speech and even paused while she turned a couple of pages. Fletcher was surprised that such a seasoned campaigner hadn't calculated that the occasional burst of applause would cut into her time. Fletcher's opening remarks were timed at just over five minutes. "Better to finish a few seconds early than have to rush toward the end," Harry had warned him again and again. Mrs. Hunter's peroration closed a few seconds after the second bell had rung, making it sound as if she had been cut short. Nevertheless, she still received rapturous applause from half of the audience, and courteous acknowledgment from the remainder.

"I'll now ask Mr. Davenport to make his opening statement."

Fletcher slowly approached the lectern on his side of the stage, feeling like a man just a few paces away from the gallows. He was somewhat relieved by the warm reception he received. He placed his five-page, double-spaced, large-type script on the lectern and checked the opening sentence, though in truth he had been over the speech so many times he virtually knew it by heart. He looked down at the audience and smiled, aware that the moderator wouldn't start the clock until he'd delivered his first word.

"I think I've made one big mistake in my life," he began. "I wasn't born in Hartford." The ripple of laughter helped him, "But I made up for it. I fell in love with a Hartford girl when I was only fourteen." Laughter and applause followed. Fletcher relaxed for the first time and delivered the rest of his opening remarks with a confidence that he hoped belied his youth. When the bell for five minutes rang, he was just about to begin his peroration. He completed it with twenty seconds to spare, making the final bell redundant. The applause he received was far greater than he had been greeted with when he first approached the lectern, but then the opening statement was no more than the end of the first round.

He glanced down at Harry and Jimmy, who were seated in the second row. Their smiles suggested he had survived the opening skirmish.

"The time has now come for the question session," said the moderator, "which will last for forty minutes. The candidates are to give brief responses. I'll start with Charles Lockhart of the *Hartford Courant.*"

"Does either candidate believe the educational grants system should be reformed?" asked the local editor crisply.

Fletcher was well prepared for this question, as it had come up again and again at local meetings, and was regularly the subject of editorials in Mr. Lockhart's paper. He was invited to respond as Hunter had spoken first.

"There should never be any discrimination that makes it harder for someone from a poor background to attend college. It is not enough to believe in equality, we must also insist on equality of opportunity." This was greeted with a sprinkling of applause and Fletcher smiled down at the audience.

"Fine words," responded Mrs. Hunter, cutting into the applause, "but you out there will also expect fine deeds. I've sat on school boards so you don't have to lecture me on discrimination, Mr. Davenport, and if I am fortunate enough to be elected senator, I will back legislation that supports the claims of all men," she paused, "and women, to equal opportunities." She stood back from the lectern while her supporters began cheering. She turned her gaze on Fletcher. "Perhaps someone who has had the privilege of being educated at Hotchkiss and Yale might not be able to fully grasp that."

Damn, thought Fletcher, I forgot to tell them that Annie sat on a school board, and they had just enrolled Lucy in Hartford Elementary, a local public school. When there had only been twelve in the audience, he had remembered every time.

Questions on local taxes, hospital staffing, public transportation and crime predictably followed. Fletcher recovered from the opening salvo and began to feel that the session would end in a draw, until the moderator called for the last question.

"Do the candidates consider themselves truly independent, or will their policies be dictated by the party machine, and their vote in the Senate dependent on the views of retired politicians?" The questioner was Jill Bernard, weekend anchor of a local radio talk show, which seemed to have Barbara Hunter on every other day.

Mrs. Hunter replied immediately. "All of you in this hall know that I had to fight every inch of the way to win my party's nomination, and unlike some, it wasn't handed to me on a plate. In fact, I've had to fight for everything in my life, as my parents couldn't afford silver spoons. And may I remind you that I haven't hesitated to stand firm on issues whenever I believed my party was wrong. It didn't always make me popular, but no one has ever doubted my independence. If elected to the Senate, I wouldn't be on the phone every day seeking advice on how I should vote. I will be making the decisions and I will stand by them." She finished to rapturous applause.

The knot in his stomach, the sweat in the palms of his hands, and the weakness in his legs had all returned as Fletcher tried to collect his thoughts. He looked down at the audience to see every eye boring into him.

"I was born in Farmington, just a few miles away from this hall. My parents are longstanding active contributors to the Hartford community through their professional and voluntary work, in particular for St. Patrick's Hospital." He looked down at his parents, who were sitting in the fifth row. His father's head was held high, his mother's was bowed. "My mother sat on so many nonprofit boards, I thought I must be an orphan, but they have both come along to support me tonight. Yes, I did go to Hotchkiss, and Mrs. Hunter is right. It was a privilege. Yes, I did go to Yale, a great

Connecticut university. Yes, I did become president of the college council, and yes, I was editor of the *Law Review,* which is why I was invited to join one of the most prestigious legal firms in New York. I make no apology for never being satisfied with second place. And I was equally delighted to give all that up so that I could return to Hartford and put something back into the community where I was raised. By the way, on the salary the state is offering, I won't be able to afford many silver spoons and so far, no one's offered me anything on a plate." The audience burst into spontaneous applause. He waited for the applause to die down, before he lowered his voice almost to a whisper. "Don't let's disguise what this questioner was getting at. Will I regularly be on the phone to my father-in-law, Senator Harry Gates? I expect so, I am married to his only daughter." More laughter followed. "But let me remind you of something you already know about Harry Gates. He's served this constituency for twenty-eight years with honor and integrity, at a time when those two words seem to have lost their meaning, and frankly," said Fletcher, turning to face his Republican rival, "neither of us is worthy to take his place. But if I am elected, you bet I'll take advantage of his wisdom, his experience and his foresight; only a blinkered egotist wouldn't. But let me also make one thing clear," he said, turning back to face the audience, "I will be the person who represents you in the Senate."

Fletcher returned to his place with over half of the audience on their feet cheering. Mrs. Hunter had made the mistake of attacking him on ground where he needed no preparation. She tried to recover in her closing remarks, but the blow had been landed.

When the moderator said, "I'd like to thank both candidates," Fletcher did something Harry had recommended at lunch the previous Sunday. He immediately walked across to his opponent, shook her by the hand, and paused to allow the *Courant*'s photographer to record the moment.

The following day, the picture of the two of them dominated the front page, and achieved exactly what Harry had hoped for— the image of a six-foot-one man, towering over a five-foot-seven woman. "And don't smile, look serious," he'd added. "We need them to forget how young you are."

Fletcher read the words below the picture—*nothing between them.* The editorial said that he had held his own in the debate, but Barbara Hunter still led the opinion polls by two percent with only nine days to go.

32

"Do you mind if I smoke?"

"No, it's only Su Ling who doesn't approve of the habit."

"I don't think she approves of me either," said Julia Kirkbridge, as she flicked on her lighter.

"You have to remember that she was brought up by a very conservative mother," said Tom. "She even disapproved of Nat to begin with, but she'll come around, especially when I tell her . . ."

"Shh," said Julia, "for now that must remain our little secret." She inhaled deeply, and then added, "I like Nat; you two obviously make a good team."

"We do, but I'm keen to close this deal while he's on vacation, especially after his triumph in taking over our oldest rival."

"I can understand that," said Julia, "but how do you rate our chances?"

"It's beginning to look as if there are only two or three serious bidders in the field. The restrictions set out in the council's offer document should eliminate any cowboys."

"Restrictions?"

"The council is demanding not only that the bidding must be by public auction, but that the full amount has to be paid on signature."

"Why are they insisting on that?" asked Julia, sitting up in bed. "In the past, I've always put ten percent down and assumed I would be given at least twenty-eight days before I had to complete."

"Yes, that would be normal practice, but this site has become a political hot potato. Barbara Hunter is insisting there be no holdups, because one or two other deals have fallen through recently when it was discovered that a speculator didn't have the necessary resources to complete the agreement. And don't forget, we're only days away from an election, so they are making sure that there can be no comebacks later."

"Does that mean I'll have to deposit another three million with you by next Friday?" asked Julia.

"No, if we secure the property, the bank will cover you with a short-term loan."

"But what if I renege on the deal?" asked Julia.

"It doesn't matter to us," said Tom. "We would sell it on to the under-bidder, and still have your five hundred thousand to cover any loss."

"Banks," said Julia as she stubbed out her cigarette and slid under the sheets. "You never lose."

—◇—

"I want you to do me a favor," said Su Ling as the plane began its descent into Los Angeles airport.

"Yes, little flower, I'm listening."

"See if you can go a whole week without phoning the bank. Don't forget this is Luke's first big trip."

"Mine too," said Nat, putting his arm around his son, "I've always wanted to visit Disneyland."

"Now stop teasing, you made a deal, and I expect you to keep to it."

"I would like to keep an eye on the deal that Tom's trying to close with Julia's company."

"Don't you think Tom just might like to have a little triumph of his own, one that hadn't been double-checked by the great Nat Cartwright? It was you, after all, who decided to trust her."

"I take your point," said Nat, as Luke clung to him as the plane touched down. "But do you mind if I phone him on Friday afternoon just to find out if our bid on the Cedar Wood project was successful?"

"No, as long as you do leave it until Friday afternoon."

"Dad, will we travel in a Sputnik?"

"You bet," said Nat, "why else would you go to LA?"

—◦—

Tom met Julia off the train from New York and drove her straight to City Hall. They walked in to find the cleaners just leaving after the debate the previous evening. Tom had read in the *Hartford Courant* that over a thousand people attended the event, and the paper's editorial had suggested there wasn't much to pick between the two candidates. He'd always voted Republican in the past, but he thought that Fletcher Davenport sounded like a decent man.

"Why have we arrived so early?" asked Julia, breaking into his thoughts.

"I want to be familiar with the layout of the room," explained Tom, "so that when the bidding starts, we can't be taken by surprise. Don't forget, the whole thing could all be over in a few minutes."

"Where do you think we should sit?"

"Halfway back on the right. I've already told the auctioneer what sign I intend to use when I'm bidding."

Tom looked up toward the stage and watched as the auctioneer mounted the rostrum, tapped the microphone, and stared down at the tiny audience, checking everything was in place.

"Who are all these people?" asked Julia, looking around the hall.

"A mixture of council officials, including the chief executive, Mr. Cooke, representatives from the auctioneer's, and the odd person who's got nothing better to do on a Friday afternoon. But as far as I can see, there are only three serious bidders." Tom checked his watch. "Perhaps we should sit down."

Julia and Tom took their places about halfway back on the end of the row. Tom picked up the sales brochure on the seat beside him, and when Julia touched his hand, he couldn't help wondering how many people would work out that they were lovers. He turned the page and studied an architect's mock-up of what the proposed mall might look like. He was still reading through the small print when the auctioneer indicated he was ready to begin. He cleared his throat.

"Ladies and gentlemen," he said, "there is only one item to come under the hammer this afternoon, a prime site on the north side of the city known as Cedar Wood. The city council is offering this property with approval for commercial development. The terms of payment and regulatory requirements are detailed in the brochure to be found on your seats. I must stress that if any of the terms are not adhered to, the council is within its rights to withdraw from the transaction." He paused to allow his words to sink in. "I have an opening bid of two million," he declared, and immediately looked in Tom's direction.

Although Tom said nothing and gave no sign, the auctioneer announced, "I have a new bidder at two million two hundred and fifty thousand." The auctioneer made a show of glancing around the room, despite the fact he knew exactly where the three serious bidders were seated. His eyes settled on a well-known local lawyer in the second row, who raised his brochure. "Two million five hundred thousand, it's with you, sir." The auctioneer turned his attention back to Tom, who didn't even blink. "Two million seven hundred and fifty thousand." His eyes returned to the lawyer, who waited for some time before he once again raised his brochure. "Three million," said the auctioneer, and immediately looked in Tom's direction before saying, "Three million two hundred and fifty thousand." He returned to the lawyer, who seemed to hesitate. Julia squeezed Tom's hand between the chairs. "I think we've got it."

"Three million five hundred thousand?" suggested the auctioneer, his eyes fixed on the lawyer.

"Not yet we haven't," Tom whispered.

"Three million five hundred thousand," repeated the auctioneer hopefully. "Three million five hundred thousand," he repeated gratefully as the brochure rose for a third time.

"Damn," said Tom, taking off his glasses, "I think we must have both settled on the same upper limit."

"Then let's go to three six," said Julia. "That way at least we'll find out."

Although Tom had removed his glasses—the sign that he was no longer bidding—the auctioneer could see that Mr. Russell was in deep conversation with the lady seated next to him. "Have we finished bidding, sir? Or . . ."

Tom hesitated and then said, "Three million six hundred thousand."

The auctioneer swung his attention back to the lawyer, who had placed his brochure on the empty seat beside him. "Can I say three million seven hundred thousand sir, or are we all finished?"

The brochure remained on the seat. "Any other bids from the floor?" asked the auctioneer as his eyes swept the dozen or so people who were seated in a hall that had held a thousand the night before. "One last chance, otherwise I will let it go at three million six hundred thousand." He raised his hammer and, receiving no response, brought it down with a thud. "Sold for three million six hundred thousand dollars to the gentleman at the end of the row."

"Well done," said Julia.

"It's going to cost you another hundred thousand," said Tom, "but we couldn't have known that two of us would settle on the same upper limit. I'll just go and sort out the paperwork and hand over the check, then we can go off and celebrate."

"What a good idea," said Julia, as she ran a finger down the inside of his leg.

"Congratulations, Mr. Russell," said Mr. Cooke. "Your client has secured a fine property which I am sure in the long term will yield an excellent return."

"I agree," said Tom, as he wrote out a check for three point six million dollars and handed it across to the council's chief executive.

"Is Russell's Bank the principal in this transaction?" inquired Mr. Cooke as he studied the signature.

"No, we are representing a New York client who banks with us."

"I am sorry to appear to be nitpicking about this, Mr. Russell, but the terms of the agreement make it clear that the check for the full amount must be signed by the principal and not by his or her representative."

"But we represent the company, and are holding their deposit."

"Then it shouldn't be too difficult for your client to sign a check on behalf of that company," suggested Mr. Cooke.

"But why . . ." began Tom.

"It's not for me to try and fathom the machinations of our elected representatives, Mr. Russell, but after the debacle last year over the Aldwich contract and the questions I have to answer daily from Mrs. Hunter," he let out a sigh, "I have been left with no choice but to keep to the letter, as well as the spirit, of the agreement."

"But what can I do about it at this late stage?" asked Tom.

"You still have until five o'clock to produce a check signed by the principal. If you fail to do so, the property will be offered to the under-bidder for three point five million, and the council will look to you to make up the difference of one hundred thousand dollars."

Tom ran to the back of the room. "Have you got your check-book with you?"

"No," said Julia. "You told me that Russell's would cover the full amount until I transferred the difference on Monday."

"Yes, I did," said Tom, trying to think on his feet. "There's nothing else for it," he added, "we'll just have to go straight to the bank." He checked his watch, it was nearly four o'clock. "Damn," he added, painfully aware that if Nat hadn't been on holiday, he would have spotted the subclause and anticipated its consequences. On the short walk from City Hall to Russell's Bank, Tom explained to Julia what Mr. Cooke had insisted on.

"Does that mean I've lost the deal, not to mention a hundred thousand?"

"No, I've already thought of a way around that, but it will need your agreement."

"If it will secure the property," said Julia, "I'll do whatever you advise."

As soon as they entered the bank, Tom went straight to his office, picked up a phone and asked the chief teller to join him. While he waited for Ray Jackson to arrive, he took out a blank checkbook and began writing out the words three million six hundred thousand dollars. The chief teller knocked on the door and entered the chairman's office.

"Ray, I want you to transfer three million one hundred thousand dollars to Mrs. Kirkbridge's account."

The chief teller hesitated for a moment. "I'll need a letter of authorization before I can transfer such a large amount," he said. "It's way above my limit."

"Yes, of course," said the chairman, and removed the standard form from his top drawer and quickly filled in the relevant figures. Tom didn't comment on the fact that it was also the largest sum he had ever authorized. He passed the form across to the chief teller, who studied the details carefully. He looked as if he wanted to query the chairman's decision, and then thought better of it.

"Immediately," emphasized Tom.

"Yes, sir," said the chief teller, and departed as quickly as he had arrived.

"Are you sure that was sensible?" asked Julia. "Aren't you taking an unnecessary risk?"

"We have the property and your five hundred thousand, so we can't lose. As Nat would say, it's a win-win proposition." He turned the checkbook around and asked Julia to sign it and print beneath her signature the name of her company. Once Tom had checked it he said, "We'd better get back to City Hall as quickly as possible."

Tom tried to remain calm as he dodged in and out of the traffic while crossing Main Street before jogging up the steps to City Hall. He kept having to wait for Julia, who explained it wasn't easy to keep up with him in high heels. When they reentered the building, Tom was relieved to find Mr. Cooke was still seated behind his desk at the far end of the hall. The chief executive rose when he saw them heading toward him.

"Hand over the check to the thin man with the bald head," said Tom, "and smile."

Julia carried out Tom's instructions to the letter, and received a warm smile in return. Mr. Cooke studied the check carefully. "This seems to be in order, Mrs. Kirkbridge, if I could just see some form of identification."

"Certainly," said Julia, and took a driver's license out of her handbag.

Mr. Cooke studied the photo and the signature. "It's not a flattering picture of you," he said. Julia smiled. "Good, now all that is left for you to do is sign all the necessary documents on behalf of your company."

Julia signed the council agreement in triplicate and handed a copy over to Tom. "I think you'd better hold on to this until the money is safely transferred," she whispered.

Mr. Cooke looked at his watch. "I shall be presenting this check first thing on Monday morning, Mr. Russell," he said, "and I would be obliged if it were cleared as quickly as is convenient. I don't want to give Mrs. Hunter any more ammunition than is necessary only days before the election."

"It will be cleared on the same day it's presented," Tom assured him.

"Thank you, sir," said Mr. Cooke to a man he regularly had a round of golf with at their local club.

Tom wanted to give Julia a hug, but restrained himself. "I'll just run back to the bank and let them know that it all went smoothly, then we can go home."

"Do you really have to?" asked Julia. "After all, they won't be presenting the check until Monday morning."

"I guess that's right," said Tom.

"Damn," said Julia, bending down to take off one of her shoes, "I've broken the heel running up those steps."

"Sorry," said Tom, "that was my fault, I shouldn't have made you rush back from the bank. As it turned out we had more than enough time."

"It's not a problem," said Julia, smiling, "but if you could fetch the car, I'll join you at the bottom of the steps."

"Yes, of course," said Tom. He jogged back down and across to the parking lot.

He was back outside City Hall a few minutes later, but Julia was nowhere to be seen. Perhaps she had slipped back inside? He waited a few moments, but she still didn't appear. He cursed, leaped out of the illegally parked car and ran up the steps and into the building to find Julia in one of the phone booths. The moment she saw him, she hung up.

"I've just been telling New York about your coup, darling, and they've instructed our bank to transfer the three million one hundred thousand before close of business."

"That's good to hear," said Tom, as they strolled back to the car together. "So shall we have supper in town?"

"No, I'd rather go back to your place and have a quiet meal on our own," said Julia.

When Tom pulled up in his driveway, Julia had already removed her coat, and by the time they reached the bedroom on the second floor, she had left a trail of clothes in her wake. Tom was down to his underwear and Julia was peeling off a stocking when the phone rang.

"Leave it," Julia said as she fell to her knees and pulled down his boxer shorts.

⋯⋯

"There's no reply," said Nat, "they must have gone out for dinner."

"Can't it wait until we get back on Monday?" asked Su Ling.

"I suppose so," admitted Nat reluctantly, "but I'd like to have known if Tom managed to close the Cedar Wood deal, and if so, at what price."

33

"Too Close to Call" ran the banner headline in the *Washington Post* on election morning. "Neck and Neck" was the opinion of the *Hartford Courant*. The first referred to the national race between Ford and Carter for the White House, the second to the local battle between Hunter and Davenport for the State Senate Chamber. It annoyed Fletcher that they always put her name first, like Harvard before Yale.

"All that matters now," said Harry as he chaired the final campaign meeting at six that morning, "is getting our supporters to the polls." No longer was there any need to discuss tactics, press statements, or policy. Once the first vote had been cast, everyone seated around the table had a new responsibility.

A team of forty would be in charge of the car pool, armed with a list of voters who required a lift to their nearest polling place, the old, the infirm, the downright lazy and even some who took a vicarious pleasure in being taken to the poll just so they could vote for the other side.

The next team, and by far the largest, were those who manned the bank of phones back at headquarters.

"They'll be on two-hour shifts," said Harry, "and must spend their time contacting known supporters to remind them that it's election day, and then later to make sure they've cast their vote. Some of this group will need to be called three or four times before the polls close at eight this evening," Harry reminded them.

The next group, whom Harry described as the beloved amateurs, ran the counting houses all over the borough. They would keep a minute-by-minute update on how the voting was going in their district. They could be responsible for as few as a thousand voters or as many as three thousand, depending on whether theirs was a built-up or a rural area. "They are," Harry reminded Fletcher, "the backbone of the party. From the moment the first vote is cast, they'll have volunteers sitting outside the polling stations ticking off names of the voters as they go to the polls. Every thirty minutes those lists will be handed over to runners, who will take them back to the house where the full register will be laid out on tables or pinned to a wall. That list will then be marked up—a red line through the name for any Republican voter, blue for Democrats, and yellow for unknown. One glance at the boards at any time, and the captain of the precinct will know exactly how the vote is progressing. As many of the captains have done the same job for election after election, they'll be able to give you an immediate comparison with any past poll. The details, once 'boarded,' are then relayed through to headquarters so that the phoners don't keep bothering a pledge who has already cast their vote."

"So what's the candidate supposed to do all day?" asked Fletcher, once Harry had come to the end of his briefing.

"Keep out of the way," said Harry, "which is why you have a program of your own. You will visit the forty-four counting houses, because they all expect to see the candidate at some time during the day. Jimmy will act as your driver, known as 'the candidate's friend,' because we certainly can't afford any spare workers wasting their time on you."

Once the meeting had broken up, and everyone had dashed off to their new assignments, Jimmy explained just how Fletcher would spend the rest of the day, and he spoke with some experience, because he'd carried out the same exercise for his father during the previous two elections.

"First the no-no's," said Jimmy when Fletcher joined him in the front of the car. "As we have to visit all forty-four houses between now and eight o'clock this evening when the polls close, everyone will offer you a coffee, and between 11:45 and 2:15 lunch, and after 5:30 a drink. You must always reply with a polite but firm no to any such offer. You will only drink water in the car, and we'll have lunch at 12:30 for thirty minutes back at headquarters, just so they realize they've got a candidate, and you won't eat again until after the polls close."

Fletcher thought he might become bored, but each visit produced a new cast of characters and a new set of figures. For the first hour, the sheets showed just a few names crossed out, and the captains were quickly able to tell him how the turnout compared with past elections. Fletcher was encouraged by how many blue lines had appeared before ten o'clock, until Jimmy warned him that the time between seven and nine was always good pickings for the Democrats as the industrial and night-shift workers vote before they start, or after they have finished work. "Between ten and four, the Republicans should go into the lead," Jimmy added, "while after five and up until the close of the polls is always the time when the Democrats have to make their comeback. So just pray for rain between ten and five, followed by a fine warm evening."

By 11 A.M. all the captains were reporting that the poll was slightly down compared with the last election when it had closed on fifty-five percent. "Anything below fifty percent, we lose, over fifty and we're in with a shout," said Jimmy, "above fifty-five and it's yours by a street."

"Why's that?" asked Fletcher.

"Because the Republicans traditionally are more likely to turn out in any weather, so they always benefit from a low turnout. Making sure our people vote has always been the Democrats' biggest problem."

Jimmy stuck rigidly to his schedule. Just before arriving he would hand Fletcher a slip of paper with the basic facts on the household running that district. Fletcher would then commit the salient points to memory before he reached the front door.

"Hi, Dick," he said when the door was opened, "good of you to allow us to use your house again, because of course this is your fourth election." Listen to reply. "How's Ben, is he still at college?" Listen to reply, "I was sorry to hear about Buster—yes, Senator Gates told me." Listen to reply. "But you have another dog now, Buster Junior—is that right?"

Jimmy also had his own routine. After ten minutes he would whisper, "I think you ought to be leaving." At twelve, he would begin to sound a little anxious and dispense with think, and at fourteen, he became insistent. After shaking hands and waving, it always took another couple of minutes before they could finally get away. Even with Jimmy keeping to a rigorous schedule, they still arrived back at campaign headquarters twenty minutes late for lunch.

Lunch was a snack rather than a meal, as Fletcher grabbed a sandwich from a table that was heaped with food. He took the occasional bite as he and Annie moved from office to office, shaking hands with as many of the workers as possible.

"Hi, Martha, what's Harry up to?" asked Fletcher as he entered the phone room.

"He's outside the old State House doing what he does best, pressing the flesh, dispensing opinions, and making sure people haven't forgotten to vote. He should be back at any moment."

Thirty minutes later Fletcher passed Harry in the corridor on his way out, as Jimmy had insisted that, if they were still going to visit every counting house, then they had to leave by 1:10. "Good morning, Senator," said Fletcher.

"Good afternoon, Fletcher, glad you were able to find time to eat."

The first house they visited after lunch showed that the Republicans had gone into a slight lead, which continued to increase during the afternoon. By five o'clock there were still fifteen captains left to visit. "If you miss one of them," said Jimmy, "we'll never hear the end of it, and they sure won't be there for you next time around."

By six o'clock the Republicans had a clear lead, and Fletcher tried not to show that he was feeling a little depressed. "Relax," said Jimmy, and promised him it would look better in a couple of hours' time; what he didn't mention was that by this time in the evening, his father always had a small lead and therefore knew he'd won. Fletcher envied those who were running for seats where they weighed the votes.

"How much easier to relax if you knew you were certain to win, or certain to lose."

"I wouldn't know how that feels," said Jimmy, "Dad won his first election by 121 votes before I was born, and during the past thirty years built up his majority to just over 11,000, but he always says if sixty-one people had voted the other way, he would have lost that first election, and might never have been given a second chance." Jimmy regretted the words the moment he said them.

By seven, Fletcher was relieved to see a few more blue lines appearing on the sheets and although the Republicans were still in the lead, the feeling was that it would go to the line. Jimmy had to cut the last six houses down to eleven minutes each, and even then he didn't reach the final two until after the poll had closed.

"What now?" asked Fletcher as he walked away from the last house.

Jimmy checked his watch. "Back to HQ and listen to the tallest stories you've ever heard. If you win, they will become folklore, and if you lose, they will be disowned and quickly forgotten."

"Like me," commented Fletcher.

Jimmy turned out to be right, because back at HQ everyone was talking at once, but only the foolhardy and naturally optimistic were willing to predict what the result would be. The first exit poll was broadcast minutes after the last vote had been cast and showed that Hunter had won by a whisker. The national polls were predicting that Ford had beaten Carter.

"History repeating itself," said Harry as he walked into the room. "Those same guys were telling me that Dewey was going to be our next president. They also said I'd lose by a whisker, and we cut both those whiskers off, so don't worry about straw polls, Fletcher, they're for straw men."

"What about the turnout?" asked Fletcher, recalling Jimmy's words.

"Too early to be sure, it's certainly over fifty percent, but not fifty-five."

Fletcher looked around at his team and realized that it was no longer any use thinking about how to gather in votes, as the time had come to count them.

"There's not much else we can do now," said Harry, "except to make sure that our tellers register at City Hall before ten. The rest of you should take a break, and we'll all meet up at the count later. I have a feeling it's going to be a long night."

In the car on the way to Mario's, Harry told Fletcher he couldn't see a lot of point in them turning up much before eleven, "so let's have a quiet meal and follow the party's fortunes in the rest of the country on Mario's television."

Any chance of a quiet meal evaporated when Fletcher and Harry entered the restaurant, and several of the diners rose to their feet and applauded the two men all the way to their table in the corner. Fletcher was pleased to find his parents had already arrived, and were enjoying a drink.

"So what can I recommend?" asked Mario once everybody had settled down.

"I'm too tired to even think about it," said Martha. "Mario, why don't you go ahead and choose for us, as you've never taken any notice of our opinion in the past."

"Of course, Mrs. Gates," said Mario, "just leave it to me."

Annie stood up and waved when Joanna and Jimmy walked in. As Fletcher kissed Joanna on the cheek, he glanced over her shoulder to see Jimmy Carter on Mario's television arriving back at his ranch, and moments later President Ford stepping onto a helicopter. He wondered what sort of a day they'd had.

"Your timing is perfect," said Harry as Joanna took the seat next to him, "we've only just arrived. How are the children?"

Within minutes, Mario returned carrying two large plates of antipasti, while a waiter followed with two carafes of white wine. "The wine is on the house," declared Mario, "I think maybe you make it," he said as he poured a glass for Fletcher to taste. Someone else who wasn't willing to predict the result.

Fletcher put a hand under the table and touched Annie's knee. "I'm going to say a few words."

"Must you?" said Jimmy, pouring himself a second glass of wine. "I've heard enough speeches from you to last a lifetime."

"It will be short, I promise you," Fletcher said as he rose from his place, "because everyone I want to thank is at this table. Let me start with Harry and Martha. If I hadn't sat next to their dreadful little brat on my first day at school, I would never have met

Annie, or indeed Martha and Harry, who have changed my whole life, although in truth it is my mother who is to blame, because it was she who insisted that I went to Hotchkiss rather than Taft. How different my life might have been if my father had had his way." He smiled at his mother. "So thank you." He sat down just as Mario reappeared at their table carrying another bottle of wine.

"I don't remember ordering that," said Harry.

"You didn't," said Mario, "it's a gift from a gentleman sitting on the far side of the room."

"That's very kind of him," said Fletcher, "did he leave his name?"

"No, all he said was that he was sorry not to be able to give you more help during the election, but he's been involved in a takeover. He's one of our regulars," added Mario, "I think he's something to do with Russell's Bank."

Fletcher looked across the restaurant and nodded when Nat Cartwright raised a hand. He had a feeling that he'd seen him somewhere before.

34

"HOW DID SHE manage it?" asked Tom, his face ashen.

"She chose her victim well and, to be fair, she paid meticulous attention to detail."

"But that doesn't explain . . ."

"How she knew we would agree to transfer the money? That was the easy part," said Nat. "Once all the other pieces had fallen neatly into place, all Julia had to do was call Ray and instruct him to move her account to another bank."

"But Russell's closes at five, and most of the staff leave before six, especially at a weekend."

"In Hartford."

"I don't understand," said Tom.

"She instructed our chief cashier to transfer the full amount to a bank in San Francisco, where it was still only two in the afternoon."

"But I only left her alone for a few minutes."

"Long enough for her to make a phone call to her lawyer."

"Then why didn't Ray contact me?"

"He tried to, but you weren't in the office and she took the phone off the hook when you got home, and don't forget when I called you from LA, it was three thirty, but it was six thirty in Hartford and Russell's was already closed."

"If only you hadn't been on vacation."

"My bet is she took that into consideration as well," said Nat.

"But how?"

"One call to my secretary asking for an appointment that week, and she would have known I would be in LA, and no doubt you confirmed as much soon after you'd met her."

Tom hesitated. "Yes, I did. But it doesn't explain why Ray didn't refuse to action the transfer."

"Because you'd deposited the full amount in her account, and the law is very clear in a case like this: if she asks for a transfer, we have no choice but to carry out her instructions. As her lawyer pointed out when he called Ray at four fifty, by which time you were on your way back home."

"But she'd already signed a check and handed it over to Mr. Cooke."

"Yes, and if you had returned to the bank and informed our chief teller about that check, he might have felt able to hold off any decision until Monday."

"But how could she be so confident that I would authorize the extra money to be placed in her account?"

"She wasn't, that's why she opened an account with us and deposited $500,000, assuming we would accept that she had more than sufficient funds to cover the purchase of Cedar Wood."

"But you told me that her company checked out?"

"And it did. Kirkbridge and Company is based in New York and made a profit of just over a million dollars last year, and surprise, surprise, the majority shareholder is a Mrs. Julia Kirkbridge. And it was only because Su Ling thought she was a phony that I even called to check and see if the company was having a board meeting that morning. When the switchboard operator informed me that Mrs. Kirkbridge couldn't be disturbed as she was in that meeting, the last piece of the jigsaw fell neatly into place. Now that's what I mean by attention to detail."

"But there's still a missing link," said Tom.

"Yes, and that's what turns her from an ordinary flim-flam artist into a fraudster of true genius. It was Harry Gates's amendment to the finance bill that presented her with a hoop that she knew we would have to jump through."

"How does Senator Gates get in on the act?" asked Tom.

"It was he who proposed the amendment to the property bill

stipulating that all future transactions enacted with the council should be paid in full on signature of the agreement."

"But I told her that the bank would cover whatever surplus proved necessary."

"And she knew that wouldn't be sufficient," said Nat, "because the senator's amendment insisted that the principal beneficiary," Nat opened the brochure at a passage he had underlined, "had to sign both the check and the agreement. The moment you rushed back to inquire if she had a checkbook with her, Julia knew she had you by the balls."

"But what if I'd said the deal is off unless you can come up with the full amount?"

"She would have returned to New York that night, transferred her half million back to Chase, and you would never have heard from her again."

"Whereas she pocketed three point one million dollars of our money and held on to her own $500,000," said Tom.

"Correct," said Nat, "and by the time the banks open in San Francisco this morning, that money will have disappeared off to the Cayman Islands via Zurich or possibly even Moscow, and although I'll obviously go through the motions, I don't believe we have a hope in hell of retrieving one cent of it."

"Oh, God," said Tom, "I've just remembered that Mr. Cooke will be presenting that check this morning, and I gave him my word that it would be cleared the same day."

"Then we shall have to clear it," said Nat. "It's one thing for the bank to lose money, quite another for it to lose its reputation, a reputation which your grandfather and father took a hundred years to establish."

Tom looked up at Nat. "The first thing I must do is resign."

"Despite your naïveté, that's the last thing you should do. Unless, of course, you want everyone to find out what a fool you've made of yourself and immediately transfer their accounts to Fairchild's. No, the one commodity I need is time, so I suggest you take a few days off. In fact, don't mention the Cedar Wood project again, and if anyone should raise the subject, you simply refer them to me."

Tom remained silent for some time, before he said, "The true irony is that I asked her to marry me."

"And her true genius is that she accepted," replied Nat.

"How did you know that?" asked Tom.

"It would have all been part of her plan."

"Clever girl," said Tom.

"I'm not so sure," said Nat, "because if you two had become engaged, I was ready to offer her a place on the board."

"So she had you fooled as well," said Tom.

"Oh yes," replied Nat, "with her grasp of finance she wouldn't have been a passenger, and had she married you she would have made a lot more than three point one million, so there must be another man involved." Nat paused. "I suspect he was the one on the other end of the phone." Nat turned to leave. "I'll be in my office," he said, "and remember, we only ever discuss this matter in private, nothing in writing, never on the phone."

Tom nodded as Nat closed the door quietly behind him.

"Good morning, Mr. Cartwright," said Nat's secretary as he walked into his office, "did you have a good vacation?"

"Yes, I did, thank you, Linda," he replied cheerily. "I'm not sure who enjoyed Disneyland more, Luke or myself." She smiled. "Any real problems?" he asked innocently.

"No, I don't think so. The final documents for the takeover of Bennett's came through last Friday, so from January first, you'll be running two banks."

Or none, thought Nat. "I need to speak to a Mrs. Julia Kirkbridge, the director of . . ."

"Kirkbridge and Company," said Linda. Nat froze. "You asked for the details of her company just before you went on vacation."

"Of course I did," said Nat.

Nat was rehearsing what he would say to Mrs. Kirkbridge, when his secretary buzzed through to tell him that she was on the line.

"Good morning, Mrs. Kirkbridge, my name is Nat Cartwright, I'm the chief executive of Russell's Bank in Hartford, Connecticut. We have a proposition we thought your company might be interested in, and as I'm in New York later today, I hoped you would be able to spare me a few minutes."

"Can I call you back, Mr. Cartwright?" she replied in a crisp English accent.

"Of course," said Nat, "I look forward to hearing from you."

He wondered how long it would take Mrs. Kirkbridge to discover that he was the chief executive of Russell's Bank. She was obviously checking, because she didn't even ask for his telephone number. When the phone rang again his secretary said, "Mrs. Kirkbridge on the line."

Nat checked his watch; it had taken her seven minutes.

"I could see you at two thirty this afternoon, Mr. Cartwright; would that suit you?"

"Suits me just fine," said Nat.

He put the phone down and buzzed Linda. "I'll need a ticket on today's eleven-thirty train to New York."

Nat's next call was to Rigg's Bank in San Francisco, who confirmed his worst fears. They had been instructed to send the money to Banco Mexico only moments after it had been deposited with them. From there, Nat knew it would follow the sun until it finally disappeared over the horizon. He decided it would be pointless to call in the police unless he wanted half the banking community let in on the secret. He suspected that Julia, or whatever her real name was, had also worked that out.

Nat got through a great deal of the backlog caused by his absence before leaving the office to catch the train to New York. He made it to the offices of Kirkbridge & Co. on 97th Street with only moments to spare. He hadn't even had time to take a seat in reception before a door opened. He looked up to see an elegant, well-dressed woman standing in the doorway. "Mr. Cartwright?"

"Yes," he said, rising from his seat.

"I'm Julia Kirkbridge; would you like to come through to my office?" The same crisp English accent. Nat could not recall how long ago it was that a director of any company had come to collect him in the reception area rather than sending a secretary, especially one working out of New York.

"I was intrigued by your call," said Mrs. Kirkbridge as she ushered Nat through to a comfortable seat by the fireplace. "It's not often a Connecticut banker comes to New York to visit me."

Nat took some papers out of his case, as he tried to assess the woman sitting opposite him. Her clothes, like those of her impersonator, were smartly tailored, but far more conservative, and although she was slim and in her mid-thirties, her dark hair and dark eyes were a total contrast to the blond from Minnesota.

"Well, it's quite simple really," began Nat. "Hartford City Council has put another site on the market that has planning approval for a shopping mall. The bank has purchased the land as an investment and is looking for a partner. We thought you might be interested."

"Why us?" asked Julia.

"You were among the original companies that bid for the Robinson's site, which, incidentally, has proved to be a great success, so we thought you might want to be involved in this new venture."

"I'm somewhat surprised that you didn't think of approaching us before you made your bid," said Mrs. Kirkbridge, "because had you done so, you would have discovered that we had already considered the terms far too restrictive." Nat was taken by surprise. "After all," continued Mrs. Kirkbridge, "that is what we do."

"Yes, I know," said Nat, buying time.

"May I ask how much it went for?" asked Mrs. Kirkbridge.

"Three point six million."

"That was way above our estimate," said Mrs. Kirkbridge, turning a page of the file on the table in front of her.

Nat had always considered himself a good poker player, but he had no way of knowing if Mrs. Kirkbridge was bluffing. He only had one card left. "Well, I'm sorry to have wasted your time," he said, rising from his place.

"Perhaps you haven't," said Mrs. Kirkbridge, who remained seated, "because I'm still interested in listening to your proposal."

"We're looking for a fifty-fifty partner," said Nat, resuming his seat.

"What does that mean exactly?" asked Mrs. Kirkbridge.

"You put up $1.8 million, the bank finances the rest of the project, and once the debt has been recouped, all the profits will be divided fifty-fifty."

"No bank fees, and the money loaned at prime rate?"

"I think we would consider that," said Nat.

"Then why don't you leave all the details with me, Mr. Cartwright, and I'll come back to you. How long have I got before you need a decision?"

"I'm meeting two other possible investors while I'm in New York," said Nat. "They were also bidders for the Robinson's site."

From the expression on her face, there was no way of telling if she believed him.

Mrs. Kirkbridge smiled. "Half an hour ago," she said, "I had a call from the chief executive of the Hartford City Council, a Mr. Cooke." Nat froze. "I didn't take the call as I thought it would be prudent to see you first. However, I find it hard to believe that this was the type of case study they expected you to analyze at Harvard Business School, Mr. Cartwright, so perhaps the time has come for you to tell me why you *really* wanted to see me."

35

ANNIE DROVE HER husband to City Hall, and it was the first time they had been alone all day. "Why don't we just go home?" said Fletcher.

"I expect every candidate feels that way just before the count."

"Do you know, Annie, we haven't once discussed what I'm going to do if I lose."

"I've always assumed you'd join another law firm. Heaven knows enough have been knocking on your door. Didn't Simpkins and Welland say they needed someone who specializes in criminal law?"

"Yes, and they've even offered me a partnership, but the truth is that politics is what I enjoy doing most. I'm even more obsessed than your father."

"That's not possible," said Annie. "By the way, he said to use his parking space."

"No way," said Fletcher, "only the senator should occupy that spot. No, we'll park down one of the side streets." Fletcher glanced out of the window to see dozens of people walking up City Hall steps.

"Where are they going?" asked Annie. "They can't all be close relations of Mrs. Hunter."

Fletcher laughed. "No, they're not, but the public are allowed to watch the count from the gallery. It's evidently an old Hartford tradition," he added as Annie finally found a parking space some distance from City Hall.

Fletcher and Annie held hands as they joined the crowds heading into the hall. Over the years, he had watched countless politicians and their wives holding hands on election day, and often wondered how many performed the ritual simply for the cameras. He squeezed Annie's hand as they strolled up the steps trying to look relaxed.

"Do you feel confident, Mr. Davenport?" asked a local newscaster, thrusting a microphone into his face.

"No," said Fletcher honestly. "Nervous as hell."

"Do you think you've beaten Mrs. Hunter?" tried the reporter again.

"I'll be happy to answer that question in a couple of hours' time."

"Do you believe it's been a clean fight?"

"You'd be a better judge of that than me," said Fletcher as he and Annie reached the top step and walked into the building.

As they entered the hall, there was a ripple of applause from some of those seated in the gallery. Fletcher glanced up, smiled and waved, trying to look confident, even though he didn't feel it. When he glanced back down, the first face he saw was Harry's. He looked pensive.

How different City Hall felt from the day of the debate. All the chairs had been replaced by a horseshoe of long tables. In the center stood Mr. Cooke, who had presided over seven previous elections. This would be his last, as he was due to retire at the end of the year.

One of his officials was checking the black boxes, which were lined up on the floor inside the horseshoe. Mr. Cooke had made it clear during the briefing he had given both candidates the previous day that the count would not begin until all forty-eight ballot boxes had arrived from their polling stations and had been authenticated. As the poll closed at 8 P.M. this procedure usually took about an hour.

A second ripple of applause broke out, and Fletcher glanced around to see Barbara Hunter enter the room, also displaying a smile of confidence as she waved to her supporters in the gallery.

Once all forty-eight boxes had been checked, their seals were broken by the officials and the votes emptied onto the tables ready for counting. Seated on either side of the horseshoe were the hundred or so counters. Each group consisted of one representative from the Republican party, one from the Democrats and a neutral observer standing a pace behind them. If an observer was unhappy about anything once the counting had begun, he or she would raise a hand and Mr. Cooke or one of his officials would go to that table immediately.

Once the votes had been emptied onto the tables, they were separated into three piles—a Republican pile, a Democratic pile and a third, smaller pile of disputed ballot papers. Most of the constituencies around the nation now carried out this entire process by machine, but not Hartford, although everyone knew that would change the moment Mr. Cooke retired.

Fletcher began walking around the room, watching as the different piles grew. Jimmy carried out the same exercise, but strolled in the opposite direction. Harry didn't move as he watched the boxes being unsealed, his eyes rarely straying from what was taking place inside the horseshoe. Once all the boxes had been emptied, Mr. Cooke asked his officials to count the votes and place them in piles of one hundred.

"This is where the observer becomes important," Harry explained as Fletcher came to a halt by his side. "He has to be sure that no ballot is counted twice, or two aren't stuck together." Fletcher nodded, and continued his perambulation, occasionally stopping to watch a particular count, one moment feeling confident, the next depressed, until Jimmy pointed out that the boxes came from different districts and he could never be sure which ones had come from a Republican stronghold and which from a Democratic area.

"What happens next?" asked Fletcher, aware that Jimmy was attending his fourth count.

"Arthur Cooke will add up all the ballots and announce how many people have voted, and calculate what percentage that is of the electorate." Fletcher glanced up at the clock—it was just after eleven, and in the background, he could see Jimmy Carter on the big screen, chatting to his brother Billy. The early polls suggested that the Democrats were returning to the White House for the first time in eight years. Would he be going to the Senate for the first time?

Fletcher turned his attention back to Mr. Cooke, who appeared to be in no hurry as he went about his official business. His pace did not reflect the heartbeat of either candidate. Once he had gathered up all the sheets, he went into a huddle with his officials, and transferred his findings onto a calculator, his only concession to the 1970s. This was followed by the pressing of buttons, nods and mutters, before two numbers were written neatly on a separate piece of paper. He then walked across the floor and up onto the stage at a stately pace. He tapped the microphone, which was enough to bring silence, as the crowd was impatient to hear his words.

"God damn it," said Harry, "it's been over an hour already. Why doesn't Arthur get on with it?"

"Calm down," said Martha, "and try to remember that you're no longer the candidate."

"The number of people who cast votes in the election for the Senate is 42,429, which is a turnout of 52.9%." Mr. Cooke left the stage without another word, and returned to the center of the horseshoe. His team then proceeded to check the piles of one hundreds, but it was another forty-two minutes before the chief executive climbed back onto the stage. This time he didn't need to tap the microphone. "I have to inform you," he said, "that there are seventy-seven disputed ballots, and I will now invite the two candidates to join me in the center of the room so that they can decide which ones should be considered valid."

Harry ran for the first time that day and grabbed Fletcher before he joined Mr. Cooke in the horseshoe. "That means that whichever one of you is in the lead, it must be by less than seventy-seven votes, otherwise Cooke wouldn't be bothering to go through this whole rigmarole of seeking your opinions." Fletcher nodded his agreement. "So you must select someone to check over those crucial votes for you."

"That's not a difficult choice," Fletcher replied, "I select you."

"I don't think so," said Harry, "because that will put Mrs. Hunter on her guard, and for this little exercise you'll need someone whom she won't feel threatened by."

303

"Then how about Jimmy?"

"Good idea, because she's bound to think that she can get the better of him."

"Not a hope," said Jimmy as he appeared by Fletcher's side.

"I may need you to," said Harry mysteriously.

"Why?" asked Jimmy.

"It's just a hunch," replied Harry, "no more, but once it comes to deciding those few precious votes, Mr. Cooke will be the man to watch, not Barbara Hunter."

"But he won't try anything with four of us standing over him," said Jimmy, "not to mention all those staring down from the gallery."

"And he wouldn't dream of doing so," said Harry. "He's one of the most punctilious officials I've ever dealt with, but he detests Mrs. Hunter."

"For any particular reason?" asked Fletcher.

"She's been on the phone to him every day since this campaign began, demanding statistics on everything from housing to hospitals, even legal opinions on planning permits, so my bet is he'll not relish the idea of her becoming a member of the Senate. He's got quite enough to be worrying about without the likes of Barbara Hunter taking up every spare moment of his time."

"But, as you said, there's nothing he can do."

"Nothing that's illegal," said Harry. "But should there be any disagreement over a vote, he will be asked to arbitrate, so whatever he recommends, just say 'Yes, Mr. Cooke,' even if you think at the time it favors Mrs. Hunter."

"I think I understand," said Fletcher.

"I'm damned if I do," said Jimmy.

◄◦►

Su Ling checked the dining-room table. When the front doorbell rang, she didn't bother to call up for Nat, because she knew he was rereading *The Cat in the Hat*. "Read it again, Dad," Luke always demanded when they reached the last page. Su Ling opened the door to find Tom clutching a bunch of parrot tulips. She gave him a big hug, as if nothing had happened since they last met.

"Will you marry me?" asked Tom.

"If you can cook, read *The Cat in the Hat*, answer the door and set the table all at the same time I'll give serious consideration to your proposal." Su Ling took the flowers. "Thank you, Tom," she said, giving him a kiss on the cheek. "They'll look beautiful on the dining table." Su Ling smiled, "I'm so sorry about Julia Kirkbridge, or whatever her real name was."

"Never mention that woman to me again," said Tom. "In future, our dinners will just be the three of us, a *ménage à trois;* sadly without the *ménage.*"

"Not tonight," said Su Ling. "Didn't Nat tell you? He's invited a business colleague to join us. I assumed you knew all about it and I, as usual, was the only person he informed at the last minute."

"He didn't mention anything about it to me," said Tom as the doorbell rang.

"I'll get it," said Nat, as he came bounding down the stairs.

"Now, promise me you won't talk shop all evening, because I want to hear all about your trip to London . . ."

"How nice to see you again," said Nat.

"It was just a short break," said Tom.

"Let me take your coat," said Nat.

"Yes, but did you manage to see any theater?"

". . . yes, I saw Judi . . ." began Tom as Nat ushered his guest into the living room.

"Let me first introduce you to my wife, Su Ling. Darling, this is Julia Kirkbridge, who, as I'm sure you know, is our partner in the Cedar Wood project."

"How nice to meet you, Mrs. Cartwright."

Su Ling recovered more quickly than Tom. "Please call me Su Ling."

"Thank you, and you must call me Julia."

"Julia, this is my chairman, Tom Russell, who I know has been looking forward to meeting you."

"Good evening, Mr. Russell. After all Nat has told me about you, I've been looking forward to meeting you too." Tom shook her hand, but couldn't think of anything to say.

"A glass of champagne, I think, to celebrate the signing of the contract."

"The contract?" mumbled Tom.

"What a nice idea," said Julia. Nat opened the bottle and poured three glasses, while Su Ling disappeared into the kitchen. Tom continued to stare at the second Mrs. Kirkbridge as Nat handed them both a glass of champagne.

"To the Cedar Wood project," said Nat, raising his glass.

Tom just managed to get out the words, "The Cedar Wood project."

Su Ling reappeared, smiled at her husband, and said, "Perhaps you'd like to bring our guests in for dinner?"

"Now, I think it's only fair, Julia, that I should explain to my wife and Tom that you and I have no secrets."

Julia smiled. "None that I can think of, Nat, especially after signing a confidentiality agreement concerning the details of the Cedar Wood transaction."

"Yes, and I think it should stay that way," said Nat, smiling across at her, as Su Ling placed the first course on the table.

"Mrs. Kirkbridge," said Tom, not touching his lobster bisque.

"Please call me Julia; after all we have known each other for some time."

"Have we?" said Tom, "I don't . . ."

"That's not very flattering, Tom," said Mrs. Kirkbridge, "after all, it was only a few weeks ago, when I was out jogging that you invited me for a drink and then to dinner at the Cascade the following evening. That's when I first told you about my interest in the Cedar Wood project."

Tom turned to Nat. "This is all very clever, but you seem to have forgotten that Mr. Cooke, the auctioneer, and our chief teller, have all come into contact with the original Mrs. Kirkbridge."

"The first Mrs. Kirkbridge, yes, but not the original," said Nat. "And I have already given that problem some considerable thought. There is no reason why Mr. Cooke should ever meet Julia, as he retires in a few months' time. As for the auctioneer, it was you who did the bidding, not Julia, and you needn't worry about Ray because I'm going to move him to the Newington branch.

"But what about the New York end?" said Tom.

"They know nothing," said Julia, "other than that I have closed a very advantageous deal." She paused. "This is lovely lobster bisque, Su Ling. It's always been my favorite."

"Thank you," said Su Ling as she cleared away the soup bowls and returned to the kitchen.

"And, Tom, can I just say while Su Ling is out of the room, that I would prefer to forget any other little indiscretions that are rumored to have taken place during the past month."

"You bastard," said Tom, turning to face Nat.

"No, to be fair," said Julia, "I did insist on being told everything before I signed the confidentiality agreement."

Su Ling returned carrying a serving dish. The smell of roast lamb was tantalizing. "I've now worked out why Nat asked me to serve exactly the same meal a second time, but I'm bound to ask, how much more do I need to know if I'm to keep up this charade?"

"What would you like to know?" asked Julia.

"Well, I've worked out that you're the real McCoy, and there- fore must be the majority shareholder of the Kirkbridge company, but what I'm not sure about is, did you at your husband's request jog over building sites on a Sunday morning and then report back to him?"

Julia laughed. "No, my husband didn't expect me to do that, as I already have an architecture degree."

"And may I ask," continued Su Ling, "did Mr. Kirkbridge die of cancer and then leave the company to you, having taught you everything he knew?"

"No, he's very much alive, but I divorced him two years ago, when I discovered he was siphoning off the company's profits for his personal use."

"But wasn't it his company?" asked Tom.

"Yes, and I wouldn't have minded so much if he hadn't been lavishing those profits on another woman."

"Would that woman by any chance be around five foot eight, blond, like expensive clothes, and claim to hail from Minnesota?"

"You've obviously met her," said Julia, "and I expect it was also my ex-husband who called you from a bank in San Francisco claiming to be Mrs. Kirkbridge's lawyer."

"You've no idea where the two of them are at the moment, by any chance?" asked Tom. "Because I'd like to kill them."

"Absolutely no idea," said Julia, "but should you find out, please let me know. Then you can kill her and I can kill him."

"Anyone for *crème brûlée?*" asked Su Ling.

"How did the other Mrs. Kirkbridge answer that question?" inquired Julia.

—◦—

Members of the public were leaning over the balcony observing every move, and Mr. Cooke seemed to want everyone in the hall to witness what was going on. Fletcher and Jimmy left the senator to join Mrs. Hunter and her representative inside the horseshoe.

"There are," said Mr. Cooke, addressing both candidates, "seventy-seven disputed ballot papers, of which I believe forty-three are invalid, however there remain difficulties over the other thirty-four." Both candidates nodded. "First I am going to show you the forty-three," said the returning officer, placing his hand on the larger of the two piles, "which I consider to be invalid. If you agree, I shall then go through the remaining thirty-four that are still in dispute," his hand transferring across to the smaller pile. Both candidates nodded again. "Just say no if you disagree," said Mr. Cooke, as he began to turn over the ballot papers in the larger pile, only to reveal that no vote had been registered on any of them. As neither candidate put up any objection, he completed this part of the exercise in under two minutes.

"Excellent," said Mr. Cooke, pushing those ballot papers to one side, "but now we must consider the crucial thirty-four." Fletcher noted the word crucial, and realized just how close the final result must be. "In the past," continued Mr. Cooke, "if both parties were unable to agree, then the final decision would be left to a third party." He paused.

"If there is any dispute," said Fletcher, "I am quite happy to abide by your decision, Mr. Cooke."

Mrs. Hunter didn't immediately respond and began whispering to her aide. Everyone waited patiently for her response. "I am also happy that Mr. Cooke should act as the arbitrator," she finally conceded.

Mr. Cooke gave a slight bow. "Of the thirty-four votes in the disputed pile," he said, "eleven I believe can quickly be dealt with, as they are what I would call, for lack of a better description, the Harry Gates supporters." He then laid out on the table eleven votes that had "Harry Gates" written across the ballot paper. Fletcher and Mrs. Hunter studied them one by one.

"They are obviously invalid," said Mrs. Hunter.

"However, two of them," continued Mr. Cooke, "also have a cross against Mr. Davenport's name."

"They must still be invalid," said Mrs. Hunter, "because as you can see, Mr. Gates's name is clearly written across the paper, making them invalid ballots."

"But . . ." began Jimmy.

"As there is obviously some disagreement on these two ballots," said Fletcher, "I'm happy to allow Mr. Cooke to decide."

Mr. Cooke looked toward Mrs. Hunter and she nodded reluctantly. "I concur that the one with 'Mr. Gates should be president' written across it is indeed invalid." Mrs. Hunter smiled. "However, the one that has a cross by Mr. Davenport's name with the added comment, 'but I'd prefer Mr. Gates,' is in my view under election law, a clear indication of the voter's intention, and I therefore deem it to be a vote for Mr. Davenport." Mrs. Hunter looked annoyed but, aware of the crowd peering down from the gallery, managed a weak smile. "Now we can turn to the seven votes where Mrs. Hunter's name appears on the ballot."

"Surely they must all be mine," said Mrs. Hunter as Mr. Cooke laid them out neatly in a row so that the two candidates could consider them.

"No, I don't think so," said Mr. Cooke.

The first had written on it, "Hunter is the winner," with a cross against Hunter.

"That person clearly voted for Mrs. Hunter," said Fletcher.

"I agree," said Mr. Cooke as a ripple of applause emanated from the gallery.

"That boy's honesty will be the death of him," said Harry.

"Or the making of him," said Martha.

"Hunter would be a dictator," was written across the next with no cross against either name. "I believe that to be invalid," said Mr. Cooke. Mrs. Hunter reluctantly nodded.

"Despite being accurate," said Jimmy under his breath.

"Hunter is a bitch," "Hunter should be shot," "Hunter is mad," "Hunter is a loser," "Hunter for pope" were also declared invalid. Mrs. Hunter did not bother to suggest that any of these wanted her to be Hartford's next senator.

"Now we come to the final group of sixteen," said Mr. Cooke. "Here the voter did not use a cross to indicate his or her preference." The sixteen votes had been placed in a separate pile, and the top one had a tick in the box opposite the name "Hunter."

"That is clearly a vote for me," insisted the Republican candidate.

"I have a tendency to agree with you," said Mr. Cooke. "The voter appears to have made his wishes quite clear; however I will need Mr. Davenport to accept that judgment before I can proceed."

Fletcher looked outside the horseshoe and caught Harry's eye. He gave a slight nod. "I agree that it is clearly a vote for Mrs. Hunter," he said. Applause once again broke out in the gallery from the pro-Hunter supporters. Mr. Cooke removed the top ballot paper to reveal that the one underneath also had a tick in the box opposite "Hunter."

"Now that we've agreed on the principle," said Mrs. Hunter, "that must also count as my vote."

"I have no quarrel with that," said Fletcher.

"Then those two votes go to Mrs. Hunter," said Mr. Cooke, who removed the second voting slip to reveal a tick by Fletcher's name on the one underneath. Both candidates nodded.

"Two–one in favor of Hunter," said Mr. Cooke before he removed that vote, to show the next had a tick in the "Hunter" box.

"Three–one," she said, unable to hide a smirk.

Fletcher began to wonder if Harry might have miscalculated. Mr. Cooke removed the next ballot paper to reveal a tick by Fletcher's name.

"Three–two," Jimmy said as the chief executive began to remove the votes from the pile more quickly. As each one showed a clear tick, neither candidate was able to object. The crowd in the gallery began to chant—three–all, four–three—in Fletcher's favor—five–three, six–three, seven–three, eight–three, eight–four, nine–four, ten–four, eleven–four, ending on twelve–four in Fletcher's favor.

Mrs. Hunter couldn't hide her anger as Mr. Cooke, looking up at the gallery, proclaimed, "And that completes the checking of invalid ballot papers, making an overall position of fourteen for Mr. Davenport and six for Mrs. Hunter." He then turned back to the candidates and said, "May I thank you both for your magnanimous approach to the whole proceedings."

Harry allowed himself a smile as he joined in the renewed applause that followed Mr. Cooke's statement. Fletcher quickly left the horseshoe and rejoined his father-in-law on the outside.

"If you win by fewer than eight votes, my boy, we'll know whom to thank, because now there's nothing Mrs. Hunter can do about it."

"How long before we find out the result?" asked Fletcher.

"The vote? Only a few minutes," said Harry, "but the result, I suspect, won't be sorted out for several hours."

Mr. Cooke studied the figures on his calculator, and then transferred them to a slip of paper, which all four of his officials dutifully signed. He returned to the stage for a third time. "Both sides having agreed on the disputed ballots, I can now inform you that the result of the election to the Senate for Hartford County is: Mr. Fletcher Davenport 21,218, Mrs. Barbara Hunter, 21,211." Harry smiled.

Mr. Cooke made no attempt to speak during the uproar that followed, but once he had regained the attention of the floor, he announced, "There will be a recount," even before Mrs. Hunter could demand one.

Harry and Jimmy circled the room, uttering only one word to each of their observers. Concentrate. Fifty minutes later, it was found that three of the piles only had ninety-nine votes, while another four had one hundred and one. Mr. Cooke checked all seven offending piles for a third time, before returning to the stage.

"I declare the result of the election to the Senate for Hartford

County to be as follows: Mr. Davenport 21,217, Mrs. Hunter 21,213."

Mr. Cooke had to wait for some time before he could be heard above the noise. "Mrs. Hunter has once again called for a recount." This time some boos mingled with the cheers, as the gallery settled down to watch the counters begin the entire process again. Mr. Cooke was punctilious in making sure that each pile was checked and double-checked, and if there was any doubt he went over it again himself. He didn't walk back onto the stage until a few minutes after one in the morning, when he asked both candidates to join him.

He tapped the microphone to be sure it was still working. "I declare the result of the election to the Senate for Hartford County, to be Mr. Fletcher Davenport 21,216, Mrs. Barbara Hunter 21,214." The cheers and boos were even louder this time, and it was several minutes before order could be restored. Mrs. Hunter leaned forward and suggested to Mr. Cooke in a stage whisper that as it was past one, the council workers should be allowed to go home, and a further recount should take place in the morning.

He listened politely to her protestations, before returning to the microphone. However, he had clearly anticipated every eventuality. "I have with me," he said, "the official election handbook." He held it up for all to see as a priest might the Bible. "And I refer to a ruling on page ninety-one. I will read out the relevant passage." The hall fell silent as they waited for Mr. Cooke's deliberations. "In an election for the Senate, if any one candidate should win the count three times in a row, by however small a majority, he or she will be declared the winner. I therefore declare Mr. . . . ." But the rest of his words were drowned by Fletcher's cheering supporters.

Harry Gates turned around and shook Fletcher by the hand. He could hardly make out the former senator's words above the uproar.

Fletcher thought he heard Harry say, "May I be the first to congratulate you, Senator."

BOOK FOUR

ACTS

36

NAT WAS ON the train back from New York when he read the short piece in the *New York Times*. He had attended a board meeting of Kirkbridge & Co., where he was able to report that the first stage of building on the Cedar Wood site had been completed. The next phase was to lease the seventy-three shops, which ranged in size from a thousand to twelve thousand square feet. Many of the successful retailers currently on the Robinson's site had already shown an interest, and Kirkbridge & Co. were preparing a brochure and application form for several hundred potential customers. Nat had also booked a full-page ad in the *Hartford Courant* and agreed to be interviewed about the project for the weekly property section.

Mr. George Turner, the council's new chief executive, had nothing but praise for the enterprise, and in his annual report, singled out Mrs. Kirkbridge's contribution as project coordinator. Earlier in the year, Mr. Turner had visited Russell's Bank, but not before Ray Jackson had been promoted to manager of their Newington branch.

Tom's progress was somewhat slower as it had taken him seven months before he plucked up the courage to invite Julia out for dinner. It took her seven seconds to accept.

Within weeks Tom was on the 4:49 P.M. train to New York every Friday afternoon, returning to Hartford on Monday morning. Su Ling kept asking for progress reports, but Nat seemed unusually ill-informed.

"Perhaps we'll find out more on Friday," he said, reminding her that Julia was down for the weekend, and they had both accepted an invitation to join them for dinner.

Nat reread the short piece in the *New York Times,* which didn't go into any detail, and left the impression that there was a lot more behind the story. *William Alexander of Alexander Dupont & Bell, has announced his resignation as senior partner of the firm founded by his grandfather. Mr. Alexander's only comment was that for some time he had been planning to take early retirement.*

Nat looked out of the window at the Hartford countryside speeding by. He recognized the name, but couldn't place it.

—◦—

"Mr. Logan Fitzgerald is on line one, Senator."

"Thank you, Sally." Fletcher received over a hundred calls a day, but his secretary only put them through when she knew they were old friends or urgent business.

"Logan, how good to hear from you. How are you?"

"I'm well, Fletcher, and you?"

"Never better," Fletcher replied.

"And the family?" asked Logan.

"Annie still loves me, heaven knows why, because I rarely leave the building before ten, Lucy is at Hartford Elementary and we've put her down for Hotchkiss. And you?".

"I've just made partner," said Logan.

"That's no surprise," said Fletcher, "but many congratulations."

"Thanks, but that wasn't why I was calling. I wanted to check if you'd spotted the piece about Bill Alexander's resignation in the *Times.*" Fletcher felt a chill go through his body at the mere mention of the name.

"No," he said, as he leaned across the desk and grabbed his copy of the paper. "Which page?"

"Seven, bottom right."

Fletcher quickly flicked through the pages until he saw the headline, *Leading lawyer resigns.* "Hold on while I just read the piece." When he'd come to the end, all he said was, "It doesn't add up. He was married to that firm, and he can't be a day over sixty."

"Fifty-seven," said Logan.

"But the partners' mandatory retirement age is sixty-five, and even then they keep you on as an in-house advisor until you're seventy. It doesn't add up." Fletcher repeated.

"Until you dig a little."

"And when you dig a little, what do you find?" asked Fletcher.

"A hole."

"A hole?"

"Yes, it seems that a large sum of money went missing from a client's account when . . ."

"I have no time for Bill Alexander," Fletcher cut in, "but I do not believe that he would remove one penny from a client's account. In fact I'd stake my reputation on it."

"I agree with you, but what will interest you more is that the *New York Times* didn't bother to report the name of the other partner who resigned on the same day."

"I'm listening."

"Ralph Elliot, no less."

"They both went on the same day?"

"They sure did."

"And what reason did Elliot give for resigning? It certainly can't have been because he was planning to take early retirement."

"Elliot gave no reason; in fact their PR spokeswoman is reported to have said that he was unavailable for comment, which must be a first."

"Did she add anything?" asked Fletcher.

"Only that he was a junior partner, but she failed to point out that he was also Alexander's nephew."

"So a large sum of money goes missing from a client's account, and Uncle Bill decided to take the rap rather than embarrass the firm."

"That sounds about right," said Logan.

Fletcher could feel the sweat on the palms of his hands as he put the phone down.

—◇—

Tom burst into Nat's office. "Did you spot the piece in the *New York Times* about Bill Alexander's resignation?"

"Yes, I recalled the name, but couldn't remember why."

"It was the law firm Ralph Elliot joined after he left Stanford."

"Ah yes," said Nat, putting down his pen, "so is he the new senior partner?"

"No, but he *is* the other partner who resigned. Joe Stein tells me that half a million has gone missing from a client account, and the partners had to cover the sum out of their own earnings. The name on the street is Ralph Elliot."

"But why would the senior partner have to resign if Elliot's name is in the frame?"

"Because Elliot's his nephew, and Alexander pushed for him to be the youngest partner in the firm's history."

"Sit still and revenge will visit thine enemies."

"No, I don't think so," said Tom, "but it might revisit Hartford."

"What do you mean?" asked Nat.

"He's telling everyone that Rebecca is missing her friends, so he's bringing his wife back home."

"His wife?"

"Yeah. Joe says they were married at City Hall quite recently, but not before she also resembled a big apple."

"I wonder who the father is," said Nat almost to himself.

"And he's opened an account at our Newington branch, obviously unaware that you're the bank's chief executive."

"Elliot knows only too well who the bank's chief executive is. Just let's be sure he doesn't deposit half a million," Nat added with a smile.

"Joe says there's no proof, and what's more, Alexander's has a reputation for being tight-lipped, so don't expect to hear anything more from that quarter."

Nat looked up at Tom. "Elliot wouldn't come home unless he had a job to go to. He's too proud for that. But just who's been foolhardy enough to employ him?"

—◇—

The senator picked up line one. "Mr. Gates," said his secretary.

"Business or pleasure?" Fletcher asked when Jimmy came on the line.

"Certainly not pleasure," replied Jimmy. "Have you heard Ralph Elliot is back in town?"

"No. Logan rang this morning to tell me that he'd resigned

from AD and B but he didn't say anything about him returning to Hartford."

"Yeah, he's joining Belman and Wayland as the partner in charge of corporate business. In fact, part of his agreement is that the firm will in the future be known as Belman Wayland and Elliot." Fletcher didn't comment. "Are you still there?" asked Jimmy.

"Yes, I am," said Fletcher. "You do realize they're the law firm that represents the council?"

"As well as being our biggest rival."

"And I thought I'd seen the last of him."

"You could always move to Alaska," said Jimmy, "I read somewhere that they're looking for a new senator."

"If I did, he'd only follow me."

"There's no need for us to lose any sleep over it," said Jimmy. "He'll assume we know about the missing five hundred thousand and realize he'll have to lie low until the rumors have died down."

"Ralph Elliot doesn't know the meaning of lying low. He'll ride into town with both guns blazing, with us lined up in his sights."

―◇―

"What else have you found out?" asked Nat, looking up from behind his desk.

"He and Rebecca already have a son and I'm told they've put him down for Taft."

"I hope to God he's younger than Luke, otherwise I'd send the boy to Hotchkiss."

Tom laughed. "I mean it," said Nat. "Luke's a sensitive enough child without having to cope with that."

"Well, there are also consequences for the bank of his joining Belman and Wayland."

"And Elliot," added Nat.

"Don't forget that they were the lawyers overseeing the Cedar Wood project on behalf of the council, and if he ever found out . . ."

"There's no reason he should," said Nat. "However, you'd better warn Julia, even though it's been a couple of years, and don't forget Ray has also moved on. Only four people know the full story, and I'm married to one of them."

"And I'm going to marry the other," said Tom.

"You're what?" said Nat in disbelief.

"I've been proposing to Julia for the past eighteen months, and last night she finally gave in. So I'll be bringing my fiancée for dinner tonight."

"That's wonderful news," said Nat, sounding delighted.

"And Nat, don't leave it until the last moment to tell Su Ling."

"It's just a shot across our bow," said Harry in reply to Fletcher's question.

"It's a bloody cannon," responded Fletcher. "Ralph Elliot doesn't deal in shots, so we'll need to find out what the hell he's up to."

"I've no idea," said Harry. "All I can tell you is that I had a call from George Turner to alert me that Elliot had asked for all the papers that the bank has ever been involved with, and yesterday morning he called again asking for more details on the Cedar Wood project, and in particular the original terms of agreement that I recommended to the Senate."

"Why the Cedar Wood project? That's proving to be a huge success story, with a rush of applications to lease space. Just what is he up to?"

"He's also asked to see copies of all my speeches, and any notes I'd made at the time of the Gates Amendment. No one has ever asked me for copies of my old speeches before, let alone my notes," said Harry. "It's very flattering."

"'He only flatters to deceive,'" said Fletcher. "Remind me of the finer points of the Gates Amendment?"

"I insisted that any purchaser of council land valued at over one million dollars be named and not be able to hide his or her identity behind the offices of a bank or a law firm so we'd know exactly who we were dealing with. They were also required to pay the full amount on the signing of any contract to prove they were a viable company. That way there would be no holdups."

"But everyone now accepts that as good practice. In fact, several other states have followed your lead."

"It could just be an innocent inquiry."

"You've obviously never dealt with Ralph Elliot before," said Fletcher. "Innocent is not part of his vocabulary. However, in the past he has always selected his enemies carefully. Once he's driven past the Gates Library a few times, he may decide you're not someone to cross. But be warned, he's up to something."

"By the way," said Harry, "has anyone told you about Jimmy and Joanna?"

"No," said Fletcher.

"Then I'll keep my mouth shut. I'm sure Jimmy will want to tell you in his own time."

―◦►

"Congratulations, Tom," said Su Ling, as she opened the front door. "I'm so pleased for both of you."

"That's kind of you," said Julia, as Tom handed his hostess a bunch of flowers.

"So when are you going to get married?"

"Sometime in August," said Tom, "we haven't settled on a date, in case you and Luke were booked for another trip to Disneyland, or Nat was off for a spell of night ops with the reserves."

"No, Disneyland is a thing of the past," said Su Ling, "Can you believe Luke's now talking about Rome, Venice and even Arles— and Nat's not due down at Fort Benning until October."

"Why Arles?" asked Tom.

"It's where Van Gogh ended his days," said Julia as Nat walked into the room.

"Julia, I'm glad you're here, because Luke needs to consult you on a moral dilemma."

"A moral dilemma? I didn't think you started worrying about those until after puberty."

"No, this is far more serious than sex, and I don't know the answer."

"So what's the question?"

"Is it possible to paint a masterpiece of Christ and the Virgin Mary if you are a murderer?"

"It's never seemed to worry the Catholic Church," said Julia. "Several of Caravaggio's finest works are hanging in the Vatican, but I'll go up and have a word with him."

"Caravaggio, of course. And don't stay up there too long," added Su Ling, "there are so many questions I want to ask you."

"I'm sure Tom can answer most of them," said Julia.

"No, I want to hear your version," said Su Ling as Julia disappeared upstairs.

"Have you warned Julia what Ralph Elliot is up to?" asked Nat.

"Yes," Tom replied, "and she can't foresee any problems. After all, why should it ever occur to Elliot that there were two Julia Kirkbridges. Don't forget, the first one was only with us for a few days and has never been seen or heard of since, whereas Julia has been around for a couple of years now, and everybody knows her."

"But it's not her signature on the original check."

"Why's that a problem?" asked Tom.

"Because when the bank cleared the $3.6 million, the council asked for the check to be returned to them."

"Then it will be tucked away in a file somewhere, and even if Elliot did come across it, why should he be suspicious?"

"Because he has the mind of a criminal. Neither of us thinks like him." Nat paused. "But to hell with that, let me ask you, before Julia and Su Ling return, am I looking for a new chairman, or has Julia agreed to settle in Hartford and wash dishes?"

"Neither," said Tom, "she's decided to accept a takeover bid from that fellow Trump, who's been after her company for some time."

"Did she get a good price?"

"I thought this was meant to be a relaxed evening to celebrate . . . ?"

"Did she get a good price?" repeated Nat.

"Fifteen million in cash, and a further fifteen million in Trump shares."

"That's a PE ratio of about sixteen. Not bad," said Nat, "although Trump obviously believes in the potential of the Cedar Wood project. So does she plan to open a real estate company in Hartford?"

"No, I think she ought to tell you what she has in mind," said Tom as Su Ling returned from the kitchen.

"Why don't we invite Julia to join the board?" asked Nat, "and put her in charge of our property division. That would free me up to spend more time concentrating on the banking side."

"I think you'll find she considered that scenario at least six months ago," said Tom.

"Did you by any chance offer her a directorship if she agreed to marry you?" asked Nat.

"Yes, I did originally, and she turned both down. But now I've convinced her to marry me, I'll leave it to you to persuade her to join the board because I have a feeling she has other plans."

37

FLETCHER WAS ON the floor of the chamber listening to a speech on subsidized housing when the proceedings were interrupted. He'd been checking through his notes, as he was due to speak next. A uniformed officer entered the chamber and passed a slip of paper to the presiding member, who read it, and then read it again, banged his gavel and rose from his place. "I apologize to my colleague for interrupting proceedings, but a gunman is holding a group of children hostage at Hartford Elementary. I am sure Senator Davenport will need to leave, and, given the circumstances, I believe it would be appropriate to adjourn for the day."

Fletcher was on his feet immediately and had reached the door of the chamber even before the presiding member had closed the proceedings. He ran all the way to his office, trying to think on the move. The school was in the middle of his district, Lucy was a pupil and Annie was head of the PTA. He prayed that Lucy wasn't among the hostages. The whole of the State House seemed to be on the move. Fletcher was relieved to find Sally standing by the door to his office, notebook in hand. "Cancel all of today's appointments, call my wife and ask her to join me at the school, and please stay by the phone."

Fletcher grabbed his car keys and joined the flood of people hurrying out of the building. As he drove out of the members' parking lot, a police car shot in front of him. Fletcher pressed his foot down hard on the accelerator and swung into the police car's slipstream as they headed toward the school. The line of cars became longer and longer, with parents making their way to pick up their offspring, some looking frantic after hearing the news on their car radios, others still blissfully unaware.

Fletcher kept his foot on the accelerator, staying only a few feet away from the rear bumper in front of him, as the police car shot down the wrong side of the road, lights blinking, sirens blaring. The policeman in the passenger seat used his loudspeaker to warn the pursuing vehicle to drop back, but Fletcher ignored the ultimatum, knowing they wouldn't stop. Seven minutes later both came to a screeching halt at a police barrier outside the school, where a group of hysterical parents was trying to find out what was going on. The policeman in the passenger seat leaped out of his car and ran toward Fletcher as he slammed his door closed. The officer drew his pistol and shouted, "Put your hands on the roof." The driver, who was only a yard behind his colleague, said, "Sorry, Senator, we didn't realize it was you."

Fletcher ran to the barrier. "Where will I find the chief?"

"He's set up headquarters in the principal's office. I'll get someone to take you there, Senator."

"No need," said Fletcher, "I know my way."

"Senator . . ." said the policeman, but it was too late.

Fletcher ran down the path toward the school, unaware that the building was surrounded by military guards, their rifles all aimed in one direction. It surprised him to see how quickly the public stood to one side the moment they saw him. A strange way to be reminded that he was their representative.

"Who the hell's that?" asked the chief of police as a lone figure came running across the yard toward them.

"I think you'll find it's Senator Davenport," said Alan Shepherd, the school's principal, looking through the window.

"That's all I need," said Don Culver. A moment later Fletcher came charging into the room. The chief looked up from behind the desk, trying to hide his "that's all I need" look, as the senator came to a halt in front of him.

"Good afternoon, Senator."

"Good afternoon, chief," Fletcher replied, slightly out of breath. Despite the wary look, he rather admired the paunchy, cigar-smoking chief of police, who wasn't known for running his force by the book.

Fletcher gave a nod to Alan Shepherd, and then turned his attention back to the chief. "Can you bring me up to speed?" he asked as he caught his breath.

"We've got a lone gunman out there. It looks as if he strolled up the main path in broad daylight a few minutes before school was due to come out." The chief turned to a makeshift ground-floor plan taped to the wall, and pointed to a little square with ART ROOM printed across it. "There appears to be no rhyme or reason why he chose Miss Hudson's class, other than it was the first door he came to."

"How many children in there?" Fletcher asked, turning his attention back to the principal.

"Thirty-one," replied Alan Shepherd, "and Lucy isn't one of them."

Fletcher tried not to show his relief. "And the gunman, do we know anything about him?"

"Not a lot," said the chief, "but we're finding out more by the minute. His name is Billy Bates. We're told his wife left him about a month ago, soon after he lost his job as the night watchman at Pearl's. Seems he was caught drinking on duty once too often. He's been thrown out of several bars during the past few weeks, and, according to our records, even ended up spending a night in one of our cells."

"Good afternoon, Mrs. Davenport," said the principal, rising from his place.

Fletcher turned to see his wife, "Lucy wasn't in Miss Hudson's class," were his first words.

"I know," said Annie, "she was with me. When I got your message, I dropped her off with Martha and came straight over."

"Do you know Miss Hudson?" asked the chief.

"I'm sure Alan has told you that everyone knows Mary, she's an institution. I think she's the longest-serving member of staff." The principal nodded. "I doubt if there's a family in Hartford who doesn't know someone who's been taught by her."

"Can you give me a profile?" asked the chief, turning to face Alan Shepherd.

"In her fifties, single, calm, firm and well respected."

"And something you left out," added Annie, "much loved."

"What do you think she'd be like under pressure?"

"Who knows how anyone would react under this sort of pressure," said Shepherd, "but I've no doubt she'd give up her life for those children."

"That's what I feared you'd say," said the chief, "and it's my job to make sure she doesn't have to." His cigar was no longer glowing. "I've got over a hundred men surrounding the main block and a sniper on top of the adjacent building who says he occasionally gets a sighting of Bates."

"Presumably you're trying to negotiate?" said Fletcher.

"Yes, there's a phone in the room which we've been calling every few minutes, but Bates refuses to pick it up. We've set up a loudspeaker system, but he's not responding to that either."

"Have you thought of sending someone in?" asked Fletcher as the phone on the principal's desk rang. The chief pressed the intercom button.

"Who's this?" Culver barked.

"It's Senator Davenport's secretary, I was hoping . . ."

"Yes, Sally," said Fletcher, "what is it?"

"I've just seen a report on the news that says the gunman is called Billy Bates. The name sounded familiar, and it turns out that we have a file on him—he's been to see you twice."

"Anything helpful in his case notes?"

"He came to lobby you on gun control. He feels very strongly on the subject. In your notes you've written 'restrictions not tough enough, locks on triggers, sale of firearms to minors, proof of identification.'"

"I remember him," said Fletcher, "intelligent, full of ideas but no formal education. Well done, Sally."

"Are you sure he isn't just crazy?" asked the chief.

"Far from it," said Fletcher. "He's thoughtful, shy, even timid, and his biggest complaint was that no one ever listened to him.

Sometimes that sort of person feels they have to prove a point when every other approach has failed. And his wife leaving him and taking the children, just when he's lost his job, may have tipped the balance."

"Then I've got to take him out," said the chief, "just like they did with that guy in Tennessee who locked up all those officials in the revenue office."

"No, that's not a parallel case," insisted Fletcher, "that man had a record as a psychopath. Billy Bates is a lonely man who's seeking attention, the type that regularly comes to see me."

"Well, he's sure grabbed my attention, Senator," responded the chief.

"Which could be precisely why he's gone to such extremes," said Fletcher. "Why don't you let me try and speak to him?"

The chief removed his cigar for the first time; junior officers would have warned Fletcher that meant he was thinking.

"OK, but all I want you to do is to get him to pick up the phone, then I'll take over any negotiations. Is that understood?" Fletcher nodded his agreement. The chief turned to his number two and added, "Dale, tell them that the senator and I are going out there, so hold their fire." The chief grabbed the megaphone and said, "Let's do it, Senator."

As they started walking down the corridor, the chief added firmly, "You're only to step a couple of paces outside the front door, and don't forget your message needs to be simple, because all I want him to do is pick up the phone."

Fletcher nodded as the chief opened the door for him. He took a few steps before he came to a halt and held up the megaphone. "Billy, this is Senator Davenport, you've been to see me a couple of times. We need to speak to you. Could you please pick up the phone on Miss Hudson's desk?"

"Keep repeating the message," barked the chief.

"Billy, this is Senator Davenport, would you please pick up . . ."

A young officer came running toward the open door, "He's picked up the phone, Chief, but he says he'll only speak to the senator."

"I'll decide who he talks to," said Culver. "No one dictates to me." He disappeared through the door and almost ran back to the principal's study.

"This is Chief Culver. Now listen, Bates, if you imagine . . ." The phone went dead. "Damn," said the chief as Fletcher walked back into the room. "He hung up on me, we're going to have to try again."

"Perhaps he meant it when he said he would only speak to me."

The chief removed his cigar again. "OK, but the moment you've calmed him down, you pass the phone over."

Once they'd returned to the playground Fletcher spoke over the megaphone again. "Sorry, Billy, can you call again, and this time I'll be on the other end of the line?" Fletcher accompanied Don Culver back to the principal's study to find Billy already on the speaker-phone.

"The senator's just walked back into the room," the principal assured him.

"I'm right here, Billy, it's Fletcher Davenport."

"Senator, before you say anything, I'm not budging while the chief has all those rifles trained on me. Tell them to back off if he doesn't want a death on his hands."

Fletcher looked at Culver, who removed his cigar once again before nodding.

"The chief's agreed to that," said Fletcher.

"I'll call you back when I can't see one of them."

"Right," said the chief, "tell everyone to back off, except for the marksman on the north tower. There's no way Bates could spot him."

"So what happens next?" asked Fletcher.

"We wait for the bastard to call back."

—◆—

Nat was answering a question on voluntary redundancies when his secretary came rushing into the boardroom. They all realized that it had to be urgent as Linda had never interrupted a board meeting before. Nat immediately stopped speaking when he saw the anxious look on her face.

"There's a gunman at Hartford Elementary . . ." Nat went cold, ". . . and he's holding Miss Hudson's class hostage."

"Is Luke . . ."

"Yes he is," she replied. "Luke's last lesson on a Friday is always Miss Hudson's art class."

Nat rose unsteadily from his chair and walked toward the door. The rest of the board remained silent. "Mrs. Cartwright is already on her way to the school," Linda added as Nat left the room. "She said to tell you she'll meet you there."

Nat nodded as he pushed open a door that led into the underground parking garage. "Stay by the phone," was the last thing he said to Linda as he climbed into his car. When he nosed up the ramp and out onto Main Street, he hesitated for a moment before turning left instead of his usual right.

The phone rang. The chief touched the speaker and pointed to Fletcher.

"Are you there, Senator?"

"Sure am, Billy."

"Tell the chief to allow the TV crews and press inside the barrier; that way I'll feel safer."

"Hey, wait a minute," began the chief.

"No, you wait a minute," shouted Billy. "Or you'll have your first body in the playground. Try explaining to the press that it only happened because you didn't let them inside the barrier." The phone went dead.

"You'd better go along with his request, Chief," said Fletcher, "because it looks like he's determined to be heard one way or the other."

"Let the press through," said Culver, nodding to one of his deputies. The sergeant quickly left the room, but it was several minutes before the phone rang again. Fletcher touched the console.

"I'm listening, Billy."

"Thank you, Mr. Davenport, you're a man of your word."

"So what do you want now?" barked the chief.

"Nothing from you, Chief, I prefer to go on dealing with the senator. Mr. Davenport, I need you to come across and join me; that's the only way I have a chance of getting my case heard."

"I can't allow that to happen," said the chief.

"I don't believe it's your call, Chief. It's up to the senator to decide, but I guess you'll have to sort that out among yourselves. I'll call back in two minutes." The phone went dead.

"I'm happy to agree to his demand," said Fletcher. "Frankly there doesn't seem to be a lot of choice."

"I don't have the authority to stop you," said the chief, "but maybe Mrs. Davenport can spell out the consequences."

"I don't want you to go in there," said Annie. "You always think the best of everyone, and bullets aren't that discriminating."

"I wonder how you'd feel if Lucy was one of the children trapped in there?"

Annie was about to reply when the phone rang again. "Are you on your way, Senator, or do you need a body to help you make up your mind?"

"No, no," said Fletcher, "I'm on my way." The phone went dead.

"Now listen carefully," said the chief, "I can cover you while you're in the open, but you're on your own once you're in that classroom." Fletcher nodded and then took Annie in his arms, holding her for several seconds.

The chief accompanied him along the corridor. "I'm going to phone the classroom every five minutes. If you get a chance to talk, I'll tell you everything that's happening on our end. Whenever I ask a question, just answer yes or no. Don't give Bates any clues as to what I'm trying to find out." Fletcher nodded. When they reached the door, the chief removed his cigar. "Let me take your jacket, Senator." Fletcher looked surprised. "If you're not concealing a gun, why give Bates any reason to believe you might be?" Fletcher smiled as Culver held the door open for him. "I didn't vote for you last time, Senator, but if you get out alive, I just might consider it next time. Sorry," he added, "just my warped sense of humor. Good luck."

Fletcher stepped out onto the playground and began to walk slowly down the path toward the main classroom building. He could no longer spot any of the sharpshooters, but he sensed that they weren't far away. Although he couldn't see the TV crews, he could hear their tense chatter as he stepped into the light of their massive arc lamps. The path that led to the classrooms couldn't have been more than a hundred yards. To Fletcher it felt like walking a mile-long tightrope in the blazing sun.

Once he'd reached the other side of the playground he climbed the four steps to the entrance. He entered a dark, empty corridor and waited until his eyes became accustomed to the gloom. When he reached a door stenciled with the words MISS HUDSON in ten different colors, he knocked quietly. The door was immediately yanked open. Fletcher stepped inside to hear the door slam behind him. When he heard the muffled sobbing, Fletcher glanced across to see a group of children huddled on the floor in one corner.

"Sit there," commanded Bates, who looked as nervous as Fletcher felt. Fletcher squeezed into a desk built for a nine-year-old on the end of the front row. He looked up at the disheveled man, whose ill-fitting jeans were torn and dirty. A paunch hung over his waistline, despite the fact that he couldn't have been more than forty. He watched carefully as Bates crossed the room and stood behind Miss Hudson, who remained seated at her table in the front of the class. Bates held the gun in his right hand, while placing his left arm on her shoulder.

"What's happening out there?" he shouted, "what's the chief up to?"

"He's waiting to hear from me," said Fletcher in a quiet voice. "He's going to phone in every five minutes. He's worried about the children. You've managed to convince everyone out there you're a killer."

"I'm no killer," said Bates. "You know that."

"Perhaps I do," said Fletcher, "but they might be more convinced if you were to release the children."

"If I do that, then I won't have anything to bargain with."

"You'll have me," said Fletcher. "Kill a child, Billy, and everyone will remember you for the rest of their lives; kill a senator, and they'll have forgotten by tomorrow."

"Whatever I do, I'm a dead man."

"Not if we were to face the cameras together."

"But what would we tell them?"

"That you've already been to see me twice, and you'd put forward some sensible and imaginative ideas on gun control but no one took any notice. Well, now they're going to have to sit up and listen, because you're going to be given the chance to speak to Sandra Mitchell on prime-time news."

"Sandra Mitchell? Is she out there?"

"Sure is," replied Fletcher, "and she's desperate to interview you."

"Do you think she'd be interested in me, Mr. Davenport?"

"She hasn't come all this way to talk to anyone else," said Fletcher.

"Will you stay with me?" asked Bates.

"You bet, Billy. You know exactly where I stand on gun control. When we last met you told me you had read all of my speeches on the subject."

"Yes I have, but what good did that do?" asked Billy. He took his arm off Mary Hudson's shoulder and began walking slowly toward Fletcher, the gun pointed directly at him. "The truth is that you're only repeating exactly what the chief has told you to say."

Fletcher gripped the sides of the desk, never taking his eyes off Billy. If he was going to risk it, he knew he needed to draw Billy in as close as possible. He leaned forward slightly while still holding firmly to the lid of the desk. The phone by Miss Hudson began ringing. Billy was now only a pace away, but the ringing sound caused him to turn his head for a split second. This gave Fletcher the chance to jerk the lid of the desk up in a sudden movement, crashing it into Billy's right hand. Billy momentarily lost his balance, and as he stumbled, he dropped the gun. They both watched it hurtle across the floor, coming to a halt just a few feet away from Miss Hudson. The children began to scream as she fell on her knees, grabbed the gun and pointed it straight at Billy.

Billy rose slowly and advanced toward her as she remained kneeling on the floor, the gun pointing at his chest. "You're not going to pull the trigger, are you, Miss Hudson?"

With each step Billy took toward her, Miss Hudson trembled more and more violently. Billy was only a foot away from her when she closed her eyes and pulled the trigger. There was a click. Billy looked up, smiled, and said, "No bullets, Miss Hudson. I never intended to kill anyone, I just wanted someone to listen for a change."

Fletcher slid out from behind the desk, ran to the door and yanked it open. "Out, out," he yelled, his right hand gesturing in a sweeping movement at the terrified children. A tall girl with long pigtails stood up and ran toward the open door and out into the corridor. Two more followed closely behind her. Fletcher thought he heard a piping voice say "Go, go," as he held the door open. All but one of the children came rushing toward him, disappearing out of sight within moments. Fletcher stared toward the corner at the one remaining child. The boy slowly rose from his place and walked to the front of the class. He leaned down, took Miss Hudson by the hand, and led her toward the door, never once looking at Billy. When he reached the open door, he said, "Thank you, Senator," and accompanied his teacher out into the corridor.

—◦—

A loud cheer went up as the tall girl with long black pigtails came charging through the front door. Searchlights beamed down on her and she quickly placed a hand over her eyes, unable to see the welcoming crowd. A mother broke through the cordon and ran across the playground to take the girl in her arms. Two boys followed closely behind, as Nat placed an arm around Su Ling's shoulder, desperately searching for Luke. A few moments later, a larger group came running out of the door, but Su Ling couldn't hold back the tears once she realized Luke was not among them.

"There's still one more to come," she heard a journalist reporting on the early evening news, "along with his teacher."

Su Ling's eyes never left the open door for what she later described as the longest two minutes of her life.

An even bigger cheer went up when Miss Hudson appeared in the doorway clutching Luke's hand. Su Ling looked up at her husband, who was vainly attempting to hold back the tears.

"What is it with you Cartwrights," she said, "that you always have to be the last out?"

—◦—

Fletcher remained by the door until Miss Hudson was out of sight. He then closed it slowly, and walked across to pick up the insistent phone.

"Is that you, Senator?" demanded the chief.

"Yes."

"Are you OK? We thought we heard a crash, maybe even a shot."

"No, I'm just fine. Are all the children safe?"

"Yes, we've got all thirty-one of them," said the chief.

"Including the last one?"

"Yes, he's just joined his parents."

"And Miss Hudson?"

"She's talking to Sandra Mitchell on *Eyewitness News*. She's telling everyone that you're some kind of hero."

"I think she's talking about someone else," said Fletcher.

"Are you and Bates planning to join us sometime?" asked the chief, assuming he was just being modest.

"Give me a few more minutes, Chief. By the way, I've agreed that Billy can also talk to Sandra Mitchell."

"Who's got the gun?"

"I have," said Fletcher. "Billy won't be causing you any more trouble. The gun wasn't even loaded," he added, before putting the phone down.

"You know they're going to kill me, don't you, Senator?"

"No one's going to kill you, Billy, not as long as I'm with you."

"Do I have your word on that, Mr. Davenport?"

"You have my word on it, Billy. So let's go out and face them together."

Fletcher opened the classroom door. He didn't need to search for a light switch as there were so many megawatts beaming in from the playground that he could clearly see the door at the far end of the passage.

He and Billy walked down the corridor together without a word passing between them. When they reached the main door that led onto the playground, Fletcher opened it tentatively and stepped into a beam of light, to be greeted by another huge cheer from the crowd. But he couldn't see their faces.

"It's going to be all right, Billy," said Fletcher, turning back toward him. Billy hesitated for a moment, but finally took a tentative step forward and stood by Fletcher's side. They walked slowly down the path together. He turned and saw Billy smile. "It's going to be all right," Fletcher repeated, just as the bullet ripped through Billy's chest. The sheer impact threw Fletcher to one side.

Fletcher pushed himself up off his knees and leaped on top of Billy, but it was too late. He was already dead.

"No, no, no," Fletcher screamed. "Didn't they realize that I gave him my word?"

38

"SOMEONE IS BUYING our shares," said Nat.

"I do hope so," said Tom, "we are, after all, a public company."

"No, chairman, I mean that someone is *aggressively* buying them."

"For what purpose?" asked Julia.

Nat put down his pen. "To try and take us over would be my bet." Several of the board began to speak at once, until Tom tapped the table. "Let's hear Nat out."

"For some years now, our policy has been to buy up small ailing banks and add them to our portfolio, and overall that has proved a worthwhile enterprise. All of you know my long-term strategy is to make Russell's the largest banking presence in the state. What I hadn't planned for was that our success would, in turn, make us attractive to an even larger institution."

"And you're convinced someone is now trying to take us over?"

"I most certainly am, Julia," said Nat, "and you're partly to blame. The most recent phase of the Cedar Wood project has been such a massive success that our overall profits nearly doubled last year."

"If Nat is right," said Tom, "and I suspect he is, there's only one question that needs to be answered. Are we happy to be taken over or do we want to put up a fight?"

"I can only speak for myself, chairman," said Nat, "but I'm not yet forty and I certainly wasn't planning on early retirement. I suggest we have no choice but to fight."

"I agree," said Julia, "I've been taken over once already, and I'm not going to let it happen a second time. In any case, our share-holders will not expect us to roll over."

"Not to mention one or two of the past chairmen," said Tom, looking up at the paintings of his father, grandfather and great-grandfather staring down at him from the surrounding walls. "I don't think we need to vote on this," continued Tom, "so why don't you take us through the options, Nat."

The chief executive opened one of the three files on the table in front of him.

"The law in these circumstances couldn't be clearer. Once a company or individual owns six percent of the target company, they must declare their position to the Securities and Exchange Commission in Washington, D.C., and state within twenty-eight calendar days if it is their intention to make a takeover bid for the rest of the shares. And if so, what price they are willing to offer."

"If someone is trying to take us over," said Tom, "they won't wait the statutory month. Once they've hit six percent they'll make a bid the same day."

"I agree, Mr. Chairman," said Nat, "but until then, there is nothing to stop us buying our own shares, although they are priced a little on the high side at the moment."

"But won't that alert the opposition to the fact that we know what they're up to?" asked Julia.

"Possibly, so we must instruct our brokers to buy soft, and that way we'll quickly find out if there's one big purchaser in the market."

"How much stock do we own between us?" asked Julia.

"Tom and I each hold ten percent," said Nat, "and you are currently holding," he checked some figures in a second file, "just over three percent."

"And how much cash do I still have on deposit?"

Nat turned the page, "Just over eight million dollars, not to mention your Trump shares, which you've been liquidating whenever there's a strong demand."

"Then why don't I pick up any soft shares, which wouldn't be quite so easy for any predators to trace?"

"Especially if you only dealt through Joe Stein in New York," said Tom, "and then ask him to let us know if his brokers can identify any particular individual or company who's buying aggressively." Julia began taking notes.

"The next thing we have to do is select the sharpest takeover lawyer in the business," said Nat. "I've talked to Jimmy Gates, who's represented us in all our previous takeover bids, but he says this one is out of his league, and recommends a guy from New York called," he checked the third file, "Logan Fitzgerald, who specializes in corporate raids. I thought I'd travel up to New York before the weekend and find out if he'll represent us."

"Good," said Tom, "anything else we ought to be doing in the meantime?"

"Yes, keep your eyes and ears open, chairman. I need to find out as quickly as possible who it is we're up against."

◄◊►

"I'm very sorry to hear that," said Fletcher.

"It's nobody's fault," said Jimmy, "and I can't pretend it's been going well for some time, so when UCLA invited Joanna to head up their history department, it just brought matters to a head."

"How are the children taking it?"

"Elizabeth's just fine, and now that Harry Junior's at Hotchkiss, they both seem grown up enough to handle the situation. In fact, Harry rather likes the idea of spending his summer vacations in California."

"I am sorry," repeated Fletcher.

"I think you'll find it's the norm nowadays," said Jimmy. "It won't be long before you and Annie are in the minority. The principal told me that around thirty percent of the children at Hotchkiss come from broken homes. Do you know when we were there, I can't remember more than one, perhaps two, of our contemporaries whose parents were divorced." He paused. "And the good thing is, if the children are in California during the summer, I'll have more time to spend on your reelection campaign."

"I'd rather you and Joanna were still together," said Fletcher.

"Any idea who you'll be up against?" asked Jimmy, obviously wanting to change the subject.

"No," said Fletcher, "I hear Barbara Hunter is desperate to run yet again, but the Republicans don't seem to want her as their candidate if they can find a half-decent alternative."

"There was a rumor circulating," said Jimmy, "that Ralph Elliot was considering running, but frankly after your Billy Bates triumph, I don't think the Archangel Gabriel could unseat you."

"Billy Bates was not a triumph, Jimmy. That man's death haunts me even now. He could still be alive today if I'd only been firmer with Chief Culver."

"I know that's how you see it, Fletcher, but the public feels otherwise. Your reelection last time proved that. All they remember is that you risked your life to save thirty-one children and their favorite teacher. Dad says if you had run for president that week you'd be living in the White House right now."

"How is the old buzzard?" asked Fletcher. "I'm feeling a bit guilty because I haven't had a chance to visit him recently."

"He's fine, likes to believe he's still running everything and everybody, even if he's only planning your career."

"What year has he got me running for president?" asked Fletcher with a grin.

"That all depends on whether you're first considering running for governor. By the time you've done four terms as senator, Jim Lewsam will just about have completed his second term."

"Perhaps I don't want to be governor."

"Perhaps the pope isn't a Catholic."

—◦—

"Good morning," said Logan Fitzgerald as he looked around the boardroom table. "Before you ask," he continued, "the answer is Fairchild's."

"Of course," said Nat. "Damn it, I should have worked it out for myself. When you think about it, they are the obvious predator. Fairchild's is the largest bank in the state; seventy-one branches with almost no serious rivals."

"Someone on their board obviously considers we are a serious rival," said Tom.

"So they've decided to eliminate you before you think of doing the same thing to them," said Logan.

"I can't blame them," said Nat, "it's exactly what I'd do if I were in their position."

"And I can also tell you that the original idea didn't come from a member of their board," continued Logan. "The official notification to the SEC was signed on their behalf by Belman Wayland and Elliot, and there are no prizes for guessing which of the three partners' signature appears on the dotted line."

"That means we've got one hell of a fight on our hands," said Tom.

"True," said Logan, "so the first thing we have to do is start playing the counting game." He turned his attention to Julia. "How many shares have you picked up in the last few days?"

"Less than one percent," she replied, "because someone out there keeps pushing the price up. When I asked my broker yesterday evening, he told me at close of business the shares had touched $5.20."

"That's way above their realistic value," said Nat, "but there's no way back for either of us now. I've asked Logan to join us this morning so he can give us his assessment of our chances of survival, as well as take us through what's likely to happen during the next few weeks."

"Let me bring you up to date as of nine o'clock this morning, Mr. Chairman," continued Logan. "In order to avoid a takeover, Russell's must have in their possession, or pledged to them in writing, fifty point one percent of the bank's shares. The board currently holds just over twenty-four percent, and we know Fairchild's already has at least six percent. On the face of it, that looks satisfactory. However, as Fairchild's are now offering $5.10 a share for a period of twenty-one days, I feel it's my duty to point out that should you decide to sell your shares, the cash value alone would net you in the region of twenty million dollars."

"We've already made our decision on that," said Tom firmly.

"Fine, then you're left with only two choices. You can either make a higher offer than Fairchild's $5.10 a share, remembering your chief executive's judgment that they are already way above their realistic value, or you can contact all your shareholders, asking them to pledge their stock to you."

"The latter," said Nat, without hesitation.

"As I anticipated that would be your response, Mr. Cartwright, I've studied the list of stockholders carefully—as of this morning, there were 27,412 in all, mostly holding small amounts, a thousand or less shares. However, five percent remains in the portfolios of three individuals, two widows residing in Florida who own two percent each, and Senator Harry Gates, who is in possession of one percent."

"How's that possible?" asked Tom. "Harry Gates is known to have spent his entire public life living on a senator's salary."

"He has his father to thank for that," said Logan. "It seems that he was a friend of the founder of the bank, who offered him one percent of the company in 1892. He purchased one hundred shares for one hundred dollars, and the Gates family has held on to them ever since."

"What are they worth now?" asked Tom.

Nat tapped his calculator. "Close to half a million, and he probably doesn't even realize it."

"Jimmy Gates, his son, is an old friend of mine," said Logan, "in fact I owe my present job to him. And I can tell you that once Jimmy finds out that Ralph Elliot is involved, those shares will immediately be pledged to us. If you can lay your hands on them, and reel in the two old ladies from Florida, you'll be close to controlling thirty percent, which still means you'll need another twenty point one percent before anyone can relax."

"But from my experience of past takeovers, at least five percent won't get back in touch with either of us," said Nat, "when you consider changes of address, trust funds, and even those like Harry Gates who don't bother to check their portfolios from year to year."

"I agree," said Logan, "but I won't rest easy until I know you control over fifty percent."

"So how do we go about getting our hands on that extra twenty percent?" asked Tom.

"Damned hard work, and hours of it," said Logan. "To start with, you will have to send out a personal letter to all your shareholders, just over twenty-seven thousand in all. This is the sort of thing I have in mind." Logan handed copies of a letter to each of the board members. "You'll see that I've concentrated on the bank's strengths, long history in the community, highest growth of any financial institution in the state. I've asked if they want one bank to end up with a monopoly."

"Yes," said Nat. "Ours."

"But not yet," said Logan. "Now, before we agree on this letter, I'd welcome your input, as it has to be signed by your chairman or chief executive."

"But that's over twenty-seven thousand signatures?"

"Yes, but you can split them between you," said Logan with a smile. I wouldn't suggest such a Herculean task if I wasn't fairly sure our rivals will send out a circular headed "Dear Shareholder" with a stylized signature above the name of their chairman. The personal touch might well make the difference between survival and extinction."

"Can I help in any way?" asked Julia.

"You certainly can, Mrs. Russell," replied Logan. "I've designed a totally different letter for you to sign that should be sent to every female shareholder. Most of them are either divorced or widowed and probably don't check their portfolios from one year to the next. There are nearly four thousand such investors, so that should take care of your weekend." He pushed a second letter across the table. "You'll see I've referred to your particular expertise in having run your own company, as well as being a board member of Russell's for the past seven years."

"Anything else?" asked Julia.

"Yes," said Logan, passing her two more sheets of paper. "I want you to visit the two widows from Florida."

"I could go early next week," said Julia, checking her diary.

"No," said Logan firmly. "Phone them this morning and fly down to see them tomorrow. You can be sure that Ralph Elliot has already paid them a visit."

Julia nodded, and began checking through the file to find how much was known of Mrs. Bloom and Mrs. Hargaten.

"And finally, Nat," continued Logan, "you're going to have to get yourself involved in a fairly aggressive media campaign; in other words, let it all hang out."

"What do you have in mind?" asked Nat.

"Local boy made good, Vietnam hero, Harvard scholar who returned to Hartford to build up the bank with his closest friend. Even throw in your cross-country experience—the nation is going through a bout of jogging mania at the moment—and one or two of them might even be shareholders. And if anyone wants to interview you from *Cycling News* to *Knitting Weekly*, just say yes."

"And who will I be up against?" asked Nat. "The chairman of Fairchild's?"

"No, I don't think so," said Logan, "Murray Goldblatz is an astute banker, but they won't risk putting him on television."

"Why not?" asked Tom. "He's been the chairman of Fairchild's for over twenty years, and he's one of the most respected financiers in the business."

"I agree, chairman," said Logan. "But don't forget that he had a heart attack a couple of years back, and worse, he stutters. It may not worry you because you've become used to it over the years, but the chances are that if he goes on television, the public will only see him once. He may be the most respected banker in the state, but stuttering spells dithering. Unfair, but you can be sure that they'll have thought that through."

"So I guess it will be Wesley Jackson, my opposite number?" mused Nat. "He's about the most articulate banker I've come up against. I even offered him a place on our board."

"You may well have," said Logan. "But he's black."

"This is 1988," said Nat angrily.

"I'm aware of that," said Logan, "but well over ninety percent of your shareholders are white, and they will have taken that into consideration as well."

"So who do you think they'll put up?" asked Nat.

"I don't have any doubt that you'll be up against Ralph Elliot."

—◇—

"So the Republicans have ended up endorsing Barbara Hunter after all," said Fletcher.

"Only because no one else wanted to run against you," Jimmy replied. "Once they realized you were nine points ahead in the polls."

"I hear they begged Ralph Elliot to throw his hat in the ring, but he said he couldn't consider it while he was in the middle of a takeover bid for Russell's Bank."

"A good excuse," said Jimmy, "but there was no way that man would have allowed his name to go forward unless he knew he had a reasonable chance of beating you. Did you see him on television last night?"

"Yes," said Fletcher with a sigh, "and if I hadn't known better, I might have fallen for that 'be assured of your future by joining the largest, safest and most respected bank in the state.' He's lost none of his old charisma. I only hope your father didn't fall for it."

"No, Harry's already pledged his one percent to Tom Russell, and is telling everyone else to do the same thing, though he was shocked when I told him how much his shares were worth."

Fletcher laughed. "I see the financial journalists are speculating that both sides now have around forty percent, with only another week to go before the offer closes."

"Yes, it's going to be close. I only hope Tom Russell realizes just how dirty it will become now that Ralph Elliot is involved," said Fletcher.

"I couldn't have made it clearer," said Jimmy quietly.

—◇—

"When was this sent out?" Nat asked as the rest of the board studied the latest missive circulated to all shareholders by Fairchild's.

"It's dated yesterday," said Logan, "which means we have three days left to respond, but by then I fear the damage will have been done."

"Even I wouldn't have believed Elliot was capable of sinking this low," said Tom as he studied the letter signed by Murray Goldblatz:

Things you didn't know about Nathaniel Cartwright,
the Chief Executive of Russell's Bank

—Mr. Cartwright was neither born nor raised in Hartford;

—he was rejected by Yale after cheating in the entrance exam;

—he left the University of Connecticut without a degree, after losing the election for student president;

—he was sacked from J P Morgan after losing the bank $500,000;

—he's married to a Korean girl whose family fought against the Americans during the war;

—the only job he could find after being sacked by Morgan's was with an old school friend, who just happened to be chairman of Russell's Bank.

Pledge your shares to Fairchild's: be sure your future is secure.

"This is the response that I propose we send out by express mail today," said Logan, "allowing Fairchild's no time to respond to it." He slid a copy across to each board member.

> Things you ought to know about Nat Cartwright,
> the Chief Executive of Russell's Bank

—Nat was born and raised in Connecticut;

—he won the Medal of Honor in Vietnam;

—he completed his undergraduate degree at Harvard (summa cum laude), before going on to Harvard business school;

—he resigned from Morgan's, having made a profit for the bank of over a million dollars;

—during his nine years at Russell's as Chief Executive, he has quadrupled the bank's profits;

—his wife is Professor of Statistics at UConn, and her father was a master sergeant in the American Marines.

Stay with Russell's: the bank that cares about you and takes care of your money.

"Can I release it immediately?" asked Logan.

"No," said Nat, tearing it up. He didn't speak for some time. "It takes a lot to get me angry, but I am about to kill off Ralph Elliot once and forever, so listen carefully."

Twenty minutes later, Tom ventured the first comment, "That would be taking one hell of a risk."

"Why?" asked Nat, "if the strategy fails, we'll all end up multimillionaires, but if it succeeds, we'll take control of the biggest bank in the state."

—◇—

"Dad's livid with you," said Jimmy.

"But why?" asked Fletcher, "when I won."

"That's the problem, you won by over twelve thousand votes, which was tactless of you," said Jimmy as he watched Harry Junior running down the wing, the ball at his feet. "Don't forget that he only managed eleven thousand once in twenty-eight years, and that was when Barry Goldwater was running for president."

"Thanks for the warning," said Fletcher. "I guess I'd better avoid the next couple of Sunday lunches."

"You'd better not, it's your turn to be told how he made a million overnight."

"Yes, Annie warned me that he'd sold his shares in Russell's Bank. I thought he'd made a pledge not to release them to Fairchild's at any cost?"

"He did, and he would have kept to it, but the day before the offer was due to close, and the shares had peaked at $7.10, he had a call from Tom Russell, advising him to sell. He even suggested that he get in touch with Ralph Elliot direct so the deal would go through quickly."

"They're up to something," said Fletcher. "There's no way Tom Russell would have told your father to deal with Ralph Elliot unless there's another chapter still to be written in this particular saga." Jimmy said nothing. "So can we therefore assume that Fairchild's has secured over fifty percent?"

"I asked Logan the same question, but he explained that because of client confidentiality, he couldn't say anything until Monday, when the official figures would be released by the SEC."

"Ouch," said Jimmy, "did you see what that Taft kid just did to Harry Junior? He's lucky Joanna's not here, otherwise she would have run onto the field and whacked him."

—◇—

"Those in favor?" asked the chairman.

Every hand around the table rose, though Julia seemed to hesitate for a moment. "Then it's unanimous," declared Tom and, turning to Nat, added, "perhaps you should take us through what's likely to happen next."

347

"Certainly, chairman," said Nat. "At ten o'clock this morning, the SEC will announce that Fairchild's has failed to secure control of Russell's Bank."

"What percentage do we think they'll end up with?" asked Julia.

"They had 47.89 percent at midnight on Saturday, and may have picked up a few more shares on Sunday, but I doubt it."

"And the price?"

"At close of business on Friday they were $7.32," said Logan, "but after this morning's announcement, all pledges are automatically released and Fairchild's cannot make another bid for at least twenty-eight days."

"That's when I plan to put a million of Russell's shares on the market," said Nat.

"Why would you do that?" asked Julia, "when our shares would be certain to fall sharply."

"So will Fairchild's because they own nearly fifty percent of us," said Nat, "and they can do nothing about it for twenty-eight days."

"Nothing?" repeated Julia.

"Nothing," confirmed Logan.

"And if we then use the extra cash to buy Fairchild's shares as they begin dropping . . ."

"You would have to inform the SEC the moment you reached six percent," said Logan, "and at the same time let them know that it's your intention to make a full takeover bid for Fairchild's."

"Good," said Nat, as he pulled the phone toward him and dialed ten digits. No one spoke as the chief executive waited for the phone to be answered. "Hi, Joe, it's Nat, we're going ahead as planned. At one minute past ten, I want you to place a million of the bank's shares on the market."

"You realize they'll drop like a stone," said Joe, "because you're about to turn everyone into a seller."

"Let's hope you're right, Joe, because that's when I want you to start mopping up Fairchild's shares, but not until you think they've bottomed out. And don't stop until you've got hold of five point nine percent."

"Understood," said Joe.

"And, Joe, just be sure you keep an open line night and day, because you're not going to get much sleep during the next four weeks," added Nat before replacing the receiver.

"Are you sure we're not breaking the law?" asked Julia.

"Certain," said Logan, "but if we pull it off, my bet is that Congress will have to rewrite the legislation on takeovers in the very near future."

"And do you consider what we're doing is ethical?" asked Julia.

"No," said Nat, "and it wouldn't have even crossed my mind to behave this way if we hadn't been dealing with Ralph Elliot." He paused. "I did warn you that I was going to kill him. I just didn't tell you how."

39

"YOU'VE GOT THE chairman of Fairchild's on line one, Joe Stein on line two, and your wife on line three."

"I'll take the chairman of Fairchild's. Ask Joe Stein to hold and tell Su Ling I'll call back."

"Your wife said it was urgent."

"I'll call her back in a few minutes."

"I'm putting Mr. Goldblatz through."

Nat would have liked a few moments to compose himself before he spoke to the chairman of Fairchild's; perhaps he should have told his secretary that he would call him back. For a start, how should he address him: Mr. Goldblatz, Mr. Chairman or sir? After all, he had been chairman of Fairchild's when Nat was still at Harvard Business School doing case studies on banking.

"Good morning, Mr. Cartwright."

"Good morning, Mr. Goldblatz, how can I help you?"

"I wondered if perhaps we could meet." Nat hesitated because he wasn't quite sure what to say. "And I think it would be wise if it were just the two us," he added. "Jus . . . jus . . . just the two of us."

"Yes, I'm sure that would be all right," said Nat, "but it will have to be somewhere no one would recognize us."

"Might I suggest St. Joseph's Cathedral?" said Mr. Goldblatz, "I don't think anyone will recognize me there."

Nat laughed. "When did you have in mind?" he asked.

"I would have thought sooner rather than later."

"I agree," said Nat.

"Shall we say three o'clock this afternoon? I can't imagine there will be that many people in church on a Monday afternoon."

"St. Joseph's, three o'clock, I'll see you there, Mr. Goldblatz." No sooner had Nat put the phone down than it rang again.

"Joe Stein," said Linda.

"Joe, what's the latest?"

"I've just picked up another hundred thousand of Fairchild's stock, which takes you up to twenty-nine percent. They're currently around $2.90, which is less than half their high point. But you do have a problem," said Joe.

"And what's that?"

"If you don't get hold of fifty percent by next Friday, you'll be facing exactly the same problem Fairchild's had a fortnight ago, so I hope you know what your next move is."

"It may become clearer after a meeting I'm having at three o'clock this afternoon," said Nat.

"That sounds interesting," said Joe.

"It could well be," said Nat, "but I can't say anything at the moment because even I'm not sure what it's all about."

"Curiouser and curiouser," said Joe. "I'll look forward to hearing more. But what do you expect me to do in the meantime?"

"I want you to go on buying every Fairchild's share you can lay your hands on until close of business tonight. Then let's talk again just before the market opens tomorrow morning."

"Understood," said Joe, "then I'd better leave you and get back on the floor."

Nat let out a long sigh, and tried to think what Murray Goldblatz could possibly want to see him about. He picked up the phone again, "Linda, get me Logan Fitzgerald—he'll be on his New York number."

"Your wife did stress that it was urgent and she called back again while you were speaking to Mr. Stein."

"Right, I'll phone her while you try and find Logan."

Nat dialed his home number and then began strumming his fingers on the desk as he continued to think about Murray Goldblatz and what he could possibly want. Su Ling's voice interrupted his thoughts.

"Sorry I didn't—call you straight back," said Nat, "but Murray . . ."

"Luke's run away from school," said Su Ling. "No one's seen him since lights out last night."

—◦—

"You've got the chairman of the Democratic National Committee on line one, Mr. Gates on line two, and your wife on line three."

"I'll take the party chairman first. Would you ask Jimmy to hold and tell Annie I'll call her right back."

"She said it was urgent."

"Tell her I'll only be a couple of minutes."

Fletcher would have liked a little more time to compose himself. He'd only met the party chairman a couple of times, in a corridor at the national convention, and at a cocktail party in Washington, D.C. He doubted if Mr. Brubaker would remember either occasion. And then there was the problem of how to address him, Mr. Brubaker, Alan, or even sir. After all, he'd been appointed chairman before Fletcher had even run for the Senate.

"Good morning, Fletcher, Al Brubaker."

"Good morning, Mr. Chairman, how nice to hear from you. How can I help?"

"I need to have a word with you in private, Fletcher, and wondered if you and your wife could possibly fly down to Washington and join Jenny and me for dinner one evening."

"We'd be delighted to," said Fletcher, "when did you have in mind?"

"How's the evening of the eighteenth looking? That's next Friday."

Fletcher quickly flicked through the pages of his appointment book. He had a caucus meeting at noon, which he shouldn't miss now that he was deputy leader, but nothing was penciled in for that evening. "What time would you like us to be there?"

"Eight suit you?" asked Brubaker.

"Yes, that will be fine, Mr. Chairman."

"Good, then eight o'clock it is, on the eighteenth. My home is in Georgetown, 3038 N Street."

Fletcher wrote it down in the space below the caucus meeting. "I look forward to seeing you then, Mr. Chairman."

"Me too," said Brubaker. "And Fletcher, I would prefer if you didn't mention this to anyone."

Fletcher put the phone down. It would be tight, and he might even have to leave the caucus meeting early. The intercom buzzed again.

"Mr. Gates," said Sally.

"Hi, Jimmy, what can I do for you?" asked Fletcher cheerily, wanting to tell him about his invitation to have dinner with the chairman of the party.

"It's not good, I'm afraid," said Jimmy. "Dad's had another heart attack and they've rushed him into St. Patrick's. I'm just about to leave, but I thought I'd give you a call first."

"How bad is he?" asked Fletcher quietly.

"Hard to tell until we hear what the doctor has to say. Mom wasn't exactly coherent when she got in touch with me, so I won't know a lot more until I've been to the hospital."

"Annie and I will be with you as soon as we can," said Fletcher. He touched the bridge of his telephone and then dialed his home number. It was busy. He replaced the phone and began tapping his fingers. If it was still busy when he tried again he decided he would drive straight home and pick Annie up so they could go over to the hospital together. For a moment, Al Brubaker flashed back into his mind. Why would he want a private meeting that he would prefer not to be mentioned to anyone else? But then his thoughts returned to Harry and he dialed his home number a second time. He heard Annie's voice on the end of the line.

"Have you heard?" she asked.

"Yes," said Fletcher, "I've just spoken to Jimmy. I thought I'd go directly to the hospital so we could meet there."

"No, it's not just Dad," said Annie. "It's Lucy, she had a terrible fall when she was out riding this morning. She's concussed and has broken her leg. They've put her in the infirmary. I don't know what to do next."

⟶◦⟵

"I blame myself," said Nat. "Because of the takeover battle with Fairchild's I haven't been to see Luke once this term."

"Me neither," admitted Su Ling. "But we were going to the school play next week."

"I know," said Nat. "As he's playing Romeo, do you think the problem might be Juliet?"

"Possibly. After all, you met your first love at the school play, didn't you?" asked Su Ling.

"Yes, and that ended in tears."

"Don't blame yourself, Nat. I've been just as preoccupied with my graduate students these last few weeks, and perhaps I should have questioned Luke more closely about why he was so silent and withdrawn during term break."

"He's always been a bit of a loner," said Nat, "and studious children rarely gather a lot of friends around them."

"How would you know?" asked Su Ling, glad to see her husband smile. "And both our mothers have always been quiet and thoughtful," Su Ling added as she drove onto the highway.

"How long do you think it will take us to get there?" asked Nat as he glanced at the clock on the dashboard.

"At this time of day, about an hour, so I expect we should arrive around three o'clock," said Su Ling, as she took her foot off the accelerator, once she'd touched fifty-five.

"Three, oh hell," said Nat, suddenly remembering, "I'll have to let Murray Goldblatz know that I won't be able to make his meeting."

"The chairman of Fairchild's?"

"No less, he requested a private meeting," said Nat as he picked up the car phone. He quickly checked Fairchild's number in his phone book.

"To discuss what?" asked Su Ling.

"It has to be something to do with the takeover, but beyond that I haven't a clue." Nat pressed the eleven digits. "Mr. Goldblatz, please."

"Who shall I say is calling?" asked the switchboard operator.

Nat hesitated, "It's a personal call."

"I will still need to know who it is," the voice insisted.

"I have an appointment with him at three o'clock."

"I'll put you though to his secretary." Nat waited.

"Mr. Goldblatz's office," said a female voice.

"I have a three o'clock appointment with Mr. Goldblatz, but I fear I am going . . ."

"I'll put you through, Mr. Cartwright."

"Mr. Cartwright."

"Mr. Goldblatz, I must apologize, a family problem has arisen and I won't be able to make our meeting this afternoon."

"I see," said Goldblatz, not sounding as though he did.

"Mr. Goldblatz," said Nat, "I'm not in the habit of playing games, I have neither the time nor the inclination."

"I wasn't suggesting you did, Mr. Cartwright," said Goldblatz curtly.

Nat hesitated. "My son has run away from Taft and I'm on my way to see the principal."

"I'm so . . . so . . . sorry to hear that," Mr. Goldblatz said, his tone immediately changing. "If it's any consolation, I also ran away from Taft, but once I'd spent all my pocket money I decided to go back the following day."

Nat laughed. "Thank you for being so understanding."

"Not at all, perhaps you'd give me a call and let me know when it's convenient for us to meet."

"Yes of course, Mr. Goldblatz, and I wonder if I might ask a favor."

"Certainly."

"That none of this conversation is reported to Ralph Elliot."

"You have my word on that, but then, Mr. Cartwright, he has no idea that I planned to meet you in the first place."

When Nat put the phone down, Su Ling said, "Wasn't that a bit of a risk?"

"No, I don't think so," said Nat. "I have a feeling that Mr. Goldblatz and I have discovered something we have in common."

As Su Ling drove through the Taft gates, memories came flooding back to Nat: his mother being late, having to walk down the center aisle of a packed hall when his knees were knocking, sitting next to Tom, and twenty-five years later, accompanying his son back on his first day. Now he only hoped his boy was safe and well.

Su Ling parked the car outside the principal's house, and

before she had turned the engine off, Nat spotted Mrs. Henderson coming down the steps. He felt his stomach churn until he saw the smile on her lips. Su Ling jumped out of the car.

"They've found him," Mrs. Henderson said. "He was with his grandmother, helping her with the laundry."

—◦—

"Let's both go straight to the hospital and see your father. Then we can decide if one of us should go on to Lakeville and check up on Lucy."

"Lucy would be so sad if she knew," said Annie. "She has always adored Grandpa."

"I know, and he's already begun planning her life," said Fletcher. "Perhaps it would be better not to tell her what has happened, especially as she obviously won't be able to visit him."

"You may be right. In any case, he did go and see her last week."

"I didn't know that," said Fletcher.

"Oh yes, those two are plotting something," said Annie as she drove into the hospital parking lot, "but neither of them is letting me in on the secret."

When the elevator doors opened, the two of them walked quickly down the corridor to Harry's room. Martha stood up the moment they walked in, her face ashen. Annie took her mother in her arms as Fletcher touched Jimmy's shoulder. He looked down at a man whose flesh was drawn and sallow, his nose and mouth covered with a mask. A monitor beeped beside him, the only indication that he was still alive. This was the most energetic man Fletcher had ever known.

The four of them sat around the bed in silence, Martha holding her husband's hand. After a few moments she said, "Don't you think one of you should go and see how Lucy is getting on? There's not a lot you can do here."

"I'm not moving," said Annie, "but I think Fletcher ought to go."

Fletcher nodded his agreement. He kissed Martha on the cheek, and looking at Annie said, "I'll drive straight back just as soon as I've made sure that Lucy is OK."

Fletcher couldn't recall much of the journey to Lakeville as his mind wondered from Harry to Lucy, and for a moment to Al

Brubaker although he found that he was no longer preoccupied with what the chairman of the party wanted.

When he reached the road sign announcing the intersection for Hotchkiss, Fletcher's thoughts returned to Harry and how they had first met at the football game. "Please God let him live," he said out loud as he drove into his old school and brought the car to a halt outside the entrance to the infirmary. A nurse accompanied the senator to his daughter's bedside. As he walked down the corridor of empty beds, he could see in the distance a plastered leg, hooked high into the air. It reminded him of when he had run for the school presidency and his rival had allowed the voters to sign his cast on the day of the election. Fletcher tried to remember his name.

"You're a fraud," said Fletcher even before he saw the huge smile on Lucy's face and the bottles of soda and bags of cookies scattered all around her.

"I know, Dad, and I even managed to miss a calculus exam, but I must be back on campus by Monday if I'm to have any chance of becoming class president."

"So that's why Grandpa came down to see you, the sly old buzzard," said Fletcher. He kissed his daughter's cheek and was eyeing the cookies when a young man walked in and stood nervously on the other side of the bed.

"This is George," said Lucy. "He's in love with me."

"Nice to meet you, George," said Fletcher smiling.

"You too, Senator," the young man said as he extended his right hand across the bed.

"George is running my campaign for class president," said Lucy, "just like my godfather ran yours. George thinks that the broken leg will help bring in the sympathy vote. I'll have to ask Grandpa for his opinion when he next comes up to visit me— Grandpa's our secret weapon," she whispered, "he's already terrified the opposition."

"I don't know why I bothered to come down to see you at all," said Fletcher, "you so obviously don't need me."

"Yes I do, Dad. Could I get an advance on next month's allowance?"

Fletcher smiled and took out his wallet. "How much did your grandfather give you?"

"Five dollars," said Lucy sheepishly. Fletcher extracted another five-dollar bill. "Thanks, Dad. By the way, why isn't Mom with you?"

—◦—

Nat agreed to drive Luke back to school the following morning. The boy had been very uncommunicative the previous evening, almost as if he wanted to say something, but not while both of them were in the room.

"Perhaps he'll open up on the way back to school, when it's only the two of you," suggested Su Ling.

Father and son set out on the journey back to Taft soon after breakfast, but Luke still said very little. Despite Nat's trying to raise the subjects of work, the school play and even how Luke's running was going, he received only monosyllabic replies. So Nat changed tactics and also remained silent, hoping that Luke would, in time, initiate a conversation.

His father was in the passing lane, driving just above the speed limit, when Luke asked, "When did you first fall in love, Dad?" Nat nearly hit the car in front of him, but slowed down in time before drifting back into the middle lane.

"I think the first girl I really took any serious interest in was called Rebecca. She was playing Olivia to my Sebastian in the school play." He paused. "Is it Juliet you're having the problem with?"

"Certainly not," said Luke, "she's dumb—pretty, but dumb." This was followed by another long silence. "And how far did you and Rebecca go?" he finally asked.

"We kissed a little, if I remember," said Nat, "and there was a little of what we used to call in those days petting."

"Did you want to touch her breasts?"

"Sure did, but she wouldn't let me. I didn't get that far until our freshman year at college."

"But did you love her, Dad?"

"I thought I did, but that bombshell didn't truly hit me until I ran into your mother."

"So was Mom the first person you made love to?"

"No, there had been a couple of other girls before her, one in Vietnam, and another while I was at college."

"Did you get either of them pregnant?"

Nat moved across to the inside lane and fell well below the speed limit. He paused. "Have you got someone pregnant?"

"I don't know," said Luke, "and neither does Kathy, but when we were kissing behind the gym, I made a terrible mess all over her skirt."

◄○►

Fletcher spent another hour with his daughter before he drove back to Hartford. He enjoyed George's company. Lucy had described him as the brightest kid in the class. "That's why I chose him as my campaign manager," she explained.

Fletcher was back in Hartford an hour later, and when he walked into Harry's hospital room the tableau hadn't changed. He sat down next to Annie and took her hand.

"Any improvement?" he asked.

"No, nothing," said Annie, "he hasn't stirred since you left. How about Lucy?"

"A complete fraud, as I told her. She'll be in a plaster cast for around six weeks, which doesn't seem to have cramped her style; in fact she seems convinced it will help her chances of becoming class president."

"Did you tell her about Grandpa?"

"No, and I had to bluff a little when she asked where you were."

"Where was I?"

"Chairing a meeting of the school board."

Annie nodded. "True, just the wrong day."

"By the way, did you know she had a boyfriend?" asked Fletcher.

"Do you mean George?"

"You've met George?"

"Yes, but I wouldn't have described him as a boyfriend," said Annie, "more a devoted slave."

"I thought Lincoln abolished slavery in 1863?" said Fletcher.

Annie turned to face her husband, "Did it worry you?" she asked.

"Certainly not, Lucy's got to have a boyfriend sooner or later."

"That's not what I meant, and you know it."

"Annie, she's only sixteen."

"I was younger when I first met you."

"Annie, have you forgotten that when we were at college we marched for civil rights, and I'm proud that we've passed that conviction on to our daughter."

40

WHEN NAT DROPPED his son off at Taft and returned to Hartford, he felt guilty about not having enough time to visit his parents. But he knew he couldn't miss the meeting with Murray Goldblatz two days in a row. When he said goodbye to Luke, at least the boy no longer appeared shrouded in the world's woes. Nat promised his son that he and his mother would be back on Friday evening for the school play. He was still thinking about Luke when the car phone rang—an innovation that had changed his life.

"You were going to call before the market opened," said Joe. He paused. "With some possible news?"

"I'm sorry not to have called, Joe; a domestic crisis came up and I simply forgot."

"Well, are you able to tell me more?"

"Tell you more?"

"Your last words were, 'I'll know more in twenty-four hours.' "

"Before you burst out laughing, Joe, I'll know more in twenty-four hours."

"I'll accept that, but what are today's instructions?"

"The same as yesterday, I want you to go on buying Fairchild's aggressively until the close of business."

"I hope you know what you're doing, Nat, because the bills are going to start coming in next week. Everyone knows Fairchild's can ride out this sort of storm, but are you absolutely certain you can?"

"I can't afford not to," said Nat, "so just keep on buying."

"Whatever you say, boss, I just hope you've got a parachute, because if you haven't secured fifty percent of Fairchild's by Monday morning at ten o'clock it's going to be a very bumpy landing."

As Nat continued his journey back to Hartford, he realized that Joe was doing no more than stating the obvious. By this time next week he knew he could well be out of a job, and more important, have allowed Russell's to be taken over by their biggest rival. Was Goldblatz already aware of this? Of course he was.

As Nat drove into the city, he decided not to return to his office, but to park a few blocks from St. Joseph's, grab a snack and consider all the alternatives Godblatz might come up with. He ordered a bacon sandwich in the hope that it would put him in a fighting mood. He then began to write out a list of the pros and cons on the back of the menu.

At ten to three, he left the deli and started to make his way slowly toward the cathedral. Several people nodded or said "Good afternoon, Mr. Cartwright," as they passed, reminding him how well known he'd become recently. Their expressions were of admiration and respect, and he only wished he could advance the reel by one week to see how the faces would react then. He checked his watch—four minutes to three. He decided to circle the block and walk into the cathedral from the quieter south entrance. He climbed the steps in twos and entered the south transept a couple of minutes before the cathedral clock chimed the hour. Nothing would be gained by being late.

It took Nat a few moments to accustom himself to the darkness of the candle-lit cathedral after the strong light of the mid-afternoon sun. He looked down the center aisle that led to the altar, dominated by a massive gilded cross studded with semi-precious stones. He transferred his attention to the rows and rows of dark oak pews that stretched out in front of him down the nave. They were indeed almost empty as Mr. Goldblatz had predicted, save for four or five old ladies shrouded in black, one of them holding a rosary and chanting, "Hail Mary, full of Grace, the Lord is with you, blessed art thou . . ."

Nat continued down the center aisle, but could see no sign of Goldblatz. When he reached the great carved wooden pulpit, he stopped for a moment to admire the craftsmanship, which reminded him of his trips to Italy. He felt guilty that he'd been unaware of such beauty in his own city. He looked back down the aisle, but the only occupants remained the cluster of old ladies, heads bowed, still mumbling. He decided to make his way to the far side of the cathedral and take a seat near the back. He checked his watch again. It was one minute past three. As he walked, he became aware of the echoing sound his feet made on the marble floor. It was then that he heard a voice say, "Do you wish to confess, my son?"

Nat swung to his left to see a confessional box with the curtain drawn. A Catholic priest with a Jewish accent? He smiled, took a seat on the small wooden bench and drew the curtain closed.

—◇—

"You're looking very smart," said the majority leader as Fletcher took his place on Ken's right. "Anyone else and I'd have said you had a mistress."

"I do have a mistress," said Fletcher, "and her name is Annie. By the way, I may have to leave around two."

Ken Stratton glanced down the agenda. "That's fine by me; other than the education bill there doesn't seem to be a lot that involves you except perhaps candidates for the next election. We've all assumed you will be running again for Hartford, unless Harry plans to make a comeback. By the way, how is the old buzzard?"

"He's a little better," said Fletcher. "Restless, interfering, irascible and opinionated."

"Not much change then," said Ken.

Fletcher considered the agenda. Fund-raising was all he would be missing, and that item had been on every agenda since the day he was elected, and would still be there long after he'd retired.

As twelve struck, the majority leader called for order and asked Fletcher to present his timetable for the education bill. For the next thirty minutes Fletcher outlined his proposals, going into considerable detail about those clauses he anticipated the Republicans would oppose. After five or six questions from his colleagues, Fletcher realized that it would require all his legal and debating skills if he was to get this piece of legislation through the Senate. The last question predictably came from Jack Swales, the longest-serving member of the Senate. He always asked the last question, which was a sign that it was time to move on to the next item on the agenda.

"How much is this all going to cost the taxpayer, senator?"

Other members smiled as Fletcher performed the ritual: "It's covered in the budget, Jack, and was part of our platform at the last election."

Jack smiled and the majority leader said, "Item number two, candidates for the next election."

Fletcher had intended to slip out as soon as the discussion got under way, but like everyone else in the room, was taken by surprise when Ken went on to say, "I have to inform my fellow members, with some regret, that I shall not be running at the next election."

A half-sleepy group meeting suddenly became a powder keg, with "whys?" and "surely nots" and "who?" until Ken raised a hand. "I don't have to explain to you why I feel the time has come to retire."

Fletcher realized the immediate consequence of Ken's decision was that he was now the favorite to become majority leader. When his name was called, Fletcher made it clear that he would be running for reelection. He slipped out when Jack Swales began a speech on why he felt it was nothing less than his duty to seek reelection at the age of eighty-two.

Fletcher drove the half-mile to the hospital, and ran up the stairs to the second floor rather than wait for the elevator. He walked in to find Harry laying down the law on impeachment to an attentive audience of two. Martha and Annie turned to face him as he entered the room.

"Anything happen at the party caucus that I ought to know about?" Harry asked.

"Ken Stratton won't be running at the next election."

"That's no surprise. Ellie's been ill for some time, and she's the only thing he loves more than the party. But what it does mean, is that, if we can hold on to the Senate, you could well be the next majority leader."

"What about Jack Swales? Won't he consider it his by right?"

"In politics, nothing is yours by right," said Harry. "In any case, my bet is that the other members wouldn't back him. Now don't waste any more time talking to me, I know you've got to be in Washington for your meeting with Al Brubaker. All I want to know is when you think you'll be back."

"First thing tomorrow morning," said Fletcher. "We're only staying overnight."

"Then drop in on your way from the airport; I want a blow-by-blow account of why Al wanted to see you, and make sure you give him my regards, because he's the best chairman the party's had in years. And ask him if he got my letter."

"Your letter?" said Fletcher.

"Just ask him," said Harry.

"I thought he looked a lot better," said Fletcher as he and Annie drove to the airport.

"I agree," said Annie, "and they've told Martha that they may even let him go home next week if, and only if, he promises to take things easy."

"He'll promise," said Fletcher, "but just be thankful the election's not for another ten months."

The shuttle to the capital took off fifteen minutes late, but Fletcher had allowed for that, so when they touched down, he felt confident they would still have enough time to check into the Willard Hotel, shower, and be in Georgetown by eight.

Their cab pulled up outside the hotel at seven ten. The first thing Fletcher asked the porter was how long it would take to get to Georgetown.

"Ten, maybe fifteen minutes," he replied.

"Then I'd like to book a cab for seven forty-five."

Annie somehow managed to shower and change into a cocktail dress, while Fletcher paced around the room looking at his watch every few moments. He opened the cab door for his wife at 7:51.

"I need to get to 3038 N Street in," he checked his watch, "nine minutes."

"No, you don't," said Annie, "if Jenny Brubaker is anything like me, she'll be grateful if we're a few minutes late."

The cabbie wove his way in and out of the evening traffic and managed to pull up outside the chairman's house at two minutes past the hour. After all, he knew who would be paying the fare.

"It's nice to see you again, Fletcher," Al Brubaker said as he opened the front door. "And it's Annie, isn't it? I don't think we've met, but of course I know about your work for the party."

"The party?" said Annie.

"Don't you sit on the Hartford school board as well as the hospital committee?"

"Yes, I do," said Annie, "but I've always looked on that as working for the community."

"Just like your father," said Al. "By the way, how is the old bruiser?"

"We've just left him," said Fletcher. "He was looking a lot better, and sends his best wishes. By the way, he wanted to know if you received his letter."

"Yes I did. He never gives up, does he?" added Brubaker with a smile. "Why don't we go through to the library and I'll fix you both a drink. Jenny should be down shortly."

◦

"How's your boy?"

"He's fine, thank you, Mr. Goldblatz. His absence turned out to be caused by an affair of the heart."

"How old is he?"

"Sixteen."

"A proper age to fall in love. Now, my son, do you have anything to confess?"

"Yes, father, by this time next week I will be the chairman of the largest bank in the state."

"By this time next week, you might not even be the chief executive of one of the smaller banks in the state."

"What makes you think that?" asked Nat.

"Because what might have turned out to be a brilliant coup could have backfired, leaving you overextended. Your brokers must have warned you that there is no chance of your laying your hands on fifty percent of Fairchild's by Monday morning."

"It's going to be a close-run thing," said Nat, "and I still believe we can make it."

"Thank heavens neither of us is a Catholic, Mr. Cartwright, otherwise you would be blushing, and I would be recommending a penance of three Hail Marys. But fear not, I see redemption for both of us."

"Do I need redemption, father?"

"We both do, which is wh . . . wh . . . why I asked to see you. This battle has done neither of us any favors and if it continues beyond Sunday, it will harm both the institutions we serve, and possibly even close yours."

Nat wanted to protest, but he knew that Goldblatz was right. "So what form does this redemption take?" he asked.

"Well, I think I've come up with a better solution than three Hail Marys, which may cleanse us both of our sins and might even show us a little profit."

"I await your instructions, father."

"I've watched your career with interest over the years, my son. You're very bright, extremely diligent and ferociously determined, but what I admire most about you is that you're straight—however much one of my legal advisors would have me believe otherwise."

"I'm flattered, sir, but not overwhelmed."

"And neither should you be. I am a realist, and I think that if you don't succeed this time, you might well try again in a couple of years, and go on trying until you do succeed. Am I right?"

"You may well be, sir."

"You have been frank with me, so I shall respond in kind. In eighteen months' time I will be sixty-five, when I wish to retire to the golf course. I would like to hand over to my successor a thriving institution, not an ailing patient continually returning to the hospital for more treatment. I believe you may be the solution to my problem."

"I thought I was the cause."

"All the more reason for us to try and pull off a coup that is both bold and imaginative."

"I thought that's exactly what I was doing."

"And you still may, my son, but for political reasons I need the whole thing to be your idea, which means, Mr. Cartwright, that you're going to have to trust me."

"It's taken you forty years to build your reputation, Mr. Goldblatz. I can't believe you'd be willing to trade it in just months before you're due to retire."

"I too am flattered, young man, but, like you, not overwhelmed. Therefore might I suggest that it was you who requested this meeting to put forward your proposal that, rather than continue to fight each other, we should in fact work together."

"A partnership?" said Nat.

"Call it what you will, Mr. Cartwright, but if our two banks were to merge, no one will have lost out, and more important, all our shareholders will benefit."

"And what terms are you suggesting that I should recommend to you, not to mention to my board?"

"That the bank be called Fairchild-Russell, and that I remain chairman for the next eighteen months, while you are appointed my deputy."

"But what will happen to Tom and Julia Russell?"

"Obviously they would both be offered a place on the board. If you become chairman in eighteen months' time, it would be up to you to appoint your own deputy, although I think you might be wise to keep Wesley Jackson on as your chief executive. But as you invited him to join your board some years ago, I can't believe you'd find that a setback."

"No, I wouldn't, but that doesn't solve the problem of stock allocation."

"You currently hold ten percent of Russell's, as does your chairman. His wife, who incidentally I think should manage our combined property portfolios, did at one point possess as much as four percent of the stock. But I suspect that it has been her shares that you have been releasing onto the open market for the past few days."

"You could be right, Mr. Goldblatz."

"In turnover and profits Fairchild's is rou . . . rou . . . roughly five times the size of Russell's, so I would suggest that when you put forward your proposal, you and Mr. Russell ask for four percent and settle for three. In the case of Mrs. Russell, I would have thought one percent would be appropriate. All three of you will of course retain your present salaries and benefits."

"And my staff?"

"The status quo should remain for the first eighteen months. After that, the decision will be yours."

"And you want me to approach you with this offer, Mr. Goldblatz?"

"Yes, I do."

"Forgive me for asking, why don't you simply make the proposal yourself, and let my board consider it?"

"Because our legal advisors would recommend against it. It seems that Mr. Elliot has only one purpose in this takeover, and that is to destroy you. I also have only one purpose, and that is to maintain the integrity of the bank I have served for over thirty years."

"Then why not just sack Elliot?"

"I wanted to, the day after he sent out that infamous letter in my name, but I couldn't afford to admit we might have an internal disagreement only days before we were facing a takeover. I can just imagine what the press would make of that, not to men . . . men . . . mention the shareholders, Mr. Cartwright."

"But once Elliot hears the proposal has come from me," said Nat, "he'll immediately advise your board against it."

"I agree," said Goldblatz, "which is why I sent him to Washington yesterday so that he can report directly back to me once the Securities and Exchange Commission announces the outcome of your takeover bid on Monday."

"He'll smell a rat. He knows only too well that he doesn't need to sit around in Washington for four days. He could fly down on Sunday night, and still brief you on the Commission's decision on Monday morning."

"Funny you should mention that, Mr. Cartwright, because it was my secretary who sp . . . sp . . . spotted that the Republicans are having their midterm get-together in Washington ending with a dinner at the White House," he paused, "I had to call in more than one favor to ensure that Ralph Elliot received an invitation to that august gathering. So I think you'll find he's fairly preoccupied at the moment. I keep reading in the local press about his political ambitions. He denies them, of course, so I assume it has to be true."

"So why did you employ him in the first place?"

"We've always used Belman and Wayland in the past, Mr. Cartwright, and until this takeover, I hadn't come across Mr. Elliot. I blame myself, but I am at least attempting to rectify the mistake. You see, I didn't have your advantage of losing to him twice in the past."

"*Touché*," said Nat, "so what happens next?"

"I have enjoyed meeting with you, Mr. Cartwright, and I shall put your proposal to my board later this afternoon. Sadly one of our members is in Washington, but I would still hope to be able to phone you back with our reaction later this evening."

"I'll look forward to that call," said Nat.

"Good, and then we can meet face-to-face, and I suggest as quickly as possible, as I would like an agreement signed by Friday evening subject to due diligence." Murray Goldblatz paused. "Nat," he said, "yesterday you asked me to do you a favor; I would now like one in return."

"Yes, of course," said Nat.

"The monsignor, a shrewd man, asked for a two-hundred-dollar donation for the use of this box, and I feel now that we are partners you should pay your share. I only mention this because it will amuse my board, and allow me to keep a reputation among my Jewish friends of being ruthless."

"I shall make sure I'm not the reason you lose that reputation, father," Nat assured him.

Nat slipped out of the box and quickly made his way to the south entrance, where he saw a priest standing by the door dressed in a long black robe and biretta. Nat removed two fifty-dollar bills from his wallet and handed them over.

"God bless you, my son," the monsignor said, "but I have a feeling I could double your contribution if only I knew which of the two banks the church should be investing in."

—◦—

By the time coffee had been served, Al Brubaker still hadn't given any clue as to why he'd wanted to see Fletcher.

"Jenny, why don't you take Annie through to the drawing room, as there's something I need to discuss with Fletcher. We'll join you in a few minutes." Once Annie and Jenny had left them Al said, "Care for a brandy or a cigar, Fletcher?"

"No thank you, Al. I'll stick with the wine."

"You chose a good weekend to be in Washington. The Republicans are in town preparing for the midterms. Bush's throwing a party for them at the White House tonight, so we Democrats have to go into hiding for a few days. But tell me," said Al, "how's the party shaping up in Connecticut?"

"The caucus met today to discuss picking our candidates, and inevitably finance."

"Will you be running again?"

"Yes, I've already made that clear."

"And I'm told you could be the next majority leader?"

"Unless Jack Swales wants the job; he is, after all, the longest-serving member."

"Jack? Is he still alive? I could have sworn I'd attended his funeral. No, I can't believe the party will get behind him, unless . . ."

"Unless?" said Fletcher.

"You decide to run for governor." Fletcher put his glass of wine back on the table, so that Al couldn't see that his hand was shaking. "You must have considered the possibility."

"Yes, I have," said Fletcher, "but I assumed the party would get behind Larry Connick."

"Our esteemed lieutenant governor," said Al as he lit his cigar. "No, Larry's a good man, but he's aware of his limitations, thank God, because not many politicians are. I had a word with him last week at the governor's conference in Pittsburgh. He told me that he would be happy to remain on the ticket but only if we felt it would assist the party." Al took a puff of his cigar and enjoyed the moment, before adding, "No, Fletcher, you're our first choice, and if you agree to throw your hat into the ring, you have my word that the party will get behind you. The last thing we need is a bruising election for our candidate. Let's leave the real scrap for when we have to fight the Republicans, because their candidate will be trying to ride on Bush's coattails, so we can expect a tough battle if we hope to hold on to the governor's mansion."

"Do you have any view on who the Republicans might put up?" asked Fletcher.

"I was rather hoping you'd tell me," said Al.

"There seem to be two serious contenders who come from different wings of the party. Barbara Hunter, who sits in the House, but her age and record are against her."

"Record?" said Al.

"She hasn't made a habit of winning," said Fletcher, "although she has over the years built up a strong base in the party, and as Nixon showed us after losing in California, you can never count anyone out."

"Who else?" said Al.

"Does the name Ralph Elliot mean anything to you?"

"No," said the chairman, "but I did notice that he's a member of the Connecticut delegation that's having dinner at the White House tonight."

"Yes, he's on their state central committee, and if he becomes their candidate, it could turn out to be a very dirty campaign. Elliot's a bare-knuckle boxer who scores most of his points between rounds."

"In which case he may turn out to be as much of a liability as an asset."

"Well, I can tell you one thing, he's a hell of a street-fighter and doesn't like losing."

"That's exactly what they say about you," said Al with a smile. "Anyone else?"

"Two or three other names are being bandied about, but so far nobody's come forward. Let's face it, few people had even heard of Carter until New Hampshire."

"And what about this man," said Al, holding up the cover of *Banker's Weekly*.

Fletcher stared at the headline NEXT GOVERNOR OF CONNECTICUT? "But if you read the article, Al, you'll see he's strongly tipped to become the next chairman of Fairchild's if the two banks can agree on terms. I glanced through the piece on the plane."

Al flicked through the pages. "You obviously didn't get as far as the last paragraph," he said, and read aloud, "*Although it's assumed when Murray Goldblatz retires he would be succeeded by Cartwright, this position could just as easily be filled by his close friend, Tom Russell, should the CEO of Russell's decide to allow his name to be put forward as the Republican candidate for governor."*

--◦--

Once he and Annie had returned to their hotel and gone to bed, Fletcher couldn't sleep, and it wasn't just because the bed was more comfortable and the pillows softer than he was used to. Al needed to know his decision by the end of the month, as he was keen to get the party up and running behind their candidate.

Annie woke just after seven. "Did you have a good night's sleep, darling?" she asked.

"I hardly slept a wink."

"I slept like a log, but then I didn't have to worry about whether you should run for governor."

"Why not?" asked Fletcher.

"Because I think you should go for it, and can't imagine why you would have any reservations."

"First, I need a long session with Harry, because one thing's for sure, he'll already have given the idea a lot of thought."

"I wouldn't be so sure of that," said Annie. "I think you'll find he's more preoccupied with Lucy for class president."

"Well, perhaps I'll be able to grab a moment of his undivided attention to discuss the governorship of Connecticut." Fletcher leaped out of bed. "Would you mind if we skipped breakfast and caught an early flight? I want to have a word with Harry before going on to the Senate."

Fletcher barely spoke on the journey back to Hartford, as he read and reread the article in *Banker's Weekly* on Nat Cartwright, the possible new deputy-chairman of Fairchild's or the next governor of Connecticut. Once again, he was struck by how much they had in common.

"What are you going to ask Dad?" said Annie as their plane circled Bradley Field.

"For a start, am I too young?"

"But as Al pointed out, there is already one governor younger than you, and two about the same age."

"Second, how does he rate my chances?"

"He wouldn't be willing to answer that until he knows who your opponent is."

"And third, am I capable of doing the job?"

"I know what his answer will be to that question, because I've already discussed it with him."

"Thank God we didn't take this long to land when we flew in to Washington last night," said Fletcher as they circled the airport for a third time.

"Will you still stop by and see Dad before you go to the Capitol?" asked Annie. "He's bound to be sitting up in bed waiting to hear your news."

"I always intended to make Harry my first stop," said Fletcher as he drove his car out of the airport and onto the highway.

It was a bright autumnal morning when Senator Davenport arrived back in town. He decided to drive up the hill and past the Capitol before cutting across to the hospital.

As they came over the brow of the hill, Annie stared out of the car window, and began weeping uncontrollably. Fletcher pulled over to the hard shoulder. He took his wife in his arms, as he looked over her shoulder at the Capitol building.

The United States flag was flying at half mast.

41

MR. GOLDBLATZ ROSE from his place at the center of the table and glanced down at his prepared statement. On his right sat Nat Cartwright, and on his left, Tom Russell. The rest of the board was seated in the row behind him.

"Ladies and gentlemen of the press, it is my great pleasure to announce the merger of Fairchild's and Russell's, creating a new bank which will be known as Fairchild Russell. I shall remain as chairman, Mr. Nat Cartwright will be my deputy chairman, and Tom and Julia Russell will join the board. Mr. Wesley Jackson will continue as the new bank's chief executive. I am able to confirm that Russell's Bank has withdrawn its takeover bid, and a new ownership structure for the company will be announced in the near future. Both Mr. Cartwright and I will be happy to answer your questions."

Hands shot up all over the room. "Yes," said the chairman, pointing to a woman in the second row, with whom he had pre-arranged the first question.

"Is it still your intention to resign as chairman in eighteen months' time?"

"Yes, it is, and there are no prizes for guessing who I expect to succeed me."

He turned and looked at Nat as another journalist shouted, "How does Mr. Russell feel about that?"

Mr. Goldblatz smiled, as it was a question they had all antici-pated. He turned to his left and said, "Perhaps Mr. Russell should answer that question."

Tom smiled benevolently at the journalist. "I'm delighted by the coming together of the two leading banks in the state, and honored to have been invited to join the board of Fairchild Russell as a non-executive director." He smiled. "I'm rather hoping Mr. Cartwright will consider reappointing me in eighteen months' time."

"Word perfect," whispered the chairman as Tom resumed his place.

Nat quickly rose from the other side to deliver an equally well-scripted response, "I most certainly will be reappointing Mr. Russell, but not as a nonexecutive director."

Goldblatz smiled and added, "I am sure that will not come as a total surprise to anyone who follows these matters closely. Yes?" he said, pointing to another journalist.

"Will there be any layoffs caused by this merger?"

"No," said Goldblatz. "It is our intention to retain all of Russell's staff, but one of Mr. Cartwright's immediate responsibilities will be to prepare for a complete restructuring of the bank during the next twelve months. Though I would like to add that Mrs. Julia Russell has already been appointed to head up our new combined property division. We at Fairchild's have watched with admiration her handling of the Cedar Wood project."

"Can I ask why your legal counsel, Ralph Elliot, is not present today?" said a voice from the back of the room.

Another question Goldblatz had anticipated, even though he couldn't quite see where it had come from. "Mr. Elliot has been in Washington, D.C. Last night he dined with President Bush at the White House, otherwise he would have been with us this morning. Next question?" Goldblatz made no reference to the "frank exchange of views" he'd had with Elliot on the phone in the early hours of the morning.

"I spoke to Mr. Elliot earlier today," said the same journalist, "and I wonder if you would care to comment on the press statement he has just released?"

Nat froze as Goldblatz rose more slowly. "I'd be happy to comment if I knew what he'd said."

The journalist looked down at a single sheet of paper and read from it: *"I am delighted that Mr. Goldblatz felt able to take my advice and bring the two banks together rather than continue a bruising and damaging battle from which no one would have profited."* Goldblatz smiled and nodded. *"In eighteen months' time there will be three members of the board available to replace the current chairman, but as I consider one of them quite unsuitable to hold a post that requires financial probity, I have been left with no choice but to resign from the board and withdraw as the bank's legal advisor. With that one reservation, I wish the company every success in the future."*

Mr. Goldblatz's smile quickly disappeared, and he was unable to contain his rage. "I have no comment to make at the present t . . . t . . . time, and that ends this press con . . . con . . . conference." He rose from his place and marched out of the room with Nat following a pace behind him. "The bastard broke his agreement," said Goldblatz furiously, as he strode down the corridor toward the boardroom.

"Which was what precisely?" asked Nat, trying to remain calm.

"I agreed to say that he was a party to the successful negotiations, if in turn he would resign and withdraw as the legal representative of the new company, and make no further comment."

"Do we have that in writing?"

"No, I agreed to it over the phone last night. He said he would confirm it in writing today."

"So once again Elliot comes out smelling of roses," said Nat.

Goldblatz came to a halt outside the boardroom door and turned to face Nat. "No, he does not. I think the smell is more akin to manure," he added, "and this time, he's chosen the wrong man to cro . . . cro . . . cross."

—◇—

The popularity of an individual in life often only manifests itself in death.

The funeral service for Harry Gates, held at St. Joseph's Cathedral, was filled to overflowing, long before the choir had left the vestry. Don Culver, the chief of police, decided to cordon off the block in front of the cathedral, so that mourners could sit on the steps or stand in the street, while they listened to the service being relayed over loudspeakers.

When the cortège came to a halt, an honor guard carried the coffin up the steps and into the cathedral. Martha Gates was accompanied by her son, while her daughter and son-in-law walked a pace behind them. The throng of people on the steps made a passage to allow the family to join the other mourners inside. The congregation rose as an usher accompanied Mrs. Gates to the front pew. As they walked down the aisle, Fletcher noted the coming together of Baptists, Jews, Episcopalians, Muslims, Methodists and Mormons, all unified in their respect for this Roman Catholic.

The bishop opened the service with a prayer chosen by Martha, which was followed by hymns and readings that Harry would have enjoyed. Jimmy and Fletcher both read lessons, but it was Al Brubaker, as chairman of the party, who climbed the steps of the wooden pulpit to deliver the address.

He looked down at the packed congregation and remained silent for a moment. "Few politicians," he began, "inspire respect and affection, but if Harry could be with us today, he would see for himself that he was among that select group. I see many in this congregation I have never come across before," he paused, "so I have to assume they're Republicans." Laughter broke out inside the cathedral, and a ripple of applause outside in the street. "Here was a man who, when asked by the president to run for governor of this state, replied simply, 'I have not completed my work as the senator for Hartford,' and he never did. As chairman of my party, I have attended the funerals of presidents, governors, senators, congressmen and congresswomen, along with the powerful and mighty, but this funeral has a difference, for it is also filled with ordinary members of the public, who have simply come to say thank you.

"Harry Gates was opinionated, verbose, irascible and maddening. He was also passionate in the pursuit of causes he believed in. Loyal to his friends, fair with his opponents, he was a man whose company you sought out simply because it enriched your life. Harry Gates was no saint, but there will be saints standing at the Gates of Heaven waiting to greet him.

"To Martha, we say thank you for indulging Harry and all his dreams, so many achieved; one still to be fulfilled. To Jimmy and

Annie, his son and daughter, of whom he was inordinately proud. To Fletcher, his beloved son-in-law, who has been given the unenviable burden of carrying the torch. And to Lucy his grand-daughter, who became class president a few days after he died. America has lost a man who served his country at home and abroad, in war and in peace. Hartford has lost a public servant who will not easily be replaced.

"He wrote to me a few weeks ago," Brubaker paused, "begging for money—what a nerve—for his beloved hospital. He said he'd never speak to me again if I didn't send a check. I considered the pros and cons of that particular threat." It was a long time before the laughter and applause died down. "In the end, my wife sent a check. The truth is, that it never crossed Harry's mind that if he asked, you wouldn't give, and why? Because he spent his whole life giving, and now we must make that dream a reality and build a hospital in his memory of which he would have been proud.

"I read in the *Washington Post* last week that Senator Harry Gates had died, and then I traveled to Hartford this morning and drove past the senior citizens' center, the library and the hospital foundation stone that bears his name. I shall write to the *Washington Post* when I return tomorrow and tell them, 'you were wrong. Harry Gates is alive and still kicking.'" Mr. Brubaker paused as he looked down into the congregation, his eyes settling on Fletcher. *"Here was a man, when comes such another?"*

On the cathedral steps, Martha and Fletcher thanked Al Brubaker for his words.

"Anything less," said Al, "and he would have appeared in the pulpit next to me, demanding a recount." The chairman shook hands with Fletcher. "I didn't read out the whole of Harry's last letter to me," he said, "but I knew you would want to see the final paragraph." He slipped a hand into an inside pocket, removed the letter, unfolded it and passed it across to Fletcher.

When Fletcher had read Harry's last words, he looked at the chairman and nodded.

—◇—

Tom and Nat walked down the cathedral steps together and joined the crowds as they quietly dispersed.

"I wish I'd known him better," said Nat. "You realize that I asked him to join the board when he retired from the Senate?" Tom nodded. "He wrote—hand-wrote—such a charming letter explaining the only board he would ever sit on was the hospital's."

"I only met him a couple of times," said Tom, "he was mad, of course, but you have to be if you choose to spend your life pushing boulders up a hill. Don't ever tell anyone, but he's the only Democrat I've ever voted for."

Nat laughed. "You as well?" he admitted.

"How would you feel if I recommended that the board should make a donation of fifty thousand to the hospital fund?" asked Tom.

"I would oppose it," said Nat. Tom looked surprised. "Because when the senator sold his Russell's shares, he immediately donated a hundred thousand to the hospital. The least we can do is respond in kind."

Tom nodded his agreement and turned back to see Mrs. Gates standing on the top of the cathedral steps. He would write to her that afternoon enclosing the check. He sighed. "Look who's shaking hands with the widow."

Nat swung around to see Ralph Elliot holding Martha Gates's hand. "Are you surprised?" he said. "I can just hear him telling her how pleased he was that Harry took his advice and sold those shares in Russell's Bank, and made himself a million."

"Oh, my God," said Tom, "you're beginning to think like him."

"I'm going to have to if I'm to survive during the coming months."

"That's no longer an issue," said Tom. "Everyone at the bank accepts that you'll be the next chairman."

"It's not the chairmanship I'm talking about," said Nat. Tom came to a halt in front of the steps of the bank and turned to face his oldest friend.

"If Ralph Elliot puts his name forward as the Republican candidate for governor, then I shall run against him." He looked back toward the cathedral. "And this time I will beat him."

BOOK FIVE

JUDGES

42

"LADIES AND GENTLEMEN, Fletcher Davenport, the next governor of Connecticut."

It amused Fletcher that within moments of being selected as the Democratic candidate, he was immediately introduced as the next governor; no suggestion of an opponent, no hint that he might lose. But he recalled only too well Walter Mondale continually being introduced as the next president of the United States, and ending up as ambassador to Tokyo while it was Ronald Reagan who moved into the White House.

Once Fletcher had called Al Brubaker to confirm that he was willing to run, the party machine immediately swung behind him. One or two other Democratic heads appeared above the parapet, but like ducks at a shooting range they were quickly flattened.

In the end, Fletcher's only opposition turned out to be a congresswoman who had never done any harm—or enough good—for anyone else to notice. Once Fletcher had defeated her in the September primary, his party machine suddenly turned her into a formidable opponent who had been soundly beaten by the most impressive candidate the party had produced in years. But Fletcher privately acknowledged that she hadn't been much more than a paper opponent, and the real battle would begin once the Republicans had selected their standard bearer.

Although Barbara Hunter was as active and determined as ever, no one really believed she was going to head up the Republican ticket. Ralph Elliot already had the backing of several key party members, and whenever he spoke in public or private, the name of his friend, and even occasionally his close friend, Ronnie, fell easily from his lips. But Fletcher repeatedly heard rumors of just as large a group of Republicans who were searching for a credible alternative; otherwise they were threatening to abstain, even vote Democrat. Fletcher found it nerve-racking waiting to discover who that opponent would be. By late August, he realized that if there was to be a surprise candidate, they were leaving it tantalizingly late to come forward.

Fletcher looked down at the crowd in front of him. It was his fourth speech that day, and it wasn't yet twelve o'clock. He missed Harry's presence at those Sunday lunches, where ideas could be tested and found wanting. Lucy and George were happy to add their contributions, which only reminded him how indulgent Harry had been when he had come up with suggestions the senator must have heard a hundred times before, but never once hinted as much. But the next generation certainly left Fletcher in no doubt of what the Hotchkiss student body expected of their governor.

Fletcher's fourth speech that morning didn't differ greatly from the other three: to the Pepperidge Farm plant in Norwalk, the Wiffle Ball headquarters in Shelton and the Stanley tool-workers in New Britain. He just altered the occasional paragraph to acknowledge that the state's economy would not be in such good shape without their particular contribution. On to lunch with the Daughters of the American Revolution, where he failed to mention his Scottish ancestry, followed by three more speeches in the afternoon, before attending a fund-raising dinner, which wouldn't produce much more than ten thousand dollars.

Around midnight he would crawl into bed and put his arms around his sleeping wife and occasionally she would sigh. He'd read somewhere that once, when Reagan was out on the stump, he had been found cuddling a lamppost. Fletcher had laughed at the time, but no longer.

—◦—

"Romeo, Romeo, wherefore art thou Romeo?"

Nat had to agree with his son's assessment. Juliet was beautiful, but not the sort of girl Luke was likely to fall for. With five other females in the cast, he tried to work out which one it could possibly be. When the curtain came down for the interval, he thought that Luke had given a moving performance, and felt a glow of pride as he sat there in the audience listening to the applause. His parents had seen the play the night before, and told him that they'd felt the same pride as when he had performed Sebastian in the same hall.

Whenever Luke left the stage, Nat found his mind wandering back to the phone call he'd taken from Washington that morning. His secretary assumed it was Tom playing one of his practical jokes when he was asked if he was available to speak to the president of the United States.

Nat had found himself standing when George Bush came on the line.

The president congratulated him on Fairchild and Russell's being voted Bank of the Year—his excuse for the call—and then added the simple message, "Many people in our party hope you will allow your name to go forward as governor. You have a lot of friends and supporters in Connecticut, Nat. Let's hope we can meet soon."

The whole of Hartford knew within the hour that the president had called, but then switchboard operators also have a network of their own. Nat only told Su Ling and Tom, and they didn't seem all that surprised.

"The exchange of thy love's faithful vow for mine."

The father's mind switched back to the play.

Nat found that people began to stop him in the street and say, "I hope you'll run for governor, Nat"—Mr. Cartwright—even sir. When he and Su Ling had entered the hall that evening, heads had turned and he sensed a buzz all around him. In the car on the way to Taft he didn't ask Su Ling if he should run, simply, "Do you think I can do the job?"

"The president seemed to think so," she replied.

When the curtain came down following the death scene, Su Ling remarked, "Have you noticed that people are staring at us?" She paused. "I suppose we'll just have to get used to our son being a star."

How quickly she could bring Nat back down to earth, and what a governor's wife she would make.

The cast and the parents were invited to join the principal for supper, so Nat and Su Ling made their way over to his house.

"It's the nurse."

"Yes, she gave a very sensitive performance," said Nat.

"No, you fool, the nurse must have been the one Luke's fallen for," said Su Ling.

"What makes you so sure of that?" asked Nat.

"Just as the curtain came down, they held hands, and I'm fairly sure that wasn't in Shakespeare's original stage directions," said Su Ling.

"Well, we're about to find out if you're right," said Nat as they entered the principal's house.

They found Luke sipping a Coke in the hallway. "Hi, Dad," he said turning to face them. "This is Kathy Marshall; she played the nurse." Su Ling tried not to smirk. "And this is my mother. Wasn't Kathy fantastic? But then she plans to major in drama at Sarah Lawrence."

"Yes she was, but you weren't bad yourself," said Nat. "We were both very proud of you."

"Have you seen the play before, Mr. Cartwright?" asked Kathy.

"Yes, when Su Ling and I visited Stratford. The nurse was played by Celia Johnson, but I don't suppose you've even heard of her."

"*Brief Encounter*," Kathy responded immediately.

"Noël Coward," Luke said.

"And Trevor Howard played opposite her," said Kathy. Nat nodded at his son, who was still dressed as Romeo.

"You must be the first Romeo to have fallen for the nurse," said Su Ling.

Kathy grinned. "It's his Oedipus complex," she said. "And how did Miss Johnson translate the part? When my drama teacher saw it as an undergraduate with Dame Edith Evans, she said she played the nurse like a school matron—strict and firm, but loving."

"No," said Su Ling, "Celia Johnson portrayed her as slightly dotty, erratic but also loving."

"What an interesting idea. I must look up the director. Of course I would like to have played Juliet, but I'm just not good-looking enough," she added matter-of-factly.

"But you're beautiful," said Luke.

"You're hardly a reliable judge on that subject, Luke," she said, taking his hand. "After all, you've been wearing glasses since the age of four."

Nat smiled, and thought how lucky Luke was to have Kathy as a friend.

"Kathy, would you like to come and spend a few days with us during the summer vacation?" asked Nat.

"Yes, if it's not going to cause you too much trouble, Mr. Cartwright," Kathy replied. "Because I wouldn't want to be in your way."

"Be in my way?" queried Nat.

"Yes, Luke tells me that you'll be running for governor."

—◇—

LOCAL BANKER RUNS FOR GOVERNOR ran the banner headline in the *Hartford Courant*. An inside page was given over to a profile of the brilliant young financier who, twenty-five years earlier, had been awarded the Medal of Honor, bringing his career up to date with the role he'd played in the merger between the small family bank of Russell's, with its eleven local branches, and Fairchild's with its one hundred and two establishments spread right across the state. Nat smiled when he recalled the confessional at St. Joseph's, and the graceful way Murray Goldblatz continued to convey the impression that the original idea had been Nat's. Nat had continued to learn from Murray, who never lowered his guard or his standards.

The *Courant*'s editorial suggested that Nat's decision to run against Ralph Elliot for the Republican nomination had opened up the contest, as both were outstanding candidates at the top of their professions. The editorial did not come out in favor of either man, but promised to report fairly on the duel between the banker and the lawyer, who were known not to like each other. "*Mrs. Hunter will also run*," they added in the final paragraph almost as an afterthought, which summed up the *Courant*'s view on her chances now that Nat had allowed his name to go forward.

Nat felt well satisfied with the press and television coverage that followed his announcement, and even more pleased by the favorable public reaction on the street. Tom had taken a two-month leave of absence from the bank to run Nat's campaign, and

387

Murray Goldblatz sent a substantial check for the campaign fund.

The first meeting was held at Tom's home that evening, when Nat's chief of staff explained to his carefully selected team what they would be up against during the next six weeks.

Rising before the sun each morning, and collapsing in bed after midnight had few compensations, but an unexpected one for Nat was Luke's fascination with the electoral process. He spent his vacation accompanying his father everywhere, often with Kathy by his side. Nat grew to like her more and more as each day passed.

Nat took a little time getting used to the new routine, and being reminded by Tom that you can't bark out instructions to volunteers, and you must always thank them, however little they've done and however badly they've done it. But even with six speeches and a dozen meetings a day, the learning curve proved steep.

It quickly became clear that Elliot had been out on the stump for several weeks, hoping his early groundwork would give him an unassailable advantage. Nat soon realized that although the first caucus in Ipswich would only yield seventeen electoral votes, its importance was disproportionate to the numbers involved, as in New Hampshire at a presidential election. He visited every one of the caucus voters and never left in any doubt that Elliot had been there before him. Although his rival had already locked up several delegates, there remained a few waverers who were undecided or simply didn't trust the man.

As the days slipped by, Nat discovered that he was always expected to be in two places at once because the primary in Chelsea was only two days after the caucus in Ipswich. Elliot was now spending most of his time in Chelsea, as he considered he'd already wrapped up the Ipswich caucus.

Nat returned to Ipswich on the night of the caucus vote, to hear the local chairman announce that Elliot had captured ten of the votes while he had secured seven. Elliot's team, while claiming it as a clear-cut victory, were unable to hide their disappointment. As soon as he'd heard the result, Nat ran to his car and Tom had him back in Chelsea by midnight.

To his surprise, the local papers discounted the result in

Ipswich, saying that Chelsea, with an electorate of over eleven thousand, would be much more of an indicator as to how the public felt about the two men rather than reading anything into the views of a handful of party *apparatchiks*. And Nat certainly felt more relaxed out on the streets, in the shopping malls, at the factory gates, and in the schools and clubs than he had been in smoke-filled rooms listening to people who believed it was their "God-given right" to select the candidate.

After a couple of weeks of pressing the flesh, Nat told Tom that he was very encouraged by how many voters were saying they would support him. But was Elliot receiving the same response, he wondered.

"I've no idea," said Tom as they drove off to yet another meeting, "but I can tell you that we are fast running out of money. If we're soundly beaten tomorrow, we may have to withdraw from the race, having taken part in one of the shortest campaigns in history. We could of course let the world know that Bush is backing you, because that would be sure to swing a few votes."

"No," said Nat firmly. "That was a private call, not an endorsement."

"But Elliot never stops talking about his trip to the White House with his old friend George, as if it was a dinner for two."

"And how do you feel the rest of the Republican delegation feel about that?"

"That's far too subtle for the average voter," suggested Tom.

"Never underestimate them," said Nat.

―◇―

Nat couldn't recall much about the day of the Chelsea primary, except that he never stopped moving. When it was announced just after midnight that Elliot had won by 6,109 votes to 5,302 for Cartwright, Nat's only question was, "Can we afford to go on now that Elliot has gained a twenty-seven to ten lead among the delegates?"

"The patient is still breathing," Tom replied, "but only just, so it's on to Hartford, and if Elliot wins that one as well, we won't be able to stop his bandwagon rolling all over us. Just be thankful you have a day job to go back to," he added with a smile.

Mrs. Hunter, who had only picked up two electoral college votes, conceded defeat and said she was withdrawing from the race and would be announcing in the near future which candidate she would be supporting.

Nat enjoyed returning to his hometown, where the people in the streets treated him as a friend. Tom knew how much effort had to be put into Hartford, not only because it was their last chance, but as the state capital it carried the most electoral votes, nineteen in all, with the prehistoric rule of winner takes all, so if Nat topped the poll, he would go into the lead, 29:27. If he lost, he could unpack his bags and stay at home.

During the campaign, the candidates were invited to attend several functions together, but whenever they did, they rarely acknowledged each other's presence, and certainly never stopped for a chat.

With three days to go to the primary, a poll in the *Hartford Courant* put Nat two points ahead of his rival, and they reported that Mrs. Barbara Hunter was throwing her support behind Cartwright. This was exactly the boost Nat's campaign needed. The following morning, he noticed that far more workers were with him on the street, and many more passersby came up to shake him by the hand.

He was in Robinson's Mall when the message came through from Murray Goldblatz, "I need to see you urgently." Murray was not a man to use the word urgent unless that was exactly what he meant. Nat left his team to go on canvassing, assuring them that he would return shortly. They didn't see him again that day.

When Nat arrived at the bank, the receptionist told him that the chairman was in the boardroom with Mr. and Mrs. Russell. Nat walked in and took his usual place opposite Murray, but the expressions on the faces of his three colleagues didn't harbor glad tidings. Murray came quickly to the point. "I understand that you have a town meeting tonight which both you and Elliot will be addressing?"

"Yes," said Nat, "it's the last major event before the vote tomorrow."

"I have a spy in the Elliot camp," said Murray, "and she tells me that they have a question planned for tonight that will derail your campaign, but she can't find out what it is, and daren't be too inquisitive, in case they become suspicious. Do you have any idea what it might be?"

"No, I don't," said Nat.

"Perhaps he's found out about Julia," said Tom quietly.

"Julia?" said Murray, sounding puzzled.

"No, not my wife," said Tom. "The first Mrs. Kirkbridge."

"I had no idea there was a first Mrs. Kirkbridge," said Murray.

"No reason you should," said Tom. "But I've always dreaded the thought that the truth might come out." Murray listened attentively as Tom recalled how he'd met the woman who passed herself off as Julia Kirkbridge, and how she had signed the bank's check and then removed all the money from her account.

"Where is that check now?" asked Murray.

"Somewhere in the bowels of City Hall, would be my guess."

"Then we must assume that Elliot's got his hands on it, but were you technically breaking the law?"

"No, but we didn't keep to our written agreement with the council," said Tom.

"And the Cedar Wood project went on to be a huge success, making everyone involved a handsome return," added Nat.

"So," said Murray, "we are left with a choice. You either make a clean breast of it and prepare a statement this afternoon, or wait until the bomb drops tonight and hope you have an answer to every question that's thrown at you."

"What do you recommend?" said Nat.

"I would do nothing. First, my informant could be wrong, and second, the Cedar Wood project may not be the curve ball, in which case you will have opened that can of worms unnecessarily."

"But what else could it be?" said Nat.

"Rebecca?" said Tom.

"What do you mean?" asked Nat.

"That you made her pregnant and forced her to have an abortion."

"That's hardly a crime," said Murray.

"Unless she tries to claim you raped her."

Nat laughed. "Elliot's never going to raise that particular subject, because he might well have been the father himself, and abortion is not part of his holier-than-thou image."

"Have you considered going on the attack yourself?" asked Murray.

"What do you have in mind?" asked Nat.

"Didn't Elliot have to resign from Alexander Dupont and Bell on the same day as the senior partner because half a million went missing from a client account?"

"No, I will not stoop to his level," said Nat. "In any case, Elliot's involvement was never proved."

"Oh yes, it was," said Murray. Tom and Nat stared across at the chairman. "A friend of mine was the client in question, and phoned to warn me the moment he heard that Elliot was repre-senting us in the takeover."

Nat sighed. "That may well be the case, but the answer is still no."

"Good," said Murray, "then we'll beat him on your terms, which means that we'll have to spend the rest of the afternoon preparing answers to whatever you imagine might be the questions."

At six o'clock, Nat left the bank feeling wrung out. He phoned Su Ling and told her what had happened. "Do you want me to come along tonight?" she asked.

"No, little flower, but can you keep Luke well occupied? If it's going to be unpleasant, I'd rather he wasn't around. You know how sensitive he can be, and he always takes it all so personally."

"I'll take him to a movie—there's a French film playing at the Arcadia that he and Kathy have been pressing me to see all week."

Nat tried not to appear nervous when he arrived at Goodwin House that night. He walked into the hotel's main dining room to find it was packed with several hundred local businessmen chat-ting to each other. But who were they supporting, he wondered? He suspected many of them still hadn't made up their minds, as the polls kept reminding them that 10 percent were still unde-cided. The headwaiter directed him to the top table, where he found Elliot chatting to the local party chairman. Manny Fried-man swung around to welcome Nat. Elliot leaned across and made a public show of shaking hands. Nat sat down quickly and began to make notes on the back of a menu.

When the chairman called for order he introduced "the two heavyweights both well qualified to be our next governor," and then invited Elliot to make his opening remarks. Nat had never heard him speak so poorly. The chairman then asked Nat to reply and when he resumed his place, he would have been the first to admit he hadn't done much better. The first round, he thought, had ended in a no-points draw.

When the chairman called for questions, Nat wondered when the missile would be launched and from which direction. His eyes swept the hall as he waited for the first question.

"How do the candidates feel about the education bill that is currently being debated in the Senate?" came from someone sitting at the top table. Nat concentrated on the provisions in the bill that he felt should be amended, while Elliot kept reminding them that he had completed his undergraduate degree at the University of Connecticut.

The second questioner wanted to know about the new state income tax, and whether both candidates would guarantee not to raise it. Yes and yes.

The third questioner was interested in the policy on crime, and with a particular reference to young offenders. Elliot said they should all be locked up and taught a lesson. Nat was less sure that prison was the answer to every problem, and that they should perhaps consider some of the innovations which Utah had recently introduced into their penal system.

When Nat resumed his seat, the chairman rose and looked around the room for another question. As soon as the man stood up without actually looking at him, Nat knew this had to be the plant. He glanced at Elliot, who was scribbling notes, pretending to be oblivious of his presence. "Yes, sir," said the chairman, pointing at him.

"Mr. Chairman, may I ask if either of the candidates has ever broken the law?"

Elliot was on his feet immediately. "Several times," he said. "I've had three parking tickets in the past week, which is why I'll be easing parking restrictions in town centers the moment I'm elected." Word perfect, thought Nat; even the timing had been rehearsed. A splattering of applause broke out.

Nat rose slowly and turned to face Elliot. "I shall not be changing the law to accommodate Mr. Elliot, because I believe there
should be fewer vehicles in our city centers, not more. It may not
be popular, but someone has to stand up and warn people that
their future will be bleak if we build bigger and bigger cars that
consume more and more gas and then spit out more and more
toxic fumes. We owe our children a better heritage than that, and
I have no interest in being elected on glib remarks that will be
quickly forgotten once I'm in power." He sat down to loud
applause and hoped that the chairman would move on to another
questioner, but the man remained standing.

"But, Mr. Cartwright, you didn't answer my question as to
whether you'd ever broken the law."

"Not that I'm aware of," replied Nat.

"But isn't it true that you once cleared a check for three million
six hundred thousand dollars from Russell's Bank, when you knew
that the funds had already been misappropriated and that the signature on the check was fraudulent?"

Several of the audience began chattering at once, and Nat had
to wait for some time before he could reply.

"Yes, Russell's was swindled out of that money by a very clever
fraudster, but as that exact sum was owed to the local council, I
felt that the bank had no choice but to honor the debt and pay the
council the amount in full."

"Did you inform the police at the time that the money had been
stolen? After all, it belonged to the customers of Russell's Bank
and not to you," continued the questioner.

"No, because we had every reason to believe that the cash had
been transferred abroad, so we knew that there would be no possibility of retrieving it." Nat realized as soon as he had finished
speaking that his answer would not placate the questioner or several others in the audience.

"If you were to become governor, Mr. Cartwright, would you
treat the taxpayers' money in the same cavalier fashion?"

Elliot was immediately on his feet. "Mr. Chairman, that was a
disgraceful suggestion and nothing more than innuendo and slur;
why don't we move on?" He sat down to loud applause while Nat

remained standing. He had to admire the sheer nerve of Elliot setting up the question and then being seen to come to his opponent's defense. He waited for complete silence.

"The incident you refer to occurred over ten years ago. It was a mistake on my part that I regret, although it is ironic that it turned out to be a massive financial success for all those involved, because the three point six million the bank invested in the Cedar Wood project has been a boon to the people of Hartford, not to mention the city's economy."

The questioner still wouldn't sit down. "Despite Mr. Elliot's magnanimous comments, may I ask him if he would have reported such a misappropriation of funds to the police?"

Elliot rose slowly. "I would prefer not to comment without knowing all the details of this particular case, but I am happy to take Mr. Cartwright's word when he says that he did not commit any offense, and bitterly regrets not reporting the matter to the appropriate authorities at the time." He paused for some time. "However, if I am elected governor, you can be assured of open government. If I make a mistake, I will admit it at the time and not ten years later." The questioner sat down, his job completed.

The chairman found it difficult to bring the meeting back to order. There were several more questions, but they were not listened to in silence, as those seated in the body of the hall continued to discuss Nat's revelation.

When the chairman finally brought the meeting to a close, Elliot left the room quickly while Nat remained in his place. He was touched by how many people came up and shook him by the hand, many agreeing that the Cedar Wood project had proved beneficial for the city.

"Well, at least they didn't lynch you," Tom said as they left the room.

"No, they didn't, but there will only be one subject on the voters' minds tomorrow. Am I a suitable person to occupy the governor's mansion?"

43

THE CEDAR WOOD SCANDAL was the headline in the *Hartford Courant* the following morning. A photograph of the check and Julia's real signature had been placed side by side. It didn't read well, but luckily for Nat half the voters had gone to the polls long before the paper hit the streets. Nat had earlier prepared a short withdrawal statement should he lose, which congratulated his opponent, but fell short of endorsing him for governor. Nat was in his office when the result was announced from Republican head-quarters.

Tom took the call and rushed in without knocking. "You won, you won, 11,792 to 11,673—it's only by a hundred and nineteen votes, but it still puts you in the lead in the electoral college, 29–27."

The next day, the leader in the *Hartford Courant* did point out that no one had lost any money by investing in the Cedar Wood project, and perhaps the voters had made their intentions clear.

Nat still had to face three more caucuses and two more primaries before the candidate was finally selected. He was therefore relieved to find that Cedar Wood quickly became yesterday's news. Elliot won the next caucus 19–18, and Nat the primary four days later, 9,702–6,379, which put him even further ahead as they approached the final primary. In the electoral college, Nat now led 116–91 and the polls were showing him seven points ahead in the town of his birth.

On the streets of Cromwell, Nat was joined by his parents, Susan and Michael, who concentrated on the older voters, while Luke and Kathy tried to persuade the young to turn out. As each day passed, Nat became more and more confident that he was going to win. The *Courant* began to suggest that the real battle lay ahead for Nat when he would have to face Fletcher Davenport, the popular senator for Hartford. However, Tom still insisted that they take the television debate with Elliot seriously.

"We don't need to trip up at the final hurdle," he said. "Clear that, and you'll be the candidate. But I still want you to spend Sunday going over the questions again and again, as well as preparing for anything and everything that might come up during the debate. You can be sure that Fletcher Davenport will be sitting at home watching you on TV and analyzing everything you say. If you stumble, he will have issued a press statement within minutes."

Nat now regretted that some weeks before he'd agreed to appear on a local television program and debate with Elliot the night before the final primary. He and Elliot had settled on David Anscott to conduct the proceedings. Anscott was an interviewer who was more interested in coming over as popular than incisive. Tom didn't object to him as he felt the occasion would act as a dry run for the inevitably more serious debate with Fletcher Davenport scheduled for some time in the future.

Reports were coming back to Tom each day that volunteers were deserting Ralph Elliot in droves and some were even switching over and joining their team, so by the time he and Nat arrived at the television studio they both felt quietly confident. Su Ling accompanied her husband, but Luke said he wanted to stay at home and watch the debate on television so he could brief his father on how he came over to the larger audience.

"On the sofa with Kathy, no doubt," suggested Nat.

"No, Kathy went back home this afternoon for her sister's birthday," said Su Ling, "and Luke could have joined her, but to be fair he's taking his role as your youth advisor very seriously."

Tom came rushing into the green room and showed Nat the latest opinion poll figures. They gave him a six percent lead. "I think only Fletcher Davenport can now stop you becoming governor."

"I won't be convinced until the final result has been announced," said Su Ling. "Never forget the stunt Elliot pulled with the ballot boxes after we'd all assumed the count was over."

"He's already tried every stunt he can think of and failed," said Tom.

"I wish I could be so confident of that," said Nat quietly.

Both candidates were applauded by the small television audience as they walked out onto the stage for a program billed as "The Final Encounter." The two men met in the center of the stage and shook hands, but their eyes remained fixed on the camera.

"This will be a live program," David Anscott explained to the audience, "and we'll be going on air in around five minutes. I will open with a few questions, and then turn it over to you. If you have something you want to ask either candidate, make it short and to the point—no speeches, please."

Nat smiled as he scanned the audience, until his eyes came to rest on the man who had asked the Cedar Wood question. He was sitting in the second row. Nat could feel the sweat on the palms of his hands, but even if he was called, Nat was confident he could handle him. This time he was well prepared.

The television arc lights were switched on, the titles began to roll, and David Anscott, smile in place, opened the show. Once he'd introduced the participants, both candidates made a one-minute opening statement—sixty seconds can be a long time on television. After so many sound bites, they could have delivered such homilies in their sleep.

Anscott began with a couple of warm-up questions which had been scripted for him. Once the candidates had given their replies, he made no attempt to follow up anything they had said, but simply moved on to the next question as it appeared on the autocue in front of him. Once the interviewer had come to the end of his set piece, he quickly turned it over to the audience.

The first question turned into a speech on choice, which pleased Nat as he watched the seconds ticking away. He knew Elliot would be indecisive on this subject, as he was willing to offend neither the women's movement nor his friends in the Roman Catholic church. Nat made it clear that he supported unequivocally a woman's right to choose. Elliot, as he suspected, was evasive. Anscott called for a second question.

Watching from home, Fletcher made notes on everything Nat Cartwright said. He clearly understood the underlying principle of the education bill and, more important, he obviously thought the changes Fletcher wanted to bring about were quite reasonable.

"He's very bright, isn't he," said Annie.

"And cute too," said Lucy.

"Anyone on my side?" asked Fletcher.

"Yes, I don't think he's cute," said Jimmy. "But he has thought a great deal about your bill and he obviously considers it an election issue."

"I don't know about cute," said Annie, "but have you noticed that at certain angles he looks a little like you, Fletcher?"

"Oh no," said Lucy, "he's much better looking than Dad."

The third question was on gun control. Ralph Elliot stated that he backed the gun lobby and the right of every American to defend himself. Nat explained why he would like to see more control of guns, so that incidents like the one his son had experienced while at elementary school could never occur again.

Annie and Lucy started clapping, along with the studio audience.

"Isn't someone going to remind him who it was in that classroom with his son?" asked Jimmy.

"He doesn't need reminding," said Fletcher.

"One more question," said Anscott, "and it will have to be quick, because we're running out of time."

The plant in the second row rose from his place right on cue. Elliot pointed at him in case Anscott was considering anyone else.

"How would the two candidates deal with the problem of illegal immigrants?"

"What the hell's that got to do with the governor of Connecticut?" asked Fletcher.

Ralph Elliot looked straight at the questioner and said, "I'm sure I speak for both of us when I say that America should always welcome anyone who is oppressed and in need of help, as we have always done throughout our history. However, those who wish to enter our country must, of course, abide by the correct procedure and meet all the necessary legal requirements."

"That sounded to me," said Fletcher, turning to face Annie, "overprepared and overrehearsed. So what's he up to?"

"Is that also your view on illegal immigrants, Mr. Cartwright?" asked David Anscott, a little puzzled as to what the questioner was getting at.

"I confess, David, that I haven't given the matter a great deal of thought, as it has not been high on my priorities when I consider the problems currently facing the state of Connecticut."

"Wrap it up," Anscott heard the producer say in his earpiece, just as the questioner added, "But you must have given it some thought, Mr. Cartwright. After all, isn't your wife an illegal immigrant?"

"Hold on, let him answer that," said the producer. "If we go off the air now we'll have a quarter million people phoning in to find out his response. Close-up on Cartwright."

Fletcher was among those quarter of a million who waited for Nat's reply as the camera panned across to Elliot, who had a puzzled look on his face.

"You bastard," said Fletcher, "you knew that question was coming."

The camera returned to Nat, but his lips remained pursed.

"Wouldn't I be right in suggesting," continued the questioner, "that your wife entered this country illegally?"

"My wife is the Professor of Statistics at the University of Connecticut," said Nat, trying to disguise a tremble in his voice.

Anscott listened on his earpiece to find out how the producer wanted to play it, as they had already overrun their time slot.

"Say nothing," said the producer, "just hang in there. I can always run the credits over them if it gets boring." Anscott gave a slight nod in the direction of the head-on camera.

"That may well be the case, Mr. Cartwright," continued the questioner, "but didn't her mother, Su Kai Peng, enter this country with false papers, claiming to be married to an American serviceman, who had in fact died fighting for his country some months before the date on the marriage license?"

Nat didn't reply.

Fletcher was equally silent as he watched Cartwright being stretched on the rack.

"As you seem unwilling to answer my question, Mr. Cartwright, perhaps you can confirm that on the marriage license your mother-in-law described herself as a seamstress. However, the fact is that before she landed in America, she was a prostitute plying her trade on the streets of Seoul, so heaven knows who your wife's father is."

"Credits," said the producer. "We've run out of time and I daren't break into *Baywatch,* but keep the cameras running. We may pick up some extra footage for the late-night news."

Once the monitor on the stage showed credits rolling, the questioner quickly left the studio. Nat stared down at his wife sitting in the third row. She was pale and shaking.

"It's a wrap," said the producer.

Elliot turned to the moderator and said, "That was disgraceful, you should have stopped him a lot earlier," and looking across at Nat added, "believe me, I had no idea that . . ."

"You're a liar," said Nat.

"Stay on him," said the director to the first cameraman, "Keep all four cameras rolling, I want every angle on this."

"What are you suggesting?" asked Elliot.

"That you set the whole thing up. You weren't even subtle about it—you even used the same man that questioned me on the Cedar Wood project a couple of weeks ago. But I'll tell you one thing, Elliot," he said, jabbing a finger at him, "I will still kill you."

Nat stormed off the stage and found Su Ling waiting for him in the wings. "Come on, little flower, I'm taking you home." Tom quickly joined them as Nat put an arm around his wife.

"I'm sorry, Nat, but I have to ask," said Tom. "Was any of that garbage true?"

"All of it," said Nat, "and before you ask another question, I've known since we were first married."

"Take Su Ling home," said Tom, "and whatever you do, don't talk to the press."

"Don't bother," said Nat. "You can issue a statement on my

behalf saying that I'm withdrawing from the race. I'm not having my family dragged through any more of this."

"Don't make a hasty decision that you may well later regret. Let's talk about what needs to be done in the morning," said Tom.

Nat took Su Ling by the hand, walked out of the studio and through a door leading into the parking lot.

"Good luck," shouted one supporter as Nat opened the car door for his wife. He didn't acknowledge any of the cheers as they drove quickly away. He looked across at Su Ling, who was thumping the dashboard in anger. Nat took a hand off the steering wheel and placed it gently on Su Ling's leg. "I love you," he said, "and I always will. Nothing and no one will ever change that."

"How did Elliot find out?"

"He's probably had a team of private detectives delving into my past."

"And when he couldn't come up with anything about you, he switched his sights onto me and my mother," whispered Su Ling. There was a long silence before she added, "I don't want you to withdraw; you must stay in the race. It's the only way we can beat the bastard." Nat didn't reply as he joined the evening traffic. "I just feel so sorry for Luke," Su Ling eventually said. "He will have taken it so very personally. I only wish Kathy had stayed on for another day."

"I'll take care of Luke," said Nat. "You'd better go and collect your mother and bring her back to our place for the night."

"I'll call her just as soon as we get in," said Su Ling. "I suppose it's just possible that she didn't watch the program."

"Not a hope," said Nat as he pulled into the driveway, "she's my most loyal fan and never misses any of my TV appearances."

Nat put his arm around Su Ling as they walked toward the front door. All the lights in the house were off except for one in Luke's bedroom. Nat turned the key in the lock and as he opened the door, said, "You phone your mother, and I'll pop up and see Luke."

Su Ling picked up the phone in the hallway as Nat walked slowly up the stairs, trying to compose his thoughts. He knew Luke would expect every question to be answered truthfully. He walked down the corridor and knocked gently on his son's door. There was no reply, so he tried again, saying, "Luke, can I come in?" Still no reply. He opened the door a little and glanced inside, but Luke wasn't in bed and none of his clothes were laid out neatly over the usual chair. Nat's first reaction was that he must have gone across to the shop to be with his grandmother. He turned out the light and listened to Su Ling talking to her mother. He was about to go down and join her when he noticed that Luke had left a light on in the bathroom. He decided to switch it off.

Nat walked across the room and pushed open the bathroom door. For a moment he remained transfixed as he stared up at his son. He then collapsed onto his knees, unable to get himself to look up a second time, although he knew he would have to remove Luke's hanging body so that it wouldn't be the last memory Su Ling would have of their only child.

—◇—

Annie picked up the phone and listened. "It's Charlie from the *Courant* for you," she said, handing the phone across.

"Did you watch the program?" the political editor asked the moment Fletcher came on the line.

"No, I didn't," said Fletcher, "Annie and I never miss *Seinfeld*."

"*Touché*, so do you want to make any statement about your rival's wife being an illegal immigrant and her mother a prostitute?"

"Yes, I think that David Anscott should have cut off the questioner. It was obviously a cheap setup from the start."

"Can I quote you?" said Charlie. Jimmy was shaking his head vigorously.

"Yes, you most certainly can, because that made anything Nixon's got up to look like the *The Muppet Show*."

"You'll be glad to hear, Senator, that your instincts are in line with public opinion. The station's switchboard has been jammed with calls of sympathy for Nat Cartwright and his wife, and my bet is that Elliot will lose by a landslide tomorrow."

"Which will make it that much tougher for me," said Fletcher, "but at least one good thing comes out of it."

"And what's that, Senator?"

"Everybody has finally found out the truth about that bastard Elliot."

"I wonder if that was wise?" said Jimmy.

"I'm sure it wasn't," said Fletcher, "but it's no more than your father would have said."

◄○►

When the ambulance arrived Nat decided to accompany his son's body to the hospital, while his mother tried helplessly to comfort Su Ling.

"I'll come straight back," he promised, before kissing her gently.

When he saw the two paramedics sitting silently on either side of the body, he explained that he would follow in his own car. They just nodded.

The hospital staff tried to be as sympathetic as possible, but there were forms to be filled in, and procedures to be carried out. Once that had been completed, they left him alone. He kissed Luke on the forehead and turned away at the sight of the red and black bruises around his neck, aware that the memory would remain with him for the rest of his life.

Once they had covered Luke's face with a sheet, Nat left his beloved son, passing bowed heads murmuring their sympathy. He must get back to Su Ling, but before that, he knew there was someone else he had to visit first.

Nat drove away from the hospital on automatic pilot, his anger not diminishing as each mile clocked up. Although he had never been to the house before, he knew exactly where it was, and when he eventually turned into the driveway, Nat could see some lights coming from the ground floor. He parked the car and began to walk slowly toward the house. He needed to be calm if he was to see it through. As he approached the front door he could hear raised voices coming from inside. A man and a woman were arguing, unaware of the visitor outside. Nat banged on the knocker and the voices suddenly went silent, as if a television had been switched off. A moment later, the door swung open and Nat came face-to-face with the man he held responsible for his son's death.

Ralph Elliot looked shocked, but recovered quickly. He tried to slam the door in his face, but Nat had already placed a shoulder firmly against it. The first punch Nat threw landed on Elliot's nose and sent him reeling backward. Elliot stumbled, but regained his balance quickly, turned and ran down the corridor. Nat strode after him, following Elliot into his study. He looked around for the other raised voice, but there was no sign of Rebecca. He turned his attention back to Elliott, who was pulling open a drawer in his desk. He grabbed a gun and pointed it at Nat.

"Get out of my house," he shouted, "or I'll kill you." Blood was streaming from his nose.

Nat advanced toward him. "I don't think so," he said. "After that stunt you pulled tonight, no one will ever take your word again."

"Yes, they will, because I have a witness. Don't forget that Rebecca saw you barge into our home making threats and then assaulting me."

Nat advanced, ready to take a second punch, causing Elliot to step back and momentarily lose his balance as he stumbled across the arm of the chair. The gun went off, and Nat leaped on Elliot, knocking him to the ground. As they fell to the floor, Nat jerked his knee into Elliot's groin with such force that his rival bent double, letting go of the gun. Nat grabbed it and pointed the barrel at Elliot, whose face was contorted with fear.

"You planted that bastard in the audience, didn't you?" said Nat.

"Yes, yes, but I didn't know he would go that far, surely you wouldn't kill a man because . . ."

"Because he was responsible for the death of my son?"

All the color drained from Elliot's face.

"Yes, I would," Nat said, pressing the barrel of the gun against Elliot's forehead. Nat stared down at a man who was now on his knees whimpering and begging for his life. "I'm not going to kill you," said Nat, lowering the gun, "because that would be the easy way out for a coward. No, I want you to suffer a much slower death—year upon year of humiliation. Tomorrow you're going to discover what the people of Hartford really think of you, and then you'll have to live with the final ignominy of watching me take up residence in the governor's mansion."

Nat rose to his feet, calmly placed the gun on the corner of the desk, turned and left the room to find Rebecca cowering in the hallway. As soon as he had passed her she ran into the study. Nat strode on through the open door and climbed into his car.

He was driving out of the gates when he heard the shot.

—◇—

Fletcher's phone was ringing every few minutes. Annie took all the calls, explaining that her husband had no further comment to make, other than that he had sent his condolences to Mr. and Mrs. Cartwright.

Just after midnight, Annie unplugged the phone and made her way upstairs. Although the light was on in their bedroom, she was surprised to find that Fletcher wasn't there. She went back downstairs to check the study. The usual papers were piled up on his desk, but he wasn't sitting in his chair. She climbed slowly back up the stairs and noticed a light shining under Lucy's door. Annie turned the handle slowly and quietly pushed the door open in case Lucy had fallen asleep, leaving her light on. She looked inside to see her husband sitting on the bed, clinging to their sleepy daughter. Tears were streaming down his cheeks. He turned and faced his wife. "Nothing's worth that," he said.

—◇—

Nat arrived back home to find his mother sitting on the sofa with Su Ling. Su Ling's face was ashen, her eyes sunken; she had aged ten years in a few hours. "I'll leave you with her now," said his mother, "but I'll come back first thing in the morning. I'll see myself out."

Nat bent down, kissed his mother goodbye and then sat next to his wife. He held her slight body in his arms, but said nothing. There was nothing to say.

He couldn't remember how long they had been sitting there when he heard the police siren. He assumed that the grating noise would quickly disappear into the distance, but it became louder and louder, and didn't stop until a car came to a screeching halt on the gravel outside their front door. He then heard a door slam, heavy footsteps, followed by a loud banging on the front door.

He removed his arm from around his wife's shoulder and made his way wearily to the front door. He opened it to find Chief Culver with a police officer standing on either side of him.

"What's the problem, Chief?"

"I'm sorry about this, remembering what you've already been through," said Don Culver, "but I have no choice but to place you under arrest."

"What for?" asked Nat in disbelief.

"For the murder of Ralph Elliot."

44

IT WAS NOT the first time in American history that a dead candidate's name was listed on the ballot, and it was certainly not the first time an arrested candidate had stood for election, but search as they might, the political historians were unable to find both on the same day.

Nat's one call that the chief permitted was to Tom, who was still wide awake despite it being three in the morning. "I'll get Jimmy Gates out of bed and join you at the police station as soon as I can."

They had only just finished taking his fingerprints when Tom arrived, accompanied by his lawyer. "You remember Jimmy," said Tom, "he advised us during the Fairchild's takeover."

"Yes, I do," said Nat as he continued to dry his hands after removing the traces of black ink from his fingers.

"I've talked to the chief," said Jimmy, "and he's quite happy for you to go home, but you'll have to appear in court at ten o'clock tomorrow morning to be formally charged. I shall apply for bail on your behalf, and there is no reason to believe it won't be granted."

"Thank you," said Nat, his voice flat. "Jimmy, you'll recall that before we began the takeover bid for Fairchild's, I asked you to find me the best corporate lawyer available to represent us?"

"Yes, I do," said Jimmy, "and you've always said that Logan Fitzgerald did a first-class job."

"He certainly did," said Nat quietly, "but now I need you to find me the Logan Fitzgerald of criminal law."

"I'll have two or three names for you to consider by the time we meet up tomorrow. There's a guy in Chicago who's exceptional, but I don't know what his schedule's like," he said as the chief of police walked over to join them.

"Mr. Cartwright, can one of my boys drive you home?"

"No, that's good of you, Chief," said Tom, "but I'll take the candidate home."

"You say candidate automatically now," said Nat, "almost as if it was my Christian name."

On the journey home, Nat told Tom everything that had taken place while he was at Elliot's house. "So in the end it will come down to your word against hers," commented Tom as he pulled up outside Nat's front door.

"Yes, and I'm afraid my story won't be as convincing as hers, even though it's the truth."

"We can talk about that in the morning," said Tom. "But now you need to try and get some sleep."

"It is the morning," said Nat as he watched the first rays of sunlight creeping across the lawn.

Su Ling was standing by the open door. "Did they for a moment believe . . . ?"

Nat told her everything that had happened while he was at the police station, and when he finished, all Su Ling said was, "Such a pity."

"What do you mean?" asked Nat.

"That *you* didn't kill him."

Nat climbed the stairs and walked through the bedroom straight on into the bathroom. He stripped off his clothes and threw them in a bag. He would dispose of the bag later so that he would never have to be reminded of this terrible day. He stepped into the shower and allowed the cold jets of water to beat down on him. After putting on a new set of clothes he rejoined his wife in the kitchen. On the sideboard was his election-day schedule; no mention of a court appearance on arraignment for murder.

Tom turned up at nine. He reported that the voting was going briskly, as if nothing else was happening in Nat's life. "They took a poll immediately following the television interview," he told Nat, "and it gave you a lead of sixty-three to thirty-seven."

"But that was before I was arrested for killing the other candidate," said Nat.

"I guess that might push it up to seventy-thirty," replied Tom. No one laughed.

Tom did his best to focus on the campaign and try to keep their minds off Luke. It didn't work. He looked up at the kitchen clock. "Time for us to go," he said to Nat, who turned and took Su Ling in his arms.

"No, I'm coming with you," she said. "Nat may not have murdered him, but I would have, given half a chance."

"Me too," said Tom gently, "but let me warn you that when we get to the courthouse it's bound to be a media circus. Look innocent and say nothing, because anything you say will end up on every front page."

As they left the house, they were greeted by a dozen journalists and three camera crews just to watch them climb into a car. Nat clung to Su Ling's hand as they were driven through the streets, and didn't notice how many people waved the moment they spotted him. When they arrived at the steps of the courthouse fifteen minutes later, Nat faced the largest crowd he'd encountered during the entire election campaign.

The chief had anticipated the problem and detailed twenty uniformed officers to hold back the crowd, and make a gangway so that Nat and his party could enter the building without being hassled. It didn't work, because twenty officers weren't enough to control the phalanx of photographers and journalists who shouted and jostled Nat and Su Ling as they tried to make their way up the courtroom steps. Microphones were thrust in Nat's face, and questions came at them from every angle.

"Did you murder Ralph Elliot?" demanded one reporter.

"Will you be withdrawing as candidate?" followed next, as a microphone was thrust forward.

"Was your mother a prostitute, Mrs. Cartwright?"

"Do you think you can still win, Nat?"

"Was Rebecca Elliot your mistress?"

"What were Ralph Elliot's last words, Mr. Cartwright?"

When they pushed through the swing doors, they found Jimmy Gates standing on the far side, waiting for them. He led Nat to a bench outside the courtroom and briefed his client on the procedure he was about to face.

"Your appearance should only last for about five minutes," Jimmy explained. "You will state your name, and having done so, you will be charged, and then asked to enter a plea. Once you've pleaded not guilty, I shall make an application for bail. The state is suggesting fifty thousand dollars at your own recognizance, which I've agreed to. The moment you've signed the necessary papers, you will be released and you won't have to appear again until a trial date has been fixed."

"When do we anticipate that might be?"

"It would normally take about six months, but I've asked for the whole process to be speeded up on account of the upcoming election." Nat admired his counsel's professional approach, remembering that Jimmy was also Fletcher Davenport's closest friend. However, like any good lawyer, Nat thought, Jimmy would understand the meaning of client privilege.

Jimmy glanced at his watch. "We ought to go in, the last thing we need is to keep the judge waiting."

Nat entered a packed courtroom and walked slowly down the aisle with Tom. He was surprised by how many people thrust out their hands and even wished him luck, making it feel more like a party meeting than a criminal arraignment. When they reached the front, Jimmy held open the little wooden gate dividing the court officials from the simply curious. He then guided Nat to a table on the left, and ushered him into the seat next to his. As they waited for the judge to make his entrance, Nat glanced across at the state's attorney, Richard Ebden, a man he'd always admired. He knew that Ebden would be a formidable adversary, and wondered who Jimmy was going to recommend to oppose him.

"All rise, Mr. Justice Deakins presiding."

The procedure Jimmy had described took place exactly as he

predicted, and they were back out on the street five minutes later, facing the same journalists repeating the same questions and still failing to get any answers.

As they pushed their way through the crowd to their waiting car, Nat was once again surprised by how many people still wanted to shake him by the hand. Tom slowed them down, aware that this would be the footage seen by the voters on the midday news. Nat spoke to every well-wisher, but wasn't quite sure how to reply to an onlooker who said, "I'm glad you killed the bastard."

"Do you want to head straight home?" asked Tom as his car slowly nosed its way through the melee.

"No," said Nat, "let's go across to the bank and talk things through in the boardroom."

The only stop they made on the way was to pick up the first edition of the *Courant* after hearing a newsboy's cry of "Cartwright charged with murder." All Tom seemed to be interested in was a poll on the second page showing that Nat now led Elliot by over twenty points. "And," said Tom, "in a separate poll, seventy-two percent say you shouldn't withdraw from the race." Tom read on, suddenly looked up but said nothing.

"What is it?" asked Su Ling.

"Seven percent say they would happily have killed Elliot, if only you'd asked them."

When they reached the bank, there was another hustle of journalists and cameramen awaiting them; again they were met with the same stony silence. Tom's secretary joined them in the corridor and reported that early polling was at a record high as Republicans obviously wished to make their views known.

Once they were settled in the boardroom, Nat opened the discussion by saying. "The party will expect me to withdraw, whatever the result, and I feel that might still be my best course of action given the circumstances."

"Why not let the voters decide?" said Su Ling quietly, "and if they give you overwhelming support, stay in there fighting, because that will also help convince a jury that you're innocent."

"I agree," said Tom. "And what's the alternative—Barbara Hunter? Let's at least spare the electorate that."

"And how do you feel, Jimmy? After all, you're my legal advisor."

"On this subject I can't offer an impartial view," Jimmy admitted. "As you well know, the Democratic candidate is my closest friend, but were I advising him in the same circumstances, and I knew he was innocent, I would say stick in there and fight the bastards."

"Well, I suppose it's just possible that the public will elect a dead man; then heaven knows what will happen."

"His name will remain on the ballot," said Tom, "and if he goes on to win the election, the party can invite anyone they choose to represent him."

"Are you serious?" said Nat.

"Couldn't be more serious. Quite often they select the candidate's wife, and my bet is that Rebecca Elliot would happily take his place."

"And if you're convicted," said Jimmy, "she could sure count on the sympathy vote just before an election."

"More important," said Nat, "have you come up with a defense counsel to represent me?"

"Four," responded Jimmy, removing a thick file from his briefcase. He turned the cover. "Two from New York, both recommended by Logan Fitzgerald, one from Chicago who worked on Watergate, and the fourth from Dallas. He's only lost one case in the last ten years, and that was when his client had committed the murder on video. I intend to call all four later today to find out if any of them is free. This is going to be such a high-profile case, my bet is that they will all make themselves available."

"Isn't there anyone from Connecticut worthy of the shortlist?" asked Tom. "It would send out a far better message to the jury."

"I agree," said Jimmy, "but the only man who is of the same caliber as those four simply isn't available."

"And who's that?" asked Nat.

"The Democratic candidate for governor."

Nat smiled for the first time. "Then he's my first choice."

"But he's in the middle of an election campaign."

"Just in case you haven't noticed, so is the accused," said Nat, "and let's face it, the election isn't for another nine months. If I turn out to be his opponent, at least he'll know where I am the whole time."

"But . . ." repeated Jimmy.

"You tell Mr. Fletcher Davenport that if I become the Republican candidate, he's my first choice, and don't approach anyone else until he's turned me down, because if everything I've heard about that man is true, I feel confident he'll want to represent me."

"If those are your instructions, Mr. Cartwright."

"Those are my instructions, counselor."

—◦—

By the time the polls had closed at eight P.M. Nat had fallen asleep in the car as Tom drove him home. His chief of staff made no attempt to disturb him. The next thing Nat remembered was waking to find Su Ling lying on the bed beside him, and his first thoughts were of Luke. Su Ling stared at him and gripped his hand. "No," she whispered.

"What do you mean, no?" asked Nat.

"I can see it in your eyes, my darling, you wonder if I would prefer you to withdraw, so that we can mourn Luke properly, and the answer is no."

"But we'll have the funeral, and then the preparations for the trial, not to mention the trial itself."

"Not to mention the endless hours in between, when you'll be brooding and unbearable to live with, so the answer is still no."

"But it's going to be almost impossible to expect a jury not to accept the word of a grieving widow who also claims to have been an eyewitness to her husband's murder."

"Of course she was an eyewitness," said Su Ling. "She did it."

The phone on Su Ling's bedside table began to ring. She picked it up and listened attentively before writing two figures down on the pad by the phone. "Thank you," she said. "I'll let him know."

"Let him know what?" inquired Nat.

Su Ling tore the piece of paper off the pad and passed it across to her husband. "It was Tom. He wanted you to know the election result." Su Ling handed over the piece of paper. All she had written on it were the figures "69/31."

"Yes, but who got sixty-nine percent?" asked Nat.

"The next governor of Connecticut," she replied.

Luke's funeral was, at the principal's request, held in Taft School's chapel. He explained that so many pupils had wanted to be present. It was only after his death that Nat and Su Ling became aware just how popular their son had been. The service was simple, and the choir of which he was so proud to be a member sang William Blake's "Jerusalem" and Cole Porter's "Ain't Misbehavin'." Kathy read one of the lessons, and dear old Thomo another, while the principal delivered the address.

Mr. Henderson spoke of a shy, unassuming youth, liked and admired by all. He reminded those present of Luke's remarkable performance as Romeo, and how he had learned only that morning that Luke had been offered a place at Princeton.

The coffin was borne out of the chapel by boys and girls from the ninth grade who had performed with him in the school play. Nat learned so much about Luke that day that he felt guilty he hadn't known what an impact his son had made on his contemporaries.

At the end of the service, Nat and Su Ling attended the tea party given in the principal's house for Luke's closest friends. It was packed to overflowing, but then as Mr. Henderson explained to Su Ling, everyone thought they were a close friend of Luke's. "What a gift," he remarked simply.

The headboy presented Su Ling with a book of photographs and short essays composed by his fellow pupils. Later, whenever Nat felt low, he would turn a page, read an entry and glance at a photograph, but there was one he kept returning to again and again: *Luke was the only boy ever to speak to me who never once mentioned my turban or my color. He simply didn't see them. I had looked forward to him being a friend for the rest of my life. Malik Singh (16).*

As they left the principal's house, Nat spotted Kathy sitting alone in the garden, her head bowed. Su Ling walked across and sat down beside her. She put an arm around Kathy and tried to comfort her. "He loved you very much," Su Ling said.

Kathy raised her head, the tears streaming down her cheeks. "I never told him I loved him."

45

"I can't do it," said Fletcher.

"Why not?" asked Annie.

"I can think of a hundred reasons."

"Or are they a hundred excuses?"

"Defend the man I'm trying to defeat," said Fletcher, ignoring her comment.

"Without fear or favor," quoted Annie.

"Then how would you expect me to conduct the election?"

"That will be the easy part." She paused. "Either way."

"Either way?" repeated Fletcher.

"Yes. Because if he's guilty, he won't even be the Republican candidate."

"And if he's innocent?"

"Then you'll rightly be praised for setting him free."

"That's neither practical nor sensible."

"Two more excuses."

"Why are you on his side?" asked Fletcher.

"I'm not," insisted Annie. "I am, to quote Professor Abrahams, on the side of justice."

Fletcher was silent for some time. "I wonder what he would have done faced with the same dilemma?"

"You know very well what he would have done . . . *but some people will forget those standards within moments of leaving this university . . .*"

"*. . . I can only hope that at least one person in every generation,*" said Fletcher, completing the professor's oft-repeated dictum.

"Why don't you meet him," said Annie, "and then perhaps that will persuade you . . ."

—◇—

Despite abundant caution from Jimmy and vociferous protests from the local Democrats—in fact from everyone except Annie—it was agreed that the two men should meet the following Sunday.

The chosen venue was Fairchild and Russell, as it was felt few citizens would be strolling down Main Street early on a Sunday morning.

Nat and Tom arrived just before ten, and it was the chairman of the bank who unlocked the front door and turned off the alarm for the first time in years. They only had to wait a few minutes before Fletcher and Jimmy appeared on the top step. Tom ushered them quickly through to the boardroom.

When Jimmy introduced his closest friend to his most important client, both men stared at each other, not sure which one of them should make the first move.

"It's good of you . . ."

"I hadn't expected . . ."

Both men laughed and then shook each other warmly by the hand.

Tom suggested that Fletcher and Jimmy sit on one side of the conference table, while he and Nat sat opposite them. Fletcher nodded his agreement, and once seated, he opened his briefcase and removed a yellow notepad, placing it on the table in front of him, along with a fountain pen taken from an inside pocket.

"May I begin by saying how much I appreciate you agreeing to see me," said Nat. "I can only imagine the opposition you must have faced from every quarter and am well aware that you did not settle for the easy option." Jimmy lowered his head.

Fletcher raised a hand. "It's my wife you have to thank." He paused. "Not me. But it's me that you have to convince."

"Then please pass on my grateful thanks to Mrs. Davenport, and let me assure you that I will answer any questions you put to me."

"I only have one question," said Fletcher, as he stared down at the blank sheet of paper, "and it's the question a lawyer never asks because it can only compromise his or her ethical position. But on this occasion I will not consider discussing this case until that question has been answered."

Nat nodded, but didn't respond. Fletcher raised his head and stared across the table at his would-be rival. Nat held his gaze.

"Did you murder Ralph Elliot?"

"No, I did not," replied Nat, without hesitation.

Fletcher looked back down at the blank sheet of paper in front of him, and flicked over the top page to reveal a second page covered in row upon row of neatly prepared questions.

"Then let me next ask you . . ." said Fletcher, looking back up at his client.

⋅◇⋅

The trial was set for the second week in July. Nat was surprised by how little time he needed to spend with his newly appointed counsel once he had gone over his story again and again, and that stopped only when Fletcher was confident he had mastered every detail. Although both recognized the importance of Nat's evidence, Fletcher spent just as much time reading and rereading the two statements that Rebecca Elliot had made to the police, Don Culver's own report on what had taken place that night, and the notes of Detective Petrowski, who was in charge of the case. He warned Nat. "Rebecca will have been coached by the state's attorney, and every question you can think of she will have had time to consider and reconsider. By the time she steps onto the witness stand, she'll be as well rehearsed as any actress on opening night. But," Fletcher paused, "she still has a problem."

"And what's that?" asked Nat.

"If Mrs. Elliot murdered her husband, she must have lied to the police, so there are bound to be loose ends that they are unaware of. First we have to find them, and then we have to tie them up."

Interest in the gubernatorial race stretched far beyond the boundaries of Connecticut. Articles on the two men appeared in journals as diverse as the *New Yorker* and the *National Inquirer*, so that by the time the trial opened, there wasn't a hotel room available within twenty miles of Hartford.

With three months still to go before election day, the opinion polls showed Fletcher had a twelve-point lead, but he knew that if he was able to prove Nat's innocence, that could be reversed overnight.

The trial was due to open on July 11, but the major networks already had their cameras on top of the buildings opposite the courthouse and along the sidewalks, as well as many more hand-helds in the streets. They were there to interview anyone remotely connected with the trial, despite the fact it was days before Nat would hear the words "All rise."

Fletcher and Nat tried to conduct their election campaigns as if it was business as usual, although no one pretended it was. They quickly discovered that there wasn't a hall they couldn't fill, a rally they couldn't pack, a clambake they couldn't sell twice over, how-ever remote the district. In fact, when they both attended a char-ity fund-raiser in support of an orthopedic wing to be added to the Gates Memorial Hospital in Hartford, tickets were changing hands at five hundred dollars each. This was one of those rare elections when campaign contributions kept pouring in. For sev-eral weeks they were a bigger draw than Frank Sinatra.

Neither man slept the night before the trial was due to open, and the chief of police didn't even bother to go to bed. Don Cul-ver had detailed a hundred officers to be on duty outside the courthouse, ruefully remarking how many of Hartford's petty criminals were taking advantage of his overstretched force.

Fletcher was the first member of the defense team to appear on the courthouse steps, and he made it clear to the waiting press that he would not be making a statement or answering any ques-tions until the verdict had been delivered. Nat arrived a few min-utes later, accompanied by Tom and Su Ling, and if it hadn't been for police assistance, they might never have got into the building.

Once inside the courthouse, Nat walked straight along the mar-ble corridor that led to court number seven, acknowledging onlookers' kind remarks, but only nodding politely in response as instructed by his counselor. Once he'd entered the courtroom, Nat felt a thousand eyes boring into him as he continued on down the center aisle, before taking his place on the left of Fletcher at the defense table.

"Good morning, counselor," said Nat.

"Good morning, Nat," replied Fletcher, looking up from a pile of papers, "I hope you're prepared for a week of boredom while we select a jury."

"Have you settled on a profile for the ideal juror?" Nat asked.

"It's not quite that easy," said Fletcher, "because I can't make up my mind if I should select people who support you or me."

"Are there twelve people in Hartford who support you?" asked Nat.

Fletcher smiled. "I'm glad you haven't lost your sense of humor, but once the jury's sworn in, I want you looking serious and concerned. A man to whom a great injustice has been done."

Fletcher turned out to be right, because it wasn't until Friday afternoon that the full complement of twelve jurors and two alternatives were finally seated in their places, following argument, counterargument and several objections being raised by both sides. They finally settled on seven men and five women. Two of the women and one of the men were black, five from a professional background, two working mothers, three blue-collar workers, one secretary and one unemployed.

"How about their political persuasions?" asked Nat.

"My bet is, four Republicans, four Democrats, and four I can't be sure of."

"So what's our next problem, counselor?"

"How to get you off, and still grab the votes of the four I'm not sure of," said Fletcher as they parted on the bottom step of the courthouse.

Nat found that, whenever he went home in the evening, he would quickly forget the trial, as his mind continually returned to Luke. However much he tried to discuss other things with Su Ling, there was so often only one thought on her mind. "If only I'd shared my secret with Luke," she said again and again, "perhaps he would still be alive."

46

ON THE FOLLOWING MONDAY, after the jury had been sworn in, Judge Kravats invited the state's attorney to make his opening statement.

Richard Ebden rose slowly from his place. He was a tall, elegant, gray-haired man, who had a reputation for beguiling juries. His dark blue suit was the one he always wore on the opening day of a trial. His white shirt and blue tie instilled a feeling of trust.

The state's attorney was proud of his prosecution record, which was somewhat ironic because he was a mild-mannered, church-going family man, who even sang bass in the local choir. Ebden rose from his place, pushed back his chair, and walked slowly out into the open well of the court, before turning to face the jury.

"Members of the jury," he began, "in all my years as an advocate, I have rarely come across a more open-and-shut case of homicide."

Fletcher leaned across to Nat and whispered, "Don't worry, it's his usual opening—*but despite this*, comes next."

"But despite this, I must still take you through the events of the late evening and early morning of February twelfth and thirteenth."

"Mr. Cartwright," he said, turning slowly to face the accused, "had appeared on a television program with Ralph Elliot—a popular and much respected figure in our community and, perhaps more importantly, favorite to win the Republican nomination, which might well have taken him on to be governor of the state we all love so much. Here was a man at the pinnacle of his career, about to receive the accolades of a grateful electorate for years of unselfish service to the community, and what was to be his reward? He ended up being murdered by his closest rival.

"And how did this unnecessary tragedy come about? Mr. Cartwright is asked a question as to whether his wife was an illegal immigrant—such is the stuff of robust politics—a question I might add that he was unwilling to answer, and why? Because he knew it to be the truth, and he had remained silent on the subject for over twenty years. And having refused to answer that question, what does Mr. Cartwright do next? He tries to shift the blame onto Ralph Elliot. The moment the program is over, he starts to shout obscenities at him, calls him a bastard, accuses him of setting up the question, and the most damning of all, says, 'I will still kill you.'" Ebden stared at the jury, repeating the five words slowly, "I will still kill you."

"Don't rely on my words to convict Mr. Cartwright, for you are about to discover that this is not rumor, hearsay or my imagination, because the entire conversation between the two rivals was recorded on television for posterity. I realize this is unusual, your honor, but under the circumstances, I'd like to show this tape to the jury at this juncture." Ebden nodded toward his table and an assistant pressed a button.

For the next twelve minutes, Nat stared at a screen that had been set up opposite the jury, and was painfully reminded just how angry he had been. Once the tape had been switched off, Ebden continued with his opening statement.

"However, it is still the responsibility of the state to show what actually took place after this angry and vindictive man had charged out of the studio." Ebden lowered his voice. "He returns home to discover that his son—his only child—has committed suicide. Now all of us can well understand the effect that such a tragedy might have on a father. And as it turned out, members of the jury, this tragic death triggered a chain of events that was to end in the cold-blooded murder of Ralph Elliot. Cartwright tells his wife that after he has been to the hospital, he will return home immediately, but he has no intention of doing so, because he has already planned a detour that will take him to Mr. and Mrs. Elliot's house.

And what could possibly have been the reason for this nocturnal visit at two A.M.? There can only have been one purpose, to remove Ralph Elliot from the gubernatorial race. Sadly for his family and our state, Mr. Cartwright succeeded in his mission.

"He drives over uninvited to the Elliots' family home at two A.M. The door is answered by Mr. Elliot, who has been in his study working on an acceptance speech. Mr. Cartwright barges in, punching Mr. Elliot so hard on the nose that he staggers back into the corridor, only to see his adversary come charging in after him. Mr. Elliot recovers in time to run into his study and retrieve a gun that he kept in a drawer in his desk. He turns just as Cartwright leaps on him, kicking the gun out of his hand, thus ensuring that Mr. Elliot has no chance of defending himself. Cartwright then grabs the pistol, stands over his victim and without a moment's hesitation, shoots him through the heart. He then aims a second shot into the ceiling to leave the impression that a struggle had taken place. Cartwright then drops the gun, runs out of the open door and, jumping into his car, drives quickly back to his home. Unbeknownst to him, he left behind a witness to the entire episode—the victim's wife, Mrs. Rebecca Elliot. When she heard the first shot, Mrs. Elliot ran from her bedroom to the top of the stairs and moments after hearing the second shot, she watched in horror as Cartwright bolted out of the front door. And just as the television camera had recorded every detail earlier in the evening, Mrs. Elliot will describe to you with the same accuracy, exactly what took place later that night."

The state's attorney turned his attention away from the jury for a moment and looked directly at Fletcher. "In a few moments' time, defense counsel will rise from his place and with all his famed charm and oratory will attempt to bring tears to your eyes as he tries to explain away what really happened. But what he can't explain away is the body of an innocent man murdered in cold blood by his political rival. What he can't explain away is his television message, 'I will still kill you.' What he can't explain away is a witness to the murder—Mr. Elliot's widow, Rebecca."

The prosecutor transferred his gaze to Nat. "I can well understand you feeling some sympathy for this man, but after you have heard all the evidence, I believe you will be left in no doubt of Mr.

Cartwright's guilt, and with no choice but to carry out your duty to the state and deliver a verdict of Guilty."

There was an eerie silence in the courtroom when Richard Ebden resumed his place. Several heads nodded, even one or two on the jury. Judge Kravats made a note on the pad in front of him, and then looked down toward the defense counsel's table.

"Do you wish to respond, counselor?" asked the judge, making no attempt to hide the irony in his voice.

Fletcher rose from his place and, looking directly at the judge, said, "No thank you, your honor, it is not my intention to make an opening statement."

Fletcher and Nat sat in silence looking directly in front of them amid the pandemonium that broke out in the courtroom. The judge banged his gavel several times, trying to bring the proceedings back to order. Fletcher glanced across at the state attorney's table, to see Richard Ebden, head bowed, in a huddle with his prosecution team. The judge tried to hide a smile once he realized what a shrewd tactical move the defense had made; it had thrown the state's team into disarray. He turned his attention back to the prosecution.

"Mr. Ebden, that being the case, perhaps you'd like to call your first witness?" he said matter-of-factly.

Ebden rose, not quite as confidently now that he'd worked out what Fletcher was up to. "Your honor, I would in these unusual circumstances seek an adjournment."

"Objection, your honor," cried Fletcher, rising quickly from his place. "The state has had several months to prepare their case; are we now to understand they cannot even produce a single witness?"

"Is that the case, Mr. Ebden?" asked the judge. "Are you unable to call your first witness?"

"That is correct, your honor. Our first witness would have been Mr. Don Culver, the chief of police, and we did not want to take him away from his important duties until it was entirely necessary."

Fletcher was on his feet again. "But it is entirely necessary, your honor. He is the chief of police, and this is a murder trial, and I therefore ask that this case be dismissed on the grounds there is no police evidence available to place before the court."

"Nice try, Mr. Davenport," said the judge, "but I won't fall for it. Mr. Ebden, I shall grant your request for an adjournment. I shall reconvene this court immediately after the lunch break, and if the chief of police is unable to be with us by then, I shall rule his evidence inadmissible." Ebden nodded, unable to hide his embarrassment.

"All rise," said the clerk, as Judge Kravats glanced at the clock before leaving the courtroom.

"First round to us, I think," remarked Tom, as the state's team hurriedly left the courtroom.

"Possibly," said Fletcher, "but we'll need more than Pyrrhic victories to win the final battle."

⟞⟶

Nat hated the hanging around, and was back in his seat long before the lunch break was up. He looked across at the state's table to see Richard Ebden also in his place, knowing he wouldn't make the same mistake a second time. But had he yet worked out why Fletcher had risked such a bold move? Fletcher had explained to Nat during the adjournment that he believed his only hope of winning the case was to undermine Rebecca Elliot's evidence, and therefore he couldn't afford to let her relax even for a moment. Following the judge's warning, Ebden would now have to keep her waiting in the corridor, perhaps for days on end, before she was finally called.

Fletcher took his seat next to Nat only moments before the judge was due to reconvene. "The chief's out there in the corridor storming up and down fuming, while Mrs. Elliot is sitting alone in a corner biting her nails. I intend to keep that lady hanging around for several days," he added as the clerk called, "All rise, Judge Kravats presiding."

"Good afternoon," said the judge, and turning to the chief prosecutor added, "Do you have a witness for us, Mr. Ebden?"

"Yes, I do, your honor. The state calls Police Chief Don Culver."

Nat watched as Don Culver took his place on the stand and repeated the oath. Something was wrong, but he couldn't work out what it was. Then he saw the second and third fingers of Culver's right hand twitching, and realized it was the first time he'd seen him without his trademark cigar.

"Mr. Culver, would you tell the jury your present rank?"

"I'm the chief of police for the city of Hartford."

"And how long have you held that position?"

"Just over fourteen years."

"And how long have you been a law enforcement officer?"

"For the past thirty-six years."

"So it would be safe to say that you have a great deal of experience when it comes to homicide?

"I guess that's right," the chief said.

"And have you ever come into contact with the defendant?"

"Yes, I have, on several occasions."

"He's stealing some of my questions," Fletcher whispered to Nat, "but I haven't yet worked out why."

"And had you formed an opinion of the man?"

"Yes, I had, he's a decent law-abiding citizen, who, until he murdered . . ."

"Objection, your honor," said Fletcher, rising from his place, "it is up to the jury to decide who murdered Mr. Elliot, not the chief of police. We don't live in a police state yet."

"Sustained," said the judge.

"Well, all I can say," said the chief, "is that until all this happened, I would have voted for him." Laughter broke out in the court.

"And after I've finished with the chief," whispered Fletcher, "he sure won't be voting for me."

"Then you must have had some doubt in your mind that such an upstanding citizen was capable of murder?"

"Not at all, Mr. Ebden," said the chief. "Murderers aren't run-of-the-mill criminals."

"Would you care to explain what you mean by that, Chief?"

"Sure will," said Culver. "The average murder is a domestic affair, usually within the family, and is often carried out by someone who not only has never committed a crime before, but probably never will again. Once they're in custody, they are often easier to handle than a petty burglar."

"Do you feel Mr. Cartwright falls into this category?"

"Objection," said Fletcher from a seated position, "how can the chief possibly know the answer to that question?"

"Because I've been dealing with murderers for the past thirty-six years," Don Culver responded.

"Strike that from the record," said the judge. "Experience is all very well, but the jury must in the end deal only with the facts in this particular case."

"Then let's move on to a question that does deal with fact in this particular case," said the state's attorney. "How did you become involved in this case, Chief Culver?"

"I took a call at my home from Mrs. Elliot in the early hours of February twelfth.

"She called you at home? Is she a personal acquaintance?"

"No, but all candidates for public office are able to get in touch with me directly. They are often the subject of threats, real or imagined, and it was no secret that Mr. Elliot had received several death threats since he'd declared he would run for governor."

"When Mrs. Elliot called you, did you record her exact words?"

"You bet I did," said the chief. "She sounded hysterical, and was shouting. I remember I had to hold the phone away from my ear, in fact she woke my wife." A little laughter broke out in the court for a second time, and Culver waited until it had died down before he added, "I wrote down her exact words on a pad I keep next to the phone." He opened a notebook.

Fletcher was on his feet. "Is this admissible?" he asked.

"It was on the agreed list of prosecution documents, your honor," Ebden intervened, "as I feel sure Mr. Davenport is aware. He's had weeks to consider its relevance, not to mention importance."

The judge nodded to the chief. "Carry on," he said as Fletcher resumed his seat.

"'My husband has been shot in his study, please come as quickly as possible,'" said the chief, reading from his notebook.

"What did you say?"

"I told her not to touch anything, and I'd be with her just as soon as I could get there."

"What time was that?"

"Two twenty-six," the chief replied after rechecking his notebook.

"And when did you arrive at the Elliots' home?"

"Not until three nineteen. First I had to call the station and tell them to send the most senior detective available to the Elliots' residence. I then got dressed, so that when I eventually made it, I found two of my officers had already arrived—but then they didn't have to get dressed." Once again laughter broke out around the courtroom.

"Please describe to the jury exactly what you saw when you first arrived."

"The front door was open, and Mrs. Elliot was sitting on the floor in the hallway, her knees hunched up under her chin. I let her know I was there, and then joined Detective Petrowski in Mr. Elliot's study. Mr. Petrowski," the chief added, "is one of the most respected detectives on my force, with a great deal of experience with homicide, and as he seemed to have the investigation well under way. I left him to get on with his job, while I returned to Mrs. Elliot."

"Did you then question her?"

"Yes, I did," replied the chief.

"But wouldn't Detective Petrowski already have done that?"

"Yes, but it's often useful to get two statements so that one can compare them later and see if they differ on any essential points."

"Your honor, these statements are hearsay," Fletcher interjected.

"And did they?" Ebden hurriedly asked.

"No, they did not."

"Objection," Fletcher emphasized.

"Overruled, Mr. Davenport. As has already been pointed out, you have had access to these documents for several weeks."

"Thank you, your honor," said Ebden. "I would like you to tell the court what you did next, Chief."

"I suggested that we go and sit in the front room, so that Mrs. Elliot would be more comfortable. I then asked her to take me slowly through what had happened that evening. I didn't hurry her, as witnesses are quite often resentful of being asked exactly the same questions a second or third time. After she'd finished her cup of coffee, Mrs. Elliot eventually told me that she had been asleep in bed when she heard the first shot. She switched on the light, put on her robe and went to the top of the stairs and that was when she heard the second shot. She then watched as Mr. Cartwright ran out of the study toward the open door. He turned to look back, but couldn't have seen her in the darkness at the top of the stairs, although she recognized him immediately. She then ran down-stairs and into the study where she found her husband lying on the floor in a pool of blood. She immediately called me at home."

"Did you continue to question her?"

"No, I left a female officer with Mrs. Elliot while I checked over her original statement. After a farther consultation with Detective Petrowski, I drove to Mr. Cartwright's home accompanied by two other officers, arrested the defendant and charged him with the murder of Ralph Elliot."

"Had he gone to bed?"

"No, he was still in the clothes he had been wearing on the tele-vision program that night."

"No more questions, your honor."

"Your witness, Mr. Davenport."

Fletcher walked across to the witness box with a smile on his face. "Good afternoon, Chief. I won't detain you for long, as I'm only too aware how busy you are, but I do nevertheless have three or four questions that need answering." The chief didn't return Fletcher's smile. "To begin with, I would like to know what period of time passed between your receiving the phone call at your home from Mrs. Elliot, and when you placed Mr. Cartwright under arrest."

The chief's fingers twitched again while he considered the ques-tion. "Two hours, two and a half at the most," he eventually said.

"And when you arrived at Mr. Cartwright's house, how was he dressed?"

"I've already told the court that—in exactly the same clothes as he was wearing on television that night."

"So he didn't open the door in his pajamas and dressing gown looking as if he had just got out of bed?"

"No, he didn't," said the chief, puzzled.

"Don't you think that a man who had just committed a murder might want to get undressed and into bed at two o'clock in the morn-ing, so that should the police suddenly turn up on his doorstep, he could at least give an impression of having been asleep?"

The chief frowned. "He was comforting his wife."

"I see," said Fletcher. "The murderer was comforting his wife, so let me ask you, Chief, when you arrested Mr. Cartwright, did he make a statement?"

"No," the chief replied, "he said he wanted to speak to his lawyer first."

"But did he say anything at all that you might have recorded in your trusty notebook?"

"Yes," said the chief, and flipped back some pages of the notebook before carefully studying an entry. "Yes," he repeated with a smile, "Cartwright said, 'but he was still alive when I left him.'"

"But he was still *alive* when I left him," repeated Fletcher. "Hardly the words of a man who is trying to hide the fact that he had been there at all. He doesn't get undressed, he doesn't go to bed, and he openly admits he was at Elliot's house earlier that evening." The chief remained silent. "When he accompanied you to the police station, did you take his fingerprints?"

"Yes, of course."

"Did you carry out any other tests?" asked Fletcher.

"What did you have in mind?" asked the chief.

"Don't play games with me," said Fletcher, his voice revealing a slight edge. "Did you carry out any other tests?"

"Yes," said the chief. "We checked under his fingernails to see if there was any sign that he had fired a gun."

"And was there any indication that Mr. Cartwright had fired a gun?" asked Fletcher, returning to his more conciliatory tone.

The chief hesitated. "We could find no powder residue on his hands or under his fingernails."

"There was no powder residue on his hands or under his fingernails," said Fletcher, facing the jury.

"Yes, but he'd had a couple of hours to wash his hands and scrub his nails."

"He certainly did, Chief, and he also had a couple of hours to get undressed, go to bed, turn off all the lights in the house, and come up with a far more convincing line than, 'but he was still alive when I left him.'" Fletcher's eyes never left the jury. Once again, the chief remained silent.

"My final question, Mr. Culver, is something that's been nagging at me ever since I took on this case, especially when I think about your thirty-six years of experience, fourteen of them as chief of police." He turned back to face Culver. "Did it ever cross your mind that someone else might have committed this crime?"

"There was no sign of anyone else having entered the house other than Mr. Cartwright."

"But there was already someone else in the house."

"And there was absolutely no evidence of any kind to suggest that Mrs. Elliot could possibly have been involved."

"No evidence of any kind?" repeated Fletcher. "I do hope, Chief, that you will find time in your busy schedule to drop in and hear my cross-examination of Mrs. Elliot, when the jury will be able to decide if there was absolutely no evidence of any kind to show she might have been involved in this crime." Uproar broke out in the courtroom as everyone began talking at once.

The state's attorney leaped to his feet, "Objection, your honor," he said sharply. "It's not Mrs. Elliot who is on trial." But he could not be heard above the noise of the judge banging his gavel as Fletcher walked slowly back to his place.

When the judge had managed to bring some semblance of order back to proceedings, all Fletcher said was, "No more questions, your honor."

"Do you have any evidence?" Nat whispered as his counsel sat down.

"Not a lot," admitted Fletcher, "but one thing I feel confident about is that if Mrs. Elliot did kill her husband, she won't be getting a lot of sleep between now and when she enters that witness stand. And as for Ebden, he'll be spending the next few days wondering what we've come up with that he doesn't yet know about." Fletcher smiled at the chief as he stepped down from the witness stand, but received a cold, blank stare in response.

The judge looked down from the bench at both attorneys. "I think that's enough for today, gentlemen," he said. "We will convene again at ten o'clock tomorrow morning, when Mr. Ebden may call his next witness."

"All rise."

47

WHEN THE JUDGE made his entrance the following morning, only a change of tie gave any clue that he had ever left the building. Nat wondered how long it would be before the ties also began to make a second and even a third appearance.

"Good morning," said Judge Kravats as he took his place on the bench and beamed down at the assembled throng as though he were a benevolent preacher about to address his congregation. "Mr. Ebden," he said, "you may call your next witness."

"Thank you, your honor. I call Detective Petrowski."

Fletcher studied the senior detective carefully as he made his way to the witness stand. He raised his right hand and began to recite the oath. Petrowski could barely have passed the minimum height the force required of its recruits. His tight-fitting suit implied a wrestler's build, rather than someone who was overweight. His jaw was square, his eyes narrow and his lips curled slightly down at the edges, leaving an impression that he didn't smile that often. One of Fletcher's researchers had found out that Petrowski was rumored to be the next chief when Don Culver retired. He had a reputation for sticking by the book, but hating paperwork, much preferring to be visiting the scene of the crime than sitting behind a desk back at headquarters.

"Good morning, Captain," said the state's attorney once the witness had sat down. Petrowski nodded, but still didn't smile. "For the record, would you please state your name and rank."

"Frank Petrowski, chief of detectives, City of Hartford Police Department."

"And how long have you been a detective?"

"Fourteen years."

"And when were you appointed chief of detectives?"

"Three years ago."

"Having established your record, let us move on to the night of the murder. The police log shows that you were the first officer on the scene of the crime."

"Yes, I was," said Petrowski, "I was the senior officer on duty that night, having taken over from the chief at eight o'clock."

"And where were you at two thirty that morning when the chief called in?"

"I was in a patrol car, on the way to investigate a break-in at a warehouse on Marsham Street, when the desk sergeant phoned to say the chief wanted me to go immediately to the home of Ralph Elliot in West Hartford, and investigate a possible homicide. As I was only minutes away, I took on the assignment and detailed another patrol car to cover Marsham Street."

"And you drove straight to the Elliots' home?"

"Yes, but on the way I radioed in to headquarters to let them know that I would be needing the assistance of forensics and the best photographer they could get out of bed at that time in the morning."

"And what did you find when you arrived at the Elliots' house?"

"I was surprised to discover that the front door was open and Mrs. Elliot was crouched on the floor in the hallway. She told me that she had found her husband's body in the study, and pointed to the other end of the corridor. She added that the chief had told her not to touch anything, which was why the front door had been left open. I went straight to the study, and once I had confirmed that Mr. Elliot was dead, I returned to the hallway and took a statement from his wife, copies of which are in the court's possession."

"What did you do next?"

"In her statement, Mrs. Elliot said that she had been asleep when she heard two shots coming from downstairs, so I and three other officers returned to the study to search for the bullets."

"And did you find them?"

"Yes. The first was easy to locate because after it had passed through Mr. Elliot's heart it ended up embedded in the wooden panel behind his desk. The second took a little longer to find, but we eventually spotted it lodged in the ceiling above Mr. Elliot's bureau."

"Could these two bullets have been fired by the same person?"

"It's possible," said Petrowski, "if the murderer had wanted to leave the impression of a struggle, or the victim had turned the gun on himself."

"Is that common in a homicide case?"

"It's not unknown for a criminal to try and leave conflicting evidence."

"But can you prove that both bullets came from the same gun?"

"That was confirmed by ballistics the following day."

"And were any fingerprints found on the firearm?"

"Yes," said Petrowski, "a palm mark on the handle of the gun, plus an index finger on the trigger."

"And were you later able to match up these samples?"

"Yes," he paused. "They both matched Mr. Cartwright's prints."

A babble of chatter erupted from the public benches behind Fletcher. He tried not to blink as he observed the jury's reaction to this piece of information. A moment later he scribbled a note on his yellow pad. The judge banged his gavel several times as he called for order, before Ebden was able to resume.

"From the entry of the bullet into the body, and the burn marks on the chest, were you able to ascertain what distance the murderer was from his victim?"

"Yes," said Petrowski. "Forensics estimated that the assailant must have been standing four to five feet in front of his victim, and from the angle which the bullet entered the body, they were able to show that both men were standing at the time."

"Objection, your honor," said Fletcher, rising from his place. "We have yet to prove that it was a man who fired either shot."

"Sustained."

"And when you had gathered all your evidence," continued Ebden as if he had not been interrupted, "was it you who made the decision to arrest Mr. Cartwright?"

"No, by then the chief had turned up, and although it was my case, I asked if he would also take a statement from Mrs. Elliot, to make sure her story hadn't changed in any way."

"And had it?"

"No, on all the essential points, it remained consistent."

Fletcher underlined the word *essential* as both Petrowski and the chief had used it. Well rehearsed or a coincidence, he wondered.

"Was that when you decided to arrest the accused?"

"Yes, it was on my recommendation, but ultimately the chief's decision."

"Weren't you taking a tremendous risk, arresting a gubernatorial candidate during an election campaign?"

"Yes, we were, and I discussed that problem with the chief. We often find to our cost that the first twenty-four hours are the most important in any investigation, and we had a body, two bullets and a witness to the crime. I considered it would have been an abrogation of my duty not to make an arrest simply because the assailant had powerful friends."

"Objection, your honor, that was prejudicial," said Fletcher.

"Sustained," said the judge, "and strike it from the record." He turned to Petrowski and added, "Please stick to facts, detective, I'm not interested in your opinions."

Petrowski nodded.

Fletcher turned to Nat. "That last statement sounded to me as if it had been written in the DA's office." He paused, looked down at his yellow pad and commented that "abrogation," "essential points," and "assailant" were delivered as if they had been learned by heart. "Petrowski won't have the opportunity to deliver rehearsed answers when I cross-examine him."

"Thank you, Captain," said Ebden, "I have no more questions for Detective Petrowski, your honor."

"Do you wish to question this witness?" asked the judge, preparing himself for another tactical maneuver.

"Yes, I most certainly do, your honor." Fletcher remained seated while he turned a page of his legal pad. "Detective Petrowski, you told the court that my client's fingerprints were on the gun."

"Not just his fingerprints, also a palm print on the butt as confirmed in the forensic report."

"And didn't you also tell the court that in your experience, criminals often try to leave conflicting evidence in order to fool the police?"

Petrowski nodded, but made no reply.

"Yes or no, Captain?"

"Yes," said Petrowski.

"Would you describe Mr. Cartwright as a fool?"

Petrowski hesitated while he tried to work out where Fletcher was attempting to lead him. "No, I would say he was a highly intelligent man."

"Would you describe leaving your fingerprints and a palm print on the murder weapon as the act of a highly intelligent man?" asked Fletcher.

"No, but then Mr. Cartwright is not a professional criminal, and doesn't think like one. Amateurs often panic and that's when they make simple mistakes."

"Like dropping the gun on the floor, covered in his prints, and running out of the house leaving the front door wide open?"

"Yes, that doesn't surprise me, given the circumstances."

"You spent several hours questioning Mr. Cartwright, Captain; does he strike you as the type of man who panics and then runs away?"

"Objection, your honor," said Ebden, rising from his place, "how can Detective Petrowski be expected to answer that question?"

"Your honor, Detective Petrowski has been only too willing to give his opinion on the habits of amateur and professional criminals, so I can't see why he wouldn't feel comfortable answering my question."

"Overruled, counselor. Move on."

Fletcher bowed to the judge, stood up, walked over to the witness stand and came to a halt in front of the detective. "Were there any other fingerprints on the gun?"

"Yes," said Petrowski, not appearing to be fazed by Fletcher's presence, "there were partials of Mr. Elliot's prints, but they have been accounted for, remembering that he took the gun from his desk to protect himself."

"But his prints were on the gun?"

"Yes."

"Did you check to see if there was any powder residue under his fingernails?"

"No," said Petrowski.

"And why not?" asked Fletcher.

"Because you'd need very long arms to shoot yourself from a distance of four feet." Laughter broke out in the court.

Fletcher waited for silence before he said, "But he could well have fired the first bullet that ended up in the ceiling."

"It could have been the second bullet," rebutted Petrowski.

Fletcher turned away from the witness box and walked over to the jury. "When you took the statement from Mrs. Elliot, what was she wearing?"

"A robe—as she explained, she had been asleep at the time when the first shot was fired."

"Ah yes, I remember," said Fletcher before he walked back to the table. He picked up a single sheet of paper and read from it. "It was when Mrs. Elliot heard the second shot that she came out of the bedroom and ran to the top of the stairs." Petrowski nodded.

"Please answer the question, detective, yes or no?"

"I don't recall the question," said Petrowski, sounding flustered.

"It was when she heard the second shot that Mrs. Elliot came out of the bedroom and ran to the top of the stairs."

"Yes, that's what she told us."

"And she stood there watching Mr. Cartwright as he ran out of the front door. Is that also correct?" Fletcher asked, turning around to look directly at Petrowski.

"Yes it is," said Petrowski, trying to remain calm.

"Detective, you told the court that among the professionals you called in to assist you was a police photographer."

"Yes, that's standard practice in a case like this, and all the photographs taken that night have been submitted as evidence."

"Indeed they have," said Fletcher as he returned to the table and emptied a large package of photographs onto his table. He selected one, and walked back to the witness stand. "Is this one of those photographs?" he asked.

Petrowski studied it carefully, and then looked at the stamp on the back. "Yes, it is."

"Would you describe it to the jury?"

"It's a picture of the Elliots' front door, taken from their driveway."

"Why was this particular photograph submitted as evidence?"

"Because it proved that the door had been left open when the murderer made good his escape. It also shows the long corridor leading through to Mr. Elliot's study."

"Yes, of course it does, I should have worked that out for myself," said Fletcher. He paused. "And the figure crouched in the corridor, is that Mrs. Elliot?"

The detective took a second look, "Yes it is, she seemed calm at the time, so we decided not to disturb her."

"How considerate," said Fletcher. "So let me ask you finally, detective, you told the district attorney that you did not call for an ambulance until your investigation had been completed?"

"That is correct, paramedics sometimes turn up at the scene of a crime before the police have arrived, and they are notorious for disturbing evidence."

"Are they?" asked Fletcher. "But that didn't happen on this occasion, because you were the first person to arrive following Mrs. Elliot's call to the chief."

"Yes, I was."

"Most commendable," said Fletcher." "Do you have any idea how long it took you to reach Mrs. Elliot's home in West Hartford?"

"Five, maybe six minutes."

"You must have had to break the speed limit to achieve that," said Fletcher, with a smile.

"I put my siren on, but as it was two in the morning, there was very little traffic."

"I'm grateful for that explanation," said Fletcher. "No more questions, your honor."

"What was all that about?" muttered Nat when Fletcher had returned to his place.

"Ah, I'm glad you didn't work it out," said Fletcher. "Now we must hope that the state's attorney hasn't either."

48

"I CALL REBECCA ELLIOT to the stand."

When Rebecca entered the courtroom, every head turned except Nat's. He remained staring resolutely ahead. She walked slowly down the center aisle, making the sort of entrance that an actress looks for in every script. The court had been packed from the moment the doors were opened at eight o'clock that morning. The front three rows of the public benches had been cordoned off, and only the presence of uniformed police officers kept them from being colonized.

Fletcher had looked around when Don Culver, the chief of police, and Detective Petrowski had taken their seats in the front row, directly behind the state's attorney's table. At one minute to ten, only thirteen seats remained unoccupied.

Nat glanced across at Fletcher, who had a little stack of yellow legal pads in front of him. He could see that the top sheet was blank and prayed that the other three unopened pads had something written on them. A court officer stepped forward to show Mrs. Elliot into the well of the court and guide her to the witness stand. Nat looked up at Rebecca for the first time. She was wearing her widow's weeds—fashionable black tailored suit, buttoned to the neck, and a skirt that fell several inches below the knee. Her only jewelry other than her wedding and engagement ring was a simple string of pearls. Fletcher glanced at her left wrist and made the first note on his pad. As she took the stand, Rebecca turned to face the judge, and gave him a shy smile. He nodded courteously. She then haltingly took the oath. She finally sat down and,,turning

439

to face the jury, gave them the same shy smile. Fletcher noticed that several of them returned the compliment. Rebecca touched the side of her hair, and Fletcher knew where she must have spent most of the previous afternoon. The state's attorney hadn't missed a trick, and if he could have called for the jury to deliver their verdict before a question had been asked, he suspected that they would have happily sentenced him, as well as his client, to the electric chair.

The judge nodded, and the state's attorney rose from his place. Mr. Ebden had also joined in the charade. He was dressed in a dark charcoal suit, white shirt and a sober blue tie—the appropriate attire in which to question the Virgin Mother.

"Mrs. Elliot," he said quietly, as he stepped on into the well of the court. "Everyone in this courtroom is aware of the ordeal you have been put through, and are now going to have to painfully relive. Let me reassure you that it is my intention to take you through any questions I might have as painlessly as possible, in the hope that you will not have to remain in the witness stand any longer than is necessary."

"Especially as we have been able to rehearse every question again and again for the past five months," murmured Fletcher. Nat tried not to smile.

"Let me begin by asking you, Mrs. Elliot, how long were you married to your late husband?"

"Tomorrow would have been our seventeenth wedding anniversary."

"And how did you plan to celebrate that occasion?"

"We were going to stay at the Salisbury Inn, where we had spent the first night of our honeymoon, because I knew Ralph couldn't spare more than a few hours off from his campaign."

"Typical of Mr. Elliot's commitment and conscientious approach to public service," said the state's attorney as he walked out into the well of the court and across to the jury. "I must, Mrs. Elliot, ask you to bear with me while I return to the night of your husband's tragic and untimely death." Rebecca bowed her head slightly. "You didn't attend the debate that Mr. Elliot took part in earlier that evening: Was there any particular reason for that?"

"Yes," said Rebecca, facing the jury, "Ralph liked me to stay at home and watch him whenever he was on television, where I could make detailed notes that we would discuss later. He felt that if I was part of the studio audience, I might be influenced by those sitting around me, especially once they realized that I was the candidate's wife."

"That makes a great deal of sense," said Ebden. Fletcher penned a second note on the pad in front of him.

"Was there anything in particular you recall about that evening's broadcast?"

"Yes," said Rebecca. She paused and bowed her head. "I felt sick when Mr. Cartwright threatened my husband with the words 'I will still kill you.'" She slowly raised her head and looked at the jury, as Fletcher made a further note.

"And once the debate was over your husband returned home to West Hartford?"

"Yes, I had prepared a light supper for him which we had in the kitchen, because he sometimes forgets." She paused again. "I'm so sorry, forgot, to take a break from his arduous schedule to eat."

"Do you recall anything in particular about that supper?"

"Yes, I went over my notes with him, as I felt strongly about some of the issues that had been raised during the debate." Fletcher turned the page and made another note. "In fact, it was over supper that I learned Mr. Cartwright had accused him of setting up the last question."

"How did you react to such a suggestion?"

"I was appalled that anyone could think Ralph might have been involved in such underhanded tactics. However I remained convinced that the public would not be taken in by Mr. Cartwright's false accusations, and that his petulant outburst would only increase my husband's chances of winning the election the following day."

"And after supper did you both go to bed?"

"No, Ralph always found it difficult to sleep after appearing on television." She turned to face the jury again. "He told me that the adrenalin would go on pumping for several hours, and in any case, he wanted to put some finishing touches to his acceptance speech,

so I went to bed while he settled down to work in his study."
Fletcher added a further note to his script.

"And what time was that?"

"Just before midnight."

"And after you had fallen asleep, what was the next thing you
remember?"

"Being woken by a shot, and not being certain if it was real or
just part of a dream. I turned on the light and checked the time by
the clock on my bedside table. It was just after two o'clock, and I
remember being surprised that Ralph still hadn't come to bed.
Then I thought I heard voices, so I walked over to the door and
opened it slightly. That was when I first heard someone shouting
at Ralph. I was horrified when I realized it was Nat Cartwright.
He was screaming at the top of his voice, and once again threatening to kill my husband. I crept out of the bedroom to the top of the
stairs and that was when I heard the second shot. A moment later
Mr. Cartwright came running out of the study, continued on down
the corridor, opened the front door and disappeared into the
night."

"Did you chase after him?"

"No, I was terrified."

Fletcher scribbled yet another note as Rebecca continued. "I
ran downstairs, and straight into Ralph's study, fearing the worst.
The first thing I saw was my husband on the far side of the room
slumped in the corner, blood trickling from his mouth, so I immediately picked up the phone on his desk and called Chief Culver at
home."

Fletcher turned yet another page and continued writing furiously. "I'm afraid I woke him, but the chief said he would come
over as quickly as possible and that I was to touch nothing."

"What did you do next?"

"I suddenly felt cold and sick to my stomach, and I thought I
was going to faint. I staggered back out into the corridor and collapsed on the floor. The next thing I remember was a police siren
in the distance and a few moments later someone came running
through the front door. The policeman knelt down by my side and
introduced himself as Detective Petrowski. One of his officers

made me a cup of coffee and then he asked me to describe what had happened. I told him all I could remember, but I'm afraid I wasn't very coherent. I recall pointing to Ralph's study."

"Can you remember what happened next?"

"Yes, a few minutes later I heard another siren, and then the chief walked in. Mr. Culver spent a long time with Detective Petrowski in my husband's study, and then returned and asked me to go over my story once again. He didn't stay for very long after that, but I did see him in deep conversation with the detective before he left. It wasn't until the following morning that I discovered that Mr. Cartwright had been arrested and charged with the murder of my husband." Rebecca burst into tears.

"Right on cue," said Fletcher as the chief prosecutor removed a handkerchief from his top pocket and handed it over to Mrs. Elliot. "I wonder how long they took rehearsing that?" he added as he turned his attention to the jury and noticed that a woman in the second row was also quietly crying.

"I'm sorry to have put you through such an ordeal, Mrs. Elliot." Ebden paused, "Perhaps you would like me to ask the court for an adjournment so you have a little time to compose yourself?"

Fletcher would have objected, but he already knew what her answer would be, because they were so obviously sticking to a well-worn script.

"No, I'll be fine," said Rebecca, "and in any case I'd rather get it over with."

"Yes, of course, Mrs. Elliot," Ebden looked up toward the judge, "I have no more questions for this witness, your honor."

"Thank you, Mr. Ebden," said the judge. "Your witness, Mr. Davenport."

"Thank you, your honor." Fletcher removed a stopwatch from his pocket and placed it on the table in front of him. He then slowly rose from his place. He could feel the eyes of everyone in the courtroom boring into the back of his head. How could he even consider questioning this helpless, saintly woman? He walked over to the stand and didn't speak for some time. "I will try not to detain you for longer than is necessary, Mrs. Elliot, remembering the ordeal you have already been put through." Fletcher spoke softly. "But I must ask you one or two questions, as it is my client who is facing the death penalty, based almost solely on your testimony."

"Yes, of course," Rebecca replied, trying to sound brave as she wiped away the last tear.

"You told the court, Mrs. Elliot, that you had a very fulfilling relationship with your husband."

"Yes, we were devoted to each other."

"Were you?" Fletcher paused again. "And the only reason you did not attend the television debate that evening was because Mr. Elliot had asked you to remain at home and make some notes on his performance, so that you could discuss them later that evening?"

"Yes, that is correct," she said.

"I can appreciate that," said Fletcher, "but I'm puzzled as to why you did not accompany your husband to a single public function during the previous month?" He paused. "Night or day."

"I did, I feel sure I did," she said. "But in any case you must remember that my main task was to run the home, and make life as easy as possible for Ralph, after the long hours he spent on the road campaigning."

"Did you keep those notes?"

She hesitated, "No, once I'd gone over them with him, I gave them to Ralph."

"And on this particular occasion you told the court that you felt very strongly about certain issues?"

"Yes, I did."

"May I ask which issues in particular, Mrs. Elliot?"

Rebecca hesitated again. "I can't remember exactly." She paused. "It was several months ago."

"But it was the only public function you took an interest in during his entire campaign, Mrs. Elliot, so one would have thought you might just have remembered one or two of the issues you felt so strongly about. After all, your husband was running for governor and you, so to speak, for first lady."

"Yes, no, yes—health care, I think."

"Then you'll have to think again, Mrs. Elliot," said Fletcher as he returned to the table and picked up one of his yellow notepads.

"I also watched that debate with more than a passing interest, and was somewhat surprised that the subject of health care was not raised. Perhaps you'd like to reconsider your last answer, as I did keep detailed notes on every issue that was debated that night."

"Objection, your honor. Defense counsel is not here to act as a witness."

"Sustained. Keep to your brief, counselor."

"But there was one thing you felt strongly about, wasn't there, Mrs. Elliot?" continued Fletcher. "The vicious attack on your husband when Mr. Cartwright said on television, 'I will still kill you.'"

"Yes, that was a terrible thing to say with the whole world watching."

"But the whole world wasn't watching, Mrs. Elliot, otherwise I would have seen it. It wasn't said until after the program had ended."

"Then my husband must have told me about it over supper."

"I don't think so, Mrs. Elliot. I suspect that you didn't even see that program, just as you never attended any of his meetings."

"Yes, I did."

"Then perhaps you can tell the jury the location of any meeting you attended during your husband's lengthy campaign, Mrs. Elliot?"

"How could I be expected to remember every one of them, when Ralph's campaign started over a year ago?"

"I'll settle for just one," said Fletcher, turning to face the jury.

Rebecca started crying again, but on this occasion the timing was not quite as effective, and there was no one on hand to offer her a handkerchief.

"Now let us consider those words, 'I will still kill you,' spoken off air the evening before an election." Fletcher remained facing the jury. "Mr. Cartwright didn't say 'I will kill you,' which would have indeed been damning; what he actually said was 'I will *still* kill you,' and everyone present assumed he was referring to the election that was taking place the following day."

"He killed my husband," shouted Mrs. Elliot, her voice rising for the first time.

"There are still a few more questions that need to be answered before I come to who killed your husband, Mrs. Elliot. But first allow me to return to the events of that evening. Having watched a television program you can't remember, and had supper with your husband to discuss in detail issues that you don't recall, you went to bed while your husband returned to his study to work on his acceptance speech."

"Yes, that is exactly what happened," said Rebecca, staring defiantly at Fletcher.

"But as he was significantly behind in the opinion polls, why waste time working on an acceptance speech he could never need hope to deliver?"

"He was still convinced he would win, especially following Mr. Cartwright's outburst and . . ."

"And?" repeated Fletcher, but Rebecca remained silent. "Then perhaps you both knew something the rest of us didn't," said Fletcher, "but I'll come to that in a moment. You say you went to bed around midnight?"

"Yes, I did," said Rebecca, sounding even more defiant.

"And when you were woken by a gunshot, you checked the time by looking at the clock on your side of the bed?"

"Yes, it was just after two."

"So you don't wear a wristwatch in bed?"

"No, I lock away all my jewelry in a little safe Ralph had installed in the bedroom. There have been so many burglaries in the area recently."

"How wise of him. And you still think it was the first shot that woke you?"

"Yes, I'm sure it was."

"How long was it between the first and second shot, Mrs. Elliot?" Rebecca didn't answer immediately. "Do take your time, Mrs. Elliot, because I wouldn't want you to make a mistake that, like so much of your evidence, needs correcting later."

"Objection, your honor, my client is not . . ."

"Yes, yes, Mr. Ebden, sustained. That last comment will be struck from the record," and turning to Fletcher, the judge repeated, "stick to your brief, Mr. Davenport."

"I will try to, your honor," said Fletcher, but his eyes never left the jury to make sure it wasn't struck from their minds. "Have you had enough time to consider your reply, Mrs. Elliot?" He waited once again before repeating, "How long was it between the first and second shots?"

"Three, possibly four minutes," she said.

Fletcher smiled at the chief prosecutor, walked back to his table and picked up the stopwatch, which he placed in his pocket. "When you heard the first shot, Mrs. Elliot, why didn't you phone the police immediately, why wait for three or four minutes until you heard the second shot?"

"Because to begin with I wasn't absolutely sure that I had heard it. Don't forget, I'd been asleep for some time."

"But you opened your bedroom door and were horrified to hear Mr. Cartwright shouting at your husband and threatening to kill him, so you must have believed that Ralph was in some considerable danger, so why not lock your door, and immediately phone the police from the bedroom?" Rebecca looked across at Richard Ebden. "No, Mrs. Elliot, Mr. Ebden can't help you this time, because he didn't anticipate the question, which, to be fair," said Fletcher, "wasn't entirely his fault, because you've only told him half the story."

"Objection," said Ebden, jumping to his feet.

"Sustained," said the judge. "Mr. Davenport, stick to questioning Mrs. Elliot, not giving opinions. This is a court of law, not the Senate Chamber."

"I apologize, your honor, but on this occasion I do know the answer. You see the reason Mrs. Elliot didn't call the police was because she feared that it was her husband who had fired the first shot."

"Objection," shouted Ebden, leaping to his feet as several members of the public began talking at once. It was some time before the judge could gavel the court back to order.

"No, no," said Rebecca, "from the way Nat was shouting at Ralph I was certain he'd fired the first shot."

"Then I will ask you again, why not call the police immediately?" Fletcher repeated, turning back to face her. "Why wait three or four minutes until you heard the second shot?"

"It all happened so quickly, I just didn't have time."

"What is your favorite work of fiction, Mrs. Elliot?" asked Fletcher quietly.

"Objection, your honor. How can this possibly be relevant?"

"Overruled. I have a feeling we're about to find out, Mr. Ebden."

"You are indeed, your honor," said Fletcher, his eyes never leaving the witness. "Mrs. Elliot, let me assure you that this is not a trick question, I simply want you to tell the court your favorite work of fiction."

"I'm not sure I have a particular one," she replied, "but my favorite author is Hemingway."

"Mine too," said Fletcher, taking the stopwatch out of his pocket. Turning to face the judge, he asked, "Your honor, may I have your permission to briefly leave the courtroom?"

"For what purpose, Mr. Davenport?"

"To prove that my client did not fire the first shot."

The judge nodded. "Briefly, Mr. Davenport."

Fletcher then pressed the starter button, placed the stopwatch in his pocket, walked down the aisle through the packed courtroom, and out of the door. "Your honor," said Ebden, jumping up from his place, "I must object. Mr. Davenport is turning this trial into a circus."

"If that turns out to be the case, Mr. Ebden, I shall severely censure Mr. Davenport the moment he returns."

"But, your honor, is this kind of behavior fair to my client?"

"I believe so, Mr. Ebden. As Mr. Davenport reminded the court, his client faces the death penalty solely on the evidence of your principal witness."

The chief prosecutor sat back down, and began to consult his team, while chattering broke out on the public benches behind him. The judge started tapping his fingers, occasionally glancing at the clock on the wall above the public entrance.

Richard Ebden rose again, at which point the judge called for order. "You honor, I move that Mrs. Elliot be released from further questioning on the grounds that the defense counsel is no longer able to carry out his cross-examination as he has left the courtroom without explanation."

"I shall approve your request, Mr. Ebden," the state's attorney looked delighted, "should Mr. Davenport fail to return in under four minutes." He smiled down at Mr. Ebden, assuming they had both worked out the significance of his judgment.

"Your honor, I must . . ." continued the state's attorney, but he was interrupted by the court doors being flung open and Fletcher marching back down the aisle and up to the witness stand. He handed a copy of *For Whom the Bell Tolls* to Mrs. Elliot, before turning to the judge.

"Your honor, would the court judicially note the length of time I was absent?" he said, handing over the stopwatch to the judge.

Judge Kravats pressed the stopper and, looking down at the stopwatch, said, "Three minutes and forty-nine seconds."

Fletcher turned his attention back to the defense witness. "Mrs. Elliot, I had enough time to leave the courthouse, walk to the public library on the other side of the street, locate the Hemingway shelf, check out a book with my library card, and still be back in the courtroom with eleven seconds to spare. But you didn't have enough time to walk across your bedroom, dial 911 and ask for assistance when you believed your husband might have been in mortal danger. And the reason you didn't is because you knew your husband had fired the first shot, and you were fearful of what he might have done."

"But even if I did think that," said Rebecca, losing her composure, "it's only the second bullet that matters, the one that killed Ralph. Perhaps you've forgotten that the first bullet ended up in the ceiling, or are you now suggesting that my husband killed himself?"

"No, I am not," said Fletcher, "so why don't you now tell the court exactly what you did when you heard the second shot."

"I went to the top of the stairs and saw Mr. Cartwright running out of the house."

"But he didn't see you?"

"No, he only glanced back in my direction."

"I don't think so, Mrs. Elliot. I think you saw him very clearly when he calmly walked past you in the corridor."

"He couldn't have walked past me in the corridor because I was at the top of the stairs."

"I agree that he couldn't have seen you if you had been at the top of the stairs," said Fletcher as he returned to the table and selected a photograph, before walking back across to the witness stand. He passed the photograph over to her. "As you will see from this picture, Mrs. Elliot, anyone who left your husband's study, walked into the corridor and then out of the front door could not have been observed from the top of the stairs." He paused so that the jury could take in the significance of his statement, before continuing, "No, the truth is, Mrs. Elliot, that you were not standing at the top of the stairs, but in the hallway when Mr. Cartwright came out of your husband's study, and if you would like me to ask the judge to adjourn so that the jury can visit your home and check on the veracity of your statement, I would be quite happy to do so."

"Well, I might have been halfway down the stairs."

"You weren't even *on* the stairs, Mrs. Elliot, you were in the hallway, and you were not, as you also claimed, in your robe, but in a blue dress that you had worn to a cocktail party earlier that evening, which is why you didn't see the television debate!"

"I was in a robe and there's a picture of me to prove it."

"Indeed there is," said Fletcher, once again returning to the table and extracting another photograph, "which I am happy to enter as evidence—item 122, your honor."

The judge, prosecution team and the jury began to rummage through their files as Fletcher handed over his copy to Mrs. Elliot.

"There you are," she said, "it's just as I told you, I'm sitting in the hallway in my robe."

"You are indeed, Mrs. Elliot, and that photograph was taken by the police photographer, and we've since had it enlarged so we can consider all the details more clearly. Your honor, I would like to submit this enlarged photograph as evidence."

"Objection, your honor," said Ebden, leaping up from his place. "We have not been given an opportunity to study this photograph."

"It's state's evidence, Mr. Ebden, and has been in your possession for weeks," the judge reminded him. "Your objection is overruled."

"Please study the photograph carefully," said Fletcher as he walked away from Mrs. Elliot and passed the state's attorney a copy of the enlarged photo. A clerk handed one to each member of the jury. Fletcher then turned back to face Rebecca. "And do tell the court what you see."

"It's a photograph of me sitting in the hallway in my robe."

"It is indeed, but what are you wearing on your left wrist and around your neck?" Fletcher asked, before turning to face the jury, all of whom were now studying the photograph intently.

The blood drained from Rebecca's face.

"I do believe they're your wristwatch and your pearl necklace," said Fletcher answering his own question. "Do you remember?" He paused. "The ones you always locked away in your safe just before going to bed because there had been several burglaries in the area recently?" Fletcher turned to face Chief Culver and Detective Petrowski, who were seated in the front row. "It is, as Detective Petrowski reminded us, the little mistakes that always reveal the amateur." Fletcher turned back and looked directly at Rebecca, before adding, "You may have forgotten to take off your watch and necklace, Mrs. Elliot, but I can tell you something you didn't forget to take off, your dress." Fletcher placed his hands on the jury box rail before saying slowly and without expression. "Because you didn't do that until after you'd killed your husband."

Several people rose at once, and the judge carried on banging his gavel before it was quiet enough for the state's attorney to say in a loud voice, "Objection. How can wearing a wristwatch prove that Mrs. Elliot murdered her husband?"

"I agree with you, Mr. Ebden," said the judge and turning to Fletcher suggested, "That's quite a quantum leap, counselor."

"Then I will be happy to take the state's attorney through it step by step, your honor." The judge nodded. "When Mr. Cartwright arrived at the house, he overheard an argument going on between Mr. and Mrs. Elliot, and after he'd knocked on the door, it was Mr. Elliot who answered it, while Mrs. Elliot was nowhere to be seen. I'm willing to accept that she did run up to the top of the stairs so that she could overhear what was going on while not being observed, but the moment the first shot was fired, she came back down into the corridor and listened to the quarrel taking place between her husband and my client. Three or four minutes later, Mr. Cartwright walked calmly out of the study and passed Mrs. Elliot in the corridor, before opening the front door. He looked back at Mrs. Elliot, which is why he was able to tell the police questioning him later that night that she was wearing a low-cut blue dress and a string of pearls. If the jury studies the photograph of Mrs. Elliot, if I'm not mistaken, she is wearing the same string of pearls as the ones she has on today." Rebecca touched her necklace as Fletcher continued. "But let's not rely on my client's word, but on your own statement, Mrs. Elliot." He turned another page of the state's evidence, before he began reading. "I ran into the study, saw my husband's body slumped on the floor and then called the police."

"That's right, I did ring Chief Culver at home, he's already confirmed that," interjected Rebecca.

"But why did you call the chief of police first?"

"Because my husband had been murdered."

"But in your evidence, Mrs. Elliot, given to Detective Petrowski only moments after your husband's death, you stated that you saw Ralph slumped in the corner of his study, blood coming from his mouth, and immediately called the chief of police."

"Yes, that's exactly what I did," shouted Rebecca.

Fletcher paused before turning to face the jury. "If I saw my wife slumped in a corner with blood coming from her mouth, the first thing I would do is to check to see if she was still alive and, if she was, I wouldn't call for the police, I'd call for an ambulance. And at no time did you call for an ambulance, Mrs. Elliot. Why? Because you already knew that your husband was dead."

Once again there was uproar in the body of the court, and the reporters who weren't old-fashioned enough to take shorthand struggled to get down every word.

"Mrs. Elliot," continued Fletcher, once the judge had stopped banging his gavel, "allow me to repeat the words you said only a few moments ago when questioned by the state's attorney." Fletcher picked up one of the yellow pads from his desk and began reading. "'I suddenly felt cold and sick to my stomach, and I thought I was going to faint. I staggered back out into the corridor and collapsed on the floor.'" Fletcher threw the notepad down on his desk, stared at Mrs. Elliot and said, "You still haven't even bothered to check if your husband is alive, but you didn't need to, did you, because you knew he was dead; after all, it was you who had killed him."

"Then why didn't they find any traces of gunpowder residue on my robe?" Rebecca shouted above the banging of the judge's gavel.

"Because when you shot your husband, you weren't in your robe, Mrs. Elliot, but still in the blue dress you'd been wearing that evening. It was only after you had killed Ralph that you ran upstairs to change into your nightgown and robe. But unfortunately Detective Petrowski switched on his car siren, broke the speed limit, and managed to be with you six minutes later, which is why you had to rush back downstairs, forgetting to take off your watch or pearls. And even more damning, not leaving yourself enough time to close the front door. If, as you have claimed, Mr. Cartwright had killed your husband, and then run out of the door, the first thing you would have done would be to make sure that it was closed so he couldn't get back in to harm you. But Detective Petrowski, conscientious man that he is, arrived a little too quickly for you, and even remarked how surprised he was to find the front door open. Amateurs often panic, and that's when they make simple mistakes," he repeated almost in a whisper. "Because the truth is that once Mr. Cartwright had walked past you in the hallway, you then ran into the study, picked up the gun and realized this was a perfect opportunity to be rid of a husband you'd despised for years. The shot Mr. Cartwright heard as he was driving away from the house was indeed the bullet that killed your husband, but it wasn't Mr. Cartwright who pulled the trigger, it was you. What Mr. Cartwright did do was give you the perfect alibi, and a solution to all your problems." He paused and, turning away from the jury, added, "If only you had remembered to remove your wristwatch and pearls before you came downstairs, closed the front door and then phoned for an ambulance, rather than the chief of police, you would have committed the perfect murder, and my client would be facing the death penalty."

"I didn't kill him."

"Then who did? Because it can't have been Mr. Cartwright, as he left some time *before* the second shot was fired. I feel sure you recall his words when confronted by the chief—'he was still alive when I left him,' and by the way, Mr. Cartwright didn't find it necessary to change out of the suit he'd been wearing earlier that evening." Once again Fletcher turned to face the jury, but they were now all staring at Mrs. Elliot.

She buried her head in her hands and whispered, "Ralph's the one who should be on trial. He was responsible for his own death."

However firmly Judge Kravats called the court to order, it was still some time before he was able to restore calm. Fletcher waited until he had complete silence, before he delivered his next sentence.

"But how is that possible, Mrs. Elliot?" he asked. "After all, it was Detective Petrowski who pointed out that it's quite difficult to shoot yourself from four feet away."

"He made me do it."

Ebden leaped to his feet as the public began repeating the sentence to each other.

"Objection, your honor, the witness is being . . ."

"Overruled," said Judge Kravats firmly. "Sit down, Mr. Ebden, and remain seated." The judge turned his attention back to the witness. "What did you mean, Mrs. Elliot, by 'he made me do it'?"

Rebecca turned to the judge, who looked down at her with concern. "You honor, Ralph was desperate to win the election at any cost, and after Nat told him that Luke had committed suicide, he knew he no longer had any hope of becoming governor. He kept pacing around the room repeating the words, 'I will still kill you,' then he snapped his fingers and said, 'I've got the solution, you're going to have to do it.'"

"What did he mean by that?" asked the judge.

"To begin with I didn't understand myself, your honor, then he started shouting at me. He said, 'There's no time to argue, otherwise he'll get away, and then we'll never be able to pin it on him, so I'll tell you exactly what you're going to do. First, you'll shoot me in the shoulder, and then you'll call the chief at home and tell him that you were in the bedroom when you heard the first shot. You came rushing downstairs when you heard the second shot, and that's when you saw Cartwright running out of the front door.' "

"But why did you agree to go along with this outrageous suggestion?" asked the judge.

"I didn't," said Rebecca. "I told him if there was any shooting to be done, he could do it himself, because I wasn't going to get involved."

"And what did he say to that?" asked the judge.

"That he couldn't shoot himself because the police would be able to work that out, but if I did it, they would never know."

"But that still doesn't explain why you agreed to go through with it?"

"I didn't," repeated Rebecca quietly. "I told him I would have nothing to do with it, Nat had never done me any harm. But then Ralph grabbed the gun and said, 'If you're not willing to go through with it, then there's only one alternative, I'll have to shoot you.' I was terrified, but all he said was, 'I'll tell everyone that it was Nat Cartwright who killed my wife when she tried to come to my rescue, then they'll be even more sympathetic when I play the part of the grieving widower.' He laughed, and added, 'Don't think I wouldn't do it.' He then took a handkerchief out of his pocket and said, 'Wrap this around your hand, so your fingerprints won't be on the gun.' " Rebecca was silent for some time before she whispered, "I remember picking up the gun and pointing it at Ralph's shoulder, but I closed my eyes just as I pulled the trigger. When I opened them, Ralph was slumped in the corner. I didn't need to check to know that he was dead. I panicked, dropped the gun, ran upstairs and called the chief at home just as Ralph had told me to. Then I started to undress. I'd just put on my robe when I heard the siren. I looked through the curtains and saw a police car turning into the driveway. I ran back downstairs as the car was pulling up outside the house, which didn't leave me enough time to close the front door. I slumped down in the hallway just before Detective Petrowski came rushing in." She bowed her head and this time the weeping was genuine and unrehearsed. Whispering turned to chattering as everyone in the courtroom began to discuss Rebecca's testimony.

Fletcher turned to face the state's attorney, who was in a huddle, consulting his team. He made no attempt to hurry them, and returned to take his seat next to Nat. It was some time before Ebden eventually rose from his place. "Your honor."

"Yes, Mr. Ebden?" said the judge.

"The state withdraws all charges against the defendant." He paused for some time. "On a personal note," he added as he turned to face Nat and Fletcher, "having watched you as a team, I can't wait to see what will happen when you're up against each other."

Spontaneous applause broke out from the public benches, and the noise was such that they did not hear the judge release the prisoner, dismiss the jury, and declare the case closed.

Nat leaned across and almost had to shout, "Thank you," before adding, "two inadequate words as I'll spend the rest of my life in your debt without ever being able to properly repay you. But nevertheless, thank you."

Fletcher smiled. "Clients," he said, "fall into two categories: those you hope never to see again, and just occasionally those who you know will be friends for the rest . . ."

Su Ling suddenly appeared by her husband's side and threw her arms around him.

"Thank God," she said.

"Governor will do," said Fletcher, as Nat and Su Ling laughed for the first time in weeks. Before Nat could respond, Lucy came bursting through the barrier and greeted her father with the words, "Well done, Dad, I'm very proud of you."

"Praise indeed," said Fletcher. "Nat, this is my daughter Lucy, who fortunately isn't yet old enough to vote for you, but if she were . . ." Fletcher looked around, "so where's the woman who caused all this trouble in the first place?"

"Mom's at home," replied Lucy. "After all, you did tell her it would be at least another week before Mr. Cartwright would be on the stand."

"True," said Fletcher.

"And please pass on my thanks to your wife," said Su Ling. "We will always remember that it was Annie who persuaded you to represent my husband. Perhaps we can all get together in the near future, and . . ."

"Not until after the election," said Fletcher firmly, "as I'm still hoping that at least one member of my family will be voting for me." He paused, and turning to Nat said, "Do you know the real reason I worked so hard on this case?"

"You couldn't face the thought of having to spend the next few weeks with Barbara Hunter," said Nat.

"Something like that," he said, with a smile.

Fletcher was about to go across and shake hands with the state's team, but stopped in his tracks when he saw Rebecca Elliot still sitting in the witness stand waiting for the court to clear. Her head was bowed, and she looked forlorn and lonely.

"I know it's hard to believe," said Fletcher, "but I actually feel sorry for her."

"You should," said Nat, "because one thing's for certain, Ralph Elliot would have murdered his wife if he had thought it would win him the election."

BOOK SIX

REVELATION

49

FLETCHER SAT IN his Senate office reading the morning papers the day after the trial.

"What an ungrateful lot," he said, passing the *Hartford Courant* across to his daughter.

"You should have left him to fry," said Lucy as she glanced at the latest opinion poll figures.

"Expressed with your usual elegance and charm," said Fletcher. "It does make me wonder if all the money I've spent sending you to Hotchkiss has been worthwhile, not to mention what Vassar is going to cost me."

"I may not be going to Vassar, Dad," said Lucy in a quieter voice.

"Is that what you wanted to talk to me about?" asked Fletcher, picking up on his daughter's change of tone.

"Yes, Dad, because even though Vassar has offered me a place, I may not be able to accept it."

Fletcher couldn't always be certain when Lucy was kidding and when she was serious, but as she had asked to see him in his office and not to mention the meeting to Annie, he had to assume she was in earnest. "What's the problem?" he asked quietly, looking across the desk at her.

Lucy didn't meet his stare. She bowed her head and said, "I'm pregnant."

Fletcher didn't reply immediately as he tried to take in his daughter's confession. "Is George the father?" he eventually asked.

"Yes," she replied.

"And are you going to marry him?"

Lucy thought about the question for some time before replying. "No," she said. "I adore George, but I don't love him."

"But you were willing to let him make love to you."

"That's not fair," said Lucy. "It was the Saturday night after the election for president, and I'm afraid we both had a little too much to drink. To be honest, I was sick of being described by everyone in my class as the virgin president. And if I had to lose my virginity, I couldn't think of anyone nicer than George, especially after he admitted that he was also a virgin. In the end I'm not sure who seduced whom."

"How does George feel about all this? After all, it's his child as well as yours and he struck me as rather a serious young man, especially when it came to his feelings for you."

"He doesn't know yet."

"You haven't told him?" said Fletcher in disbelief.

"No."

"How about your mother?"

"No," she repeated. "The only person I've shared this with is you." This time she did look her father in the eye, before adding, "Let's face it, Dad, Mom was probably still a virgin on the day you married her."

"And so was I," said Fletcher, "but you're going to have to let her know before it becomes obvious to everyone."

"Not if I were to have an abortion."

Again, Fletcher remained silent for some time, before saying, "Is that what you really want?"

"Yes, Dad, but please don't tell Mom, because she wouldn't understand."

"I'm not sure I do myself," said Fletcher.

"Are you pro-women's choice for everyone except your daughter?" asked Lucy.

—◇—

"It won't last," said Nat, staring at the headline in the *Hartford Courant*.

"What won't?" said Su Ling as she poured him another coffee.

"My seven-point lead in the polls. In a few weeks' time the electorate won't even remember which one of us was on trial."

"I guess *she'll* still remember," said Su Ling quietly as she glanced over her husband's shoulder at a photograph of Rebecca Elliot walking down the courtroom steps, every hair no longer in place. "Why did she ever marry him?" she said almost to herself.

"It wasn't me who married Rebecca," said Nat. "Let's face it, if Elliot hadn't copied my thesis and prevented me going to Yale, to start with we would never have met," said Nat, taking his wife's hand.

"I just wish I'd been able to have more children," said Su Ling, her voice still subdued. "I miss Luke so much."

"I know," said Nat, "but I'll never regret running up that particular hill, at that particular time, on that particular day."

"And I'm glad I took the wrong path," said Su Ling, "because I couldn't love you any more. But I'd have willingly given up my life if it would have meant saving Luke's."

"I suspect that would be true of most parents," said Nat, looking at his wife, "and you could certainly include your mother, who sacrificed everything for you, and doesn't deserve to have been treated so cruelly."

"Don't worry about my mother," said Su Ling, snapping out of her maudlin mood. "I went to see her yesterday only to find the shop packed with dirty old men bringing in their even dirtier laundry, secretly hoping that she's running a massage parlor upstairs."

Nat burst out laughing. "And to think we kept it secret for all those years. I would certainly never have believed that the day would come when I would be able to laugh about it."

"She says if you become governor, she's going to open a string of shops right across the state. Her advertising slogan will be 'we wash your dirty linen in public.'"

"I always knew that there was some overriding reason I still needed to be governor," said Nat as he rose from the table.

"And who has the privilege of your company today?" asked Su Ling.

"The good folk of New Canaan," said Nat.

"So when will you be home?"

"Just after midnight would be my guess."

"Wake me," she said.

—◦—

"Hi, Lucy," said Jimmy as he strolled into her father's office. "Is the great man free?"

"Yes, he is," said Lucy as she rose from her chair.

Jimmy glanced back as she slipped out of the room. Was it his imagination or had she been crying? Fletcher didn't speak until she'd closed the door. "Good morning, Jimmy," he said as he pushed the paper to one side, leaving the photograph of Rebecca staring up at him.

"Do you think they'll arrest her?" asked Jimmy.

Fletcher glanced back down at the photograph of Rebecca. "I don't think they've been left with much choice, but if I were sitting on a jury I would acquit, because I found her story totally credible."

"Yes, but then you know what Elliot was capable of. A jury doesn't."

"But I can hear him saying, *If you won't do it, then I'll have to kill you, and don't think I wouldn't.*"

"I wonder if you would have remained at Alexander Dupont and Bell if Elliot hadn't joined the firm."

"One of those twists of fate," said Fletcher, as if his mind were on something else. "So what have you got lined up for me?"

"We're going to spend the day in Madison."

"Is Madison worth a whole day?" asked Fletcher, "when it's such a solid Republican district?"

"Which is precisely why I'm getting it out of the way while there's still a few weeks to go," said Jimmy, "though ironically their votes have never influenced the outcome of the election."

"A vote's a vote," said Fletcher.

"Not in this particular case," said Jimmy, "because while the rest of the state now votes electronically, Madison remains the single exception. They are among the last districts in the country who still prefer to mark their ballots with a pencil."

"But that doesn't stop their votes from being valid," insisted Fletcher.

"True, but in the past those votes have proved irrelevant, because they don't begin the count until the morning after the election, when the overall result has already been declared. It's a bit of a farce, but one of those traditions that the good burgers of Madison are unwilling to sacrifice on the altar of modern technology."

"And you still want me to spend a whole day there?"

"Yes, because if the majority were less than five thousand, suddenly Madison would become the most important town in the state."

"Do you think it could be that close while Bush still has a record lead in the polls?"

"Still is the operative word, because Clinton's chipping away at that lead every day, so who knows who'll end up in the White House, or in the governor's mansion for that matter?"

Fletcher didn't comment.

"You seem a little preoccupied this morning," said Jimmy. "Anything else on your mind that you want to discuss with me?"

—◦—

"It looks as if Nat's going to win by a mile," said Julia from behind the morning paper.

"A British prime minister once said that 'a week's a long time in politics,' and we've still got several more of them left before the first vote is cast," Tom reminded his wife.

"If Nat becomes governor, you'll miss all the excitement. After all you two have been through, returning to Fairchild's may turn out to be something of an anticlimax."

"The truth is that I lost any interest in banking the day Russell's was taken over."

"But you're about to become chairman of the biggest bank in the state."

"Not if Nat wins the election, I won't," said Tom.

Julia pushed the paper aside. "I'm not sure I understand."

"Nat has asked me to be his chief of staff if he becomes governor."

"Then who will take over as chairman of the bank?"

"You, of course," said Tom. "Everyone knows you'd be the best person for the job."

"But Fairchild's would never appoint a woman as chairman, they're far too traditional."

"We're living in the last decade of the twentieth century, Julia, and thanks to you, nearly half our customers are women. And as for the board, not to mention the staff, in my absence most of them think you already *are* the chairman."

"But if Nat were to lose, he'll quite rightly expect to return to Fairchild's as chairman, with you as his deputy, in which case the question becomes somewhat academic."

"I wouldn't be so sure of that," said Tom, "don't forget that Jimmy Overman, Connecticut's senior senator, has already announced that he'll not be running for reelection next year, in which case Nat would be the obvious choice to replace him. Whichever one of them becomes governor, I feel sure the other will be going to Washington as the state's senator." He paused, "I suspect it will only be a matter of time before Nat and Fletcher run against each other for president."

"Do you believe I can do the job?" asked Julia quietly.

"No," said Tom, "you have to be born in America before you can run for president."

"I didn't mean president, you idiot, but chairman of Fairchild's."

"I knew that the day we met," said Tom. "My only fear was that you wouldn't consider I was good enough to be your husband."

"Oh, men are so slow on the uptake," said Julia. "I made up my mind that I was going to marry you the night we met at Su Ling and Nat's dinner party." Tom's mouth opened and then closed.

"How different my life would have been if the other Julia Kirkbridge had come to the same conclusion," she added.

"Not to mention mine," said Tom.

50

FLETCHER STARED DOWN at the cheering crowd and waved enthusiastically back at them. He had made seven speeches in Madison that day—on street corners, in market places, outside a library—but even he had been surprised by his reception at the final meeting in the town hall that night.

COME AND HEAR THE WINNER was printed in bold red and blue letters on a massive banner that stretched from one side of the stage to the other. Fletcher had smiled when the local chairman told him that Paul Holbourn, the independent mayor of Madison, had left the banner in place after Nat had spoken at the town hall earlier that week. Holbourn had been the mayor for fourteen years, and didn't keep getting reelected because he squandered the taxpayers' money.

When Fletcher sat down at the end of his speech, he could feel the adrenaline pumping through his body, and the standing ovation that followed was not the usual stage-managed affair, where a bunch of well-placed party hacks leap up the moment the candidate has delivered his last line. On this occasion, the public were on their feet at the same time as the hacks. He only wished Annie could have been there to witness it.

When the chairman held up Fletcher's hand and shouted into the microphone, "Ladies and gentlemen, I give you the next governor of Connecticut," Fletcher believed it for the first time. Clinton was neck and neck with Bush in the national polls and Perot's independent candidacy was further chipping away at the Republican's support. It was creating a domino effect for Fletcher. He only hoped that four weeks was enough time to make up the four-point deficit in the polls.

It was another half hour before the hall was cleared, and by then Fletcher had shaken every proffered hand. A satisfied chairman accompanied him back to the parking lot.

"You don't have a driver?" he said, sounding a little surprised.

"Lucy took the night off to see *My Cousin Vinny,* Annie's attending some charity meeting, Jimmy's chairing a fund-raiser, and as it was less than fifty miles, I felt I could just about manage that by myself," explained Fletcher as he jumped behind the wheel.

He drove away from the town hall on a high, and began to relax for the first time that day. But he'd only driven a few hundred yards before his thoughts returned to Lucy, as they had done whenever he was alone. He faced a considerable dilemma. Should he should tell Annie that their daughter was pregnant?

⟶

Nat was having a private dinner with four local industrialists that night. Between them they were in a position to make a significant contribution to the campaign coffers, so he didn't hurry them. During the evening they had left him no doubt what they expected from a Republican governor, and although they didn't always go along with some of Nat's more liberal ideas, a Democrat wasn't moving into the governor's mansion if they had anything to do with it.

It was well past midnight when Ed Chambers of Chambers Foods suggested that perhaps the candidate should be allowed to go home and get a good night's sleep. Nat couldn't remember when he'd last had one of those.

This was the usual cue for Tom to stand up, agree with whoever had made the suggestion, and then go off in search of Nat's coat. Nat would then look as if he were being dragged away, shaking hands with his hosts before telling them that he couldn't hope to win the election without their support. Flattering though the sentiment might sound, on this occasion it also had the merit of being true.

All four men accompanied Nat back to his car, and as Tom drove down the long winding drive from Ed Chambers's home, Nat tuned in to the late news. Fletcher's speech to the citizens of Madison was the fourth item, and the local reporter was highlighting some of the points he'd made about neighborhood watch schemes, an idea Nat had been promoting for months. Nat began to grumble about such blatant plagiarism until Tom reminded him that he'd also stolen some of Fletcher's innovations on education reform.

Nat switched off the news when the weather forecaster returned to warn them about patchy ice on the roads. Within minutes Nat had fallen asleep, a trick Tom had often wished he could emulate, because the moment Nat woke, he was always backfiring on all cylinders. Tom was also looking forward to a decent night's sleep. They didn't have any official function before ten the following morning, when they would attend the first of seven religious services, ending the day with evensong at St. Joseph's Cathedral.

He knew that Fletcher Davenport would be covering roughly the same circuit in another part of the state. By the end of the campaign, there wouldn't be a religious gathering where they hadn't knelt down, taken off their shoes, or covered their heads in order to prove that they were both God-fearing citizens. Even if it wasn't necessarily their own particular God being revered, they had at least demonstrated willingness to stand, sit and kneel in His presence.

Tom decided not to switch on the one o'clock news, as he could see no purpose in waking Nat only to hear a regurgitation of what they had listened to thirty minutes before.

They both missed the newsflash.

—◦—

An ambulance was on the scene within minutes, and the first thing the paramedics did was to call in the fire department. The driver was pinned against the steering wheel, they reported, and there was no way of prying open his door without the use of an acetylene torch. They would have to work quickly if they hoped to get the injured man out of the wreck alive.

It wasn't until the police had checked the license plate on their computer back at headquarters that they realized who it was trapped behind the wheel. As they felt it was unlikely that the senator had been drinking, they assumed he must have fallen asleep.

There were no skid marks on the road and no other vehicles involved.

The paramedics radioed ahead to the hospital, and when they learned the identity of the victim the duty physician decided to page Ben Renwick. Remembering his seniority, Renwick didn't expect to be woken if there was another surgeon available to do the job.

"How many other people in the car?" was Dr. Renwick's first question.

"Only the senator," came back the immediate reply.

"What the hell was he doing driving himself at that time of night?" muttered Renwick rhetorically. "What is the extent of his injuries?"

"Several broken bones, including at least three ribs and the left ankle," said the duty physician, "but I'm more worried about the loss of blood. It took the fire boys nearly an hour to cut him out of the wreck."

"OK, make sure my team is scrubbed up and ready by the time I arrive. I'll call Mrs. Davenport." He hesitated for a moment. "Come to think of it," he said, "I'll call both Mrs. Davenports."

Annie was standing in the biting wind by the hospital emergency entrance when she saw the ambulance speeding toward her. It was the accompanying police squad cars that made her think that it had to be her husband. Although Fletcher was still unconscious, they allowed her to clutch his limp hand as they wheeled him through to the operating room. When Annie first saw the condition Fletcher was in, she didn't believe anyone could save him.

Why had she attended that charity meeting when she should have been in Madison with her husband? Whenever she was with Fletcher, she always drove him home. Why had she ignored his protestations when he'd insisted that he'd enjoy the drive—it would give him some time to think, and in any case, it was such a short distance, he'd added. He'd only been five miles from home when he'd driven off the road.

Ruth Davenport arrived at the hospital a few moments later,

and immediately set about finding out as much as she could. Once she had spoken to the duty administrator, Ruth was able to reassure Annie of one thing. "Fletcher couldn't be in better hands than Ben Renwick. He's quite simply the best in the state." What she didn't tell her daughter-in-law was that they only got him out of bed when the odds of pulling a patient through were low. Ben Renwick wasn't a betting man.

Martha Gates was the next to arrive, and Ruth repeated everything that she'd picked up. She confirmed that Fletcher had three broken ribs, a broken ankle and a ruptured spleen, but it was the loss of blood that was causing the professionals to be anxious.

"But surely a hospital as large as St. Patrick's has a big enough blood bank to cope with that sort of problem?"

"Yes would be the usual answer," replied Ruth, "but Fletcher is AB negative, the rarest of all the blood groups, and although we've always maintained a small reserve stock, when that school bus careered off Route 95 in New London last month and the driver and his son turned out to be AB negative, Fletcher was the first to insist that the entire batch should be shipped out to the New London hospital immediately, and we just haven't had enough time to replace it."

An arc lamp was switched on and lit up the hospital entrance. "The vultures have arrived," said Ruth, looking out of the window. She turned and faced her daughter-in-law. "Annie, I think you should talk to them, it just might be our only chance of locating a blood donor in time."

—◦—

When she rose on Sunday morning, Su Ling decided not to wake Nat until the last possible moment; after all, she had no idea what time it was when he'd crept into bed.

She sat in the kitchen, made herself some fresh coffee, and began to scan the morning papers. Fletcher's speech seemed to have been well received by the citizens of Madison, and the latest opinion poll showed the gap between them had narrowed by another point, bringing Nat's lead down to three percent.

Su Ling sipped her coffee and pushed the paper to one side. She always switched on the television just before the hour to catch the weather forecast. The first person to appear on the screen even before the sound came on was Annie Davenport. Why was she standing outside St. Patrick's, Su Ling wondered? Was Fletcher announcing some new health care initiative? Sixty seconds later she knew exactly why. She dashed out of the kitchen and up the stairs to wake Nat and tell him the news. A remarkable coincidence. Or was it? As a scientist, Su Ling gave scant credence to coincidence. But she had no time to consider that now.

A sleepy Nat listened as his wife repeated what Annie Davenport had just said. Suddenly he was wide awake, leaped out of bed quickly and threw on yesterday's clothes, not bothering to shave or shower. Once dressed, he ran downstairs, pulling on his shoes only when he was in the car. Su Ling was already behind the wheel with the engine running. She took off the moment Nat slammed the car door.

The radio was still tuned into the 24-hour news station, and Nat listened to the latest bulletin while trying to tie up his laces. The on-the-spot reporter couldn't have been more explicit: Senator Davenport was on a ventilator, and if someone didn't donate four pints of AB negative blood within hours, the hospital feared for his survival.

It took Su Ling twelve minutes to reach St. Patrick's by simply ignoring the speed limit—not that there was a lot of traffic on the road at that time on a Sunday morning. Nat ran into the hospital while Su Ling went in search of a parking space.

Nat spotted Annie at the end of the corridor and immediately called out her name. She turned and looked startled when she saw him charging toward her. *Why was he running?* was her first reaction.

"I came just as soon as I heard," shouted Nat, still on the move, but all three women just continued to stare at him, like rabbits caught in a headlight. "I'm the same blood group as Fletcher," Nat blurted out as he came to a halt by Annie's side.

"You're AB negative?" said Annie in disbelief.

"Sure am," said Nat.

"Thank God," said Martha. Ruth quickly disappeared into the

intensive care unit, and returned a moment later with Ben Renwick by her side.

"Mr. Cartwright," he said thrusting out his hand, "My name is Dr. Renwick, and I'm . . ."

"The hospital's senior consultant, yes, I know you by reputation," said Nat, shaking his hand.

The surgeon gave a slight bow. "We have a technician ready to take your blood . . ."

"Then let's get on with it," said Nat, pulling off his jacket.

"To begin with we'll need to run some tests and check if your blood is an exact match, and then screen it for HIV and hepatitis B."

"Not a problem," said Nat.

"But I'm afraid, Mr. Cartwright, I'll also need at least three pints of your blood if Senator Davenport is to have any chance of survival, and that will require several indemnity forms signed in the presence of a lawyer."

"Why a lawyer?" asked Nat.

"Because there's an outside chance you might suffer severe side effects, and in any case, you'll end up feeling pretty weak yourself, and it may prove necessary to keep you in the hospital for several days just to administer extra fluids."

"Are there no extremes that Fletcher will not go to to keep me off the campaign trail?"

All three women smiled for the first time that day as Renwick quickly led Nat off to his office. Nat turned around to speak to Annie, to find her being comforted by Su Ling.

"Now I have another problem to consider," admitted Renwick as he took a seat behind his desk and began sorting through some forms.

"I'll sign anything," repeated Nat.

"You can't sign the form I have in mind," said the consultant.

"Why not?" asked Nat.

"Because it's an absentee ballot, and I'm no longer certain which one of you to vote for."

51

"LOSING THREE PINTS of blood doesn't seem to have slowed down Mr. Cartwright," said the duty nurse as she placed his latest chart in front of Dr. Renwick.

"Maybe not," said Renwick, flicking through the pages, "but it sure made one hell of a difference to Senator Davenport. It saved his life."

"True," said the nurse, "but I've warned the senator that despite the election, he'll have to stay put for at least another two weeks."

"I wouldn't bet on that," said Renwick, "I anticipate that Fletcher will have discharged himself by the end of the week."

"You could be right," said the nurse with a sigh, "but what can I do to prevent it?"

"Nothing," said Renwick, turning over the file on his desk so that she couldn't read the names Nathaniel and Peter Cartwright printed in the top-right corner. "But I do need you to make an appointment for me to see both men as soon as possible."

"Yes, doctor," replied the nurse, making a note on her clipboard before leaving the room.

Once the door was closed, Ben Renwick turned the file back over and read through its contents once again. He'd thought about little else for the past three days.

When he left later that evening, he locked the file away in his private safe. After all, a few more days wouldn't make a great deal of difference, after all what he needed to discuss with the two men had remained a secret for the past forty-three years.

Nat was discharged from St. Patrick's on Thursday evening, and no one on the hospital staff imagined for a moment that Fletcher would still be around by the weekend, despite his mother trying to convince him that he should take it easy. He reminded her there were now only two weeks to go before election day.

During the longest week in his life, Ben Renwick continued to wrestle with his conscience, just as Dr. Greenwood must have done forty-three years before him, but Renwick had come to a different conclusion; he felt he'd been left with no choice but to tell both men the truth.

The two combatants agreed to meet at six A.M. on Tuesday morning in Dr. Renwick's office. It was the only time before election day that both candidates had a clear hour in their agendas.

Nat was the first to arrive, as he had hoped to be in Waterbury for a nine o'clock meeting, and perhaps even squeeze in a visit to a couple of commuter stations on the way.

Fletcher hobbled into Dr. Renwick's office at five fifty-eight, annoyed that Nat had made it before him.

"Just as soon as I get this cast off," he said, "I'm going to kick your ass."

"You shouldn't speak to Dr. Renwick like that, after all he's done for you," said Nat, with a grin.

"Why not?" asked Fletcher. "He filled me up with your blood, so now I'm half the man I was."

"Wrong again," said Nat. "You're twice the man you were, but still half the man I am."

"Children, children," said the doctor, suddenly realizing the significance of his words, "there is something a little more serious that I need to discuss with you."

Both men fell silent after hearing the tone in which they had been admonished.

Dr. Renwick came from behind his desk to unlock his safe. He removed a file and placed it on the desk. "I have spent several days trying to work out just how I should go about imparting such confidential information to you both." He tapped the file with his right index finger. "Information that would never have come to my attention had it not been for the senator's near-fatal accident and the necessity to check both your files." Nat and Fletcher glanced at each other, but said nothing. "Even whether to tell you separately or together became an ethical issue, and at least on that, it will now be obvious what decision I came to." The two candidates still said nothing. "I have only one request, that the information I am about to divulge should remain a secret, unless both of you, I repeat, both of you, are willing, even determined, to make it public."

"I have no problem with that," said Fletcher, turning to face Nat.

"Neither do I," said Nat, "I am, after all, in the presence of my lawyer."

"Even if it were to influence the outcome of the election?" the doctor added, ignoring Nat's levity. Both men hesitated for a moment, but once again nodded. "Let me make it clear that what I am about to reveal is not a possibility or even a probability; it is quite simply beyond dispute." The doctor opened the file and glanced down at a birth certificate and a death certificate.

"Senator Davenport and Mr. Cartwright," he said, as if address-ing two people he'd never met before, "I have to inform you that, having checked and double-checked both your DNA samples, there can be no questioning the scientific evidence that you are not only brothers," he paused, his eyes returning to the birth cer-tificate, "but dizygotic twins." Dr. Renwick remained silent as he allowed the significance of his statement to sink in.

Nat recalled those days when he still needed to rush to a dic-tionary to check the meaning of a word. Fletcher was the first to break the silence. "Which means we're not identical."

"Correct," said Dr. Renwick, "the assumption that twins must look alike has always been a myth, mainly perpetrated by romantic novelists."

"But, that doesn't explain . . ." began Nat.

"Should you wish to know the answer to any other questions you might have," said Dr. Renwick, "including who are your natu-ral parents, and how you became separated, I am only too happy that you should study this file at your leisure." Dr. Renwick tapped the open file in front of him once again.

Neither man responded immediately. It was some time before Fletcher said, "I don't need to see the contents of the file."

It was Dr. Renwick's turn to register surprise.

"There's nothing I don't know about Nat Cartwright," Fletcher explained, "including the details of the tragic death of his brother."

Nat nodded. "My mother still keeps a picture of both of us by her bedside, and often talks of my brother Peter and what he might have grown up to be." He paused and looked at Fletcher. "She would have been proud of the man who saved his brother's life. But I do have one question," he added, turning back to face Dr. Renwick, "I need to ask if Mrs. Davenport is aware that Fletcher isn't her son?"

"Not that I know of," replied Renwick.

"What makes you so sure?" asked Fletcher.

"Because among the many items I came across in this file was a letter from the doctor who delivered you both. He left instructions that it was only to be opened if a dispute should arise concerning your birth that might harm the hospital's reputation. And that letter states that there was only one other person who knew the truth, other than Dr. Greenwood."

"Who was that?" asked Nat and Fletcher simultaneously.

Dr. Renwick paused while he turned another page in his file. "A Miss Heather Nichol, but as she and Dr. Greenwood have since died, there's no way of confirming it."

"She was my nanny," said Fletcher, "and from what I can remember of her, she would have done anything to please my mother." He turned to look at Nat. "However, I would still prefer that my parents never find out the truth."

"I have no problem with that," said Nat. "What purpose can be served by putting our parents through such an unnecessary ordeal? If Mrs. Davenport became aware that Fletcher was not her son, and my mother were to discover that Peter had never died, and she had been deprived of the chance of bringing up both of her children, the distress and turmoil that would quite obviously follow doesn't bear thinking about."

"I agree," said Fletcher. "My parents are now both nearly eighty, so why resurrect such ghosts of the past?" He paused for some time. "Though I confess I can only wonder how different our lives might have been, had I ended up in your crib, and you in mine," he said, looking at Nat.

"We'll never know," Nat replied. "However, one thing remains certain."

"What's that?" asked Fletcher.

"I would still be the next governor of Connecticut."

"What makes you so confident of that?" asked Fletcher.

"I had a head start on you and have remained in the lead ever since. After all, I've been on earth six minutes longer than you."

"A tiny disadvantage from which I had fully recovered within the hour."

"Children, children," admonished Ben Renwick a second time. Both men laughed as the doctor closed the file in front of him. "Then we are in agreement that any evidence proving your relationship should be destroyed and never referred to again."

"Agreed," said Fletcher without hesitation.

"Never referred to again," repeated Nat.

Both men watched as Dr. Renwick opened the file and first extracted a birth certificate which he placed firmly into the shredder. Neither spoke as they watched each piece of evidence disappear. The birth certificate was followed by a three-page letter dated May 11, 1949, signed by Dr. Greenwood. After that came several internal hospital documents and memos, all stamped 1949. Dr. Renwick continued to place them one by one through the shredder until all he was left with was an empty file. On top were printed the names *Nathaniel and Peter Cartwright*. He tore the file into four pieces before offering the final vestige of proof to the waiting teeth of the shredder.

Fletcher rose unsteadily from his place, and turned to shake hands with his brother. "See you in the governor's mansion."

"You sure will," said Nat, taking him in his arms. "The first thing I'll do is put in a wheelchair ramp so you can visit me regularly."

"Well, I have to go," said Fletcher, turning to shake hands with Ben Renwick. "I've got an election to win." He hobbled toward the door, trying to reach it before Nat, but his brother jumped in front and held it open for him.

"I was brought up to open doors for women, senior citizens and invalids," explained Nat.

"And you can now add future governors to that list," said Fletcher, hobbling through.

"Have you read my paper on disability benefits?" asked Nat, as he caught up with him.

"No," Fletcher replied, "I've never bothered with impractical ideas that could never reach the statute books."

"You know, I will regret only one thing," said Nat, once they were alone in the corridor and could no longer be overheard by Dr. Renwick.

"Let me guess," said Fletcher as he waited for the next quip.

"I think you would have been one hell of a brother to grow up with."

52

Dr. Renwick's prediction turned out to be accurate. Senator Davenport had discharged himself from St. Patrick's by the weekend, and a fortnight later no one would have believed he had been within hours of dying only a month before.

With only a few days left before the election, Clinton went farther ahead in the national polls as Perot continued to eat into Bush's support. Both Nat and Fletcher went on traveling around the state at a pace that would have impressed an Olympic athlete. Neither waited for the other to challenge them to a debate, and when one of the local television companies suggested they should face each other in three encounters, both accepted without needing any persuasion.

It was universally agreed that Fletcher came off better in the first duel, and the polls confirmed that impression when he went into the lead for the first time. Nat immediately cut down on his travel commitments, and spent several hours in a mock-up television studio being coached by his staff. It paid off, because even the local Democrats conceded that he had won the second round, when the polls put him back into the lead.

So much rested on the final debate that both men became overanxious not to make a mistake, and it ended up being judged as a stalemate or, as Lucy described it, "dullmate." Neither candidate was distressed to learn that a rival station had aired a football game that had been watched by ten times as many viewers. The polls the following day put both candidates at forty-six percent, with eight percent undecided.

"Where have they been for the past six months?" demanded Fletcher as he stared at the figure of eight percent.

"Not everyone is as fascinated by politics as you are," suggested Annie over breakfast that morning. Lucy nodded her agreement.

Fletcher hired a helicopter and Nat chartered the bank's small jet to take them around the state during the final seven days, by which time the don't-knows had fallen to six percent, shedding one point to each rival. By the end of the week, both men wondered if there was a shopping mall, factory, railway station, town hall, hospital or even street that they hadn't visited, and both accepted that, in the end, it was going to be the organization on the ground that mattered. And the winner would be the one who had the best-oiled machine on election day. No one was more aware of this than Tom and Jimmy, but they couldn't think of anything they hadn't already done or prepared for, and could only speculate as to what might go wrong at the last minute.

For Nat, election day was a blur of airports and main streets, as he tried to visit every city that had a runway before the polling booths closed at eight P.M. As soon as his plane touched down, he would run to the second car in the motorcade, and take off at seventy miles an hour, until he reached the city limits, where he would slow down to ten miles an hour, and start waving at anyone who showed the slightest interest. He ended up in the main street at a walking pace, and then reversed the process with a frantic dash back to the airport before taking off for the next city.

Fletcher spent his final morning in Hartford, trying to get out his core vote before taking the helicopter to visit the most densely populated Democratic areas. Later that night, commentators even discussed who had made the better use of the last few hours. Both men landed back at Hartford's Brainard airport a few minutes after the polls had closed.

Normally in these situations, candidates will go to almost any lengths to avoid one another, but when the two teams crossed on the tarmac, like jousters at a fair, they headed straight toward each other.

"Senator," said Nat, "I will need to see you first thing in the morning as there are several changes I will require before I feel able to sign your education bill."

"The bill will be law by this time tomorrow," replied Fletcher. "I intend it to be my first executive action as governor."

Both men became aware that their closest aides had fallen back so that they could have a private conversation, and they realized that the banter served little purpose if there was no audience to play to.

"How's Lucy?" asked Nat. "I hope her problem's been sorted out."

"How did you know about that?" asked Fletcher.

"One of my staff was leaked the details a couple of weeks ago. I made it clear that if the subject was raised again he would no longer be part of my team."

"I'm grateful," said Fletcher, "because I still haven't told Annie." He paused, "Lucy spent a few days in New York with Logan Fitzgerald, and then returned home to join me on the campaign trail."

"I wish I'd been able to watch her grow up, like any other uncle. I would have loved to have a daughter."

"Most days of the week she'd happily swap me for you," said Fletcher. "I've even had to raise her allowance in exchange for not continually reminding me how wonderful you are."

"I've never told you," said Nat, "that after your intervention with that gunman who took over Miss Hudson's class at Hartford School, Luke stuck a photograph of you up on his bedroom wall, and never took it down, so please pass on my best wishes to my niece."

"I will, but be warned that if you win, she's going to postpone college for a year and apply for a job in your office as an intern, and she's already made it clear that she won't be available if her father is the governor."

"Then I look forward to her joining my team," said Nat, as one or two aides reappeared and suggested that perhaps it was time for both of them to be moving on.

Fletcher smiled. "How do you want to play tonight?"

"If either of us gets a clear lead by midnight, the other will call and concede?"

"Suits me," said Fletcher, "I think you know my home number."

"I'll be waiting for your call, Senator," said Nat.

The two candidates shook hands on the concourse outside the airport, and their motorcades whisked off in different directions.

A designated team of state troopers followed both candidates home. Their orders were clear. If your man wins, you are protecting the new governor. If he loses, you take the weekend off.

Neither team took the weekend off.

53

NAT SWITCHED ON the radio the moment he got into the car. The early exit polls were making it clear that Bill Clinton would be taking up residence in the White House next January, and that President Bush would probably have to concede before midnight. A lifetime of public service, a year of campaigning, a day of voting, and your political career becomes a footnote in history. "That's democracy for you," President Bush was later heard to remark ruefully.

Other pollsters across the country were suggesting that not only the White House, but both the Senate and Congress would be controlled by the Democrats. CBS's anchor man, Dan Rather, was reporting a close result in several seats. "In Connecticut, for example, the gubernatorial race is too close to call, and the exit polls are unable to predict the outcome. But for now it's over to our correspondent in Little Rock, who is outside Governor Clinton's home."

Nat flicked off the radio as the little motorcade of three SUVs came to a halt outside his home. He was greeted by two television cameras, a radio reporter and a couple of journalists—how different from Arkansas, where over a hundred television cameras and countless radio and newspaper journalists waited for the first words of the president-elect. Tom was standing by the front door.

"Don't tell me," said Nat as he walked past the press and into the house. "It's too close to call. So when can we hope to hear a result involving some real voters?"

"We're expecting the first indicators to come through within the hour," said Tom, "and if it's Bristol, they usually vote Democrat."

"Yes, but by how much?" asked Nat as they headed toward the kitchen, to find Su Ling glued to the television, a burning smell coming from the stove.

—◦—

Fletcher stood in front of the television, watching Clinton as he waved to the crowds from the balcony of his home in Arkansas. At the same time he tried to listen to a briefing from Jimmy. When he'd first met the Arkansas governor at the Democratic convention in New York City, Fletcher hadn't given him a prayer. To think that only last year, following America's victory in the Gulf War, Bush had enjoyed the highest opinion poll ratings in history.

"Clinton may be declared the winner," said Fletcher, "but Bush sure as hell lost it." He stared at Bill and Hillary hugging each other, as their bemused twelve-year-old daughter stood by their side. He thought about Lucy and her recent abortion, realizing it would have been front-page news if he had been running for president. He wondered how Chelsea would cope with that sort of pressure.

Lucy came dashing into the room. "Mom and I have prepared all your favorite dishes, as it will be nothing but public functions for the next four years." He smiled at her youthful exuberance. "Corn on the cob, spaghetti bolognese, and if you've won before midnight, *crème brûlée*."

"But not all together," begged Fletcher, and, turning to Jimmy, who had rarely been off the phone since the moment he'd entered the house, he asked, "When are you expecting the first result in?"

"Any minute now," Jimmy replied. "Bristol prides itself on always announcing first, and we have to capture that by three to four percent if we hope to win overall."

"And below three percent?"

"We're in trouble," Jimmy replied.

—◦—

Nat checked his watch. It was just after nine in Hartford, but the image on the screen showed voters still going to the polls in California. BREAKING NEWS was plastered across the screen. NBC was the first to declare that Clinton would be the new president of the United States. George Bush was already being labeled by the networks with the cruel epitaph "one-termer."

The phones rang constantly in the background, as Tom tried to field all the calls. If he thought Nat ought to speak to the caller personally, the phone was passed across to him, if not, he heard Tom repeating, "He's tied up at the moment, but thank you for calling, I'll pass your message on."

"I hope there's a TV wherever I'm 'tied up,'" said Nat, "otherwise I'll never know whether to accept or concede," he added as he tried valiantly to cut into a burned steak.

"At last a real piece of news," said Tom, "but I can't work out who it helps, because the turnout in Connecticut was fifty-one percent, a couple of points above the national average." Nat nodded, turning his attention back to the screen. The words "too close to call" were still being relayed from every corner of the state.

When Nat heard the name Bristol, he pushed aside his steak. "And now we go over to our eyewitness correspondent for the latest update," said the news anchor.

"Dan, we're expecting a result here at any moment, and it should be the first real sign of just how close this gubernatorial race really is. If the Democrats win by . . . hold on, the result is coming over on my earpiece . . . the Democrats have taken Bristol." Lucy leaped out of her chair, but Fletcher didn't move as he waited for the details to be flashed across the bottom of the screen. "Fletcher Davenport 8,604 votes, Nat Cartwright 8,379," said the reporter.

"Three percent. Who's due up next?"

"Probably Waterbury," said Tom, "where we should do well because . . ."

"And Waterbury has gone to the Republicans, by just over five thousand votes, putting Nat Cartwright into the lead."

Both candidates spent the rest of the evening leaping up, sitting down and then leaping back up again as the lead changed hands sixteen times during the next two hours, by which time even the commentators had run out of hyperboles. But somewhere in between the results flooding in, the local anchor man found time to announce that President Bush had phoned Governor Clinton in Arkansas to concede. He had offered his congratulations and best wishes to the president-elect. Does this herald a new Kennedy era? The politicos were asking . . . "But now back to the race for governor of Connecticut, and here's one for the statistics buffs, the position at the moment is that the Democrats lead the Republicans by 1,170,141 to 1,168,872, an overall lead for Senator Davenport of 1,269. As that is less than one percent, an automatic recount would have to take place. And if that isn't enough," continued the commentator, "we face an added complication because the district of Madison maintains its age-old tradition of not counting its votes until ten o'clock tomorrow morning."

Paul Holbourn, the mayor of Madison, was next up on the screen. The septuagenarian politician invited everyone to visit this picturesque seaside town, which would decide who would be the next governor of the state.

"How do you read it?" asked Nat, as Tom continued to enter numbers into his calculator. "Fletcher leads at the moment by 1,269 and at the last election, the Republicans took Madison by 1,312."

"Then we must be favorites?" ventured Nat.

"I wish it was that easy," said Tom, "because there's a further complication we have to consider."

"And what's that?"

"The present governor of the state was born and raised in Madison, so there could be a considerable personal vote somewhere in there."

"I should have gone to Madison one more time," said Nat.

"You visited the place twice, which was once more than Fletcher managed."

"I ought to call him," said Nat, "and make it clear that I'm not conceding."

Tom nodded his agreement as Nat walked over to the phone. He didn't have to look up the senator's private number because he had dialed it every evening during the trial.

"Hi," said a voice, "this is the governor's residence."

"Not yet it isn't," said Nat firmly.

"Hello, Mr. Cartwright," said Lucy, "were you hoping to speak to the governor?"

"No, I wanted to speak to your father."

"Why, are you conceding?"

"No, I'll leave him to do that in person tomorrow, when, if you behave yourself, I'll be offering you a job."

Fletcher grabbed the telephone, "I'm sorry about that, Nat," he said, "I presume you're calling to say all bets are off until tomorrow when we meet at high noon?"

"Yes, and now you mention it, I'm planning to play Gary Cooper," said Nat.

"Then I'll see you on Main Street, sheriff."

"Just be thankful it's not Ralph Elliot you're up against."

"Why?" asked Fletcher.

"Because right now he would be in Madison filling up ballot boxes with extra votes."

"It wouldn't have made any difference," said Fletcher.

"Why not?" asked Nat.

"Because if Elliot had been my opponent, I would have already won by a landslide."

BOOK SEVEN

NUMBERS

54

It took Nat about an hour to drive to Madison, and when he reached the outskirts of the town, he could have been forgiven for thinking the little borough had been chosen as the venue for the seventh game in the World Series.

The highway was filled with cars festooned with emblems of red, white and blue, with donkeys and elephants staring blankly out of numerous back windows. When he took the turnoff for Madison, population 12,372, half the vehicles left the highway like steel filings drawn toward a magnet.

"If you take away those who are too young to vote, I presume the turnout should be around five thousand," said Nat.

"Not necessarily. I suspect it will prove to be a little higher than that," Tom replied. "Don't forget Madison is where retired people come to visit their parents, so you won't find it full of youth clubs and discos."

"Then that should benefit us," said Nat.

"I've given up predicting," said Tom with a sigh.

No signpost was needed to guide them to the town hall, as everyone seemed to be heading in the same direction, confident that the person in front of them knew exactly where they were going. By the time Nat's little motorcade arrived in the center of the town, they were being overtaken by mothers pushing strollers. When they turned into Main Street, they were continually held up by pedestrians spilling onto the road. When Nat's car was over-taken by a man in a wheelchair, he decided the time had come to get out and walk. This slowed his progress down even more, because the moment he was recognized, people rushed up to shake him by the hand, and several asked if he would mind posing for a photograph with his wife.

"I'm glad to see that your reelection campaign has already begun," teased Tom.

"Let's get elected first," said Nat as they reached the town hall. He climbed the steps, continuing to shake hands with all the well-wishers as if it were the day before the election, rather than the day after. He couldn't help wondering if that would change when he came back down the steps and the same people knew the result. Tom spotted the mayor standing on the top step, looking out for him.

"Paul Holbourn," whispered Tom. "He's served three terms and at the age of seventy-seven has just won his fourth election unopposed."

"Good to see you again, Nat," said the mayor, as if they were old friends, though in fact they had only met on one previous occasion.

"And it's good to see you too, sir," said Nat, clutching the mayor's outstretched hand. "Congratulations on your re-election—unopposed, I'm told."

"Thank you," said the mayor. "Fletcher arrived a few minutes ago, and is waiting in my office, so perhaps we ought to go and join him." As they walked into the building, Holbourn said, "I just wanted to spend a few moments taking you both through the way we do things in Madison."

"That's fine by me," said Nat, knowing that it wouldn't make a blind bit of difference if it wasn't.

A crowd of officials and journalists followed the little party down the corridor to the mayor's office, where Nat and Su Ling joined Fletcher and Annie and around thirty other people who felt they had the right to attend the select gathering.

"Can I get you some coffee, Nat, before we proceed?" asked the mayor.

"No thank you, sir," said Nat.

"And how about your charming little wife?" Su Ling shook her head politely, not fazed by the tactless remark of a past generation. "Then I'll begin," the mayor continued, turning his attention to the crowded assembly that had squeezed into his office.

"Ladies and gentlemen," he paused, "and future governor," he tried to look at both men at once. "The count will commence at ten o'clock this morning, as has been our custom in Madison for over a century, and I can see no reason why this should be delayed simply because there is a little more interest in our proceedings than usual." Fletcher was amused by the understatement, but wasn't in any doubt that the mayor intended to savor every moment of his fifteen minutes of fame.

"The township," continued the mayor, "has 10,942 registered voters, who reside in eleven districts. The twenty-two ballot boxes were, as they always have been in the past, picked up a few minutes after the polls closed, and then transferred into the safe custody of our chief of police, who locked them up for the night." Several people politely laughed at the mayor's little joke, which caused him to smile and lose his concentration. He seemed to hesitate, until his chief of staff leaned forward and whispered in his ear, "Ballot boxes."

"Yes, of course, yes. The ballot boxes were collected this morning and brought to the town hall at nine o'clock, when I asked my chief clerk to check that the seals had not been tampered with. He confirmed that they were all intact." The mayor glanced around to observe his senior officials nodding their agreement. "At ten o'clock, I shall cut those seals, when the ballots will be removed from the boxes and placed on the counting table in the center of the main hall. The first count will do no more than verify how many people have cast their votes. Once that has been established, the ballots will then be sorted into three piles. Those who have voted Republican, those who have voted Democrat, and those that might be described as disputed ballots. Though I might add, these are rare in Madison, because for many of us, this might well be our last chance to register a vote." This was greeted by a little nervous laughter, though Nat wasn't in any doubt he meant it.

"My final task as the election officer will be to declare the result, which in turn will decide who is elected as the next governor of our great state. I hope to have completed the entire exercise by midday." Not if we continue at this pace, thought Fletcher. "Now, are there any questions before I accompany you through to the hall?"

Tom and Jimmy both began speaking at the same time, and Tom nodded politely to his opposite number, as he suspected that they would be asking exactly the same questions.

"How many counters do you have?" asked Jimmy.

The official once again whispered in the mayor's ear. "Twenty, and all of them are employees of the council," said the mayor, "with the added qualification of being members of the local bridge club." Neither Nat nor Fletcher could work out the significance of this remark, but were not inclined to ask for further clarification.

"And how many observers will you be allowing?" asked Tom.

"I shall permit ten representatives from each party," said the mayor, "who will be allowed to stand a pace behind each counter and must at no time make any attempt to talk to them. If they have a query, they should refer it to my chief of staff and if it remains unresolved, he will consult me."

"And who will act as arbitrator should there be any disputed ballots?" asked Tom.

"You will find that they are rare in Madison," repeated the mayor, forgetting that he had already expressed this sentiment, "because for many of us this could well be our last chance to register a vote." This time no one laughed, while at the same time the mayor failed to answer Tom's question. Tom decided not to ask a second time. "Well, if there are no further questions," said the mayor, "I'll escort you all to our historic hall, built in 1867, of which we are inordinately proud."

The hall had been built to house just under a thousand people, as the population of Madison didn't venture out much at night. But on this occasion, even before the mayor, his executives, Fletcher, Nat and their two respective parties had entered the room, it looked more like a Japanese railroad station during the rush hour than a town hall in a sleepy coastal Connecticut resort. Nat only hoped that the senior fire officer was not present, as there couldn't have been a safety regulation that they weren't breaking.

"I shall begin proceedings by letting everyone know how I

intend to conduct the count," said the mayor, before heading off in the direction of the stage, leaving the two candidates wondering if he would ever make it. Eventually the diminutive, gray-haired figure emerged up onto the platform and took his place in front of a lowered microphone. "Ladies and gentlemen," he began. "My name is Paul Holbourn, and only strangers will be unaware that I am the mayor of Madison." Fletcher suspected that most people in that room were making their first and last visit to the historic town hall. "But today," he continued, "I stand before you in my capacity as elections officer for the district of Madison. I have already explained to both candidates the procedure I intend to adopt, which I will now go over again . . ."

Fletcher began looking around the room and quickly became aware that few people were listening to the mayor as they were busy jostling to secure a place as near as possible to the cordoned-off area where the vote would be taking place.

When the mayor had finished his homily, he made a gallant effort to return to the center of the room, but would never have completed the course if it hadn't been for the fact that proceedings could not commence without his imprimatur.

When he eventually reached the starting gate, the chief clerk handed the mayor a pair of scissors. He proceeded to cut the seals on the twenty-two boxes as if he were performing an opening ceremony. This task completed, the officials emptied the boxes and began to tip the ballots out onto the elongated center table. The mayor then checked carefully inside every box—first turning them upside down, and then shaking them, like a conjuror who wishes to prove there's no longer anything inside. Both candidates were invited to double-check.

Tom and Jimmy kept their eyes on the center table as the officials began to distribute the voting slips among the counters, much as a croupier might stack chips at a roulette table. They began by gathering the ballots in tens, and then placing an elastic band around every hundred. This simple exercise took nearly an hour to complete, by which time the mayor had run out of things to say about Madison to anyone who was still willing to listen. The piles were then counted by the chief clerk, who confirmed that there were fifty-nine, with one left over containing fewer than a hundred ballots.

In the past at this point, the mayor had always made his way back up onto the stage, but his chief clerk thought it might be easier if the microphone was brought to him. Paul Holbourn agreed to this innovation and it would have been a shrewd decision had the wire been long enough to reach the cordoned-off area, but at least the mayor now had a considerably shorter journey to complete before having to deliver his ultimatum. He blew into the microphone, producing a sound like a train entering a tunnel, which he hoped would bring some semblance of order to the proceedings.

"Ladies and gentlemen," he began, checking the piece of paper the chief clerk had placed in his hand, "5,934 good citizens of Madison have taken part in this election, which I am informed is fifty-four percent of the electorate, being one percent above the average for the state."

"That extra percentage point might well turn out to our advantage," Tom whispered in Nat's ear.

"Extra points usually favor the Democrats," Nat reminded him.

"Not when the electorate has an average age of sixty-three," rebutted Tom.

"Our next task," continued the mayor, "is to separate the votes of both parties before we can begin the count." No one was surprised that this exercise took even longer, as the mayor and his officials were regularly called on to settle disputes. Once this task had been completed the counting of the votes began in earnest. Piles of tens in time multiplied into hundreds before being placed in neat little lines like soldiers on a parade ground.

Nat would have liked to circle the room and follow the entire process, but the hall had become so crowded that he had to satisfy himself with the regular reports relayed back to him by his lieutenants in the field. Tom did decide to fight his way around and came to the conclusion that although Nat looked as if he was in the lead, he couldn't be sure if it was sufficient to make up the 118-vote advantage that Fletcher currently enjoyed following the recount of the overnight ballots.

It was another hour before the counting had been completed,

and the two piles of slips were lined up facing each other. The mayor then invited both candidates to join him in the cordoned-off area in the center of the room. There he explained that sixteen ballots had been rejected by his officials, and he therefore wished to consult them before deciding if any should be considered valid.

No one could accuse the mayor of not believing in open government, because all sixteen ballots had been laid out on the center of the table for everyone to see. Eight appeared to have no mark on them at all, and both candidates agreed that they could be rejected. "Cartwright should have been sent to the electric chair," and "no lawyer is fit to hold public office," were also dismissed just as quickly. Of the remaining six, all had marks other than crosses against one of the names, but as they were equally divided, the mayor suggested that they should all be validated. Both Jimmy and Tom checked the six votes and could find no fault with the mayor's logic.

As this little detour had yielded no advantage to either candidate, the mayor gave the green light for the full count to begin. Stacks of hundreds were once again lined up in front of the counters, and Nat and Fletcher tried from a distance to gauge if they had won or lost enough to change the wording on their letterhead for the next four years.

When the counting finally stopped, the chief clerk passed a piece of paper to the mayor with two figures printed on it. He didn't need to call for silence, because everyone wanted to hear the result. The mayor, having abandoned any thought of returning to the stage, simply announced that the Republicans had won by a margin of 3,019 to 2,905. He then shook hands with both candidates, obviously feeling that his task had been completed, while everyone else tried to work out the significance of the figures.

Within moments, several of Fletcher's supporters were leaping up and down once they realized that, although they had lost Madison by 114, they had won the state by four votes. The mayor was already on his way back to his office, looking forward to a well-earned lunch, by the time Tom had caught up with him. He explained the real significance of the local result, and added that on behalf of his candidate, he would be requesting a recount. The mayor made his way slowly back into the hall to be greeted with chants of *recount, recount, recount,* and, without consulting his officials announced that was what he had always intended to do.

Several of the counters who had also begun to pack up and leave quickly sidled back to their places. Fletcher listened carefully as Jimmy whispered in his ear. He considered the suggestion for a few moments, but replied firmly, "No."

Jimmy had pointed out to his candidate that the mayor had no authority to order a recount, as it was Fletcher who had lost the vote in Madison, and only a losing candidate could call for a recount. The *Washington Post* wrote in a leader the following morning that the mayor had also exceeded his authority on another front, namely that Nat had beaten his rival by over one percent, also rendering a recount unnecessary. However, the columnist did concede that rejecting such a request might well have ended in a riot, not to mention interminable legal wrangles, which would not have been in keeping with the way both candidates had conducted their campaigns.

Once again, the stacks were counted and recounted, before being checked and double-checked. This resulted in the discovery that three piles contained 101 votes, while another had only ninety-eight. The chief clerk did not confirm the result until he was sure that the calculators and the hand count were in unison. Then he once again passed a piece of paper to the mayor with two new figures for him to announce.

The mayor read out the revised result of 3,021 for Davenport to 2,905 for Cartwright, which cut the Democrat's overall lead to two votes.

Tom immediately requested a further recount, although he knew he was no longer entitled to do so. He suspected that as Fletcher's majority had fallen, the mayor would find it difficult to turn down his request. He crossed his fingers as the chief clerk briefed the mayor. Whatever it was that the chief clerk had advised, the mayor simply nodded, and then made his way back to the microphone.

"I shall allow one further recount," he announced, "but should the Democrats retain an overall majority for a third time, however small, I shall declare Fletcher Davenport to be the new governor of Connecticut." This was greeted by cheers from Fletcher's supporters, and a nod of acquiescence from Nat as the counting procedure cranked back into action.

Forty minutes later, the piles were all confirmed as being correct, and the battle looked to be finally over, until someone noticed one of Nat's observers had his hand held high in the air. The mayor walked slowly across to join him, with the chief clerk only a pace behind, and inquired what the query was. The observer pointed to a pile of one hundred votes on the Davenport side of the table, and claimed that one of the votes should have been credited to Cartwright.

"Well, there's only one way of finding out," said the mayor as he began to turn the ballots over, with the crowd chanting in unison, "one, two, three . . ."

Nat felt embarrassed and muttered to Su Ling, "He'd better be right."

"Twenty-seven, twenty-eight . . ." Fletcher said nothing as Jimmy joined in the counting.

"Thirty-nine, forty, forty-one. . . ." And suddenly there was a hush; the observer had been correct, because the forty-second ballot had a cross against Cartwright's name. The mayor, the chief clerk, Tom and Jimmy all checked the offending ballot and agreed that a mistake had been made, and therefore the overall result was a tie. Tom was surprised by Nat's immediate response.

"I wonder how Dr. Renwick voted."

"I think you'll find he abstained," whispered Tom.

The mayor was looking exhausted, and agreed with his chief of staff that they should call for a recess, to allow the counters and any other officials to take an hour's break, before the next recount at two o'clock. The mayor invited Fletcher and Nat to join him for lunch, but both candidates politely declined, having no intention of leaving the hall or even straying more than a few feet from the center table, where the votes were stacked up.

"But what happens if it remains a tie?" Nat heard the mayor ask the chief clerk as they made their way toward the exit. As he didn't hear the reply, he asked Tom the same question. His chief of staff already had his head buried in the *Connecticut State Elections Manual*.

~⋄~

Su Ling *did* slip out of the hall and walked slowly down the corridor, remaining just a few paces behind the mayor's party. When she spotted LIBRARY printed in gold letters on an oak door, she came to a halt. She was pleased to find the door unlocked and stepped quickly inside. Su Ling took a seat behind one of the large bookcases, leaned back and tried to relax for the first time that day.

"You too," said a voice.

Su Ling looked up to see Annie sitting in the opposite corner. She smiled. "The choice was another hour in that hall or . . ."

". . . or lunch with the mayor, and further epistles of the apostle Paul on the virtues of Madison." They both laughed.

"I only wish it had all been decided last night," said Su Ling. "Now one of them is bound to spend the rest of his life wondering if he should have canvassed another shopping mall . . ."

"I don't think there was another shopping mall," said Annie.

"Or school, hospital, factory or station, come to think of it."

"They both should have agreed to govern for six months each year, and then let the electorate decide who they wanted in four years' time."

"I don't think that would have settled anything."

"Why not?" asked Annie.

"I have a feeling this will be the first of many contests between them that will prove nothing until the final showdown."

"Perhaps the problem for the voters is that they are so alike it's impossible to choose between them," Annie suggested, looking carefully at Su Ling.

"Perhaps it's just that there is nothing between them," said Su Ling, returning her gaze.

"Yes, my mother often comments on how alike they are whenever they're both on TV, and the coincidence of their shared blood group has only emphasized that feeling."

"As a mathematician I don't believe in quite so many coincidences," said Su Ling.

"It's interesting that you should say that," ventured Annie, "because whenever I raise the subject with Fletcher, he simply clams up."

"Snap," said Su Ling.

"I suspect if we combined our knowledge . . ."

"We would only live to regret it."

"What do you mean?" asked Annie.

"Only that if those two have decided not to discuss the subject, even with us, they must have a very good reason."

"So you feel we should remain silent as well."

Su Ling nodded. "Especially after what my mother's been put through . . ."

"And my mother-in-law would undoubtedly be put through," suggested Annie. Su Ling smiled and rose from her place. She looked directly at her sister-in-law. "Let's just hope that they don't both stand for president, otherwise the truth is bound to come out."

Annie nodded her agreement.

"I'll go back first," said Su Ling, "and then no one will ever realize this conversation took place."

—◦—

"Did you manage to get some lunch?" asked Nat.

Su Ling didn't have to reply as her husband was distracted by the reappearance of the mayor clutching a piece of paper in his right hand. He looked far more relaxed than when last seen disappearing in the direction of his office. On reaching the center of the room, the mayor gave an immediate order that another recount should commence. The satisfied look on his face was not the result of good food and even better wine; in fact the mayor had forgone lunch to phone the justice department in Washington and seek the advice of the attorney general's office on how they should proceed in the event of a tie.

The tellers were, as ever, thorough and meticulous, and forty-one minutes later came up with exactly the same result. A tie.

The mayor reread the attorney general's fax, and to everyone's disbelief, called for a further recount, which, thirty-four minutes later, confirmed the deadlock.

Once the chief clerk had reported this to his elected representative, the mayor began to make his way toward the stage, having asked both candidates to join him. Fletcher shrugged his shoulders when he caught Nat's eye. So keen were the onlookers to discover what had been decided that they quickly stood aside to allow the three men to pass, as if Moses had placed his staff on the Madison waters.

The mayor stepped up onto the platform with the two candidates in close attendance. When he came to a halt in the center of the stage, the candidates took their places on each side of him, Fletcher on his left, Nat on his right, as befitted their political persuasion. The mayor had to wait a few more moments for the microphone to be returned to its original position before he could address an audience that had not diminished in size despite the holdups.

"Ladies and gentlemen, during the lunch break, I took the opportunity to telephone the justice department in Washington, D.C., to seek their advice as to what procedure we should follow in the event of a tie." This statement elicited a silence that until that moment had not been achieved since the doors opened at nine o'clock that morning. "And to that end," the mayor continued, "I have a fax signed by the attorney general confirming the due process of law that must now take place." Someone coughed, and in the hush that had overcome the assembled gathering it sounded like Vesuvius erupting.

The mayor paused for a moment before returning to the attorney general's fax. "If in an election for governor, any one candidate wins the count three times in a row, that candidate shall be deemed to be the winner, however small his or her majority. But should the vote end in a tie for a third time, then the result shall be decided," he paused, and this time no one coughed, "by the toss of a coin."

The tension broke and everyone began speaking at once, as they tried to take in the significance of this revelation, and it was some time before the mayor was able to continue.

He once again waited for complete silence before producing a silver dollar from his waistcoat pocket. He placed the coin on his upturned thumb before glancing at the two contestants as if seeking their approval. They both nodded.

One of them called, "Heads," but then he always called heads.

The mayor gave a slight bow before spinning the coin high in the air. Every eye followed its ascension, and its even quicker descent, before it finally bounced up and down on the stage, ending up at the mayor's feet. All three men stared down at the thirty-fifth president, who resolutely returned their gaze.

The mayor picked up the coin and turned around to face the two candidates. He smiled at the man now standing on his right, and said, "May I be the first to congratulate you, Governor."